ALFA
INVESTIGATIONS
SERIES

Publisher © Chelle Bliss
Editor: Lisa A. Hollett
Proofreaders: Rosarita Reader & Fiona Wilson
Cover Design © Chelle Bliss
Formatted by Chelle Bliss

SINFUL INTENT

ALFA INVESTIGATIONS BOOK ONE

WALL STREET JOURNAL & USA TODAY BESTSELLING AUTHOR

CHELLE BLISS

CHAPTER I

FAMILY

MORGAN

"All right, Ma." I dig through the pile of unopened mail to find the invitation I'd ignored.

"You need to see your family. It'll do you good to be around the Gallo side."

"Why?" I don't know why I asked. I already knew the answer. They were her side and, therefore, superior.

My Ma, Fran DeLuca, had been on my back since the day I'd come home from the army. I loved the hell out of the woman, but she could be a major pain in my ass.

"They have their lives together. Sal knew how to raise boys."

My jaw tightened. "Are you saying I'm not a good man, Ma?"

"Morgan, you know that's not what I meant. You need to get out of this city for a little while and clear your head. Plus," she added, drawing out the S, "I need you to accompany me on the trip. You know I hate traveling alone. The suitcase is always too heavy for me to lift, and I get lost easily."

I closed my eyes and exhaled. "Fine, Ma. I'll take you to Izzy's wedding. But I won't be happy about it."

"Thank you, baby. I'll call now and tell your aunt Maria to expect us. I want to get there a couple of days early. I'll book the airfare. You just show up sober enough to be allowed on the plane, Morgan. Understand?"

She showed up at my place, without calling, after I'd had a few beers while watching football. She immediately jumped to the conclusion that I was a closet drinker and I've never been able to convince her otherwise.

"Ma, I'm not a drunk, for Christ's sake." I pinched the bridge of my nose.

"I love you," she said as she disconnected the call.

Fan-fucking-tastic.

I hadn't seen the Gallos in ages. Izzy had been a gawky teenager with a sharp tongue, and the boys...they were Gallo through and through. They were tough, rough, and always looking for an angle.

I wouldn't say that I was very different from them, but the bloodline had been watered down with the addition of my father's side. They were the better half of the family tree.

At least I could spend a couple of days in the sunshine instead of freezing my balls off in Chicago. My mother would have my full attention and use the time to chew my ear off about why didn't I find a good woman to settle down with already—it was the same conversation we'd had almost every day for the last month.

Before I could even get up from the table, my phone rang again.

"What now, Ma?" I pushed the chair back.

"I spoke to your aunt and everything is set. You're going to stay with Joe while we're there, and I'll stay with Mar and Sal."

"Do I get a choice in this?" I stood, wandering over to the floor-to-ceiling windows that overlooked the city.

"Nope. Everyone else is full. Joey will be happy to have you."

"I'm going to get a hotel."

I hated staying with people, especially when I hadn't seen that person in ten years. I knew them as well as I knew my father, and he walked out of our lives the day I graduated from high school.

"No, you're not. That would be such a slap in the face. You'll stay with Joe and Suzy."

"We'll talk about it later. I have shit to do."

"Start packing, Morgan. I'll book our tickets for the day after tomorrow." *Click.*

Ma was the queen of hanging up before I could say anything more.

Staring out at Lake Michigan, I rolled my neck and counted to ten. I could handle a few days with the family.

Maybe they'd help get my mind off all the fucked-up shit I'd seen. My faith in humanity had evaporated while I'd been in combat, but the silence and calm of being a civilian had me climbing the freaking walls.

I needed to get out of here.

Old friends, the kind who were trouble, had been lighting up my phone since the day I returned. They weren't the type of people I needed to be hanging out with.

As a kid, I found myself in trouble more times than I liked to remember—small crimes, petty theft, and other bullshit things kids do. The last straw came when we stole a car and were quickly popped for the crime.

Instead of spending time in jail, I was given an option—enter the service and turn my life around or head to the slammer and do some time.

The military seemed like the better choice. At least I'd be free and see the world. But the only part of the world I'd seen resembled a barren wasteland, not even close to the tropical paradise the brochures promoted.

I'll say one thing about the military—it did straighten my ass out and made me a man. I wasn't the same punk who'd left for basic training.

The last thing I needed was to hook up with my *buddies* who had never left "the life." I knew they were still pulling jobs that could land them in prison for much of their natural life. I'd finally been given my freedom back, and there was no way in hell I'd give it up to make a quick buck.

Spending quality time with my quiet family should help me unwind and figure out my future, right?

Who was I kidding?

The Gallos had never been quiet a day in their lives. They were loud and obnoxious, but they were my family, and it would be nice to spend time with them.

It was time to get my shit in order, head down to the Florida sunshine, and get the fuck away from the Windy City.

CHAPTER 2

OPPORTUNITIES

MORGAN

"I'm so excited to see Sal and Mar," Ma chattered as she stared out the window, watching the palm trees whiz by as I drove.

"I hope she has food. I'm starving. What's with the peanuts on a three-hour flight?" I glanced at the GPS.

We were close, within ten minutes of their house.

"Do you think about anything but food?"

"Yep." There was so much on my mind, but in that moment, all I could think of was a home-cooked meal. The thing I remembered the most about Aunt Mar was her food. Ma wasn't a good cook, but we made do. When we'd visit the Gallos, I made sure to memorize every taste until the next trip. "But right now I need to eat."

"I can't wait to wrap my arms around my brother. It's a shame I haven't been back in so long." She fidgeted clicking her fingernails together.

"Why haven't you, Ma? We used to come here all the time, and then you stopped visiting."

She placed her hand on my arm. "I felt ashamed after your father left. I couldn't bring myself to face them."

"Ma, if they judge you—"

"No, no, Morgan." She brushed her fingers against my skin. "They aren't like that. It was all in my head. Then you left for the army and I was scared to go anywhere."

I glanced at her. "What do you mean you were scared?"

"I always waited for the man to come tell me that my son died serving his country. I was too petrified to go anywhere in case I'd miss that."

"Jesus." I gripped the steering wheel tighter. "That's the dumbest shit I've ever heard."

Her hand flew from my arm and smacked me upside the head. "You just had to sign up for the army," she nagged as her voice grew nasally. "You couldn't go off to college like the rest of the kids. I had enough stress in my life besides having my only child serve during a time of war."

That was classic Fran DeLuca.

Hard-core nag and guilt-tripper extraordinaire.

I cursed the gods every day for making me an only child. She gave me all of her attention. Sure, it had been great when I was a little kid, but now? Not so much.

When my father left, I knew she'd be up my ass. That's one of the reasons I decided to join the army. I wanted to get away from every-thing, including her attention. I couldn't imagine if I ended up in jail— she'd probably visit every day to yell at me.

"Can you be any more dramatic?" I shifted my eyes, glancing at her.

"I saw the names of the soldiers killed in action as I watched the news each night. Do you know what that does to a mother?" Her voice was almost shrill.

"I'm sure you're gonna tell me."

"You're lucky I love you." She stared out the window again.

"Uh-huh," I replied as I pulled onto the freeway exit, getting one step closer to the Gallos.

This entire week, my mother would be out of my hair. She'd be too wrapped up in her brother and sister-in-law to care about what I did.

The rest of the way, we drove in silence.

"You have arrived," the robotic GPS voice stated.

"I remember it being bigger." I took in the sight of their house.

"It's the same, but you were small."

"I was never small." I put the car in park.

"You're so full of shit, Morgan. Let's go. I can't sit here another minute." She opened the door and climbed out quicker than I'd seen her move in years.

Turning off the car, I started to pray as I climbed out. "God grant me the serenity."

"Franny!" Aunt Mar came running out the front door with her arms outstretched. Uncle Sal strolled behind her like his usual cool self, looking like it was just another day and he was heading to the grocery store.

"Mar!" Ma yelled back, jogging toward her.

It was going to be one of those weeks. Loud, loving, and sweet enough to make my teeth hurt. I leaned against the car with my arms crossed and watched the scene unfold.

I couldn't remember the last time I'd seen my mother as happy as she looked in that moment.

One by one, my cousins piled out of the house, but a few new faces followed them.

"Yo!" Mike stalked down the driveway toward me.

The boy had grown into a man. He was beyond jarhead size; the man was built like a brick shithouse. Then I spotted a drop-dead gorgeous brunette standing next to him.

"Hey, shithead," I replied as he got closer. "Lookin' bigger than ever."

"Fuck off, dickface. Gimme a hug, big man." He held out his arms to me.

I rolled my eyes as he put his arms around me. "You people are way too touchy-feely for me," I muttered as he smashed my body.

Mr. Ray DeLuca hadn't been a hugger. My mother showered love on me, but rarely did I ever experience it from another man. Only when we visited Ma's side of the family did I realize I'd missed out.

"You're such a whiny bitch, Morgan."

"I've heard you've turned into quite the pussy." I jabbed him in the ribs.

"Was that a fly or did you hit me?" He backed away, holding my shoulders and laughed. "It's so good to see you, li'l cousin."

"You too, Mikey."

He slapped me on the shoulder, almost throwing me off-kilter. "You're still an asshole. That's why you're my favorite cousin," he said with a grin.

Peering over his shoulder, I gawked at his woman. She had pink cheeks, wild curls that fell over her shoulders, and matching warm brown eyes that sparkled in the sunlight. "Who do we have here?" I asked, giving her my best smile.

Mike cleared his throat; his glare was inescapable as he wrapped his arm tightly around her waist. "This is my wife, Mia." He emphasized the wife part.

"It's a pleasure meeting you, Mia." I reached for her hand.

"She's mine," Mike warned, pulling Mia toward him.

She gave me a playful smirk. "Hey, handsome."

Mike pulled her closer. "Mia," he snarled.

"Get over yourself, Michael. It's your cousin," she told him, motioning toward me as she pried herself from his grip.

"Oh, I like her already."

"Hey, little cousin." Thomas pulled me into a bear hug with a beautiful redhead standing behind him. "It's so good to see you, man."

"It's nice to see you made it out alive." His years undercover had aged him, but his getting out in one piece was nothing short of miraculous.

"I could say the same to you. I want you to meet my wife, Angel."

"Hi, Morgan. It's wonderful to meet you." She held her hand out.

Instead of taking her hand, I did it the Gallo way and wrapped her in my arms. "It's wonderful to meet you, Angel," I whispered before releasing her.

"Morgan!" a woman screeched from behind Angel, pushing her out of the way. "I've missed you!"

"Izzy?" I looked down at her and shook my head, shocked that she was no longer the little girl I'd pictured.

My little cousin Izzy had always been beautiful—well, maybe not during that awkward teenage phase. When she was little, she'd follow us around, trying to do whatever we were. I couldn't imagine dealing with a little sister all the time. I would've gone batshit crazy.

"You've grown more beautiful with age," I teased, but it was the truth.

"You're still a bullshitter, DeLuca." She kicked the dirt near her feet much like she had when she was a little girl.

"Where's my hug from the bride-to-be?"

She flung herself into my arms. As I squeezed her, I watched as Ma greeted everybody with a giant smile on her face.

"You're like hugging a damn hard teddy bear." Izzy's fingers dug into my back.

"Must be a Gallo thing," I replied, noticing that I was similar in size to her brothers.

"Choking me," she whined with a strangled voice.

"Sorry, babe." I set her feet on the ground.

"You're a big lug." She laughed as Auntie Mar approached us.

There was something weird about seeing my family after having been apart for many years. Although they were different people and had grown older, we fell in like old times. The familiarity hadn't vanished. We shared memories of the way things used to be, and that drew us together, making us one.

The number of new names I'd have to remember was daunting. Angel was Thomas's wife, James was Izzy's husband-to-be, Max was Anthony's wife, Suzy was Joe's wife, and Mia was Mike's. Plus, they each had children. Maybe by the end of the trip I'd have the names down pat. It was enough to make my head spin.

"Hey, Auntie Mar. I've missed you."

"Hey, kiddo." She smiled, tilting her head up and looking at me. "Morgan, my dear, you just want to eat my food. I haven't forgotten," she said as she rubbed my stomach.

"True, but that doesn't mean I didn't miss you too." I rubbed my stomach where her hand had just been. "But your sauce is something that can't be explained, and based on my Ma's cooking, it can't be replicated either." I waited for Ma to slap me again.

Scanning the yard, I noticed that Ma was too far to hear or reach me even if she had.

"You're lucky she didn't hear you." Aunt Mar wrapped her arms around my waist and rested her head on my chest. "I'm so happy you're home safe. We were so worried about you."

I hugged her back, feeling a bit warm and fuzzy inside. I'd always loved Auntie Mar the most out of any of my relatives. "I made it out alive."

"You're the last thing your Ma has." She peered up at me. "If something were to happen to you, she'd lose it."

I refrained from rolling my eyes. "Thanks for more of a guilt trip, Auntie Mar."

"It's a family thing."

"Yeah, and something I could do without."

"Let's get some food in you and maybe you won't feel so grumpy."

"Couldn't think of anything more perfect." I kissed the top of her head.

We headed up the driveway along with my cousins and their other halves. The crew had quadrupled if I counted the kids.

Suddenly, I felt behind in the family department.

Shit. Was I going to be stuck with Ma as my plus-one for an eternity?

I COLLAPSED ON THE COUCH. Why hadn't I worn sweat pants? I had known I'd overeat, but I hadn't wanted to greet my family looking like a slob. Let's be real. If I'd shown up to the airport in sweats, Fran would've had a conniption.

Being in the living room, looking around at my family, I felt genuinely happy. When I was a kid, I used to beg my parents to let me stay with Auntie Mar for the summer just so I could feast on her amazing cooking, but Ma always said no. She claimed that they had enough children to worry about without having to feed me every day.

"So, what are you doing with yourself now?" Joe asked as I yawned.

Joe had always been a tough-lookin' guy. Even as a teenager, he had the look that had others cower around him. His tattoos, his wide torso, and fuck-off look that had become permanently etched on his face made him even more intimidating.

"Trying to digest. Other than that, not a damn thing." I closed my eyes.

"Must you always be a smartass?" Anthony asked.

He was the oldest of the Gallo kids. He'd always been artsy, interested in music at a young age, and had shied away from the bullshit Joe and I had found ourselves in as kids. He was an old soul, but he wasn't the touchy-feely type. The one thing he had a talent for besides music was women. His cup overflowed with pussy, and he made no apologies.

"That's ripe coming from you." I could feel the food coma starting to grip my body.

Anthony had always been the biggest smartass. He'd never been as physically big as his brothers, or as athletic, but he used his words as weapons. His calling me a smartass was the funniest damn thing in the world.

"Have you found a job?" Thomas sat down next to me.

The wear and tear from Thomas's time undercover lined his face. He looked older than the others now, the stress permanently etched on his tanned skin.

"Nothing yet. I haven't even bothered to look, really. I'm just trying to settle back into civilian life."

"It's freaky shit, isn't it? Nothing feels right anymore. Happened to me when I finished working undercover for the DEA. It took me a good year before things felt normal again."

"Yeah," I replied, too tired to say anything more. I stretched, trying to wake myself up. I needed to sit up to stay awake. This was utterly ridiculous.

"What did you do in the army?" Izzy sat down next to her fiancé James.

James was the perfect partner for her. I could tell. I'd always thought I had a knack for reading people. James obviously didn't put up with her bullshit. She needed a man more overbearing than her brothers or she'd eat him alive. James and Thomas had become best friends when they'd worked together in the DEA, and they'd started a business together a year ago.

I leaned forward and took a deep breath. "I was a cavalry scout and did recon work."

"Interesting." James rubbed his chin and stared at me.

"Sometimes it could be. Basically, I was the eyes and ears for the troops on the battlefield."

James turned to Thomas and raised an eyebrow. "You know what I'm thinking?"

"Yep, and we'll talk about it later," Thomas replied as he rubbed his hands together, glancing at me.

They nodded to each other, and James turned his attention back to me. "How long did you serve?"

"Served eight years."

"Thanks for your service," Suzy, Joe's girl, said as she held their daughter, Gigi.

"Any time, beautiful." Out of the corner of my eye I could see Joe staring at me. "It's impressive that each of you found a beautiful woman."

"Looks aren't everything, man," Anthony said.

"Says the man with the exotic beauty in the next room," I teased him. "I'm not being a dick. I'm just making an observation."

"Well, you can keep those thoughts to yourself, buddy," Mike warned, puffing out his chest.

They were so uptight.

"Let me say this. They are your women. I'll never try anything or get in between you. I respect your relationships entirely. I'm just making a statement. You've all done well for yourselves. I'm hoping that, someday, I'm lucky enough to find someone for myself. We're family. I'd never fuck with family."

"Watch your mouth." Ma smacked my head.

My body jolted and I cursed under my breath. I hadn't seen her enter the room behind me. I swear she'd lurk in the shadows just to whack me.

"Yes, Ma." I turned toward Joe. "Thanks for letting me stay with you."

"I'm pretty close to rethinking that now, Morgan." He smirked, running his hand up Suzy's leg.

"Come on, man. I'll be a perfect gentleman." I meant every word of it, too.

I'd never try anything with their ladies. I knew I could be a total jackass, but that was beyond even my level of assholishness.

Suzy set Gigi on the floor and climbed into Joe's lap. "Stop being so serious all the time. He can help with Gigi while you're at work."

I shook my head and waved my hands. "Oh, no. I couldn't. I'm not good with kids anyway." Fuck, I'd never really been around little ones.

"You'll be fine. Gigi likes you."

"No, she doesn't," I replied, staring at Gigi, who couldn't have cared less about me as she played with a Barbie.

"She likes everyone." Suzy smiled at Joe.

"Just like her mother." Joe's eyes shot up toward the ceiling as he mumbled something and rubbed his face.

"Joseph," Suzy warned, "you'll be nice to our guest this week."

"Anything for you, sugar." He gave her a kiss and brought her closer to his body.

"I can get a hotel," I interrupted, feeling like a third wheel.

He tucked his face into her neck. "Nah, man. Stay with us. We have plenty of room. We actually have a guesthouse on the property. You'll have it to yourself."

I whistled, impressed that my cousin had a pad swanky enough to have a guesthouse.

"Suzy's friends used to rent it, but it's been empty since they moved out."

"I may never leave," I teased.

"Dessert!" Auntie Mar yelled from the dining room.

My stomach growled, and I looked down, trying to figure out how I'd fit another bite of food in my body. "How do you guys stay so damn fit with her cooking?"

"It's a challenge, bro." Thomas walked past and slapped me on the shoulder. "Lots of working out and physical activity."

It took me two attempts to push myself off the couch before I was able to stagger to my feet. "I'd have to spend all my free time at the gym if I ate her food every day."

"You won't have that problem with Suzy's cooking," Izzy teased as she followed me into the dining room.

"She lured me by other means," Joe said before he pulled Suzy into his arms and gave her a deep kiss.

Being around the Gallos kind of made my head hurt and my heart ache. They never stopped talking or teasing each other, but the amount of love in the house made me long for something I'd never had.

I grabbed a slice of cake and headed back to the living room, trying to get a moment's peace. Before my ass hit the couch cushion, Mike strolled into the room.

"So," he said before he stuffed a forkful of cake in his mouth. "I know you have some shit going on up there. Fess up." Small crumbs fell from his lips, landing on his lap as he spoke.

"Not a thing, Mike," I replied before scooping the frosting off the cake and shoving it in my mouth.

"Liar. Back in the game?" He cocked an eyebrow.

"Nope."

He stared at me as if he were trying to figure out if I was bullshitting him or not. "Fine. Are you getting back in, then?"

I shook my head. "Nah. I'm too old to do any time in the joint, man. It's not worth it anymore. I was given my one chance at redemption, and I doubt I'd get a second if I got caught."

Mike laughed. "You always were a lucky SOB. I mean, we had to move because of all the shit you started to get Joe involved in. Ma did not want him to be a criminal."

"Oh, please. Joe would've never been a criminal."

"Don't be so sure. He's still scary as fuck. Hey, why don't you move down here, dude? I mean, the weather sucks in Chicago. You don't have a job. You'd have us. What could be bad?"

I savored another bite of cake, wishing I could eat like this every week. "I don't know. I don't think my mother would survive without me."

"She'll be fine."

"Dude, you clearly don't know Fran that well. She's up in my shit all the time." I scraped my fork against the plate, gathering every morsel left before putting it in my mouth. "She'd go bananas if I moved away," I mumbled.

"Have her come too." He shrugged, not meeting my eyes.

"Chicago is a big city. I could get lost and not see her for weeks if I wanted to. Here, it's a little too close for comfort, if ya know what I mean."

"Yeah." He leaned back and polished off the cake.

"What are you talking about in here?" Thomas walked in, rubbing his gut.

"I'm trying to get Morgan to move down here, T," Mike replied, setting his empty plate on the coffee table.

"James and I were just talking about that. We could use another guy on our team. You have the skills we need and you're family," Thomas said as he sat across from me in his father's chair and leaned forward.

"What do you do again?" I asked, forgetting what Ma had told me.

"James and I started a private investigations company a while back. It's become such a success that we have a backlog of cases and often have to turn people away. So what do you say?"

I could easily be a PI. It didn't seem like that hard of a job. The army had given me the skills necessary for the part.

"I'll think about it." I chewed my lip, mulling his words over. "I need a few days to make a decision."

"The offer stands." Thomas reached into his pocket and pulled a business card out. "When you have a decision, call me or stop by the office."

I took the card and read it.

Thomas Gallo

Owner

ALFA Private Investigation

Underneath was the contact information for the office and his cell phone number.

I flipped it in my fingers and nodded. "I'll let you know as soon as I figure shit out. Don't mention a word of it to Fran."

The last thing I wanted was for her to go berserk before the wedding. Thomas and Mike both laughed.

"We got your back," Thomas said.

Suzy and Joe had been gracious hosts. They had made sure I'd wanted for nothing while I'd stayed with them. Most likely out of fear that word would get back to Auntie Mar.

I'd always thought of my big cousin Joe as somewhat of a badass when we were kids. Spending a couple of days with him had me learning about the real man.

He was always kind to his wife, showing the utmost patience and care. He was over the top with his daughter and never became flustered. He was everything I looked up to in a man and nothing I'd grown up having.

I'd gained mad respect for him in the three days I'd spent with them waiting for the wedding. I'd tried to get lost during the day, not wanting to be the new babysitter. Every evening, Joe and I would enjoy a beer and chat before we both headed to bed.

"You know, if you stay," he said as he tossed his beer can in the trash can while we sat on the stone patio of the guesthouse, "you can rent this until you find a place of your own."

"Thanks, Joe. It's kind of you to still want me around." I grinned.

"I learned that you aren't as big of an asshole as you make yourself out to be."

"Joe," I said as I stood, "don't tell anyone that. I like for people to think I'm a giant prick."

"I won't let your secret out as long as you don't tell people about me."

"I know. I figured that out already."

"I gotta hit the sack. Ma will have my head if I'm late to the wedding tomorrow."

I nodded, knowing we'd all have hell to pay if we didn't arrive on time. "Sleep well, cousin."

He walked back toward the main house, giving me time alone. I'd built a small fire in the pit earlier, and I decided to watch it as it burned out.

The night sky in Florida was different than back home. The bright lights of the city drowned out the twinkle of the stars. Here, underneath the country sky, with the nearest city miles away, every small star seemed to sparkle.

There was a quiet there that I hadn't experienced since I was a kid. The smallest rustle of a little animal moving through the woods was audible.

I closed my eyes and listened to the nothingness around me. I'd never thought I'd enjoy it, especially after growing up surrounded by the sounds of the city.

I knew in that moment that I didn't want to leave. The serenity that surrounded me sucked me in, and I couldn't imagine going back to the frigid city with no job in sight.

I pulled my phone out of my pocket and sent a message to Thomas.

Me: We'll talk after the wedding, but I want to hear more about the business.

Staying there would send my mother over the edge, but this was my life to live.

I walked inside and pulled off my clothes before I dropped them on the floor and climbed into bed. I stared at the ceiling and thought about my possible move and new career path.

I'd just have to find a way to break it to my ma. Leaving her behind was something she'd throw in my face for the rest of my life. She'd probably fall at my feet or hang on to my bumper as I drove out of the city, screaming for me not to leave her.

I was sure my imagination was just a tad overactive; she'd wish me well and kiss me goodbye.

Who the hell was I kidding? Fran was gonna have a meltdown.

CHAPTER 3
SHIT-FACED DRUNK
MORGAN

Fran was plastered. I mean completely shit-faced. Talking nonstop, smiling more than usual, and smoking like a train.

She'd never been a drinker, but at weddings, something inside her shifted. She'd consume more than her fair share of alcohol and suddenly turn into a chain smoker.

It was the perfect time to drop the news, that I'd be moving, in her lap. Maybe her drunkenness would extend her reaction time and give me a chance to escape before she tried to beat me to death.

That was the thing about her.

She loved me, and often she was overbearing, melodramatic, and fiercely protective. Not only would she beat the crap out of anyone who hurt me, she'd willingly do the same to me if she thought it was for my own good.

No matter how many times Ma had hit me, I'd never thought about striking her back. She'd raised me to respect women, and I knew that, if I ever did raise a hand to her, my uncle would end my life.

My size made her ability to actually hurt me impossible, but I knew that it was how she'd react. She wouldn't throw a right hook, but she'd pound on my chest and beg me not to leave. Hopefully, giving her the news at the wedding would stop her from causing a scene.

"Hey, Ma." I pulled out the chair next to her. I glanced at Uncle Sal, who was kicked back and just enjoying life now that his only daughter was married off.

"Hey, baby." She looked up at me with a sloppy smile, a cigarette between her fingers with ash an inch too long hanging from the end. "Whatcha doin'?" she asked as she hiccupped.

"I wanted to talk to you about something." I sat down and pulled my chair close to her.

Uncle Sal cleared his throat, standing quickly. "I'm going to leave you two alone."

"Thanks, Uncle." I nodded.

"Sal." Ma reached out and grabbed his hand. "Be a dear and get me another one of those fruity things." She looked up at him, grinning.

He nodded, patting her hand before he disappeared through the crowd and left us to talk.

I fidgeted with my drink as I thought about how to break the news to her. There wasn't an easy way to say it. I needed to man up and just...

"Just spill it, Morgan." She took a long, slow drag of her cigarette and let the smoke waft out of her mouth.

"I found a job," I blurted out, figuring it was best to lead with something positive.

"Does it have anything to do with those criminals back home?" She rested her elbow on the table, holding the cigarette in the air like an old-school Hollywood actress as the ash tumbled to the plate in front of her.

"No. Thomas actually asked me to come work for him."

A smile crept across her face. "Thank God, honest work. I didn't know he was opening a Chicago branch." She took another drag, almost missing her mouth in the process.

Uncle Sal stood behind her, listening to our conversation. I nodded at him before he set the drink in front of her.

She grabbed the glass and took a sip. "Thank you, brother."

He walked away quickly, knowing that the real bomb hadn't been dropped yet.

"He's not opening an office in Chicago, Ma." I swallowed hard as I looked around the backyard.

Her eyes narrowed. "What do you mean?" She set the drink on the table too hard, causing some of the liquid to slosh out of the glass.

"I'm going to move here as soon as we get back and I pack up my things." I leaned back in the chair and out of arm's reach.

"Move?" she asked, placing her hand on her chest. "You can't move."

"I am." I crossed my arms over my chest, standing my ground.

Here we go.

I braced myself and waited for her to embarrass the hell out of me in front of my entire family. Big Fran was ready to blow.

"You have nowhere to live," she argued.

"I'm going to rent Joe's guesthouse until I find a place."

"You're going to leave me all alone in Chicago?"

There was the guilt trip—right on cue.

"Seriously, Ma. You've been alone for years. I promise to come visit all the time." I knew this was going to be a battle.

"Alone," she whined. "Don't leave me alone." She face-planted on the table, one hand on the drink and the other still holding the cigarette.

If I hadn't been trying to avoid a battle, I'd have laughed. Drunk Ma was funny as hell and kind of cute, although I'd never admit it.

I closed my eyes, took a deep breath, and opened them again. "You have a bunch of friends. You'll be fine."

She sat upright and tapped her cigarette against the ashtray. "If you're moving here, then so am I," she said, looking really happy about the situation.

Oh my God.

No.

She was following me.

I wanted to face-plant now, but instead I took it in an entirely different direction.

I looked up toward the starry sky and cursed under my breath before I said, "That's a great idea, Ma."

Please, please God, tomorrow when the drinks had worn off, make her see the error of her ways.

If she decided to follow me, she'd at least have Uncle Sal and Auntie Mar to keep her busy and out of my hair. Maybe being around the family would take some of the heat off me.

It could end up being a good thing in the end.

What the hell was I thinking? It was going to be a clusterfuck of awesomeness.

"It's settled, then." She stubbed her cigarette out. "When are you going to get married?" she threw at me out of left field.

"I have to find a woman first," I shot back.

"You're getting old, baby. Don't wait too long, or you'll be alone forever."

"Hold up, woman." I held my hand up, shushing her. "Look around. Joe was older when he married. All of my cousins were older than I am now when they found love and settled down."

"Not Izzy," she replied, pursing her lips.

"Izzy's a girl."

"So? I want to be a grandmother before I'm dead."

There it was. The baby topic. I had known it was coming. Being around the kids all week had put her in baby mode.

How freaking lucky was I?

I swear she'd been dying since I was a kid. Every time she wanted to get her way, she'd talk about how her end was near.

"It'll be years before I have a kid. I'm not ready. So you'll have to hold off on dying."

"I just look around and see how happy Sal and Mar are with their grandbabies, and it makes my womb ache."

"Then maybe you should adopt. Think of all the fun and happiness you could have raising another child."

Never mind the fact that she'd have someone else to pester all the time.

"You were enough to last a lifetime. You weren't the easiest child to raise."

"Womb isn't aching that bad, is it?" I teased her.

"Everything okay?" Auntie Mar mouthed as she approached the table.

I nodded to her. "Hey, Auntie Mar. I just told Ma that I'm moving to Florida."

"Oh." She tried to act surprised. "Are you okay, Frannie?" Aunt Mar sat down next to her, placing her hand on Ma's arm.

"I couldn't be better, Maria. I've decided I'm going to move here too. I've spent too long away from you guys." Ma laid her hand over Aunt Mar's, both women plastered but sharing a moment.

"That makes me a happy woman. Sunday dinners at my house just got a whole lot more fun," Aunt Mar sang, swaying in her chair.

"We wouldn't miss it for the world," Ma answered for us both.

Normally it would have pissed me off, but I loved Aunt Mar's food too much to ever miss out on a Sunday dinner, and Ma was just too damn drunk to be angry with her.

"Are you two enjoying the wedding?" Aunt Mar glanced around the backyard.

"It was a beautiful ceremony, and the yard looks amazing," Ma said as she skimmed the crowd, trying to focus.

It really did look spectacular. Tables lined the perimeter of the grass, with a dance floor in the center. Lanterns and candles illuminated the backyard, creating a warm glow for the guests. Everyone seemed to be having a great time; most people were sufficiently drunk by now anyway.

"It's been a busy few days, but everything turned out perfectly," Aunt Mar replied.

"Izzy has turned into quite the beauty. You have to be so proud of her." Ma's eyes landed on Izzy, who was on the dance floor, dancing in her father's arms.

"She was the hardest of my children to raise. She's so full of piss and vinegar, and naturally the last to get married."

"She's like you, Mar. Headstrong and tough."

"Well, ladies, I'm going to let you two gab a bit while I find my cousins."

"They're at the bar," my aunt replied as I stood.

"Perfect." I leaned down and gave them each a kiss on the cheek.

As I started to walk away, Aunt Mar asked, "Does he have a girlfriend?"

"No, and he isn't getting any younger, either," Ma complained as her voice trailed off.

I shook the insult off. I wasn't even thirty yet and they wanted me to settle down. The last thing I was thinking about now was a relationship.

Winding my way through the crowd, I spotted Thomas and James at the bar doing shots.

"Gentlemen," I said as I approached. "Care if I join you?"

"Have a drink." James held a shot glass out. "Let's celebrate."

"Thanks. What are we drinking to?" I took the shot from his hands.

"The future." Thomas raised his glass. "Both in love and success in work."

"I'll drink to that."

"Thinking about joining us?" James asked.

"I put some thought into it and I've decided I want to work for you. I love Florida, and I'm sick of the shitty weather in Chicago anyway. I'd like to give it a try."

"Fantastic." Thomas pumped his fist. "Let's drink to another important member of our team. We're going to kick some major ass, men." He held his glass high in the air as we tapped ours to his and drank.

I winced as the liquid slid down my throat, burning a path to my stomach. "What the hell was that?"

"Moonshine." James wiped his mouth with the back of his hand.

"Fuck," I coughed, trying to fill my lungs with air as my throat felt like it was closing.

"It'll wear off." James slapped me on the back.

I coughed again, trying to clear my throat, but with no luck. I swallowed it down, trying to cool the burn with my saliva.

"Another?" James asked with a cocky grin and a raised eyebrow.

"I think I'll stick with vodka. It's a bit smoother," I whispered.

"Pussy." James called over to the bartender. "We'll take a bottle of vodka."

"A bottle, sir?" the man asked with a perplexed look on his face.

James nodded, holding his hand out. "Yes. The entire bottle and six shot glasses."

"It's going to be one of those nights, isn't it?" I realized I'd probably have a pounding headache tomorrow. "Do you want to be drunk on your wedding night?"

"It's going to take more than splitting a bottle of vodka with the guys to get me drunk." He grabbed the bottle, leaving us standing there.

"Okay, then," I said to Thomas as we grabbed the shot glasses and followed James toward a table where Joe, Mike, and Anthony were sitting.

"Hey, boys." James placed the bottle in the center of the table. "It's time to celebrate."

Joe pulled his bow tie off and tossed it before cracking his neck. "Finally. Is it after ten yet?"

"Yeah, dude. It's way after ten," Anthony answered.

"Thank fuck," Joe mumbled. "Pour me a shot."

"What the hell does ten have to do with anything?" I was completely confused.

"Ma made us all promise not to have more than two drinks before ten," Joe replied. "None of us felt like hearing her bullshit if we didn't follow her rules."

"Mothers."

"They're a pisser." James grabbed the bottle and poured us each a shot.

We toasted to various things, drinking shot after shot until the bottle was empty. I listened to my cousins talk. They'd never been so happy in their entire lives.

I didn't know if I'd ever feel that way. Finding a woman who was willing to put up with my shit would be a difficult endeavor. I hadn't given up on love, but I didn't think I was ready.

For now, I'd bury myself in my work and enjoy learning the Floridian way of life. Everything there, and it would take some getting used to.

The rest of the evening breezed by. We danced and drank until most of the guests left. When I'd had enough, I found Ma still sipping on a "fruity drink." She was too drunk to care.

"Night, baby," she slurred.

"Night, Ma. Love you." I gave her a kiss.

"Love you too," she whispered.

I wandered to the front yard and grabbed a taxi. Auntie Mar, in all of her wisdom, had hired a horde of them to take guests home who were too smashed to drive home.

Tomorrow was a new beginning. I'd make a plan and meet with Thomas at the office while James and Izzy jetted off to their honeymoon.

Life was looking up, and change was on the horizon.

CHAPTER 4
SUNSHINE
MORGAN

It wasn't hard to say goodbye to Chicago. After I served in the army, it didn't feel like home anymore. It took me a week to gather my things and head south.

Four days after I'd arrived in Florida with all of my belongings in tow and passed the exam for my Florida PI license, I was ready for my first day of work.

I stopped in front of the doorway to ALFA PI and cracked my neck, shaking my hands to calm my nerves. Even though my cousin owned the company, I didn't want to fuck shit up.

When I pushed the door open, Angel had the phone resting on her shoulder as she jotted down a note.

"I'll have Mr. Gallo call you as soon as his meeting is over, sir." She held a finger up.

The wall behind her desk had the company logo with the words *Aggressive-Loyal-Fearless-Accurate* inscribed underneath. I stared at it for a moment before taking in the rest of the office. Modern interior, gray and black walls, and not a knickknack or file visible. Sunlight streamed in from the wall of windows that comprised the eastern side of the building.

"Hey, Morgan," Angel said as she hung up. "Thomas is expecting you, and I'm excited to have you here."

"Thanks, Angel. I hope my cousin is happy too."

She smiled, rising from her seat. "Oh, he is. They've been so busy we've had to turn away cases. I know they sure could use your help." She motioned for me to follow. "Let me show you to his office."

As we walked down a hallway, a door caught my eye and I stopped.

It read:

Morgan DeLuca

Intelligence Services & Surveillance Specialist

I couldn't help but feel my insides warm.

"I told you he's happy to have you," she whispered.

"I guess so." I grinned.

Angel touched my arm, breaking my trance. "Come on. You can check your office out after you talk with the boss." She knocked lightly before entering.

"We'll see you tomorrow." Thomas put his feet down. "Morgan is here. I'll catch ya later. Glad you're back, man."

"Thomas." I walked toward him.

He tossed his cell phone on top of the desk, letting it bounce. He rose to his feet and came around the desk. "It's good to see you. That was James." He shook my hand. "He'll be in tomorrow."

"I heard."

"Hey, beautiful." He extended his arm to Angel.

She walked to him, snuggled into his side, and kissed his jaw. "You want any coffee or anything, baby?" She looked up at him with a small smile.

"No, thanks, love. Morgan?" he asked before he kissed her head.

"No, thanks. I'm good." I took a seat across from my new boss.

One thing I noticed with the Gallo men: They held their women close and often showered them with kisses. I envied them, but I'd never admit it.

Angel walked out, closing the door behind her as Thomas sat back down and I looked around the office.

"See your new office?" He put his feet back up on the desk, resting his hands behind his head.

I nodded. "I did. Thanks, man. It was beyond cool seeing that."

"You came at the perfect time. We hadn't even thought about you until I heard you were coming to the wedding. I did your background check before you arrived."

"Isn't that illegal?"

"I have friends who helped me work around the legalities. That's part of this job. Sometimes we're on the fringe of breaking laws. I assume you don't have any problem with that?" he asked with a raised eyebrow.

I shook my head. "Never been an issue for me before. I don't know why it would be now."

"Sometimes when we have to get information, we use all means necessary."

"Am I going to be stuck in that office all day?" I wondered if my job title meant "trapped in front of a computer screen."

"Hell no. God, that would be horrible. You're going to be going out on jobs like the rest of us. What I had put on your door is your specialty."

"Gotcha." I relaxed a little into the chair.

"I already have a case picked out for you, if you're willing to start as soon as possible."

"I'm all yours."

I was ready.

I'd never been the type for idleness, and after having been home for over a month, I wanted nothing more than to dive headfirst into my first case.

I was now Morgan, P.I. More handsome than Magnum, and hopefully, I'd do a better job at solving the cases. Maybe I should have grabbed myself one of those flowery shirts he always wore on television. Nah, I'd look like a giant douche. I liked my classic style of blue jeans and T-shirts.

He shuffled through the files on his desk and pulled one out. "Here she is. Her name is Race True." He handed it to me. "She came in a couple of days ago."

I opened the folder and scanned the first page. "What's her situation?"

"I don't have the entire story. She stated she'd only divulge it to the PI working her case. Basically, she's been getting harassed, and the messages have become more aggressive."

"Oh." I read through her questionnaire.

Thomas's phone rang and I continued reading as he began speaking with a client.

Race True was a twenty-seven-year-old woman who worked as a senior contract manager at a downtown communications firm. She'd lived in the Tampa area her entire life, except when she'd attended NYU. She held a master's degree in business and lived on her own in Clearwater. Not too much information, but at least it narrowed our possible suspects down.

I rested the file on my leg and stared out the window. What could have had this girl jumpy enough about an e-mail to cause her to seek help? Why not just go to the police, report the situation, and let them follow up on the threats?

Thomas rubbed his forehead as he hung up the phone.

"What's wrong?" I studied his face.

"Just bullshit from a case I worked on last week. It's a wife who suspected her husband of cheating. Long story. What do you think of Race?" he asked as he fidgeted in his chair, rocking back and forth.

"Not too much to go on."

He nodded, setting his lips in a firm line. "I know. Why don't I show you to your office, tell you a little bit about our rules, and then you can set up a meeting with her?"

I closed her file and stood. "I want to get working right away."

"Then let's get you settled," he said as he rose from his chair and walked around the desk. As he slapped me on the back, he said, "Welcome to the team, Morgan."

"It's good to be part of something again."

"Ms. TRUE, PLEASE," I said to the woman on the other end of the line.

"This is she. With whom am I speaking?" she asked in the sexiest Southern voice I'd ever heard.

"Morgan DeLuca from ALFA P.I. I was given your case, ma'am."

She hissed loud enough for it to catch me off guard. "I hate being called that."

I made a quick mental note not to make that mistake again. "Sorry." I gritted my teeth. "Just trying to be polite, Ms. True."

"It's fine. So, you're my guy?"

"Yes. I'd like to schedule a meeting to discuss the details you left off your questionnaire."

"Ah. If you're going to be working for me, then I'll share them with you, but no one else."

"That's fine." I tapped the pencil against my desktop. "When are you available?"

"I can meet you tomorrow for lunch. Let's say noon at the Blue Martini. Do you know where that is?"

"Yes," I lied. "I'll be there at noon." I'd lived here for a total of ninety-six hours, but I'd find it without trouble.

"Mr. DeLuca." She cleared her throat. "Please be prompt. I don't have time to waste waiting around for you."

"Yes, ma'am," I replied before hanging up. I grimaced, knowing she'd probably cursed me because I'd called her that again.

I leaned back in my chair, taking in my new digs. The walls matched the gray ones in the waiting room. On the opposite wall from my desk there was a modern black leather couch, and two chairs were immediately in front of my desk.

My eyes stung from the endless hours of staring at a computer, trying to learn the new programs. I climbed to my feet and stretched before I grabbed my keys. I looked around my office, finally letting it sink in. I had a new purpose and could start a brand-new life. Wanting to say goodbye to Thomas, I headed to his office before leaving.

"Hey." I opened the door and froze, seeing more than I expected.

Thomas had Angel bent over the desk with her skirt pulled up and was banging the hell out of her.

Their eyes met mine as I stood in the doorway, unable to move. "Sorry." I finally found my footing and took a step backward. I closed the door and took a deep breath. "Fuck," I muttered as I looked up at the ceiling. "I'll be back later!"

"Take the afternoon off!" Thomas yelled back.

"Thanks." I had to look like a kid who'd walked in on his parents.

Since I was diving right into work, I figured I'd better get my ass home, my car unpacked, and settle in.

I planned to be there for a very long time.

CHAPTER 5
HOTTIE IN HEELS
MORGAN

I overslept and missed my workout. I had to haul ass to make it on time to the Blue Martini. I texted Thomas in the morning, still slightly embarrassed, and told him I'd be in the office after my meeting with Ms. True.

Walking toward the restaurant, I peered down at my clothes, feeling out of place. While the rest of the crowd was wearing suits and business casual, I had my usual jeans and T-shirt on.

I stood in the doorway, surveying the bar and trying to pick Ms. True out of the crowd.

A woman peered up from her phone and looked back down.

Whoever she was, she was fucking gorgeous. She sat there with her spine straight, blond hair in a perfect bun, and a crisp black dress shirt tucked into a gray pencil skirt. Her high cheekbones almost kissed her deep-green eyes.

I wanted to saunter up to her, ask her for her number, and beg that on our first date she wear the red stilettos she had on, which made my cock instantly hard.

She glanced up, caught me staring, and waved me over.

Well, hell. Maybe she wanted my number too.

Keep calm and act natural.

Her eyes remained down, concentrating on her phone, as I approached.

"Mr. DeLuca, I presume." She glanced up for a moment, her emerald eyes flickering. "Take a seat."

Disappointment flooded me. The beautiful creature in front of me wasn't calling me over to get my number. She was my new client.

"Ms. True?" I let my eyes linger on her legs for a little too long but not caring.

"Yes," she said, still not making eye contact.

I grabbed the small pad of paper and pen I'd jammed in my back pocket and tossed them on the bar. "I hope you don't mind if I take notes." I tried not to stare at her legs, but failed.

"I do, actually." She dropped the phone in her purse, pinning me with her fierce, green eyes. "I'd prefer if you remember everything I tell you. I don't want a paper trail." The look on my face had to be one of total confusion, because she added, "I don't want anything possibly getting into the wrong hands."

"Okay."

"Good. Let's order and then we'll talk." She snapped her fingers to get the bartender's attention. "Do you know what you want?"

"Yeah. I come here all the time," I lied.

When the waitress approached, Race placed her order filled with special requests. She didn't like tomatoes but wanted extra cheese and only wanted grilled chicken.

I learned within five minutes that Race True wasn't easy. She seemed uptight, controlled, and unwilling to bend.

"And you, sir?" the beautiful bartender asked.

"Just a water, please."

"That's it? No giant, sloppy burger?" Ms. True asked, blinking rapidly.

"That's it." I glanced between them.

Race shrugged and waited for the bartender to reach the far end of the bar before she started to speak. "I thought I'd buy you lunch while we talked."

"I'd rather keep this strictly professional, Ms. True."

Lie number three.

I did want to be professional, but sitting here and staring at her had my mind going a million different ways, and most of them were sexual.

Fuck. I needed to get laid or everything could derail in a hurry. Why couldn't she have been unattractive? As I watched her, I wanted to know if she was as difficult to please in bed as she was at having a simple meal. I wondered if she screamed when she was fucked or what her hair looked like when her bun was taken down.

Race had pouty red lips, the whitest teeth I'd ever seen on a human being other than movie stars, and eyes the shade of emeralds. She was average size, with fabulous tits that peeked out from the neckline of her blouse and drew my attention. The pencil skirt accentuated her hips and made her legs seem a mile long.

"So, Morgan. Tell me a little bit about your background before I tell you about my problem. I want to know that you're the right man for the job." She sipped her wine, keeping her green eyes pinned on me.

It wasn't going to be easy to keep my thoughts from straying from the purpose of the meeting. Hopefully, our contact would be minimal and mainly over the phone so I wouldn't have to risk a slap in the face from gawking at her tits.

"I recently left the army after serving eight years. I worked the last four years gathering intel for the troops on the battlefield."

"Oh," she interrupted, placing the glass on the bar and resting her hand near mine. "That's impressive."

"Not really, ma'am."

She stiffened and rubbed the bridge of her nose.

"Sorry. It's a military thing. Everyone is a ma'am or a sir. It has nothing to do with me thinking you're anything like your grandmother, but I'm sure she's a lovely woman."

"She's a conniving hag. I'm nothing like her."

"Got it."

"Continue." She grabbed her glass again, averting her eyes.

"I became a civilian again about a month ago."

"What makes Mr. Gallo so sure you're the right man for the job?" she questioned, eyeing me with speculation.

I turned to face her, resting my arm on the bar. I didn't like that I had to defend my qualifications to her. "Listen, Ms. True. If you're not comfortable with me working your case, I can ask for someone else to be assigned to you. Right now, we don't have the manpower for another investigator to take over right away. If you're willing to wait, I'm sure we can find you a more suitable replacement. Someone more to your…liking. But no one will work as hard as I will."

"No." Her voice was louder than before. "I just need to have someone work on this case who knows their shit. I can't have some hack trying to clear my good name and fuck shit up." Her jaw clenched as she pinned me with her stare.

My dick twitched—honest to God, moved inside my pants from her filthy mouth.

"As long as you can promise me that you have the skills I need to find out who's behind this, then you're my guy." She placed her hand on my arm.

I smirked, feeling a bit playful. "I have the skills you desire." I glanced down, feeling the coolness of her touch on my warm skin. "I'm your man. I have more training in intelligence gathering than anyone else in my office. I was trained by the best the military had to offer. I have no doubt I'll find the perpetrator."

She nodded, brushing her fingertips across my skin before removing her hand slowly. "Fine. I'm sorry if I came off bitchy there for a moment. I know you're new. You weren't there when I went to the office to seek help. I just want to make sure I don't have the newbie who's learning on the job."

"Why don't you tell me about what's going on? Your file lacked anything to help me start identifying my plan of attack. I promise you this, Ms. True: I'll give your case my full attention and the utmost privacy."

She glanced around the bar, checking our surroundings. "The messages started about a year ago. First they were just strange. You know, the type you delete and forget about." She waved her hands in the air near her shoulder. "But then," she whispered as her eyes grew large, "then the person started mentioning personal stuff that only someone I knew would know."

"Like what type of details?"

"I wasn't always this put-together lady you see in front of you today." She fidgeted. "I made questionable decisions in college."

"That's part of the college experience," I said in a soothing tone. "You were a normal kid. Do you know anyone from college who would want to cause you harm?" I tapped the pen against the paper, wishing I could take notes.

She shook her head, slowly bringing her eyes to mine. "Not that I can think of, but obviously, there's someone." She said the last word with a look that let me know she thought I wasn't the brightest light bulb in the fixture.

"I promise I'll find the person." I dropped the pen on the paper. "I'll need access to your e-mail or any other means of communication they've used to reach you. Also, I'll need you to make a list of your known associates from college."

"I don't know." Her eyes shifted.

"Listen, Ms. True. The only thing that matters to me is solving your case and having you walk away satisfied."

She stared at me as her lips parted.

I cleared my throat, shifting in my seat. "A satisfied customer. That's what I meant." I settled back in my chair and smirked.

She swallowed hard as her eyes dipped to my hands. "Fine, Morgan."

Not only did her attitude ooze from her body, it slipped from her lips like it was part of her. There wasn't one piece of her that didn't exude class or social status. I was the grunt in this situation, and she didn't let that fact slide.

"I'll gather the information for you and have it delivered to your office," Race said as she looked back up at the motion of the approaching server.

The bartender placed Race's meal in front of her and asked if I wanted anything, but I waved her off.

"If you trust someone enough to bring it on your behalf." I stood, not letting her off the hook so easily.

"Fuck," she whispered. "I don't. I'll bring it to your office in a day or so. Where are you going?" She pursed her lips.

"I gotta get back to the office. You enjoy your lunch, Ms. True." I threw enough to cover the bill on the bar. "I look forward to working with you."

"I'll see you in a couple of days, Mr. DeLuca, but I'm more than capable of paying for my own lunch."

Jesus, she was a stubborn.

"I know, but I got it." I didn't add anything else as I started to stride away. "See you in a couple of days, Race," I said over my shoulder, taking in her beauty one more time.

Race True was used to getting her way.

I'd take every chance to remind her that I was in charge of this investigation. I might have been working on her behalf, but shit was going to go down the way I wanted it to go.

If I failed, her life could be ruined and I could be out of a job before I'd even started.

CHAPTER 6

SECRETS

RACE

For two days, I thought about nothing but *him*.

Morgan DeLuca was a cocky son of a bitch, but it didn't stop me from fantasizing about him. He was a bossy prick. I knew the type from working in the corporate world, but Morgan had a kindness in his eyes. I couldn't forget his face. His distinctive features would be forever etched in my brain. I don't mean just a guy I'd give a second look to when walking by.

He had the package.

Strong, chiseled face lined with dark stubble. Lips so full that I'd feel them long after a kiss had ended, muscles that bulged from places that shouldn't be legal, and eyes so blue that I could get lost in them for hours.

Oh, seriously.

I needed to get a fucking grip. It wasn't like it had been that long since I'd had sex.

Had it?

I'd been too busy trying to climb the corporate ladder to even bother with any type of relationship. Plus, the men I worked with just didn't do it for me. I liked them rough around the edges with a hint of beautiful underneath.

Like Morgan.

I walked into his office two days later with an envelope filled with possible suspects, copies of the e-mails, and other information I thought he needed.

Their receptionist spoke on the phone as I tapped my fingernails against the desk, waiting for her.

She kept holding up her finger. I looked at my watch, wondering how long I'd have to stand here.

She was a pretty little thing with long red hair that flowed over her shoulders. I hadn't paid much attention to her when I had been there the first time. Maybe she was Morgan's type—pretty and perky, with a natural beauty and casual attire.

"Sorry, ma'am. Can I help you?" she asked as she hung up the phone.

I righted myself, trying not to feel a pang of jealousy. "I'm here to see Mr. DeLuca."

"And you are?" Her eyes raked over my upper body.

Oh my God. Was she checking me out like I had her?

"Ms. True," I said with an overly sweet voice.

She pushed back from the desk, popped up from her seat, and left me alone in the waiting room.

Moments later, she returned with Morgan following close behind her.

"Ah, Race."

"Ms. True," I corrected him, pushing my shoulder back.

His eyes dropped to my chest as he smirked. "Let's talk in my office where it's more… private."

I followed him to his office, staring at his ass as we walked. When he held the door open, he barely left me enough space to pass by without touching him.

My shoulder brushed against his and his scent hit me. I closed my eyes, taking in the rich cologne he was wearing, trying to memorize it.

"Please sit." He pushed the door closed with his body.

I fidgeted with the envelope as he sat across from me, leaning back in his chair. He looked handsome today, but the stubble on his jaw had disappeared.

Pity, really, because I liked how it had looked.

He placed his hands flat on the desk as he sat. "What did you bring for me?"

I blinked twice, clearing my mind before I tossed the envelope on the desk, not trusting my voice.

He glanced down. "Did you bring everything I told you to?" He eyed me.

"Yes. It's my e-mails, including the first message I received. I erased it right after I printed it," I said, feeling foolish, tugging on the edge of my skirt.

"Why don't you tell me what it says?" He cocked his head to the side as he held the envelope without opening it.

I grimaced, squirming in my seat. "It's embarrassing, Mr. DeLuca."

"I don't care what it is. I'm not here to judge you. It would help if I knew what the real issue is. What the hell does this person have on you that is freaking you out so bad?"

Covering my face with my hands, I dug my index fingers into the corners of my eyes. "Oh, God," I whispered, trying to breathe through my nose.

"I promise not to laugh," he said in a steady, calm voice.

"I wish it were funny," I mumbled as my stomach started to knot and my eyes met his.

"Did you sell drugs?" The side of his jaw ticked.

I blinked rapidly at him. "Are you kidding me?"

He shrugged. "No. I'm just trying to come up with what the hell it could possibly be." He rubbed his chin, studying me. "Did you cheat?"

"No." I shook my head, absently stroking my throat.

"Get pregnant and not have the baby?" He raised an eyebrow.

"No. Jesus," I muttered, shaking my head.

"Let's start with something easier. What did the first e-mail say and why did you erase it?" He crossed his arms over his chest.

"I thought it was bullshit. So I just erased it and pretended it never happened." My chest tightened as I peered up at him. "Promise me you won't judge me?" I winced.

"Just spill it, Race. I won't think differently of you, unless you killed someone. We all have a checkered past."

I looked down at my lap. "I was seeing this guy for about a year. I thought we were in love." My stomach churned just from thinking about him.

"And?"

"One night we were partying and—God, this is so stupid." I shook my head, covering my face with my hands. "He convinced me to make a sex video as a memento of our time together."

"That's it?" he said. "It's nothing to be ashamed of."

I dropped my hands as I straightened. "But how many people get a threat that it would be sent to their boss?"

He slapped the desk. "Why didn't you tell me that? It's simple. Has to be your ex-boyfriend."

I shook my head, pursing my lips. "Nope. It's not him. He died after we graduated. But someone claims to have the video." I gave a long, low sigh.

"It's just a job, Race."

Rubbing my temples, I lifted my head to meet his gaze. "It's all I have, Morgan. I worked my ass off to get where I am today. There's no way in hell I'm going to let anyone destroy it."

"Hmm," he muttered, rubbing his chin. "Okay. It has to be someone who had access to your ex's things after he died. Tell me more about him."

"He was an engineering major, and we met sophomore year. Things between us heated up quickly, and we spent every waking minute together before we broke up at the end of my junior year."

He stared at me for a moment without speaking, continuing to stroke his chin. "Keep going."

"His name was Shane. I bumped into him one day while he was waiting for his cousin after class." I glanced out the office window, thinking about how much easier my life had been then.

"Do you remember his cousin's name?"

I shook my head, looking up at the ceiling. "They weren't close. His cousin was a jerk. I want to say it was something like Kyle or Tyler." I shrugged.

"It's a start, princess."

"I'm really sorry." I blew out a heavy breath. "I wish I could tell you more, but I never spoke to the guy."

"What happened with Shane? Maybe it'll help tie everything together."

I dragged my eyes to him. "I caught him in bed with my best friend. We ended that night. He was the last boyfriend I ever had. Is that good enough?" My cheeks heated as I averted my eyes.

"What a bastard," he growled. "It's okay. I'll see what we can dig up. What was Shane's last name?" he asked, grabbing his cell phone off his desk.

"McGovern."

"Hey, Thomas," Morgan said as he put the phone on his shoulder. "I need you to do some digging if you have time today, or put one of the other guys on it."

His eyes darted to mine. "Yeah. Race just told me about a possible lead. Dig in to Shane McGovern. He's deceased, but I think his cousin has something to do with the threats."

I thought Shane was a nice guy.

I thought he was the one.

It had been six years, and I still hadn't allowed myself to get involved with anyone. My ability to trust had been completely shattered.

"His name is Tyler or Kyle."

I stared at him as he spoke, taking a good look at him without being bombarded with questions.

His muscles bulged underneath the sleeves of the clean white dress shirt, which were rolled up, resting against the middle of his forearms. The top of his hair was longer than the sides, a little grown out since his time in the military. The strands were brown in color but verging on black, with each strand in place.

"You okay?"

"Yeah." I drew my knees together and dragged my eyes to his face. "Sorry. I was thinking about work. What did you ask?"

"I need your account information. I have copies of the e-mails, but the original messages hold information that's critical to tracking the source."

I sank into the chair, crossing my legs. "I don't give that out to anyone." God, I needed to get laid, or else I'd be squeezing my legs together every time I met with him.

He crossed his arms, narrowing his eyes. "I'm not just anyone."

I swallowed hard, wishing he'd been an ugly man closer to sixty instead of the man sitting in front of me. "Sorry. My mind is just elsewhere."

"Haven't we been over this before? I need the information." He leaned forward, clasping his hands together as he rested them on the desk. "Why bother hiring me if you won't trust me enough to do my job?"

"I'm sorry I'm being so difficult." I shifted in my chair, feeling both horny as hell and uncomfortable.

He clenched his jaw. "I just want to help you."

"I know. I'm sorry."

I never usually apologized for my behavior, but with him it was starting to become the norm.

I'd honed my bitch skills right after college.

I'd had to.

I'd walked into work the first day filled with happiness and feeling perkier than ever. I'd landed my dream job and was beyond excited. The cold reality of corporate America had slapped me in the face within five minutes.

From that day forward, I'd put on my best resting bitch face and perfected my go-fuck-yourself stare. I'd never let anyone treat me that way again. I'd become the woman I was that day in Morgan's office. Confident and powerful, and nothing in the world would make me change, including the cocksucker who was trying to blackmail me.

"I promise I will only look at the e-mails that pertain to your case. Your privacy is very important to me, Race." He spoke in a soothing tone.

I nodded, scooted forward in the chair, and grabbed a pen. On a piece of scrap paper that was lying nearby, I wrote down my e-mail log-in information and the website address he'd need to access the account. "Here." I pushed it toward him, giving him a weak smile.

"Was that so hard?"

I tilted my head to the side. "Be careful, Mr. DeLuca. I can still fire you."

"But you won't." He smirked.

I bit my lip, holding back the comment that sat on the edge of my tongue. I stood quickly, smoothing my skirt. "Call me when you figure out who's sending the messages, and I'll handle it from there."

He hopped to his feet and came around the desk before I made it to the door. "Once I have the name, I'll be in contact and *we'll* decide together the best course of action."

I stared up at him, my nostrils flaring. God, he smelled so good. I wanted to rub against him and find out if his entire body was as hard as it looked.

I had to snap out of it.

This is business, Race.

"Race?" He touched my arm.

I jerked my arm away. "Call me once you have a name and we'll discuss it then," I replied, backing up and bumping into the chair with the backs of my knees. I cleared my throat. "Damn," I mumbled.

"Would you like me to show you out?"

"No," I answered, wanting to put some distance between us. I needed to. "Thank you. I know the way." I turned around, warmth creeping up my chest and neck.

He'd turned me into a clumsy idiot.

"I'll see you soon, Race," he called as I walked out.

I didn't turn around as I closed the door. Then collapsed against it as I bowed my head.

"You okay out there?" he yelled from the other side of the door.

I winced, feeling lightheaded. "Just checking my messages!" I yelled. I pushed off the door and practically jogged out of the building.

When I walked outside, I could smell him still.

Damn it.

I'd have to spend the entire day smelling him, and it would be wasted with fantasies of Morgan DeLuca and his powerful body mingling with mine as I surrendered all control to him.

God, I was so fucked that it wasn't even funny.

I needed to get to the gym and run off some of the pent-up energy. Being near him had me feel something that I didn't like to feel.

Vulnerable.

CHAPTER 7

THE WEEKEND

MORGAN

It was early, and the sun still hung low as it streamed through the trees, casting shadows on the grass. Standing outside, I watched a wild turkey walk through the backyard as I sipped on a cup of coffee and thought about my day.

I went through a checklist of shit I needed to get accomplished. The top of my list: Race True.

It had been a week since our last meeting. I wanted to let her know that I had made headway in her case. I'd e-mailed her last night asking her to meet me tonight.

There were a few assumptions I'd made about Race during our two interactions. She didn't like to be bossed around, but I wondered if there was ever a time she gave up her control.

Race acted like she didn't like me much, but I could tell that she did. I'd caught her more times than I could count checking me out.

No matter what came out of her mouth, I knew that her attraction to me was as great as mine was to her.

She was strong, independent, and self-assured, but there was more to her. Something sweet and kind that had been tamped down over time was hidden under the surface.

Something inside me wanted to find out.

Plus, I needed a little fun. I lived in the sticks, and there wasn't a damn thing to do around here. The last thing I wanted to do tonight was sit by the fire and watch the stars pass overhead again.

I figured I'd meet with Race and see where the night took us. I wanted to dig deeper and find out what made her tick.

My phone chimed as I dumped my coffee into the sink, ready to start the day.

Race: I'll be there at 5 sharp. Don't keep me waiting.

I stared at the screen. I'd been waiting since I'd seen her a week ago. The real Race True would reveal herself tonight.

As I climbed into my car, I replied.

Me: Change of plans. Meet me at the Fly Bar around 5. I'll be waiting for you.

I tossed my phone on the passenger seat, revved the engine, and turned the radio up before I pulled away.

I could tell that this was going to be a kickass day and the best way to start the weekend.

THOMAS TOSSED a file onto his desk. "We need to hire someone else," he told James, avoiding eye contact.

James nodded, collapsing on the couch. "You're right. Any ideas who?"

"I don't know." Thomas dragged his hands through his hair.

"Morgan, you know anyone?" James asked.

I shook my head. "I don't know anyone around here."

"The only person I can think of is…" Thomas started, rubbing his chin.

"Don't." James waved him off.

Thomas slapped the desk, glaring at James. "Come on, man. So much time has passed. She's your wife now, for shit's sake."

"You know I don't like him, Thomas." James wrinkled his nose.

"James, get the fuck over it already. Sam and Izzy are only friends. She's in love with you, and Sam has a woman."

"How do you know?" James sat up.

Thomas kicked his feet up on the desk and reclined in his chair. "We've been in contact."

I looked between them both as they stared each other down. "Um, who the fuck is Sam?"

Thomas glanced at me. "Izzy's friend," he replied.

"Her old fuck buddy," James said, curling his lip.

"Oh." My mouth fell open.

"I'll never forgive him for putting her in danger, Thomas."

Thomas nodded, placing his hands behind his head. "I know, but we wouldn't have been able to save Angel and Izzy without him."

"We wouldn't have had to rescue Izzy if it weren't for his dumb ass."

Thomas glared at James. "You wouldn't be married to Izzy if it weren't for his mistake."

A small smile crept across James's face as he puffed his chest out. "True," he said as his cheeks filled before he blew out a long breath. "I hadn't thought about it that way."

"Stop being such an asshole all the time. Sam has the qualifications, and from what I can tell from his e-mails, he's not enjoying life in the Big Easy that much." Thomas rocked back and forth as he stared at the ceiling.

I glanced down at my watch. I had one hour until I had to meet Race. The minutes seemed to slow the later in the day it became.

"You said he's found a woman?" James asked with a wrinkled brow.

"Yeah. He said he's never been so in love. Her name's Fiona, and she's a nurse in the city."

"Hmm," James muttered. "Good to know he's moved on."

"Are you threatened by him? Think Izzy would leave you for him?" Thomas teased.

"No. Izzy loves me. She knows I'd never let her go without a fight."

Thomas glanced at him, giving him the evil eye. "If my sister wanted to leave you, I'd make sure she got her way. Remember, I'll always take my sister's side."

"You know I would never hurt her. I love the woman."

"I'm just sayin'. I love you like a brother, but she'll always be my sister."

"Thomas." James threw a ball of paper at him. "I wouldn't expect anything less."

"So, are we okay with Sam?" Thomas asked, his face softening.

"If you think we need him."

I pulled another file from the stack, ignoring their conversation. Maybe a little work would make the minutes tick by quicker.

"We do. He'll be a great addition to the team. Trust me. He's over Izzy."

"If you say so. I think Sam and I will have a little chat," James said, balling up another piece of paper.

"I'm sure everyone will want to have a little talk with him."

"You know that everyone may have a coronary if you invite him to be part of this business."

Thomas shook his head, rolling his eyes much like Izzy often did. "Dude, they'll get the fuck over it just like you."

James laughed. "Yeah. I'm sure they will," he said, tossing the paper ball in the air and catching it again. "Make the call and see if you can get him back here, then."

"I'll call him over the weekend. I told Angel I'd take her to dinner tonight. We're making Friday our date night."

"Aww, that's so sweet it makes my teeth hurt," James teased, smirking at Thomas.

"What are you doing tonight?" Thomas asked him, changing the subject. "Izzy is probably dying to go out."

"Oh, we have plans. We're hitting the club tonight."

I looked up and caught Thomas glaring at James with his lips set in a firm line.

"James." Thomas sat upright in the chair as his body grew rigid. "I told you I don't want to know a damn thing about it. Didn't I make myself clear?"

"Sometimes it sucks being married to your sister. I can never share the good stuff with you," James complained with a pained expression.

"You better not be sharing the *good stuff* with anyone," Thomas replied, not taking his eyes off James.

"What club?" I asked, interrupting their conversation.

Maybe I could get Race to head over there after the bar tonight. I'd love to see if she could dance. I hadn't been to a nightclub since I was too young to drink.

I missed so much shit from having been away for eight years.

"It's not your type of club." Thomas's eyes slowly moved to mine.

"What type of club is it?"

James chuckled. "It's not a nightclub."

"A strip club?" I asked, raising an eyebrow.

"Nope," James said in a clipped tone.

"I'm lost. Swingers club?" I turned around to face him fully. "Tell me you don't have my cousin sleeping with random dudes?"

"I'd never let anyone touch her but me," James glanced at me before glaring at Thomas.

"Then what? Can someone clue me the fuck in?"

James laughed louder. "Why don't I walk you out and I'll tell you. Thomas gets kind of testy when I talk about it." James rolled off the couch, climbing to his feet.

"Sure, man."

"Fucker," Thomas hissed.

"Dude, get the fuck over it, as you said earlier." James walked toward the door.

Thomas glared at James's back as his nostrils flared. "Have a good meeting, Morgan."

I stood, rubbing the back of my neck. They had such an interesting relationship.

"I'll see you on Sunday?" I asked.

Thomas glanced at me, finally cracking a smile. "Yeah."

"Good. I better run before I'm late."

"Don't do anything I wouldn't do," he said as he waved me away.

"Sounds like I want to do whatever James is doing," I replied, seeing the smile drop from his face.

When I turned around, James laughed, holding his stomach. "I can't believe you just said that."

"He was too damn serious." I wondered if Thomas was about to march out of the office and smack me upside the head. "So, where are you headed tonight?"

"Well," he said as we started to walk down the hallway, glancing over his shoulder, "it's a BDSM club."

My mouth fell open.

Oh my God. My little cousin was into that stuff?

"Like chains and whips?" I asked, trying to pick my jaw up off the floor.

James laughed harder, shaking his head as he slapped me on the back. "Something like that. It's more about dominance and submission."

"Izzy bosses you around a lot?"

"No, young man." James's face turned very serious. "I boss her around."

"But I thought…"

James grinned. "I'm the dominant in that relationship."

"Izzy is so bossy though." I gawked at him.

"She acts out all the time. I think she does it on purpose just so I'll punish her."

I swallowed hard, trying to wipe that mental image from my mind. "I don't want to know." I fully understood why Thomas didn't want to hear about it. "She's my little cousin, man."

"Not into it?" he asked as we walked into the reception area.

"I never said that. I just don't want to hear about you and Izzy there though."

"James, are you and Izzy going to the place that shall not be named?" Angel teased, standing from her desk and walking over to us with a playful smile.

"Yeah, Angel. Tonight's our night out."

"Lucky bitch." Angel laughed. "Mention that in front of Thomas?" She chewed her lip, peering down the hallway.

"I may have."

"Fuck," she said, shaking her head. "Now he's going to be all pissy."

James bent down and kissed her cheek. "I'm sure you can put a smile back on his face, darling."

"True." She practically skipped toward his office.

"If you ever want to go there, just let me know. I can introduce you to a bunch of people. I'm sure you'd be a big hit there," James offered.

"I don't know much about it." I couldn't say that my interest wasn't piqued.

"I can teach you the ropes."

"You know there's so much shit I can say with all the double meaning I'm getting from you." I shook my head.

"I know. Just think about it."

"I will." I pushed the front door open. "Catch ya Sunday, man."

"Have a good night," he said as he stood in the lobby, his chest inflated and his feet shoulder-width apart, a smug smirk on his face.

"Not as good as you, I'm sure," I replied as the door swung closed behind me.

If I went any longer without a little excitement, I might have to take James up on his offer.

Life was getting dull.

CHAPTER 8

CLUSTERFUCK
RACE

I stomped down the sidewalk to the Fly Bar, my high heels clicking against the cement, barely missing the divots in the shitty sidewalk. I swear to God, if I fell, I'd kick him in the balls for making me come to this dive.

I'm the one who hired him, not the other way around.

By the time I walked inside, my clothes were damp and my throat was so dry. I needed a gallon of water to quench my thirst.

I shook the thoughts of his balls out of my mind as I walked toward the bar. He was leaning back in his chair and sipping a drink, oblivious to my presence.

I cleared my throat as I approached. I needed to be tough or at least act like the pit bull I'd become known as. I couldn't show weakness.

Not to him or any other man or I'd be eaten alive.

I squared my shoulders, shifting slightly. "Mr. DeLuca."

"Race." He didn't turn around.

I took a moment and studied him. His shoulders looked broader than I had fantasized about this week. The corded muscles of his neck looked more taut and strained where they connected. I wanted to touch him, feel the strength underneath his clothes.

I pushed my thoughts away before I sat down, tossing my purse on the bar. "I'm here as ordered."

"Good." He stared at the television screen. "Cubs are doing crappy this year," he mumbled as he tossed some peanuts in his mouth. His stubble was back, giving him the look I'd come to love. The tiny hairs dotting his face moved together as if in a choreographed dance as he chewed.

I wanted to reach out and run my fingers across them to see if they were as coarse as they looked. "I hate baseball," I muttered, looking around the bar, trying not to stare at him.

"Such a shame." He glanced at me. "You're flushed. Are you okay?" He tilted his head, studying me.

I peered at him out of the corner of my eye. "It's hotter than hell outside. I just walked two blocks in high heels from where I parked to get here. Naturally, I'm flushed." I fanned myself, playing off the attraction I could no longer deny.

"Well, let's get you a cold drink to help cool you off." He snapped his fingers and the bartender walked toward us quickly.

I shook my head, blowing out a breath.

All he had to do to get service was beckon her, but me—I had to wait to be noticed.

"Thanks," I mumbled through gritted teeth.

She leaned over the bar, showing off her tits as she rested her chin in her hand. "Can I get you another?"

"I'll take a martini, extra dirty," I snarled.

She glanced at me and turned her attention back to him. "And you, handsome?" She batted her eyelashes, ignoring me.

Seriously.

It took everything in me not to reach over the bar and crack her. Women like her were the reason I had the problems I did at work.

"He'll take another, sweetheart," I snapped, the vein in my temple pulsing.

"Just another beer, Lisa."

She nodded, glaring at me as she began to walk away.

Fuck, he was on a first-name basis with her.

Does he like her?

"She's probably going to spit in my drink."

"You'd kind of deserve it if she does."

I looked at him, trying to remain calm. "I didn't need to see her tits hanging out. I just wanted to order a drink and speak with the man I hired about my case. We're here for work, not tits."

He stared at me, not saying a word as Lisa set our drinks down.

I ignored Lisa as she lingered a little too long. "This is a business meeting." I kept my gaze locked on his, wringing my hands together in my lap.

"I know, but you don't have to be so uptight. It's Friday, we're at a bar, and I'm in good company. Unwind a little. We have a lot to talk about," he said. Then his tongue darted out and swept across his lips.

My eyes dropped to his mouth. My skin flushed as his tongue swept across his lip. I fisted my fingers and kept them in my lap.

When his tongue disappeared, a grin spread across his face. "Can we drink to that?" he asked.

My eyes shot up to his. "To what?"

"Unwinding and good company?" He smirked, holding his glass up and covering his lips with the liquid.

"I'll drink to something cold and a tit-free zone." My eyes wandered down his arm to his biceps. I swallowed hard, noticing the way the T-shirt cut into his flesh.

"Fine." He chuckled. "To titless women and cold company."

I raised my glass, not realizing exactly what he'd said, and swallowed a mouthful.

As I set my glass down, I averted my eyes. "So, what news do you have to share with me?" I asked as I tapped the olive-laden toothpick against the rim of the glass.

He explained every procedure and boring fact he'd uncovered. At some point, I think I zoned out, because the next thing I knew, a new drink appeared in front of me.

Without interrupting him, I sipped my drink and listened to him babble on about tech bullshit. I let him go on and on and stared at his lips as they moved with each word. By the time I'd nearly finished the second drink, he was ready to give me the information I'd been waiting to hear.

"I tracked the IP address from your e-mail and used other methods to find the culprit. I was shocked to find that the IP originated not in New York, but from right here in Tampa."

I recoiled, my mouth falling open. "Tampa?"

He nodded, turning the beer in his hands. "Yeah. I was surprised. I thought, based on the information you gave me, that it would be from New York too. It doesn't mean that it couldn't be someone on the list you gave me, but we need to expand our search parameters."

"Fuck," I mumbled. "This is a complete clusterfuck." I bit my lip.

"I'll get it solved, Race. Don't ever fear that." He gave me a sweet smile. "Who here would want to harm your reputation?"

I winced as I shook my head. "The question is who doesn't."

His face fell. "Are you that unlikeable?"

"I work in a male-dominated industry. I'm not the type of girl to take shit from anyone," I said as I rubbed my face, barely having any feeling in my cheeks. "I've made a lot of enemies at work. No one likes a woman executive, especially the men who think they're better than I am."

"Is it really that brutal?"

"More brutal than you could ever imagine, Morgan," I said.

He stroked his lip. "Let's start with your competition at work first. Anyone who would be threatened by your success?"

I swirled the last of the liquid in my glass, trying to avoid looking at him. "I could fill a notebook." I started to feel sorry for myself. "I think I need another." I tipped my glass, noticing that it was basically empty.

God, I had so many haters.

Was it because I was a bitch? I hated the term. I thought I was tough, but I heard the murmurs in the office and the whispers about being the biggest bitch in the company when I walked by.

I never put much thought into people liking me. I didn't give a shit if I made friends, either. The only thing I cared about was being successful and doing a good job. Now, I had to watch my back and wonder about who wished for my failure enough to threaten me.

"Write down their names." He pushed the paper in front of me.

I jotted down twenty names, mostly males, of people I could picture wanting to see me crash and burn.

"Do you have any friends, with a list of enemies that long?" he asked, pushing the drink closer to me.

I dropped the pen and clasped my hands together. "Not really."

"Too busy trying to get ahead?"

For some reason, his statement made me giggle. "Yeah, something like that." I giggled again as I glanced at him.

He wrinkled his nose. "Maybe I should cut you off." He put his hand over the glass and started to pull it toward him.

I scowled and moved quickly, placing my hand over his. "Don't you dare. I need that drink. I earned that drink this week, goddammit."

"Whatever you say," he whispered.

The warmth of his hands had my thoughts drifting to the feel of them caressing my breasts. My face flushed as I realized he was staring at me.

"You feeling okay, Race?" The corner of his mouth twitched.

I cleared my throat. "Just a little warm from the weather still. I can't seem to cool off." I fanned myself, pulling on the collar of my blouse.

"Sure." He grinned, pulling his hand from my drink. "You want ice water instead? Maybe that would help cool you off." He raised an eyebrow.

"Nope, just another martini." I brought the glass to my mouth, watching Morgan over the rim as I polished it off.

I needed to get myself together.

I didn't have time to fantasize.

There was someone after me, and I needed to focus on that. One slipup and whoever had it in for me would probably pounce on my shit and use it as an opportunity to ruin me.

I made a mental note—all future conversations were to take place over the telephone.

One-on-one contact could be hazardous to my health.

CHAPTER 9
MARTINI MADNESS
MORGAN

"You're really purdy," she slurred with a lopsided grin, running her finger down my cheek.

"That's it. No more drinks for you." I dragged the glass away from her.

"No! I've only had three." She lurched forward, pulling the drink out of my hands. "I'm enjoying myself. I've had a bitch of a week and I deserve to let loose a little."

I held my hands up. "You've actually had four martinis, but anything you want, princess."

Her eyes grew into little slits. "I'm not your princess."

My cheeks hurt as I smiled. "I'm going to take you home now. I think you need to sleep it off."

"Last time I checked," she said before hiccupping, "you're not my daddy." A slow smile crept across her face. She scooted closer and whispered, "Unless that's your thing." She tried to wink, but both eyes closed, one after the other.

I leaned into her space, a breath away from her lips. "It's not my thing, but I'm happy to act out your fantasies. But I don't think you want to cross that line. Once you go there, there's no going back." I stared into her eyes.

"Oooh." Her eyes grew wide. "Is that supposed to scare me, Mr. DeLuca?"

I didn't move. "I'm just giving you fair warning. You've had a few drinks, and I won't take advantage of that. I'm just telling you how it is."

"You're full of yourself." Her warm, sweet breath caressed my lips as she spoke.

All I wanted to do was reach out, pull her face to mine, and kiss her full, beautiful lips. "I'm sure of myself and confident in my abilities, yes. That's entirely different than being full of myself." I licked my lips, testing her.

Her eyes dropped to my mouth as her lips parted.

"Another?" Lisa interrupted.

"We're good." I kept my eyes pinned to Race and waving Lisa off.

"Pfft," Lisa scoffed, stomping away.

Race glared in Lisa's direction. "She wants you."

Was she jealous?

"I don't want her."

"She's a sure thing though."

I leaned closer, leaving very little space between us. "I never liked easy."

"All men like easy." Her body swayed, moving so close our lips almost brushed.

Yep, she was definitely jealous.

I reached out, steadying her. "Maybe for a cheap fuck, but nothing more."

Her body jolted as someone bumped into her chair and she tumbled forward, her face landing against my chest.

"Watch it, asshole," I barked.

"Fuck off," the drunk asshole called out as he staggered away.

"Don't," she muttered into my chest, her hands squeezing my thighs.

I grabbed her arms, starting to stand.

"No," she yelled into my chest, trying to hold me in place. "Don't start a fight."

I grunted, staying in my chair. I didn't want the night to end already. I couldn't risk Race getting upset with me.

I grabbed her shoulders and tried to prop her upright.

"Gimme a minute," she said, her voice muffled by my shirt.

"He should apologize to you," I growled, trying to find him in the sea of people.

Her fingertips dug into my skin as she felt my thighs. She nestled her face deeper into my chest, her warm breath coming through my shirt.

"Come on, big girl. Let's get you home." I lifted her, pushing her against the chair.

"I'm not ready to go home though," she whined as her eyes tried to focus on me but crossed instead.

"I think it's best for us both if I take you home."

"I'll grab a cab." She straightened and started to tip sideways.

I shook my head and held her up with one hand. "I'd feel better if I took you home."

"I'd feel better with you in my home too." She leaned into my touch.

"Okay, Race. That's it." I stood, reached in my pocket for a fifty, and tossed it on the bar. "Come on, lightweight. Let's get you to bed."

"Mmm." She tried to stand. "Bed sounds perfect."

I held her by the waist as she stumbled out of the restaurant on unsteady feet. When we hit the sidewalk, I lifted her into my arms.

"Oh my God," she screeched, batting at my chest. "Put me down."

I held her tight as she started to wiggle. "You can't walk in those heels on this shitty, cracked sidewalk. You'll fall and break your neck. Stop wigglin', woman, or I'll drop you," I lied.

She weighed nothing, but I'd use it as an excuse to hold her for a little while. Relaxing, she laid her head on my shoulder.

"Are you smelling me?" she asked as we approached my car.

"No." I moved my face away from her head, knowing I'd been caught. I couldn't get enough of her sweet scent.

"Surrre." She snuggled into me.

"We're here." I looked down at her and smiled.

"I'm so tired," she mumbled, sagging closer to me, "and comfortable."

"I'm going to put you down now," I warned her before releasing my grip.

She slid down my body, letting her face press against my chest. I didn't bother to hide my amusement. I pushed her back and propped her against the car as I unlocked it and opened the door. "In ya go." I held her by the arm, making sure she got in without banging her head.

"You're really a nice guy," she said, blinking slowly, out of sync, as her body swayed.

"Let's keep that our little secret." I lifted her legs inside and closed the door. "Lord give me strength not to fuck this up." I glanced upward as I walked around the car. "I cannot sleep with her."

The hard dick inside my pants begged to differ, but I knew I couldn't take advantage of her. That was what I'd be doing if I let tonight get out of control.

I can't fuck her tonight.

CHAPTER 10
IT'S NOW OR NEVER
RACE

"Morgan," I whispered as he carried me inside my house.

"Yeah?" he asked, staring down at me.

"I'm not that drunk," I whispered.

"But you are, princess." He opened my bedroom door and carried me inside.

"I'm not," I argued, sliding my hand up his neck and holding his cheek, slowly stroking the fresh stubble.

"What are you doing?" His fingers dug into my hip.

"I want you." I brushed my lips across his chin.

"We shouldn't, Race," he told me.

"I don't care what we should do. Don't you want me?" I murmured against his skin.

He closed his eyes, inhaling deeply. "I do, but you're going to regret it in the morning," he said, giving me another chance to back out.

There was no way in hell I'd say no.

I wanted Morgan DeLuca.

After a week of fantasizing about nothing but him, I had my chance to make it a reality.

"I wanted you the moment I saw that big guy standing in the doorway, looking like he was ready to kick someone's ass. I wanted to grab your muscles"—I held his forearm, squeezing it gently—"taste your skin, and feel you inside me."

"I wanted you before I knew your name." He laid me down on the bed.

I looped my arms around his neck, bringing his face closer. "Kiss me, then," I murmured, moving my mouth toward his.

Hell yes.

His nostrils flared as his breath grew harsh. He crushed his lips to mine, breathing me in as he kissed me. His mouth was softer than I'd fantasized, with the perfect amount of tongue and lip.

I moaned into his mouth, feeling my body tingle all over. It was so cliché, but it happened.

I ran my fingers through his hair, dragging my nails against his scalp. He shuddered, moaning and driving forward into my mouth. His tongue swept inside, tasting me as I wrapped my legs around his back, holding him against my body.

He was hard. Rock hard. As he pressed against me, I ground my pussy against his length, loving the friction as our bodies rubbed together.

"Don't," he murmured into my mouth.

I smiled against his lips. "Why?"

"I want you so badly. I don't want this to be over before it starts," he growled.

I groaned, pretending to be sad, but his words made me wet. Morgan DeLuca was kissing me. He was in my bed, on top of me, and he wanted me. I unhooked my legs from his body, instantly missing the contact.

His hand slid down my body, finding my breast. As his finger swept across my hardened nipple, I felt the air leave my body. He inhaled it, bringing it into him.

"Morgan," I moaned with the last ounce of breath I had.

He grunted as his hand skated across my torso and found the edge of my shirt, slipping underneath. Tiny sparks skidded across my skin as his hand swept over my stomach on a collision course with my breasts.

My belly flipped when his finger stroked the edge of my bra. The warmth of his palm didn't stop the goose bumps that erupted across my skin.

When the front closure to my bra popped, my breasts sprang free.

"Mm." He cupped my breast, sweeping a thumb across my nipple. "So fucking soft."

As his hand vanished, I whimpered, missing the contact. Had he changed his mind? My eyes popped open as his lips left mine. My body stiffened as my stomach flipped and he sat back, resting his body on his heels.

He stared down at me with a sly grin. "Sit up," he whispered. "I need you naked."

Relief flooded my body. The butterflies that had been floating around my insides transformed. I sat up and started to lift my shirt.

He placed his hands over mine, stopping me. "No." He peered down at me. "I want to undress you."

My damn system went into overdrive. Morgan DeLuca wanted to undress me. He wanted to fuck me. If I'd been sober, I might have thought about the repercussions, but the alcohol helped me relax enough to share my true feelings.

I could no longer deny that I wanted him. I couldn't deny him any longer. I had hoped for a kiss when the night ended, but I was getting so much more.

I lifted my arms, glancing up at him as my shirt and bra were quickly removed and tossed to the floor. If I'd been sober, I might have covered myself up. Between the liquor and the burning in his eyes, I did the opposite. I soaked in the way he was looking at me as he slid my skirt down my legs.

"Morgan," I blurted out, feeling a bit self-conscious, but not about my body.

"Yeah?" he asked as he threw my panties and skirt in the same place as my top. As he crawled off the bed and removed his shirt, I couldn't help but stare.

His chest looked harder and bigger than it had underneath the formfitting T-shirts he wore. My eyes raked over every ripple of his six-pack and I felt my mouth water as he unzipped his jeans.

I knew I wasn't going to be disappointed, but seeing it and feeling it were entirely different. I'd felt him between my legs, hard and big. But it had been so long since I'd had sex, and I wanted Morgan so much that I wondered if it was a mirage. When his dick sprang free, I was secretly scared.

There's such a thing as too big. Especially when I hadn't fucked anyone in a year. I read somewhere that a pussy snaps back to virginal tightness after being empty for so long. I wouldn't be shocked if mine was sealed closed with cobwebs inside.

As I swallowed hard, he crawled onto the bed and settled between my legs, pressing his eight inches of hardness against me.

"I want to warn you," I said with a raspy voice.

He shook his head, leaning forward and placing his finger over my lips. "I don't want to know. Stop thinking so much."

"But I…" I mumbled against his fingers, staring up at him.

"Let it go. It doesn't matter." He placed a hand against my belly, coaxing me flat against the mattress. "All that matters is I want to bury myself so deep inside you that everything else disappears."

All thoughts vanished as his lips found my neck. When his teeth sank into my shoulder, I shivered. That was my spot. The special one that made my entire body burst into flames.

As his mouth carved a path of ecstasy down my torso, I closed my eyes and enjoyed the feel of him on me. His mouth sizzled as he stroked my nipple with his tongue, and I opened my legs wider, needing more.

"So fucking beautiful," he muttered against the skin right above my pubic hair.

The tiny hairs swayed as his breath drifted down. Each one moved, sending a tingle down my legs. I could feel the wetness between my legs. I didn't think I'd ever been so turned on in my life.

When he placed his mouth against my pussy, kissing me more fiercely than he had my mouth, I almost exploded. My body arched as the ache between my legs grew more intense.

"Morgan." My eyes rolled back in my head.

He mumbled against my clit and my body trembled in response. As he slipped a single, thick digit inside me, I fisted the sheets.

"Oh God." I relished the fullness I felt and moaned again.

He stroked my insides as his mouth caressed my skin. I needed to come so badly, but just as it was about to break free, he stopped. I lifted my head and stared at him, ready to scream.

"Not yet," he said. "Don't tense."

I tossed my head back against the pillow, and tried to relax. He slipped his fingers out as his mouth found me again. As he rubbed two fingers against my opening, I braced myself for impact, waiting for the familiar stretch I knew was coming from my unused body.

Inch by inch, he drove them forward, stretching me. To my surprise, I relished in the feel of the fullness. After a few more sweeps of his tongue against my clit, my body grew taut.

When his fingers curled inside me, rubbing my G-spot, I couldn't hold it together. I exploded. The orgasm ripped through my body as my pussy clamped down against his fingers. I couldn't breathe as the room spun. I never wanted the feeling to end.

I couldn't yell out or moan. I lay here stiff as my body rode out the wave of ecstasy crashing over me. As my body relaxed, I basked in the pleasure, and then he slipped his fingers out. Instantly, my core felt abandoned but deliciously used by him.

As he climbed up me, I sucked in air, trying to catch the tiny breaths I'd missed during the throes of passion.

"You got a condom?" He brushed his lips against mine.

Only me.

The condoms I had were older than the sour milk I had in the fridge. "No." I tasted myself on his mouth.

"I'm clean, Race. I was just tested and I haven't been with anyone since." He looked down on me with soft eyes.

I'd been on the pill to help control my cramps, so I wasn't worried about pregnancy. At my last checkup I got a clean bill of health, and I hadn't been with anyone besides my vibrator. I knew I was clean. "I'm clean too, and I'm on the pill," I announced, feeling his hard length settling between my legs.

"Is this okay? Do you trust me?" He rubbed the tip of his cock against my wetness.

In my infinite wisdom to get drunk and fuck Morgan DeLuca, I hadn't thought about protection. I'd assumed he was the type of guy who carried one around in his wallet, ready for action at a moment's notice.

Did I trust Morgan enough to let him fuck me without protection? Staring up into his eyes, I believed every word he'd whispered. I did trust him. I trusted him with my life and my body.

"I do," I whispered, swallowing down the lump that started to work its way down my throat.

Without another word, his cock poked my opening, and he drove the tip inside. The delicious ache returned, and I felt my body stretch to accommodate him. Every worry fell away, replaced by the need to feel him in my body.

When he shoved his dick inside me, I started to cry out as his mouth collided with mine and stole my breath once again.

His pelvis reared back and slammed into me. My back arched, driving him deeper as I stared, completely in awe.

Seeing each of his abdominal muscles ripple made my fingertips ache to touch them. I slid my hands down his back, finding the edge of the muscles and feeling them move underneath my fingers.

I stilled as he tugged on my legs, sat up slightly, and grabbed my ankles. I watched with wide eyes as he pulled them to the sides, creating a giant V.

His cock slammed, nothing stopping him from seating himself inside me fully. I closed my eyes, unable to watch as he stroked my insides.

"Open your eyes," he commanded in a stern but soft voice. "Look at me as I fuck you."

Without hesitation, I opened my eyes and watched him fuck me. Pleasure and lust burned in his eyes as he stared down at me and worked his cock in and out of my body. His lower body swayed as his shoulders remained still, and he gyrated his hips in the most delicious way.

"Touch yourself. I want to see you make yourself come as I fuck you."

I'd never touched myself in front of someone else, but with the way he was looking at me, I didn't hesitate. After sliding my hand down my midsection, I found my clit and began to caress around it.

The slickness from his mouth still lingered, making my fingers slide easily against my flesh. Every time he drove his cock inside, I moaned, moving my fingers closer to my clit.

Unable to resist, I circled my clit, letting the strokes grow harsher with each pass. I wanted this orgasm more than I'd needed the one he'd already given me. With the way his cock swept inside me, I couldn't wait any longer.

"That's it, baby. Come on my cock."

No one had ever dirty-talked me in bed before, and I suddenly realized its appeal.

I closed my eyes, concentrating on my strokes.

"Look at me when you come," he growled softly.

My eyes flew open as my finger brushed against my clit more deliberately. As he snaked his hips and I stroked between my legs, a burst of pleasure zipped throughout my body.

My toes curled; my head lifted from the pillow as my fingers faltered. The orgasm ripping through my system was greater than every previous orgasm I'd had in my life combined.

I tried to breathe, but I couldn't. My body locked, lungs and all, as the crest crashed down, pulling the life out of me. Morgan moaned, following me over the cliff and shuddering.

I clenched down, pulling him deeper as the aftershocks racked his body, matching my own.

We gasped for air, growing limp as he crushed his body against mine. My legs were stiff, aching from the unfamiliar position as they flopped on the bed. My body was spent, my mind hazy as I tried to bring the oxygen into my system.

When he rolled onto his side and pulled me against him, I went willingly. I nestled against him, sated, and drifted off to sleep with nothing on my mind but him.

CHAPTER 11

I'M SO FUCKED

MORGAN

I slept with my client.

No. I fucked Race True.

The memory of last night came back to me as I opened my eyes. The way she had called out my name, the sound of her moans, and the massive orgasm that had ripped through me made me smile.

Race True was more than I'd bargained for. I'd known the moment I saw her that I wanted her.

She stirred, pulling the comforter against her chest.

Sitting up, I watched her as soft snores fell from her lips.

There was so much about the woman I didn't know. The one thing I knew for sure was that I wanted to know everything about her.

Last night wasn't the end.

It couldn't be.

I'd been with plenty of women in my life, but no one like her.

I'm so fucked.

I slept with my client.

If she woke up and regretted last night, she could have me fired. Thomas would probably murder me if he found out. Anxiety gripped me.

"Morning," she whispered, stretching her arms.

"Morning, beautiful." I felt instantly relieved.

"I slept like a rock." She kicked the covers back, contorting her body like I'd never seen as she yawned.

"Me too."

Last night, I'd passed out cold, holding her body and twirling my fingers in her hair.

"Come here, Race." I patted my leg, wanting to touch her.

"You want me to suck your dick already?" Her eyes widened.

"If you're offering." I laughed. "I just want to talk."

"Oh," she mumbled before setting her head on my thigh.

I dug my fingers into her hair, stroking the yellow silk. "I want to talk about last night."

She rolled over and peered up at me. "What's to talk about?"

"Are you okay?" I swallowed hard, stilling my hands in her hair. "I mean, are we okay?"

"Do you think I regret it? Or that I was too drunk to know what I was doing?"

I bit my lip and took a deep breath. "Yeah."

"Morgan," she whispered, rubbing her cheek against my thigh, "I don't regret a minute of last night."

"Phew." I started to stroke her hair again, loving the way it fell through my fingertips. "Because it was fan-fucking-tastic."

She giggled, nodding her head. "It was, and I told you I wasn't drunk," she said, relaxing against me.

"You were pretty drunk."

"By the time we got back here, I'd sobered enough to know what I was asking for. I don't regret a minute of it."

I closed my eyes, resting my head against the headboard. "You shouldn't. I was pretty spectacular." I peeked at her with one eye.

"You're an asshole." She slapped my stomach. "Morgan," she whispered, tracing the contours of my abdomen with her fingers where her hand had just swatted.

"Yeah?" I asked, getting lost in the pattern.

"Do you think we should stop working together? I mean, can you still work on my case after what we did?" Her finger stilled, remaining flush against my skin.

I didn't answer right away as I thought about it. "Yeah, Race. I want to finish your case. There's nothing more that I want than for you to be safe." I knew that no one else would work as hard for her. "No one has more to gain by the case being over than I do."

She lifted herself, glancing up at me as the creases in her forehead deepened. "What do you have to gain, Mr. DeLuca?"

"You, Ms. True," I said matter-of-factly. "I have everything to lose if I don't get it right and more than I deserve if I solve your case."

"How do you know I didn't just want to sleep with you and be done?" She smirked.

"Come on, princess. I saw how you looked at me when you came with my dick buried inside you."

"Sweetie, that was lust."

I shook my head, pursing my lips. "That was more than lust."

"I like you, Morgan, but let's not go overboard." She laid her head back down. "Although, I'll admit, I do love your cock."

"It's a start," I lied, because although she couldn't say the words, her body betrayed her. "You can lie to yourself all you want, but I know the truth." I winked at her.

"I have to go into the office," she muttered, closing her eyes.

"It's Saturday."

"So? Are you going to work today?" She stroked the V on my abdomen.

"Yeah. After I find a place to live."

"See. We're both workaholics," she teased, raking her fingernails across my skin.

"Only because I want to solve your case."

"Good answer."

I glanced at the clock, realizing I had an hour. "I have to go, but I don't feel like moving."

"Mmm," she mumbled.

"I have an appointment with my realtor."

She sat up. "You better go, then." She let the sheets fall from her body as she smirked.

I stared at her chest as my morning boner grew larger, ready to break off. "I have a little time." I leaned forward. "Do you?" I murmured against her skin.

"I can make time."

"I see that look in your eye," I told her, sweeping my tongue across her neck.

"Morgan," she whispered, her voice breathy, "just fuck me and shut up."

I bit down on her neck. "I like a woman who knows what she wants."

"Shh." She palmed my dick. "Less talking."

I fucked Race one more time before I left. I didn't know if it would be the last time I'd have her. I memorized every angle, storing it away for later.

I walked outside on unsteady legs, perfectly spent.

Things had shifted between us, and my life seemed to be falling into place.

Maybe I was reading more into it than I should've been. But there's a look I know, one that conveys every emotion that's left unspoken. I saw it in her eyes.

She wanted to know me as much as I wanted to find out who the real Race True was, and it made me happy.

I walked down the driveway and climbed in my car, savoring the memory of her calling my name.

Life was good.

CHAPTER 12

HOW DID THAT HAPPEN?

RACE

Oh my God. I slept Morgan DeLuca.

Actually, he'd fucked me, and I wasn't ashamed to admit that I'd loved every minute of it.

He'd cuddled me too. Held me in his arms all night, and I fucking loved it.

"What's that grin about?" Cara asked as she walked into my office.

"Oh, nothing." I rocked back and forth in my chair.

"I've worked for you long enough to know you." She cocked an eyebrow as she started to tidy my desk.

Cara had been assigned to me my first day on the job. As I'd climbed the ranks, she'd come with me and remained forever loyal. I didn't think it could be possible to have a better secretary than her. More importantly, she was my best friend, and I always confided in her.

She glanced at me. "It's that man, isn't it?"

"Who?" My voice squeaked.

"You've had two meetings now with that man from the investigation company."

"He's nice." I fidgeted with my pen.

"Sure. Why are you so red now that I've mentioned him?" She tilted her head, smirking.

"It's hot in here."

"It's not. So, you like him?" she asked. "Have you kissed him?"

"Cara." I tried not to smile.

She shook her head and giggled. "It doesn't matter. Whatever he's done, I like seeing you happy."

"Yeah." I couldn't look her in the eye.

"Don't forget what today is." She grabbed a stack of folders from the outgoing bin on the bureau.

"I know." A knot formed in my stomach.

"Did you want me to grab some flowers for you?" she asked, stopping at the door.

"No. I'll do it." I shook my head. "Why don't you leave early today? There's no reason for you to work on the weekends with me, Cara."

"I like spending time with you, Race. You know that. My kids are grown, my husband passed, and I can't just sit at home all day. I'd go crazy."

"Well, I love having you around, Cara. You're more than just my secretary."

"I know, kid. I know. I think you should take the day off too." She held the door open as she balanced the stack of files in her arms.

I glanced over my desk, realizing I didn't have anything else to do. "I'll head out soon."

"See you Monday," she said before leaving.

"Monday," I repeated, grabbing my purse and following her into the lobby.

———

TODAY WAS the anniversary of my father's death.

Where did fifteen years go?

Even though time had passed, the soul-crushing sadness of losing my dad hadn't diminished. Every day I thought about him. There were times when I missed him more than others, but there wasn't a moment that passed that I didn't long to be in his arms.

Tears fell from my eyes, plopping on the grass as I stood in front of his grave. "Daddy," I whispered as I collapsed into the grass. "I'm so sorry," I wailed, covering my face. "I should've come sooner."

As each year passed, I came to visit less and less. The guilt I experienced when I came sucked the life out of me. I couldn't spend my weekends here, feeling the weight of his death on my shoulders.

He had been my entire world, and the only one in my family who had shown me unconditional love. He'd brought me everywhere with him, much to my mother's dismay. We'd secretly snuck to the racetrack on weekends, enjoying our time out of the city together.

My dad had been my best friend. There was nothing I'd loved more than being his little girl. When he died, a piece of me was buried with him.

My mother grew more hateful with each passing day. By the time I'd gone to college, we'd stopped speaking. Really, I'd stopped talking to her because I couldn't take her bullshit anymore. Somehow she'd come to the conclusion that it was my fault my father had died.

He died instantly one day after work when he'd come to pick me up from school. She'd said that his need to make me happy by not requiring me to take the school bus was the cause. Not the semi that had plowed through the back of his SUV, but me. In her mind, I was the one who killed him.

After placing the flowers on his grave, I pushed myself up and kissed his headstone. "I love you, Daddy," I whispered, another wave of sobs breaking free.

I would've given anything to hear him call my name again.

I knew loss.

It was part of me.

My father was my first love—and the first one to leave me behind.

Everyone left me.

I couldn't let myself feel anything for Morgan. I didn't think I could take another heartbreak without losing myself completely in the blackness.

CHAPTER 13

FAMILY DINNER

MORGAN

"How's work going?" Uncle Sal asked.

"Good. Good."

"He's been a huge help, Pop." Thomas gave me a brief nod. "We really needed him. Hell, we still could use a few guys to help pick up the slack."

"It's always good to be in demand, son."

I should've felt guilty about Friday night, but I didn't. I didn't regret a moment I'd spent with Race.

"Yeah. James and I are throwing around a couple names of people we could recruit to join us." Thomas put his feet up on the coffee table.

"Anyone I know?" Uncle Sal raised an eyebrow.

"You do, but I don't want to talk about work today. I'm still trying to convince James that he's the right man for the job."

"Sam?"

James mashed his hands together and gritted his teeth. "You know I hate him."

Thomas looked over at James and grinned. "We've already been over this."

"Have you talked to your mom today, Morgan?" Auntie Mar walked into the living room.

"Not today. Something happen?" My heart began to beat erratically.

"She said she'd be here by next weekend." She smiled as she sat on the arm of the couch.

"Great," I said in a quiet voice through closed teeth.

"You're a horrible liar." Auntie Mar hit me with the kitchen towel.

"I love her, but the woman is so overbearing sometimes."

"We're mothers. We're supposed to be."

That was always the excuse my mother gave me. It was their job to be annoying and nosy as hell.

"But it would be nice if she could let go just a little."

Aunt Mar laughed. "Never going to happen," she said before she stood and headed back to the kitchen.

Joe nudged me with his elbow. "You just have to learn how to handle them."

"Yep," Mike agreed from the chair in the corner, nodding slowly.

"Pretend like you're listening and learn to ignore her. That's what I do with Ma." Anthony pulled his wife, Max, into his lap.

"I can hear you," Auntie Mar yelled from the kitchen.

"Ma isn't that bad," Thomas added.

All eyes turned to him.

"That's because you were gone so long. If it weren't for that, you'd get the same bullshit we all do." Joe's eyes darted toward the kitchen.

"Oh, please. She just loves us." Thomas puffed his chest out.

"Lies. All lies." Izzy slid between James's legs on the floor.

I felt envious of the Gallos.

They had each other.

I'd been alone my entire life, with no brothers or sister to tease or have my back. I missed my ma, but I'd never admit it. And if I was being entirely truthful, I wished Race were here with me.

"What's wrong?" Joe asked.

I blinked a couple of times and focused on him. "Me?" I scrunched my nose.

"Yeah, you."

"Nothing, man."

"Something's on your mind, cousin. Spit it out," Joe said, running his finger across his lip.

I scrubbed my hands across my face. "Just thinking about how lucky you are to have each other."

"Dude, it must've sucked being an only child," Mike chimed in, shaking his head as he winced.

I shrugged. "At times, it was great. I didn't have to share shit with anyone, but then at other times…"

"Yeah. It has to be lonely," Mike said.

"I call bullshit. I'd love to be an only child," Izzy blurted out. "I'd want all the attention. Plus, I wouldn't have had to put up with your asses my entire life."

"Izzy." Anthony gave her a nasty look, "Please stop with your crap. You've been treated like an only child for years. You're a girl, and that's afforded you a pretty charmed existence."

"That's such a crock of crap." She rolled her eyes.

In the other room, the older kids played in the new playroom Auntie Mar had made for them. The Gallos were creating a small army. Izzy had twin boys about six months before her wedding and named them Rocco and Carmello, but everyone called him Mello. Thomas and Angel had a little boy, Nick, who was just learning to walk. Anthony, Joe, and Mike each had little girls named Tamara, Gigi, and Lily respectively.

"I better go get Nick up so he's ready to eat, baby," Angel said to Thomas before kissing him on the cheek and heading upstairs.

"James." Izzy glanced at him.

"What?"

"I need help carrying those two beasts you helped create." Izzy stood and put her hands on her hips.

"I got ya. I'll get them both, love. You rest." He pulled her back down onto the floor and nuzzled his face into her neck. "I love waking the boys up," he mumbled against her skin.

"Nah. I want to help you." She giggled as she climbed to her feet and pulled James with her.

The living room thinned quickly. I took it as a cue to go see if

Auntie Mar needed any help. The least I could do was pitch in, since she had been gracious enough to invite me.

"Hey, Auntie Mar." I walked into the kitchen, finding her spooning the meatballs into a giant bowl. "Let me help you."

"You're such a dear, Morgan." She turned and gave me a magnificent smile. "Can you finish this while I get the gnocchi ready?"

"Hell yeah." Gnocchi was my favorite. The shit sat in my stomach like a ton of bricks, but it was amazingly soft.

She handed me the spoon. "You're really a good man. You've changed so much since you were a teenager."

"I hope so. I was a punk back then."

"We all have to grow up sometime. You just took the harder road." She bent over and pulled a strainer that could fit at least three pounds of pasta in it without a problem out of the cupboard.

"Joining the army was the best thing for me. My mom would disagree, but I don't know if I'd be alive today if it weren't for them."

She placed the strainer in the sink and turned toward me. "Morgan." She placed her hand on my shoulder. "Your mom knows it was the best thing for you. She just likes to complain. Plus," she added as she turned her attention back to the pasta, "it's the job of a mother to make her children feel guilty." She was surrounded by a cloud of steam as she dumped the boiling water and pasta into the sink.

I dropped the last meatball in the bowl and watched as she shook the water out of the pasta. "You're all crazy."

"We'd be boring if we weren't. Be a dear and go set those meatballs on the dining room table. We're just about done here."

"Yes, ma'am." I saluted her.

"Smartass. You're all the same."

"Touché, Aunt Mar." I wished I had used a potholder to carry the damn bowl.

For the first time in forever, I felt like I had a family again. I belonged somewhere. Although they were my cousins, I loved them like we were more. We'd spent our youth together, tearing shit up and causing trouble in the neighborhood.

That was until Joe and I had gotten into just enough trouble to make Auntie Mar and Uncle Sal pack the kids up and leave town. It was the worst feeling ever.

I stared around the dining room table, looking at each of the chairs, and said to myself, "I'm a lucky son of a bitch." I left out the bit about Race.

Just then, Aunt Mar yelled, "Dinner!" as she carried the gnocchi into the dining room with the potholders I'd decided not to use.

"Thanks," I said as I turned to her.

"For what?" She set the bowl on the table.

"For being my family." I gave her a kiss on the cheek.

"Who knew you were such a softy, Morgan?"

"This doesn't go any further. Got me?"

"Too late," Joe said as he walked in the room. "I'm going to buy your ass a purse to carry around all those feelings in."

"Don't you start, Joseph," Aunt Mar warned him. "You aren't as tough as you look, son. People in glass houses—"

"Yeah, yeah," he interrupted. "I got ya."

"What did I miss?" Izzy asked as she walked in behind Suzy, carrying Mello. Or maybe it was Rocco. I couldn't tell them apart yet.

"Nothing, Izzy. Let's eat." Joe pulled the chair out for his wife.

One by one, everyone entered the dining room, taking their spots at the table. Even I had my own chair. I was a full-fledged member of the family.

This time, I wouldn't do anything to fuck it up.

CHAPTER 14
I'M TOTALLY FUCKED
RACE

I hated Sundays.

They were useless.

I'd always planned to spend my Sundays on the beach, sipping wine, and reading a good book, but it never happened. Typically, I sat home, did laundry, and worked in my pajamas.

I hadn't been able to get Morgan off my mind. I knew I shouldn't want to be with him, but I wanted it more than anything in the world. I wouldn't survive him. I knew that.

When I checked my e-mail before settling down to watch a movie, what popped up on my screen rattled me.

Race,

He can't help you. No one can. You're in my crosshairs and I'm coming for you when you least expect it.

My heart started to pound as I glanced around, wondering if someone was outside my house. I grabbed my phone and texted Morgan.

Morgan: I'll be right over. Stay put.

Me: No. I'm fine. I just wanted to make you aware.

I unlocked and relocked my French doors to the back deck as I waited for his reply, and then I peeked through the blinds, trying to see if someone was outside.

Morgan: I'm coming over, Race. I need to do a perimeter check. I'll bring the others to help and stay with you for a while. No lip.

I didn't expect him to rush right over. I felt guilty for pulling him away from whatever he was doing tonight.

Me: No. There's no one here. I'm fine. Really.

Morgan: Stay inside, lock the doors, and stay away from the windows. I'll be there in twenty.

Duh! I mean, seriously. Did he think I was going to stand outside and sing a song?

Me: Yes, sir.

I turned the lights off and tried to distract myself while I waited.

I settled on the couch, watching *The Bachelor* and the train wreck that happened every episode. It was always good for a laugh. I started to drift off during the rose ceremony, my eyes feeling heavy and starting to sting.

My doorbell rang and I jumped.

"Race!" Morgan yelled as he knocked on the door. "Race, answer the goddamn door."

"Coming." I stomped toward the door. I checked my reflection in the mirror. My eyes were red, with bags underneath. Great. My pajamas were okay, but they were nothing he hadn't seen before. Really, it was just a pair of shorts and a tank top. I wasn't about to make it look like I'd made an effort.

This was business, I reminded myself as I reached for the door, not sex.

"Race. I'm going to bust this door down if you don't open it." He pounded on the door this time.

The man was such a spaz. "What the hell?" I threw my hands up after I opened the door.

His eyes were on fire as he breathed hard. "What the hell? That's all you have to say?" His hands rested on the frame with two men behind him.

"Well, yeah. I mean, I'm fine, and there's no reason to threaten to bust down my door. I yelled 'Coming.'"

"I wouldn't let a door stand between me and your safety." He gave me a halfhearted smile.

"I'm fine. I haven't been murdered." I opened the door wide enough to let them in.

"Not yet," the tall guy said, following Morgan into the house.

"Jesus. You're all such Debbie Downers," I said as I closed the door.

"We're realists, Ms. True. You have threats against you, and we are taking them very seriously."

"Fine. I'm worried too. You're right. But we don't have to go over the top here."

While I stood there, half dressed, redness crept up my chest.

I'd never been that girl.

"Over the top would've been if we came in with our guns out, ma'am," the tall man said.

I shook my head as I walked back toward the couch. "Men. You're all crazy." I collapsed onto the cushion.

"We're going to survey the perimeter while Morgan checks the house. We'll be out of your hair shortly," Thomas reassured me before he walked toward the back door.

"The sooner the better." I crossed my arms over my chest.

"I'm staying," Morgan told me as he set his feet shoulder-width apart, puffing himself out like a cat.

"No, you're not." I shot up and moved toward him.

I wanted him to stay—not because he had to, but because he wanted to.

He peered down at me. "Yes. I. Am."

"Why?" I glared at him.

His eyes darted toward my chest, and my eyes followed. For the love of God, my arms had pushed my breasts up, putting them on full display.

When I brought my eyes back to his, he was still gawking at my chest. Any embarrassment I'd had vanished. Morgan DeLuca wanted seconds. Or would it be thirds?

"Because I won't be able to sleep tonight if I think someone is attacking you."

"I have a gun."

He closed his eyes, pinching the bridge of his nose. "That doesn't put my mind at ease, princess."

I cocked my head. "Why? 'Cause I'm a girl?"

"No, Race. Let me check out the house and have a quick meeting with the guys, and I'll explain it to you."

I rolled my eyes, turning my back to him. Before I took two steps, his hand wrapped around my arm, dragging me backward.

"Excuse me," I snapped, staring at his hand.

"Listen, Race. Drop the attitude for five fucking minutes. I'm here to protect you. You can wait." He touched my chin, raising my eyes to meet his glare. "Don't get all huffy and stomp off like a child. Please let me do my job without any backtalk, woman."

"Go," I said as I shooed him away. "Do your job." I cringed, knowing that it sounded crappy.

He released my arm as his jaw tightened. "Stay here." He pointed to the floor.

I crossed my arms again. "Fine."

He marched off, moving from room to room.

Why in the hell did Morgan DeLuca make the strong business-woman in me disappear?

When I was around him, I turned into a bitch, a drunk, or a loose-lipped woman.

"Find anything good?" I called out, still standing in the same spot.

"Nope." He stalked into the kitchen, slamming the back door as he left.

I tiptoed to the kitchen, opened the blinds, and watched them. They were huddling together in the sand. No matter how hard I tried, I couldn't make out what they were saying to each other. When they broke apart and Morgan started to walk back up the steps, I ran back to my spot.

When he walked into the room, he stared at me with his eyebrow cocked. "You stayed?"

"Yes."

He narrowed his eyes at me. "Doesn't matter. The perimeter is clear and no one is inside the house. The guys have gone back home."

"Can I move now?"

"Yes."

I turned my back, moving faster this time, and fell on the couch. "I could've told you that no one was here. You didn't need to bring the guys over to check. Now that I'm safe, you can go. Your job doesn't entail guarding me." I grabbed the remote, flipped through the channels, and tried not to look at him.

He sat down, turning to glare at me. "I'm staying with you."

I stared back. "Why? You just said no one is here."

"I want to make sure you're safe tonight."

"Isn't that going above the call of duty?"

He pinched the bridge of his nose, letting out a long, hard breath. "Race," he said, peering up at me, "you're more than a job to me. Didn't the other night mean anything to you?"

"Well, I…" I mumbled, feeling like a complete asshole.

He leaned forward, resting his elbows on his knees and raking his fingers through his hair. "It meant something to me. You weren't just a one-night stand. And until I know who's after you, I'm not chancing anything happening to you. We've been over this before. Can you stop being a hard-ass for five minutes?"

"I'm sorry." I scooted closer to him. "I was going to watch a movie before bed. Do you want to watch a movie?" I asked, swallowing hard and trying to avoid temptation.

"Whatever you want." He leaned back into the couch cushion.

"*Stepmom* or *P.S. I Love You*?" Luckily for him, I had them both on DVD.

"Which one has the most action?"

I threw my head back against the cushion and smirked. "*P.S.* has more death."

"Sounds good."

"Popcorn?" I got up from the couch just as the previews started.

"Want my help?" He started to stand.

I pushed him down. "I got it. You relax."

I tossed the popcorn in the microwave and stared at it as it turned, popping slowly.

I wanted him again. Having him this close, I wanted to feel his skin against me as his mouth covered mine.

Lost in thought, I stood on my tiptoes and reached for a glass bowl. I touched the bottom edge, trying to coax it out. As if in slow motion, the bowl came barreling out of the cupboard and began to fall.

"Fuck." I flinched as I tried to grab it. As it hit the edge of the counter, it shattered, crashing to the floor in pieces, shards of glass trailing in its wake.

Before I could blink, Morgan was standing by my side, pulling me away from the wreckage of the bowl.

I jumped, yelping loudly. "Jesus, you scared the shit out of me."

"Sorry." He lifted me away from the glass.

"Damn it," I whispered as I caught a glimpse of my hands.

He pulled my hands closer. "Let me see."

Instead of pulling back, I gave in.

Blood had already began to pool in my palms and dripped from the edges.

Why did I have to try to catch the fucking bowl?

"The cuts don't look too deep." He brought my hands closer to his face and inspected them. "We need to clean the wounds and stop the bleeding."

"Are you a doctor now?" I tried to choke down the tears that were threatening to fall.

He grabbed my waist and hoisted me onto the countertop. Shocked by his strength, I just gawked at him. We stared at each other as he brushed his thumbs against my stomach, causing my insides to flip.

"Just sit there and look pretty while I bandage you up."

He thinks I'm pretty.

I felt my cheeks flush.

His muscles moved under the edges of his T-shirt sleeves, and I became transfixed by their rhythm, squeezing my legs together. "This may hurt a little." He rubbed the soap into the paper towel.

I winced, trying to pull my hands back. "Isn't there a better way to do it?" I asked.

He stepped forward, almost standing between my legs.

My heart stopped and my breathing faltered.

"I just need to clean the blood away and make sure there are no shards inside the wounds before I bandage them."

"What are you doing?" My eyes grew wide.

He glanced up and grinned. "I'm standing where I know you can't kick me in the balls."

I sighed, resting my knees against his sides.

Might as well enjoy myself.

He touched my hand and pulled my fingers flat. I grimaced, waiting for the soap to sting. As he wiped my palm, the coolness of the water felt better than I'd expected.

Maybe my brain was fuzzy from him being so near, but I didn't feel pain. My belly fluttered as he touched me.

If I leaned forward just a little bit more, I could kiss him and smell him.

"Did you just sniff me?" He peered up, holding my hand in his.

"No." I squirmed, squeezing my knees against his sides and instantly regretting our position.

"You smelled me." He looked back down with a grin.

I swallowed hard, feeling wetness pool between my legs.

"Leave your hand open to dry." He opened my right hand and repeated the process.

"Are we good?" I asked as he finished wiping the last cut. I was ready to hop down and put a little space between us.

"Yeah, but we need to bandage them up first. They're still bleeding, and if we don't, you'll get it everywhere."

"Great." I rolled my eyes. Why the fuck had I made my interior white?

"Your hands are going to be sore tomorrow." His hands rested on my thighs, scorching my skin. "Where's your first-aid kit?"

I should've shaved. "Fucking fabulous," I muttered. "In the master bathroom." I motioned toward the hallway.

"Stay put," he commanded, pointing at me.

I hunched my shoulders, placing my palms up. "Where am I going? I'm not bleeding all over my place."

He rubbed his forehead as he walked down the hallway and out of sight.

"Get your shit together, Race," I told myself before inhaling a long, deep breath. "You're a strong woman. You're an executive. You don't have time for romantic entanglements." I blew the air out of my lungs and closed my eyes. "We'd never work anyway," I told myself as I thought back to Friday night.

"What wouldn't work?"

I jumped and closed my fists. "Damn it!" I shrieked as pain sliced through my hands.

"I didn't mean to scare you," he said, setting the first-aid kit on the counter.

"I'm just jumpy," I lied as I peered down at my hands, bouncing my heels off the cabinet. "I'm sorry."

"For what? I'm the one who scared you."

I held my palms out, showing him the mess I'd made. "You're going to have to clean them again." I tried to hide my smile, 'cause in reality I'd welcome him between my legs.

"It's not a big deal, princess," he said in a calm voice, shrugging.

"Tell me more about yourself, Morgan," I said, trying to think of something other than his body and mine together, naked, sweaty.

Fuck me, I was hopeless.

"Not much to tell, Race. I told you a lot about myself the day we met."

"No, you didn't. I want to know more than you were in the army. Are you from around here?" I knew he wasn't, but damn it, getting information from him wasn't easy.

"I grew up in Chicago and just moved here right before I started working on your case."

"I was there once. It's an amazing city. The shopping is spectacular."

"I guess so. I'm not much of a shopper." He threw the bloody paper towel into the sink.

"Yeah. I can see that."

"Is that a dig?" He glanced up at me with a gleam in his eye.

I shook my head. "No. You're just a man." God, I was such an asshole sometimes. "What brought you to Florida?"

"I came for a wedding and my cousin offered me a job."

"Which one is your cousin?"

"Thomas." He opened the first-aid kit and grabbed a bandage.

"I can see the resemblance." They were both beefy men and drop-dead gorgeous. "Why did you join the army?" I knew I was always tight-lipped about my past and life, but getting information out of him was like pulling teeth.

"I got into some trouble as a kid. Judge told me I either join up or spend some time behind bars."

"What did you do? Rob someone?" I pursed my lips.

"Something like that," he mumbled.

"Huh."

"I haven't always been a good guy, Race," he said as he covered my hand with the bandage.

"We all do dumb stuff when we're young."

"You're still young."

"When we're younger." I emphasized the last word. "What exactly did you do? I want to hear this."

"Why do you want to know?"

I bit the inside of my mouth and thought about how to answer his question. "I'm just making small talk."

"I'd rather—"

"Wait," I interrupted him. "I just want to know who you are as a person. I promise not to judge you."

"You've been judging me since the day you met me."

A lump formed in my throat. "I'm sorry. I'm not going to judge you. I just want to know more about you. We all have a past, Morgan."

"I'll tell you something if you share some of yourself with me."

"Me?" I asked, a little terrified.

"Yeah. It's only fair, Race."

"Okay. You're on, but you go first." I chickened out. I wanted to hear his big, dark secret about his past life before I'd divulge anything about myself.

He started to slather antibiotic salve across my palm, but I felt nothing, too distracted listening to him. "I got mixed up with the wrong kids in high school. It started off with small things and just being bored. Eventually, our reputation made it to some higher-ups in the neighborhood."

"Higher-ups?" I swallowed hard.

"Yeah. Chicago still has a lot of organized crime. One day, we ripped off a truck full of goods."

"A truck?" I looked down at him with my mouth hanging open.

"An entire truck filled with electronics. We needed to sell the shit quick so we wouldn't get caught. The fence we used told someone, who then told someone else, and it got back to the man running things in our neighborhood."

"That doesn't sound very good." I stared down at his hands as he touched me with such tenderness that I became fixated.

"We were scared shitless at first, but once we met with the guy, we were excited. We were kids and dumb as hell, but we thought it was a great opportunity. Naturally, we were wrong, and we ended up arrested about a year later."

"That doesn't make you a bad guy, Morgan. It makes you a stupid kid."

"Nah, baby. I'm a total asshole. I didn't join the military out of some code of honor. I signed up because I didn't want to sit in jail." He pulled my hand up to his face and blew on the wetness.

Shivers ran down my spine as his breath skidded across my skin. "That doesn't make you an asshole."

"No." He grinned. "I'm just one naturally. I'm not the nicest person."

I started to giggle. "Morgan, I'm a bitch. I embrace that side of me. As long as you know who you are, the rest doesn't matter. I don't think you're an asshole anyway."

"I have my moments, Race." He opened the bandage and placed it over my palm, covering the wound.

"We all do." I watched as he carefully covered my cuts, enthralled by his movements and the feel of him against me.

"All done." He patted my knees and rested his hands on my legs.

"Thank you," I whispered, trying to close my fists.

Crap. I'd be useless like this tomorrow.

Everything would be a fucking chore.

"What's wrong?" He tilted his head.

"I was just thinking." I bit my lip as I stared at him. "Tomorrow, my hands are going to hurt. What a pain in the ass."

He nodded as his thumb started to stroke the side of my kneecap. "Yeah. It'll take a few days until the pain subsides."

"Great." My body sagged. "This is the last thing I need."

"Take the day off tomorrow. It's probably best you don't go into work tomorrow anyway."

"Morgan, I can't skip work."

"When was the last time you had a day off?" He raised an eyebrow.

"Never. I'm a workaholic."

"Well, tomorrow, you're going to play hooky. With the new threat against you, it's better not to chance it." He squeezed my knee, sending tiny shock waves down my legs.

"I don't want some jerk to stop me. They'll think they won."

"Who gives a fuck what they think? If they think they won, they may get sloppy."

"I don't like it," I grumbled, shaking my head.

"Let's get you down," he said, placing his hands on my waist.

My eyes fluttered closed. My body reacted to his touch. I wanted more Morgan.

"I can get down," I said, placing my palms flat against the counter and instantly pulling them back. "Fuck."

"Woman, can't you let me help you without trying to do shit for yourself?" He increased the pressure of his fingertips against my sides.

"I'm not used to having someone help me." I frowned, wondering if I sounded strong or pitiful.

He lifted me in the air, and I tumbled forward, but I didn't dare use my palms to catch myself. I had a split second where I could've reached out and stopped myself, but I didn't.

His body felt nice against mine.

"Sorry," I whispered into his chest. I inhaled, getting another whiff of his cologne as his body shook with laughter.

"Go sit down, and I'll clean up in here," he said to me as I finally started to find my footing.

"Okay," I whispered.

I'm totally fucked.

I'd never let anyone get to me the way he did.

I could see us burning out in fantastic fashion.

I wondered if we'd be like a nuclear explosion, destroying everything in our path, including ourselves, or if the slow burn of need I felt would smolder like an ember, eventually extinguishing.

CHICK FLICK

MORGAN

We sat in silence, our hands grazing each other's as we reached into the bowl.

A few times I got choked up, but I refused to let her see.

Why do women watch this depressing shit?

I hadn't expected it to be gut wrenching.

"I'm sorry I'm a mess." She sniffled, wiping her nose with the back of her hand.

"It's okay." I patted her knee, liking the softer side of Race, minus the hand thing. I leaned over and reached for a tissue. "Here." I handed it to her.

"It's just so sad," she said with a shaky voice as she took the tissues from my hand. She blew her nose with one and wiped her tears away with the other. "I can't get through this movie without using an entire box of Kleenex." She curled up next to me, snuggling into my side. "This part gets me every time." She wiped her face against my T-shirt.

I stroked her shoulder, letting my fingertips glide against her soft skin. Glancing down, I snuck a peek at her tits. Soft, round peaks stuck out of the top of her tank top, and I itched to taste them again.

"Are you watching?" She peered up at me, catching me staring at her chest.

I cleared my throat. "Yep."

"Watch," she demanded, lifting my chin to see the television instead of her breasts.

My eyes kept moving between the screen and her chest.

I couldn't help it.

I wanted her again.

As the final scenes closed and a new world of possibility opened for the female lead, the movie left me feeling...hopeful.

"Wasn't it amazing?" She wiped the last traces of tears off her face.

"It wasn't what I expected." Using the pad of my thumb, I brushed away a single tear that had been missed by her tissue. "Sorry," I whispered.

As I started to pull away, she said, "No. Don't."

My stomach instantly flipped. "Race," I warned, feeling my dick grow hard.

I knew what she was going to say. I could see it in her deep-green eyes. "Morgan, I can't stop thinking about us," she whispered as she touched my cheek.

"Me either." I pulled in a ragged breath.

"Stay with me tonight." She brushed her lips against my neck, sending shock waves rippling straight to my dick.

"I'm staying, princess. I told you that," I said, tangling my hand in her hair.

"No," she murmured against my skin. "I want you in my bed tonight."

I smirked, feeling my insides warm. "I'll stay wherever you want me to."

She crawled into my lap and held my face in her hands. "I want you to hold me tonight," she whispered, her eyes watery.

"Is that all?"

She shook her head, biting her bottom lip. "No. I want to feel you inside me again."

I grabbed her hips and squeezed them gently as she leaned forward and hovered over my lips.

"Please," she begged.

"I'll stay with you tonight. Not because I have to, Race, but because I want to." I captured her lips in a kiss.

She relaxed into me, wrapping her arms around my neck and kissing me back with fervor. My hands slid down her thighs, loving the feel of her soft skin against my palms.

I felt my restraint slipping as she moaned into my mouth. I slid her shorts to the side and touched the outside of her panties, feeling her body shudder in my arms.

Her legs widened, giving me access as I dipped my fingers underneath her panties, finding her already wet.

When my fingers glided over her clit, she moaned, "Yes," into my mouth.

I wanted her more than I had before. Remembering how it felt to sink myself deep inside of her, stroking her intimately, I didn't know if I could ever get enough of it.

Holding her back, I pushed two fingers inside her, instantly feeling her pussy clamp down. Positioning my thumb over her clit and using the same motion she'd used to get herself off, I worked my fingers in and out of her.

Her hand slid down my chest and palmed my dick through my jeans as I groaned. The deliciousness of it all had me hanging on by a thread. As her body grew tight, starting to milk my fingers, I withdrew.

"I. Need. Inside. You," I panted, lifting her in my arms as I stood. "Wrap your legs around me," I told her, carrying her toward her bedroom.

Her feet locked behind my back as she ground her pussy against my dick. "You're so hard," she whispered, repeating the motion.

"Hard for you, princess." I kicked her door open and carried her to her bed.

I laid her on the bed and pulled her shorts from her body. As they flew through the air, I planted my mouth against her and began to worship her with my mouth.

CHAPTER 16

THE MORNING AFTER

RACE

I tiptoed out of bed, trying not to wake him, dressing as I headed toward the kitchen.

I couldn't wipe the silly grin off my face, but I had to remember that this was nothing more than mutual attraction.

Morgan and I didn't have a future.

He hadn't promised me anything more, and I hadn't asked him to be mine.

As I grabbed the coffee pot to fill it with water, I hissed then pulled my hand back.

I stood here and glared at the empty pot. It took everything in me not to cry. Coffee was my elixir, and I felt like a zombie until I'd had at least one cup.

The floor creaked.

I glanced over, finding Morgan standing there.

"Morning," he said through a yawn, completely naked. His muscles tightened and his cock bobbed as he straightened.

Fuck me. The man was more beautiful in the daylight, every muscle taut and perfect.

"Morning," I whispered, my eyes glued to him. I swallowed hard, mesmerized.

"Need help?" He strode toward me, his cock waving.

I shook my head. "I can do it." I waved my hands.

He took a step closer, giving me a sleepy smile. "If you say so."

I reached for the coffee pot again.

I cringed as my hand slid around the handle, and I bit my lip. As I gritted my teeth, I carried it to the sink.

"Move over." He nudged my hip with his. "Let me do it."

I glared up at him. "I can do this."

"Race, you're sweating and your face is redder than an apple from carrying an empty pot. Let me do this. I've made coffee more times than I can count." His blue eyes twinkled, and his cock twitched. "Plus, I don't feel like waiting an hour for the first cup."

I rounded the island and took a seat on one of the barstools to get a better view. Watching him as he worked his magic on the coffee pot, I was enthralled by his nakedness.

"How did you know where I kept my coffee?"

He turned around to face me and leaned against the counter, pushing his cock farther out. "Lucky guess that you kept it in the cupboard above the pot. It's something most people do."

"Thanks for making it." I yawned against the back of my hand.

He pushed off the counter and his cock came toward me. "Let me take a look at your hands."

I tried to swallow, wishing I'd brushed my teeth before I'd left my room. "They're fine."

"Stop being so stubborn. I want to make sure they're healing. Last night, you couldn't stop moaning yes, and now you're back to your hard-ass self."

I straightened my back. "I'm just cranky until I get my coffee."

Overnight, the cuts had begun to scab and the blood had dried.

"You'd already have it if you would've let me make it to begin with." He cleared his throat. "We'll need to clean the dried blood off these, but they look good." He reached for the first-aid kit he'd left on the counter last night and pulled fresh bandages from the container. "First, let's have coffee, and then we'll clean them." He set the bandages off to the side. "It's best to give them some air for a little while."

"Yes, sir," I said to the side, blowing my nasty breath away from him.

"That's sexy." He chuckled quietly.

Before I could say anything, the pot beeped.

"Stay there, I'll grab you a cup." His eyes shifted to my shirt and the corner of his mouth twitched before he turned around.

I glanced down, noticing that my nipples were standing at attention. I tried to hide them, pulling my tank top away from my body, but it did nothing.

"How do you want your coffee?" He pulled two cups down, keeping his back to me.

I stared at his naked ass, studying it. "A dash of cream and two sugars, please," I mumbled.

His ass was as beautiful as the rest of him. The skin was blemish-free and smooth, sitting higher from the muscle tone. I'd say one thing about the military: It did a body good.

"Did you let work know you weren't coming in today?" He turned around and caught me as I gawked at him.

Slowly, I dragged my eyes up to his. "Yeah." I tried not to glance at his dick as he set the coffee in front of me.

I looped my fingers through the handle, holding it loosely. "You can go whenever you want. I'm just going to chill on the couch and get some work done." I kept my eyes down, peeking at him through my veiled eyelashes. Which, coincidently, were about crotch level.

"I'm going wherever you are," he said, setting his cup down.

"For the love of God," I said, but he lifted an eyebrow.

"I'm not going anywhere. So drop it. Why don't we do something today? You can work here later."

"I really need to work," I lied. I didn't know if I could spend the day in his presence without ending up in bed with him again.

"I won't keep you out long. I don't know the area well." He leaned forward, resting his hands against the counter. "You could show me around a little bit. Your hands need time to rest anyway."

"Are you sure that's a good idea?" I peeked at him from under my eyelashes.

"We'll call it a workday. I need to pick your brain a little."

I chewed my lip. "As long as it's for work. I don't want to keep you from doing your job."

"Race, no one can make me do what I don't want to. Finish your cup and then you're mine."

I wished his statement were true. "Where to first?"

"I need to stop at my place for a change of clothes."

"You can shower here."

"With you?" He grinned, running his thumb across his chin.

"If you want," I blurted out. The truth was that I wanted him to. Sitting here, watching him saunter around nude, threw my body into overdrive.

He walked around the counter, holding his hand out to me. "Oh, I want. Let's get your pretty ass wet."

I swallowed hard, wishing I could press my legs together to squash the familiar ache that amplified with his words. As I stood, sliding my hand into his, I rose up on my tiptoes and kissed him.

"Someday, you'll admit you want me for more than just my cock," he teased, brushing his nose against mine.

When I started to walk away, he smacked me on the ass, the echo reverberating through my kitchen.

"That's for being difficult."

I yelped, jumping from the impact and rubbing my ass as he followed me to the shower.

CHAPTER 17

THE REAL RACE TRUE

MORGAN

"What are you looking at?" I walked out of my bedroom, slipping on a fresh shirt.

"Is this your mother?" She glanced over her shoulder.

"Yeah, that's Ma."

I hadn't had time to decorate, but I had placed a couple of photos around the room. I'd made sure to put a picture of Ma out. I knew that, as soon as she made it to Florida, she'd drop by and take note.

"Does she live here?" Her fingertips swept across the glass as she tilted her head.

I plucked the photo from her hands and placed it back on the coffee table. "She followed me here."

"That's so sweet." She turned and started to wander around my place.

"I guess so."

"Seriously. I have no one. That's why I'm so devoted to my work. It's the only thing I have in my life anymore."

I frowned, wondering how someone got to that point in their life. "That's sad, Race."

"I know." She traced the curves of the couch as her eyes roamed. "You don't have much here."

"I just moved in. I'm still trying to get everything set up."

She stopped and faced me, clasping her hands together. "I can help with that."

"You want to decorate?" I shuddered. Fuck. I hated shopping.

"I'm pretty good at it." She shrugged, plastering an innocent smile on her face. "What else do you have planned today?" She stepped closer.

If I had my way, I'd have her bent over the sofa and screaming my name within ten minutes. "I don't even know where to go around here."

"I'll take you, but only if I drive." She held her hand out, waiting for me to give her the keys.

The woman must've lost her marbles.

No one, and I mean no one, would drive my girl. She was a Dodge Challenger SRT Hellcat. Not only was she gorgeous, she could kick serious ass.

I shook my head, crossing my arms over my chest. "No one but me drives Elvira."

She burst out laughing, holding her stomach. "Elvira?" She rolled her eyes. "You've got to be shitting me."

I puffed my chest out, setting my lips in a firm line. "It's the perfect name for my girl."

Covering her mouth, she tried to calm her giggles. "I don't think I've ever known anyone who named their car Elvira. You've got to tell me why." Her hand dropped.

Rubbing the back of my neck, I cleared my throat. "Well, I've never slept with an Elvira. I wouldn't want to be reminded of someone from my past every day when I climbed into her. Plus, when I was a kid, I used to be mesmerized by her. When I saw my black beauty, I knew the name fit. She was sleek, sexy, and dark."

Her smile vanished. "Makes sense when I hear you say it. I don't know many guys who would admit that Elvira was their childhood crush." She shrugged.

"I'll drive." I grabbed the keys off the kitchen counter.

Before I could close my fist, she plucked them from my hands.

"Gotta get them back from me if you want to drive." She moved quickly, giggling as she sprinted to the other side of the room.

"Race," I said, grabbing my head, "come on."

She dangled the keys from her fingers and shook them.

"Woman," I said, dropping my hands to my sides, "no one fucks with Elvira."

"I'll be gentle."

I stalked toward her, ready to snatch the keys from her fingertips.

She darted to the right, but I reached out, grabbed her arm, and spun her around to face me. Caging her in when she collided with the wall, I placed my arms on either side of her.

I closed my eyes, trying to steady my breathing and not think about her beautiful tits being within inches of my mouth. We'd never get out of here. "Can we be adults, princess?"

When her body began to move, I opened my eyes.

"Jesus Christ," I muttered as she placed the keys down her shirt and nestled them between her breasts.

"What are you going to do now?" She grinned, raising one eyebrow.

"Babe, you think that's going to stop me from getting them?" My eyes dipped to her chest, and I studied its beauty. I'd use my fucking teeth if I had to.

"I hope not." She smirked, blinking slowly.

"I thought we were going to keep today all business?" I asked, swallowing hard and trying not to face-plant in her cleavage.

"I think that went out the window this morning in the shower." She laughed softly.

Without saying another word, I pulled her to me and stared down into her deep-green eyes. Her breath hitched as I brought my lips down on hers and kissed her hard.

The sounds of our breathing filled the room as our mouths tried to devour each other. Her hands slid up my arms, leaving goose bumps in their path, before she grabbed the hair on top of my head and held me to her.

I grabbed her arms and pried her from me before my lips broke contact. "We can't," I said, my voice sounding winded as it cracked.

Wrinkles lined her forehead as she gawked at me. "Why not?"

"We'll never get out of here."

She sucked her lip in her mouth as her head fell forward. "Can't get enough of me?"

"I don't know if I'll ever get enough of you."

"You won't?" Her eyes grew wide.

I closed my eyes, drawing in a deep breath through my nose. "I wouldn't just fuck you to fuck you, Race."

"You don't have to lie to me, Morgan." Pushing against my chest, she put space between us.

"Listen," I said as I dragged my hands through my hair, "it's been a long time since I've liked anyone. I really like you. Lord knows why, because you can be a pain in the ass at times." I smiled, hoping she'd know I was joking. "I'm supposed to protect you and find out who is threatening you, not fuck you every chance I get."

"I started it." She glanced down at her feet. "I'll behave," she said as she pulled my keys from her shirt. "Here." The keys dangled from her fingertips.

I rubbed my forehead, feeling like the biggest tool. This girl had me in knots. She'd scrambled my brain in a few short days. I knew I was fucked.

"You keep them. I'll let you drive Elvira."

"Really?"

"Yes."

Twirling the keys in her fingers, she whistled before she yelled, "Yes."

"I see you're happy."

"Totally worth kissing you to be able to drive that baby."

"You didn't want to kiss me?" I felt my stomach plummet.

"Oh, I did, but I didn't think you'd let me drive the car. Let's hit the road." She started for the door.

I followed behind her, dragging my feet. "Let's set a few ground rules first."

She'd already climbed inside Elvira before I'd finished the sentence. "She'll be fine." She slammed the door.

Looking up at the sky, I cursed. I could swear God was trying to punish me.

Thomas had to give Race to me as my first case. It couldn't have been something easy, like a cheating spouse? No. I'd had to get the overbearing, ballbusting corporate executive who made my dick feel like a lead pipe ready to break off.

Before I settled in my seat, she had the car started and revved the engine. "Ground rules," I reminded her.

"Hit me." She gripped the steering wheel and looked like a woman possessed.

"Don't your hands hurt?"

"I was so excited to get behind the wheel that I totally forgot." She shrugged, easing her grip.

"Number one, go the speed limit. Two, no changing lanes unnecessarily, and three, be kind to my girl." I sounded like my mother rattling off commands when I'd started to drive.

I had hit asshole territory.

"I can do that," she said as she started to back up.

I fastened my seat belt and said a small prayer as I shifted in my seat.

As she put the car in drive, the wheels began to screech, causing the car to fishtail. I reached for the dashboard, my heart pounding wildly as I screamed, "Race."

"What?" she asked innocently as she glanced at me.

The car glided across the pavement, not gripping the surface.

She turned the wheel, gaining control of Elvira. "Did I ever tell you how I got my name?"

"No." I braced myself. "Slow the hell down though."

"We're good. My daddy was a huge fan of racing. He named me Race because of it. When I was a little girl, he'd take me to some of the dirt courses around here and let me speed around. I could barely see over the damn steering wheel, but I drove like a speed demon."

"Shocking."

"I could've gone pro if I'd stuck with it."

"I can't breathe." I wiped the sweat from my forehead.

"Oh, stop being such a baby. Elvira couldn't be in better hands."

When the car came to a screeching halt at the end of my street, I was ready to run out of the car and lie down in front of it just to get her to stop.

"This is the only thing I have in my name. I don't want you to fuck her up, princess."

"I promise to behave if you calm down." She looked over at me.

"Why don't I believe you?"

Using her fingers, she made an X over her heart. "I promise." Her lips parted, giving me a toothy and totally bullshit smile.

I should've demanded the keys back.

The car behind us honked, causing Race to flip them off in the rearview mirror.

My mouth fell open. "What's gotten into you?"

"It's this car. I swear I turn into a different person when I'm behind the wheel of a car with some power."

"Just go before you start shit and I have to finish it." I motioned for her to move, keeping my eyes glued to the side mirror. The last thing I wanted to do was kick someone's ass before we had even driven a mile.

She looked like a different person today.

The tank top and skinny jeans looked good on her. She looked calmer and more relaxed than I'd ever seen her. The way she held the leather wheel in her hands made it clear that she was in her element.

As she eased onto the street without causing the car to spin, I took a deep breath and tried to relax. "So why don't you race anymore?"

"When my father died, I didn't want to go to the course anymore. I miss him every day, but I just couldn't go there. I started to study harder and decided to leave that world behind."

"I'm sorry. What happened to him, if you don't mind my asking?" I watched her face change.

I knew the trauma of losing a parent. My dad hadn't died, but the bastard might as well have, since he'd dropped off the face of the Earth.

"He was hit by a semi and died instantly." Her chin trembled. "It was my fault."

I blinked. "Race, how could it be your fault?"

"It just is. Ask my mama. She'll tell you." She shrugged.

"She can't feel that way. How old were you?"

"Twelve." She tightened her grip on the steering wheel.

"You can hardly be at fault," I reassured her, placing a hand on her shoulder. "You were just a little kid."

"Anyway, he was my best friend and we spent our weekends together at the racetrack."

"You know you aren't at fault, Race, right?" I asked, concerned about her change of attitude.

"In my heart I know it, but I can still hear the words coming out of my mama's mouth."

"Sometimes parents say shit they don't mean," I said, knowing that my ma had said more than a few things I knew she wished she could take back.

"I know," she said, keeping her eyes on the road.

She weaved in and out of traffic, and I couldn't look. "It's quite a leap from race car driver to the corporate world." I swallowed hard, trying to get the lump out of my throat.

"I wanted something challenging and cutthroat, but I never expected what's happening now."

As she pulled into the IKEA parking lot, my phone rang and Thomas's number scrolled across the radio.

"Let me grab this. Thomas may have some news." I pulled my phone out of my pocket and took it off Bluetooth.

"Yeah?" I asked, hoping he had a lead.

"I think I found him," Thomas said, the excitement in his voice evident. "Come to the office this afternoon and we'll work out a game plan."

CHAPTER 18

PROBLEM

RACE

"We'll be in shortly. Thanks, man." Morgan glanced at me as I pulled my phone from my purse, needing to check my messages. "He has a lead," he whispered, covering the phone with his hand.

"Thank God," I mumbled, glancing down at my screen.

My hands began to shake as I checked my messages. I squeezed my eyes shut, trying to slow my breathing. I swallowed down the bile that had started to rise in my throat.

Race,

The time is coming. Meet me tomorrow at 7 p.m. if you want your tape back. Come alone or I'll e-mail it to your boss. I bet he'd like to hear you moaning like a whore.

I couldn't read any more.

I couldn't breathe.

"We'll stop in the office later. We're doing a few things today." There was a long pause. "Yeah, I have her with me. You told me to keep an eye on her." More silence. "Don't worry, man. I got it."

I turned my phone off and tossed it back in my purse.

"Looks like we're a step closer to solving your case," he said.

"Thank God," I replied, knowing that either way, it would be over tomorrow night.

109

"Ready to do some shopping?" Morgan asked.

Pulling at my lip, I stared at him as he spoke but didn't hear the words.

"Race." He touched my leg as his forehead scrunched.

I blinked a few times, trying to clear my head. "Sorry. I zoned out." I couldn't look at him.

"What's wrong? You look pale."

"I'm just hungry," I lied.

"You want to skip shopping and go grab some lunch?" he asked as his thumb stroked my knee.

I shook my head, still not making eye contact. "No. Let's shop and then we'll grab a bite to eat."

In my heart, I knew I should tell him about the e-mail. He needed to handle things and get the video from the bastard who had threatened me, but I couldn't risk everything going to shit and it landing in the hands of my boss.

But I wasn't ready to ruin our day together.

"Okay, Race. This is your show. I'm fine with the few items I have, but have at it."

"You need to make it more like a home." I finally brought my eyes to his.

"I'm a simple guy. A couch and a television are all I need to survive."

"Just let me get lost in a little shopping today. What's my budget?" I rubbed my hands together. I pushed all thoughts of tomorrow night out of my mind, focusing on Morgan.

Tomorrow I'd go there, retrieve the video, and be done with it.

It was that simple.

Everything would finally be over.

My life could return to normal.

"I'm not giving you a total. Let's see what you find and we'll go from there."

Retail therapy would help. Lots of retail therapy. "If you say I have one hundred dollars, I'm going to throw myself into traffic."

He reached in his back pocket and pulled his wallet out. "Let me see how much I have." He opened it, turned it upside down, and shook it until a few bills fell into his lap. "I have one hundred and seventeen dollars. Dazzle me with your ability."

"For fuck's sake." I rolled my eyes.

He stuffed the money back in his wallet. "I have a credit card, princess."

"Thank God. I know the military doesn't pay well, though, so I don't want to go crazy."

"I think I can handle anything you throw at me. It's IKEA anyway. I could probably decorate my entire place for one hundred and seventeen dollars."

"Hardly," I scoffed as I threw the keys at him. "It adds up quickly."

"Show me your mad skills." He smiled. "Hey, thanks for not wrecking Elvira."

"I would never. I can't wait to drive her home. Now, let's go spend your money."

"After you," he said as I climbed out of the car and gently closed the door. As we entered the store, his mouth fell open. "Holy shit."

"What's wrong?"

"We're going to be here all day."

"Nah. We'll make it quick. What do you need?"

"I don't know," he said as he followed behind me.

"Don't worry. We'll figure it out as we go," I reassured him, happy that I'd be able to lose myself in the wonders of IKEA.

"I'm all yours."

My chest tightened at his words.

I have a problem.

I liked Morgan.

No, that wasn't totally true.

I wanted Morgan.

Strike that.

I had a crush on Morgan.

Spending time with him had made me want him more. The moment I'd met him, I'd felt my attraction to him, but I tried to tell myself that it was only physical.

"I'm all yours," he repeated as he grabbed a cart.

He made me want to go back on the promise I'd made of swearing off relationships forever.

CHAPTER 19

PLANS

MORGAN

I still hated shopping.

Even with Race by my side.

I hated every damn minute of it.

I bought shit I didn't need because she said that it was cute.

What use did I have for decorative pillows for my bed? I never even made the damn thing, let alone decorated it.

"Thanks for lunch and the drink," she said as we pulled into the parking lot of ALFA PI.

"You seemed on edge. I thought you could use a little something."

"I just get more nervous with each passing day." Her eyes didn't meet mine when she spoke. "You think you guys have a solid lead?" She still seemed distant.

She was hiding something.

Her playful attitude from earlier had vanished.

She'd played it off like nothing happened, but I could tell.

"We won't be here long." I placed my hand on hers. "I just want to see what Thomas found."

"It doesn't matter. I've decided to not work at all today. I'm not even going to look at my phone."

Alarm bells started to ring in my head.

"Race, is there something you aren't telling me?"

Race had been glued to her phone during business hours.

"Everything is fine," she reassured me as we walked toward the building.

"Hey, Morgan," Angel greeted us.

"Hey, Angel. Is Thomas in his office?" I placed my hand on the small of Race's back just because I could.

Race didn't try to escape my touch—she stood still at my side.

"Yeah. He's expecting you. Go on back." Angel's eyes dropped to my arm.

"Thanks." I guided Race down the hallway, my hand still on her lower back. "All the way at the end."

"I remember." She walked slow enough to keep the contact between us. "Who is she?"

I looked down at Race, confused. "Who? Angel?"

She looked away, staring down the hallway. "Yes."

"She's Thomas's girl."

She was jealous.

"Oh," she said as her eyebrows shot up. "Well, that's nice."

I stopped walking, turning her body toward me. "Are you jealous, Race?"

"No." She shook her head but still not looking me in the eye.

"Do you always lie so much?"

She crossed her arms, becoming defensive. "No," she snapped, finally glancing up at me.

"Sure. But I know when you're not telling me the truth."

She gnawed on her lip. "Can we drop it?" she asked, moving her hands to her sides.

When we arrived at the door, I leaned forward, invading her personal space. "You're hiding something, and I need to know what it is. I expect you to tell me when we're done meeting with Thomas."

Her eyes dropped to the floor as her shoulders sagged. "Okay," she whispered as I opened his door.

"Hey, T," I greeted him, helping Race sit before I took the seat next to her. "Find anything out?"

He turned his attention to his computer. "I was able to figure out the name of his cousin using an obituary and college records. I haven't moved past that yet. His name is—"

A knock on the door caused him to stop mid-sentence. "Thomas," a voice said from the other side.

"Come in, Sam," Thomas called out.

I turned to catch a glimpse of the infamous Sam.

Sam slid the sunglasses to the top of his head as he looked around the room. "Sorry. I didn't mean to interrupt." He was a tower of a man, with wide shoulders, cropped hair, and a fit physique.

Thomas walked toward Sam with an extended hand. "You aren't. Sam, this is Morgan, another member of ALFA PI."

Sam gave me a quick nod. "Nice to meet you, Morgan."

"Sam." I returned the nod.

"I'm excited to start working. It's great to be home again."

"I didn't think I'd be able to lure you away from New Orleans," Thomas told him as he placed a hand on his shoulder. "Is Fiona settled?"

"Yeah. She's excited for a fresh start." Sam peered over his shoulder. "Is James here?"

"He's in his office, I believe."

Sam fidgeted with the file in his hands. "I need to talk to him."

"Go ahead. Don't worry. He's cooled down in the last couple of years."

"I'd hope so." Sam gave Thomas a weak smile. "I'm going to go have a chat with James and then get settled in my office."

"I'll come looking for you when we're done here. We need to discuss some things," Thomas told him as he held the door open.

"Nice to meet you, Morgan. You too, ma'am."

"Race."

"Race," he repeated before he closed the door.

Thomas laughed, plopping down in his chair. "This is going to be fun."

"Sure will be."

"Where was I?" Thomas asked as he scratched his head.

"The name." I glanced at Race.

She wasn't herself.

She'd been entirely too quiet for the last hour.

"Tyler O'Shea."

"Race, does that sound right?"

She seemed uninterested. "Yeah. I think so."

"I'll do some digging and see what I can come up with." I stood, holding my hand out to Race. "Thanks for getting the name for me, Thomas."

She placed her tiny palm in mine and I closed my fingers around her hand, helping her up from the chair.

"Morgan, can I talk to you in private for a moment?" Thomas asked.

Race glanced up.

"Go wait for me in my office. I'll be right there," I whispered to her. She gave me a brief nod and left.

"What's up, Thomas?" I asked as I sat back down.

"What's going on with you two?"

"Nothing," I lied, shaking my head.

"I saw how you touched her. There's something different about you two. And what the hell happened to her hands?"

"Listen." I rubbed the back of my neck, "you told me to stay with her to make sure she was safe last night. I did that."

"I also asked you to keep it in your pants, but did you do that too?" he asked, tilting his head to the side.

"Well, um, no. I didn't listen to that part. But—"

"Just get the case solved," he told me, crossing his arms in front of his chest.

"I will."

"Shopping? Really?"

"Yeah, man. She mocked my place and said I needed to decorate. She couldn't work today because she cut her hands when a bowl shattered last night. We thought it was best if she gave her hands a day to heal."

"Uh-huh," he mumbled.

I flipped him off, closed the door, and headed to my office.

As I passed James's door, I heard heated words being exchanged. I guessed not everything was water under the bridge when it pertained to Izzy.

Race had sprawled out on the small love seat. Her arm was resting against her face, her mouth slightly parted, and her legs crossed at her ankles.

I sat down, turning my computer on. "Sorry about that."

"It's okay," she whispered without moving.

"Why don't you tell me what's on your mind, princess?"

She didn't look at me. "I got another message today while you were talking to Thomas," she said, hiding behind her arm.

I froze, knowing that she'd hid it for a reason. "Fuck. What did it say?"

"I didn't read it all. Something about come alone and he wanted to meet me tomorrow."

"You're not going."

She glared at me. "It's my career, Morgan."

"I don't care what it is, Race. You're *not* going to put your life in danger. I'll get the tape for you."

"How?"

"I'm going to get my ass up and find everything I can on Tyler O'Shea. Then I'm going to get the guys together and we're going to form a plan. You are not going. I won't allow it. End of story."

"Morgan," she said before I pinned her with my eyes.

I shook my head, glaring at her. "Absolutely not."

"It's my life hanging in the balance."

"Woman, if I have to tie your ass to the bed, you're not going."

"Fine," she said, crossing her arms over her chest.

"I'm glad you're seeing things my way," I said, smirking.

"You can be a jerk," she snarled.

"I told you I was an asshole sometimes."

She didn't reply as I sat down and started researching Tyler O'Shea.

He lived in Tampa and had gotten married three years ago to a woman named Natasha. Both held business degrees, and Tyler worked at a financial firm in the area.

The thing I hadn't expected was where Natasha worked.

She had become employed two years ago with the same company Race worked for.

Her position in the company was lower, but she was in line for the same promotion as Race. If Tyler was able to destroy Race's career, Natasha would be able to climb the corporate ladder quicker.

I stood without excusing myself, and I headed straight for Thomas's office.

"We have a problem." I walked through the door without knocking again.

I saw Angel bent over the desk with a look matching my own. "Oh my God. I'm so sorry." I covered my eyes, splaying my fingers so I could peek. "Fuck. Again," I muttered as I started to back up.

"Out," Thomas yelled, pointing toward the door.

"What's he all pissy about?" James asked from behind me as I closed the door.

"He was a little busy when I walked in." I motioned toward Thomas's office. "They sure get a lot of use out of that desk."

He looked at the ceiling and shook his head. "I've told him a million times to lock the damn door. I've seen way more of him than I ever wanted to lately." James chuckled.

"Don't you knock?"

"Nah. I kind of like catching them. I think they like it too, or else he'd lock the damn door."

"Interesting." I scrubbed my hand across my face. "Can I talk to you, since Thomas is busy?"

"Step into my office and we'll chat until he's done. Don't worry. He's quick."

I followed him inside and took a seat on the couch.

Before I could speak, Thomas's door opened and closed.

"See." James motioned toward the hallway. "Quick."

"Poor girl." I snickered.

"What can I do for you?" James asked as he sat down in the leather chair across from me.

"It's about this case. I need extra eyes and hands on deck tomorrow. Do you know anything about her case?"

"I know about all the cases in the office. What's happening tomorrow?"

I spent the next five minutes explaining the e-mail that she'd received today and the background information on Tyler O'Shea.

He leaned forward, resting his elbows on his knees. "Here's what we're going to do. I'll put Sam on staking out Tyler and updating us on his movements. Thomas and I will decide the best course of action on our end, and we'll have extra bodies at the meeting point tomorrow night."

"They'll stay out of sight though, right?" I asked, my leg shaking. If this went south, it would all fall on my shoulders.

"No one will see us. You stay by Race's side until we have the douchebag and the tape in our hands."

"That may be a problem."

"Why?" His face contorted.

"She's pissed at me right now. It's going to be hell to convince her to let me stick by her side and let us handle everything."

Pinching the bridge of his nose, he leaned back in the chair and stretched his legs out. "Is there something going on with you two?" he asked.

"Well…" I winced.

"Does she like you?"

"Yes."

"Do you like her?"

"Yes."

"Make sure she doesn't want to get rid of you tonight. Keep her close. Take her to dinner. Buy her some drinks. Do something. Just don't let her out of your sight."

"Gotcha, buddy. Text me the details and keep me updated. I'm going to get Race and head out. Thanks for your help."

"I'll message you later, after I figure everything out and get it all set up. Remember, only worry about your client."

"Shit's easier said than done." I walked toward the door.

Just then there was a small knock. "Jimmy," Izzy said in a low tone.

"Looks like you better lock your door." I opened the door to my cousin, who was standing there with her fist up and about to knock.

"Hey, Morgan."

"Iz. Go easy on him."

"If we don't come out in thirty minutes, call the paramedics," she said as she walked past me and into his office.

"I'll let you two have some time alone."

"Thanks." James looked around Izzy. "Lock the door, love," he said as the door started to close.

I shook my head, wondering how I was the only person in the office not getting any at-work action. Then again, I was the only one in the office who wasn't attached.

"Race," I called out as I opened the door and walked into my office, ready to head outside. My heart jumped into my throat when I noticed the couch empty—Race was gone.

I marched into the waiting room where Angel sat, fixing her makeup in a small compact mirror. "Where is she?" I asked, squeezing my fists at my sides.

"She just walked out a minute ago. She needed some air," Angel replied, wiping the corners of her lips.

"Fuck," I muttered, smashing through the front doors in a panic. "Race," I called out as I looked around, shielding my eyes from the sun.

She was standing next to Elvira, her pale skin whiter than normal. She didn't reply, just stood like a statue looking down.

"Race." I jogged toward her. "What's wrong?"

She pointed toward the ground. "Elvira," she whispered.

Someone had slashed my tires. Each one had huge punctures, and enough air had seeped out of them that they were practically flat.

"Fuck!" I yelled, feeling my chest tighten. I wasn't upset about the car. It was just an object. If she had come out just a few minutes earlier... I couldn't think about it.

"I'm so sorry," she whispered, clutching her neck. "It's all my fault."

"It's just a car." I tried to keep my voice calm as I put my arm around her. "It can be fixed. It's not your fault."

She held a tiny piece of paper out. "Yes, it is. Look."

"'You can't save her. Keep your nose where it belongs,'" I read out loud, pulling her closer to me.

Whoever this prick was, he sure had balls as big as basketballs. To come to this office and slash my tires was extremely risky.

"Shh. It's no big deal. You're safe and that's all that matters."

Her shoulders shook as tears began to stream down her face. "I'm so sorry," she repeated, sucking in a shaky breath.

"It's only a car, princess."

Her body could've had the note for me instead of it being left on Elvira.

"Let me help you fix it," she whispered as she peered up at me.

"I'm sure Thomas has insurance for stuff like this." I could see that there were dangers to this job that I hadn't anticipated.

"I know a guy I can call."

"You know a guy?" My eyes narrowed. "Sounds ominous."

"An old racing contact of my dad's. Let me call him, please." She batted her eyelashes.

Fuck.

There was no way I could refuse her.

"Okay. Let's go inside, and you can call him while I speak with Thomas."

She nodded and leaned into my side. "We'll get your baby back in action."

"I can get a rental until she's all fixed up. Stop worrying."

"Everything okay?" Angel asked as we walked back inside.

"Yeah, Angel. Everything will be okay." I gave her a fake smile, my insides turning about what had transpired. I glanced down at Race. "Go in my office and use the phone while I speak with Thomas."

She nodded and walked down the hallway. I watched, completely transfixed by the sway of her hips. Before she opened the door, she looked over her shoulder and caught me.

"See something you like, big boy?" Angel asked from my side.

My face flushed. "I wanted to make sure she went to the right door. I wouldn't want her walking in on something she shouldn't." I arched an eyebrow and didn't bother to hide my amusement as her nose scrunched.

She coughed, "Asshole."

"Is Thomas alone?"

"As far as I know." She busied herself with the stack of paperwork at her desk.

I marched down the hallway, straight to Thomas's office.

This time, I knocked.

"Come in."

"Sorry to interrupt, but I needed to talk with you about a situation."

"What's the problem now?" Thomas peered up from behind his desk.

I dragged my hands through my hair. "I went outside to find Race, and Elvira's tires were slashed."

"I'll get James on the parking lot surveillance video right away."

"Um," I mumbled, glancing behind me toward James's door, "he's kind of busy right now."

"What the fuck is he doing?" Thomas moved around the desk.

I put up my hands, stopping him from leaving. "Just give him a few minutes. What do I do about the car?"

"Just give me the bill and we'll pay it. Insurance will cover it."

"Thanks, Thomas."

"Don't thank me yet. Since you're here, we need to discuss your relationship with Ms. True." He leaned forward, resting his elbows on the desk. "James," he called out as he walked into the room, straightening his clothes. "Shut the door, James," Thomas said as he collapsed in his chair.

"Do I want to hear this?" I knew what he was peeved about.

"Listen, smartass. Dating a client can complicate shit and open us up to a slew of lawsuits."

I set my mouth in a firm line at the insinuation that she'd be after money. "Race isn't like that."

He shook his head, throwing his body back into the chair. "Be careful. You're in very dangerous territory."

"I know. I didn't mean for anything to happen."

Thomas crossed his arms in front of his chest. "I don't want excuses. Keep her safe and close the case."

"I never set out to like her. I don't know what happened, but I'll keep her safe. And the case should be over tomorrow. She just makes me crazy."

"Women do that." James toyed with the wedding ring on his hand.

"Firsthand knowledge?" My eyes dropped to his hand.

"I didn't want to like Izzy. God, she's such a pain in the ass. I couldn't help it. One thing led to another, and here I am. Married." He shook his head. "Sometimes we can't resist fate."

"Hey, James, Hallmark wants their cheesy line back," Thomas joked.

"Shut up, man." James lifted his chin to Thomas.

"Anyway, we'll handle everything," Thomas said. "Stay with her tonight. I don't like that this person came here and vandalized your car. They're bold and could try anything. Just, for the love of God, stay on your toes."

"I won't let my guard down."

"A dead client doesn't pay," James added.

Jesus. "You know just the right shit to make me feel better, James."

"James, I need you to pull the parking lot footage for the last hour," Thomas said, tapping his finger on the desk.

"What happened?" James raised an eyebrow as he glanced at me.

"Someone slashed my tires."

"Fuck." He pushed himself up from the chair. "I'm on it."

I closed my eyes, wishing I could fast-forward to tomorrow, when hopefully, all of this would be over. "Do you need me for anything else?" I asked, needing to get back to Race.

"No. We'll get everything set and send you the details."

"Okay. I'm going to call for a rental car and get Elvira towed."

"Sounds like a plan."

"Oh, and, Morgan," Thomas said as I had one foot in the hallway.

"Yeah?" I asked, keeping my back to him and closing my eyes.

"Thanks for knocking this time, man."

Everyone laughed.

CHAPTER 20

THE GUY

RACE

"I have great news," I told Morgan as he sat down at his desk.

Rocking back and forth, he tried to muster a smile. "Hit me."

"Johnny is bringing new tires and he's going to fix Elvira in the parking lot."

"The guy?" he asked with a halfhearted grin.

I nodded, trying to contain my excitement. "The guy."

"That's great, princess." He held his hand out to me, a serious look on his face. "We gotta talk. It's about Tyler and the entire situation."

"Can I go tomorrow?" I held my breath.

"No."

I scowled, grinding my teeth.

"Do you trust me, Race?" He reached out for me.

This time, I didn't hesitate as I set my hand in his, finally giving in. "Yes."

"Good." He pulled me forward and wrapped his arms around me. "Then you aren't fucking going."

I tumbled into his lap and yelled, "Hey."

He positioned me in his lap, cocooning me against his torso.

I peered up at him, confused. "What are you doing?"

"Protecting you," he whispered in my ear.

124

My breath hitched.

For once, I was at a loss for words.

"I'm going to stay with you again tonight."

"You don't have to. I'm a big girl." I enjoyed being cradled in his arms.

Tenderly, he took my hand in his and stroked the side near the bandages. "Keep arguing and I'm going to spank you tonight."

"Oh," I whispered, butterflies filling my insides.

The vibrations of his deep laugh ricocheted through my body. "Maybe you'd like that."

"Morgan…" I relaxed into him.

"Listen, someone is after you. They came to my work and slashed my tires. I don't want to find you the same way we found Elvira. So you can't get rid of me, no matter how mouthy you are."

"Don't be silly," I said, feeling butterflies starting to float around my stomach. "You don't think someone would do that. Do you?" My heart quickened, beating feverishly inside my chest.

"I don't know, Race." His fingers trailed up my arm, running over my highly sensitive skin. "I won't take the chance."

"Okay" left my mouth a little too quickly.

I couldn't deny it any longer—at least, not to myself anymore.

Morgan DeLuca stirred all kinds of feelings inside of me.

I lusted after him.

That word might not even be enough to describe how badly I wanted him.

The moment his lips had touched mine, I had known I was a goner.

Never in my entire life had a man kissed me the way he had, let alone the way he fucked me.

"Good," he said against my hair as he traced tiny circles on my shoulder.

I sat there like a doe-eyed girl, basking in the feel of his skin against mine. "Morgan," I whispered, biting on my lip.

"Yeah?" His mouth brushed against my ear.

I shuddered. "This."

He held me tighter, resting his lips against my neck. "Listen, have you ever wanted something so badly that you never thought you'd want in a million years?"

I swallowed hard and nodded.

"I never thought I'd want to be with someone, Race. But then your bossy ass sat there on a barstool slinging all types of bullshit at me and everything inside me changed."

"You really like me?" I blinked.

Oh my God.

"Yes," he answered in a serious tone.

I stared straight ahead, not daring to make eye contact. "We don't really make sense."

"Let's take it one day at a time. I like you though. More than I ever expected or wanted to."

"I know. Me too." My cheeks heated.

He leaned forward and placed his mouth over mine. My breath was lost as he stole every bit of air inside my body, causing me to feel lightheaded and dizzy.

As his lips lingered over mine, he asked, "Do you want me in your bed?"

My mind was still hazy from the lust that had flooded my every fiber. "Yes."

Before I could take it back, he covered my mouth in another kiss.

A moment later, he backed away, holding me at arm's length. "I need you, Race, but not here," he said as his chest heaved. He tried to catch his breath, just as affected by the kiss as I had been.

"Johnny should be here soon," I said, unsure of what else to say.

"When he's done, I'll take you to dinner and then we can head home."

"What if I don't want to go home?"

"Then I'll take you anywhere you want, but eventually we'll end up at your place."

"And then?"

"Then we'll finish what we started."

Hope bloomed inside me, and self-doubt evaporated. Want flooded my system as I took in the man before me.

CHAPTER 21

BEG FOR IT

MORGAN

Her guy, Johnny, fixed Elvira in record time as the entire office gawked from behind the glass doors.

I graciously let Race drive Elvira as we headed to dinner.

Once we'd arrived at the restaurant, conversation was almost nonexistent for the first half of the meal. After she'd consumed three glasses of wine, she started to talk.

"Thanks for letting me drive your girl." She sloshed the wine around in her glass. "I really am sorry it happened because of me."

"Don't apologize any more." I wiped my mouth and tossed my napkin on the table. "It's in the past."

"Kind of like I'll be," she whispered.

"What?" I cocked my head.

"Nothing." She watched the liquid as it moved around, and her eyes became glassy. "Can I drive her home?"

"Let's get a few things clear. Shall we?" I asked, rubbing my hands against my pants. "I had a simple life. Then this blond-haired woman walked into my world with her attitude, sassy mouth, and killer body and wrecked everything."

"Well, I—"

"Every time I look into her emerald-green eyes, I feel myself falling deeper, losing a bit of my heart with each kiss. I've never felt like this before. I don't know how to act half the time. So don't toss aside my feelings for you. When your case is over, I'm far from done with you, Race True."

She sat there with her lips parted as she stroked her cleavage. "Okay." A small smile crept across her face. "Can I have more wine?"

"I want you fully lucid when I have you tonight. You'll beg for more."

"I've never begged, Morgan."

"You will tonight." I smirked.

Her throat moved as she swallowed hard and her lips parted wider. As her eyes softened, she uncrossed her arms and leaned forward.

"I don't fucking beg."

I scooted forward in my chair, moving my face as close as possible to hers. Our mouths were almost touching as her warm, wine-laden breath trailed across my lips. "You will for me tonight. That I promise you."

"Put up or shut up." The corner of her mouth twitched.

I grabbed my wallet, pulled out enough cash to more than cover the bill and tip, and stood. Holding my hand out, I stared down at her, ready to get out of there. "Let's see if you're all talk, princess."

"You're going to be the one walking funny tomorrow, big boy."

"I welcome the challenge."

"LET'S WATCH A MOVIE OR SOMETHING," I told her as we walked into her house.

She gawked at me. "Really?"

"No. Get your fine ass over here and kiss me, princess." I pointed to the floor near my feet.

"No foreplay?" She took one step forward.

"Oh, there'll be lots of that."

"No romance?"

"Dinner was the romance, and now, it's time for dessert."

"Are you sure you want to do this?" She glanced up at me from under her eyelashes.

"Do you want me?" I asked, crooking my finger at her, beckoning her forward.

"Uh, yeah."

"Or do you only want my enormous dick?" I teased, trying to lighten the mood.

"Well. I do want you, but you're not who I thought, Morgan." She took another step closer.

I leaned forward, bringing my lips close to hers. "Then kiss me, Race," I whispered, holding her chin in my hand.

Her eyes changed as I stared into them. She hesitated for a moment before her lips touched mine, hesitantly at first before her breathing changed and the kiss became more ravenous.

She wove her fingers through my hair, pulling me closer. Using both of my hands, I squeezed her ass, grinding against her. Her moans spilled into my mouth, making my cock even harder.

Leaving one hand on her ass, I fisted her hair in the other and pulled her mouth away from mine. As her head tipped back, I took the opportunity to taste her neck.

Her smooth skin smelled like sweet caramel as my tongue slid down the side of her neck. Taking my time, I explored her neck, stopping for a moment over her pulse. Her heart drummed against my lips in an erratic rhythm.

As my lips found the top of her breast, her fingernails dug into my forearms, piercing the skin. I hissed, sucking in a quick breath as my tongue darted out and slid against her silky tit.

"Don't stop," she cried out.

I'd come this far and there was nothing that would stop me now. After releasing her, I grabbed the bottom of her tank top and pulled it over her head. The delicate lace of her bra barely hid her breasts as her nipples strained against the material, yearning to be touched. I brushed the pad of my thumb against it, seeing her shudder.

Before I dropped to my knees, I unfastened her bra and tossed it to the floor. Touching the small of her back, I pulled her toward me and buried my face between her breasts. At that very moment, I wished I had more than one mouth. There wasn't a spot on her body I didn't want to devour, and patience wasn't something I had to spare.

My mouth went right and a hand cupped the left, making sure each would receive equal attention. Her hands dropped to her sides as she swayed. Her nipples grew even more taut as I sucked, and my cock strained for freedom.

When her body swayed again, I wrapped my arm around her back and held her steady. I alternated between each breast, using my teeth to give her a jolt when her body began to shake. I moaned, using the vibration to my advantage.

"You're killing me," she whined as I was about to switch sides again.

I didn't reply. Some situations didn't require words. I grazed her nipple with my teeth and undid the button on her jeans.

She wiggled as I pulled them down her legs. The girl had gone commando, and it was sexy as hell. All day she'd sat next to me with nothing between her pussy and me except for one scrap of material.

My fingers slid down her smooth mound and cupped her sex. I had to take a moment to regain my composure before I slid my fingers through her wetness. My mouth watered as the scent of her arousal finally hit me.

I groaned as I touched her pussy. Using the wetness on my fingers, I circled her clit, feeling the hardness against my fingertips. There was nothing I wanted to do more than to plunge my fingers inside her, but I wanted to tease her and make her beg for it.

I hadn't released her nipple, so I sucked on it harder as I circled her clit. Her body shook in my arms as she gripped my shoulders with shaky fingers.

"More," she moaned, pushing her pussy against my hand.

The wetness dripped from my fingers, coating them thoroughly as I prodded her opening. The last thing I wanted to do was hurt her, but I couldn't waste any more time. I needed to be inside her. It had taken everything in me to show the restraint I already had, and I wouldn't be able to hold out much longer.

Slowly, I sank one finger inside her, feeling her walls convulse around me. Touching her from the inside was almost heavenly. The only thing better would have been my dick, but there would be time for that.

"More," she called out.

Without releasing her nipple, I did as I'd been told. Dipping a second finger inside, I resisted the urge to cry out myself. My eyes rolled back in my head as the feeling of ecstasy overcame me.

I would not come in my pants. I couldn't. All credibility I had with Race would quickly go out the window. I left my fingers inside, not moving as I calmed myself down.

"More!"

She was a greedy little thing. I loved that. I wanted her to be aggressive.

"Harder."

It almost sounded like she was begging, although she'd argue that point. I did as she'd commanded, slowly moving my fingers out before plunging them back inside.

I needed to taste her.

As I worked my fingers inside her, I trailed a path down her stomach. Then I hovered just in front of her pussy. I paused, letting her musky female arousal penetrate every fiber of my being before I leaned forward and licked her.

"Fuck," she groaned, almost collapsing in my arms.

The salty sweetness of her exploded in my mouth. I swear to fuck, my dick was about to break off, and I was hanging by a thread as I fastened my mouth around her and captured her wetness with my tongue.

As I glanced up at her, her eyes rolled back and closed. I wouldn't let her come—not yet, at least. She'd have to beg for it. From the sounds coming from her throat, I knew I was on the right track, so I pushed forward and increased the pressure of my mouth against her bare flesh.

Just as her body began to shake and her breathing came out in ragged, short breaths, I pulled away.

"Don't stop."

"Beg," I demanded, still working my fingers inside her.

"Morgan," she said.

I ignored her, continuing my assault on her from the inside. After finding her G-spot, I let my fingers slide against it each time my digits retreated.

"Oh my God," she cried out, pushing her pussy toward my face. "You can't!"

"I can. God won't help you now. Only I can. Say it."

"Fuck you." Her fingers dug into my scalp, pulling my hair.

"You will."

She glared at me, still grinding against my hand. Her nipples were hard peaks and her skin was covered in goose bumps. "I hate you."

I stuck my tongue out and swept it across her clit, curling it to get maximum contact.

"Yes!"

I pulled away. "Yes what?" I hooked my fingers inside her so she couldn't move.

"Fuckin' eat me, Morgan."

Now that was sexy, but it wasn't enough. I slid a third finger inside, stretching her wide.

"Oh," she groaned. This time, her knees were weak enough that I held her up. If I moved, she'd fall back.

Her pussy clamped down. "Please, Morgan."

"Please, Morgan what?"

Now, I was just toying with her and being a total prick. I knew it, and I was sure she did too.

"Please let me come," she whispered, looking down at me with a softened face.

They all became sweet little things when their orgasms rested on their actions. If it weren't for my fingers inside her, I was sure she'd claw my eyeballs out.

Since she'd asked so nicely, I placed my mouth over her and toyed with her clit, applying just enough pressure to bring her close but nothing more.

She rose up on her tiptoes, trying to get closer to my face. I didn't protest, moving forward and burying my face in her flesh. Even if I suffocated, it would be one hell of a way to go.

Just as my jaw started to ache, her body trembled and her pussy contracted around my fingers. As she cried out my name, I increased the pressure of my mouth against her and thrust my fingers deeper inside her.

Her fingers pulled at my hair as she screamed, "Yes!"

By the time her body stopped twitching, my cock was about to explode. I could feel the blue balls slowly killing my member. I eased my fingers out, ready to get mine before there was nothing to be gotten.

I licked her off my fingers as I stood. Her eyes fluttered open and tried to focus on me. My need overcame my sensibilities as I undid my pants, leaving the zipper hanging open.

"Down you go." I pushed on her shoulders.

"Wait. What?" she asked as her knees bent from the pressure.

"I want to feel your mouth on me. Be a good girl and wrap your lips around my dick."

"Are you going to beg too?" She smirked as she slid the jeans down my legs.

"Please suck my cock, princess," I whispered as my dick sprang free and bobbed. My dick waved in her face as if taunting her.

She palmed it without hesitation, causing my junk to lurch forward. The silky warmth of her hands had me on the brink.

I needed to think about something other than my dick. I didn't want it to be over before it had even begun. As her tongue poked out, grabbing the wetness that had seeped from the tip, I almost had a heart attack.

The only thing I could think of to keep my mind off her was work. As the tip of my dick passed her lips, I wondered what the guys had done to secure backup for tomorrow night. I mentally rattled off a list of things I needed to speak to the guys about before the drop occurred.

Trying to keep my mind occupied didn't help for too long. Quickly, I ran out of shit to think about and could only feel her tongue stroking the underside of my shaft. Every time the tip of her tongue caressed the sensitive spot where the head met the stem, I shuddered.

It was my turn for my knees to feel weak. Her mouth demanded my attention as she took me deep, but not enough to swallow me whole. I couldn't take it any longer. I wanted to come. The last thing I cared about when I had my dick in her mouth was that I'd look weak if I came too quickly. I wasn't about to torture myself. We had all night, and this was just the appetizer.

"Put your hands on your knees," I commanded as I looked down.

If I were any bigger, I wouldn't have fit. There's nothing like seeing your cock buried inside a woman's mouth.

She swallowed against my cock as her hands fell to her legs and she looked at me with questioning eyes.

"You good?" I asked even though, no matter the answer, I was still going to do the same thing.

She gave a slight nod as drool started to pool at the corners of her lips.

I slid my hands down her hair and grasped it tightly in my fingers. I pushed my cock forward, slipping it down her throat just a little farther than it had been before. She gagged a little as her eyes closed. Her throat clamped down as she tried to swallow, and I almost erupted in her mouth.

When my tip bent slightly, curving down her throat, it was the most amazing feeling in the world, and I wasn't about to stop.

"Fuck, that feels so good," I murmured as I fucked her face.

She just stared up at me through teary eyes. Her tongue tried to keep up, pushing on the underside of my dick, but it wasn't necessary.

"I'm so close."

Instantly, she stopped fighting it, letting me take control of her body. Having Race on her knees, with my dick in her mouth and listening to my commands, was more than I could take. I exploded inside her.

Everything in the room went blurry. Come chills racked my body as my legs began to buckle. I gripped her hair tighter, grounding myself to her as support as I rode the wave of ecstasy.

By the time my orgasm had passed, I was breathless and panting. I couldn't get air in fast enough as I released her hair and leaned forward, completely winded.

"Jesus." I eased my softening cock from her mouth.

She wiped the corners of her mouth, pulling the last drops of me onto her tongue before swallowing.

If my dick were hard, I would've come again from seeing her do that.

"Good girl." I stroked the side of her cheek, finding a little bit she'd missed.

I placed the pad of my thumb against her mouth. "Open up. One last drop."

As I slid my finger inside, my dick twitched but quickly fell flat, totally milked and spent.

"I can't decide if you're an asshole or not," she muttered after she'd swallowed.

"But you like me anyway."

"Hardly," she shot back as she climbed to her feet.

"Your pussy says otherwise."

"Bastard."

"I bet you're still wet. Maybe wetter after sucking my cock." I grabbed her arms and pulled her toward me.

"Am not." She pushed against my chest.

Reaching down, I slid my fingers through her, feeling her wetter than before. She moaned as her mouth fell open and then she gasped. After raking her with my fingertips, I brought them back up to our faces.

"Liar," I murmured as I placed them against my tongue and brought her mouth to mine. I wanted her to taste exactly what I had—her on my tongue.

I wasn't done with her yet.

The night was still young.

CHAPTER 22

TRY ME, PRINCESS

RACE

I twirled my finger against his pec, making tiny circles. "You don't understand how I grew up."

As he stroked the side of my arm, he inched his body closer, resting his chin on top of my head. "Tell me, then."

"It's so boring."

"I don't think anything you say is boring."

"Fine," I whispered as I caressed his skin. "My mother was a total religious prude."

"Was?" He squeezed my shoulder.

"She's alive. Don't worry. We haven't spoken in years though."

"I'm sorry."

"I'm not. She was a nightmare after my father died. She had always been religious, but after he passed, she became a fanatic."

"She's one of those people. Sorry, kid." He kissed my hair before adjusting our bodies. He slid downward, making us face each other.

Fucking hell.

It was easier to confess stuff to him when I didn't have to look him in the eyes.

"She was ashamed of me. I could never do anything right in her eyes anymore. Every day, she'd tell me I was going to hell for something or other. I had enough of it after I left for college. I haven't spoken to her since the day I stepped on campus."

He brushed his fingers against my cheek. "Do you regret it?" he asked as his face softened.

I shook my head. "Not at all. I'd rather be alone than listen to her tell me I'm not good enough every day."

"Is that why your work is so important to you?"

I nodded and wished it weren't true. "It's all I have. My family has fallen apart. Some of it is my fault, but I've committed myself to my work. I'm good at it, and I want to make a name for myself."

"You will." He touched me tenderly.

"If we get the tape back," I whispered.

"There's no we, and it'll all be over tomorrow," he said. "About that." He removed his hand from my face.

"What?" My stomach dropped.

"I found a current connection between you and Tyler O'Shea."

"Oh my God, tell me."

"His wife works at your company." He winced after he spoke. "I'm sorry I didn't tell you sooner."

"Who is she?" I demanded, now going through everyone I knew from work. "I don't know anyone with the last name O'Shea."

"She never took his name when they married. I found it when I was searching through his records."

"Fuck." I grabbed my cheeks and dragged my hands down my face. "Are you going to tell me who it is?"

"Nope." He shook his head.

I glared at him. "Why the fuck not?"

"Race," he said in a soft tone, scooting forward in the bed, "I will not allow you to put yourself in danger. If I tell you who she is, you'll go after her."

"I would not. And what's with the 'you won't allow me' bullshit?" I asked, feeling my jaw tense. Who in the fuck did this man think he was?

"You hired me to do a job, and I'm going to do it."

"You're fired."

"No, I'm not," he said. "Remember, I'll tie you up before I let you put yourself at risk."

I crossed my arms over my chest. "You wouldn't."

"Try me, princess." He smirked.

I gnawed on the inside of my lip, debating my next words. "Can I help, at least?"

"No. Absolutely not."

My shoulders sagged. "But if I don't go, I'll never get the tape back." I toyed with the sheet near my feet and refused to look at him.

"Hey." He touched my chin.

"What?" I asked, trying to figure out how to get the tape back myself.

"Remember when you said you trusted me?"

"Yes," I mumbled, staring at his lips.

"You have to trust me now, Race." He brought my eyes to his.

"I do, but so much can go wrong."

"Nothing will go wrong. You have an entire team of men behind you."

"Do they have an opening for a businesswoman? Because when that tape gets released, I'll be blackballed."

"You're so dramatic." He rolled his eyes.

I straightened my back, squaring my shoulders. "Since I'm the one paying, I should be able to help out in any way I see fit."

"Baby," he murmured as he leaned forward to kiss me.

I weaved, avoiding the contact. "Don't 'baby' me."

He hovered over my lips, staring me straight in the eyes. "I'll talk to the guys and ask them if they think it's okay. All right?"

I glared at him, knowing he was just pacifying me. "Fine." I was going to find a way to be there when the shit went down.

I didn't have a choice. It was my life hanging in the balance, and no one would look out for me like I would.

No one.

I was the only person I could rely on in my life. It was how it'd been for years. I was okay with it. I had grown used to it. I couldn't just hand my future over to a man. That was how I'd gotten into this mess to begin with.

My father had taught me to trust my instincts.

DON'T LET HER RUN

MORGAN

Race's eyes grew wide, her mouth hanging open as I walked into her office. "What are you doing here?"

"Hey, princess." I took in the majesty of her office. I was totally impressed by the size. "I thought I'd drop by and see how things were going."

She glanced at her watch before glaring at me. "It's almost five. Aren't you supposed to be getting ready to go meet *him*?"

I nodded, tapping on my watch. "Plenty of time."

She sighed, pushing herself away from her desk before stalking toward me. "No, there isn't."

"Everything is set. We're just waiting for seven to roll around. The day is dragging. I thought stopping by would be a great way to pass the time."

She slid her hand up my arm and rested it on my shoulder. "Did you talk to the guys about me tagging along tonight?"

"Yeah. They said that you can meet us at six thirty at the office and we'll head out from there." I was fucking lying through my teeth.

Her eyebrows shot up. "Really?"

"Yeah," I lied again. I was going to have to do some major groveling later to make up for the bullshit falling out of my mouth.

"Thank you." She leaned forward and gave me a kiss square on the lips.

As she started to pull away, I wrapped my arms around her waist and brought her body flush with mine.

"Where are you going? I need more of that," I murmured against her lips.

"Morgan." She pushed against my chest. "I can't get caught here at work."

"Doesn't everyone knock?" I peered over her shoulder toward the door.

"Yeah, but—"

I cut her off, covering her mouth with mine and breathing her in.

She moaned into my mouth as she pulled the breath from my lungs. I pulled her tighter against me, wrapping her in my arms.

What the fuck was I doing?

I hadn't gone there to fuck her, let alone kiss her. I wanted to drop by, say hello, have a quick chat with Natasha, and then make sure Race wouldn't make the seven o'clock meeting tonight. But here I was, in a lip-lock with Race.

I broke the kiss. "I gotta stop."

"What if I don't want you to?" she asked with lipstick-smudged lips, panting.

"I just wanted to drop by and see how you were and tell you about tonight." I licked my lips, savoring every drop of her left behind.

"That's all you wanted?" She backed away as she adjusted her shirt.

"Yep. That's all," I lied.

Three times I'd lied to her face. She'd probably have me by the balls later for it, but it was the right thing to do.

"Ms. True," her secretary called through the door as she knocked.

"Fix your lips," I whispered, touching my mouth.

"Shit," she muttered, running to her desk. She grabbed a mirror and tried to fix her lipstick but failed. "Yes?"

Her secretary walked in, glancing between us as she walked toward Race's desk. She gave me a quick wink before turning her full attention to her boss. "Natasha wanted to go over the notes for your meeting tomorrow before she leaves tonight. She asked me to give them to you and to have you phone her when you're ready."

Natasha. That was Tyler's wife—and possibly an accomplice in his scheme to ruin Race's career. I hadn't told her about Natasha yet, and I still didn't feel the time was right, but I had to warn her.

Race took the notes from the woman and flipped through the pages. "I'll give them a quick read, Cara. Call her and tell her to come to my office in five."

The woman nodded and turned on her heel to face me. "Are you sure you'll be done?" Cara asked as her eyes raked over me from head to toe, and with a grin so dirty, I knew exactly what she had on her mind.

"Yes. We're done here. Mr. DeLuca was on his way out."

"Shame," Cara whispered before she sauntered toward the door and left.

Race looked up from her notes with her eyebrows knitted together. "What did she say?"

"Nothing." I shrugged.

She tossed the papers on the desk and collapsed in her chair. "Is there anything else you need, Morgan?"

"Oh, we're back to Morgan?"

"Stop." She rubbed her forehead. "I have to finish my work so I can be out of here on time tonight. There's no way I'm going to miss it."

"But it's okay if you can't make it tonight. I'd prefer it if you weren't there." It was the only truthful thing I'd said since I'd walked through her office door.

"I'm going. Don't even try to talk me out of it. Now go so I'm not late."

I waved. "Yes, ma'am," I said before I left.

As the door clicked closed, a loud bang made me jump.

"What the hell?" I asked as I turned around.

Cara walked over to me, touching my arm. More like she groped my arm as she stared up at me. "Don't mind her. Oh, you must work out." She squeezed my forearms, working her way up to just above my elbows.

"Cara..."

"I'm too old for you, Mr. DeLuca. I'm just wondering what your intentions are toward Ms. True."

"Um, I don't know."

"Honey, the woman needs a man. I saw the look on her face when I walked in the room. I saw her bee-stung lips and red lipstick still smeared on her face. I think you're just what the doctor ordered. Just perfect."

"Thanks." I laughed. "I'm trying my best."

"The woman works too much. Life's too short and she's too young to always spend it in the office. Just treat her right, Mr. DeLuca."

"Morgan," I corrected her.

"Morgan," she repeated, dropping her hand from my arm.

The sound of a person clearing their throat made us both turn.

"Am I interrupting?" the woman asked, glaring at me and giving us both a look of disgust.

Cara shook her head as she sat down and started moving papers around on the desk. "I was just saying goodbye, ma'am. You're a few minutes early, but I'm sure Ms. True is ready for you."

In front of me stood Natasha.

The vibe she threw off was that of a megabitch.

Although Race carried herself with authority, she had nothing on Natasha. Her pin-straight black hair was pulled up in a bun so tight that I wondered if it altered the look of her face. Her business suit was perfect, not a wrinkle on it, as if she'd stood all day to avoid any imperfections.

"And you are?" Natasha asked in a snotty tone as she looked me over, but not like Cara had before. Natasha looked at me like a low-class citizen who wasn't fit to breathe the same air she was breathing.

"Mr. DeLuca," I replied as I looked at her the exact same way she had me, but I held my hand out, trying to be courteous.

She glanced down and snarled. "I'm sure she's ready for me," Natasha said as she walked past me and entered Race's office without knocking.

"Wow," I muttered to myself before the door closed.

"She's a real treat," Cara said before sticking her finger in her mouth. "She's one of the ugliest people I know."

I wondered if Cara was the eyes and ears in this place. Typically, secretaries talked. If there was a bitchy boss, I wondered how much information was shared between them.

"Let me ask you something," I whispered as I leaned on Cara's desk to be close enough not to be overheard.

"Anything you want, handsome." She gazed up at me.

"Natasha. Good person or bad? I think I know the answer."

"Nothing but bad there."

"How bad?" I rubbed my chin.

"She'd sell her own mother for personal gain. She's the worst there is here. No one likes her, and poor Ms. True has to work with her. They're both in line for partnership. It's dog-eat-dog, and I worry Natasha will do anything to win."

"I'll make sure that doesn't happen," I said even though I didn't know how in the fuck I'd do that. But I knew that if Natasha were involved, I wouldn't let her destroy Race.

"Who are you, Morgan?" She rested her chin in her palm, giving me dreamy eyes.

"I may be done before anything gets started."

"Well, isn't that confusing?"

"If you see me again, I'll answer it. Right now, everything is in the air."

"Don't let her run," she whispered. "She needs a tight leash, that one." Cara covered her mouth. "Don't ever tell her I said that."

I ran my fingers across my lips and replied, "My lips are sealed."

"Cara!" a voice yelled from the other side of the closed door.

She pushed back from the desk. "You better go before we get ourselves in trouble."

I nodded. I liked Cara. I felt like we could be good friends. "I'm out. Nice chatting with you, Cara."

"Any time, handsome. Come back, ya hear?" She waved before disappearing into Race's office.

As soon as I exited the building, I dialed Johnny. "Hey, this is Race's friend from the other day."

"Hi, son. What can I do for you?"

"Race is going to call you tonight. I need a favor."

"Anything you or Race need, I'm there for you."

"Here's what I need you to do for me," I said before setting my plan into motion.

CHAPTER 24
I'M COMING, STFU
RACE

After I changed into a pair of black track pants, a formfitting, black tank top, and matching sneakers, I headed for the door. I probably looked like a complete fool, but I couldn't exactly show up in my business suit.

For once, I got out of the office on time.

I walked toward my car, feeling the summer sun beating down against my clothing as it scorched my skin underneath.

Me: I'm on my way.

I texted Morgan before I rifled through my purse to grab my keys. As I approached my car, I could see immediately that something was wrong.

I closed my eyes, drawing deep breaths through my nose.

This can't be happening. No. No.

This can't be happening.

One of my tires was flat. I wasn't going anywhere any time soon.

"Fuck." I gripped my keys hard enough that they dug into the cuts on my hands, making me wince. "Motherfucker!" I yelled out, trying to steady my breathing but finding it impossible.

I closed my eyes again. Tears started to form as I stood there, trying not to be hysterical.

Just as I was about to throw my shit everywhere in a mini fit, my phone beeped.

Morgan: When will you be here?

I replied through watery eyes, having to erase my message a few times before getting it right.

Me: As soon as I can get a cab. I have a flat tire.

Morgan: Do not leave the office.

He can't be serious.

I didn't care if I had to walk to the damn meeting spot; I was going to be there. I tried to hold the phone steady as I typed back with shaky fingers.

Me: I'm coming. STFU.

I tossed my keys in my purse, giving my car one more look before marching back toward the office building. I stopped three steps away from the front door, dialing Johnny.

He answered the phone with his same old greeting. "Johnny's Auto."

"Hey, Johnny. It's Race."

"Baby girl, twice in one week. I couldn't be so lucky."

A pang of guilt sliced through me. He seemed to like talking about my father as much as I did, and he was the only connection I had to talk with about him now.

"I'm sorry, Johnny. I should call you more."

"I know you're busy, kid. You're a high-powered businesswoman now. Your daddy would've been so proud."

"I need your help." I avoided his statement about my father. I didn't want to lose time by chatting about the olden days. There would be time for that later, but Tyler needed to be dealt with today.

"What can I do for ya?"

"I have a flat tire. I need your help, Johnny."

"Seems to be common problem this week."

"Yeah." I laughed through my tears. "Can you help me?"

"I can. I'll be there as soon as possible."

"Johnny," I said, twirling the keys on my index finger as I started through the door of the office building, "I won't be here when you get here. I'll leave the keys with security."

"Where are you going?" he asked, panic evident in his voice.

I stopped mid-step. "What does it matter?"

"It doesn't. I just don't know which car is yours."

It couldn't be true.

Did Morgan do this?

He couldn't have.

He wouldn't have.

He said I could go.

But he didn't want me to go.

Who the hell was I kidding?

Even if he had forbidden it, I would find a way to be there.

"Johnny, did Morgan call you today?" I narrowed my eyes as my nostrils flared.

"Well, um. No," he whispered.

"Fuck. Seriously. You're both working against me."

"No!" Johnny yelled. "Race, he just doesn't want you to get hurt. I don't know what kind of trouble you're in."

"Stop."

"But—"

"Johnny, I'm a grown woman. I've always dealt with my problems, and I'll do it again. No one is ever going to tell me no. Keys are with the security guard. I'll text you the address, and I drive a BMW Alpina B6. It'll be the one with the flat tire."

"Race, I don't think you should—"

I didn't hear the rest of his statement. I hit end on the screen, hanging up on Johnny.

Morgan's a fucking asshole.

I should've known he'd pull some shit to make sure I couldn't be there. I knew I could never trust a man. They all thought they knew what was best.

I only had one thing to do. I'd call a cab and go directly to the meeting location. Fuck them all. I'd get my tape back myself and show the guys that I didn't need them after all.

After I'd left my keys with security, I went outside to wait for the taxi. I paced, becoming more pissed with each passing second.

Morgan DeLuca was going to pay—right after I helped to bring Tyler O'Shea down and retrieved my video.

I had my best friend in my purse, my Beretta PX4.

Tyler would give me that video.

Anything to save my career.

I'd have to deal with Morgan another day.

He'd wish he'd never met me by the time I was done with him.

Just as I tossed the gun back in my purse, the taxi pulled in.

It was now or never.

HELL TO PAY

MORGAN

"Dude, that takes balls," Sam said as he drove to the abandoned warehouse.

Race was far from stupid. She'd figure it out sooner or later, and it wouldn't be a pretty sight when she saw me again.

Race: As soon as I can get a cab. I have a flat tire.

"I'll pay for it later." I stared out the passenger window with a knot in my stomach.

"If there is a later." Thomas slapped me on the back of the head.

"What's that supposed to mean?" I ignored the fact that he'd hit me and replied to her text.

Me: Do not leave the office.

"She'll probably never talk to you again, man." Thomas shook his head. "You lied to her. Never mind about the tire."

"Yep. You're never getting another shot with her," James added. "Izzy would murder me."

"Race will get over it," I said, shrugging it off.

"I doubt that. I've only met her a couple of times, but she doesn't seem like the type to forgive and forget," Thomas said.

"I'm not saying I won't pay dearly for it, guys, but I think I can handle her." I glanced in the backseat.

"You like this girl that much, huh?" James asked.

"I don't know why, but I do. God help me." I looked up at the roof and blew out a long breath.

"It's the magic of the tough chick," James replied as he patted my shoulder. "I know it well."

"I just can't picture my cousin dealing with your bullshit."

"My bullshit?" He snickered, clutching his chest. "Have you met your cousin? That girl has more tricks up her sleeve than Houdini."

"How do you deal with her?"

"You gotta break her."

"What?" I turned around with my mouth agape.

"James." Thomas glared at him. "You're talking about my sister here. Choose your next words *very* carefully."

James slapped Thomas on the leg. "No worries, brother." He glanced at me, lifting his chin in my direction. "We'll talk about the ladies later, Morgan."

I returned his chin lift. "I'll take you up on that offer."

"Five minutes out," Sam said. "We ready for this?" He adjusted his body, gripping the steering wheel so hard that his knuckles had turned white.

"You okay, man?" I asked Sam, placing my hand on his shoulder.

"I'm pumped. I've been on the sidelines for a bit. I'm so excited. This shit is like the olden days."

"The olden days sucked," James said, hanging his head.

"Oh, stop with your Debbie Downer shit, James," Thomas barked. "Everyone knows the plan, yeah?"

"Why don't you go over it again, because clearly we may have missed something the ten times you've already reviewed it with us," James teased.

The final minutes of the car ride were in silence. Each of us checked our equipment, removed safeties, and got mentally focused. Sam had secured permission from the owner of the next building to stash the car inside to avoid being spotted by Tyler.

After the car was hidden, we all took our positions and waited. Sam took the roof, being our lookout, while James, Thomas, and I took our spots around the building.

I was so nervous that I could barely focus. My heart was pounding in my throat and my palms felt slick from the nonstop perspiration that formed every time I wiped them on my jeans.

If this shit didn't go down right, her life could be in a shambles and it would be entirely my fault.

I couldn't let her take a chance with her life. She might be an adult, but like hell would I let her walk into a fire when I could put it out without her getting involved.

I glanced at my watch and realized more than ten minutes had passed while I'd been standing here. Tyler hadn't arrived.

"He's late," James said in my earpiece, figuring out the same thing I had.

"Let's wait ten more minutes before we call it," Thomas replied.

"I don't see anyone coming either," Sam added.

"Fuck," I said as my stomach began to sink. "I bet the fucker doesn't show." I had a feeling I couldn't explain. I'd felt it once or twice in the army, and typically shit went bad.

"What do we want to do?" James's voice echoed in my ear.

"I think you're right, Morgan. We'll wait five and leave," Thomas replied.

I crouched down, picked up tiny pebbles, and tossed them. My mind was racing, and just standing here was making me crazy. I didn't like the unknown.

I pulled my phone from my pocket, needing to check on Race.

Me: Sorry we left without you. No time to spare.

"Men, I think it's time to pack it in," Thomas said.

"Did you hear from Angel? Race said she was going to head to the office," I said, heading toward the building we'd hid the vehicle in.

"Meet at the truck. I'll call Angel on the way," Thomas replied.

"Ten-four," James said. "Something's off for sure."

"What are you thinking?" Sam asked over the radio.

"I don't know, but I know something bad is happening."

"Thomas, call Angel," I demanded as sweat lined my brow.

"I'm doing it, fucker."

Before I'd made it to the van, he said the words I didn't want to hear.

"She never made it, man."

Bile rose in my throat and I tried my best to swallow it down. "Everyone, get your ass back here."

"What are you thinking, Morgan?" James appeared at my side.

"I don't know, man, but I think we definitely got played. There is no way in hell anything would stop Race from showing up here today. I may have told her not to, but I knew she wouldn't listen." I tried to keep calm, but on the inside, I was crumbling.

"We'll find her, man." James patted me on the shoulder. "Move your asses," he barked into the radio.

"Fuck me." I shrugged his hand away. "I did this."

"Stop being a pussy," James blurted. "You didn't do shit."

I started to hyperventilate. "I did." I drew in a shaky breath, pushing down the fear that started to grip me. "If she were here, I'd know she was safe."

"Yo!" Sam yelled as he jogged into the building, Thomas right on his heels.

"We're all here. Move your asses," Thomas said, pointing toward the truck.

I pushed the fear away, readying myself for battle.

I'd get her back.

I climbed into the car, feeling on edge but ready to kick Tyler's ass.

Who was I kidding?

I planned to wring his neck until I choked the very last breath out of him.

The car ride was a whirlwind.

Thomas and James were on the phone with contacts, gathering intel and trying to find someone willing to hack into the phone records to try to pinpoint her location. I tried to text her and call her again, but she didn't respond or pick up.

Even if she were livid with me, she would have texted me back. I'd made it pretty clear how worried I was and that she was in grave danger, but nada. No reply from Race.

"She isn't responding," I said after the fifth text.

"I got a guy working on her location." James flipped the phone in his hand.

"We're just about there," Sam called out, moving his face closer to the window, sitting forward and ready to go.

When James's phone rang, the car grew silent. "Hit me," James said as he stared at me.

Please let her be okay.

"Got it. On our way there now," James said before disconnecting the call. "Last known location was her office. After that, the signal goes cold. Someone turned her phone off."

"Motherfucker." I punched the dashboard.

"Stay calm, man." Thomas grabbed my shoulder.

"Easy for you to say." I closed my eyes as my chest tightened. "I need to find my woman."

"Listen, we've done this shit more than once. We always get the girl back. Always," Thomas said in a calm, even voice.

"It's almost an inauguration of sorts around these parts. Angel was kidnapped and Izzy was abducted. Somehow, they're still alive and breathing."

"What the fuck?" I jerked my head back. "What the hell did you guys get me involved in?"

"Life isn't always pretty," James replied, giving me a shrug.

"It happens when you live your life on the edge, Morgan. You wouldn't be so upset if you didn't have feelings for Race."

"Fuck you! I'd still be pissed off that we were duped," I shot back.

"Yeah, but it stings because you fucked up and you like the girl. I promise we'll get her back," Thomas said, staring out the window, surveying the parking lot as we pulled in.

Before the truck came to a stop, I opened my door and hopped out, using the extra speed to run toward the doors.

I could see Johnny's truck in the distance near Race's car. She'd called, just like I'd assumed, but where the fuck was she?

"James," I yelled, stopping near the entrance as the guys climbed out. "Go see if Race is over there by her car."

He nodded, jogging away quickly.

"Excuse me, sir?" I asked, trying to catch my breath as I ran inside.

"Yes?" the portly security guard asked as he rose from his chair.

"Did you see a blond woman leave here about thirty minutes ago?" I leaned on the desk, ready to push off and run.

"Do you mean Ms. True?" A smile spread across his face.

"Yes." My jaw stiffened.

"Why, yes. She was waiting outside for a taxi last I saw her," he replied.

"Did she get in a taxi?"

His lips bunched as his forehead drew down. "I don't know, sir. I didn't pay attention."

"Fucking great," I muttered, squeezing my eyes shut.

"Find her?" James asked as he jogged through the doors.

"She isn't here," I replied as I made tight fists, trying not to punch something.

"Not outside, either."

"Fucking hell. We lost her." I started to pace.

James touched my shoulder. "Come on, man. Let's go to the office. We'll find her."

"We better," I whispered.

I wasn't done with Race True.

This wasn't how we were supposed to end.

CHAPTER 26

DARKNESS

RACE

Darkness surrounded me.

I lay here frozen, unable to see, as my eyes were covered by something.

My bones ached, my head throbbed, and I couldn't move. My hands and feet were bound, my torso strapped down, leaving me unable to so much as wiggle.

What the fuck happened?

The only sounds in the room were my labored breathing and the sob that was about to burst from my throat.

It all came flooding back to me.

The flat tire.

Waiting outside for the taxi.

Tossing my gun in my purse.

And then… I gasped for air. Then the attack.

I hadn't seen it, but I'd felt the blow to my jaw as the pain radiated across my face. As I'd grabbed my chin, I was struck in the head. As the world had gone dim, my knees had crumpled and I'd fallen to the ground.

I had been so consumed by my anger toward Morgan that I hadn't been aware of my surroundings.

It was my fault I was here.

I began to cry.

"Hello?" I whispered so low that I barely heard it myself.

I held my breath, waiting for a reply, but heard nothing in response as tears streamed down my cheeks.

I need to take slow breaths and keep myself calm, I told myself over and over again.

I couldn't do it.

Who the fuck could keep their wits about them in a situation like this? Seriously. I'd like to think I was pretty levelheaded, but right now images of *Texas Chainsaw Massacre* kept playing over and over again inside my head.

Pulling at the restraints, I started to hyperventilate.

My heart beat so furiously that it was all I could hear.

A door opened, making me freeze.

"Ah, you're awake," said a woman from a distance.

I held my breath, waiting for my heart to explode as her heels clicked against the floor.

"Can you help me?" I whispered, remaining still.

She cackled, slapping the bottom of my feet. "Silly, Race."

I tried to flinch, but I couldn't move an inch. The tender flesh stung where her hand had landed.

"Please. I'll do anything you ask," I said, my voice strained.

"You know, you're not as light as you look." She dragged her fingernails up the side of my leg, leaving fire in their wake. "Always the perfect skinny bitch with perfect tits and never a bit out of place."

I gasped.

I knew the voice. The acidic tone was one I'd heard before.

Natasha.

The coworker I'd thought I was friends with.

She had to be Tyler's wife.

"Where's Tyler? Did he put you up to this?" I asked, trying to swallow but not finding enough moisture to make it possible.

"You think you have everything figured out, don't you?" she snarled in my ear, sending shivers down my spine. "Tyler was never behind this, darling."

Wait. What?

"You've been the one sending me messages?" My stomach turned.

"Your hired goons didn't figure it out, did they? They pegged my husband all along." She dragged her nails down my arm, pressing harder than she had on my leg.

The skin had started to break, but I bit my lip. "Let me go, please, Natasha." I tried not to scream.

"Don't be a silly girl, Race. I've got you right where I want you." Her heels tapped against the floor as she took three short steps away from me.

The sound of metal clinking in the background put my senses on high alert. "I'll do anything."

One step.

Two steps.

Three steps.

"You don't get it, do you?" she purred in my ear.

"Tell me. I'll make it right." I turned my head toward the sound of her voice, trying to see through the dark material covering my eyes, but I saw only darkness.

"There's nothing you can do," she said calmly.

"I thought we were friends." I fought back the tears I knew I couldn't wipe away.

Cold metal touched my cheek, the sharpness of the edge biting into my flesh. "We *were* friends."

I stilled.

"Until I found Tyler watching your video." Her warm breath skidded across my face. "I thought he loved me, but it was never me that he had been thinking about."

"But you're his wife." Nothing like stating the obvious to a crazy person as she held a knife against my face—no doubt I was thinking about as clearly as she was.

"I am, but you're the one he thinks about when he touches himself. Not me!" she yelled in my ear, making me flinch.

"But I—"

She pressed the blade deeper into my skin. "Keep your fucking mouth shut! Imagine how my heart shattered when I walked in on him. He sat there, moaning as he watched you on the screen and pictured you doing *those* things to him."

I gasped.

"It's you that he fantasizes about. You're the one he makes love to. I knew it, but I didn't believe it until he said your name in his sleep."

"Natasha, I never ever knew Tyler. I swear I had no idea." My breath caught as the blade slid under the blindfold.

Squinting, I tried to focus my eyes as the material fell to the table. I blinked, trying to clear the tears away.

Natasha stood above me, shifting with the blade in her grip. She snarled as the blade turned over in her hands.

"I'm going to make you pay for what you've done to me," she growled.

I pulled at the restraints. "I didn't do anything! Please just let me go." My lips trembled.

She shook her head as she ground her teeth, clenching her jaw tight.

I squeezed my eyes shut, bracing myself.

She leaned forward with the knife, cutting through the fabric of my tank with ease.

I gasped for air as my head spun.

Using the tip, she pushed the tattered shreds to the side, exposing my bra.

I tensed, giving a guttural scream with a closed mouth.

"I'm sure he loves these." She ran the blade across the tops of my breasts and my skin broke out into goose bumps.

"Please!" I shrieked, tensing my muscles. "Please don't do this."

She wagged the knife in front of my face, taunting me. "Are you scared, Race?" She smirked.

"Yes. I'll do anything. Please," I begged, shaking my head as she leaned forward with the blade.

I closed my eyes. I couldn't look. I held my breath as tears streamed down my face.

Blazing pain, unlike anything I'd ever felt before, sliced through my body so hard that I became winded. I screamed in pain, pulling at the restraints, tossing my head back and forth. "Stop, please!" I cried out, feeling dizzy.

I prayed to black out.

Begged for mercy, but nothing.

Just uncontrollable agony that radiated throughout my body.

When she lifted the knife, blood dripped from the edge, falling to my chest. Her eyes widened as her lips parted.

"You look better already." She walked around the table.

I tried to steady my breathing, focusing on something else other than the pain. I felt the blood as it oozed from the wound, traveling down my side and pooling underneath my back.

"No. I can't." I sucked in a breath, trying to grip the table and prepare myself for more torment. "Please don't do this," I cried as my body began to shake.

"Ah, pretty, Race. Are you worried you won't be perfect anymore?" she teased as the blade came down again.

As I cried and screamed, blackness took me.

CHAPTER 27

TYLER MOTHERFUCKIN' O'SHEA

MORGAN

I kicked the front door in, jerking my head until I found him. "Where the fuck is she?" I headed straight for him, lunging at him.

"What the fuck?" He put his hands up to cover his face.

"Don't play stupid. What the fuck did you do with her?" I wrapped my fingers around his neck, holding him against the wall.

His eyes bulged out as he gasped for air. "I don't know what you're talking about!"

"What do you mean you don't know what the fuck we're talking about?" I yelled, glaring at him.

He pulled at my fingers, trying to lessen the pressure around his neck. "I don't. I swear to God."

"Listen, motherfucker. I'll choke the last breath out of you right now," I growled. "Tell me where the fuck you're keeping Race."

"Race," he whispered, his eyes growing wider.

"Race. Where the fuck is she?" I squeezed tighter.

"Wait. I love Race." He dropped his hands to his sides.

"What?" My mouth fell open.

"I wouldn't hurt her. I love her," he babbled.

I lessened the pressure against his throat enough for him to speak, but not enough for him to get out of my hold.

"I wouldn't hurt her. I swear, man."

"Morgan!" Thomas yelled from behind me. "Let him go. He can't get away, and we can't get information if you kill him."

"Dude, fuckin' let him go." James patted my arm. "We won't let him get away."

"You should listen to your friends," Tyler said in a strangled voice.

I closed my eyes and applied just enough pressure to remind him that I held his fate in my hands. "If you fuckin' say one thing I don't like, I'll break your neck."

"Yes, sir," Tyler said, trying to nod under my fingertips.

I released him, pushing his body and slamming his head into the wall in the process. "You better start fuckin' talking."

Thomas and Sam stood at the foot of the steps with their guns out and ready to shoot, and James had my back.

Tyler reached for his throat. "Why do you think I have Race?" he asked as he rubbed his skin and swallowed.

"She got your messages about the video," I snarled as I stood one foot in front of him and didn't move.

"How do you know about the video?" he asked, his eyes as wide as saucers.

"Um, again, asshole. You sent her e-mails blackmailing her. I don't have time for this shit. Where the fuck is she?" I yelled, punching him in the stomach and watching him crumple.

He crouched over, holding his stomach. "I haven't told anyone about the video. It's still in my study."

"Someone knows. If you don't have Race, then who the fuck else could know about it?" James moved closer to Tyler.

"You got this all wrong. I'd never hurt her. I loved her from the moment I laid eyes on her in college. My lucky asshole cousin dated her. When he died, I found the tape, and I've never let it out of my sight."

"Sick bastard," Sam said.

"Who else fuckin' knows?" I pushed him back against the wall.

"Only Natasha. She kind of caught me once and…" He dragged his hands through his hair, still trying to catch his breath.

"Natasha. Where the hell is she?" I asked, looking around the room. "Sam, go look for her!" I yelled, holding Tyler in my grip.

Sam nodded and disappeared.

"She's not here, fucker," Tyler said. "She hasn't come home from work yet."

"Where's the video?"

"In my office," he said, pointing to his right.

"Show me." I turned him and pushed him down the stairs. "Try anything and Thomas there will put a bullet in your head."

"Jesus. I'm not stupid, man." He walked slowly with us inches behind.

As he approached his desk, I grabbed his arm and pulled him back. "Don't even think about it," I warned, increasing my hold.

"In the top drawer, in the back. Get it yourself." He glared at me.

"I'll get it," Thomas said. He pulled the drawer out, turned it over, and reached for a disc. "Got it." he shouted, putting it in his pocket.

"Where the hell would Natasha take Race?"

Tyler flinched. "I don't know."

"I don't have time for this shit." I pulled the gun from my holster and held it against his temple. "Where's Natasha?"

Tyler began to shake as he closed his eyes. "I don't know. Maybe the beach house," he offered as his lips began to tremble.

I lowered my gun. "You're coming with us, motherfucker." I pulled him forward, placing my weapon back in the holster.

"But why?"

"Because," James answered as we walked out of the office, "you know where the house is, and if she isn't there, we'll need you some more."

"Or I may kill you." I pulled him with me.

"Fuck," he muttered.

"Stop being an asshole." Thomas walked by us both and slapped Tyler in the head. "You're the reason Race is in this mess. You're sure as fuck going to help us get her out of it."

"Fine." Tyler straightened and walked of his own volition. "I don't want anything to happen to her."

"To your wife?" James asked with one eyebrow raised.

"No." Tyler snickered. "She's a coldhearted bitch. I meant Race."

"Sam." I ignored Tyler's statement about Race. "Let's go."

I'd never let Tyler near her again.

Whether he was involved in this shit or not, he would never, ever touch her.

Just as I stuffed Tyler in the backseat, Sam appeared in the doorway and headed straight for the car.

"If one hair on her head—" I started, but James stopped me with a hand on my shoulder.

"Stay calm. We need you calm, man. She needs you calm."

"I'm as calm as I'm going to get."

"We'll get her back," he said, but I knew they were empty words.

"Drive faster," I told Sam, feeling my very sanity start to slip.

"On it," he said, adjusting himself in the seat and stepping on the gas. "We're ten minutes out."

CHAPTER 28
THE END

RACE

"Race," a voice whispered in my ear, but it sounded like it was a million miles away.

I moaned, shaking my head.

"Wake up, Race. I'm not done with you yet," she whispered again.

My eyes flew open at a burning so intense that it ripped through my chest. She'd pushed her finger against the cut on my chest.

Everything hit me like a ton of bricks.

My awareness of my surroundings, the smell of her perfume, the sheer pain from the cut, and my absolute terror.

I pulled in a ragged breath before shrieking from the pain.

I mumbled something I didn't even understand as the tears began to flow again.

"See what happens when bitches like you try to steal my husband?"

"No," I screamed, shaking my head.

Just as she started to rip my pants from my body, the door burst open and slammed against the wall.

I turned my head toward the noise, seeing Morgan run through the door. Before he could take a step inside, Natasha held the knife to my throat.

"Take one more step and I'll cut her throat." She pressed the blade against my artery.

I lifted my chin, trying to escape and prevent the crazy bitch from cutting me, and pleaded for Morgan to save me using only my eyes.

Tears streamed down, covering my cheeks as I whimpered. "Please," I whispered to Morgan.

His eyes darted to me, growing wide as he took in the sight of me.

"Put the knife down," a man said as he pushed past Morgan. Tyler O'Shea stopped as soon as he saw me. "What the hell did you do, Natasha?" he asked as his mouth hung open.

"How do you like how your whore looks now, Tyler?" she asked, holding the knife closer to my throat. "Doesn't she look pretty now?"

"Natasha," he whispered.

"Do you want to fuck her now?" She glared at him.

"Morgan," I pleaded, tears falling faster than they had before.

I stared at Morgan, trying to get lost in his eyes as a group of men gathered behind him with the same look of shock and disgust on their faces.

"Put the knife down, baby. We can talk about this. She means nothing to me," Tyler told her, taking a step closer.

"Liar. So, if I did this"—she pushed the blade into my skin and I yelped—"you wouldn't care?"

"Stop," Tyler yelled, holding his hands out.

In one quick move, Morgan pushed Tyler to the side and took aim at Natasha. I held my breath, waiting for the knife to slice my throat.

As the gun went off, I screamed and blacked out.

"Race," a voice whispered in my ear, but this time, it was a man waking me. "Princess, can you hear me?" He stroked my face.

"Mmm," I moaned, unable to speak and too fuckin' scared to open my eyes as the noises around me grew louder.

Someone was undoing my hands and feet as the man continued to touch me with tenderness. "Race, wake up. You're safe," he said in a gentle voice. "Come on, baby."

I know that voice.

Morgan is touching me.

I am safe.

I don't have to be afraid anymore.

"Morgan," I whispered as my eyes fluttered open.

Pain was etched all over his face.

Maybe it was disgust in his eyes at seeing my wounds up close, but he didn't look at me the way he had in my office earlier today.

"Natasha," I whispered as he lifted me off the table.

"She's dead." He clutched me to his chest.

I settled into his warm arms and let my eyes close. Although I was in more pain than I'd ever experienced in my life, I knew no one would hurt me anymore.

"Rest, Race. I have you," he said, walking with me in his arms and kissing my forehead.

"Morgan." I nuzzled as close to his skin as humanly possible.

"I'm here." He rested his head against mine.

"I'm sorry," I said, feeling completely exhausted.

"There's nothing to be sorry about, Race. This is all my fault," he said as he placed me on his lap.

"No." I crawled closer to his side. "Don't put me down."

"I'll never let you go," he murmured, holding me tight.

"You guys go ahead. I'll deal with the police," someone said before the car door slammed.

I jumped.

"I have you." He pulled me into his side, adjusting me in his lap and closing my blouse. "Close your eyes."

I did as he'd said, too tired to argue or try to stay awake.

It was easier when I slept—or, hell, blacked out. I didn't feel the pain from the cuts, panic didn't rattle my body, and I sure as hell didn't have to think.

The only things I needed to know were that Natasha was dead and I was in Morgan's arms.

He'd saved me.

But I wasn't the girl I was before. The look when he saw me would be forever burned in my memory.

CHAPTER 29

DREAMS AND NIGHTMARES

MORGAN

It had been three weeks since Natasha had abducted Race. I hadn't seen her since I'd carried her into the emergency room and placed her on a gurney. I'd stayed day and night at the hospital, pacing the floors and driving the staff crazy. I'd pleaded with the doctors to let me see her, but she'd left strict orders not to let anyone into her room.

After three days, I finally went home to shower, and by the time I returned, Race was gone.

I called and I texted.

I even left messages at her work, but she hadn't reached out to me.

I sulked for the first week, got pissed by week two, and by the time week three rolled around, I could barely eat.

The only thing that made me get out of bed each morning was my job. The guys were great to me, constantly reassuring me that she'd come back.

I jumped when my phone rang. "Hello?" I said, feeling butterflies in my stomach.

"Yo. Where the fuck are ya, cousin?" Mike asked as he chewed something.

I sighed, feeling a knot form where the butterflies just were. "I'm not in the mood today, Mike."

"Dude, your ma said you better get your ass over here or she's coming to get you." He covered the phone with his hand. "I told him," he said.

"Tell Ma I'll see her another day. I'm just not into family time." I stretched out on the couch, barely able to keep my eyes open.

"Oh shit," he blurted. "Now, my ma said she's coming with her. Expect company, man."

I cleared my throat, throwing my arm over my face to block the sun out. "Tell them to stay there. I'll be there next week."

"He said next week, Auntie Fran." He paused. "Yeah, I'll tell him. Your ma just said she ain't taking no for an answer. You were warned," he said, and then the call disconnected.

I dropped the phone next to my head onto the couch.

I wanted to be alone.

The only person in the world I wanted to see was Race.

I pictured her smiling face, the smell of her skin, and felt the warmth of my fingers gliding across her flesh as I dozed off, losing myself in her.

I closed my eyes, wanting to dream for the first time since I'd been released from active duty. She came to me in sleep. I'd sleep my life away if it meant seeing her.

CHAPTER 30

FRAN DELUCA

RACE

The cuts above my breasts were mostly healed, but they'd never go away.

I ran my fingers along them, feeling the difference in the skin.

I grimaced, hating how they looked.

The skin was pinker and there was a glossy sheen where she'd cut me.

I couldn't let him see me like this.

He'd called twice today and texted me three times.

No matter how many times he tried, I just couldn't answer the phone.

I wanted to hear his voice.

Being in his arms, him whispering in my ear, would make everything melt away.

But I couldn't.

I wasn't ready to see him.

Especially the way I knew we'd end up.

I'd always liked my body, but now, it was just a reminder of that day.

I let myself cry.

I shed tears over Morgan, mostly.

I missed him.

He made me feel safe. I knew he just wanted the best for me.

He hadn't done anything to hurt me.

No.

That was all Natasha.

The wicked bitch would always be with me every time I looked down at my chest.

Natasha haunted my nightmares. I'd relived the night more times than I cared to remember. Each time, I'd wake up in tears with the sheets soaked.

That was when it was the hardest not to call him. I wanted him to hold me, to chase away the demons, and to save me like he had before.

Days turned into nights and hours turned into weeks as I sat on the couch staring at the television.

When I heard a car door close in my driveway, I shot up, trying to catch a glimpse of the person before they knocked.

Butterflies fluttered inside me until I realized it wasn't him.

I'd seen a photo of her before. I opened the door, not waiting for her to knock.

"Hello," I said, my voice a bit shaky.

"Hello, Race. I'm sorry to bother you, dear, but we need to talk."

I glanced around the yard. "Is he here with you?"

She shook her head and frowned. "No. I'm sorry."

Instantly, the excitement I'd felt died. "Would you like to come in, Mrs. DeLuca?" I opened the door for her.

She looked down at her feet and back at me. "I can stay out here if it's easier for you."

"Please come in. I'd rather stay inside if that's okay with you," I said, backing away.

She closed the door, looking around my home. This gave me the opportunity to get a good look at the woman behind the man. She looked the same as her photo, maybe a few years older but just as beautiful.

She wore a pair of washed-out jeans with a black blouse and wedge heels. Her hair was much like his in color, with every hair in place and cut near her shoulders.

"You have a lovely home," she said as she set her purse down on the coffee table.

"Thank you." I sat down. "Did Morgan send you?"

She sat down next to me, patting my leg. "No, dear. He has no idea I'm here."

I sighed as my shoulders sagged. "What can I do for you, Mrs. DeLuca?"

She turned toward me, smoothing her jeans out. "I want to talk to you about my son." She smiled at me. "I hope I'm not being nosy."

"You are." I laughed. "He told me about you."

"He's a little shit."

"He can be that, but he loves you though."

She took a deep breath. "He loves you too, Race."

I swallowed hard, trying to breathe. "He loves me?" I asked.

"Yes. He's been a mess since the day he found you."

"I'm sorry," I whispered and chewed my lip.

"He won't even come to Sunday dinner anymore. He's been grouchy, not sleeping well, barely eating, and just surviving without you."

"Oh," I mumbled. "I feel horrible."

She touched my leg, resting her hand on my knee. "So does he. He's hurting without you, Race."

"I miss him. I just can't let him see me like this." I motioned toward my chest.

"Baby girl," she whispered, tilting her head. "There's nothing to be ashamed of. If a man truly loves you, things like that will never matter."

"I'm scarred," I whispered, not trusting my voice.

"Did you ever think about having a baby?" she asked, staring at me with her lips set in a firm line.

"Someday."

"When you get pregnant and your belly grows big, your entire midsection will stretch. Even after you deliver the baby, the stretch marks will be there forever. Are those scars ugly?"

"Well, no, but those are from something beautiful. They're like a badge of honor earned from giving birth to another little being."

She squeezed my knee. "They're no different than these scars on your skin, my dear. You lived through something and should be proud of yourself for being a survivor."

I shook my head, glancing down at my chest. "It's not the same."

She touched my chin, bringing my eyes to hers. "It is the same. You should be proud that you're a survivor. It's only skin. What matters is what's inside your heart, Race. Do you love him?" she asked, watching me closely.

I swallowed, understanding what she meant. "Yes," I said, giving her a weak smile. "So much it makes my heart hurt."

"You need to go to him."

"I can't." I shook my head. "Not yet."

"If you wait too long, you may lose him forever."

Tears stung my eyes and slid down my cheeks.

"Don't cry." She wrapped her arm around my shoulder and pulled my face to her chest. "He blames himself for what happened to you."

I sucked in a breath, feeling like someone had kicked me in the gut. "Why?"

The tears fell faster, dropping onto her jeans.

"He didn't get there in time to save you."

"But he did. She would've killed me," I said, clutching my throat.

"He thinks he failed you. He assumes that's why you won't talk to him." She rubbed my back. "Sometimes our head gets in the way of our heart. He's reached out to you. Now, it's time for you to talk to him. Let him know that you don't blame him."

I cried harder. I'd put him through more heartache. I needed him as much as he needed me.

I wiped the tears away, sitting up. "You're right, Mrs. DeLuca. I need to see him. He needs to know I love him and I don't blame him for anything."

"Let's get you ready. I'll take you there. We'll surprise him."

"Um, he doesn't seem like the type to enjoy surprises," I mumbled, wiping my face.

"There's no time like the present. Imagine how happy you'll make him if you show up at his door. Up you go." She pushed me off the couch.

I stood, glancing down at her. "Are you sure about this? Because—"

She nodded, climbing to her feet. "If there's one thing I know, it's my son. He's in love with you, sweet girl," she said, holding my shoulders. "I want to make him happy."

"I want him happy too," I said as she turned me around, using my shoulders to push me toward the hallway.

"Then go get ready. We have a boy to see."

CHAPTER 31

PARADISE FOUND

MORGAN

"Open the goddamn door!" Ma pounded on my door and woke me from my dream.

"Fuck." I stared at the ceiling, running my hands down my face.

She'd shown up about the same time shit had gone south with Race. I'd spent the last twenty-one days trying to avoid her as much as possible. She made it harder and harder, showing up at my house unexpectedly or "popping in" to the office to say hello.

I never thought I'd say this, but I longed for my army days when shit was simpler.

When my heart wasn't in the hands of a woman and my ma was thousands of miles away.

Everything was complicated now.

Everything.

I yearned for the simpler days.

"I'm coming." I climbed to my feet and cracked my neck.

"You better open this damn door," she yelled again, continuing her pounding.

"Coming, Ma." I thought about escaping out the back door before I flung the door open just as her hand was about to land another blow, but instead, it hit me in the chest.

"Sorry, baby," she muttered as she glanced up at me. "Jesus, you look like shit."

"Thanks, Ma. You always know the right words to say."

"Look at you." She motioned toward my face and the stubble I'd let grow since Friday. "We gotta get you cleaned up," she said as she took my hand and led me into my living room.

"Hey." Auntie Mar took a step into my house.

"Hi, Auntie Mar," I said in a less-than-enthused voice.

"We have someone here to see you. You need to look better than this." Ma dragged me toward my bedroom.

"Who?" I asked, feeling my stomach turn over and looking over my shoulder.

"A friend."

"Ma…" I wasn't in the mood for her games.

She pulled me into the bedroom and closed the door. "You seemed so sad, love. I had to do something."

I shook my head, hoping she'd stuck her nose in where I'd never wanted her to stick it before. "What did you do, Ma?"

"I had a little talk with your girl."

"What?" I was both excited and shocked. "Is she here?" I took a step toward the door, but Ma blocked it.

"She is, but she can't see you like this."

"Jesus. I look like hell," I said as I caught a glimpse of myself in the full-length mirror.

I ripped my shirt off and ran into my bathroom. "Why didn't you tell me she was here?" I mumbled as I brushed my teeth.

"It would've ruined the fun." Her laughter carried into the bathroom.

"Now isn't the time for jokes. She better be out there. So help me God, if you're joking…" Then I took a sip of water and spat it in the sink.

"She's here. Aren't you glad I'm a nosy mom now?"

I closed my eyes, hardly able to believe what I was about to say. "For once, I couldn't be happier that you're so far up my ass I can barely breathe." I ran my fingers through my hair, smelled my armpits, and winced.

God, I sure as hell wasn't fresh.

I threw some deodorant on and grabbed a shirt from the back of the bathroom door.

"Let me out there," I told her as she still stood in front of the door.

She nodded. "We're going to leave you two here alone. When you're done, come back to the house for supper."

"It's almost four, Ma. It's past Gallo time." I lifted her from in front of the door and set her to the side.

"Your aunt postponed dinner until six tonight just for you and Race."

"What?"

"We've had this up our sleeve all weekend, baby. Now, you go make up with Race and come back to us."

I grabbed the door handle and glanced over my shoulder at her. "I love her, Ma."

"I know you do. Go get her, son."

"On it," I called out as I walked into the living room.

Before I turned the corner, I could see her reflection in the hallway mirror.

Standing with her hands clutched in front of her, she didn't look like the tough chick I'd fallen for over a month ago.

I took two steps forward, clearing my throat, and waited for her eyes to meet mine.

God, she was beautiful.

The sun streamed through the windows, lighting her outline and making it look as if she were glowing.

Her head rose slowly, and she met my gaze. Across the room, I could see the tears start to form and spill down her cheeks.

"Let's leave these two kids alone." Auntie Mar pulled my ma toward the doorway. "They can handle things on their own."

"Race," I called out, stepping toward her.

"Morgan." Her bottom lip trembled.

She leaped into my arms.

I wrapped my arms around her, holding her body against mine and burying my face in her hair. She smelled just as I remembered.

"I've been worried about you, princess." I inhaled her sweetness.

"I'm sorry." She wrapped her legs around my back and rested her forehead against my chin. "I'm so sorry."

"I'm so happy that you're here. Nothing else matters."

"I'm sorry," she repeated. Then she started to sob, shaking in my arms.

"Baby," I whispered. "Shh. Don't cry." I carried her to the couch, placed her in my lap, and cradled her.

"I shouldn't have ignored you." Her arms wrapped around my neck and she nuzzled into my skin. "I've been a horrible person."

"Come on now. Stop that. You're here now. I have you. You're mine, Race." I leaned back, taking her with me.

"I know. I've been so selfish." She sobbed, tears landing on my shirt as she cried.

"Race," I whispered, rocking back and forth, trying to comfort us both. I let her cry and held her tight. I didn't care about the tears or the fact that she'd used my T-shirt as a Kleenex. I was just happy to have her in my arms.

When she stopped, she pushed herself up, using my chest as leverage. "Can you forgive me?"

I stroked her cheek with the back of my knuckles. "For what?"

"For ignoring you. You saved me and—"

I pressed my finger against her lips. "Don't say it. It's in the past. What's done is done."

"I'm sorry," she mumbled against my index finger.

There's my girl.

Race was here. She was safe, and she was in my arms.

"Are you okay?"

She nodded, giving me a small flicker of a smile. "I don't want you to see my body again."

I frowned as I stared into her eyes. "Is that what you're worried about?"

She nodded again, looking at me from under her eyelashes. "I look like a monster."

I touched her chin, bringing her eyes back to mine. "Don't ever say such a thing. You're a beautiful person. We all have scars. Some we can see and others we can't. Wear those with pride. You went through something so horrible and survived it, Race."

Tears started to form again and threatened to fall. "I've been in therapy," she said, swallowing back the tears.

"Good."

"She's helped me."

"I'm proud of you." I leaned forward and kissed her forehead. "I've missed you," I said against her skin. "Are you healed?"

"Almost. I talked with a plastic surgeon, and I'll always have them."

"Scars don't scare me." I wanted to take her pain away, remove the scars from her body, and put them on my own. I could live with them, but Race had been through so much already. "Can I see them?"

She sat up and stared at me. "Not yet, Morgan. I'm not ready for anyone to see them."

I nodded. "When you're ready. Promise me you won't disappear again. If you do, I won't let you hide."

"I won't."

"Come here." I pulled her toward me and laid her head on my chest. "I want to hold you for a little while." I reclined our bodies, placing her on top of me as I spread out on the couch.

She relaxed into me, toying with my shirt. I closed my eyes, feeling her warmth.

I didn't care if she kissed me or if we had sex. I just wanted to hold her.

When I woke, I watched her sleep. Tiny snores fell from her lips as she inhaled through her nose, followed by a tiny puff of air coming out of her mouth.

Her top had shifted while we'd slept, exposing the edge of the scars near the center of her chest.

They were faint, much lighter than I had expected.

I pushed her top back and traced the lines, feeling their smoothness under my fingertips.

Leaning forward, I touched my lips to the one above her left breast and kissed it. She stirred, and I stilled, trying to avoid waking her.

"Morgan," she whispered.

I glanced up, my lips still against her freshly healed wound. "Sorry I woke you," I murmured against her skin.

"What are you doing?" She yawned.

"I wanted to kiss you."

She shifted, trying to move away from me.

I held her tighter, looking up at her. "I wanted to see, Race. I couldn't stop from touching them."

She stiffened. "Why?"

"They're part of you. I never want to forget that I almost lost you."

"But they're ugly," she said as her lip trembled.

"No, they're not. I love every inch of your body," I said, and I laid my lips upon the very spot she hated most.

"I don't know how you can look at me."

"There isn't a spot on your body I wouldn't kiss. Everything about you is beautiful."

"You just want to get in my pants again," she whispered as she started to giggle.

"Well. That too."

"So you don't think I'm ugly?"

I nudged her shirt open with my nose, exposing more of the scars. "I love you, Race True. Every. Single. Inch," I murmured against her skin as I placed tiny kisses along the lines.

Tears started to stream down her cheeks. "I love you too, Morgan DeLuca. Will you do something for me?" She wiped away the tears from her face.

"Anything." I glanced up at her.

"Make love to me," she whispered, running her fingers through my hair.

Without waiting another moment, I moved up her body and settled my mouth over hers.

I kissed her like my life depended on it, sharing the very air we breathed.

I didn't fuck Race True.
No.
I made love to my woman.

CHAPTER 32

SWEET AS SUGAR

MORGAN

Race fidgeted with her hands. "Shit, I'm so nervous."

"Why?" I stopped walking and turned to face her. "You've met Ma and Auntie Mar, and without me, too. They're the toughest."

She shook her head. "It was different."

"You weren't mine?" A smile crept across my face and I cupped her cheek.

"Yes. I mean, this is your family," she said, glancing toward the sky. "What if they hate me?"

I brushed her lips with mine. "They won't hate you."

"Liar," she teased. "We didn't make it to dinner last week."

I couldn't hide my amusement as I chuckled. "I explained things. They understood, princess. They thought we were busy."

"Oh my God. They thought we were having sex?" Her mouth hung open.

"No." They probably did think that. "They know we fell asleep."

"Uh-huh," she muttered and then sighed.

I grabbed her hand, holding it tight. "Come on before they come outside to get us. They're probably all watching from the windows."

"You know I love your ma." She walked beside me, squeezing my hand.

"You do?" I glanced at her.

"Yeah. She calls me every day to check on me."

"Fuckin' great," I mumbled as we approached the door.

"You don't know how lucky you are to have such a loving mom."

"Is that what she is now?"

Fran found a way to weave herself into every part of my life. The only sanctuaries I now had were at work and home, and even then, she'd barge in to check on me.

"Stop being a jerk. Fran loves you." Race wrapped her arms around my waist, resting her head on my chest.

I tangled my fingers in her hair and hugged her. "I'm a little worried you're on a first-name basis with my ma," I said.

"Morgan," she whispered, peering up at me. "I don't talk to my mom, so it's nice to have yours to talk to every day."

"She has plenty of love to give, princess." Maybe if Ma focused some on Race, she'd get off my back for a little while.

The front door opened and, like clockwork, Ma appeared. "There you two are," she said, holding her arms out.

Race released me, drifting to Ma as I watched. Ma had met very few women in my life, but this was the first time she'd welcomed one.

"It's good to see you, sweetie," Ma said, patting Race on the back and sticking her tongue out at me. "We've been waiting for the both of you."

"Sorry we're late, Fran. It won't happen again," Race said as she backed away.

"Oh, honey, you're fine." Ma smiled at me, repeating the gesture and holding her arms out.

"Ma, I've missed you," I said sarcastically as I let her hug me.

"Don't be late again," she whispered in my ear. "Aunt Mar will have a cow."

"But I thought—"

"You know better than to be late."

To Race, she was as sweet as sugar, but to me, her stinger came out and the old Fran appeared.

It didn't matter.

I appreciated the fact that Ma liked Race and treated her differently, even if I received the same old treatment.

"Okay, Ma," I said, not willing to argue and ready to see the rest of the family.

I'd seen James and Thomas every day at the office, but I'd missed my other cousins and my aunt and uncle.

In Chicago, I'd barely thought about them, with scattered phone calls and greeting cards throughout the year. Now that they were back in my life, there was nothing I wanted to do more on a Sunday than have family time.

After my dad had left—don't get me started on the rat bastard—family meals were never the same. Ma and I had sat around and stared at each other before I'd headed off to basic training. Life had changed in a hurry.

I realized I needed to cut Fran some slack.

Not only had her husband left her, but in a very short time after that, I had too. Her world had crumbled. Everything she loved had disappeared, and she had been left alone.

"I love you, Ma," I blurted out, giving her a final squeeze.

"Where did that come from?" She backed away from me and gawked.

"Nowhere. Just thought I should tell you more."

"You should," she replied in true Fran fashion. "I spent hours giving birth to you. Painful hours." She guided us into the house. "They're here!" she yelled in the foyer, the sound echoing through the space.

Ma stood on her tiptoes, putting her mouth next to my ear. "I told them not to scare Race," she whispered.

I gave her a brief nod.

Ma wasn't always a pain in the ass. More often than not she was, but there was also a thoughtful side to Fran DeLuca.

Times like these reminded me why I was thankful she was mine.

I put my arm around Race's shoulder as she glanced up at me. "You're going to be fine," I told her as we walked into the living room.

"Morgan." Izzy handed one of the babies off before walking over to us. "Race, it's good to meet you." She smiled at Race and hugged her. "Good to see you too, cousin."

James held both boys in his arms, looking content. "Yo!" he said, sounding a little like Mike.

I nodded then turned my attention toward Uncle Sal.

"Son," Uncle Sal called out as he approached me, holding his hand out.

I placed my hand in his and shook. "Hey, Uncle Sal."

He pulled me against him and gave me a hug. "I'm glad you're here, Morgan. We missed you the last month."

"I know. I'm so sorry for everything that's happened."

He shook his head and stared at me, rubbing his chin. "Don't be sorry. You're here now."

"Morgan," Auntie Mar chimed from the kitchen doorway. "I made your favorite." She winked.

"You're the best, Auntie Mar." I blew her a kiss.

An elbow smashed into my ribs. "Hey now," Ma warned, poking me again with that bony thing.

"I'm kidding, Ma," I lied. Then gave her a kiss on the cheek.

"How are you, dear?" Auntie Mar hugged Race.

"I'm well, Mrs. Gallo. I head back to work tomorrow, which is a little scary."

"You'll be fine, dear. Keep your head held high," Auntie Mar said as she rubbed Race's back.

Race waved as everyone stared at her. "Hey, everyone. I'm Race," she said as she elbowed me in the ribs. "Morgan seems to have forgotten his manners."

I grimaced. "Sorry, princess."

I'd just been so happy that I'd totally forgotten she hadn't met everyone.

To my utter disbelief, I felt more content than I had in… well…forever.

———

"I ENVY YOU," Race told Mia as we sat on the lanai after dinner.

I could barely move.

My stomach hadn't consumed that much food for as long as I could remember. It was hard to resist my aunt's cooking, especially when she'd gone above and beyond this week because of Race.

"Me?" Mia placed her hand on her chest.

Race nodded as she took a sip of her wine. "You have your own business. You don't need to deal with anyone's BS."

"Mama, mama," Lily, Mia's daughter, whined next to her, holding her arms out and shaking them.

Mia smiled at Lily before looking back to Race. "Why don't you just quit?" Mia suggested as she pulled Lily into her lap.

Race scrubbed her face with her hands and sighed. "I've worked my butt off to get where I am. I can't imagine just walking away."

"Do you love it?" Mia asked.

"My work?"

"Yeah. Do you love it?"

"Ugh," Race muttered. "I used to, but I don't know anymore."

"I'm sure what you've been through changes things."

"So, dude, when are we going to go out?" Mike elbowed me.

"What?" I asked, too busy listening to the ladies talk to have heard Mike's question.

"I want to hang out."

"Oh." I glanced over at him. "I'm so busy between work and Race. Sorry I haven't been around."

Mike nodded. "I get it." He motioned toward Race. "New love."

"As soon as stuff levels out, we'll have a guys' night out."

"Maybe we can get everyone to go." He smiled, looking around at his brothers. "Kids have put a damper on everything."

I peered over at Mia after he spoke. "How would you know?" she asked, glaring at him. "It's not like you've even changed a diaper in your life."

Mike blanched. "Have you smelled what comes out of those little things? I don't have the stomach for it," Mike said, waving his hands.

"For such a big guy, you sure are a sissy," I teased Mike.

"You change her, then." He pointed at the beautiful little Lily, with her wild, curly, dark hair as she sat in her mother's lap.

"Daddy sissy," Lily said.

"Lily," Mike said.

"Daddy sissy." Lily giggled, staring up at Mia.

"Great, man. Nice job," Mike muttered as his shoulders sagged.

"Baby, Daddy isn't a sissy. Look at how big and tough he is," Mia said as she glanced over at Mike.

Growling, Mike flexed. "That's right, baby. Daddy is tough." Mike stared down at his biceps, watching them jump.

"Daddy sissy," Lily repeated as her giggles grew louder.

"Jesus." Mike scrubbed a hand down his face.

Race giggled, covering her mouth as tears started to form in her eyes. She mouthed "Thank you" to me.

We stayed on the lanai, chatting until the sun hung low in the sky and dusk started to settle across the backyard.

"We better get going, princess. You have to be up early for work." I pushed my chair back.

"But I don't want to go," she whined as she climbed from her seat.

"Be a good girl and I'll give you a reward," I said, giving her a wink. "If you're a really good girl, I'll give you a spanking."

"Mama, why would Morgan spank Race if she's good?" Tamara asked Max, her face scrunched up and her tiny nose wrinkled.

Anthony patted Tamara's head, glaring at me. "Thanks for that, Morgan."

Max knelt down, bringing herself eye level with Tamara. "Sweetheart, Morgan was just kidding."

"But when I'm bad, Daddy says he's going to spank me." Tamara looked at me from the corner of her eye. "He doesn't look like he's kidding, Mama. Morgan is kind of scary," she whispered to Max, but it was loud enough that everyone could hear.

I found the entire thing priceless.

"Don't worry, Tamara," Race said as she looked down at her. "Morgan is like a teddy bear. Don't listen to him. He just acts tough."

"Like Uncle Joey?" Tamara asked, glancing over at Joe.

"Just like him, dollface." Race tapped Tamara on the nose. "Should I give him a spanking for scaring you?" Race looked up at me, her green eyes twinkling.

Tamara pulled at her lip, nodding slowly. "You should," she replied as a lopsided smile formed on her face. "If he's been a bad boy, then he deserves it."

"Oh, baby, he's been a very bad boy." Race winked at me as she stood. "I'll take care of him."

Tamara turned her body from side to side as she giggled. "Morgan's going to get punished," she said cheerfully.

"Only if I'm lucky." I patted Tamara on the head as I kissed Max. "Sorry, babe," I whispered in her ear.

"Oh, please. Anthony says things that are ten times worse." Max kissed my cheek. "I'm sure she's going to be very confused when she gets older."

"Yeah. Or she'll realize how sick we all are."

"Ready to go home, Mara?" Anthony picked the little girl up and placed her on his hip.

She tugged at his ear, resting her head on his shoulder. "Yeah, Daddy. Will you sing for me tonight?"

"Which one, baby?" He kissed the top of her head.

"The one you and Mommy danced to at your wedding." Tamara grabbed his face between her tiny hands. "Please, Daddy."

"Anything you want, baby girl."

"Sounds like you have a busy night in front of you, cousin," I said as I walked up to him. "I'll see you next week."

He held his hand out. "I wouldn't trade nights like this for anything in the world."

"I'll take your word for it." I shook his hand.

"There's nothing like the first time your daughter says, 'I love you.' You realize there's no other love like it." He clutched Tamara a little closer.

I dropped my hands, realizing that my cousin had everything in the world. A loving wife, a child, and an amazing family.

"You're a lucky man, Anthony."

"I imagine you're not too far off from where I'm standing."

I shook my head. "I'm at the starting line."

"It's not a marathon."

"I'm not sprinting."

"Just don't wait until you're as old as I am to realize you've wasted years running from the thing that makes you the happiest."

I glanced over at Race, taking his words in and knowing he was right.

No matter what, I was nothing alone.

The one thing in the world that made me feel complete stood across the table, laughing with my family.

I wouldn't let her get away.

Being apart for three weeks made me realize that I didn't want to be alone anymore.

CHAPTER 33
HARD CHOICES
RACE

A warmth between my legs woke me from my slumber. My eyes fluttered open and a moan escaped my lips as his tongue circled my clit.

I closed my eyes, pushing my body down against his face.

This was better than any cup of coffee I'd ever had, the way I wished I could wake up every morning.

He gripped my thighs, holding my legs open as he licked me. Clutching the sheets in my hands, I arched my back and struggled to catch my breath.

As my toes started to curl, his mouth left me.

"Don't stop," I pleaded, lifting my head from the pillow.

"I have to be inside you," he murmured as he crawled up my body.

Before I started to whine, he rubbed the head of his cock through my wetness and plunged inside.

"Yes!" I cried out, the feel of his mouth on me quickly forgotten.

He placed his arm behind my back, drawing me closer to him. When his hand slid under my ass, tilting my hips, his dick went deeper.

"Oh," I breathed, loving the feel of him inside me. I wrapped my legs around his back, drawing him to me as he thrust inside me over and over again.

Our skin grew damp, both of our bodies shaking as we came together. For the first time in my life, I actually had an orgasm at the same time as the man I was with. It was like the clouds parted, the heavens shone, and the angels sang.

"Damn," he murmured against my lips, his breath skidding across my face.

"Mm," I replied, unable to say anything else.

"Now that's the way to start a week," he whispered, rolling to his side.

"Ugh. Don't remind me."

"Still don't want to go to work?" He pulled me to his side with the arm that was lodged under my back.

"No, but I have to." I nestled my cheek against his chest.

"Want me to drop by and see you today?" He brushed his lips against my forehead.

"No. I'll be okay." I didn't know if I could handle going back.

Everyone in the office knew what had happened with Natasha. There was no way to hide it, and I knew that it would be on everyone's mind today as they looked at me. I wondered if they'd ever forget.

It had made all the papers. I hadn't even left my house for a week after I'd been released from the hospital. I hadn't wanted people to stare at me. I'd figured that after ten days, people had moved on to the next big story and had forgotten all about me.

When I did venture out, I still felt like everyone was staring at me. I knew they weren't, but I couldn't convince myself otherwise.

If it weren't for Morgan, I might have become a shut-in.

Let me rephrase that. If it weren't for Morgan's mother, I might have been perfectly content to stay in my home forever. She came to me, held me while I cried, and helped me pick up the pieces.

Without her, I wouldn't have been lying in his arms and feeling the peace that had just washed over me.

"I'm just a phone call away, princess. If you need me, I'll rush to your side." His other hand touched my arm, gently rubbing it as my body was flush to his.

"It'll be okay." I didn't know if I was trying to convince him or me. "I'm tougher than this. Damn," I mumbled.

"You're one of the toughest women I know. Remember that. You can do anything you want."

"Even quit?" I asked, glancing up at him.

"Quit if you want, princess. Don't do something you don't want to anymore."

I chewed my lip, wondering if I'd have the guts to quit and never look back without regret. "Easy for you to say," I said, rolling my eyes.

"See how today goes. You may have an easier time saying those words than you think. If you can't handle it today, then don't go back. Life's too damn short to be unhappy."

"I have a meeting with my boss at eleven. I'll see how I feel then."

Months ago, I would've said that nothing in the world could make me quit, but that had changed. Looking into the face of death had made me reevaluate my life. No longer did I find joy in my work— instead, I found peace in life's simple moments.

"You call and I'll be there, babe."

"I know you will," I whispered, wrapping my arm around him and squeezing him. "I love you, Morgan."

"Princess," he whispered, dragging my face to his. As he stared down at me, he smiled. "I love you too, Race. More than I've ever loved anyone or anything in the entire world."

I reached up and gave him a kiss.

Best Monday ever.

WORST MONDAY EVER.

When the elevator doors opened this morning, it sounded like everything in the office stopped. It was like being in a movie. As I walked by, every person turned to face me, papers fluttered to the floor, and people whispered to each other.

I knew that it wasn't really happening, but it felt that way to me. I felt every eye on me as I walked toward my office door. People nodded, giving me a sad smile as if they felt sorry for me. I held my head up high, refusing to play the role of the victim as I marched toward my office.

"Hi, Cara." I stopped at her desk. "Please give me a few moments to myself."

"So glad to see you, Ms. True," she replied as she nodded. "You take all the time you need, honey."

I turned on my heel and walked into my office, closing the door quietly behind me. My back collapsed against the door as I used it to hold myself up.

I couldn't do this.

I didn't want to do this.

I hated it here.

The last time I had been in this room, Natasha was with me. Even though she was dead, her words and actions haunted me.

I didn't want to be *that* girl.

I wasn't her.

I was Race—the tough chick that people cowered in front of, the one who bossed people around and exuded confidence. Not the girl who needed a door to hold myself up as I found the strength to take another step.

I glanced at the clock on the wall behind my desk, realizing I had two hours before the meeting with Mr. Emerson. Maybe I'd feel different if I immersed myself in my work, letting my mind focus only on the task at hand.

It'll only be tough for the first day.

If I could only get through this day, tomorrow would be easier. Just one day. Just like my therapist had told me.

Even over the last four weeks, small tasks had become simpler and I'd found myself feeling like I had before the attack. But that was at home, running to the store, or spending time with Morgan.

Coming back to work was like starting again at square one. I had to take baby steps to become the kickass businesswoman I had always been.

I was Race True.

Strong.

Smart.

Feared.

"Race." Cara's muffled voice came from the other side of the door as she knocked.

I pushed off the door and strode toward my desk as I tossed my purse on the couch. "Come in," I replied, running my fingers against the cool glass of the desktop.

Cara entered. After taking two steps, she stopped. "What's wrong?" She frowned.

"Nothing, Cara," I replied, glancing out the window.

"Come on now. I can always tell when there's something you aren't saying." She walked toward her usual chair.

"I just don't feel at home here anymore." I sat down, testing my chair as I rocked back and forth.

"You were meant for bigger things," Cara said as she looked around. "You weren't meant to be cooped up in a place like this. You should be running your own company."

"Now you're just being silly, Cara." I leaned back in my chair, thinking about what she'd said. "What's my schedule today?"

She stared down at her legal pad, tapping her pencil against the surface. "It's pretty light. I didn't want to overburden you today." She glanced up at me.

I returned her smile, though mine was less believable. "Thanks. What's first?"

"You have a meeting with Sue in development at ten and Mr. Emerson at eleven. Your afternoon is free because I didn't know if you'd make it a full day," she said, peering down at the paper.

"I think I'm just nervous about meeting with Emerson. I'll feel better when that's over, I'm sure."

"I'm sure," she repeated, standing from the chair. "Would you like me to get you a cup of coffee?" she asked as she strolled toward the door.

"That would be lovely, Cara."

"Coming right up, Ms. True."

With that, she disappeared.

Maybe a little kick of caffeine would have me feeling like my old self again. Or after I listened to Sue drone on for an hour, I'd be so bored and annoyed I'd want to throat-punch someone.

It had been a long time since I'd felt that fire burn deep in my belly. The old me had it smoldering, ready to explode at any moment.

I turned my computer on, ready to bury myself in my work and find the slow burn again. I wouldn't let them defeat me.

***

"Mr. Emerson will see you now," his secretary said, raking her eyes over my body with her lips set in a firm line.

As I walked through the doors of his office, I knew exactly what I needed to do.

CHAPTER 34

A LITTLE RACE FOR LUNCH

MORGAN

"Who is he again?" I asked Thomas, glancing down at my clock.

Race and I were meeting for a late lunch today. It was her first day back at work. She promised that she'd be here at two and I shouldn't keep her waiting.

"He's one of Joey's friends from the Neon Cowboy. His name is Frisco."

"Joe vouches for him," James said, raising an eyebrow as he rested his hands behind his head.

Thomas nodded, rubbing the back of his neck.

"Well, you two are the bosses, and if Joe vouches for him, then I'm sure he's a good guy." I knew that Joe didn't like many people.

The door opened and Angel was standing there with a man behind her. "Thomas, Frisco is here." She glanced over her shoulder and stepped aside.

"Frisco." Thomas walked around his desk to greet the newcomer.

"Thomas," he replied, shaking his hand.

I gave him a quick appraisal.

He had a muscular build but a lean frame. He stood pin straight, reminding me of a military man. His eyes never left one of ours, showing he was honest.

"It's great to have you here." Thomas looked over at James. "That's James, and over there," he looked toward me, "is my cousin, Morgan. Guys, this is Frisco."

"Frank is my real name, but I go by Frisco," he said, giving us each a quick nod.

"Come on in, Frisco. We have a lot to discuss," James said.

"Thank you," Thomas said to Angel.

She waved and closed the door, leaving the four of us to speak.

"What's with the name Frisco?" James asked as Frisco sat down. "Was your mom a *General Hospital* fan?"

"I'm from San Fran. The guys at the bar like to use nicknames." He shrugged.

"*GH* is a better angle."

"Let's go over a few rules." Thomas sat down.

"Shoot," Frisco replied, relaxing into his chair.

"First things first. Angel, whom you've met already, is mine. Race, whom you will meet, is Morgan's. Hands off our ladies. Let's just get that free and clear."

He raked his fingers through his hair. "I'm having enough trouble with my woman to even bother thinking about someone else's."

"Why don't you tell us about your skills?" James said, changing the subject.

"I was a Navy man for years, serving as a SEAL. I can't go into detail. Many of my missions are still classified."

I glanced over at Thomas just as he looked at me.

We both had the same impressed look on our faces.

Even though I was an army man through and through, I still had respect for all branches of the service.

SEALs weren't pussies.

"I think I have many of the skills, if not all, that would make me a great PI."

"Full of yourself," I muttered in a low voice.

He glanced at me. "I am," he replied with a smirk. "But I can back that shit up."

"So can I."

"Gentlemen, let's save the attitudes for the bad guys," Thomas said.

"We're cool, man," I said, giving Frisco a nod. "I know that, if he was a SEAL, he can back his shit up, but even if I was only an army grunt, I can too."

"We all have skills," James said. "If any of you didn't, you wouldn't be here."

"Go on." Thomas stared at Frisco and ignored me.

"Whatever you need done, I can do it." Frisco glanced at me out of the corner of his eye. "I'm here to be a team player. I just want to dive in and get my hands dirty."

"Let's just hope your first case doesn't go down like Morgan's," James said, patting me on the back.

"I wouldn't wish that on my worst enemy."

"That bad?" Frisco asked as he grimaced.

"Someday, I'll tell you about her."

"Did you lose her?" he asked, tilting his head. "I couldn't imagine someone dying because I fucked up."

"Nah, man. I didn't lose her. My world has never been the same since the day I was assigned to her case."

"I'm sorry to hear that." Frisco winced.

I remembered how simple shit used to be. "I'm not."

He returned his attention to Thomas. "I'm a pretty straightforward guy. I shoot straight, tell the truth, and sometimes I speak before thinking."

"Sounds like you'll fit right in."

I glanced at my watch again, realizing I was about to be late to my lunch appointment with Race. "I'm gonna run, guys." I stood.

"Try not to take an extended lunch again today," Thomas warned.

"At least I take mine outside of the office," I shot back. "Word to the wise, Frisco. Always knock," I said, holding my hand out.

He gave me a confused look as Thomas and James both laughed. "What?" he asked.

I shook my head. "Never mind. You'll figure it out."

"I have to run too," Thomas said as he walked around his desk. "I have a meeting with a potential client."

"I'll show Frisco the ropes and get him situated," James said.

I snapped my fingers, turning toward Thomas. "I have a meeting tonight with a client. So I plan to take a very long lunch. I'll be back in the office around six."

"Do you need one of us here?" Thomas asked.

"Nah, I got it."

"I'll be around," James added. "Izzy's home with the kids today."

"You better not stay late. She'll murder you if you leave her all day with the boys."

"Let me worry about your sister, Thomas."

"Frisco, if James doesn't come back to work tomorrow because my sister kills him, you can have his office."

"What the fuck?" I pretended to be insulted. "I should get that office first."

"Boys," James interrupted as he headed for the door and opened it. "No one gets my office. Someday you'll learn to handle your women like I do."

Thomas and I burst into laughter.

"He's so full of shit," Thomas said.

I used that as my cue to exit. "I'm out. Catch ya guys later. Nice to meet you, Frisco."

"Bye," he said as I walked out.

As I walked toward my office, Race approached from the waiting room.

"Hey, baby." She wrapped her arms around me.

"Hey, princess. How did work go?" I kissed the top of her head.

She peered up at me. "Fantastic."

"Really?"

She nodded and kept smiling. "Not at first, but it got better."

"Let's go into my office and talk before we head to lunch. Okay?" I asked, opening the door.

"Sure," she said as she stepped inside.

"So, work wasn't as bad as you thought it would be?"

"It was worse." She laughed. "So much worse."

"Okay," I whispered and stroked my chin. "You're acting weird. Why are you so happy if it was worse?"

She sobered as she placed her hands flat on the desk and leaned over. "Because I quit!" she shouted.

"You quit?" Relief washed over me.

"Yes." She stood up, held her arms out, and began to twirl. "I marched into Mr. Emerson's office and told him I was done." She fist-pumped the air.

I'd never seen Race this free and excited about anything before, and I couldn't help but smile. "Wow. That's amazing, babe. I'm so excited for you."

I hadn't been able to get her out of my thoughts this morning. Walking into that office had to be one of the toughest things she'd ever done. Everyone knew about her case; it had been all over the news the next day. She couldn't hide from it, and if her office was as cutthroat as she claimed, I'd expected problems ahead.

She stopped spinning, dropping her arms to her sides and swaying. "I feel free for the first time ever."

I walked over to her, needing to get a little piece of happiness myself. "I'm so proud of you," I told her as I pulled her into my arms.

"We need to celebrate." She giggled as she stared up at me.

"What do you have in mind?" I leaned forward and peppered her neck with kisses.

"Oh, no you don't," she said, trying to get out of my grasp.

I chuckled against her skin. "I can't think of a better way to celebrate."

"You're taking me to lunch." She crawled out of my arms, darting behind me.

"I'd rather have a little Race for lunch," I teased.

"We can't," she said as I tried to grab her, but she moved sideways and out of reach.

"Yes, we can. I've walked in on Thomas and Angel more times than I'd like to remember." I tried to catch her again.

She stopped moving as her mouth dropped open. "You have?"

This time, I didn't miss, grabbing hold of her arms. "Gotcha," I growled. "I have. I fear my office is the only one that hasn't been christened."

She placed her hands on my chest, smiling at me. "I'm afraid that'll have to wait."

"What am I supposed to do with this?" I asked as I rubbed my crotch against her stomach, letting her feel my hard dick.

"Oh," she murmured. "We can't have you going to lunch like that."

I stared into her eyes and pouted. "It would be a shame for it to go to waste. I can't really walk out of here like this, either, princess."

"I suppose you can't," she whispered, rubbing her fingers along my stubble. "Just a quickie. I'm starving."

"Quickie works, but later I expect it long and slow." I groaned as I brushed my mouth against the skin of her face, feeling the silkiness on my lips.

"Have something in mind?" she asked as she tipped her head back, giving me access to her neck.

"I always have a plan," I murmured as I kissed my way to her collarbone, stopping before I got to her scars. "Quickie now to make you happy, and a little something extra later to make me happy," I said before I bit down on her flesh.

She thought about it, her eyes darting around the room. She nodded as she looked into my eyes. "It's a deal."

"Sometimes a deal with the devil isn't always smart." I smirked.

"I think I can take whatever you're giving."

"Don't write checks with your mouth that your ass can't cash."

"What?" she asked, scrunching her nose.

"You'll see."

She threw her head back. "I trust you," she said through her giggles.

I held her ass in my hands and squeezed. "I want to own all of you. I plan to claim every last inch of you tonight."

She gasped. "Oh," she said, her cheeks growing flushed. "You know all the pretty things to say to a lady." She placed her hand on my chest, her palm scorching my skin through the material.

I placed my mouth over hers and gave her a kiss that stole the air from my lungs.

Fuck, I loved her.

I lifted her in the air as she wrapped her legs around my back, locking our bodies together. Carrying her over to the desk, I placed my mouth on hers, quieting her moans.

Opening one eye, I found the desk and laid her out on top of it.

"Are you sure this is okay?" she asked in a breathy tone.

"Totally sure." I slid my hands up her thighs, finding her garter. "Lie back." I reached the edge of her panties.

"Oh God." She grabbed the edge of the desk.

"Perfect," I murmured as I started to undo my pants and push them down to my ankles. My cock sprang free, harder than ever and ready for action.

Without having to be told, she lifted her ass and shimmied her skirt up to her waist, giving me an amazing view.

"Those have to go." I touched the edge of her black lace panties. As I grabbed the sides, she lifted, allowing me to pull them off. I twirled them in my fingers before throwing them across the room.

"Hey." She turned her head, trying to see where they landed.

"I have a new rule." I leaned over the desk, bringing my lips to hers.

"What's that?" she asked, her breath skating across my face.

"No more panties. They're forbidden."

"You can't just make that rule."

"I did. No more," I growled, moving her mouth with mine.

My palms caressed her breasts, and I rubbed her nipple with my fingertips as I kissed her. As my hand slid down her body, her back arched, moving my hand down.

She was slick and ready when I cupped her pussy.

"This is mine," I said, not really putting it up for debate.

"It's yours," she breathed, arching her back and pushing down against my hand.

"Good girl," I said as I slipped a finger inside.

Her back arched further, pushing my finger deeper inside her. "I want more. Gimme your cock, baby!" she whisper-yelled.

I looked down at her, totally in shock. I fucking loved dirty-girl Race. "Say it again."

She spread her legs. "Fuck me, Morgan."

It wasn't the same, but it made my cock leap at her words.

"You don't have to tell me twice," I said as I pressed the tip of my cock against her wetness, removed my finger, and thrust inside.

"Jesus," she murmured as I leaned forward, pulling out and pushing back inside her with more force.

"You feel so damn good," I moaned against her neck, pounding into her.

"Yes. Yes," she chanted as I covered her mouth with my hand, quieting her.

The desk jumped, moving with each thrust as I pummeled her pussy, driving deeper with each stroke.

"Everything okay in—" James asked as he walked through the door and froze.

I looked up, burying myself inside her.

Race covered her face. "Oh God."

I smiled, feeling like I was officially a member of the team. I'd christened my office and been caught for the first time.

"Looks like you're doing okay," James said, laughing quietly. "I'll let you get back to *work*," he teased, backing up and getting one last look before closing the door.

"Oh my God," Race said, her voice muffled by her hands.

"It's okay." I started to move inside her again.

"You're going to be in trouble," she whispered as she uncovered her face.

"No, I'm not," I said, driving my cock as deep as it would go.

"We can't…"

"Just wrap your legs around me and enjoy the ride, princess," I said through gritted teeth.

Gripping her tits, I held on to her chest, squeezing them in my hands as my dick plunged in and out of her wetness.

Her body thrashed, sliding against the desk as I shoved my cock inside her. I bit my lip, quieting the moans that threatened to escape as I battered her pussy over and over again.

She bore down, gripping the desk tighter as she fucked me back, slamming her core against me. As my balls slapped her ass, I felt the familiar tightness and tingle in my spine.

"I can't last," I warned, hoping she was close.

"Just a little more." She jammed herself down on my hard length.

"Fuck," I moaned, trying to hold out just a little longer.

"Yes. Right there." Her head tipped back and her body halted, gripped by the orgasm ripping through her system and squeezing the life out of my dick.

She sent me over the edge as my vision blurred and my breath hitched in my throat. I slowed my stroke, enjoying the feel of every inch sliding in and out as I came inside her.

I collapsed, hovering over her body with my shaky arm as I tried to catch my breath.

"I can't believe we just did that," she whispered, sucking in air like a fish out of water.

"It was fuckin' amazing." I pushed myself up as my cock began to soften inside her.

She sat up on her elbows, watching me as I pulled my pants up and tucked everything inside. "I could get used to a lunch break like this," she said with a lopsided, post-orgasm smile.

"Only if you're working with me, princess," I said, zipping my pants as I walked over to retrieve her panties.

She tipped her head, watching me upside down. "I can't work with you."

"Why not?" I thought it was an amazing idea. She needed a job; why the fuck not work here with me?

"I have a few ideas, and they don't include working here."

I opened my desk drawer, dropped her panties inside, and shut it with my knee.

"Hey," she yelled, sitting up and reaching for the drawer.

"Don't," I said, shaking my head at her and keeping my leg flush against the handle.

"I need those," she whined, trying to move my leg away but not succeeding.

"No panties, remember?" I cocked an eyebrow as I stared down at her, still spread-eagle and half naked on my desk.

"Fine. I have more where those came from." She slid off the desk. "I have to clean up," she said, looking around my office.

"Here." I grabbed a few tissues off the bureau and handed them to her.

"It would be easier if I had my panties back," she said, wiping herself and tossing the tissues in the trash. "Please."

I grabbed her around the waist, pulling her close and giving her a kiss. "Oh no you don't," I told her, brushing my nose against hers. "No panties when you're with me."

"Why?" She placed a hand on my neck and looking up at me.

"Cause I want to be able to taste you whenever I want."

She chewed her lip before she nodded.

"See how easy that is when you do what I want?" I asked as I pushed her skirt down, helping her fix it.

"You can be a bully." She smoothed the black material with her fingertips.

"But you like me that way," I teased, reaching out and holding her hand.

"Eh," she muttered.

"Race," I whispered then waited for her to reply.

"Yeah?"

"I love you," I said, feeling so much happiness that I thought I'd explode.

"I love you too, Morgan."

I was the luckiest son of a bitch in the world.

CHAPTER 35

NEW BEGINNINGS

RACE

"Where are we going?" he asked, shifting in his seat.

He still wasn't comfortable with me driving Elvira. I loved messing with his head when I drove. He was too easy.

Every time he'd flinch or grab the dashboard, I'd giggle. It didn't have much to do with his darling car, but more about giving control up to me.

"I want to show you something." I glanced at him out of the corner of my eye.

"It's barren around here," he said as he looked out the window.

"There's so much open space around here. That's why it's perfect."

"What is?" He turned his attention toward me.

"My surprise."

"I hate surprises," he grumbled.

"Just sit there and enjoy the ride." I pressed down on the gas pedal and Elvira took off like a bat out of hell.

"Race," he said, reaching out to grab the dashboard.

"Are you worried I'm going to hit a cow?" I teased, gripping the steering wheel tighter as I stared straight ahead. "Look around, Morgan. There isn't a thing for miles but trees, sunshine, and open road."

"Are we almost there, at least?"

I enjoyed every moment of anxiety I was causing him. "Yes."

"Did you buy a farm?" He dragged his hand across his face.

"No. Just relax, baby. We're only two miles away," I told him, looking for the hidden drive.

"Thank God," he said, pulling his collar out and fanning himself.

As I turned down the dirt road lined with pine trees, the sign finally came in to view.

He turned toward me. "You're bringing me to the driving course?"

I nodded, bouncing in my seat. "It's not just any course," I told him, unable to wipe the smile off my face as I glanced at him. "It's the place where I spent my childhood with my father. This is Johnny's place."

"You're going to make me sit in a car and speed around a dirt course?" His face paled. "Are you trying to kill me?"

"You can drive your own car." I pulled into the empty parking lot.

"I can't ruin Elvira."

I rolled my eyes. "You can drive one of the other cars. I wanted you to see this place."

"It's important to you, huh?" He relaxed as I parked the car.

"Very." I turned the car off and sagged into the seat.

I looked around, taking in the place that held so many happy memories for me as a child. It hadn't changed a bit. It was still an out-of-the-way, hidden course for those who followed the circuit. It was where many drivers got their feet wet before heading out to join the big leagues.

"I have something to tell you. I've been waiting until now to share the news," I whispered.

His eyes grew wide as his lips parted. "Are you..." His voice trailed off as he swallowed. "Pregnant?"

I covered my eyes, shaking my head. "God, no."

"Phew," he muttered, wiping his forehead. "I mean, maybe someday, but we haven't been a couple that long."

I raised an eyebrow as a grin danced on my lips. "I didn't know we were officially a couple," I said, totally yanking his chain.

"I told you you're mine, Race."

I clasped my hands together and hunched my shoulders. "You're always so romantic."

He threw his hands up as he exhaled. "Do you want me to get down on one knee?"

It was my turn to have the blood drain from my face. "No, Morgan. I mean, I love you, but you could ask me to be your girlfriend."

"Race, do you wanna go steady?" He smirked.

"You're such an asshole sometimes." I laughed, shaking my head.

His mouth dropped open as he held his hands out. "What did I do?"

"I want to be romanced, bonehead. A little more effort than what you just did."

He clucked his tongue against the roof of his mouth and rubbed his chin. "I'll come up with a plan."

I covered my mouth. "Now that's romantic," I mumbled into my palm.

"So, what's the news?"

"I decided what I want to do with the rest of my life," I told him, glancing at the building in front of us. "I bought the track from Johnny. I'm the proud new owner."

His mouth fell open as he stared at me.

"I'm going to make this the best damn course in central Florida." I waited for his response.

"I'm speechless," he said as he looked at the building and back to me. "You bought it already?"

I nodded, unable to stop smiling. "We're here to sign the papers."

"No more corporate world?" he asked, tilting his head.

"No. I figure I can use my background to bring this baby back to life. I'll bring Cara to help me, and we'll have this sucker hopping in no time."

A slow, lazy smile spread across his face as he leaned over and took my hand. "I'm excited for you. You're finally following your dreams."

I sighed, squeezing his hand as I stared into his eyes. "For the first time in a long time, I feel like I can breathe again. I've never been so excited about anything in my life, Morgan."

He motioned toward the track. "Want to show me around your place?"

"Yes." I released his hand.

We strolled toward the offices hand in hand, and I resisted the urge to skip. I felt like a kid again as we walked the halls that hadn't changed in twenty years.

"You have a lot of work to do." Morgan glanced around.

I squeezed his hand, peering up at him. "I know, baby. I can do it," I told him.

"I know you can. You can do anything you put your mind to. You're the most amazing woman I've ever met."

My cheeks now ached from the happiness I could no longer contain.

"Ms. True," said a man as he waited in the hallway outside the conference room. "We've been waiting for you."

"Here goes nothing," I said to Morgan, taking one last breath before walking inside and changing my future forever.

———

"You did it, kid," Johnny said as he wrapped his arm around my shoulder and pulled me against him. "Your dad would be so proud of you."

I glanced up at him, feeling the bittersweet sorrow in that truth. "I know, Johnny. I wish he'd been here to see it."

"He's watching over you, Race."

I swallowed hard. "I hope so." I blinked the tears away.

"What's the first order of business?" he asked as we gazed out over the track from the grandstands.

I looked over at Morgan as he surveyed the place. "I want to take him out on the track. He needs to experience what I feel when I'm out there."

"I don't want to go out there," Morgan interrupted as he walked toward us.

"Oh, yes you do." I glanced at Johnny and winking. "Trust me."

He grumbled, rubbing the back of his neck as he watched a car speed around the bend. "As long as I get to drive."

Johnny kissed the top of my head. "I'm going to let you two kids have some fun. I'm going to clear out my office."

I reached out, touching Johnny's arm. "I wanted to talk to you about that," I said, hoping he'd say yes.

"I'm all ears."

"I want you to stay on here and work with me," I told him, stroking his arm.

"I'd love to, kid. I want to spend more time at home, but I'll be here to help with anything you need."

"Johnny, you're the last link I have to my dad. This course has been yours since before I was born. It wouldn't be right not to have you here. You have a place here, with me, for as long as you want."

"You've made me the happiest man in the world, Race," he said and hugged me tightly.

Resting my head on his chest, I imagined that my father was hugging me, like he had so many times in this place. The familiar sounds and smells brought me back to my childhood.

"Thanks, Johnny," I mumbled into his chest, trying to hold on to the memory of my father.

"You two be careful out there, you hear?" He released me, glancing between Morgan and me.

"We will be, sir," Morgan replied.

"Are you ready to have some fun?" I asked Morgan, shaking with excitement.

Morgan didn't look so sure as he glanced back at the track.

"Should I call an EMT to be on standby in case he," Johnny said in my ear, motioning at Morgan, "has a heart attack out there?" He laughed quietly, causing me to giggle.

"He'll be fine," I told him, looking over at Morgan. "Once I get him out there, he'll relax."

"What are you two whispering about?" Morgan asked, walking toward us.

"Nothing."

"Liar," he growled, wrapping his arms around my waist.

I pulled our bodies toward the stairs, unable to wait another minute to get behind the wheel. "Come on, sissy. Let's get on that track."

He brushed his lips against my forehead. "Show me what makes you tick, princess."

"Hold on to your pants, big boy. I'm about to blow your mind," I teased him, patting his belly as we walked down the steps.

"I'd rather you blow something else." He glanced down at his crotch.

"If you're a good boy, maybe I'll reward you," I teased as I let my hand slide down his back and squeezed his ass.

He peered down at me, blocking the sun from my eyes with his size. "Baby, I eat your pussy every day and you're still a pain in the ass."

"I allow you the pleasure of tasting me because I love you. Feel lucky, big boy," I teased him as we set foot on the track next to the waiting car.

"I'm the luckiest son of a bitch in the world," he muttered as he stopped next to me, looking over the sleek, sexy red car in front of us.

I patted his stomach. "You are."

"I'm driving, right?" he asked, running his hand along the hood.

"You are," I said, letting him go to walk around the vehicle. "I'll be with you. I'm going to teach you everything you need to know."

"How fast does she go?" he asked, glancing at me from the other side.

"How fast do you want to go?" I cocked an eyebrow.

"I feel the need. The need for speed."

"All right, Maverick. Climb in and buckle up," I told him. "Let's see how big your balls are."

"Princess, I know you have a set, but let's not forget whose are bigger."

"You'll have to remind me later." I smiled at him as we climbed inside and buckled ourselves in.

"You shared your fantasy with me, making it real. Tonight, I'm going to show you mine." He smirked, biting the corner of his lip.

My belly flipped from the burning in his sapphire eyes. "I don't know if I like the sound of that."

"Don't worry." He laughed. "I'm going to make you mine tonight. In every single way possible."

I laughed, laying my head against the seat. "Going to ask me to go steady again?"

"You're going to have to wait to find out. Today is a day for new beginnings and celebrations."

"Ready?" I took a deep breath.

"More than ever." He gripped the steering wheel, feeling the leather under his fingertips.

Morgan understood the happiness I felt on the track as he took the corners like a pro.

Driving around the track, leaving everything else behind, we both felt the freedom it offered.

As he drove, I took a moment to take stock of my life. So much had changed in a short amount of time. I hadn't imagined I'd quit my job and be a business owner.

On top of that, I'd never in a million years thought I'd be head-over-heels in love with the man who'd saved my life. Not just from Natasha, but also from the mundane existence I'd accepted as my reality.

CHAPTER 36
MINE
MORGAN

I'd fantasized about Race all day as we sped around the track, feeling everything else drift away. It was the best fucking day ever, but it was about to get even better.

"What's your fantasy?" She peered up at me with uncertainty in her eyes.

I undressed her slowly, taking time to appreciate all of her beautiful curves and delicious scents. I pressed her front against the wall, pulling her top over her head, breathing in the smell of her vanilla-scented hair.

"You'll see." I leaned forward and nibbled her neck.

I found the clasp to her bra and released it, letting it drop it to the floor. As I pressed my hardening cock against her, I unbuttoned and pushed her pants down.

"Not even a hint?"

"It's a surprise," I said, repeating the phrase she'd used earlier today.

"I hate surprises." She shuddered as I slowly kissed my way down her shoulders to the small of her back.

I reached up, pressing her chest against the wall and pulling her hips toward my mouth to give me better access. I slowly licked between her cheeks, to her asshole, and past it to her wet pussy.

She jumped, pressing her ass into my face. She pressed harder against my mouth as I pushed the tip of my tongue into her, penetrating her ass. I moved my hand to her entrance and inserted a finger after a few up and down strokes, and I moved two fingers inside her. Her ass was slick with saliva as I nudged a finger against the tightness.

She jumped again, yelping softly. "What are you doing?"

"Shh, baby. It won't hurt. It's only a finger. Relax."

A moment later, as I fingered her pussy, she relaxed and pressed back, allowing my finger to enter her asshole. Slowly, I moved them in rhythm, with one finger in her ass and two in her pussy, all while nibbling on her ass cheeks.

She started to gyrate her hips in unison with my hand as I gently pressed a second finger into her ass. She paused, adjusting to the added digit before she started to move back and forth with increased speed.

Just as I felt her approaching orgasm, I removed my fingers.

She peered over her shoulder, glaring at me. "I was about to come."

"Not like this, princess. I need to be inside you," I said with a grin on my face as I stood. "Lie on the bed."

She walked to the bed as I made my way to my dresser. I opened the drawer and removed the restraints. I needed her to keep still for what I had planned for her. I'd claimed most of her body, along with her soul, but I needed to know she was mine and always would be.

"What do you think you are going to do with those?" she asked with wide eyes.

I sat down, brushing my hands against her cheek. "Do you trust me, love?"

"Yes."

"Do you believe I won't hurt you?" I swallowed hard, silently praying that she'd say yes.

"Yes," she said.

"I want to tie you up so you can't squirm away from the mind-bending orgasm I am about to give to you," I said, knowing that once I had her tied down, her ass was mine for the taking. "Is that okay with you?"

She nodded, lying back. "Yes."

"Never. I'll never hurt you," I promised, moving to the right side of the bed. Holding one strap in my hand, I tossed the others on the bed.

"I know you wouldn't."

I leaned over, whispering in her ear as I placed her hand in the loop. "I promise to bring you more pleasure than you've ever had in your life. Have you ever been tied up or restrained sexually before?" I asked as I tightened the rope around both of her wrists.

"No. Never trusted a man enough to let him. I won't lie, though—I used to fantasize about it." Her cheeks turned pink as she bit her lip.

"I'll be gentle, and I won't hurt you." I attached the rope to the headboard, both hands together over her head, and moved toward her foot before taking it in my hand.

She pulled her foot from my grasp, holding it in the air. "You're not going to leave me here tied up or some shit, are you? 'Cause I swear to God, I'll kill you in your sleep."

Tough-girl Race was sexy as fuck. "I just don't want you wiggling your sweet ass away from me."

After I'd restrained her, I stood at the foot of the bed, staring down at her. There she was, spread-eagle and all mine to do with as I wished.

I took one of my pillows and slid it under her ass, elevating her for easier access. I dropped my jeans to the floor and crawled onto the bed, positioning my dick in front of her face.

"Open." I pressed the tip to her lips.

She obliged, opening wide and taking every inch as her eyes stared into mine.

I liked her like this, totally at my mercy. Maybe it was her strong personality, her need to be in control, or her smart mouth, but having her completely under my control gave me a euphoric feeling that I couldn't get enough of, and I prayed that it would never go away.

As her tongue stroked my cock, I turned, touching her nipple. It instantly hardened under my touch. Moving my hand down her belly, I brushed my fingertips along her skin until I reached her slickness.

Just as she was starting to grind her mound against my hand, I pulled my hand back and landed a gentle smack to her pussy.

"Argh," she muttered with wide eyes, my cock filling her mouth, muffling her words.

"Never had your pussy spanked before?"

She shook her head, opening her mouth and letting my dick fall from her lips.

"No?" I lightly smacked it again.

She yelped, her body rising from the bed.

"You liked that, didn't you?" I asked, watching her body flush.

"Yes," she mumbled, relaxing back into the bed.

I crawled down her body and settled between her legs, taking in her beauty. I increased my pace and the pressure of each tap as her body arched up, meeting my hand with every smack.

"Yes." She panted.

I needed to feel her from the inside again. Pressing two fingers into her wet pussy, I slowly moved them in and out. She was close, closer than she was before, as I felt her pussy clench around my fingers.

Leaning forward, I sucked her clit into my mouth, stroking it with my tongue. She pulled at the restraints, trying to get closer. Damn, she tasted so fucking good. I could've eaten her pussy all day, but that wasn't part of my plan.

I wanted the one thing no man had ever had from her before. Nothing, not even the sweetness of her on my tongue, would cause me to lose focus.

As her body started to shudder and her head tossed from side to side, I quickened my pace.

Her hips arched off the pillow as her pants grew louder and her insides began to contract. "Yes! Yes! Yes! Morgan, fuck me with your fingers."

Removing my mouth, I spanked her pussy and fingered her as she came. "That's it, baby. Come for me. Feel me deep inside you," I murmured, forcing my fingers deeper as I pushed on her G-spot.

Liquid gushed from her pussy as she writhed. "Oh my God!" she wailed as her breathing faltered. She gasped for air. "What the hell was that?" she asked as she tried to pull a breath in.

I kept my fingers inside until her muscles stilled. "You squirted," I replied, completely shocked. I'd never in my life experienced something so...so spectacular. It was a complete turn-on.

I'd heard of women squirting, but I had never experienced it firsthand.

"Oh. My. God. I have never done that before," she mumbled, closing her eyes.

My cock was about to break off as I sat there, letting her catch her breath and come down from her high. Leaning forward, I drew her wetness into my mouth.

"Delicious."

If I didn't come, I was afraid my balls would be permanently blue. I moved between her legs, rubbing the head of my cock on her entrance, and then pushed it in to the hilt. She was so fucking wet that I almost lost it.

I stilled before I pulled back and slammed myself deeper. I thrust into her, each stroke a little harder as she arched her back to accommodate my length.

"Jesus, you're so tight," I whispered. Her pussy hadn't relaxed yet, still tense from the orgasm that had gripped her body moments ago.

"Fuck me, Morgan. Fuck me hard." Her body met my thrusts. "I love how your cock fills me," she murmured before I kissed her lips, silencing her.

Doing as she'd asked, I crashed into her—over and over until she came again. But even though my plan was to take her in the one way she hadn't been taken, I couldn't resist. The feel of her pussy milking my cock drove me over the edge and had me grunting through the pleasure that racked my body.

My legs trembled, every hair on my body stood up at attention, and my breathing stopped completely. As I spilled into her, my vision blurred and tiny sparks burst behind my closed eyes. I tried to hold myself up, not wanting to crush her under my weight. As my arms shook from the pressure, I rode the last wave of the orgasm that I hadn't been able to stop from happening.

"Fuck." I rolled to her side, trying to get air in my lungs.

"What's wrong?" she asked, her panting matching mine.

"That's not how I wanted that to go," I said, wiping the sweat from my brow.

Her body shook as she giggled. "I think it turned out pretty well for both of us."

"Says the woman who squirted all over the bed." I sat up and untied her feet.

"Sometimes we get what we need and not what we plan. You taught me that, Morgan."

"Oh, I need that." I reached over and stroked the side of her ass. "Turn over," I commanded, giving her thigh a quick slap.

"I don't think I could come again," she whined. "Plus, I still have this," she said as she wiggled her arms in the restraints above her head.

I unfastened her ankles, rubbing the red marks left behind by the ropes. "That's not a problem." I flipped her onto her belly.

"Well, fuck," she blurted, pulling on the single restraint that held her hands. "But I—"

"You will. I'm going to give you so many orgasms that you'll never want to leave me."

"I'll die if you give me another," she mumbled into the pillow, burying her face in the material.

"Baby, it's the only way to go." I ran my hands along her ass cheeks.

She looked at me over her shoulder. "Morgan?"

"Yeah, princess?"

"I'm never leaving you, orgasms or not. You don't have to do this," she whispered as she glanced at her ass.

I squeezed the cheeks in my hands, feeling their softness. "But I do. I won't feel like you're mine unless I have every inch of your body."

"Just this once," she said. "I don't know if I'll like it."

"I'm going to give you an orgasm so intense I'm going to have to perform CPR on you when I'm done." I was going to do everything in my power to make her heart stop from bliss.

"I'm yours. Take me."

I stroked my shaft, making myself hard again as I kissed the silky skin of her back. I took her gentler than I ever had before, letting her adjust to the intrusion and get used to the feeling of my hardness in her ass. It didn't take long before her tiny moans grew, turning into screams of pleasure.

I'd like to say that I lasted long, bringing her over the brink time and time again. But taking Race in this way, claiming all of her, had me spiraling out of control and getting lost sooner than I wanted.

"Mine," I murmured against her back as I came.

I realized that the only thing that mattered to me was her. Having her with me each night, spending my days with her, and making love to her made my life feel complete.

Race had softened me as much as I had her. She made me want to be a better version of myself. No longer needing to protect the soldiers of my past, I made her safety and happiness my priorities.

I loved her.

She completed me.

I fuckin' hated that line from the cheeseball movie she'd made me watch last night, but in that moment I understood it.

In all honesty, I hadn't saved Race True. She'd saved me. Giving me a life full of love and everything I'd always needed but never knew I'd wanted.

I was nothing without her.

CHAPTER 37
I DO
RACE

Today, I said the words, "I do."

Calm cascaded over me as I uttered the words, a peace I'd never known in my entire life.

I hadn't imagined they would be so easy to say, but they slipped from my lips like I'd always been meant to say them.

Morgan DeLuca was mine as much as I was his. He wasn't a selfish man, not the prick I'd thought he was when I met him a year ago.

At first, I'd wanted him for his looks, but when I'd really gotten to know the man and understood what made him tick, I hadn't been able to resist the pull he had over me.

How could I say no to a man who had rescued me twice? I loved him more than anyone, and I would be forever in his debt for everything he'd done to make me whole again.

His kindness and patience helped me get through the darkest days, and he still walks the journey with me now when I wake up screaming in the middle of the night.

"We did it," he said as we entered the church bridal room hand in hand.

"We did." I looked at my husband and smiled.

My husband.

It sounded foreign and perfect at the same time.

"Mrs. DeLuca." He drew me against his body.

"Husband," I murmured against his lips.

"Look at them. Think they'll make me a grandbaby tonight?" Fran asked as she walked into the tiny bridal room, interrupting our kiss.

I could feel the pink creep across my face as she spoke with Mrs. Gallo.

"If you're lucky, Franny. If you're lucky," Maria told Fran.

Morgan released my lips, turning us to face them. "Ma, seriously. What's the rush?" he asked as he shook his head, pulling me tighter against his side.

"I'm not getting any younger," Fran complained as she tapped her foot. "Just one."

"One too many," Morgan said, glancing down at me. "You want a baby right now, princess?" he asked, begging me to say no.

"Whatever Fran wants." I gave him a gigantic smile.

"Suck-up," he whispered in my ear.

"That's my girl." Fran came toward me. "Call me Ma."

"Ma," I whispered as my insides warmed.

"Just give her what she wants," Mike said as he entered the room. "Ma never shut up about it until Joe and Suzy got pregnant. Trust me," he added as he placed his arm on Morgan's shoulder. "Takes so much heat off you. It's amazing. Totally worth it."

"Says the man who won't change a diaper."

"I'm not crazy, woman," Mike replied, giving me a wink.

"Let's leave the kids alone so they can start on the baby as soon as possible," Fran said to everyone, trying to corral them out of the room.

"Ma, it's a church, for Christ's sake."

"Coming from your heathen ass, that's rich, Morgan."

"Mrs. DeLuca, let me escort you out and let the kids have a few moments," Johnny said as he grabbed Fran's hand and looped it into the crook of his arm.

Fran stared up at Johnny. "Anywhere you want to go, handsome."

Johnny took Fran out the door. He winked at me before leaving us alone.

"Don't egg her on, Race," Morgan pleaded with me, putting both arms around my back and smashing me against his chest.

"It's nice to have a mother, Morgan. You should be a little nicer to her sometimes."

"Babe, I'm as sweet as I can be with her. You give her an inch and she takes a mile."

"Did you see that?"

"What?" he asked, looking around the room.

"I think we have a new love connection."

He narrowed his eyes. "Who?"

"Your ma and Johnny."

"She needs someone in her life," Morgan said, surprising me at his coolness over the situation. "Maybe she'll forget about the babies."

"Speaking of babies." I cupped his cock in my hands. "Wanna practice?"

"Let's start right now. No time like the present, wife."

"It's a church, husband. We can't do that here."

He kissed me, nipping at my lip. "You're the one holding my balls. I think you already crossed the line. We're already going to hell. Best to make sure we have a little fun along the way."

I chuckled, letting his mouth travel down my neck and settle near my collarbone. When I'd picked the dress out, it seemed like a good idea to have a high neckline to hide my scars, but as I stood here with his mouth traveling across my skin, I regretted my decision.

"I'll follow you anywhere," I whispered, tangling my hands in his hair.

"You'll be the death of me," he murmured against my skin.

"Till death do us part." I reached out and locked the door. "I'm yours forever."

"Mine," he grunted as he lifted me into his arms and carried me to the couch in the corner.

"We're definitely going to hell," I murmured as he lifted the hem of my dress before undoing the zipper on his tux pants.

"As long as we'll be together."

My husband. My love.

My savior. My family.
My everything.

UNLAWFUL DESIRE

ALFA INVESTIGATIONS BOOK TWO

WALL STREET JOURNAL & *USA TODAY* BESTSELLING AUTHOR

CHELLE BLISS

CHAPTER 1

BYE FELICIA

"Fuck, baby," she said and reached for me, but I slipped out of her grip. "Where ya running off to?"

I grabbed my jeans off the floor and pulled them up quickly, needing to get out of here. "This was a mistake, Jeanine," I admitted without looking at her as I zipped up my pants.

She tried to pull me back toward the bed. "Come on. You know you want more," she said as she kneeled with her legs spread, giving me a full view of everything I'd already sampled and nothing I wanted again.

"It was nothing more than a moment of weakness." I shook my head, pulling out of her grip. "It won't happen again."

Her body jolted back before she narrowed her eyes at me. "You're a real asshole, Frisco."

"Babe, you knew exactly what last night was." I leaned forward and kept my eyes pinned to her. "Don't act like you're crushed."

She glared at me, crossing her arms over her chest. "But I thought—"

I put my hand up. I was done. Done with her. Done with us. Done with everything that had to do with her. "That's the problem. You didn't bother to listen."

Her nostrils flared as she flung virtual daggers with her eyes. "You said you wanted me, though."

"Yeah, I wanted to fuck you. Nothing more. We've been over for a long time." I pulled on my T-shirt, smoothing out the wrinkles with the palm of my hands. "Face reality, Jeanine. You'll never be more than a fuck to me. You made sure of it when you fucked your trainer."

The one thing I could never forgive was infidelity. She thought that her pussy was so damn good, I'd forget about her offering it up to someone other than me. When I made a commitment to someone, I fully expected the other person to follow the same rules. Jeanine hadn't felt the same way.

Maybe I treated her shitty by fucking her last night and being harsh with her this morning, but I didn't care. The hurt she caused me ran deep, and the pain hadn't dulled in the three months since the truth had come out.

I ducked just as her high heel landed near my head. "Get the fuck out of here. You were the biggest mistake of my life."

I grinned as I slid on my boots. "I'm the best man you'll ever have, babe. You'll never forget the way I fucked you, how deeply I loved you, and how caring I was with you. You'll crawl back to me someday, begging for it again."

She closed her eyes, dropping her head. "Just leave, Frisco."

I stopped in the doorway, glancing over my shoulder. "Call me when you're missing my cock."

"Fuck you!" she yelled, reaching over the edge of the bed, and I took that as my cue to get the hell out of there.

"Never again. That I promise you." I headed down the hallway, feeling a freedom I hadn't felt before. I'd never let her talk me into spending another night in her bed. I wouldn't even fuck her in a bathroom stall if she offered me pussy with no strings attached.

I jumped when a loud thud echoed through the small space. I guessed I'd hit a chord with my ex.

I'd spent three months feeling sorry for myself. Jeanine had ripped my heart out. We'd been together for two years, and just when I was about to propose to her, I caught her fucking *him*. She begged for my forgiveness, swore it had only happened once, and that it would never happen again, but I told her to hit the road.

It wasn't that I swore off women, but I couldn't even think about a relationship. The ladies at the Neon Cowboy, my favorite bar and hangout, were more than happy to share my bed without ties.

I walked out of her house knowing it was time for me to move on. Jeanine was my past, and who the fuck knew where my future would lead me.

I'd been given a fresh start.

For the first time in a long time, I felt ready to conquer the world. I had a kick-ass job at ALFA Private Investigations, a great group of new friends, and my buddies at the Neon Cowboy. Pussy was in abundance.

Life couldn't be any fuckin' better.

I'd never needed anyone to make me feel whole. I'd spent years in the military, traveling to countries most people only read about, and served as a member of one of the most elite fighting forces—the Navy SEALs. The men I surrounded myself with were my family and everything in the world to me. We'd looked out for each other.

Now, I had a new team. The guys at ALFA were my new family, and we had each other's backs just like my brothers in the SEALs did when I served.

Right now, work was the name of the game.

Pussy was a recreational activity.

Variety is the spice of life, right?

Who wanted to be nailed down to one woman?

I sure as hell didn't.

"Aren't those the same clothes you wore yesterday?" Thomas asked when I sat down.

"Shit happens."

"Who was it last night?" James dropped a stack of files on the conference table with a smug grin on his face.

"You don't wanna know." Sam began to laugh.

James shook his head, knowing the answer already. "You didn't?"

"She offered. I took." A slow grin spread across my face.

"Never go back." Thomas rubbed his forehead like he was trying to remove a spot from his skin. "It never ends well."

I leaned back in the conference chair, twisting from side to side and thought about his words. "Ended well for me." I laughed, remembering how pissed off Jeanine had been when I left. Fuck her feelings. She hadn't been thinking of mine when she cheated.

"Let's start the meeting and forget about Jeanine." Her name sounded like acid coming from Thomas's mouth.

"Please." Her smell still lingered on my fingers, taunting me as I rubbed my chin.

The guys hadn't stopped giving me shit about *her*. Every time I said her name, they'd tell me to get the fuck over her and find a new woman.

The problem was, I found too many.

"Let's welcome our newest member, Bear." Thomas gave Bear a nod.

"I'm happy to be here," he replied without a smile as everyone greeted him.

That was Bear—serious as a heart attack, funny as fuck, and scary as hell. We'd been friends for years. We were regulars at the Neon Cowboy and both friends of Thomas's brother Joe. We both jumped at the chance to work for a PI firm in town when Joe mentioned they were looking for new guys to hire for the crew.

"Frisco." James snapped his fingers, annoying the hell out of me.

I dragged my eyes to him. "What's up?"

He slid a folder down the long, black table, and it stopped right in front of me. "New case for you this week."

"What is it?"

"Someone wants proof that their spouse is cheating."

I looked up at James's grinning face and gritted my teeth. "Getting a kick out of this aren't ya, man?" I asked. Really, I'd been given a free pass for too long and could handle the job, but it was nice being offered the better cases.

"Shit happens every day to people. Just do your job and get the proof."

"Fine," I grumbled, reading over her details, and pretending to be upset.

"Sam, where are you with your case?" Thomas changed the subject and left me to study my next assignment.

I hadn't taken a cheating case in three months. Thomas and James had been kind enough to pass them along to the other guys.

I read the information that Mary Green had written while cases were assigned to everyone else around the table. There wasn't anything unusual. Her husband had started staying later at work, began dressing differently, changed his cologne, and added a password lock to his phone. She suspected he was cheating and wanted proof.

"Can I just ask something real quick?" Bear rubbed the back of his neck and seemed uneasy. I'd never worked with Bear, but he wasn't acting like his self-assured asshole self I knew.

"Shoot." James motioned toward Bear with a quick nod.

"When the fuck did we start calling him Sam?" His eyes moved to Sam before anyone could answer the question. "You'll always be Flash to me. Sam just sounds so, so...fucking old."

Sam's face turned pink. "I dropped the nickname years ago, Bear."

Sam, aka Flash, had worked with James and Thomas years ago. They were undercover DEA agents and Sam worked for the FBI. They worked together, not always nicely, to take down one of the biggest motorcycle gangs in Florida. Afterward, they were all sick of the life and the lies they had to tell, and that's how ALFA came to fruition.

"It suits you, though, pretty boy. I'm calling your ass Flash. Just putting it out there," Bear said and crossed his arms over his chest as he stood his ground.

Sam never seemed to sound right, but he tried to throw out the nickname. I didn't know much about the guy, but I knew that he'd had a thing with James's wife before they were a couple. The tension between James and Flash was often so intense that I could almost see the anger radiate from James.

Sam would laugh it off and try to smooth the waters, but James never got rid of the chip on his shoulder. Sam had a woman, Fiona, and was madly in love with her. Izzy, James's wife, was happily married and didn't want anything more than a friendship from Sam. James being James let the past lie, but he didn't forget everything entirely.

"Whatever you want." Sam held his hands up and gave Bear the killer smile he'd been nicknamed for.

"Glad that's settled," Morgan chimed in, tapping his fingers on the table, looking completely bored. "We done here?"

"Are you good, Frisco?" James asked, ignoring Morgan.

I nodded, giving him a fake smile while I closed the file. "I got this. Easy case."

"If it's too soon, I can give it to one of the other guys," he offered.

"What the fuck?" Morgan complained, rolling his eyes, and groaning.

I lifted my chin to him before I glanced at Morgan. "I'm not a pussy, man. I got it."

"About damn time," Morgan said with a smile. "You back finally, brother?"

"I'm back." I stood and glanced around the table. Each of the men around the table had my back. They treated me with kid gloves during the entire breakup. I wouldn't have made it through with my sanity if it hadn't been for them. "And better than ever," I added before I walked out of the room.

As I headed down the hallway toward my office, I could hear the guys hooting and laughing. I felt the truth in those words when I spoke them. I was no longer the man I had been even the day before.

I was better, a different version of my former self.

I was a self-described asshole, but I had a kind heart, too.

One thing I knew for sure: I'd never be anyone's doormat again.

"So it's really over?" Bear called down the hallway, following close on my heels.

I stopped at my office door and turned to face him. "Finished."

He fist-pumped the air and whooped before he spoke. "That bitch didn't deserve you."

"I know." My happiness had been written all over me since I'd left her place, unable to wipe the grin off my face. She fucking didn't. I knew that before I caught her with that steroid-filled douchebag.

"Drinks tonight to celebrate my first case?"

"Sure, Bear. Neon Cowboy?"

"Fuck yeah. Where else, man?"

"I'll be there. Now get to work so they don't fire your ass before you start."

"Pussy," he whispered and disappeared into his office.

Bear always knew how to put shit in perspective. He'd never liked Jeanine, but then again, I never cared what his opinion of someone had been before. Closing the door behind me, I tossed the file on my desk from across the room, and took a deep breath.

Tonight was a night to celebrate.

CHAPTER 2

MY THING...MY BUSINESS

My thing...My business

I walked through the doors of the Neon Cowboy and glanced around, scanning the crowd for Jeanine. Not because I wanted to see her, but because I didn't want to deal with her shit tonight.

"Hey, Frisco," Brandy, the waitress I flirted with often and fucked sometimes, greeted me.

Brandy and I had an agreement. We'd spent some nights together, enjoyed each other's bodies, and didn't need anything more. She was easy and didn't make my head hurt with her bullshit.

I buried my face in her hair. "Hey yourself, beautiful. How you doin' tonight?" My lips brushed against her ear, and she shivered in my arms.

"I'm better now that you're here," she whispered.

"Want me to wait around for you tonight? I can give you a ride home?"

"Yeah. I could use a ride," she replied with a small laugh.

"Let me hang out with the guys and then find me when you're ready to get off."

"I plan on it." She dragged her lips against my cheek before she backed up a step.

Tonight I'd get a piece of ass without hearing shit about it in the morning. That had been the best part of being single. No one expected anything from me.

"Look who finally decided to show his face," City said when I approached the table. He wrapped his arm tightly around his wife, Sunshine, before he took a sip of his beer.

We'd been friends for as long as I could remember. Unlike the other guys we hung out with at the Neon Cowboy, City and I had an understanding. I'd even say we were cut from the same cloth. We both believed in fidelity and loyalty above all else, and we knew how to treat our women until they needed to be tossed to the curb.

City had the look of a man you didn't fuck with. He was big, wide, and dark. His piercing blue eyes were haunting against his olive skin and dark hair, and his appearance unsettled many people who crossed his path. Much like me, his skin was covered in tattoos, but his were part of his trade.

"If your brother didn't work me to death, I'd be here more often." I pulled out a chair and collapsed. "Hey, Sunshine."

She gave me a lopsided smile and swirled the drink around in her glass. "Hey, Frisco. I haven't seen you in so long. How are ya, sweetie?" Her blond hair cascaded down her shoulders, kissing the edge of her cleavage, but I didn't dare stare.

I watched the way she curled into her husband's side, always touching him. "Just perfect, babe."

When I'd first met Sunshine, I didn't think she had a chance in hell of lasting with City. They were complete opposites—him a badass biker who inked for a living, and her a prissy schoolteacher with more issues and rules than I had back in Catholic school. But here they were, happily married.

"Are you over *her*?" Her eyes shifted when she referred to Jeanine.

"Yeah, babe. She's in the past." I looked around the table and my eyes stopped on Bear, who had a look that screamed *bullshit*.

He held the beer bottle in front of his face and stared at me down the glass. "Where was your dick last night?"

Motherfucker. Bear always had to throw me under the fucking bus.

I glared at him, grinding my teeth. "There's a lady at the table." I leaned forward in my chair, resting my elbows on the table, and glaring at him.

He glanced around before looking at me. "Who?"

I shook my head, wondering if he'd had a few too many already. "Sunshine," I snapped, motioning toward her with my fingers.

He laughed. "She's one of the guys now. I've heard her say some pretty nasty shit. Ain't that right, Sunshine?" He winked at her, causing her to giggle.

"Yeah." A straw clung to her bottom lip. "So where was it?"

There it was.

The innocence.

We'd all teased her about her inability to use cuss words, and she hadn't changed. But every so often, when you got her mad enough, she'd let them fly.

Everyone was fishing. They all wanted me to admit what I tried to hide, wanted to hide. I don't know if I was ashamed of the night before or just didn't want to hear their comments. I could see that no matter what I said, they weren't going to drop it until I fessed up.

"Where was what?" I asked Sunshine, trying to get her to say the word.

"Your thing," she replied as she set her drink down.

The entire table erupted in laughter. Sunshine had been a good girl —hell, she still was. She may have hung around with a crowd that cursed as if it was our only language, but she still couldn't use the words herself.

"See." I pointed at her, unable to contain my smile. "She's still an innocent."

I wanted someone like her.

Scratch that.

Although I loved her to pieces, I needed someone with a little more bite.

Scratch that too. I didn't want anyone. Didn't need them.

City choked on his beer and wiped his lips with the back of his hand. "She's far from that, man."

Bear slapped the table, tears forming in his eyes as he laughed. "Stop stalling. Since you're over *her*, why don't you tell us where your *thing* was last night?" He raised an eyebrow, challenging me to answer even though he knew I wouldn't back down.

"Fuck off, Bear." I waved my hand in front of my face.

"Hey, guys." Brandy held her tray against her hip and bounced slightly on her heels. "Another round?"

"I'll take a shot of Jack and a beer, Brandy."

"You got it, Frisco." She winked at me.

"Another round for everyone, including Sunshine. Make hers a double." Bear nudged City with his elbow. "We'll get you laid tonight."

City laughed, pushing Bear back. "She isn't as much of a lightweight as she used to be, Bear, and I don't need to liquor my girl up. What do you want, sugar?" He stroked her shoulder with his hand.

"I'll take another, but not a double." Sunshine pushed her empty glass toward Brandy. "I have a kid to take care of."

"Coming right up," Brandy said before sauntering off.

Bear watched her walk away. "I'd love to sink my teeth into that."

"You'd sink your *thing* into anything, Bear. Who the fuck are you kidding, you old bastard?"

"You think you have more game than me, buddy?" he challenged, adjusting himself in the chair and leaned forward.

"I think I can get more pussy than you. In a fuckin' heartbeat."

"Yo, fuckers!" Tank yelled as he walked up to the table and tossed his cigarettes in front of his open seat.

"Tank," everyone replied without looking.

"What the fuck did I miss?" His eyes swept around the table.

I laughed and pointed my thumb at Bear. "He thinks he can get more pussy than me."

Tank slammed his hand down on the table and broke out into laughter. "That old fucker thinks he can beat you in a pussy contest?" Tank looked at Bear, shaking his head. "You senile or some shit?"

"No, asshole," Bear snapped, his top lip snarling. "I can get any pussy in this room."

Tank laughed harder, holding his side with one hand. "You should get your ass checked for that dementia. Frisco has a good fifteen years on your ass, and he knows how to treat a woman. Plus, his face doesn't hurt either."

Bear recoiled and his expression hardened. "What the fuck is wrong with my face?" He ran his fingers through his beard before smoothing it.

Tank slapped the table again, doubling over in laughter. "I can't," he said, trying to catch his breath. "You've got to be fucking joking me."

Bear's face softened as he looked around the table. "I'm pretty."

"Scary," City added, joining in on the laughter.

Bear crossed his arms over his chest, pushing back his shoulders. "Fuck you guys. You're all assholes."

Sunshine leaned in front of City, looking Bear straight in the face. "I think you're pretty."

City looked down at her. "You can't be fuckin' serious?"

She peered up at him, giving him a warm smile. "Everyone is beautiful, babe."

He dragged his hand across his face. "Jesus. The woman likes everyone." Glancing toward the ceiling, City let out a loud sigh.

Bear slapped him on the back, laughing. "Lucky for you, man. How else did you get yourself such a wonderful girl?" Bear gave City's shoulder a tight squeeze.

A grin crept across City's face. "That was my *thing*."

Everyone broke out into laughter.

Sunshine rested her head on his chest as she looked up at him. "That sealed the deal, baby."

Bear blanched and turned his eyes on me. "You up for the challenge, little man?"

I pushed my chest out, squared my shoulders, and smiled. "You're on, old fuck," I said with a gleam in my eye.

"You boys are bad. You shouldn't treat girls that way," Sunshine added as she glanced between Bear and me with her mouth agape.

I cleared my throat, leaning back in my chair. "We won't treat them any other way than they want to be treated, sweetheart. Not every woman is looking for a relationship."

She nodded slowly, giggles bubbling out of her. "Works for me."

"What's our target?" I rubbed my chin and thought about the best way to go about this. Really, no matter how we did it, I'd win. I'd never lost at anything. "Quantity or—"

"Here's your drinks, guys," Brandy interrupted, placing her tray on the table before handing them out.

"Thanks, Brandy." Bear leaned forward and cleared his throat. "Can I ask you something?"

Here we go. I knew what was coming. Bear had been sweet on her, but then again he was sweet on a lot of girls. He didn't know a thing about Brandy and me. We kept our arrangement on the down low. It wasn't anyone's business but our own.

She looked up at him, chewing her lip. "Sure, Bear. What's up?"

"Well…" His eyes shifted. "Tank here wanted to know if you're taken."

Brandy blushed, glancing down at the floor. "No, I'm single," she whispered as her face turned red.

"Brandy." Tank's voice was soft as he reached out and touched her arm. "It wasn't me asking, but don't be ashamed, babe. You're a beautiful woman."

Her eyes met Tank's. "Thanks, Tank. You're really sweet." She winked at him and turned her attention toward Bear. "Anything else?" she asked as her body straightened.

"We're good." City dragged a beer in front of him and barely hid his amusement. "Thanks, Brandy. You can leave before one of these assholes says something else."

She nodded and hugged her tray before she walked away.

"You're assholes." Sunshine shook her head.

The entire table turned to her and gawked.

"Mark this day in the books, men—Sunshine swore," Bear announced, pretending to write a note on his palm.

"Fuck off. Stop harassing my woman," City ordered, kissing the top of her head, and pulling her closer while glaring at Bear.

"Fine. Back to what we were talking about before. Are we going for quantity or do you want to go head-to-head?"

Tank cleared his throat before he choked on his beer. "That didn't sound right," he said in a strangled voice.

"Sick fuck," Bear snapped. "So what'll it be, Frisco? Are you man enough?"

I leaned forward, rubbing my hands together, ready for the challenge. "I can beat your ass head-to-head any day. What's the target?"

Bear leaned forward too, glancing around the table and spoke quietly. "Brandy."

My eyebrows rose as I caught a glimpse of her across the room. "Brandy?" I asked, keeping my voice low. "Seriously? You think you can land her after that bullshit you just pulled? Her body language when she left didn't say *fuck me*." I laughed, knowing I had this one in the bag.

Bear smirked, toying with the scruff of hair hanging from his chin. "She wants me."

"Clueless," Tank mumbled before he brought the beer bottle to his lips.

I studied him and almost felt sorry for what was about to happen, but the feeling quickly passed. "What am I going to win when I crush the hell out of you?" This shit would be way too easy. Some would say it was cheating, but this was Bear and it was like taking candy from a baby.

"Fifty bucks."

"Cheap fucker," City muttered.

"One hundred, then," Bear said.

I grabbed my beer, took a sip, and studied Bear. "You're on, man. Ready to go down quicker than a hooker lookin' for a fix?" The corner of my mouth twitched as I tried to hide my amusement.

"In your dreams, prick," Bear shot back and cracked his neck, readying himself for victory. "Watch how it's done." He pushed his chair back and stood, zeroing in on his target. "I'm going to end this before it gets started."

I motioned toward Brandy, trying not to laugh. Bear looked so damn serious and confident. "Have at it, man. Let's see what game you got."

"Watch and learn, little boy." He straightened, smoothing his shirt and beard before he marched off toward her.

"You're already meeting her after work, aren't you?" City asked as we stared at Bear, waiting for the scene to play out.

I nodded, unable to hide my laughter anymore. "Yeah, I talked to her when I walked in."

Tank turned toward me. "How often you hitting that fine piece of ass?"

I glanced at him and crossed my arms in front of me, feeling a little protective. "As often as she wants."

Tank patted me on the back, a smile creeping across his face. "That's my boy."

"I wish I had fuckin' popcorn." City shook his beer, checking how full the bottle was before slamming it back.

"Me too, man. Me too." I tried to watch, but I kept looking away, guilt gnawing at my insides. The poor guy was about to lose and fall hard. But the one thing I knew about Bear was that he never let it affect him. The man would get knocked down and hop right back up, bigger and better than before.

"I missed you guys." Sunshine watched Bear intently, barely breathing.

Tank glanced over at her. "Eh, we're assholes, babe," he muttered. "You make us better men, though."

"Clearly that's a lie," she mumbled, toying with the pink umbrella resting on the rim of her drink. "You guys are up to the same nonsense as always."

"That's why you love us," I reminded her before I leaned forward, resting my elbow on the table, and watching the train wreck unfold before my eyes.

"Yeah, that must be it," she muttered. "Poor Bear."

"Oh, please. He's an asshole," City said.

Bear tried to wrap an arm around Brandy and sweet-talk her the same way I had when I walked in, but she slipped from his grip.

"It's not lookin' so good for him." Tank laughed. "I should record this shit."

"Sick fuck. That would just be cruel," City said, watching as stoically as the rest of us.

Bear tried again, caging Brandy against the bar as she leaned back. If she were mine, I would've already been on top of him, teaching him how to treat a woman. But I knew Brandy could handle herself. Working at a country biker bar like the Neon Cowboy, she had to deal with assholes all the time.

Brandy dipped under his arms, sliding out of his hold, and squaring her shoulders. She glared at him, her hands waving in front of his face, and she laid into him.

He replied, but I couldn't read his lips. Suddenly her hand flew through the air, striking him in the face. His body recoiled as he grabbed his cheek, stunned.

I jumped from my seat, moving quickly to her aid, and grabbed him by the shoulder.

"Bear," I warned.

"Dude, what?" he said, still holding his cheek with fire in his eyes as he glared at Brandy.

"Watch it."

He turned his glare on me. "You think I'd fucking hit her?" His mouth dropped open and he shook my hand off.

I gave him a weak smile. "I don't know, man." But I did. The one thing I knew about Bear is that he'd never hit a woman. He had always been the one to step in and stop us from doing something we'd regret later.

"I deserved the slap."

"I'm sorry, Bear." Brandy glanced down at the floor, hiding her face behind her brown hair.

"Nah, Brandy. I was a dick. Forgive me?"

She brought her eyes to his but didn't smile. "I'm still not fucking you, Bear."

"Can't blame a guy for trying," Bear replied before walking away and leaving us behind.

"What the fuck was that about?" she asked, shaking the sting from her palm, and peering over my shoulder.

Grabbing her hand, I massaged her tender flesh. "I'll tell you later."

"It better be good." Her shoulders sagged as I continued to rub her fingers. "That feels so good."

"I'll make ya feel better, sweetheart," I promised, giving her a smirk that I could only describe as carnal.

A greedy smile spread across her face. "I know you will, handsome."

I released her hand and gave her a kiss on the cheek. "Get back to work and let me deal with Bear."

"I'm counting the hours," she whispered, turning her face to brush her lips against mine.

"Me too." I pulled away, letting our fingertips touch as I took a step backward before turning and heading for the table.

I couldn't hide the smile on my face. Bear's posture said it all. He was pissed.

"I smell defeat," I teased as I sat down and rubbed my hands together.

His eyes narrowed. "I call bullshit, Frisco. You had her before we made the bet."

I glanced around the table, glaring at everyone. "Who fuckin' opened their big mouth?"

The only person at the table smiling was Sunshine. She never could keep a secret, especially after a few drinks. I sighed, rubbing the back of my neck because what was done was done.

"Don't be mad at me," she whispered, displaying a sweet, innocent, bullshit smile on her face.

I shook my head and sighed. "I could never be mad at you, babe."

"He just looked so sad. I couldn't help myself." She drew her shoulders up near her ears in an exasperated shrug. "Sorry, Frisco."

I waved her off. "It's cool. I'm still the winner in the end. I'll be going home with Brandy, and Bear will only go home to a handy." I laughed, but I winced when City grimaced. "Sorry, man. Too much?"

His piercing blue eyes softened. "A little."

Sunshine just laughed and gave him a quick, playful swat to the chest. "Oh, stop. I've heard worse from his brothers."

"Let's not forget Izzy," Bear chimed in.

City turned slowly as he pinned Bear with his glare. "Forget she exists."

Bear swallowed hard, all color draining from his face. "Forgotten."

"I better go get a drink at the bar. I don't think Brandy will be coming back."

"Grab a round while you're up." Tank shook his empty bottle.

"I'll put it on Bear's tab," I called out over my shoulder.

"Fucker," he mumbled.

"I plan to," I added, turning around to hide my laughter.

Bear wanted to beat my ass. It was a good thing he's my best friend or I would've been laid out already.

"Hey," Brandy said from beside me as I leaned against the bar. "I'm getting off early. Bar's slow. Wanna leave in an hour?"

I licked my lips and raked my eyes over her body, leaning into her space. The heels she had on showed off her calves beautifully and caught my eye. "I'm ready when you are. I can't wait to sink my teeth into you and taste your sweetness," I whispered in her ear. The line had been cheesy; I'd admit that. Brandy didn't need to be wined and dined. We had the same goal—to get off.

"You know all the right things to say to me."

"Uh-huh," I mumbled, sucking her earlobe into my mouth, and biting it gently. "Now be a doll and bring us another round, and I'll make all the misery melt away when I eat your sweet pussy later."

"Yes," she said, shivering in my arms.

I kissed her on the cheek. "Good girl."

As I started to walk away, she took the liberty of smacking my ass. The loud music of the bar mixed with the chatter of the crowd drowned out the thwack of her hand. I laughed, shaking my head as I walked back toward the assholes I'd have to kill an hour with.

CHAPTER 3

CUPCAKES AND CUTIES

"I don't know why the fuck I'm here," Bear said as he grabbed a cupcake off the dessert table.

I slapped him on the back and he jolted forward. "Because City is your friend and it's his kid's birthday party, dumbass. Can't you be a happy bastard one day in your life?"

He cracked a smile, barely visible behind all the facial hair. "I'm always happy." He scraped the pink frosting off with his index finger, eyeing it with curiosity. "How was Brandy Friday night, you lucky bastard?" He stuck his finger in his mouth and closed his eyes.

I widened my stance, feeling my muscles tense. "I don't kiss and tell, Bear."

He waved me off. "You're such a liar." He looked ridiculous with a small dollop of pink frosting stuck in his beard.

"I didn't see you leaving the bar alone. So don't pretend you didn't get a piece of ass."

City cleared his throat behind us. "Can we watch our language? There are children around."

I grimaced and knew better. Sunshine would've smacked me for such language. "Sorry, City. It won't happen again."

"I'm just fucking with you."

"Great party, man," Bear mumbled before he shoved the entire cupcake into his mouth.

City glanced around the yard and radiated confidence. "It turned out better than I thought." He placed his hands on his hips, puffing out his chest as his eyes roamed the crowd. "Suzy pulled it off."

The yard had been transformed into a pink princess wonderland. Round tables had baby-pink tablecloths with bright pink flowers as centerpieces. Pink lanterns, pink balloons, and pink streamers were tied everywhere. Pink threw up in City's yard, but his daughter Gigi seemed to be ecstatic as she ran around the party squealing.

Bear whistled. "I thought you decorated this masterpiece."

"Don't be an asshole, Bear."

There was a light tap on my shoulder. "Frisco," Sunshine said from behind me in a soft voice. She was up to something. I'd known the woman long enough to know when her sweetness had a purpose or a victim.

I turned, giving her a smile. "Hey, babe." I wrapped my arms around her. "Thanks for inviting me."

Her tiny hands rubbed my back when she curled into my body. "You guys are like family."

"The side we don't talk about, of course," City added.

"Dick," Bear mumbled.

City smacked Bear on the shoulder. "Language, fucker."

"What the—" Bear started, but City silenced him with a single look.

"Everything looks great, Sunshine," I told her after I let her go.

"Thanks, Frisco. So, I wanted to ask you…" She clasped her hands in front of her as she started to shift on her feet, ready to hit me with her request. "I know things didn't end that long ago with Jeanine, but I think—" She stopped talking and glanced at City.

He placed his arm around her shoulder. "Tell him, sugar."

I tried like hell not to make a facial expression that would make her feel bad. I knew where this was going—the classic fix-up for the poor guy who couldn't get a date.

Suzy Sunshine was always trying to fix everything. Sometimes the heart couldn't be fixed; it needed to mend on its own…or never.

Sunshine peered up at me through her eyelashes. "I have a friend I'd love for you to meet." There it was.

I had become everyone's charity case.

I rubbed the back of my neck, trying to find the words that wouldn't make me seem like a complete asshole. "I don't know, Sunshine. I don't know if I'm ready for anything yet." I gave her a half-hearted smile as my hands dropped to my sides.

She cocked her head, raising an eyebrow. "You were ready to go home with Brandy the other night." Her foot tapped rapidly on the grass as she stared at me.

"Well, that was different," I lied.

Sunshine poked me in the chest, her eyes piercing me. "It is not. Now, you listen to me, Frisco, and listen good." She poked me harder and stepped closer. "Georgia is a lovely girl. I work with her, and I think you two would really hit it off."

"Georgia?" Bear interrupted, bursting into laughter and regrouping. "She sounds hot."

Sunshine turned slowly and glared at him. "Suck it, Bear."

Bear repeated "Georgia, Georgia" over and over again quietly so only I could hear.

"Sunshine…" I shifted on my feet, trying to think of something brilliant to say. "I just don't think it's a good idea. I'm not really looking for a relationship right now."

In all honesty, a girl with the name Georgia probably wasn't my bag of chips. I liked Brandys, Candys, and Trixies right now. I knew what I was in for, they knew what I offered, and it kept shit simple.

Sunshine laid her hand on my chest, looking up at me with her big baby blues. "Will you at least meet her? Please," she said, pleading with me.

"Give it up, man. She won't stop until she gets what she wants," City said.

I'd known her long enough to know that she wasn't a quitter. "Fine," I growled. I didn't have a fucking choice in the matter, and I might as well get it over with.

"Yes!" she cheered, fist-pumping the air. "Stay right there." She pointed to the ground with wide eyes before shuffling off. "I'm going to go get her."

"Yay!" I chanted sarcastically and clapped my hands.

This wouldn't end well.

Fix-ups never did.

Bear nudged me in the ribs. "Hope you and Georgia have fun."

"Shut up," I grumbled. Watching Suzy walk across the yard toward a giant group of women huddled under a tree, I held my breath.

City slapped my shoulder. "Dude, you'll like her," he promised before he walked away.

I couldn't breathe. It felt like my throat was closing, like I was having an allergic reaction.

"I mean, she sounds hot," Bear said, causing me to glance at him. "Probably a teacher like Suzy Sunshine and likes to sit home with her twenty cats on the weekend." Bear wiped the tears away from his eyes.

"Fuckin' great." My gaze flickered upward before zeroing in on Sunshine. "Clusterfuck."

"This is going to be fun."

"Don't you have somewhere to be?"

"I ain't going anywhere now. Shit's about to get good. You've never been able to say no to Sunshine."

"Don't act like you don't have a soft spot for her too," I snapped. Bear would take a bullet for Suzy. He'd kill for her if need be. Not because he wanted her, but because he loved her like family.

We all did. Hence why my dumbass hadn't taken off. I stood here, waiting for her to introduce me to her friend, and felt a sense of impending doom.

Staring across the yard, I watched as Suzy spoke to the group. Which one was she? They weren't bad-lookin' ladies, but none of them looked to be my type.

That was a lie.

I didn't really have a type, other than a woman who could keep her legs closed for five damn seconds when out of my presence. I was game for just about anyone. Color didn't matter, ethnicity didn't factor, even size. I loved women who were comfortable with themselves above all else.

Dating a friend's friend complicated shit. There was nothing in the world I'd want to do to fuck up the friendship I had with Sunshine and City.

Suzy glanced at me and I waved her over. I had to put a stop to this before it ended badly. I'd just have to tell her that I couldn't meet Georgia.

"Yeah?" she asked as she approached, her sundress swaying as she tried to hold the hem from blowing up with the wind.

I peered over her shoulder, noticing the group of women staring in silence. "I don't think this is a good idea."

She recoiled, taking a step backward before recovering. "Oh no, you don't, buddy. You're going to meet her." Her lips were set in a firm line when she grabbed my hand.

"Suzy." I tried to pull away but failed. "It won't end up well. I'm not made for a schoolteacher, babe."

She rolled her eyes. "Frisco, she's not a schoolteacher."

"Oh?" My eyebrows shot up. I'd just assumed she was, not that it was a bad thing. Most teachers I knew were actually freaks in the sack, but being that she was Sunshine's friend told me she had to be innocent like her.

"Stop being a baby. We aren't all like *her*." I loved that Sunshine referred to the cheating whore as *her*. She was like an outcast who didn't deserve a name.

"I know," I said, squeezing her hand gently.

"Come on." She turned around and tugged me forward.

I dug my heels into the ground, but the woman didn't listen. She pulled me forward, yanking me by the arm like a woman possessed, and I let her.

"Suzy," I said.

"Have fun, man!" Bear called out.

"Don't listen to him. You're gonna love Georgia."

"Georgia," I whispered, choking on the word. I swallowed hard when ten sets of eyes swept over me.

"Everyone," she said, releasing my hand, and motioning toward me, "this is Frisco."

I waved like a moron. "Hi, ladies." I suddenly felt self-conscious when I noticed a few of them lick their lips.

"I'm going to borrow Georgia for a little bit." Sunshine reached through the crowd, and my eyes followed her every movement, waiting to see her.

Everything seemed to stop.

Maybe it was the redhead with the glasses who looked like she hadn't been fucked properly in her entire life. We'd never get past first base.

What was I thinking coming to this damn party?

A woman stepped through the crowd and waved. "Hey," she said, sounding like an angel. Her look, on the other hand, was anything but heavenly. Don't get me wrong. She was hot as hell, but she didn't look an ounce of innocent.

My jaw dropped open and the air in my lungs disappeared. I closed my mouth, trying to find my words. Before I could speak, I reached out and brought her hand to my lips. "It's nice to meet you, Georgia," I whispered, peering into her rich, dark eyes.

She blushed and batted her eyelashes. "You too, Frisco."

"Why don't you two go sit and chat a while?" Sunshine suggested as she touched our arms and moved us forward. "Go spend some time learning about each other."

"She's bossy," Georgia said before her shiny red lips turned up in a smile.

I laughed, nodding in agreement, and mesmerized by her mouth. "You have no idea."

Sunshine waved her hands dismissively at us. "Scoot, you two."

I gave Sunshine a peck on the cheek before turning toward Georgia.

I held out my hand to her, trying to be a complete gentleman. "Can I get you a drink?" I asked.

She slid her fingers into my palm and took a step closer. "I'd love a drink."

As we walked toward the makeshift patio bar, I caught a glimpse of Bear. His eyes were bulging out of his head and his jaw was almost touching the grass.

Eat your heart out, buddy. I smirked and gave him a chin lift.

"Fucker," he mouthed. He shook his head and grabbed another cupcake, drowning his envy in desserts.

She leaned close and whispered, "Your friend?" She motioned toward Bear with her head, and her black locks shimmered in the sunlight.

"Some people call him that." I held her hand, helping to stabilize her on the grass until our feet touched the concrete patio. "What would you like?" I asked and released her tiny hand.

"Hmmm." She tapped her chin and stared at the bottles behind the bar while I watched her. "I'll take a Bellini."

I couldn't stop my face from contorting. "A what?"

"A Bellini."

"A Bellini…" I stammered as I spoke to the bartender. He nodded, and I was happy as hell that he knew what the hell it was, because I'd sure as fuck never heard of it. "And a beer for me, please."

"Sure thing," the man in the pink tuxedo said before he reached into the cooler and grabbed my drink.

"So, Georgia…" I rested one arm against the bar, thinking I looked calm, but inside I was anything but. "Do you work with Sunshine?"

Great, I already sounded like a douchebag.

"Sunshine?" She looked at me confused with the cutest tiny crinkles in her forehead. Actually there wasn't a wrinkle on her face. Not one. Nothing even around her eyes when her face softened.

"Sorry," I said. I needed to remember that only the guys at the Cowboy called her that. "Suzy."

"Yeah," she replied. She took the champagne flute off the bar and studied the liquid before turning her attention to me. "I just started working with her this year."

"Are you a teacher?"

She grinned against the rim of her glass. "No."

Just as I was about to take a sip, I paused with the glass in front of my lips. "I was going to say. Teachers have changed since I was a kid."

As I gulped down the beer, she said, "Yeah. I'm a librarian."

I choked, almost spitting all over the bar. "A librarian?" My eyes widened.

When the fuck did librarians become hot?

Georgia did not look like the woman who used to read me *Charlotte's Web* when I was in school. I always thought of librarians as old ladies with gray hair and business suits.

That didn't describe Georgia. She had on a hot little sundress, classic fifties style with a V-neckline, and shoes with skulls. Her cleavage wasn't enormous, but her tits were enough to fit in my hands. Her long black hair and thick black eyeliner didn't fit the bookworm type.

"You're shitting me?" I tried not to eye-fuck her over my beer bottle.

She shook her head, blushing while she sipped her Bellini. "Nope. I'm a total nerd," she admitted and looked away.

"The last thing I'd call you is a nerd." Where in the hell had this girl come from, and why had Sunshine been holding out on me? "Want to sit down?" I asked, glancing at her shoes, and noticing her heels had to easily be five inches.

She sighed and shifted on her feet. "I'd love to. My feet are killing me in this heat."

We stole glances at each other as we walked toward an empty table.

She sat and crossed her ankles, holding the champagne glass in her lap. "So what do you do, Frisco?"

I turned my chair to face her, wanting to be closer. "I'm a private investigator."

"Oh, that sounds like fun."

"It can be."

She fidgeted with the glass, turning it between her fingers. "My dad's a retired police officer, which can be scary sometimes."

I should've run away as soon as she mentioned her father being a retired cop.

I definitely wasn't her type.

I wasn't a criminal, never had been, and never would be, but the people I associated with weren't always cop-loving folks. "Being a PI isn't scary. It's mostly boring work and stakeouts to grab photos of cheating spouses or tracking down someone who doesn't want to be found."

"Suzy speaks very highly of you," she said as she continued to fidget with her glass.

My back stiffened. "She does?"

Georgia's bright white teeth gleamed against her cherry-red lipstick when she spoke. "Yep. She said you're one of the good ones."

My face heated. "I don't know about that."

"May I?" she asked as she hovered her hand above my arm.

"Yes." I nodded, staring at her hand when it touched my skin.

Her fingertips slowly traced the ink on my forearm, following the lines. "This is amazing stuff. Where did you get it done?"

The feel of her against my skin was something I couldn't describe, and my stomach did this odd flip-flop thing that threw me for a loop.

"Some of it at Inked and a few at Cherry Bomb."

"Me too," she said, her eyes flickering up at me.

"How old are you?" I couldn't stop myself from asking the question.

I knew it was wrong.

A woman should never be asked her age, but I couldn't help myself. She didn't have the small lines near her eyes. I'd had them since I was twenty-five, and now that I was creeping up on thirty-one, they were almost caverns.

"Twenty-two."

Fuck.

She was way too young for me. I shouldn't even be talking to her. What the fuck was Sunshine thinking trying to hook us up?

My leg began to bounce uncontrollably. "Can you excuse me for a moment?" I asked.

"Surrre," she drawled, pulling her hand away from my arm but keeping her eyes on me.

I set my beer down on the table and stood. "I'll be right back."

"'Kay," she mumbled, frowning behind her Bellini.

I marched straight for Sunshine, needing her to explain her thinking. A twenty-two-year-old was a baby. Georgia had her entire life ahead of her, and I was used, older, and broken.

"Sunshine," I whispered and tapped her on the shoulder. "Can I speak to you?"

She turned around, giving me her full attention. "Don't you just love Georgia?" she asked and bounced from foot to foot, her blond hair swaying.

"She's a nice girl, babe. But that's just it. She's still a girl." I blinked rapidly, trying to stop a weird twitch that had started in the corner of my eye.

She poked me square in the chest with her bony little finger and stood on her tiptoes. "Don't call her that. She's a grown woman, Frisco."

Running my fingers through my hair, I groaned. "She's twenty-two, for Christ's sake."

"Oh, shut up." She rolled her eyes. "She's legal. I wouldn't have introduced you if you two weren't perfect for each other. So just go over there and be the man I know you are."

"What, a cradle robber?"

"A man who needs a loyal woman," she shot back before slapping me on the arm.

"Fuck," I muttered and rubbed the spot her hand had just hit. "I'm not looking for a girlfriend."

She waved her hand in front of my face. "Neither was City when I met him, but here we are."

"When shit goes bad, I'm blaming you." I gritted my teeth and pointed at her with narrowed eyes.

"You'll be thanking me." She grabbed my sides and tried to turn my body around. "Go back over there before you look like a complete jerk."

I cleared my throat. I had already made myself look like one when I walked away from Georgia. "I think I already fucked up." I winced and glanced over my shoulder at her.

She sat in the same spot, sipping her drink, and watching us. I waved, giving her a smile, and, much to my surprise, she reciprocated.

"Nah," Suzy whispered and shook her head. "Go already."

"Fine," I muttered before I walked back toward the table. My eyes were glued to her. She looked like a vision, but a fucking young one. She'd be a perfect pinup model, and she came straight out of my wet dreams. "Sorry about that." I took my seat, fidgeting with my shirt, and averting my eyes.

She set her glass on the table and clasped her hands in her lap. "Everything okay?"

I nodded and dragged my eyes to her. "I just needed to tell Sunshine something."

"Are you worried about my age?" she asked point-blank, and her gaze flickered toward me.

I sighed, pinching the bridge of my nose. "A little. I'm not really in the frame of mind for a relationship here, Georgia. My head's all fucked up."

She grabbed my hand, taking it away from my face, and placed it in her lap. "I'm not looking to get married."

"You'd be shit out of luck, babe."

She patted my hand before leaning back in her chair. "Suzy thought we could become friends."

"That I can do," I said and rubbed my free hand against my jeans.

"How old are you, Gramps?" She covered her mouth with the palm of her hand, hiding her grin.

"You're a smartass."

She nodded and laughed. "I am. So fess up. Are you forty?"

My mouth fell open and my eyes widened. Forty? Fuck me, I wasn't even close. "No! Jesus, do I look that fuckin' old?"

She nudged my knee with hers. "No. How old are you, really?"

"I'm thirty-one." I closed my eyes, waiting for her to stalk off from my geezer ass.

"Well, you're not my daddy's age, so we're golden."

I slumped in my chair, thankful I wasn't the same age as her father. That would be weird and fucked up. "Unbelievable."

"Have you been a PI for a long time, or did you do something else before?" She tilted her head and studied me.

I grabbed my beer to have something to hold, because I felt off my game. I felt fidgety and a little unsure of the entire situation. "I haven't been a PI for long. I used to be in the service. I served ten years."

"What branch?"

"Navy," I replied, using the opportunity to take a sip of my luke-warm beer and quell the dryness that had settled in my mouth.

"My dad was in the Marines."

It just kept getting better and better. He'd hate me because I was a Navy man, plus, with my affiliation with the Neon Cowboy crew, I wouldn't be an ideal match for his baby daughter.

"That's nice," I replied, trying to find a smile.

"Were you an officer?"

I lifted my chin, the familiar pride I'd always felt when I said the words settling inside me. "I was a SEAL."

She gasped, leaning forward. "Wow. I wouldn't have guessed it. You don't look like what I picture as a SEAL."

"'Cause I'm not built like The Rock?" I cocked an eyebrow and flexed my arms, showing her my muscles.

"You're built, but yeah, just not as *big* as I thought."

"I've been out for a couple years. I've slimmed down a bit. But, Georgia—" I flexed my arms again "I can assure you, I'm all muscle."

She giggled, throwing her head back.

City whistled. "It's time to sing 'Happy Birthday'!" He motioned toward the dessert table.

"We better go," Georgia said, setting her glass on the table, and standing. "Can you walk with all those muscles? I wouldn't want you to tip over."

"I can do a whole lot more than walk with all this awesomeness."

She blushed. "You're an interesting man."

"More like a handful." I smirked, waggling my eyebrows like an idiot as I stood.

"Well, I…" she stammered.

"Yeah," I replied, knowing I threw her off. "Let's get some cake." I placed my hand on the small of her back and guided her toward the dessert table.

"Sure." She looked up at me through her thick black eyelashes. "Cake."

When we approached the table, her friends called her over and she excused herself. I couldn't help but catch stolen glances as the crowd sang to Gigi. Georgia smiled as she listened to her friend whisper in her ear.

"You're fucked." Bear nudged me in the ribs and looked toward Georgia.

"I am not." But I fucking was.

"So fucked," he whispered.

We clapped as little Gigi blew out her candles. She'd grown so quickly, and I thought of her as a niece instead of as just my friend's kid. She was a doll and meant the world to me.

"Gonna hook up with her?" Bear asked.

Georgia turned her back and I instantly missed her smile. "Nah, man. She's just a kid."

"Can't handle her," he teased, slapping me on the back.

"If she weren't Sunshine's friend, I wouldn't have a problem getting a piece of ass and walking away, but I just can't do it."

"You're losing your touch, dude."

"Maybe so, or maybe I'm getting a conscience."

"Fuck that. Who needs it?"

I motioned toward the bar with my head. "Want another?"

"Only if you do a shot with me."

"I don't think it's that kind of party."

"Kids," he muttered and rolled his eyes.

"Frisco." Thomas walked up to us but didn't look me in the eye.

"Hey, T. What's up?"

He peered around, looking uneasy. "I need you to meet Mrs. Green at the office."

"Now?" I scratched my neck and searched for Georgia.

"Yes. She called in a panic. I'd go, but she's your client and this is my niece's party."

I sighed. "It's fine. I'll go, man. No problem. I was getting ready to head out anyway. Tell Sunshine I'm sorry I had to leave."

"I will. I'm sorry to do this to you on a weekend."

"Work always comes first. I'll take care of it," I said as I rubbed the back of my neck. "Catch ya later, Bear."

"Maybe I'll go find Georgia." Bear smirked and started searching the crowd.

"If you think you got a shot, knock yourself out." I didn't mean a word of it, but I wasn't about to admit that she'd captured my attention and had me intrigued.

He rubbed his chin as his eyes stopped on her. "Dumbass, I'll tell her you got called away on business."

I wanted to poke him in the eyes to keep him from virtually fucking her in his mind.

This wasn't good.

I needed to step away.

Staying at the party would only lead me back to Georgia. Being called in to work was probably for the better. She was too young for me. I was too broken for her, and in the end, it would be a complete clusterfuck.

"Don't forget to tell Sunshine," I called over my shoulder as I walked toward the front yard. Thomas gave me a thumbs-up and nodded.

Just as I was about to round the corner and disappear from view, I saw Georgia waving at me and the smile fell from her face.

I wanted to run to her and tell her she'd be better off, but instead I tucked my hands in my pockets and left without so much as a goodbye.

CHAPTER 4

SOMEONE'S GETTING IT

"Labor Day has always confused me," Tank said as he sat down with a beer in hand and relaxed.

"Me too. What the hell is it for?" Bear scratched his beard and stared across the room.

"It's to celebrate workers," I told them, shaking my head at their lack of knowledge. "Something you two know very little about."

"Oh, fuck off, dude. Just because you have Google doesn't make your ass smart." Bear leaned back, crossing his arms over his chest.

Tank rubbed his hands together. "Speaking of work. How was it this week? Anything juicy?"

"Boring-ass week. A cheating husband and a couple meetings."

"Oh, but that could be good. Was he fuckin' his secretary?"

I rolled my eyes. "I've told you before. I can't talk about my work."

"Who the fuck am I going to tell?" he asked, placing his hand against his chest.

"Don't care, and still isn't fuckin' happening." I sipped my beer as my phone beeped.

City: Save us an extra seat. We're on our way.

I set my beer down, wiping my lips with the back of my hand.

Me: Will do.

"Grab an extra chair. City's on the way."

Bear reached back and dragged a chair across the floor. "Who's he bringing?"

"Probably one of his brothers."

"I'm hoping to see that hot piece of ass from the party," he said after he tucked the chair underneath the table.

Fuck.

I closed my eyes and my heart started to beat uncontrollably.

Georgia.

I hadn't even thought about that. I couldn't see her. I was an asshole for leaving without saying goodbye.

"Fuck. I gotta go." I started to stand before Bear grabbed my hand.

He held me in place. "You're not going anywhere, pussy."

"What piece of ass?" Tank asked, looking between us.

"Georgia." My head began to spin from even saying her name. "Sunshine tried to fix me up with her. If they're bringing her, I can't see her."

"Sit your ass down," Tank ordered, pointing toward the chair. "I never thought you'd be afraid of a piece of tail."

I gritted my teeth and glowered. "I'm not. I just don't want to get involved with her."

"You're acting like a pussy. Sit your ass down. He's probably bringing Mikey with him."

I pulled my hand out from under Bear's and rubbed my shoulder. "Maybe he is."

"Nah, he's bringing the girl. You gotta see her, Tank. She's a fine little thing with perky tits and that trampy look we love. She's off-the-charts fuckable."

I leaned forward into his space, baring my teeth. "Don't you talk about her that way. If you even look at her funny, I'll knock your teeth out."

He moved closer and stared me straight in the eyes. "Someone's panties are in a wad. What's wrong, Frisco, you in love?"

I slammed my fist down on the table, my eyes boring into him. "I know you're a pig. She's a good girl and doesn't deserve your bullshit."

"I was going to give her my dick, not bullshit." He laughed.

Before I could stop myself, my fist flew forward and connected with his jaw. "Jackass!" I yelled, and his head recoiled.

He rubbed his jaw, trying to shake it off. "What the fuck, man?"

I pointed at him, narrowing my eyes. "I warned ya. Georgia is off-limits."

"He's in love." Tank slapped the table and whooped. "Mr. Lover Boy is back."

My knuckles ached from Bear's bony jaw, and I shook my fist. "I'm not. She's too damn young for me, and I don't want a relationship."

"Ah, you sound like City. Especially with the threats about a woman you claim to not even like," Bear muttered and held his jaw.

I sat, glancing between the two smiling dumbasses. *Fuck.* Were they right? Was I fuckin' doomed and didn't even know?

"Hey, guys." Sunshine's sweet voice came from behind me. I cringed, closing my eyes, afraid to turn around. I swallowed hard, gave myself a pep talk, and glanced at Bear.

"See," Bear whispered to Tank.

Tank's eyes were bulging out of his head, and I knew then that it was her standing behind me. "Yeah. Take a seat, ladies," he said, motioning toward the chairs.

"Fuck," I mumbled.

The empty chair next to me moved, but I didn't look, staring straight ahead. Bear looked so ecstatic I thought he may start clapping.

Please let it be City. Please let it be City.

"Hey, Frisco," Georgia said as she scooted forward, giving me an amazing view of her tits in the V-neck dress she wore.

"Hey, Georgia, right?" I asked, because I was a complete asshole and wanted to play it cool.

Her lip curled. "Yeah, from the party."

"Right." I nodded. "I remember."

"Dick," she whispered under her breath and looked away.

"I'll grab us a round." City rested his hand on Suzy's shoulder, standing behind her.

I shot out of my seat. "I'll come with you."

City walked off and I followed close on his heels. When he reached the bar, he leaned forward, waiting for me. "What the fuck is your problem?"

I hung my head and my stomach rolled. "I don't know, City. Something about that girl gets to me. I can't believe Sunshine wants us to hook up."

"Two beers, two shots of tequila, and a Sunny drink," City told the bartender. Sunshine was the only girl in the bar who ordered those shitty drinks with the umbrellas. They knew exactly what she wanted when we called it a Sunshine drink.

"Coming right up," the bartender said as he wandered away.

"Stop acting like an idiot." He turned toward me, looking over at the table. "She likes you."

I smiled, pretending to misunderstand. "Sunshine?"

"You're pushing it, fucker." He cracked his knuckles. "Georgia."

"Oh, fuck. This can't be happening. I can't fuck her, City." I clenched my jaw and fisted my hands at my sides. Everything inside me was coiled tight.

"You need to get a damn grip, Frisco. What's your problem?"

"It's just the shit with Jeanine. I'm not ready for anything more than a casual fuck. If that's what she wants, then I'm her man. Anything more, and I'm out."

"You tell her that. Stop being an asshole and man up," he told me as he grabbed a few of the drinks. "Get the shots."

I picked the rest up, following behind him, and heading straight toward disaster...I mean, Georgia.

I set them down in front of City before taking my seat. Glancing at Georgia, I turned my beer in my palm.

"A toast." Sunshine held her umbrella drink in the air.

"What are we celebrating, Sunshine?" Tank asked as he lifted his beer to join hers.

"To friends and love," she said, giving me a mischievous smile.

My jaw ticked uncontrollably and my palms began to sweat. "To friendship," I repeated, lifting my drink.

"And love." City clinked his drink to mine.

I glared at him, gnashing my teeth together. They were fucking setting me up. City would do anything Sunshine asked him to. In all the years I'd known him, I thought he had a pair of balls bigger than anyone I knew, but not when it came to her.

"Hear, hear." Georgia tapped her glass to mine.

I peered out of the corner of my eye, not trusting myself enough to look at her. I brought my drink to my lips, swallowing hard and long. I tried to calm myself the fuck down. I just needed to be honest. I wasn't looking for a girlfriend. I wanted nothing from her other than what she had between her legs.

She wiped her mouth, put the lime between her teeth, and swallowed. When she placed the lime on the table, I was still staring at her mouth. "I needed that," Georgia said before she grabbed her beer and chugged it. When she set it down, she turned toward me. "Can we talk in private?"

"Someone's getting it," Bear said from across the table.

I scowled at him. The fucker was pushing the envelope and wouldn't let his foot off my throat. I swallowed down my pride and turned my attention back to her, softening my face. "Sure."

"At the bar," she demanded. She stood and walked away, leaving me behind.

I slid my beer against the table. "Fuck."

"Go get 'er, tiger," Sunshine said, playing with the straw on her tongue.

I pointed at her. "This is all your fault." But I didn't know if I was angry or happy. Maybe a little of each.

"If you don't go, man, I will," Bear offered and started to stand.

I leaned across the table, moving closer to him. "Sit the fuck down before I put your ass back in that chair for you."

"He's in love," Bear said to Sunshine with the biggest smile I'd ever seen on his face.

Her eyes moved from me to Georgia. "I hope so."

"Fuck me," I mumbled before I stomped away from the table. As I approached Georgia, my breathing quickened and my pulse followed, small beads of sweat forming near my hairline.

She leaned back against the bar with her tits jutting out and her arms crossed underneath. "What's your problem with me? Did I do something to you, Frisco?"

Caught off guard by her question, my body jerked backward. "N-no," I stuttered.

She tapped her foot. "You ditched me, marched off when you heard my age, and tonight, you seem less than happy that I'm here. What the fuck gives?"

I cleared my throat, trying to find my voice and a reasonable explanation. "I don't have anything against you." I was in so much trouble.

"Let's cut the shit, Frisco. I'm a big girl. What's the problem? Would you rather I leave?" Her body oozed attitude.

I cringed. I never wanted to hurt anyone, but I knew that I had hurt her feelings. "No. Don't go. I'm sorry. It's just that Sunshine..." My chest tightened. "She's trying to fix us up."

Georgia filled her cheeks with air before slowly exhaling. "Is that so bad?" She narrowed her eyes. "If I'm not your type, it's cool. But otherwise, what's the issue? I thought we had a nice time up until you left the party. I'm a big girl. Just be honest with me. I'm not into playing games."

I wanted to play games. Naked games that ended with us against a wall, tangled together like we'd played the sexiest game of Twister.

"Listen, Georgia." I held my hands up because I didn't want to fight. "I like you. You're beautiful. But I'm not looking for a relationship right now. My head isn't right. Plus, there's the issue with your age."

"Hold up." She gave me the hand, shushing me. "First off, who gives a fuck what age I am? It's a number and nothing more. Secondly, who said I wanted a relationship? Are you that full of yourself that you think every woman wants to spend eternity with you?"

"Well, I...um." I touched her arm and felt that damn flip-flop in my stomach, followed by a spark. "G, come on. You just want to fuck me?" I asked, raising an eyebrow.

Say yes. Please say yes.

Her face tightened. "I thought we could be friends."

Kiss of death!

I didn't want to be friends. I had enough friends and didn't need one with tits and sweet lips I'd like to see sucking on my cock.

No. Friends wouldn't be possible.

"Men and women can never be just friends."

Her head snapped back and her eyes widened. "Why the fuck not?"

I liked her—she was fuckin' hot, smart, and probably had everything I'd ever wanted in a woman. But there was no way I'd risk my friendship with Sunshine and City over a woman.

"Because every time I see you, all I'll think about is fucking you and nothing else," I whispered in her ear.

She gasped "So what? Think what you want. That doesn't have to affect our friendship." She gaped at me as I backed away.

I rubbed my lips, watching her eyes follow their path. "I'll want to act on it."

"If you want me that badly, why not take me on a date?" She pursed her lips. "Maybe you'll get lucky."

"Why the hell do you want to go on a date with me?"

"I had a bad breakup, and you're the complete opposite of my last boyfriend. I thought you could be fun."

Fun. I could be fun.

"Babe, I'm so much fun you'd never be able to go back to your bland men again."

She rolled her eyes. "God, he was so boring. Watching paint dry was more entertaining than spending time with Brent."

"Brent?" I asked, almost choking. "The name alone says it all."

"I know." Her eyes flickered to the floor. "But if you're not man enough to take me on a date, I get it."

"I don't think it's a good idea. I'm pretty irresistible."

The corner of her mouth twitched and her eyes twinkled. "You're okay."

"I'll give you one date. That's it. It'll get Sunshine off my back, and you'll realize that I'm the worst thing for you right now."

"Why?"

"Because you won't be able to get enough of me. If you fall in love, that's on you." My eyes slid down her body, slowly and with purpose.

She swatted my shoulder. "You're so full of shit."

I threw my hands up, looking toward the floor, and shook my head. "I warned ya."

"I think I can handle a night with you and not fall in love. I'm over love."

"Me too," I muttered.

"How about…" Her hand settled on my arm, her red fingernails looking spectacular against my skin. I bet they'd look better wrapped around my dick with her matching lips working the tip in and out of her mouth. "Are you listening to me?" She dug her nails into my skin.

I nodded and gave her my full attention. "Yeah, I'm just waiting to see what you're going to say," I lied.

"Let's go out, have some drinks, and celebrate our newfound freedom. What do you say?"

"How do you know mine's new?" I cocked my head, furrowing my brow.

"Suzy told me. So, you in?"

Fucking Suzy and her trap. "You're gonna wanna fuck me," I told her and licked my lips, wishing I could do her right now. Maybe I'd get her out of my system that way. It took everything in me not to stare at her breasts. Why couldn't she wear a fuckin' turtleneck or some shit?

"I'm a hundred percent certain that I can resist your charms."

"We'll see. Don't say I didn't warn you."

"Whatcha two talking about?" Sunshine asked.

I jumped, clutching my chest. "Fuck, you scared me."

"Oh, stop. So, when's the date?" She bumped me with her body.

I glanced at Georgia, deflecting the question. "You tell her."

"Well…" Georgia paused and chewed on her lip. "We haven't set a date, but we're going to celebrate our shitty exes."

Sunshine's smile faded and she moved her face between us. "But that's not sexy."

"Oh, it is," I argued.

"I'll never understand people," Sunshine said and rolled her eyes. "You two are crazy."

"Maybe, Sunshine. Maybe."

She walked away, shaking her head, and moving her hands around in the air. Probably ranting and raving about how I was an asshole, and she'd be right.

"I'll give you my number, and when you're ready for a little action, you can call me."

The corner of that sexy mouth curved up. "Is it little?" she asked, turning her head, and bringing her ear near my mouth. "You can tell me."

"Baby, it's so big it would split your fine little ass in two."

She threw her head back, held her stomach, and laughed. "You're a funny man." Her white teeth glistened despite the dim lighting of the Neon Cowboy.

Even her laugh made me hard. I had a huge problem. She could be my worst nightmare and my biggest regret. Georgia needed to not be on my mind.

"You want a drink while we're here?"

She wiped the tears from her eyes, carefully working around her eyeliner. "Tequila."

"I didn't know librarians liked tequila."

"We're people too." She wrinkled her nose and finally looked at me like I was a douche.

"I know. I know." I leaned against the bar and hailed the bartender before ordering our drinks.

She rested her stomach on the bar with her chin in her palm. "Looking at you, I could make a few assumptions that probably aren't true." She tapped her nails against the bar.

"Like what?" I fanned my hands against the bar and dug them into the surface, bracing myself.

She smirked, raking her eyes over my face and arms. "Well, you look like an asshole." She laughed, dropping her head forward.

"Cheap shot."

"You're probably a roughneck. Most likely, you fuck anything with two legs."

"Not true," I said as our drinks were placed on the bar. I handed her the tequila and I grabbed my beer, taking a quick sip. All the talking had made my throat dry and scratchy, or maybe it was Georgia.

"How so?" she asked before slamming back the tequila and setting the glass down.

I gawked at her. I'd never seen a lady drink tequila like she had. It didn't seem to affect her. "I don't fuck dudes."

She rolled her eyes. "Another," she called out to the bartender and waved her arm, pointing at her empty glass.

"Don't you think you should take it easy?"

"You do you, and I'll do me."

I leaned over, bringing my mouth close to her ear. "I can't even begin to describe how sexy that statement is. When you do you, can I watch?" My lips brushed against her ear.

She shivered. "Never going to happen."

"You never know," I whispered.

"I don't do the bad-boy thing. I can already tell that you aren't the right kind of man for me."

"I'm all kinds of wrong, Georgia, but in the best way possible." I stroked my fingertips over the top of her hand. I tried to get rid of her and my kindness didn't work. Maybe if my other side came out, I'd run her off, screaming for the hills.

She swallowed hard, lifted the second tequila shot to her lips with her free hand, and paused. "We better get back to the group before Suzy comes after us."

"I got you scared."

"Hardly. I'm here to meet new friends, not monopolize your time."

I glanced at the table, seeing all eyes on us. "After you." I held my arm out, waiting for her to walk first.

"You just want to look at my ass," she teased. She straightened her back, took a step in front of me, and shook her ass.

"Maybe." My eyes were glued to her ass, and I was totally busted when she turned around. "View isn't bad from here." Dear God, I'd forgotten how amazing the ass of a chick in her early twenties truly was; I bet I could bounce a quarter off it.

"Hey, Frisco." A smirk spread across her face. "Don't fall in love." She winked and my knees weakened.

This wasn't me. I wasn't ready.

So far my master plan of being a dick of epic proportions hadn't worked. Maybe if I tasted her, I'd be cured.

I mean, it could totally work. Right?

As we sat back down, dragging our chairs closer, Bear stared at me. "So?" He leaned into my space, waiting for me to spill the dirt.

"What?" I asked, slowly turning my head to face him.

"You gonna get a piece, or can I?" He waggled his eyebrows, grinning like a doofus.

I clenched my fist and closed my eyes, swallowing my anger. "Bear, shut the fuck up," I muttered and opened my eyes.

"That's what I thought. You're totally hooked on the broad."

"What's up?" Tank asked.

"Just asking Frisco here about his little lady."

I glared at him, too embarrassed to glance at Georgia. "I'm gonna knock your teeth out," I whispered.

"Pussy," he teased, turning around, and crossing his arms like nothing had ever happened.

"This is going to be so much fun," Tank said.

I cleared my throat, finally looking back at Georgia. "I'm so sorry," I mouthed, sliding my beer against the table, unable to stop fidgeting.

She smiled, looking over my shoulder at Bear. "So tell me about yourself, Bear."

He coughed, choking on the beer that had been halfway down his throat. He placed his hand over his mouth and set the bottle on the table. "Not much to tell, G. When I'm not here drinking, I'm working with Frisco."

"Not married?"

"Nope."

"Shocking," she teased.

Bear shifted in his chair. "I used to be."

"What happened?" Georgia's face softened.

"She died," he replied flatly, sadness all over his face, and his shoulders slumped forward.

Georgia placed her hand on his and stroked his fingers. "I'm so sorry."

"Fuck." He leaned back in his chair, trying to shake his sadness. "Frisco, if you don't want her, I'll take her."

"Why?" I let him have his fun and change the subject. I knew he didn't want to talk about his wife. She was the love of his life. Bear had been smitten. Gone. But that changed the day she was ripped from his life, along with his unborn child.

"'Cause she has a slick tongue, and I'm wondering what else it can do," he said.

"Bear baby, you couldn't handle what I have to deliver," she shot back.

"Fuck me," I grumbled. "You won't get another warning, and she isn't mine."

"Then what fuckin' gives?"

"She ain't ever going to be yours either," I told him.

"Frisco." Georgia touched my shoulder gently. "I can speak for myself. Don't speak for me again."

"Oh, damn." City laughed. "She put you in your place."

"The best night ever," Sunshine said with the straw between her lips.

"I need a shot, anyone else?" I pulled on the collar of my shirt, trying to calm down.

"I'm in," Georgia replied, brushing her finger down my forearm.

The tiny hairs on my arm rose, moving toward her, and craving more. "Anyone else?"

Tank shook his head. "Fuck no. We're going to watch you two get shitfaced and see what happens."

"I can outdrink everyone at this table," Georgia said.

"No one can outdrink Frisco. Right, man?" Bear asked, totally being an asshole.

Now I had to play the game. "I can put tequila away like it's water."

"This I have to see," Georgia said, her nails dragging against my flesh. "You're behind by a few. Better get crackin', buddy."

"Are you seriously challenging me to a drinking contest?" I studied her face and could tell she wasn't joking.

"Fuck yeah." She nodded enthusiastically.

I rubbed my forehead. "I'll regret it tomorrow, but I can't lose to a girl."

"You're going down." Georgia looked me in the eyes before slamming her open palms on the table. "Bring on the shots."

"Coming right up," Tank replied and his hand shot up in the air to get the waitress's attention. Thankfully, it was Brandy's night off.

Imagine the happy clusterfuck that could've been.

"If you're not careful, Georgia, you'll be the one going down," I told her and lifted my chin.

"Ha!" she yelped. "I've never lost."

The night was about to get real interesting.

SHOCK AND AWE

My brain buzzed from the six tequila shots I'd had before I called uncle. Georgia didn't seem drunk at all. When she called the waitress over, ready to order shot number seven, I gave in.

The entire time we drank, we talked and laughed. One thing I learned was that not only was she drop-dead gorgeous, but she was witty. She'd be a deadly combination to my heart. I had to keep reminding myself that she was too young. I couldn't let myself touch her.

City and Sunshine decided to drive us home. As I slid out of the car, Georgia followed, catching me totally by surprise.

"What are you doing?" I asked, turning around just as the rain began to fall.

"I live far and you're closer to the bar." Her body swayed in the raindrops. "I thought, in the morning, you could take me to get my car." Her chin dipped before she averted her gaze. Her face was almost hidden by the wet strands of her hair, but I could see her smile.

My reply should've been, "Get your ass back in the car and sleep it off at Sunshine's." But that wasn't the case.

I was horny and buzzed and her dress had started to soak through.

As she stood there with her nipples erect, her outfit drenched, and my dick hard as a fuckin' rock, I said, "Sounds good to me."

Way to go, genius.

We weren't even inside my house five minutes before our mouths collided. Fireworks went off behind my eyelids, the nerve endings in my body became hyperaware of her touch, and my buzz amplified when I tasted her.

Taking a step forward, I backed her up against the wall and kissed her with more force and need than I'd ever experienced before.

The coolness of our damp skin as our hands ravaged each other made her warm mouth even more delectable.

It wasn't a sweet kiss.

No. There was nothing sweet about it—this was entirely primal.

My body craved her warmth, her taste, and her flesh. As her hands slid under my shirt and her fingernails raked across my stomach, my breathing faltered.

"Fuck," I said, trying to find air to fill my lungs.

"Don't stop," she whispered, digging her nails into my flesh.

Using my weight, I crushed her body harder against the wall, causing her hands to find their way to my back. They inched up my skin and rested on my shoulder blades.

We shared air, feeding each other with our lips, and passed it back and forth. I held her face in my hands as I ravaged her mouth.

I couldn't take it any longer.

I wanted more.

I needed it.

My lips left hers, blazing a trail down her chin to her neck. When my tongue met her flesh, her nails raked down my back, scratching me. I cried out when my skin broke and the warm blood started to trickle from the cuts.

"Jesus, Georgia," I said against her neck before tugging her skin between my teeth.

She hissed, tipping her head back and giving me better access. Her skin slipped between my lips and I tasted her flesh. I loved every minute of it—her softness, her warmth, her smell that was so intoxicating I couldn't get enough. My hands trailed a path down her shoulders, finding her breasts with the sides of my thumbs.

"Wait," she whispered and grabbed my sides.

"What's wrong, baby?" My mouth moved past her collarbone, making a beeline for her cleavage.

"I can't do thisss," she stammered, tensing in my arms.

I dipped my tongue between her tits. "Can't do what?" I asked, praying she wasn't going to leave me hanging with a hard-on the size of a Louisville Slugger.

"We can't have sex," she yelped, trying to pushing me away.

I froze and my stomach plummeted, but not in that good flip-flop way. "Why not?" I stood up, looking her in the eyes. "You don't want me?"

"It's not that, Frisco. I want you more than I've ever wanted anyone."

"I would never force myself on you. I just have to know why." I backed away and dropped my hands from her body.

"Well, I'm a vir—" she started and looked up at the ceiling, exhaling slowly.

"No," I groaned, shaking my head like a madman.

No fucking way.

"Yes," she whispered before her head fell forward and she stared at the floor. "I'm a virgin, Frisco. I've been saving myself for the right man."

Her words couldn't be true.

I hadn't kissed a virgin since high school, and she did not kiss like they did. Georgia screamed sex, and to think that no one had been inside her was unfathomable.

I clutched my forehead. "Wow." I dragged my hand down my face, wishing she had been joking. How could this be happening?

"I know," she whispered and looked at me with sadness in her eyes. "We can kiss; I'm just not ready for more."

"It's okay," I told her and adjusted my cock in my pants. How could I be pissed?

"Do you hate me?" Her sad eyes found mine.

Please let this be a test and not the truth. "No, babe. I don't hate you. I could kiss you all night and be a happy man," I said, lying through my teeth.

She took a step forward, resting her hands on my arms. "We can fool around and kiss, but no fucking."

I kissed her lips, gentler than I had before. "I can live with that." I pulled my face away and wondered exactly what fooling around meant. "Can I touch your pussy?" It sounded more like I was begging her. Which I probably was at this point—but I'd never admit it.

She giggled, running her hands up my arms, and tucking them inside my sleeves. "You can. I'm so horny I may explode at any damn second. Virginity is a bitch."

"I'd have to agree."

I tried to block out the knowledge that she was a virgin, but it was impossible. With more trepidation than I'd had since I was a kid, I kissed a path to her cleavage, finding the spot where she'd dropped the news on me.

Her breasts were perfectly lush and made to be touched. She clawed at my skin as I licked between her breasts, finding the rain-drops that had settled there. My hands glided down her dress, settling near the hem.

Fuck.

The pressure of knowing she was a virgin had me on edge and uneasy. I kissed the tops of her breasts, nipping them with my teeth while I debated touching her pussy. Before I could make a decision, she placed her hand over mine, pulling our hands up her thigh.

"Don't be afraid," she whispered.

I swallowed hard, wanting to protest. I wasn't scared, was I?

I hadn't felt fear with a woman since the first time I touched one, but knowing that she hadn't been with a man sure as fuck made me nervous. I wasn't afraid I'd hurt her. I was afraid that once I tasted her sweetness, I wouldn't be able to fucking stop.

With my face still planted in her cleavage, I murmured against her breast, "I'm not afraid, babe. I'm just savoring the moment."

She spread her legs wider, begging without words for me to touch her. Sliding my hand between her legs, I cupped her pussy, feeling the warmth radiating through her lace panties.

My already rock-hard dick grew bigger inside my already too tight jeans. The poor thing was shit out of luck tonight. Georgia wasn't going to be a wild fuck. If I was lucky, I'd get a hand job out of the deal or I'd end up giving myself one tonight to get some relief.

I pushed her panties to the side. She wasn't just wet—she was dripping for me when I touched her.

She wanted this as much as I did.

As my fingertips glided across her silkiness, my eyes rolled back in my head. With the combination of her moans, the feel of her cunt, and the way my prick was about to break off, I thought I'd pass out. I'd never wanted to be inside someone as much as I wanted to be inside her with no chance of it ever happening.

I worked my way back to her mouth, needing to quiet her moans before I lost all control. I swallowed her gasp as I inched one digit inside her. I'd told women before that they were tight, but it had always been bullshit. Her pussy clamped down hard on my finger, and I knew there was no way in hell I'd get another one inside without hurting her.

My finger curled, touching her G-spot. I worked it in and out of her. Her back arched as her mouth grew slack against mine.

"Fuck yes," she mumbled, spreading her legs wider.

I wrapped my arm around her, trying to keep her upright as I finger-fucked her.

Kissing her as a distraction wasn't working. My entire body had grown tense and even more rigid than the cock in my pants. I needed to taste her, lose myself in her pussy, and lick my way to happiness.

I broke the kiss and let my finger slide out of her. "I have to taste you," I told her before I dropped to my knees.

She nodded, staring down at me with her lips parted and bee-stung.

I set one of her legs on my shoulder, bringing my face directly in front of the place I wanted to bury myself in the most. Her breathing changed as my warm breath skidded across her panties. I should've removed them before I started to prop her up on my shoulder, but I wasn't about to start over again. Before I drew her other leg up, I reached under her dress, grabbed the side of her panties, and pulled. There wasn't time for formalities. They shredded easily, falling from her skin, and pooling in my fist.

"Well, fuck." She smacked her head on the wall and groaned.

I glanced up at her and winked. "I won't let anything come between me and eating your pussy like my very life depends on it, Georgia. Just relax."

She nodded, closing her eyes.

I steadied her, holding her ass a little tighter when I lifted her other leg over my shoulder, walking backward on my knees to get better access.

Using my shoulders to hold her up, I placed her dress over my head and moved in for the kill. Her scent hit me first, causing my mouth to water. There's nothing sweeter than the smell of pussy.

As my tongue touched her wetness, I knew I'd never tasted something so divine. It was probably my imagination, but fuck me, I could've drunk at the fountain of Georgia and lived off it alone.

My fingertips dug into her ass and I licked her clit, stroking it gently at first. She shuddered in my arms, tangling her fingers in my hair. I regretted the position, wishing I had laid her down.

Her scent and smell made my brain cloudy with want. Finding her tight opening dripping with need, I cupped it in my tongue and swallowed each drop. The overly sweet liquid pooled in my mouth and mixed with my saliva.

I drove forward, licking harder than I had before, unable to control my desire. She writhed in my arms, pushing her pussy farther into my face. The damn dress was in the way of me seeing her face clearly. I wanted to see her come undone in my arms.

Within moments, her breathing changed and her body grew rigid. As her fingers gripped my hair like a vise, her body quaked, and her breathing halted.

I didn't let up, sucking her clit into my mouth and swirling my tongue around it as she rode the wave of ecstasy. When her body dipped and she sucked in a breath, I knew I'd done my job and done it like a fuckin' champ.

I knew I'd never be in this position again—between her legs, drunk on lust for her. This was a one-time thing. I'd never fuck a virgin and be the asshole they regretted their entire life.

Slowly I placed her legs back on the floor and held her waist. She swayed, and I stood before her, transfixed. Her pupils were dilated, lips parted, and cheeks pinked in the afterglow I'd caused.

"You okay?" I asked before licking her wetness from my lips.

"Yeah." Her voice was airy and light. "I couldn't be better."

I wanted to say that at least one of us was, but I kept my mouth shut.

As I backed away, she reached out and grabbed my hand. "Where ya going?"

"I don't know," I answered honestly. My only thought was to get away from her before my cock took over and I ended up trying to talk her into fucking me.

Her eyes dropped to the obvious bulge in my pants. "What about you?"

I reached in my pants, trying to get it to lay a different way. "I'll be fine."

"Frisco." She pushed herself off the wall and took a step toward me. "I said I was a virgin, not a newbie. I can suck a mean cock." A sinful smile spread across her face as she lifted an eyebrow. "Interested?"

My knees weakened at the thought of her beautiful red lips wrapped around my shaft, working me for everything she was worth. "Oh." Seriously, she wasn't a teenager. Why did I have a vision of her never being touched before in my head? Naturally, she'd done other things.

She kicked off her heels and dropped to her knees right in front of me. My heart stopped before it jumped back to life, beating uncontrollably.

She glanced up and grabbed my jeans, pulling me forward. Working the zipper like a pro before she yanked the denim down my hips and my cock sprang free, slapping her face.

Fuckin' thing had a mind of its own, and it knew exactly where it wanted to be—nestled in her warm, sweet mouth.

She giggled, staring up at me when it continued to bob. After it finally stopped moving, her eyes dropped and she froze.

"Oh, someone has some jewels."

"I wouldn't call it jewelry." I placed my hands on my hips and stared down at her.

"Whatever it is—" she reached out and touched my dick, "it's beautiful."

While I loved the chitchat about my beautiful manhood, all I wanted was for it to be in her mouth. I didn't want to talk about my ampallang piercing or all the things it could've done to her. I just wanted to come and feel the same ecstasy that still buzzed through her veins while I stood here in agony.

"You don't have to do this." I didn't mean a fucking word. I didn't want to say, "Just put it in your mouth already," because that would make me a jerk, which I was.

She passed my hardened shaft back and forth between her palms and licked the tip. Motherfucking fireworks exploded in my head. My dick twitched, aching for more attention, and nudged her lips.

When she finally placed it in her mouth, everything in the world disappeared. I became lost in sensations. She worked my shaft in her mouth, caressing the tip with her tongue with each stroke.

I shuddered, trying to stop my body from swaying from the overwhelming need I felt. I couldn't concentrate. She stroked my cock with both hands and sucked it like it wasn't the first one in her mouth.

Don't think about that.

I was a mess.

I didn't want to think about her virginity, but I also didn't want to think about every other loser she'd had in her mouth. I was at a complete and utter loss.

I pushed the thoughts from my mind and felt the orgasm building inside me. My balls tightened, my thighs burned, and everything inside me was ready to burst. Not even two minutes into the blow job and I growled through the most amazing orgasm of my life.

Through my hazy vision, I watched as her lips popped off my tip, causing my entire body to spring forward, instantly missing the feel of her tender skin on mine.

I stood here, unable to move or speak as I watched her swallow.

She wiped her lips, sucking her finger into her mouth.

Georgia was more than I'd ever imagined and everything I couldn't have.

Tomorrow morning, I'd set shit straight and get on with my life.

CHAPTER 6
THE BIG V

"Did ya nail her?" Bear asked before I had both feet inside the office.

"What?"

"Georgia. Did you nail her?" he repeated before he plopped his ass in the chair across from my desk.

I dropped my briefcase under my desk and took a deep breath. I gritted my teeth, trying to stave off my building anger when I sat down. "It's none of your business."

He leaned back, placing his hands behind his head. "You're losing your touch, buddy. It's okay. We can't all hit a home run every time."

"Bear, it's more complicated than that."

"Sure."

I rubbed my forehead, trying to work out the stress that had settled there since Georgia walked out my front door. I wasn't angry at Bear for being his normal asshole self—that, I always expected—but I was angry at myself for being an asshole to Georgia. "Seriously. It's complicated, and you wouldn't understand."

"What's complicated?" James asked, walking into my office with a bagel hanging from his mouth and files in his hands.

Privacy at ALFA PI was almost impossible unless there was a client meeting. Although the office was filled with men, they were more gossipy than a church-lady group.

"Frisco struck out with Georgia," Bear told him.

James sat down next to him and pulled the bagel out of his mouth. "That hot, pinup-looking chick at Gigi's party?"

I dropped my head onto my desk, wishing I could start this day over. "Can everyone just leave?"

"Nah," James replied. "We have to talk about Georgia."

I lifted my head and stared at them. "Don't we have work to do?"

"It can wait. We have a meeting in ten minutes. What happened with the girl?" James stuffed part of the bagel in his mouth.

"I just told her I couldn't see her again."

Bear's mouth dropped open, and James stopped mid-chew and gawked.

"It wouldn't work out between her and me. I made sure to put an end to it before anything started." There was truth to my words, but there was no way in hell I'd tell them she was a virgin.

Not happening. Ever.

If Bear found out, he'd be all over her like a rabid dog looking for fresh meat. I certainly wasn't going to let him have her, even if I wouldn't allow myself to traverse those waters.

"Are you not over your shit with Jeanine yet, man? Get the fuck over what happened with that whore."

I pointed at Bear and snarled. "Keep your mouth shut."

"Fucker." He leaned forward and batted at my hand. "Get your dick out of your ass and get over her. It's time to move on. Georgia would be a great comeback."

I threw myself back in my chair, crossing my arms over my chest.

Georgia was more than a comeback—she was like the freakin' World Series and Super Bowl rolled into one.

I didn't know how many times I'd told myself that. I don't know if I was buying my bullshit or if I was trying to make myself believe it as the truth.

I shook my head, trying to clear my thoughts. "It has nothing to do with Jeanine. I hadn't even thought about her."

I hadn't realized it before, but she hadn't entered my mind since the moment Georgia walked into the Neon Cowboy. The woman, and I use that term loosely, who had ripped my heart out hadn't even been a fleeting thought over the last thirty-six hours. Thoughts of Georgia had replaced her.

"Tell us what happened." Bear tried to get me to answer him again, looking at me with concern. Really, the fucker wanted to hear the juicy details.

"Didn't you get laid this weekend?" I asked, changing the subject. "Why don't you regale us with your conquests?"

"Just another trashy biker broad."

"Classy," I mumbled and ran my fingers through my hair.

Thomas popped his head into the office, slapping the wall. "Let's go, guys."

"Let's hit it." James stood and stuffed the rest of the bagel in his mouth.

I had been saved, at least for a little while.

"This shit isn't over," Bear told me before we walked into the hallway.

"It's done and in the past."

"Uh-huh."

I took a deep breath and entered the conference room. Thankfully, I'd have something else to think about for the next hour.

Who the fuck was I kidding? Georgia was like a hurricane that smashed into my borders and created mayhem around me. Not only did she leave devastation in her wake, she caused chaos inside me.

No matter how many times I told myself not to think about her, she was the only thing on my mind.

Even on my way to work this morning, the song "Georgia" by Vance Joy started to play. Instead of turning it off, I listened to each word carefully and knew at that moment that I was totally and completely fucked.

As Thomas started the meeting, my phone beeped.

Sunshine: What the heck did you do to Georgia?

My stomach dropped. Who wasn't in my shit today about her?

Me: Nothing, Sun. I swear to God.

I turned my screen off and ignored her.

"How's the case with the wife?" James asked.

"Good," I replied without skipping a beat. "I'm going to wrap it up this week. I have to get a better photo of them together, but she's almost completely satisfied."

"At least one person is," Bear mumbled.

I kept my eyes glued to James. "Good. Here are three more cases we'd like you to take a look at and contact the clients." He slid the files across the table.

I grabbed the papers, pulling them in front of me. "I'm on it."

Another beep made me glance down.

Sunshine: She's in tears. She just keeps mumbling your name.

What the fuck?

I pinched the bridge of my nose and closed my eyes. The last thing I wanted was Sunshine and, in turn, City pissed off at me. I just wanted to end things with Georgia before they started.

I guess technically the moment I placed my mouth against her soft, wet mouth things could have officially started, but I refused to believe it. I turned the phone over in my hand, debating on how to answer her.

Me: In a meeting. Can't talk.

I took the coward's way out. I set my phone on the table and started to rifle through the cases James had assigned to me. My eyes flickered to my phone when the screen turned on.

Sunshine: We aren't done.

I grimaced but didn't make a sound or reply. The last thing I wanted to do had been to draw more attention to myself. The gossip girls were around the table, and I wasn't going to be on top of today's list of people to make fun of.

I read through the files front to back as cases were doled out around the table.

"Any other business before we adjourn?" Thomas asked when I looked up.

"Nope," I replied, glancing back down at my papers.

"Well…" Bear cleared his throat.

"Bear," I said through clenched teeth.

"Nothing here." He laughed.

"Smart," I mumbled.

"Then let's get to work. We have more new clients coming in today and more work to give out later this week. It may be Tuesday, but there's too much to do without slackin' off." James's tone was serious.

I wanted to laugh. Although we all pulled our weight and worked our asses off for the company, they always found time to slack. That was the number one thing I loved about working here. It wasn't business all the time. I felt at home here, the camaraderie much like a brotherhood or a family.

I was the first one to grab my papers and head for the door. When I stepped into the hallway, I stopped mid-step. City stood outside my office door, leaning against the wall with his arms crossed, and looking angry.

"City." I tried to keep my voice from betraying the shock and worry I felt at him being here. "What's up, man?"

"We gotta talk."

"Surrre," I said, motioning toward my office. "Let's go inside."

He opened the door and I trailed behind, keeping my distance.

Sweat started to form on my brow line. I had never been afraid of City, but I sure as hell never wanted to piss him off.

"What's up?" I asked, walking around my desk.

"Listen, Frisco," he said as he rubbed his forehead and sat down. "Sorry for the display out there."

"What do you mean?"

"I'm not pissed at you. Suzy asked me to talk with you, and I know she'll call Angel to see if I did. I had to make sure I looked angry so word wouldn't get back to the wife. Got me?" He laughed and shook his head. "Fuckin' women."

Suddenly the lump that had formed in my throat vanished. "Thank God. I thought you were here to beat my ass."

"Nah, bud. What happened with G? I thought you liked her." He leaned back in the chair, his shoulders and body relaxing.

"City, what do you know about her?"

"Not much, but if you say she has a dick, I'm not going to believe you."

"Nothing like that, fucker."

"I only know that Suzy loves her and thinks you two would be great together. When my wife calls upset, I act on it."

"I know." I blew out a hard breath. "She's different than other girls."

"You found one of those?"

"One of what?" I asked, straightening my back, and playing stupid.

"A girl you can't imagine life without."

I held my hands up. "Wait a minute. I'm not saying that. She's just different."

"So was my Suzy. That's why I wanted her so badly. I knew the moment I found out she was different that I wanted no one but her in my life."

"Don't put words in my mouth." I gripped the armrests, feeling the blood drain from my knuckles.

"Stop lying to yourself. What's so different about Georgia that you threw her ass out? You've never thrown anyone away. I know you, Frisco," he said as he leaned forward, placing his elbows on his knees. "You never burn a bridge to pussy heaven."

I laughed, caught completely off guard by his statement. It didn't sound like something I'd heard him say in a long, long time. "It's not that."

"Well, stop telling me what it isn't and start spilling your guts about what it is. Why is this girl in knots today, and why in the fuck am I getting calls from my wife telling me she's going to kick you in the balls?"

"I didn't throw Georgia out of my house. I swear to God, that didn't happen. I just told her we couldn't see each other again."

"Ever?" City asked, resting his index finger against his lips as he stared at me. "I mean, there's more. You have the woman in tears."

"My cock is just that amazing." It was not my place to tell the story of Georgia's sex life, or lack thereof.

City rolled his eyes and smashed his hands together. "I can see I'm going to get nothing out of you."

"My lips are sealed."

"Did you do something that would make me want to kick your ass?"

I shook my head and frowned. "I was such a gentleman, you'd give me a pat on the back."

His eyebrows drew together. "You didn't fuck her?"

"Nope. I didn't."

"Then what the fuck is she so upset about?"

I cleared my throat and decided to spill the beans. "I'll tell you, but it does not leave this room."

"Swear." He held up two fingers, giving me a bullshit scout's honor.

"She's a virgin," I blurted.

His eyebrows shot up and almost grazed his hairline. "A what?"

"A virgin," I repeated, speaking more slowly.

"Well, fuck." He scrubbed his hands over his face.

I nodded and closed my eyes, taking a moment to let that reality set in. "Yeah. It's a total clusterfuck."

He stood and started to pace in front of my desk. "But then I don't get why she's so upset."

"We messed around a little, and in the morning, I told her I couldn't see her again."

He stopped dead in his tracks and turned to face me. "You what?"

I rubbed my forehead, trying to ease the tension that I could feel building. "I can't see that girl again."

"She's like the Holy motherfuckin' Grail, Frisco. I would've killed to have had Suzy be a virgin when I met her."

His reaction matched that of probably eighty percent of the male population in the world, but not mine.

"You married Sunshine. I have no plans on settling down with Georgia—or anyone. I'm not going to be the one to take her virginity either."

"Georgia isn't Jeanine."

I resisted the urge to do a face-plant on my desk. "I know. Jeanine couldn't keep her legs closed."

He rested his hands on the desk. "Just listen to me for a minute." He paused, holding his hand up before he stood. "You wanted a relationship. You're a lot like me, but you're waiting for the right girl.

What's better than a virgin? You won't have to worry about her fucking around. I really like Georgia. I think she's perfect for you."

"City." My voice was laced with warning. "I just need to stay away from anything involving commitment. Georgia is a great girl, but just not for me."

He walked toward the door and paused. "I got ya." He opened the door, and when he walked out, I swear he mumbled, "We'll see about that."

I set my face in my hands, pressing the fleshy part of my palms into my eyes. I could see no one was going to let sleeping dogs lie. I'd do everything in my power to make everyone realize I wasn't the guy for her.

CHAPTER 7

TRICKS

Georgia wouldn't do me the way Jeanine had. Hell, she hadn't done anyone at all. I mulled over the words City said in my office earlier in the day.

Before Jeanine, I would've said I wanted a relationship. But now, the thought of it made my stomach twist into knots. Any trust I'd had in the female gender evaporated.

I wasn't the right person for Georgia based on that fact alone. She didn't deserve my issues cast onto her.

Sitting in my car outside the Silver Sands Motel, waiting for Mrs. Green's husband to show his ugly ass with his secretary, didn't do much for my faith in relationships. I'd met with Mrs. Green a few times since I'd been assigned her case. She was a sweet woman, only about ten years older than me, and in a complete shambles over the unfaithfulness of her husband.

I needed to capture a few more shots to help seal her case against him. They wouldn't be permissible in court, but she planned to use them to get her way in the divorce.

As I tossed a potato chip in my mouth, Mr. Jackass Green walked outside with his mistress, pawing her. *Fucking asshole.*

She tossed her head back and giggled as he buried his face in her neck. I grabbed my camera, taking shot after shot as they kissed and groped each other in public.

If it weren't for the fact that they were having an affair, I would've been jealous. The happiness on their faces made me long for someone by my side. But when I remembered why I'd been snapping photos, all thoughts of it evaporated.

Tomorrow, I'd hand-deliver the evidence to Mrs. Green and close another case off my roster. This was just one in an endless line of cheating spouses and assholes trying to hide something from someone.

I sat in the parking lot for a moment. I didn't feel like being home, especially after an evening like tonight. As I pulled onto the road, heading toward the Neon Cowboy, my phone beeped.

City: Can you drop by? I need help.

I couldn't even believe it was a coincidence that he'd text me to drop by tonight of all nights. The last time City had needed help, he'd been injured and needed me to move some furniture. I smelled bull-shit, but I never said no to a friend in need.

When I stopped at the red light, I texted him back and said the only thing I knew would be right.

Me: On my way.

God fucking help me. I already knew I was walking into a trap. Sunshine would probably be waiting at the front door to kick me in the balls.

As I pulled in, I turned off my headlights and let the car glide to a quiet stop. Much to my surprise, there were no other cars in the drive-way. I expected Georgia to be here waiting for me along with Sunshine.

Before I knocked, the front door opened and Sunshine stood there with her hands on her hips.

"Hey." I tucked my hands in my pockets.

"Hey." Her eyes narrowed. "That's all you have to say for yourself. Just 'hey'?"

Rocking back and forth on my heels, I glanced down at the ground. "Let me explain—"

"Save it." She stepped to the side. "Come in."

I swallowed the lump that had lodged in my throat before I looked her in the eyes. "Maybe I should just go."

"Get your ass in here," City yelled from inside the house.

I turned my body slightly and tried to shuffle by, making sure my family jewels were safe from a possible kick ready to be hurled my way. "Fine," I mumbled, walking by Sunshine.

She slammed the door. "He's in the living room." Sunshine followed close behind me, making me feel uneasy. I thought he was a tough customer this morning in my office, but little Suzy Sunshine wasn't a pushover.

"Thanks."

City sat on the couch, and Gigi played Barbies on the floor by his feet. "You made good time."

"I came as soon as you asked. What's up, buddy?" I sat down across from him and toyed with the edge of the armrest.

"We need to have a chat about Georgia."

"Fuck." He'd tricked me to get me here, and now I was a captive audience, with Sunshine by his side. "What is there to talk about? I thought we went over this already."

"We have a way you can make it up to Georgia," Sunshine said as she sat on the back of the couch and put her arm around City's.

I held up my hands, halting them in their tracks. "What do I have to make up for?"

"For making her cry."

If they weren't looking at me like I was the biggest asshole, I would've laughed. "I did nothing wrong."

"Women don't cry for no reason." Sunshine pursed her lips, the same familiar glare on her face.

"Sugar, that's not true."

"Okay," she said. Her shoulders sagged as she leaned into him. "Georgia doesn't cry for no reason."

"She's a v—" I started to say and stopped mid-sentence when City started to shake his head. "What do I have to do to make things right?"

I should've stood my ground. The only thing I cared about was getting the hell out of their place.

"Take her to dinner. That's it."

"Dinner," I repeated. "That's all I have to do?"

"Yes," City replied, rubbing Sunshine's arm with a dopey grin. "After that, what's done is done."

I should've argued the point. If anything, everyone should be thanking me for not ruining the girl. If I hadn't been a gentleman, she'd be in tears for other reasons. "I'll take her to dinner. I'll call her and set it up."

"No need," Sunshine said and stood. "She's on her way here. You can take her out tonight and apologize." Clearly Sunshine didn't have any boundaries, especially when it came to other people. Maybe I'd misjudged her after all this time. I always thought of her as meek and mild, but she had been as conniving as other women I'd known.

"I can't believe this." I rubbed my hands together in front of me.

"It's happening, buddy."

"But I look like shit and I've worked all day."

"Stop being such a girl," Sunshine told me.

I looked at City, giving him a "you gotta be kidding" look. I needed to remember he'd sell me out in a heartbeat to his wife.

The front door opened just as I was about to bail. "Suzy, I'm here. What's wrong?" Georgia's voice echoed as the door slammed closed.

I closed my eyes, realizing that she had been lied to as much as I had. At least she hadn't been okay with tricking me into seeing her.

"In here!" Sunshine yelled. A giant smile spread across her face when she looked at me.

Georgia walked into the room, jamming her cell phone in her purse before she looked up. She froze as her eyes caught a glimpse of me. "What the hell?" she asked, her eyes darting between Suzy and myself. She looked amazing, wearing a black polka-dot dress with wedge heels. Her hair was partially up, with strands falling around her shoulders.

"Georgia," I said, standing from the couch, and moving toward her.

"What's going on here? I thought you had an emergency."

Even only after being apart for a few short hours, my belly flopped. My cock instantly hardened. Too bad—no matter what, I wasn't going to get any action.

"I did have an emergency. A love emergency." Sunshine approached Georgia, giggling louder the closer she came.

"Suzy. I don't like being tricked."

"You weren't." Sunshine wrapped her arms around a stiff-backed Georgia. "Frisco dropped by and said he wanted to take you to dinner."

My mouth fell open, and my eyes grew wide at her statement. I'd always underestimated little Suzy Sunshine. We were both being tricked into this situation.

"He did?" Georgia whispered, peering at me over Sunshine's shoulder.

Snapping my mouth closed, I nodded like the fucking idiot I always seemed to turn into when she was around.

Sunshine grabbed Georgia by the shoulders. "Let him buy you a nice dinner and make up for being an asshole."

My eyes darted to City. "What the fuck?" I mouthed.

He shrugged before laughing softly.

"He wasn't really an asshole." Georgia's eyes found me, soft and warm.

"Don't ruin this," Suzy whispered back but not softly enough that I didn't hear.

Moments like these made me thankful I didn't grow up with sisters.

"Georgia, I'd love to take you to dinner."

Sunshine turned, giving me a smile over her shoulder. I wouldn't forget that she'd hustled me. Someday, I'd find a way to return the favor.

"You don't have to, Frisco." Georgia stepped forward and stopped a few feet from me.

"I haven't eaten, and you've come all this way. It's the least I can do."

"Don't put yourself out or anything."

I shook my head, realizing I sounded like an asshole. Again. It was my thing lately. "That's not how I meant it. Fuck, you make me nervous." My cheeks filled with air before I exhaled.

"Daddy, can you read me a story?" Gigi asked City, tugging on his pant leg, and breaking the tension in the room.

City picked her up, placing her in his lap before kissing her chubby cheeks. "Sure, baby. As soon as our company leaves."

I walked toward Georgia and held my hand out. "Please. I'd love to take you to dinner. Will you allow me the pleasure of your company?"

She slid her palm into mine and smiled softly. "I'd love to go to dinner with you."

"You two go have some fun and get to know each other," Sunshine said.

"I think I know a lot already," I said, smirking at Georgia.

Her cheeks turned pink and she averted her eyes. "Um..." she mumbled.

I leaned to the side, bringing my lips toward Sunshine's ear. "I'll get you for this, Sunny," I told her in a quiet tone.

"Okay. You better go. It's a school night. You don't want to keep G out too late."

For fuck's sake.

If I didn't already feel like a cradle robber, reminding me that she had school tomorrow made me feel dirty. So dirty I didn't know if I'd be able to scrub that image from my mind.

"Have fun, kids," City said as we started walking toward the front door.

"Got it, Pops," I called out over my shoulder.

Next time I saw him, we were having some words about getting into other people's business. Wife or not, it wasn't his place.

"Have fun," Sunshine said before we walked outside.

I stopped on the stoop, still holding Georgia's hand. "You don't have to come to dinner with me."

She hung her head and my heart instantly tugged. "You don't have to go out with me."

I touched her chin, bringing her eyes to mine. "Georgia." I waited for her to look at me. "I'd love to take you to dinner. I'm sorry for the way things ended. We can at least be friends. Right?"

But how? I still remembered how she tasted, how she felt in my mouth, and the sound of her moans when she came. How could I do the friends thing?

She nodded and sighed. "We can be friends."

"Good. Do you want to drive with me or follow me?"

She pulled away from my touch. "I'll follow you."

"Where to?" I asked, glancing toward my car, feeling uncomfortable.

"I need a drink, really. There's a bar down the street. Is that okay?"

"You remember what happened last time we had a few drinks?" I asked, fishing my keys out of my pocket, and adjusting my already hardening dick with my fingertips.

"I do." She giggle-snorted. "It's kind of unforgettable."

I'd say. "Just follow me," I said.

Tonight wouldn't be easy.

CHAPTER 8

COMPLICATIONS

"I get why you don't want to see me," Georgia said before taking a sip of her beer.

My stomach back flipped. "It's not that I don't want to see you." I placed my hands flat on the table, rubbing the surface. "I just don't think I'm right for you, G."

"You aren't," she said around the rim of the glass. "I know that." Her eyes twinkled, the dark brown sparkling like stars in the darkest sky.

"Thanks."

She stared at me and played with the rim of her glass. "You think of me as a kid, don't you?"

I had to be truthful. "I do. I'm sorry." I leaned back in the chair, stretching my legs out underneath the table.

"When you had your hands in my pants, did I feel like a little girl?" she asked with a playful smile.

I coughed, almost choking on my own saliva. "Didn't help that you're smooth as a baby's ass down there, babe."

She rolled her eyes. "I heard it makes everything more sensitive."

The choking came back, this time more violent. "Fuck," I said with a strangled voice, adjusting my ever-growing cock in my pants, and tried to clear my throat.

"It did, you know."

"Did what?" I asked, trying not to think about her pussy that had tasted better than anything I'd ever had in my mouth.

"Being bare." She glanced down. "Made everything feel so much better."

She was the unicorn everyone searched for but never found. Perfection. Where on earth, besides in front of me, could I find an educated, beautiful, and dirty virgin? This was how my luck seemed to roll.

"I know you're not a child, but it's hard for me."

"It was hard for me too." She winked before a totally naughty grin tugged at her lips.

I closed my eyes and took a slow, deep breath through my nose. *I will not get wood. I will not get wood. Fuck!* She did that to me. My brain may have been screaming to keep away from her—she was too young, too inexperienced—but my dick thought otherwise.

The fucker in my pants wanted to explore her depths. Plunge deep inside and see what it felt like to be the first to claim a woman. Not the girls I'd been with in high school, but someone who saved herself for someone worthy of being the first.

"Just admit that you like me."

I opened my eyes slowly and saw her grin. "I want you," I said in a low voice, keeping my tone firm.

She flushed, sucking in a breath through parted lips that I wanted to kiss. "I want you too." Her tongue darted out, sweeping across her bottom lip, and all I could do was stare.

I clenched my hands into fists, resisting the temptation to jump over the table and kiss her. "Don't do that."

"What?"

"You're trying to tempt me into doing something I don't feel is right."

"Fuck right, Frisco. Seriously? Are you worried what others will think if you date me? I never took you for a pussy."

I leaned forward. "I'm not a pussy, G. I don't give a fuck what other people think about me. But—" I inched my hands closer to hers. "I'm not the man for you."

She pulled her hands back into her lap and glared at me. "Shouldn't I be the one to make that judgment?"

"You're a good girl and deserve a good guy."

"Fuck that. I had what I thought was a good guy. He turned out to be an asshole. I don't think if you were an asshole, you'd announce it."

"Maybe I'm just truthful."

"Maybe you're scared."

My body jerked backward. "Scared?"

"Yep," she said in a clipped tone before crossing her arms in front of her chest with a smug look. "You're scared to admit that you may not just want me, but you honestly like me. You're afraid of what might happen."

"I am not," I lied.

"You are. If you're not a pansy, then take me on a date."

"You're daring me to take you out to prove my manhood?" I held in my laughter at the insanity.

She nodded with a smug, all-knowing grin. "I'm daring you to prove me wrong. Show me you aren't a pussy, and prove to me all the ways you're bad for me."

"Babe—"

"Pussy," she coughed, brushing her hands across her lips.

"Goddamn," I whispered and pushed aside my apprehension. "Fine. I'll show you exactly why you don't want to be mine."

"Who said anything about being yours? I'm just talking about a little fun. Worried you can't keep up with me?" Her eyes sparkled as she stared at me, serious and not backing down.

"Fine."

"Fine."

This girl couldn't be for real.

CHAPTER 9

BUZZING

"I don't know what you did, but Georgia is, as Sunshine says, 'absolutely buzzing' for tonight," City told me over the phone.

"Jesus." I stared at myself in the mirror, putting him on speaker, and setting the phone on the counter.

"I'm glad you finally came to your senses."

"I think the opposite." I ran my razor under the water and tapped it against the sink.

"Even if you don't fuck her, she's perfect for you."

"When did you become Dr. Ruth?"

"Go fuck yourself."

"It would be a hell of a lot less complicated than tonight." I dried my face with a towel and cursed into the material so only I could hear.

"Dude, you're full of shit."

"Banging virgins in high school was great and all, but as an adult, it's a hell of a lot of pressure."

City laughed. "Why?"

"I could mess everything up royally."

"What the hell do you care?"

I stood here leaning against the sink and thought about his question.

299

Why did I care? I never really gave a fuck, especially after Jeanine. Maybe I'd been lying to myself and I really liked Georgia.

Could that be possible?

Maybe through my hate-induced haze, I'd missed all the cues about my true feelings.

"I don't know," I admitted.

"Look at it this way—she won't know if you suck in the sack."

"Shut the fuck up."

"I better run. Suzy will have my balls if you're late because of me."

"She already has them."

"What?"

"Nothing, man. I'll talk to you soon."

"Oh, you will," he said. "Go get 'er, tiger."

"Don't call me again. We've talked on the phone more lately than ever before. We're turning into two old hags."

"Speak for yourself, fucker."

I hit end and took a deep breath.

I'd probably be the one getting fucked in the end.

I THOUGHT I'd planned a great first date. I don't remember the last time I had one. She wasn't a bar troll or Jeanine, so I wanted to do something different.

When I showed up at her house, she didn't look ready for what I had planned. Mini golf and dinner, I figured, would be innocent. There was nothing sexy about it, and it would keep my ass out of trouble—and my cock too.

But when she opened the door in sky-high cherry red peep toe heels, I knew I was in trouble. Georgia didn't play fair. I knew that about her in the short amount of time we'd spent together. Peeking out were her toes, shiny and painted black.

My eyes slowly traveled up her legs, catching a spectacular view of her legs before landing on her chest. It's not that I typically ogled a woman's cleavage, but the V-neck dress she wore showed everything off.

Instantly, my mouth watered at the sight. I wanted to taste her skin. I'd touched it before, but it wasn't enough.

"Am I dressed okay?" she asked. She looked down, following where my eyes had landed.

I blinked and broke my trance with her breasts before dragging my eyes to hers. "Uh," I stammered, swallowing hard. "Yeah."

Her eyes drifted down my body, slowing as they took in my arms before traveling the length of my body. "I think I'm overdressed."

"We're going to play mini golf," I blurted out and let my eyes drop back to her magnificent tits.

"Well, fuck. I can golf in these," she said, tipping her shoes, and tensing her calf muscles.

There wasn't an inch of her body that wasn't impeccable. Her calves were toned, sleek, and craving to be touched. I wanted to feel them wrapped around my back, pulling my dick deeper inside.

My fingers began to tingle and I shook them out, trying to get rid of my need to touch her. "I'm ready if you're ready."

She closed the door and smiled before sauntering down the walkway in front of me. Did I talk about her ass—tight as shit in all its round glory? I closed my fists and clenched them tightly.

I would not touch her. At least not yet. Resist the urge, I told myself. I had willpower. I learned how to hone it in the military.

There was a problem with my plan. I hadn't thought about her bending over and waving her ass in my face every hole. Eighteen holes, multiple attempts, and every time she did it, I had to tell my dick that it was a no go.

She didn't make it easy either. No. Georgia wouldn't be that kind. Behind her innocence was a vixen dying to be set free.

Every time she bent over, she hadn't been ladylike. She didn't bend at the knees and scrunch down to retrieve her ball. Nope. She kept her legs straight, bending at the waist, and gave me a full view of her upper thighs and perky ass each time. Not one time did she take it easy on me.

She knew exactly what she was doing. Her small smiles, pretend apologies the entire time were all bullshit.

Every opportunity she had, she'd brush against my body, giving me just enough to drive me crazy. The smell of her perfume and the feel of her body against mine drove me crazy.

By the time we sat down at dinner, I didn't know if I could walk another step. My dick felt like a baseball bat inside my pants, ready to splinter if I moved any farther.

"Are you all right?" she asked when the waitress put our entrees on the table.

I shifted in my seat, placing the napkin on my lap, and pushing my cock down between my legs. "Yeah. I couldn't be better."

"You look a little flushed."

I glanced up at her just as she placed a French fry in her mouth, wrapping her lips around it like a dick, and suckling it.

She pulled the fry out slowly, toying with the tip of it with her tongue. "Your face is all red."

I closed my eyes and tried to think of something sad—anything to make the raging boner in my pants go away. I didn't look at her as I picked up my fork. "I'm good," I said, my voice betraying me when it cracked.

Her moans drew my attention just as I was about to place a forkful of whatever I'd ordered in my mouth. She had closed her eyes, slowly sucking on the French fry, and fucking moaning.

Every ounce of air in my lungs disappeared, and I couldn't do anything but stare. My lips were half open, waiting to be fed, and my brain couldn't communicate with my hand. I just sat here. Staring at her. Gawking as she moaned, totally breathless and dumbfounded.

After she swallowed and glanced at me, a small smile played on her lips. "You want a taste?"

I shoved the fork in my mouth, needing to put something inside to stop me from answering. I stabbed at my food as she laughed softly. "Enjoying yourself, aren't you?"

"Nah."

I didn't risk a glance. I couldn't. "You are."

"Why are you fighting it so badly?"

I still wouldn't look. Because I knew why I fought it. She wasn't right for me, and I sure as fuck wasn't right for her. "It's not right. Plain and simple."

"Frisco." Her voice was soft and sultry when she spoke my name. "Do you think I'm weak?"

I stopped chewing, peering up at her. "I don't."

"Then stop treating me like I'm fragile."

She had me there. I did think it was my duty to protect her from me, but really, I was keeping myself safe. "I don't mean to."

"The words that you say do not match what your body tells me."

Setting my fork down, I leaned back and stared at her. "What are you talking about?"

She continued to eat, speaking between bites. "You can't keep your eyes off me."

"Well, you're beautiful."

"When I brush against you, I can feel how hard you are for me."

My lips twisted and my dick twitched, reminding me that she had a point. "I can't help what happens when you touch me."

"I'm not asking for a lifetime here. Stop being so full of yourself and assuming you're going to break my heart and steal my virginity."

"Well, I never—"

She waved her fork in front of her and silenced me. "First off, I won't willingly give away my virginity. I've held on to it too long. It's sacred and I'll only give it to someone who is special to me. So you don't have to worry about taking it."

I'd be lying if I didn't admit that her words gave me a funny feeling. Like when you're sitting in an airplane to skydive for the first time, that kind of belly flop slash nausea that overcomes someone.

The thought of her just offering it up on a platter made me angry. It shouldn't have. She wasn't mine to feel jealousy over, but there it was. Sitting in my gut, twisting away like a knife.

"But I like you."

The words lodged in my throat. Thoughts swirled through my mind about Georgia. I liked her too. Liked everything about her. Okay, that was a lie. I hated that she was so young, too young, I thought, for me. But she wasn't a college kid looking to chug beer at a frat party. She was a woman. One hell of a woman who oozed sex appeal from every pore and could make the strongest-willed man bend to her desires.

I grabbed my gin, swallowing it down, and grimacing. I couldn't hold it back anymore. I had to say it. Free myself from the restraint. "I like you too."

She smiled and stared at me with soft, playful eyes. "Glad you finally admitted it. Now eat up. Because I want you to do that thing you did with your mouth."

I coughed into my glass, choking on the gin that had barely passed my tongue.

"And your fingers. God, they're so thick and long."

"Stop," I warned her, feeling my control slipping.

She leaned forward, placing her tits closer to me and on full display. "I may be a virgin and want to keep it that way, but it doesn't mean I don't want to wrap my lips around your cock and taste your want for me."

"You're playing a dangerous game."

"I know exactly what I want, and I'll do anything to get it."

I set down my drink, clasped my hands in front of me on the table, and leaned forward, close to her. "I gave you a chance to get away, Georgia. I warned you what I am, but you kept coming. I'm sick of running and fighting my attraction to you." I licked my lips, watching her eyes drop to my mouth and getting a little thrill. "I'm done being a gentleman. I know what I want. Who I want. And I'll put my mouth anywhere you want it. I'll give you so much pleasure, you'll never want another man in your life."

"Promise?" she asked, bringing her face closer, and looking me straight in the eye.

I leaned over and brushed my lips against hers. Peering into her eyes, I whispered, "You can bet your ass on it."

Too many drinks, a lot of flirting and innuendo, and a taxi ride spent kissing and touching that led us back to her place.

Unable to contain myself by the time we walked through the door, I tossed her over my shoulder and carried her to the bedroom. She giggled, half drunk, and squealed when I tossed her on the bed.

Her dress flipped up, covering her face as she giggled. My pulse quickened at the sight of her bare pussy. In one quick motion, I pulled my shirt off and slid onto the bed, right between her legs. I planned to give her exactly what she wanted and I needed.

I wrapped my arms around her thighs and pulled her to my face. She gasped at the contact and twitched in my arms when I clamped my mouth down against her.

I buried my face in her, suffocating myself but loving every minute of it. I hadn't let myself think about how badly I wanted her since the last time I touched her.

As I lay here with my face between her legs, sucking and licking like I'd never had pussy before, I realized how much I wanted her. No matter what, I didn't want to spend time with anyone else. Just her. Only Georgia.

Her hands found my hair as she sucked in air and her body shook in my arms. I held her to me, didn't let her escape as I devoured every ounce of her until she was writhing in the bed and screaming my name. By the time that happened, my dick was harder than steel.

When her breathing evened out and she stilled, I climbed up her body and licked my lips to capture every last drop. I hovered over her, watching her try to focus on my face.

"Well, fuck. That was—" She inhaled deeply and closed her eyes.

"Fucking amazing."

"The best," she whispered as her eyes fluttered open.

I settled between her legs and pressed my length against her. "I need to feel your lips on me, Georgia."

She smiled, reached up, and ran her fingers through my hair. "I can help you out with that," she said, rubbing her pussy against my jeans and almost making me come in my pants. "But first," she whispered, bringing her lips close to mine. "I want you to make me come again." She tugged at my head and pushed me down.

I laughed softly and didn't hide the smile on my face. Georgia may have been a virgin, but she wasn't innocent. She knew what she wanted and had no issue demanding it. Lucky for her, I was more than happy to serve. I'd worship at her altar and feast on her soul for an eternity if she'd allow me, as long as it meant she'd quench her thirst by wrapping her lips around my cock and drink me down.

When I perched myself between her legs, I took a moment to take in her majesty—the soft, bare flesh that held so much pleasure and had never been tapped. My fingers lightly grazed her velvety skin, damp with need. I closed my eyes, memorizing her scent and the feel of my body on hers.

The noises she made in the back of her throat drove me forward and kept me going. My dick may not have been allowed inside her, but my fingers were itching to rub her in just the right way that she'd be screaming my name until her voice turned hoarse.

I inched backward, pulling her with me because this position wouldn't work for what I had planned.

"What are you doing?" she asked, lifting her head, and staring down her body.

"Just lie back and enjoy," I told her and winked before I settled on the floor.

Her body hung over the edge and she did as I asked, gripping the comforter nervously in her hands. I removed her shoes, tossing them over my head before I placed her feet flat on the bed, giving me the most amazing view.

I scooted forward, sitting on my knees before I dragged my tongue lightly against her pussy. Her knees began to turn inward and I pushed them apart, leaving my hands on her legs and opening her to me.

While rubbing my fingers against her, priming her for the finger-fuck of a lifetime, I dipped my head forward and licked her folds. Slowly and softly touching her with my mouth and feeling her try to bring her body closer, wanting more than I gave.

I pushed my fingers inside and licked her pussy harder.

"Yes," she moaned.

My eyes moved over her body and watched as she toyed with her breast, matching the rhythm of my tongue. If I couldn't fuck her with my cock, I'd do it with my fingers.

I twisted them as I pulled out, bringing her new sensations with my tongue twirling around her clit and barely making contact. She chased my mouth, driving her pussy down on my hand in the process.

It may have been the most erotic moment of my life. Watching the virginal Georgia fuck my fingers, smashing her pussy on my face, and moaning out her pleasure.

Within seconds, her insides squeezed down on my fingers when she came, but I didn't relent. I wouldn't let up until she had another. Until she was so sated that she wouldn't deny me the relief I needed to survive.

I sucked harder and she thrashed about the bed, but she didn't tell me to stop. There were lots of *fucks* and *hell yesses* coming from her mouth, but I wanted more.

I wanted to give her something mind-blowing and unforgettable. I had other reasons too. I wanted it to be so good she didn't ask for another before I could feel her warm, wet mouth wrapped around my dick.

When my mouth left her body, she whimpered and blinked through her lust-induced haze. I shook my head as a warning and positioned myself in front of her. Before I slid my fingers back inside her, I pushed down on her pelvis and inched them inside her slowly.

"Oh," she moaned, feeling the difference.

"Tell me if it gets too much," I said, seating my fingers fully inside her. I knew it could be overwhelming. Even though she boasted that she wasn't new to foreplay, not all women could handle a real finger-fuck.

She looked up at me and blinked a few times before nodding. I added another finger, needing to fill her and make her feel everything my fingers were doing inside her.

After thrusting them in and out of her a few times, I added a twist, moving my wrist back and forth with my fingers.

Her knees pushed on my sides, holding me in place while I banged her with my hand, wishing like fuck it was my dick inside her. I pulled out slowly, thrusting back in with more determination with each stroke.

When her ass started to rise and she began the familiar chase of my fingers, wanting more than she was getting, I added a curl. Positioning the tips of my fingers against her G-spot, applying more pressure to her pelvis, and holding her down against the bed.

I mimicked the motion of my hands with my crotch and drove inside of her until she shattered. Shaking on the bed, gasping for air, and screaming my name over and over again. I couldn't help but smile, knowing I'd done it to her.

My eyes couldn't leave her. Seeing her in pieces before me was the best high I'd ever have in my entire life. Seeing her limp and exhausted may have backfired. She was spent and I'd done it.

"Gimme a minute," she whispered, throwing her arm over her face and gasping for air. "Just a minute."

I collapsed on the bed next to her and stared up at the ceiling. My curse with her would be to have forever-wood. It never softened, permanently rock hard and painful. For some unknown reason, even though we didn't fuck, I needed to give her the best damn orgasms of her life.

I'm sure Brent the Bland didn't finger-fuck her the way I had. He couldn't. She wouldn't talk about him and his dullness if he had. The problem with my need to over-please her was that she came so hard she was literally spent. I closed my eyes and tried to think of something, anything, to make my boner go down.

Before I let my mind go dark, the bed dipped and Georgia rolled to my side. "Hey," she whispered and palmed my dick through my jeans. She kissed my neck and stroked my length. "I wouldn't leave you like this." The warmth of her hand felt so amazing I didn't want her to ever stop touching me.

"Thank God," I said and laughed. "I think you better put it in your mouth before I come in my pants."

"I thought you were more of a man than that."

I smiled and pulled her face to mine. "G, I am a man. But tasting your pussy and listening to you come drove me so close to the edge, I didn't think I'd ever recover. If you don't put my dick in your mouth quick, I'm going to die."

"Technically, no one has ever died from blue balls."

I raised an eyebrow and grinned. "You risking a chance for me to be the first?"

Her eyes roamed my face while she squeezed my dick roughly.

"Well, I wouldn't want that. Who would make me come the way you do?"

"Good answer." I pulled her face down, letting her lips almost touch mine. "Wrap those beautiful red lips around my dick and make me come, baby."

Her warm breath skidded across my skin. "There's nothing I'd rather do than lick—" she stuck her tongue out and ran it over my top lip "—your cock."

My eyes rolled back slightly before I recovered. Just as I was about to push her down my body like she had me, she scooted down the bed and started to undo my jeans. Sweet Jesus, I needed this. I feared I wouldn't even be able to walk out of her place if I didn't find relief and fast.

I put my hands behind my back, watching her as she worked the zipper and opened my jeans. Instantly, my dick sprang out and searched for her mouth. She smiled and her eyes followed its movement until it stopped.

"Don't watch," she whispered and wrapped her hand around the shaft. "Close your eyes, lie back, and enjoy."

I wanted to argue because watching was half the fun. Seeing a woman with her lips wrapped around my dick, taking all I had to offer, was one of the sexiest things ever. Right now, the way I needed to come, wasn't a time to argue.

Without protesting, I put my hands behind my head and closed my eyes. Her hands, piled on top of each other, moved up and down my shaft. Hitting my piercing along the way, which caused me to twitch before groaning.

"Babe." My voice held both a warning and a plea as I looked down my body.

"I didn't tell you how to finger me, don't tell me how to suck your dick."

"I haven't felt your mouth on me yet."

"Keep it up and you won't," she shot back and stilled her hand.

"Fuck, I'm dying here," I whined and closed my eyes.

Her hands moved again, stroking my length, squeezing the tip, and striking the sensitive spot underneath. I moaned and waited for the moment. The very second when her mouth would—

Damn.

The feel of her warm, soft lips clamped around me felt like heaven. She worked my dick with her hands and mouth, trying to take my entire length to the back of her throat. Her hands twisted to the right with each upstroke and to the left with the down, over and over again.

My body tightened.

It was too soon.

I didn't want to come.

I could feel it.

I wasn't ready for it to be over.

Her tongue swirled around the tip and massaged the very spot, the one that would send me over the edge faster than anything. My breathing faltered and my muscles began to spasm. This was it. I couldn't stop it.

Being with Georgia had brought me here. Ready to come too soon and overly excited it happened. The orgasm ripped through my system. Every muscle in my body twitched as I rode the wave. It crashed over me, pulling me under while she sucked my cock like a greedy lover.

The only thing that told me I was still alive was my heart pounding inside my chest. I could hear it. It thumped erratically, slamming against my insides as I gasped for air.

Her lips moved slowly up, firmly wrapped around my cock, sliding off my tip, and taking everything I had with her.

I opened my eyes and watched her swallow it down without a sound. The smile on her face, the satisfaction it gave her, warmed my insides.

"I'm sorry," I said, wishing I'd been able to hold out longer.

She wiped her lips with the back of her hand, part of her tit hanging out of her dress. "For what?"

I pushed myself up and rested on my elbow. "For coming so soon."

Her head tipped back and she laughed. "Oh, Frisco," she said, stretching out next to me, and placing her hand on my chest. "It's flattering."

My chest tightened at her words. "It is?"

"I know this is all new to you."

It was my turn to laugh. "Blow jobs aren't new to me, G."

She slapped my chest and giggled. "I mean, messing around without fucking, asshole."

"Ahhh." I laughed. "I just want you to know I'm not always like this." Honestly, what the fuck was I saying? I sounded like a total tool.

"I'll take your word for it."

"Come here." I pulled her on top of me, and she settled against my half-hardened cock. Bad idea on my part, but I never claimed to think clearly when it came to Georgia.

"Oh." Her eyes dipped down to where our bodies connected and she blushed. "We can't."

"I know. I just wanted to kiss you," I lied. Really, I wanted to fuck her brains out, but I wouldn't do it. Not without her permission and earning it as she had said earlier.

Wait.

Hold up.

I stared up at her, into her dark, warm eyes and really looked at her. Even though her age was something I didn't think I could get past, the woman straddling me with a pink post-orgasm sheen on her face wasn't a girl. Georgia was a woman and one that I didn't want to think about being with anyone else but me.

My stomach knotted, feeling the same way it had the last time I'd been punched in the gut. The thought of Georgia having sex with anyone else pissed me off. But she wasn't mine. I didn't have any right to feel jealousy or anger, but I did.

"That was amazing," I told her before pulling her face to mine and kissing her gently.

"Yeah," she said and pushed herself off my body before settling at my side. "I can't sit like that. You're too tempting, Frisco."

"I wouldn't make you do something you didn't want, babe."

"I know," she whispered and rested her head on my chest. "I'm more worried that I'll do something before I'm ready. It's not you that'll make me do it when it happens." She pushed her cheek against my pec, burrowing deeper into my side. "I know that we're not a couple, but I don't want to fool around with anyone else."

The knots evaporated and I felt like a weight had been lifted. "I don't want to be with anyone else either," I admitted before closing my eyes.

My mind started to wander as we lay here together—her with her dress all cockeyed and me with my dick still hanging out of my pants.

"Frisco," she whispered and slid her hand underneath my shirt.

I opened my eyes, peering down at her. "Yeah?"

Her forehead crinkled, and the worry of what she was about to ask was written all over her face. "Do you like me?"

"Of course I do."

"You made it seem like you didn't."

"I'm just an asshole sometimes, babe."

Her hand stilled against my stomach, splaying out against my skin. "I'll agree with that. But do you like me, or did you only want to fuck me?" She looked across the room, breaking eye contact.

I pulled myself up, taking her with me. I adjusted myself so that I could see her face and pushed my cock back inside my jeans. "Georgia, look at me."

It took her a moment before she dragged her eyes to mine. She gnawed on her lip as she blinked slowly.

I grabbed her hand, gently rubbing the top with my fingers. "I like you. I've always liked you." I swallowed down the lump that had formed in my throat. I couldn't believe I was about to admit my feelings for her. "I liked you from the moment I saw you. Fuck, you gave me wood the first time you smiled at me."

"Then why didn't you want to see me? You made it quite clear you didn't want me around."

"You were too tempting to be around."

Her head snapped back and she frowned. "What's that mean?"

"You're younger than me, and for that simple fact, I told myself you were off-limits." I winced.

"But it's just a number." She blinked rapidly.

"I know. But you deserve more than I can offer."

"Isn't that for me to decide?"

"Yeah." I laughed, giving her hand a squeeze. "To be honest, I wanted you so badly I made myself crazy. Sunshine and City think we should be together, and they made sure to throw us together as much as possible."

"I know." A smile spread across her face. "I told her I thought you were hot."

I straightened my back, sitting up a little more confidently. "You think I'm hot?"

She waved her hand in between us. "Look at you. You're sexy as hell. You have this Keanu Reeves thing happening, but when he was sexy, not the Keanu of today. But not the pussy version of him either," she rambled as her cheeks turned pink.

"Thanks, I think."

"Keanu never had the muscles like you do, but you know. There's a look you have that I dig."

"So you want me for my looks, body, and cock?"

"I would say yes, but it would be a lie."

I started to laugh. "So you don't want me?"

"Fuck. Stop. You're confusing me. I do want you. I think you're sweet."

"I'm sweet," I repeated before blowing out a breath. "I don't know many people who have said that about me."

"Suzy does."

"Suzy likes everyone."

"Fuck no, she doesn't."

"No?"

"She told me to stay away from Bear and Tank, but that you were the one I should set my heart on. She said you were one of the best guys she knows."

"Really?" My mouth dropped open.

She pulled at her bottom lip with her fingers. "Yeah."

"But to answer your original question, I like you, Georgia. I like you more than I want to."

Her eyebrows shot up, almost touching her hairline. "You do?"

"Look at you. You're beautiful, smart, sexy, have a killer body, amazing tits, an untouched pussy."

"It's been touched now." She laughed, covering her mouth with her hand.

"Yes, it has." I chuckled, bringing her hand to my lips, and placing a kiss against her skin. "What man wouldn't want you?"

"My ex-fiancé, obviously." She shrugged.

"Oh, please. He's a bastard. Listen, my fiancée cheated on me too."

She gasped and her eyes widened. "She did?"

"Yeah." I nodded and placed our hands between us. "It happens sometimes. We give our heart to someone who isn't worthy, and they stomp all over it like it's a piece of trash. We both deserve better."

"Yeah," she whispered.

Here was my defining moment. Georgia liked me. I couldn't get enough of her. Could I take the big leap and ask her something I swore I never would? The thought of Georgia being with anyone else made my blood instantly boil. The only way to stop that from happening was to ask her a very important question.

"Georgia," I whispered, swallowing the dryness that had settled in my mouth before touching her cheek. "Will you be mine?"

Her mouth dropped open before it snapped shut. "Like *yours* yours?"

"Well, yeah." I brushed my thumb against her lip.

"Why?"

"That wasn't the response I thought I'd get," I mumbled before holding her face in my hands.

She laughed softly and kissed the tip of my thumb that rested near her mouth. "I'm sorry."

"The thought of you being with someone else makes me jealous, Georgia. I love being with you. If I were being totally honest, you make me happy. I want you to be mine and only mine. I don't want to share you with anyone."

A smile pulled at her lips. "I like that."

My heart pounded so loudly that I could hear it, and I was sure she did too. "So, is that a yes?"

"Yes!"

"Thank Christ," I muttered and closed my eyes.

"Frisco?"

I peeled open one eye and peeked at her. "Yeah?"

"What's your last name?"

"Why?" I full-on stared. She'd laugh. I knew she'd laugh.

"Because—" she swallowed, glancing up at the ceiling, "I want to change my status on Facebook, and I need to know your name for it."

"I don't use Facebook."

Her eyes widened. "What?"

"Never been my thing."

"We have to change that."

"No, we don't."

"Fine," she muttered, rolling her eyes. "What's your last name, though?"

"Jones," I said and held my breath.

My entire life I'd heard bullshit when people heard my name— Frisco Jones. My mom had been, still was to this day, a huge *General Hospital* freak. When Frisco and Felicia were a couple, she went on and on about them as if they were her friends. Lucky for me, they were the big couple when I was born. My mom couldn't resist naming me after her favorite soap opera character. The only thing I had going for me was that Georgia was most likely too young to even know who the hell they were. I always went by my middle name, Frank, when I worked. My business cards even said Frank Jones.

I had become good at telling the bullshit story of Frisco being a nickname, which it was, but Frank most certainly wasn't my legal first name.

"Can I be Felicia?" the smartass asked.

"Fucking hell," I muttered before I cracked the fuck up. "You're a ballbuster, G."

"Your ballbuster." She winked and kissed the back of my hand.

"Mine." I pulled her into my arms and kissed her, sealing the bond.

I didn't know what made me spill my guts like a pussy.

Georgia had my mind playing tricks on me.

When I fell asleep that night, I had gained a girlfriend and lost my heart.

CHAPTER 10

THE AFTERMATH

I didn't have to reach out to feel if Georgia was next to me; my nose told me she wasn't there. The smell of bacon woke me.

Rubbing my eyes, I yawned and stretched my legs. I lay here and studied her room. Bookshelves lined the room, just about two feet below the ceiling, filled with paperbacks. I expected her to have books since she was a librarian, but the quantity surprised me.

The walls were a dark gray with stark white trim. White curtains flowed down and pooled on the hardwood. There wasn't a dresser or any other furniture in the room besides the bed. My bedroom looked like a haphazard mess compared to the neatness of her room.

"Hey." She peeked her head in the door. "You're awake."

"I am." I stretched, taking the sheet off with my foot. "Are you okay?"

"I couldn't be better. Happy to see me?" Her cheeks flushed when she laughed.

I grinned, looking at her around my morning wood. "I am. You want to help me out with this?" I grabbed my cock and stroked it.

"I would." She glanced toward the kitchen before she stepped into the room with her eyes glued to my dick. "But the food is almost done, and I don't want it to burn."

I squeezed my dick. "What if I said I only wanted *you* for breakfast?"

She crawled onto the bed, climbing up my body like a cat. She batted away my hand when she came eye-to-eye with my dick. "I'd say you can have me for dessert."

I grabbed her arms and pulled her up my body, sliding her across my hardness. "I'm greedy. I want it now."

"But I have bacon," she argued with a giggle.

"I'm craving your sweetness, not bacon."

"But bacon is the greatest food ever invented."

"I beg to differ. You haven't tasted your pussy."

She placed her hands on my chest and lifted herself. "Frisco, come on. I made you a big breakfast. I need you to have enough energy for today."

I grinned and thought that whatever she had planned I would happily go along with. "What do you have in mind?"

She startled me and squirmed, causing my dick to throb. "Well…"

I closed my eyes and grabbed her waist, stilling her. "You can't do that."

She giggled, which made her body shake again and made everything worse. "Sorry," she whispered, and laughed more.

"Fuck," I mumbled, pushing her down my body and letting my cock spring free.

She glanced down and licked her lips. "I'm not telling you what we're doing today until you get out of bed."

I sat up and she pulled at my arms. "I'm up."

She looked down just as my cock touched her stomach. "I can see that."

I flexed my dick, having it twitch against her skin. "You do this to me."

"Up you go."

I glanced down and waggled my eyebrows. "I am."

She rolled her eyes. "I need food."

"Let's get up," I told her, pulling my legs out from under her, and rolling off the side of the bed.

"The bacon's probably burned by now," she said, climbing off the bed behind me.

I grabbed my boxers off the floor and started to put them on as I watched her. "I like it well done."

"How do you want your eggs?" She walked toward the door in her black silk nightie.

"Scrambled eggs are fine, but any way you want to make them." I headed toward her bathroom, needing to clean up and wash my mouth out. "I'll be right out."

"Sure. Make yourself at home. There's an extra toothbrush on the counter for you," she told me after she walked into the hall.

"Thanks," I yelled before closing the bathroom door. I hurried, not wanting to risk ruining breakfast.

I walked into the kitchen just as she set the bacon on the table. "Smells amazing in here."

She glanced up at me. "It's the bacon."

I stepped toward the stove and paused. "Do you want me to finish the eggs?"

"I'd love that. I'll finish setting the table while you do that."

I grabbed the spatula sitting next to the stove and began to fold the eggs. "I don't think anyone has ever cooked me breakfast besides my mom."

She stopped as she reached for the plates and looked over at me. "Seriously?" Tiny creases formed across her forehead.

"Seriously." I studied her face.

Morning Georgia was more beautiful than the glammed-up woman I'd grown fond of. "Hey, Georgia," I said, using my free hand to rub the back of my neck.

"Yeah?" She pulled two plates out of the cupboard.

"Don't take this wrong, but you look more beautiful this morning than I've ever seen you."

She pursed her lips. "Without my makeup?"

I grinned and let my eyes roam around her face. "You're always beautiful, but without the makeup, you're spectacular."

"Oh, you like the plain Janes."

"No, I like seeing the real woman behind the eyeliner and lipstick."

She set the plates on the counter next to me and folded her arms in front of her. "I feel naked without it sometimes."

I turned my attention back to the eggs, not wanting to ruin them. "Feel free to be naked around me anytime."

She slapped me on the arm and laughed. "You're a perv."

"I'm a man. I can't help that I love your body without anything masking its beauty."

Her cheeks turned pink. "You're really a great guy."

"I'm not; you just think I am."

"You are," she argued, slapping my ass.

I folded the eggs one last time before turning off the burner and removing the pan. "I'm an asshole."

"Nope. I won't believe it."

"So, what are we doing today?" I grabbed the plates, separating them before scooping the eggs equally between the two.

She carried the plates to the table and set them down. "It involves very little clothing."

I rubbed my hands together as I sat. "Sounds right up my alley."

She sat down and smirked. "You game for anything?"

I nodded vigorously as I grabbed a slice of bacon from the table. "How can anything with very little clothes be bad?"

She giggled when she picked up her fork and stabbed at her eggs. "How do you feel about water?"

Just as I was about to place the bacon in my mouth, I froze. "Water? I hope you mean a bath."

She shook her head. "Not a bath," she said before shoveling a forkful of eggs into her mouth.

I leaned back in my chair, dropping the bacon onto my plate. "What, then?"

She mimicked my actions, dropping her bacon on her plate, and crossing her arms. "Canoeing."

My head fell forward and I put my hands up. "Cah-what?"

"Canoeing. Y'know." She pretended to paddle through the water.

I closed my eyes and tried not to smile. "That wasn't exactly how I imagined our day."

She leaned over the table and pushed my plate toward me. "But eat quick. We have to leave soon."

"Hold up," I said, grabbing the piece of bacon I'd dropped earlier. "Where are we canoeing? In the Gulf?"

Grabbing her fork, she gawked at me. "Scared of sharks or something?"

My head jerked back. "I'm not scared of sharks, babe."

She laughed. "Everyone is scared of sharks. No, I want to go up to Weeki Wachee and canoe in the river."

I chewed slowly, thinking about the rivers up north and what lived inside. "Aren't there alligators?"

She slathered the eggs on a slice of buttered toast. "Hey, tough guy. Nothing will eat you."

"Uh-huh," I muttered with a mouthful of eggs.

She tossed a piece of bacon at me. "The water is too cold for alligators, sissy."

I glanced down, picking up the sliver as it bounced on the table. "I'm in. But you're wearing a bikini."

"Deal."

"I CAN'T BELIEVE I let you talk me into this," I huffed out, trying to stop the canoe from careening into the riverbank without Georgia's help.

She laughed, sitting with her chin resting in her palm. "It's so beautiful, though, isn't it?"

"Yeah." I glanced around and admired the creativity of Mother Nature.

The river hadn't been what I'd expected. The lushness of it with the treetop canopies and crystal-clear water shocked me. Even the temperature of it when we climbed into the canoe had me thinking twice. She left out of the part about it being a constant seventy degrees throughout the year.

Lucky for us, the river was empty. Very few people lined the shores, and no one passed us as we meandered downstream.

"Pull off to the side up here." She pointed to a clearing on the right side.

"Why?" I asked, trying to get the canoe to go in that direction.

She peered over her shoulder, giving me a sinful smile. "I want to show you something."

My stomach did that weird flop thing again. "Okay," I said through gritted teeth as I fought the current to get to the spot before we passed by.

"Don't worry. I'll make it worth your while."

"I have no doubts." I chuckled, paddling furiously to push up on the sandy shore.

She clapped and cheered as she stepped out of the canoe. "Good job, Frisco."

I wiped my brow with the back of my hand before tossing the oar to the bottom of the metal canoe. "Anytime, babe."

I needed to cool off. Even though much of the trip had been shady, the humidity was unbearable. I stepped into the water, skipping the direct route to shore, and sank down.

"Ahh." I closed my eyes and basked in the cold, clear water.

"Alligator!" Georgia screamed, pointing behind me with wide eyes.

I turned around quickly, searching in the water as I started to run backward toward shore. "Where!" I yelled, thrashing as I walked. My heart was about to burst out of my chest. If the alligator didn't get me, I might have a heart attack first.

She doubled over, laughing hysterically. "I'm totally kidding," she said, slapping her leg.

I froze. "Georgia," I said, feeling my heart pounding in my throat.

She started to sway and her laughter grew louder. "You should've seen your face."

I stepped out of the water and headed straight for her. Grabbing her above the knees, I lifted her up, and threw her over my shoulder.

"Hey!" she screamed, kicking her feet, and slapping my ass.

I swatted her ass cheek. "You're getting payback."

"Can't I blow you?" she asked, smacking my ass again.

That earned her two quick swats. "After."

"But it's cold!" she screamed as I walked into the water and fell forward, taking us both underwater.

She kicked away from me and I let her go. When she surfaced, she looked pissed as hell with her hair in disarray and water cascading down her face. "I'm so fucking getting you for this."

"Fuck me to death," I told her, wiping the water out of my eyes.

She fisted her hands at her sides, standing there like a drenched cat. "You aren't getting pussy for a long, long time."

"You think so?" I challenged her, taking a step toward her.

"Oh. I know so." She spat out the water drops that trickled into her mouth. "I think I taste manatee pee. Ugh."

I reached out, pushing the hair away from her face before wiping away the water dripping off her chin. "Jokes aren't always funny when they're on you, are they?"

She blew the water off her lips. "You're a dick."

"I know." I leaned forward and kissed her. She came closer, melting into my touch.

"What did you want to show me?" I asked after I broke the kiss and our lips were still touching.

"Forget it now," she whispered, grabbing my arms.

"Oh, no. There was a reason. Spill it."

"Well," she said, shifting from foot to foot as her body began to shiver, "I was going to take you back there." She pointed behind her to the brush. "And I was going to suck your cock."

I glanced toward the secluded spot and checked our surroundings. "You still can."

She shook her head and laughed. "No fucking way, buddy. Not after you threw me in the water."

"Please?" I pulled her against my chest. "You scared the crap out of me. You deserved it, G."

"I did, didn't I?"

I nodded, giving her puppy-dog eyes. "I almost had a heart attack. You can't do that shit to me. I'm too old to be scared."

She slapped my arm, the water making the contact sound much louder. "You're so full of shit, Frisco."

"But you can still suck my cock."

She started to stomp through the water, creating ripples across the surface. "Get your ass back in the canoe, and if you're a good boy, I'll do it later."

"But wait—" I said, following behind her toward the canoe.

"Nope. That ship has sailed." She climbed inside and grabbed the oar she'd ignored all day.

"My dick says otherwise."

She chuckled. "We have to be to the dock in an hour. Your cock will have to wait."

"Fuck me," I mumbled, sticking one leg inside the canoe.

I realized that Georgia had the perfect mixture of sassy and playful. Everything seemed to roll off her back. Even though I knew I could be a ballbuster, she gave it better than I ever had.

Maybe it was her age or her free spirit, but all I knew was I wanted more of it.

Never in my entire life had I felt the butterflies buzzing around my gut from a simple smile. With Georgia, even the most innocent look did crazy shit to my insides.

Although canoeing hadn't been on my to-do list, spending the day with Georgia was the best medicine.

CHAPTER 11

BEST STAKEOUT EVER

Waking up to a text from my ex placed a dark cloud over my day. I hadn't even rolled out of bed and I was already pissed off. Last night when I closed my eyes, I had the biggest smile on my face. Georgia put it there.

Smiling was new to me. It wasn't that I couldn't smile, but it hadn't been something I did every day. It wasn't that I'd been unhappy. No. In fact, I had a good life up until Jeanine fucked shit up.

Growing up, my parents had been pretty strict. My mother was the child of Chinese immigrants but broke from tradition when she married my father, an American boy of mixed European descent.

My grandparents had died before I was born and my mother shunned her Chinese heritage, immersing herself in American culture. Although my parents lived through the Woodstock era, people believing in free love, and the hippie culture, they never embraced it.

Even though she claimed she'd wiped any remnants of her upbringing from her mind, she hadn't. My mother had carried over the strictness of the Chinese people when it came to school and working hard.

I worked my ass off to get good grades and attend a decent college, but that was when I broke free. Once I started my freshman year at the University of Florida, I decided enough was enough.

I left college and joined the Navy. That about freaked the 'rents the fuck out. The one thing they stressed was education, and due to my ability to score high on the Armed Services Vocational Aptitude Battery, I was able to take the Physical Screening Test during boot camp.

Somehow, thank fuck, I had been accepted for entrance into the training program to become a SEAL. It changed my entire life.

As I brushed my teeth and thought back on my youth, my phone beeped. I glanced out of the corner of my eye, too scared it was Jeanine again to pick it up.

Thomas: Meeting at 8:30. Be on time.

Never in my life had I been so happy to receive a group text about work. I finished getting ready, which really consisted of washing my face after I'd brushed my teeth, and headed to the office.

As I pulled into the parking lot, my phone beeped again. I breathed a sigh of relief when I realized it wasn't Jeanine.

Georgia: Morning, Sexy. Thinking of you today.

Me: Good morning, beautiful. Can't get you off my mind.

I walked through the door at one minute before the assigned time and headed straight to the conference room. When I entered, everybody else had already been seated and was waiting for me.

"Look what the cat drug in," Bear said before he whistled.

"Dragged," I corrected.

Bear waved me off. "Whatever."

Thomas glanced at his watch before looking up at me. "Let's get started." He wanted to say something, but he couldn't.

Bear smirked at me as I sat down. Glancing out of the corner of my eye, I shook my head, telling him I wasn't in the mood.

"Frisco, where are you with Mrs. Green?" James tapped his pen against the yellow legal pad sitting in front of him, looking bored.

"Done. I just have to deliver the photos today."

Thomas pulled a file off the stack in front of him and tossed it in my direction. "Good. Here's a new case for you to start today, then."

"Thanks." I pulled the folder in front of me before opening it.

Every case I'd been assigned lately seemed to deal with marriages falling apart. My new case was no different. Instead of a cheating spouse, the wife of my new client was suspected of hiding money during a divorce. The husband had hired ALFA to keep track of his soon-to-be ex-wife's whereabouts and to see if we could find a paper trail, exposing her fraud.

As the meeting continued, I sat here studying the file, completely mesmerized. Mr. Jones had noticed changes in his wife's lifestyle shortly after they separated. She went from driving a beat-up Toyota Camry to a brand-new Lexus. She bought a bigger house than she'd lived in with her husband and upgraded her wardrobe. When confronted, she claimed that a relative had passed away and left her a small inheritance.

He called bullshit on her story about old Aunt Maud kicking the bucket. In the state of Florida, inheritance couldn't be touched during a divorce, but if she came into this windfall by any other means before their date of separation, he'd be entitled to a portion.

"Everyone have a good weekend?" James asked after all the assignments had been handed out.

I kept my head down, not wishing to discuss anything that happened.

"I think Frisco has some news." Bear nudged my arm.

I glared at him. "I stayed home all weekend."

"Lies," Bear muttered, nudging me again.

"Do that one more time, and you're going to lose that arm."

"It must not have gone well."

"It was a relaxing weekend." I clasped my hands together on top of the file after I'd closed it.

"Well, I had an amazing weekend with Izzy. We left the kids with her parents Friday night and—" James started.

Thomas put his hand in front of James's face. "Zip it. We don't wanna know."

Bear scooted forward. "Speak for yourself, T. I want to hear *all* about it."

"Everyone get your asses to work. We don't have time to sit around and talk like a group of old biddies." Thomas slid his chair back and stood.

As I stood, Bear grabbed my wrist. "What crawled up your ass and died this morning?"

Pulling my arm from his grasp, I sighed. "Jeanine texted me this morning. It wasn't how I wanted my Monday to start."

He rolled his eyes and leaned back in his chair, rocking it back and forth. "She's a nasty troll bitch."

"She needs to just leave me alone. That ship has sailed, and I'm not taking another trip."

He rubbed his chin as his eyes bounced around the room. "You know," he said, dragging his eyes to mine, "I can fuck her."

My head jerked backward. "Come again?"

He jumped up from his chair and headed for the door. "I'd do it as a favor to you."

I followed close behind, rubbing the tension from the back of my neck. "How is that a favor?"

"I figure"—he glanced over his shoulder—"I'll fuck her so good, she'll forget you exist."

When I arrived at my office, I turned to face his back as he continued down the hallway. "You're such an amazing friend."

He stopped and turned toward me. "I'd take one for the team."

"I don't care who puts his dick in her."

He rubbed his hands together and licked his lips. "I'll see if I can get her mind off you. She came into the Cowboy this weekend. When I see her again, I'll hit that shit."

As I opened the door, I shook my head and laughed. "You're truly a sick fuck."

"I never claimed to be normal," he called out as my door closed.

I pushed away the clutter on my desk and checked my calendar. By noon, I had to be on a stakeout, trying to catch a cheating wife suspected of having more than lunch with her boss. In the evening, I had another stakeout, but this time to catch a husband in the act, and I still had to drop off the photos to Mrs. Green.

All the cases that dealt with marriage made me question the possibility of there really being a happily ever after. In my line of work, I only came in contact with unhappiness and deceit. I had to remind myself that it was just a small section of the population.

I opened my new case, read over the information one more time, and called my new client. In between stakeouts, we'd meet and I'd gather the important information I'd need to ascertain if his wife had lied about how she'd gained her wealth.

I couldn't wait until my day ended. I saw a stop at the Neon Cowboy in my future. An evening with the guys was just what the doctor ordered, but before that could happen, I had to tackle my workload.

---

*GEORGIA: **What are you doing tonight?***

As soon as her text came in, I set down my camera and replied.

*Me: **Heading to the NC for a drink. You?***

*Georgia: **Maybe I'll relax with a glass of wine and read.***

Although I liked a good book as much as the next person, her night sounded boring.

*Me: **I'm on a stakeout right now and bored as hell.***

*Georgia: **Want company?***

I rubbed my chin, staring down at the screen, and thinking about her question. Sitting here with Georgia sounded a hell of a lot better than spending the next however many hours by myself, listening to the radio, and trying to stay awake.

*Me: **YES!***

*Georgia: **Where are you?***

Thankfully, I was close to her place. I gave her the directions and she texted me that she was on her way.

I checked my watch and started to count the minutes until she arrived as I kept an eye on the current love nest of my client's husband.

The couple arrived separately to the seedy motel far away from his home and work, trying to stay out of view as he cheated on his wife. Before he went inside, he glanced around, checking his surroundings and totally missing me.

When I started working at ALFA PI, I had the windows tinted as dark as legally possible. It'd been a tremendous asset, except when I needed to snap a photo. Typically, I had to do some major acrobatics and try to take it by way of the windshield. It took me a couple stakeouts to figure out just the right angle to park my car to not be seen but still be able to take photographs. Now I had that shit down pat.

Within twenty minutes, there was a knock at the passenger window. I could see the outline of Georgia's body illuminated by the streetlights behind her.

As soon as I unlocked the door, she slid inside. "Hey," she said, closing the door quietly before fixing her dress.

"Gimme a kiss." I leaned over the center console and puckered my lips.

She moved toward my waiting mouth. The kiss was tender, sweet, and left me wanting more. Her eyes were still closed when she backed away. "I needed that," she whispered.

I touched her cheek, caressing it with my thumb, and sighed. "Me too," I admitted, dragging my lips across the opposite cheek, and relishing the softness and her smell.

"So is this what you do?" she asked as her eyes fluttered open.

"What?" I murmured against her skin.

She laughed, backing away, and staring down at me. "Kiss random girls in your car when you're supposed to be working?"

"You're hardly random, and I've never had someone with me on a stakeout."

A soft smile spread across her face. "So I'm special?"

I wrapped my hand behind her neck, pulling her lips to mine again. "You're mine."

"Oh." Her lips formed a tiny circle against mine. Her eyes shifted before I had a chance to deepen the kiss. "There's a couple."

"Fuck," I said, backing away, and I reached for my camera.

"This is so exciting and kind of tragic too." She rubbed her hands together and leaned toward the windshield.

I lifted the camera, positioning the lens against the windshield to get the best photo. "They always are," I told her, holding my finger down on the button, and snapping photo after photo until they separated and sped off in their own cars.

"I feel awful." She clutched her stomach and stared out the window.

Setting the camera in the backseat, I gave her a halfhearted smile. "It's hard to see day after day. My entire life has been with unfaithful people, including my work."

She waved her hand, motioning toward the motel. "How can you believe in love when every day you see it being destroyed?"

I shrugged one shoulder and sighed, pressing my head into the headrest. "I don't know, Georgia. It's hard to have faith when I see so many of the lies."

She shook her head, peering down at her legs. "I just couldn't do it and still believe in a happily ever after." She swallowed hard, dragging her eyes to mine. "Do you think all love is doomed?"

"I don't," I lied with a straight face, wanting to believe my words were true.

"I'm not like these people." She pulled at her front lip, letting it snap back. "I could never cheat on someone. I've been the one being deceived, and I know how gut-wrenching and devastating it is. Have you ever cheated on someone?"

I shook my head vigorously. "I've never cheated. It's not my style. If I want to see someone else, I just end a relationship before jumping in bed with another woman."

She shifted in her seat, turning to face me. "Promise when you get bored of me, you'll let me down easy and say goodbye before you touch another woman."

"I promise." I reached for her hand. "Come here."

"Where?"

I patted my lap with my free hand, pulling her toward me with the other. "Climb over here."

She climbed over the console, straddled my legs, and shifted until our bodies were flush with each other.

"I would never cheat on you, Georgia. I ask the same of you, though. When you get bored of my old ass, let me down gently." I stared up into her dark eyes.

She giggled, her body shaking, and her pussy teasing my hardening dick. "You're not old and sure as hell aren't boring."

I slid my hand under her dress, feeling the edges of her lace panties. "Want to try something new?" I asked, raising an eyebrow.

Her body shuddered and her giggles evaporated. "Here?" She looked out the windows.

I dipped my finger inside the lace, finding her wet. "Here," I growled.

She adjusted in my lap and rubbed against my dick roughly. "Wait, let me get these panties off." She tried to climb off.

I grabbed her ass and pulled her against me. "Don't." I squeezed her cheeks in my hands. "I can get them off."

She rested her hands on my shoulders. "You can?"

I didn't have a magic trick, but lace panties were no match for my hands. I gripped them at the sides, giving them a quick twist before I pulled. They crumbled in my hands.

"Well played, sir." She laughed.

I gripped her hips, running my thumbs along the indentations left by her panties.

"Georgia," I growled.

"Frisco," she whispered.

"Hold the back of the seat."

Surprisingly she didn't ask any questions or argue. I pulled her up and put enough space between us for my hands. Before I let myself touch her pussy, I slowly lowered the straps of her dress and exposed her breasts. Panic filled her eyes.

"Relax. No one can see us through the tinted windows."

She closed her eyes, sealing them so tightly that little wrinkles formed near the corners. When I leaned forward and captured her hard nipple between my lips, her head tipped back, she moaned, and my dick came to life.

I couldn't focus on my need, but on hers.

Dipping my hand under her dress with my mouth still attached to her, I ran my fingers through her silkiness. She was ready for me and already turned on.

When I pushed two fingers inside of her, she gasped. I started slowly and let her body adjust before I began to hammer inside of her. Her mouth fell open and her legs began to shake against my thighs.

Just as her pussy started to contract against my hands, I slowed my movement and released her nipple.

"Please," she whispered as I straightened.

"Look at me," I told her with my fingers buried deep inside her.

She leaned forward and rested her forehead on mine before opening her eyes.

"I want to watch you come."

She swallowed hard but kept her eyes glued to mine. Her breathing quickened, matching the pace of my fingers as I thrust them inside her.

She must not have liked the speed and took over. Rocking on my hand like she would my cock. I watched her, listening to her hard, short inhales as she pounded herself down on my fingers.

"Yeah, baby. Come for me." I stared at her, completely in awe and watched her shatter in front of me. Her eyes rolled back, her mouth fell open, and her body shook in my arms as she came on my fingers.

We breathed heavily, panting for air. She collapsed against me and closed her eyes.

Neither of us spoke for a few minutes. I stroked her hair and she gulped down air until her breathing slowed.

"I'm scared, Frisco."

I squeezed her hips, stopping her from moving because I enjoyed being inside her too much for it to end. "Why?"

"I like you so much it freaks me out."

I'd be lying if I didn't admit her words hit home. Georgia had breezed into my life, giving me a happiness I'd never known. Her care-free attitude and ball-busting style made me smile. No one had ever done that before, not even Jeanine. "I know." My voice was quiet but guarded.

Her eyes opened. "What is it about you?"

"You're getting your bad boy fix, babe."

"I had that with the other guy."

"No, you didn't." I stroked the underside of her breast with my finger, letting it drift back and forth.

"He wasn't nice," she whispered, her voice ragged.

"Why, because he cheated?"

"Yeah."

"Doesn't make him a bad boy."

"What makes you one?" She pushed her chest forward, aching for more than a whisper-light touch.

I captured her lips and kissed her deeply. As I released her lips, I dragged my finger over her exposed nipples. "Where should I begin?"

Her warm breath cascaded across my face as she shivered. "I don't think you're a bad boy."

"I have a past."

"We all do," she argued, shaking her head, and jostling her breasts against my hand.

"I've used women."

"Don't most men?"

She had something to say for everything that came out of my mouth. "Look at me, G. I don't wear a suit to work, I'm covered in tats, I'm older. I'm just not the type of guy ladies bring home to meet the parents."

"It's all bullshit." She peppered my face with kisses. "We can pretend you're a bad boy, but I know what a sweetie you are."

I felt her words hit me square in the chest. No one had ever called me sweet. At least not someone I dated.

Nice?

Yeah...sometimes.

Usually when they wanted something. Being a "sweetie" wasn't what I wanted to be known for when it all ended. I'd rather be a prick so the ladies moved the fuck on and left me alone.

"Speaking of which," she said before clearing her throat, "I wanted to know if you'd meet my parents this weekend."

"Um," I mumbled, not sure how to answer that question.

It had been years since I'd met anyone's parents. Being an adult, it wasn't something that I was used to doing. Besides Jeanine, the other women I'd been with were just fuck buddies without any strings attached, and certainly no family dinners involved.

"It's okay. You don't have to." She pulled up the straps on her dress and covered her breasts.

"I didn't say I didn't want to." I was lying through my teeth. I didn't fucking want to meet her parents. We weren't at that point in our relationship. Less than three days ago, we weren't an anything.

She crawled off my lap, and I instantly missed her warmth. "It's just that I talked to my mom today," she told me as she climbed back into the passenger seat. "And mentioned I met this amazing man. She begged me to bring you to dinner this weekend."

"I don't know, babe."

"My dad is particularly interested in meeting you."

"I'm sure he is. I'm sure he wants to bash my face in too."

"No," she said quickly. "He's not like that."

"All fathers are."

"Not my dad. He's a calm guy. He loves me."

I glanced over at her and rubbed my chin as I thought of the five hundred ways this could go terribly wrong. "What's he do again?"

She smiled that fake isn't-it-great smile. "He's a retired cop."

"Right. I love meeting the father of the girl I'm fooling around with and knowing that he's carrying a weapon."

"They don't know we're 'fooling around'." She made air quotes. "Remember, I've never been that kind of girl. Plus, he doesn't carry anymore."

"Georgia." I gritted my teeth and dragged my hand through my hair. "Your dad is going to take one look at me and know I want to fuck you."

Her smile vanished. "How?"

"Your naïveté is so precious. I'm a man. It's always there, lurking in the background."

She crossed her arms over her chest and stared out the front window. "Fuck you. I resent that statement."

"Look at me, Georgia." I motioned in front of my body. "I don't look like a virgin."

"Did I?" she spat back, her lip curling.

"Point taken." I turned on the car, wishing I could take some words back. "You want to go for a drink?"

"Do you want me to, or am I too naïve for a drink?"

"Knock that shit off." I pointed at her. "I want you to come or I wouldn't ask."

She picked her purse up and started to rifle through the contents. "Fine. I'll go for *a* drink."

"That's good."

"It's a school night," she said as she pulled her keys out.

Fucking hell. That made her sound like a kid. "Yeah. Just a quick one."

"I'll meet you there." She reached for the door handle.

"Hey," I growled, grabbing her arm before she got out.

She froze, but she didn't look at me. "Yeah?"

"Give me a kiss." I tried to pull her gently down into her seat. "I want a kiss."

"We all want things," she said before pulling her wrist from my grip and slamming the door.

"Motherfucker," I said, hitting the steering wheel with my palm. "Way to fuck that up, dumbass."

Not only did I insinuate that she was still a child, but I called her innocent. It wasn't untrue, but "naïve" wasn't the best way to put it.

I'd make things right when we got to the Neon Cowboy. My chest ached from thinking that she was pissed at me.

I'd meet her parents.

What could go wrong?

CHAPTER 12

SLOW MOTION

Driving behind Georgia, I thought of a million ways to say I was sorry. I didn't think I'd ever fucked up this badly before, but I'd do everything in my power to make it right. The need was so strong to have her be happy that I had to set shit straight.

I tested out the apologies, trying to figure out which one didn't sound like I was caving, even though that's exactly what I was about to do.

"Georgia, I'm sorry. I'd love to meet your parents," I said, putting a pretend smile on my face.

I shook my head and sighed. "Pussy," I mumbled to myself.

"Georgia, I didn't mean what I said before. I'd love to meet your parents."

Rolling my eyes, I could hear the guys laughing at me.

There was more traffic on the road than most nights. Cars whizzed by as I followed her and practiced my speech. Nothing I said felt right.

"Georgia, I can't stand the thought of you mad at me," I said just as something caught my eye.

The car coming in the opposite direction was swerving, crossing the center line and overcorrecting. The driver clearly had a problem, and I could see it coming from a mile away. The road was flat and straight in this section, making it easy to see it before it happened.

I gripped the steering wheel, held my breath, and laid on the horn. I could see the outline of her body, even the strands of her hair as she peeked in the mirror. She wasn't slowing down or braking. I sucked in a breath, my chest heaving as everything started to move in slow motion.

Flashing my lights, I started to scream as the car came closer, swerving back and forth.

"Pull over, Georgia!" I punched the steering wheel and started to pull off to the side, hoping she'd follow me.

My body began to shake and my heart threatened to crawl up my throat. "Goddamn it!" I shouted.

My eyes grew wide and the air in my lungs disappeared.

I watched helplessly as the oncoming car plowed into the side of Georgia's, sending it careening off the road right in front of me and leaving me unable to drag my eyes away from the horror show before me.

Even though I screamed, nothing came out. The little bit of air I had inside me came out as a strangled yell.

Before her car came to a stop, the car that had hit her righted itself and started to drive away. I had to make a split-second decision—run for Georgia or try to get his plate.

I flew out of the car so fast he hadn't even had a chance to get up enough speed to pass me. I tried to make out his plate, getting only a partial as he passed by. Repeating it to myself over and over again in my head, I screamed for Georgia and took off toward her car.

My heart was in my throat and my stomach twisted the closer I got. Smoke was coming from the engine, the airbag had deployed, and the entire driver's side had been smashed in. The only light in the field was from my headlights shining on the section where her car had stopped.

"Georgia!" I screamed, pulling on the door handle. "Georgia!"

"Frisco." Her voice was faint and strained as she tried to lift her head.

"Don't move, babe. Goddamn it!" I tried the door handle again, but during the impact, her window had shattered. It was the quickest way to get her out. "I'm going to get you out." I batted away the airbag and gently pushed her body back into the seat.

"Oh God," she wailed. "Don't move me!" Tears streamed down her face when she closed her eyes.

"I have to move you, Georgia. It's not safe for you to stay in there."

"Call the ambulance. They'll get me out," she said, choking back tears.

Just as I pulled out my phone, flames joined the smoke licking the hood of the car. "We don't have time. I'm getting you out." I stuck the top half of my body inside the car and unhooked the seat belt.

"What's burning?" she said, her head rolling back and forth.

"Don't worry about it." I positioned my arms under her legs and behind her back. "This may hurt."

"Don't, Frisco. Everything hurts."

I didn't listen and pulled her from the car. Her sobs turned into wails when I tipped her, trying to avoid the window frame.

When her body was free from the mangled steel, she rested her head on my shoulder, barely conscious. I pulled her against my chest and walked with gentle footsteps as far away from the burning car as I could get.

I wanted to scream or break down, but I didn't let myself. I had to keep my shit together. Although my heart was about to come out of my chest, I had to focus on Georgia.

Dropping to my knees, I set her down in front of me, holding her back as she lay against me. As I pulled out my phone and dialed 911, my eyes roamed her body, checking for injuries.

I rattled off our location and stroked her arms, trying to comfort her as I kept my voice steady. I don't even remember what I said or the questions the operator asked; it was all just a blur.

After I hung up, I tossed my phone in the grass beside us. "They're on the way, G. Tell me what hurts."

"My legs are killing me," she replied, trying to lean forward and touch them.

I grabbed her hand, pulling it back into her lap. "Don't move." It was evident that her leg had been broken in the impact. The bend to it wasn't natural. "Anything else?"

She touched her cheek, hissing as her fingers danced across her face. "I'm just sore, but my face hurts too."

"The airbag hit you. What else?" I was babbling at that point. I wanted to keep her awake in case she had any internal injuries or a concussion. The last thing I wanted was for her to fall asleep.

"I think I'm okay otherwise."

All I could do was to sit here and try to comfort her. Stroking her arm, whispering calming words in her ear, and peppering the top of her head with kisses.

The overwhelming sense of guilt I felt weighed on me like a hundred-ton boulder sitting on my back. If I hadn't been such a prick about meeting her parents, maybe she wouldn't have driven and this all would've been avoided.

She began to shiver in my arms. "I'm so cold," she whispered and hugged herself.

Leaning back, I pulled off the button-down shirt I had on and wrapped it around her shoulders. "I'll keep you warm," I whispered in her ear and ran my hands down her arms.

She peered up at me as her tears ran down her face. "I'm sorry."

My hands stilled as I glanced down at her. "For what, babe?"

"For not seeing the damn car."

I shook my head, letting out a loud sigh. "It's my fault, love. Not yours."

"But—" she started but stopped when the ambulance sirens broke the silence around us.

Following behind the ambulance were a fire truck and police cruiser. In the country, especially in this area of Florida, there wasn't much action besides a car crash every so often.

When the ambulance came to a halt, one man ran to our location carrying a bag while two more grabbed the gurney inside before making a beeline for us.

The next ten minutes were a whirlwind of activity. All I could do was stand back and watch. I dragged my hands through my hair as I paced a path in the tall grass.

"Sir." The police officer interrupted my thoughts.

I stopped and turned to face him. "Yeah?"

He glanced down toward his feet. "We'll need to interview you about the accident."

I closed my eyes, fisting my hands at my sides. I glanced over at Georgia, who was now on the gurney. "Can we do it at the hospital?"

His eyes followed mine before he nodded. "Sure." He tucked his small notepad in his pocket and headed toward Georgia's mangled car. The firefighters had put out the flames, but the white smoke still filled the air.

"Frisco!" Georgia yelled, holding out her hand toward me.

Moving quickly, I headed toward her and clasped her hand in mine. "I'm here." My heart squeezed at the clear agony etched on her face.

She squeezed my hand. "Don't leave me."

"I'll be right behind the ambulance. I'm not going anywhere."

"We're taking her to Florida Hospital in Wesley Chapel if you're following us," the paramedic told me before they started to carry the gurney over the uneven terrain.

I clutched her hand, following them as they moved, and didn't let go. "I'll be right on your tail."

"Promise me," Georgia said when my fingers began to slip from hers.

I lurched forward, grasping her hand in mine. "I promise, Georgia. I'll be with you for the entire thing."

CHAPTER 13

MEET THE PARENTS

After I had been kicked out of the ER, I paced a new path in the waiting room. Wiping my sweaty hands on my shirt, I tried to calm my shit. She'd be okay. She had to be.

Just when I was about to do my hundredth pass by the reception desk, a man and a woman ran into the ER in tears. They looked exactly how I felt inside.

"We're looking for our daughter," the man said, slightly out of breath, and leaning against the desk.

The nurse glanced up, giving the man a sweet smile. "What's her name?"

"Georgia Phillips." He pulled the woman into his side, holding her close.

I closed my eyes, swallowing hard, and cautiously approached them. These were Georgia's parents. The very ones she wanted me to meet. The ones we argued over that led her to drive herself. The ones who made me act like a dumbass. The ones who led me to piss her off and made the entire night go the way it had.

"The doctors are evaluating her, sir. You'll need to take a seat, and I'll have someone come talk to you as soon as possible."

He slammed his hand down on the desk. "I want to see her *now*."

"Sir," the nurse said in a snotty voice as her sweet smile faded, "someone will be with you in a few minutes."

The woman stroked his back and glanced up at him. "Come on, honey. Let's go wait for the doctor. We don't want anyone to get angry."

"I don't give a shit about angry. I want to know how my baby is doing."

Taking another step closer, I took a deep breath and prayed this would turn out okay. If he hit me, I would totally understand and know that I deserved it.

"Mr. and Mrs. Phillips," I said with a shaky voice.

They both turned, their eyes raking over me. "Yes," the man said through gritted teeth.

I tucked my hands into my pockets, glancing down at the floor. "I'm Georgia's friend. I was with her when the accident happened."

"How is she?" her mother asked as she took a step forward.

I dragged my eyes to hers, swallowing down the lump that had been lodged in my throat since the accident. "She was awake when they kicked me out of the ER. She has a broken leg, but they're assessing her for other injuries."

She covered her mouth with her hand. "Oh, God. My poor baby."

"What the hell happened?" her father snapped as he held his wife by the shoulders and stroked her skin with his thumbs.

"I need to sit down," she said tearily.

"Come on, love." He helped her to an empty waiting room chair.

I sat next to her, feeling she was safer than sitting next to Georgia's father. "We were driving to meet some friends to have a drink."

"On a school night?"

That statement made me feel like a pedophile.

"Yes." I gritted my teeth. "I had been following her car. I saw the oncoming car in the distance. Noticed it was swerving and driving erratically. I tried to get her attention. I tried to get her to pull over, but nothing I did worked." I rubbed the back of my neck, trying to ease the perpetual tension that had settled there.

"Dear God," her mother whispered, a tear trickling down her face, following the path of her already dried tears.

"The car swiped the side of hers, causing her to lose control, and sending her car off the side of the road into a field. I got her out as quickly as possible and called 911."

Her father's eyes sliced right through me. "You shouldn't move someone after an accident."

I nodded and rubbed my hands against my jeans mindlessly. "I know, sir, but the car had caught on fire and I had no other choice but to get her out."

"Georgia Phillips's family," a woman called out from across the room.

We turned in unison, standing quickly from our chairs. "Yes," her father said. "We are." He motioned to his wife as I stood behind them.

"The doctor said you can come back now and see her."

Mrs. Phillips peered up at her husband, wrapping her arm tightly around his middle. "That's good, right?"

"I hope so, love. I hope so."

The woman looked around Mrs. Phillips and stared at me. "Family only, please."

I took a step forward, needing to see her too. "But I—"

"He's family," Mrs. Phillips told the nurse before glancing over her shoulder at me. "He's coming also."

I sighed, thankful that she'd stuck up for me.

Honestly, I was going back there no matter what.

No one would stop me.

"Fine." The nurse quickly turned on her heel and swiped her keycard before opening the door.

I leaned forward and whispered in Mrs. Phillips's ear, "Thank you."

She nodded as she and Mr. Phillips started to follow the nurse through the door, with me quick on their heels. The farther we walked, the bigger the knot in my stomach became.

"Next curtain on the right," the nurse said before leaving us.

The doctor stood outside staring at a chart as we approached. He flipped it closed as Mrs. Phillips came to a stop in front of him.

"Doctor," she said, digging her fingers into the back of her husband's shirt. "I'm Georgia's mother. How is she?" I couldn't see her face, but her voice was laced with worry.

The doctor tucked the chart into the crook of his arm. "Ah, Mrs. Phillips. She's fine. A little banged up and has a broken leg. She'll be sore for a couple of days, but she's really lucky she doesn't have more injuries."

Mrs. Phillips turned into her husband's chest, clutching him as if her life depended on it, and she began to cry.

"Thank you, Doctor. When can we take her home?" Mr. Phillips gripped his wife tightly.

"We need to set her leg and do a few more tests, but I'd say she can leave in a few hours."

Mrs. Phillips lifted her head and wiped the tears from her eyes. "May we see her?"

He nodded and moved the curtain to the side. "She's waiting for you."

"Thank you," Mrs. Phillips said before leaving Mr. Phillips's side as the doctor walked away.

Mr. Phillips turned to face me with a cold stare. "You and I are going to talk."

My eyes widened and the lump in my throat returned to join the knot in my stomach. "Yes, sir." I tried to keep my voice strong and steady.

"We're going to go in and check on her, and then I'll meet you out here."

"Okay," I whispered as he turned his back and followed his wife into the room.

I stood in the hallway alone, looking around, and rubbing my face. What a total clusterfuck. This wasn't how I wanted to meet her parents. Her dad probably wanted to string me up by the balls, and I wouldn't blame him.

This entire thing was my fault.

No matter what Georgia said, in the end, I was the one to blame.

"Frisco!" Georgia yelled.

I jumped, surprised by the strength in her voice. Without hesitation, I walked into the room. "I'm here."

For having been through such a traumatic accident, Georgia looked beautiful. "Where did you run off to? You just left me here." The girl loved busting my balls.

"They kicked me out, G."

"I thought you were tougher than that."

Mr. Phillips coughed and glared at me.

"Dad and Mom, this is Frisco. The man I told you about."

"Kinda figured that out, kid."

Oh, God! He called her kid. Fuck me.

"Don't be such a sourpuss, Dad," Georgia said, pursing her lips, and shaking her head. "Frisco saved my life tonight."

His face softened. "That's true, baby girl."

"Cut everyone some slack today," Mrs. Phillips warned him, shocking the hell out of me.

"This isn't really how I hoped to be introduced, but it's nice to meet you both." I held out my hand to her father.

He glanced down and just gawked. *Way to be an asshole.* Clearly he didn't have as high an opinion of me as his daughter, and we still had to have the "chat" in the hallway.

Mrs. Phillips batted his hand away, sliding her palm into mine. "It's great to finally meet you, Frisco. Georgia speaks very highly of you."

"Oh?" I glanced at her sideways. "It's nice to meet you, Mrs. Phillips."

"Mom," Georgia whined, covering her face with her hands. "How embarrassing."

"I mean, I could've told him what you said."

"No," Georgia said quickly.

Mrs. Phillips laughed. "George, you better shake this man's hand and stop being a hard-ass."

This was where Georgia got it. Her tough nature came from her mother. Probably some from her father, too, but she didn't have a weak woman as a role model.

A low growl escaped his lips before he thrust his hand out, snarling at me as he waited for me to shake it. I held my breath, placing my hand in his. His fingers closed around my hand and squeezed as hard as possible. It was like sticking my hand in a vise.

The man wanted to prove a point. Men did this shit all the time. Had to prove their superiority through a handshake. I'd dealt with it my entire life, and my hands were stronger than they looked. In fact, all of me was.

He released my hand before I pulled it back. There was a small smile on his face, a sense of satisfaction maybe, but I didn't dare shake out the cramp he'd given me.

"When can I bust out of here?" Georgia asked before she tried to sit up. "Fuck."

"What's wrong?" Mrs. Phillips jumped from her chair. "Should I get the doctor?"

Georgia tossed her head back into the pillow and blew out a deep breath. "No. I'm just so damn sore. It hurts to try to sit up."

I rushed to her side without a thought. "Let me help you, babe."

She looked up at me with a smile. "Thank you," she whispered.

Placing my hands under her armpits, I lifted her body forward. "Whatcha need?" I asked, standing here, holding her as her parents looked on.

Georgia winced. "This damn pillow is uncomfortable. I just need to move it."

"Let me get it." Mrs. Phillips grabbed the pillow and fluffed it.

"Can you move the bed up a little for me, Mom? My back is sore."

"Sure, doll."

For some reason, I glanced at Mr. Phillips and could see his face visibly redden. Maybe it was how close my hands were to his daughter's tits, but there was nothing sexual about it. It hadn't even entered my mind, but clearly it was on his.

I lowered her back down on her pillow, waiting for her to give me the okay. She sighed and smiled. "Better."

Mr. Phillips rubbed his temples. "Do you mind if Frisco and I step outside for a minute?"

Her eyes widened and her lips set in a firm line. "Dad, don't start your shit."

"Baby girl, watch your mouth. I'm still your father."

"Sorry, Dad. Behave. Promise?"

Using his fingers, he made an X over his heart. "I promise, kid."

"Okay." She nodded but looked at him suspiciously.

He leaned over and kissed his wife on the cheek before motioning toward the door with his head and staring at me.

"Coming. I'll be right back." I leaned over and kissed her in much the same way her father had kissed his wife.

"Good luck," Georgia said with a giggle.

"Fuck," I muttered against her cheek.

"You'll be okay." She winked, shooing me away. "Let me talk with my mom a little. You two behave."

"We will."

I kept my head held high as I followed him into the hallway. I never showed fear, especially when fathers were involved. Let them get the upper hand once, and I'd become the family whipping boy.

"What did you need to talk to me about?" I asked, keeping my eyes glued to his.

He rolled his head and cracked his knuckles. "You know I'm a retired cop, right?" Mr. Phillips was everything an old-school cop would be—giant, broad shoulders, a thick neck, jet-black hair, piercing blue eyes, and taller than the freakin' Hulk. If the Hulk were real, I'd say they could be brothers.

"Yes," I replied, straightening my shoulders, and wiping all emotion from my face.

"Have you talked to the police about the accident?"

I shook my head. "Not yet."

"Don't."

"What?" I asked.

"You heard me. Don't."

"I have to."

He glanced around the hallway, checking our surroundings. "Lie."

Um… What?

"Lie?" My mouth dropped open.

He took a step forward, speaking quietly. "The guy left the scene, right?"

"Yeah."

"Did you get the plate?"

"A partial."

"Know the make of the car?"

"Yeah."

"Then lie."

I couldn't believe what I'd heard.

"But w-why?" I asked, stammering slightly.

"Police are bogged down. Too much shit on their plate at the moment and not enough manpower to solve every case. I can track the guy down faster than they can. I'll handle it."

I shook my head because I must've heard him wrong again. "You're gonna handle it?"

"Yeah."

I tilted my head, moving my ear closer. "How?"

"Uh, I'm a retired cop."

"I know."

"Keep up, kid."

I held my hands up, trying to slow the pace of the conversation as I tried to let it all sink in. "Let me get this straight," I said before taking a deep breath.

"Yeah?"

If I'd been watching this conversation, I'd be laughing, but being the one having it wasn't funny at all. "You want me to lie to the police?"

"Just to those cops. The ones at the accident."

"But you want me to spill everything to you."

"Yeah." He looked at me like I had a screw loose.

"Okay." I shrugged, because, really, I wasn't going to argue with the guy. "Want help?" I offered, because I wanted to beat the fuck out of whoever drove Georgia off the road.

He rested his hand on my shoulder and gave it a firm squeeze. "If you want."

"Yeah."

"Good."

"Yeah."

"Nice chat," he said, slapping me on the shoulder, and leaving me in the hallway.

I stood here, completely stunned, and speechless. Somehow I'd croaked out "yeah" over and over again, but inside, I was beyond confused. I never in a million years would've thought that was what he wanted to say to me.

Before I could process everything and walk back into Georgia's room, the police officers from the scene were headed right toward me.

It was time to lie my ass off or deal with Mr. Phillips. I knew that I wanted to make him happier than I did the local authorities.

It didn't hurt that I wanted to get my hands on the prick who'd hit her and left the scene. She could've been killed, and if he was lucky, he'd be able to walk away after Mr. Phillips and I got our hands on him.

"Mr. Jones?" the uniformed officer from the accident scene asked as he approached with a serious look on his face.

"Yeah," I said, tucking my hands into my pockets, and trying to calm my insides.

"We'd like to ask you a couple of questions about the accident tonight."

"I'm an open book," I lied and nodded. "What would you like to know?"

"Did you get a license plate number?" he asked, pulling a small pad of paper from his pocket.

I grimaced and shook my head. "It happened too fast and it was too dark." I didn't blink.

This was the *start* of the lie. It was easier than I thought. I fed them more bullshit than I ever imagined possible.

CHAPTER 14
STUBBORNNESS

I struggled to unlock the door with her in my arms, but trying to stick the key in the lock became impossible. "Stop moving so much, woman," I growled, finally finding the keyhole.

She stilled and glared at me. "I could've used my crutches."

"I'd rather carry you than watch you struggle up the front stairs. Just shush it and let me do this." Turning to the side, I opened the door and kicked it wide, letting it bounce off the back wall.

"I don't see why I had to come here. I could've gone home." She placed her head against my chest.

I ignored her comment and carried her inside, using my heel to close the door. Walking past the couch, I brought her straight to my bedroom, turning the light on with my elbow.

Her fingertips brushed against the stubble along my jaw. "Are you trying to take advantage of me?"

I laughed and placed her gently on my unmade bed. "Do you want me to?"

"Um…" She pulled at her bottom lip.

I grabbed a stack of pillows and piled them against the headboard behind her. "Lean back, babe."

She yawned and closed her eyes. "I'm so tired."

350

"Do you want anything? Water? Something to eat?"

"No," she replied in a sleepy voice. "Just sleep."

Dragging my fingers through my hair, I stared at her and bit my bottom lip. "Do you want help getting undressed?"

Without opening her eyes, she tried to lean forward and failed. She blew out a breath and slammed her hands down on the mattress. "Please. If everything didn't hurt, I'd do it myself."

"No problem." I sat on the edge of the bed and moved my hands toward the buttons of her dress. Slowly I undid each one, peering up at her, and watching her close her eyes quickly. A small smile played on her lips every time I almost caught her watching.

After brushing it off the edges of her shoulders, I wrapped my arm around her back and pulled her forward, bringing her tits against my body. It gave me wood. This wasn't good. She was in no shape to have sex, and there was no way in hell I'd let my desire get the better of me.

"Bra too," she whispered in my ear.

I closed my eyes, thinking of her father as I unclasped her bra. My job tonight had been to take care of her. Nothing more.

Georgia giggled, her body shaking in my arms.

"You're getting a kick out of this, aren't you?"

"I am," she spoke softly in my ear. "Your breathing is labored. It's kind of cute."

"Georgia," I said, holding her with one hand, and dragging the strap of her bra down her arm with the other.

"I'll behave." Her voice was almost a purr, which went straight to my dick.

I sighed, working the other strap down before laying her back.

She smiled up at me, completely naked except for her underwear. "Will you sleep in the bed with me tonight?"

"Yes," I answered quickly, wondering if I should leave my clothes on.

"Naked." She giggled.

"For the love of God," I whispered and pushed myself off the bed.

As I walked around the bed, she said, "I'm serious. I'm cold and I want your body—" she coughed, covering her mouth, but I could see her smile, "heat."

I stripped off my clothes, pulled the cord on my ceiling fan, and climbed into bed next to her. Paying careful attention not to move the bed too much, I pulled the covers over us and collapsed on my back. The night had been longer than I ever imagined, and my entire body felt the exhaustion.

"Will you hold me?" she whispered, turning her head, and giving me a sad, puppy-dog face.

"I'll curl into you, but you shouldn't move around too much," I told her, moving my body around her. I placed my arm above her head, flattening my torso against her side, and placing my face next to hers. "Better?"

"Perfect," she whispered, and then sighed.

The one thing I wanted to do was to wrap my arm around her and pull her tight against me. The accident could've been the end of Georgia, and even though I wanted to deny that she meant as much to me as she did, my heart had almost stopped when the accident happened.

"You can touch me," she whispered, as if she'd read my mind.

"I don't want to hurt you."

"I'll tell you if you do. I just want to feel the safety of your arms tonight."

I didn't hesitate, moving my arm that had fallen asleep cautiously over her torso and tucking my hand underneath her back, pulling her closer. I buried my face in her hair, felt her warmth, and listened to her breath until I drifted off to sleep.

"Oh shit," she said, waking me.

I didn't open my eyes, but I knew it was morning. "What?"

"I didn't call in to work."

Pulling her a little closer, I buried my face deeper into her hair. Throughout the night, neither of us had moved. "I texted City to have Sunshine handle it, and I told the guys what's up, too."

"Oh."

"Everything is taken care of. Go back to sleep." I tried to hold in the yawn that wanted to break free.

"But it's eight."

"We didn't get home until three."

Her fingernails started making patterns on my arm. "I can never sleep past eight."

I lay here a moment, trying to open my eyes and failing. The feel of her fingers on my skin was just too good.

"I have to pee," she whined and tapped me on the arm that I still had strewn across her. "I'm kind of trapped here."

I grumbled before I moved my arm off her and rolled onto my back. "Sorry," I yawned, stretching out, and kicking away the covers.

"Can you get my crutches out of the car?" she asked, rubbing the sleep from her eyes.

"I'll carry you." I rolled off the bed and climbed to my feet.

"Oh God, no." She tried to sit up but failed.

My morning wood was on full display and being totally wasted. "I'll get the crutches after you pee, as you put it, and we'll have coffee and breakfast."

She crossed her arms over her chest and pouted. "Fine." Her eyes caught sight of my dick and zeroed in.

"Like what you see, babe?" I laughed, trying to keep the mood light.

"The sunlight bounced off the piercing," she lied.

"Liar," I said, walking around the bed to carry her to the bathroom.

She tried to push herself up, but she struggled as her arms began to shake. "This is going to suck."

"Let me help." I bent down to pick her up.

"I'm so sore today. Worse than yesterday."

"I'll be gentle," I promised as I placed an arm behind her back and under her legs, scooping her into my arms. She hissed and whimpered with every step, no matter how softly I tried to walk. "Sorry," I said as I placed her one good foot on the floor.

She stood there, staring at me.

I backed up, leaned against the doorframe, and stared back.

"What are you doing?" She crossed her arms over her chest.

I thought it had been pretty obvious. "Waiting for you."

She balanced on one foot, trying to control her laughter. "You can't stay in here."

"Why not?"

"We haven't hit that point in our relationship."

"I can't leave you alone."

She dropped her arms, squared her shoulders, and raised an eyebrow. "I'm a grown woman. I can pee on my own. Go make coffee or some shit. You are *not* going to stand there and watch." She pointed toward the door behind me. "Out!"

"You're really cute when you're mad." She really was. I mean, Georgia was drop-dead gorgeous, but when she was pissed off, her forehead wrinkled in just the perfect way, making her stunning.

"Get out," she repeated, waving her arm, and pointing toward the doorway.

I threw my hands up and took in one more vision of her nakedness. "Yell when you're ready and I'll come get you."

She flattened her hands on her face, slowly dragging them down her cheeks. "Go get my crutches and a T-shirt for me," she mumbled behind her fingers.

"I'll be right back," I told her before I left the room and headed toward my closet.

"The door!" she yelled and grunted.

I poked my head back in the door and saw her still standing, holding on to the counter as she stood near the toilet. "Sorry." I closed the door.

After I pulled on a pair of shorts, I headed to the car, grabbed her crutches, and jogged back inside. It was risky leaving her alone to hop around, especially with the soreness from the accident. There was a T-shirt hanging on the doorknob to the bedroom, and I grabbed it before knocking. "Ready?" I knocked lightly on the door.

"Almost!" she yelled. "Don't come in."

"You aren't on your feet, are you?" I held the crutches and T-shirt and waited.

"Do you have an extra toothbrush?" Something clattered to the floor.

Opening the door, I found her leaning against the counter, a razor and my toothbrush on the floor. "I do," I said as I rested the crutches against the wall and handed her the T-shirt.

"I'm sorry. I just want to be able to do things on my own." She lifted her arms, trying to put on the T-shirt, but sighed. "I can't do this on my own. Fuck me. I can't deal with this."

I stood quickly, tossing the items from the floor onto the counter. "Let me." Pulling the T-shirt over her head, I gently placed each arm in the sleeves. "We'll get you something for the pain."

"No drugs."

"Tylenol will help."

"After I brush my teeth."

I opened the medicine cabinet and grabbed a spare brush I'd saved for when I had a guest. "Here ya go."

"Always prepared." She pursed her lips.

"Don't judge—you had one too."

She shook her head with wide eyes. "I'd never!"

"Stop talking so much and brush. I need coffee."

"Nectar of the gods."

"Brush." I grabbed my toothbrush off the counter and gave it a quick rinse.

We stared at each other in the mirror and brushed our teeth. Our eyes roamed over the other but never focused elsewhere. There was a sense of comfort to it for me. Jeanine and I could never stand in a room together in silence. Never. But with Georgia, there was a calm I'd never felt. Whether it was her lying in my arms or the small breaks in conversation, I always felt at peace.

Her face had bruised overnight, the impact of the airbag leaving its mark. She'd heal in a few days, and with a little makeup, it'd be barely noticeable.

After she spat out her toothpaste in the most unladylike fashion, she turned to face me. "Will you take me home after coffee?"

I cupped my hand under the water, filled my palm, and brought it to my lips. After I swished it around and stared at her, I spat it and answered. "We'll talk about it after coffee."

"Don't make me call my dad."

"He knows you're here."

"But I'll tell him you're holding me hostage," she threatened with a small grin.

"Go ahead." I placed my toothbrush back in the cup where it belonged.

"Coffee," she said, changing the subject.

I grabbed the crutches and handed them to her. "You first. I'll follow in case you fall."

Her nostrils flared as she placed the crutches under her arms. "You're a little overbearing." She took a step forward, wobbling a little.

"I know," I admitted, reaching out, and grabbing her hips.

"The last thing I need is another overprotective man," she huffed, slowly making her way out of the bathroom.

I dashed in front of her, kicking shit that I'd left on the floor out of her way. "Hey, now. You're injured, so yes, I'm going to be protective of you."

She didn't respond as we made our way to my kitchen and I started to make coffee. I left her on her own to sit down at the island and deal with her crutches. I didn't want to suffocate her, but I glanced over my shoulder a couple of times, making sure she was okay.

"Your place is nice. I haven't looked around too much, though."

I hit start on the coffee maker. "You sound surprised."

"I am," she said, glancing around the room. "I expected it to be more…"

"Frat-like?" I raised an eyebrow.

"Maybe. It's cleaner than I thought."

"It's the military in me."

"Interesting."

A phone started to ring in the bedroom, but it wasn't my ringer. "Can you get that? It's my phone. It may be work."

I pushed off the counter and ran to the bedroom, grabbing both phones from my pants pocket. It wasn't the school calling, but her father.

"It's your dad!" I yelled from the bedroom.

"Answer it!"

"Fuck," I muttered before answering the call. "Hello."

"Frisco?"

"Yes, sir." I grimaced.

"How's my girl?"

"She seems good. Feisty as ever."

"Good to hear," he said, his voice gravelly. "Would you mind bringing her here for the day?"

I scratched my head and turned in a circle before heading back toward the kitchen. "Sure."

Georgia gave me a strange look and held out her hand.

"Georgia wants to talk to you." I started to hand the phone to her.

"Frisco!" he yelled into the phone.

I brought it back to my ear. "Yes, sir?"

"You and I have some work to do today."

I glanced at Georgia and dragged my eyes away from her. "Yeah."

"Put my baby girl on the phone."

I held the phone out to her.

She gave me a weird look as she studied me. "Hey, Daddy." She leaned forward against the counter, resting her chin in her hand as she spoke.

The knot in my stomach that had dissipated returned full force. I wasn't scared of the man or what he wanted us to do, but lying to Georgia about it didn't sit well. It wasn't an outright lie, more a lie of omission.

I poured our coffee and slid a mug in front of her as she chatted. Watching her, I sipped the warm black liquid I couldn't do without.

"We'll be there in an hour," she told him, sliding her cup closer. "Yeah, Dad. See you soon." She stared at the screen before setting her phone on the counter. As she wrapped her hands around the mug, she sighed. "Sorry about him."

"I like your dad," I lied and took another sip.

"Mm-hmm." As she tipped the cup back, taking her first sip, she closed her eyes and savored the taste.

Her father had me a bit on edge, and I'd forgotten to even ask how she wanted her coffee, but I guess she was like me, no bullshit, just caffeine. After grabbing the Tylenol from the cabinet, I set two pills down in front of her. "Take those."

She nodded and swallowed them down with her coffee before I had a chance to get her a glass of water.

"I need a shower." She pushed her empty cup toward me and smelled her hair.

"How about a sponge bath?" I asked with a grin.

"Never mind." She rolled her eyes. "I'll just wait until you take me home."

"I won't be leaving you alone for a couple of days."

"Why?"

"When you're less sore, then I'll leave you alone."

Her eyes bored holes into me. "Why?"

I could see how this conversation was going, and Georgia wasn't happy with me. "'Cause you need help."

She rose from her chair and balanced on her crutches. "I don't."

"I think you need a shower," I said, changing the subject. "Let me get a garbage bag."

She looked at me confused. "Why?"

I motioned toward the cast with one hand and pulled a bag from the cabinet. "You can't get that wet."

Her lips formed a perfect O. "Fuck, I forgot."

"Let me take care of you and stop bitching."

Her body recoiled and her eyes narrowed. "Did you just call me a bitch?"

My eyes widened and I moved toward her. "I'd never utter those words," I said, touching her cheek, and dusting my lips against hers.

"You better not. I think this cast could do a number on your balls."

I laughed into her mouth before kissing her. "Will it be that awful to shower with me for a few days?" I murmured against her lips.

"No," she muttered and sighed. "Doesn't sound so bad." Her eyes roamed over my face before I felt her smile.

"We better hurry. Wouldn't want to keep Dad waiting."

It was my turn to sigh. "No, we wouldn't want to do that."

"GEORGIA, I'm going to steal Frisco away for a few minutes." Mr. Phillips nudged my shoulder, almost knocking me off-kilter.

Her eyes darted to me. "I guess it's okay."

"Thanks, baby girl," he said, leaning forward, and kissing the top of her head before moving toward the living room.

"We'll be quick."

"What's he want with you?" She studied my face.

"Just guy talk," I lied.

"Let them go," her mother said, putting her hand on top of Georgia's before she glanced at me. "We can girl talk."

Georgia nodded, and I took it as my cue to join her father in the living room.

"Sit," he commanded and motioned toward the couch across from his chair. Coming face-to-face with a man, the father of the woman you're currently trying to bed, who you can't punch if they speak out of turn, is all kinds of scary. It's the one person in the world who can hate your fucking guts and you're helpless to defend yourself with your hands.

"Let's get a few things straight," he started as I sat down. "We didn't get to talk privately much at the hospital yesterday, and I have a few things to say."

I nodded and knew where this conversation was headed.

"I wasn't thrilled about the idea of you dating my daughter when she told us about you. For one, you're kind of old for her."

Smiling didn't feel appropriate, but I couldn't help but feel my lips twitch. "I understand. I had the same worry."

"But Georgia speaks highly of you, and she doesn't up-sell anyone. Then she tells me you're a PI. I'm not knocking the profession." He held up his hands and made a look of disgust. "But it's not a solid job."

"It is," I argued and leaned back in the chair, pretending to be relaxed.

"What's your background? I checked your criminal record, but you don't have one. I figured since you're on the fringe of law enforcement that you possibly had a criminal background."

"I attended college and served in the military."

"What branch?" He stroked his chin, waiting for my response.

"I was a SEAL, sir."

He whistled, and his hand stilled on his chin. "Impressive."

"Thank you."

"College?"

"I studied pre-law."

"Why didn't you do anything with your degree?"

"Much to the dismay of my parents, I found it too boring. Private investigation fits me better. It's a solid company run by two guys who used to work for the DEA."

"Dirty law enforcement?" he asked, raising an eyebrow.

I shook my head and grimaced. "No, sir. They were sick of working undercover and wanted to put their skills to use. They felt they could be more helpful with their own firm."

"Burned out," he said quietly and turned to stare out of the window. "It happens sometimes." He sighed before he looked back at me. "Why Frisco? It's an odd first name." He scrunched up his face.

"You'd have to ask my mother, sir." I gripped the arm of the couch tightly. I couldn't lose my cool or seem snippy. Georgia's father held a lot of clout with her, and I wasn't about to let him come between us.

"Enough of the bullshit. Let's talk about last night."

"Hit me," I muttered, grimacing, and regretting the term.

"Was a man driving?" He coughed, covering his mouth with his hand. "I can't go after a woman."

"From what I could see. It all happened so quickly but, yes, it was a man."

"Good." He nodded and pushed himself up from the chair. "I want you to write down everything you remember. Get your people on it, and I'll do some digging down at the station. I want to find this person." He leaned against the wall and looked out the window.

"But shouldn't we let the cops handle it?"

"Are you a pussy, son?" He turned to face me.

"No." I shook my head. "But—"

"No buts. We find them first. Were you scared last night?"

I nodded, remembering the feeling of fear and helplessness I'd experienced watching the accident play out in front of my eyes. "Very." My body began to shake with the amount of anger starting to boil inside me, slowly building every time I replayed the asshole driving off.

"They drove away," he said, turning back to look outside. "They didn't care about my Georgia. They're going to pay for that."

"Yeah." I closed my eyes, ignoring the gnawing ache in my gut.

I didn't get where I'd turned into a one-word wonder around this man. No man had ever intimidated me. Not even the officers who outranked me in the military. But there was something about Mr. Phillips that made me second-guess everything.

He handed me a pad of paper he'd retrieved from a cabinet near the window. "Write everything down. Don't leave one thing out."

"Okay. Can I call you George?" I remembered his wife calling him that last night at the hospital. It was all a fucking blur, but I did remember that.

"You can call me Mr. Phillips." He glared and hovered above me.

"Mr. Phillips." The prick needed to chill the fuck out. I got that he was wound up about his daughter, but at some point, especially if we were a team, he needed to not view me as an inferior person.

"Write," he growled, pointing at the paper before stalking off to the same cabinet he'd retrieved the paper from. "Drink?" he asked and removed a carafe of amber liquid.

"I don't drink this early in the morning."

"I'm too nervous not to have something to calm my nerves. If you're lucky enough to have children," he said as he glanced at me over his shoulder, "you'll understand how I feel."

I nodded, even though I already knew how he felt. Georgia wasn't my kid, but she was still mine. I'd protect her with my life if I had to. Seeing her in pain and watching her almost die before my eyes in a way that made me feel helpless would never happen again. I'd make fucking sure of it.

I started to write down the details, pausing, and looking up when I heard the clink of the carafe against the glass. His hand shook as he tried to pour the liquid into the crystal tumbler. From the outside, he seemed cool as a cucumber, but inside, he was a ball of nerves, much like me.

Every man dealt with stress differently. I didn't drown it in the bottom of a bottle; I used it to drive me forward. No matter what happened, the person would pay for what they did to Georgia.

When I finished jotting down everything I remembered, I tossed the pad on the coffee table and looked at him. He stared out the window, deep in thought, and sipped his drink. "I wrote down everything I could remember."

"Good," he said without looking. "I'm sure your company can help in the search, yeah?"

"Yeah," I replied and stood from the couch, cracking my neck to relieve the tension.

"I'll head to the station and do some digging. I can't do too much without drawing red flags. You head to the office and see what you can find. Got me?"

"But what about Georgia?" I glanced over my shoulder toward the kitchen.

"She can stay here with Rosie."

"I'm coming back for her this afternoon," I told him, unwilling to back down. I wouldn't let either of her parents run the show, and I wanted to be the one to take care of Georgia. I needed to do it to help quell my feelings of guilt over the entire situation.

"Fine." He looked at his watch. "Let's meet back here around four. We'll have dinner and discuss what we've found."

"That works."

He set down his glass and moved toward me quickly. "This stays between us. Understand?" He waved his finger in my face, and it took everything in me not to slap it away.

I tried not to lose my patience. "I got it."

"Four," he reminded me as he held out his hand to me.

"Four." I shook his hand and squeezed it as hard as he'd squeezed mine yesterday.

I'd made a decision about Mr. Phillips. He wasn't going to bully me. Georgia or not, he wasn't going to run the show. If I let him walk all over me now, there would be hell to pay in the future.

When that thought crossed my mind, I felt the blood drain from my face. The future. I hadn't thought about the future with anyone since Jeanine. Subconsciously, I'd already started to think about Georgia and where we'd be. I didn't have time to dissect my feelings or what this meant, but I knew there would be some major thinking to do and decisions to be made in the future.

I followed Mr. Phillips into the kitchen as both women glanced at us.

"How did it go?" Mrs. Phillips rose from the chair to kiss her husband.

"Great, love. Frisco has to go to work, but he'll be back for dinner at four."

Georgia's eyes widened and honed in on the clock across the room. "Four?"

"Sorry, babe. I have to run to work and take care of a few things."

"I can come," she said, reaching toward the floor to grab her crutches.

"Georgia, let me take care of you today. I haven't been able to do it in years. I want to pamper you." Rosie grabbed the crutches from Georgia's hand and put them back on the floor.

"But I—" Georgia began, but her mother placed her hand on her shoulder.

"Let the men work, and we'll cook them a feast."

Georgia glared at me. "You better come back, Frisco, or you won't have a Felicia," she mumbled.

"Oh, I miss that couple," her mother whispered, trying to hold in her giggles.

"What couple?" Mr. Phillips asked, totally out of the loop.

"No one, honey." Rosie made her way to his side. "Are you going down to the station?"

He nodded. "I told the guys I'd stop by and say hello, but I'll be back for dinner."

I walked up to Georgia and leaned over. "Sorry, babe," I said, whispering in her ear. "I promise to come back for you."

"I swear to God, if you leave me here with my helicopter parents, I'll hunt your ass down and make you regret the day you were born," she said with her lips against my cheek.

"Babe, I'll be back for you," I told her before I kissed her softly on the lips. "I have a sponge bath to give later."

"That sounds like a reward for you," she whispered in my ear.

"It may be my reward, but it's going to be your pleasure."

"I like the way you think, Mr. Jones."

"Wait for me." I started to back away.

She held up her hands, motioning as if to say, "Where the fuck am I going to go?" and I couldn't help but laugh as I headed toward the front door.

"I'm going to walk Frisco out, love. Be home soon," Mr. Phillips said before he caught up to me. He nudged me in the back and held out a business card. "Here's my number. Call me when you get anything."

"Yes, sir," I said, jamming the card into my pocket before I climbed into my car and headed toward the office.

CHAPTER 15

FOUND

"So let me get this straight," Thomas said, leaning forward in his chair after I'd explained to him and James what happened last night. "He's a retired cop."

"Yeah, and?"

"He wants to find this person, and what?" He tapped his pen against the desktop and stopped while he waited for an answer.

"He thinks we can be faster than the cops. He's kind of a scary dude."

Thomas shrugged as his lips twisted. "Sounds like my kind of guy."

"I'm so in." James clapped his hands together.

"Why do I have a sinking feeling?"

"Does Georgia know?" Thomas asked, tossing the pen off to the side, and straightening his back.

I shook my head and pinched the bridge of my nose. "No."

"Fuck me. I see a clusterfuck in your near future, my friend." James slapped me on the back and laughed.

"Thanks, guys," I said, dragging my hands down my face. "You sure know how to make me feel better."

"What's going on?" Morgan asked, sticking his head in the office.

"Frisco is going rogue," James replied, leaning back, and glancing at Morgan upside down.

"I'm in." Morgan strolled in and took a seat. "Whose ass needs to be kicked?"

"We have a partial plate, the make, model, and color, and we know the car has body damage," Thomas told him, typing furiously on his computer.

"I'll get right on it."

The printer started to spit out copies, and Thomas reached back and retrieved a couple of sheets. "Here's the info. I want all hands on deck to find the person responsible for the accident."

"You don't have to do that," I said, although I didn't mean it. We were that kind of company. Having each other's backs was what we did.

James waved his hand. "It's done."

Bear walked into the room. "Did I miss the party?"

"We have a perp to find."

"Who?" Bear took a seat on the couch.

"The fucker that ran Frisco's girl off the road."

"I'll call Tank." Bear grabbed his phone from his pocket. "He can put out some feelers to his auto repair buddies in the area."

"Smart," I said, wishing I'd thought of it first.

Typically, I knew exactly how to handle a situation, but this hit too close to home. My mind was spinning, reeling from the enormity of almost losing Georgia.

I needed to remember my training and separate myself from the situation in order to focus. The ability to step outside of myself and complete a task was what made me a great soldier. There was a new enemy, and I'd do everything in my power to hunt him down and make him pay for what he did to Georgia.

"Let's meet in the conference room in one hour to share what we've found," Thomas told everyone and handed me the stack of papers with the details I'd given.

I passed them off to James, since I had the information memorized. "Sounds good."

"On it." Morgan grabbed the paper and headed for the door.

"Yo, Tank." Bear walked out into the hallway. "I have something I need you to look into."

"Should I feel guilty?" I stopped in the doorway and turned to face James and Thomas.

"Fuck no," they responded in unison.

"I'd do the same thing if someone ran Izzy off the road and left the scene of the accident."

"I have this feeling I can't shake," I admitted, rubbing the back of my neck.

"It's not the cops you're worried about, it's Georgia." Thomas shook his head.

"Go relax and let us call our contacts to get a list of possible suspects," James told me.

I sighed and nodded before heading to my office. When I sat down, I didn't turn on my computer right away. All I wanted to do was to lie down and take a nap. The prior evening had been stressful, and I hadn't slept as well or as long as I'd hoped.

As I stifled a yawn, I moved the mouse and then took my phone out of my pocket as I waited for the computer to start. During the meeting in Thomas's office, I'd received a text but ignored it.

Georgia: You better come back for me!

I laughed as I read the message.

Me: I'll be there. I swear!

James had said to relax, but I couldn't. Everything in me felt tense. Georgia must've been as restless as I was, because she continued messaging me.

Georgia: She wants me to be Betty fuckin' Crocker.

Me: Cook me something good.

Georgia: Oh, go fuck yourself.

Me: I may have to.

Georgia: You have a greedy cock.

Me: Says the girl with the greedy pussy.

Georgia: I'll talk to it tonight.

Me: Your pussy?

Georgia: You'll never get any more pussy unless you tell me what my father wants.

I set my phone on the desk and checked my email. I felt behind and out of touch, since I'd been so focused on Georgia that I'd ignored my work. Typically, I'd check multiple times a day to make sure I didn't have a client waiting for a response. But that had been the last thing on my mind lately.

"I got news!" Bear yelled from the hallway. "Conference room!"

I hopped up from my chair, holding my chest because his voice had scared the crap out of me, and followed him down the hallway. He sat down, waiting for everyone else to arrive before he spoke.

"Good news?" I asked.

He nodded and motioned toward the door. Bear had always been a friend. Most days I wanted to punch him in the face, but he always had my back. Always. There wasn't a moment in my life that I couldn't ask him for a favor or worry that he'd say no.

"What's the word?" Thomas asked when he sat down.

"Tank found the car."

My mouth dropped open. Fuck, that only took twenty minutes. "Already?" I asked.

Bear nodded with a shit-eating grin on his face. "Dumbass brought his car to Tank's place, so it wasn't that hard."

"When?"

"This morning. The front end had been smashed in. Dude made some bullshit excuse about hitting a deer and needed it fixed as soon as possible."

"Is the guy there?" I asked, tapping my foot on the floor.

"Nope. Tank has to call him with a quote."

"I'm on it." I picked up my phone.

"You want help with this guy?" Thomas asked with a gleam in his eye.

I shook my head. "Let her dad and me handle it."

"Fuck." He slammed his hand on the conference table.

"Let us help," James pleaded, motioning around the table.

"No," I told them and narrowed my eyes. "I don't know what we're getting ourselves into, but you guys should stay out of it."

Morgan rubbed his chin and studied me intently. "Why?"

"If shit goes bad, I don't want anyone else on the hook for shit that is all my fault."

"Your fault?" Sam asked with a furrowed brow. "How is it your fault?" The guys must've filled him in with their version of the events before I arrived.

I put my hands up, trying to silence their grumbling. "She wouldn't have been driving if it weren't for me fucking shit up."

James leaned back in the chair and sighed. "Now you're talking crazy."

Rising from the chair, I leaned over the back and looked around at my friends. "It's my burden to deal with."

Morgan stood and rested his hand on my shoulder. "Dude, you're an idiot."

I dragged my eyes to him. "Thanks, man."

"You know we're all down for a good ass-kicking." He gave my shoulder a hard squeeze.

I nodded. "I'll call you if we need backup. Good?"

"Let me do some digging on the guy. Let's see what we find out before you and Rambo head into more trouble than you can handle."

"I don't think I can get him to back down. Her dad is pretty intent on handling shit himself."

"Buy me an hour, and I'll dig up everything I can. Don't call her father yet."

"Fine," I said, hanging my head, and staring at the floor, thinking about how this would all play out.

As I started to walk out of the conference room, Thomas said, "Frisco, wait to see what Morgan finds before you turn down our offer."

I nodded with a sigh before I walked to Morgan's office. "Hey," I said as I poked my head into his office. "Can you text me the info when you get it?"

He glanced at me, giving me a warm smile. "Sure, buddy. I'll text you whatever I find."

"I need to get Georgia."

"Understood," he said, shooing me away with one hand.

Without saying goodbye, I headed to my office and grabbed my keys.

"Frisco," James called out just as my hand touched the door handle. "Thomas and I want in. It's fine if you don't want the other guys, but we're coming with you."

I turned around slowly. "Why?"

James crossed his arms over his chest. "Because we look out for each other."

"Is that the only reason?"

"I don't need one," he replied with his mouth set in a firm line. "That's what friends do."

"I'll call you," I told him as I spun around, pushed open the door, and headed to Georgia's parents' house.

As I drove, I decided I'd tell Georgia. She deserved to know. I didn't think it would change anything. Her father didn't seem like the type of man who would let anyone, especially his daughter, tell him what he could or couldn't do.

All I knew was that whatever he decided, I'd have to have his back. If I wanted the man to be on my side, I'd have to stand by his.

DECISIONS

After I pushed back from the table, I rubbed my stomach. "That was fantastic. Thank you for all the hard work."

Mrs. Phillips blushed. "I just whipped it up. It's nothing."

Georgia rolled her eyes as she tossed her napkin on the table. "She lies."

I clasped Georgia's hand in mine. "Doesn't matter, babe."

"So, how was work?" Mr. Phillips asked with a raised eyebrow.

"Good. I got a lot done."

"That's good." Georgia ran her thumb along my hand. "Can we go soon? I'm tired and want to sleep in my own bed."

"Before you do that, can I have a word with you, Frisco?"

Georgia's eyes narrowed, focusing on me. She knew something was up. My woman was smart.

"Sure." My eyes never left hers. "Give me a minute to talk to your dad."

She leaned forward, bringing her mouth to my ear. "You're gonna tell me what's going on in the car, got me?"

I swallowed hard, trying to rid my mouth of the sandy feeling that had settled on my tongue. "Yep."

The chair Mr. Phillips had been sitting in scraped against the wood floor as he stood. "Let's talk in my office," he said, standing above me, casting a shadow.

"Be back." I gave her a kiss on the cheek.

Even though my back was to her, I could feel her eyes on me as I walked out of the kitchen and followed her father to his office.

"What did you find out?" he asked as he closed the door.

"The guy brought his car to my buddy's garage to be fixed."

His eyes widened as he sat down behind his desk. "That's convenient."

"I couldn't make this shit up if I tried."

"What else?" he asked, resting his elbow on the desk, and placing his index finger against his lips. "Who is he?"

I reached into my pocket for my phone and checked my email. During dinner, I'd felt my phone vibrate, alerting me that I had a new email, but I hadn't bothered to look until now.

"Morgan, my colleague at ALFA, looked him up." I scrolled down the email, reading through the message. With every new bit of information, my hands grew sweatier and my heart pounded just a little harder.

"What does it say?" His tone was sharp.

"Here." I held my phone out to him. "It'll be easier than explaining everything."

He grabbed the phone from my hand and studied the email. Morgan had dug up all kinds of shit on the person responsible for hitting Georgia.

The man wasn't an angel. He had a record a mile long, in fact. The hit-and-run wasn't even the most damning thing on his record. Recently he'd been released from prison and was currently on parole. Obviously, incarceration hadn't taught him anything, but I'd be happy to give him a prison yard beat-down to further his education.

"I fuckin' know this piece of shit," Mr. Phillips barked out without looking up. "I can't believe this." He dropped the phone onto the desk, letting it wobble before it stilled. "Fuck."

My eyebrows rose at the twist of fate. "You do?"

He gritted his teeth and I heard him growl. "I arrested this asshole years ago."

"Maybe you should step back, then." My hands coiled into fists on my lap. I'd been angry at the prick for what he did to Georgia, but now I wanted to make him pay for every bad deed he'd ever done.

Someday he'd kill someone without remorse. He could've killed Georgia if I hadn't been there. I shook the thought from my head. "Let us handle it."

"There's no way I'm letting you go without me." He bared his teeth at me.

"Listen," I said, flexing my fists, and trying to relieve some of the anger I could feel clawing at my insides. "What's your plan?"

He blew out a hard breath. "I haven't thought it all through. I want the bastard to pay. That shit I know."

I stood and began to pace in front of his desk. "I'll get a few punches in before we drop him at the door of the police station."

He cocked an eyebrow at me with a smug grin. "Is that what you've decided to do? Maybe I want more."

I froze and studied him. "You want the bastard dead?" I asked, my voice laced with shock. I'd never thought about killing the man. All I wanted to do was beat on him so badly that he felt the same fear I did when I saw him coming right for Georgia.

Mr. Phillips slammed his hands down on his desk. "Fuck," he said, letting out a long breath. "I don't want that on my conscience or yours."

I nodded, trying to keep calm. Last night when the man had run her off the road, I might have choked the life out of him if I'd been able to get my hands on him. My anger hit a point I hadn't felt since leaving the service.

"You need to stand down and let me handle this," I told him, rubbing the back of my neck.

"But I can help."

"No!" I roared, wincing as soon as I heard my own voice. "I appreciate your need to help, Mr. Phillips, but this has to be done on my terms. The guys and I will handle it."

"But—"

I held out my hand. "No. I've. Got. It."

His nostrils flared as he stared at me with narrow eyes and a red face. "Fine."

I picked up my phone from his desk and texted Thomas.

Me: We're on tonight @ 11.

"You better not fuck this up." Mr. Phillips spun around in his chair.

"I think I can handle him."

Thomas: I'll gather the guys. Meet at the office at 10:30. City's in too.

I glanced down at my phone, swallowing down the lump that had formed in my throat. I'd have to come up with a reason to leave Georgia tonight without her wanting to kick me in the balls.

"I swear to God, Frisco, if I didn't dislike you already, going easy on this douchebag will ensure my distaste for you will last a lifetime." He rubbed his face with his right hand and pinned me with his glare. "Fuck this up, and I'll make sure Georgia hates you."

I placed my fists on the desk and leaned over it, hovering above Mr. Phillips. "I won't fuck it up. Georgia's mine, and no one fucks with my girl." I seethed as my chest heaved and my stomach twisted.

"'Bout fuckin' time you say that." The brief smile he gave me quickly disappeared.

I closed my eyes, trying to steady my breath. "I will handle this and protect Georgia. You're being relieved of that duty. Don't think about getting between her and me. It won't end well," I warned him.

He nodded, twisting his lips as if he approved. "Call me when it's done. I won't sleep until I know."

"Fine." I pushed myself up and squared my shoulders. "It'll be done tonight."

Without any need for further conversation, I walked into the kitchen to find a very pissed off Georgia.

"Ready to go, babe?"

She rubbed her hands together and stared, but she didn't reply. I could almost see the wheels inside her head spinning as she tried to figure out what her father and I had cooking.

I stood in front of her and held her gaze. "G?"

"Yeah, I'm ready."

"So soon?" Rosie asked, wiping her hands on a dishtowel. "I had dessert ready."

Georgia held her hand out to me. "Maybe another time, Mom."

I helped her up and handed her the crutches. "I'll take a rain check, Mrs. Phillips."

"Where's my dad?" Georgia asked, glancing over my shoulder.

"He's in his office." I smiled the best fake smile I could muster under the situation.

"Thanks for everything, Mom." Georgia kissed her mother on the cheek before stalking off toward the door, still wobbly on the crutches. I had to fight the urge to jump in and carry her. "Let's go, Frisco. We have some talking to do," she called out over her shoulder.

Mrs. Phillips gave me a sympathetic smile as she waved goodbye. "Georgia," I called out as she tried to go down the stairs, hopping on one foot without holding on.

"I got this!" she yelled before her body started to fall forward, teetering back and forth as if on a balance beam.

Before she could fall, I grabbed her by the waist and steadied her. "Jesus," I muttered, pulling her body against mine. "Can't you wait for me to help you?"

"I'm a big girl, Frisco. I don't need anyone's help."

I looked up at the cloudy sky and cursed under my breath. "We have to talk," I told her and lifted her foot off the ground, stalking to the car with her in my arms like a rag doll.

She held the crutches against her chest, letting them swing as I carried her. "You have a lot of explaining to do."

When we made it to the car, I set her down on her good leg and used her waist to turn her body to face me. "Georgia, I can't explain everything. Just know that I would do anything to protect you."

"Anything?" she asked, quirking an eyebrow, and challenging me.

"Anything."

She leaned back against the car door and crossed her arms over her chest. "Then whatever my dad has cookin', I want you to ignore."

My head recoiled and my mouth dropped open. I stared at her for a beat before finally closing my mouth. "I don't know what you think he wants to do, but—"

"Don't lie," she said.

"I'm not lying." I took a step closer and invaded her space. Reaching out, I ran my finger along her cheek, relishing the feel of her skin against mine. "Listen, your father and I have very different ideas about how things should be handled, but I'll take care of it."

She glanced up and stared off into space. "That's what I'm afraid of," she grumbled, and her lip began to quiver.

"Hey." I cradled her face in my hands, bringing my lips against hers. "No one is going to die, if that's what you're worried about."

Her eyes darted to mine and narrowed into tiny slits. "But that doesn't mean you aren't going after the guy."

I nodded, knowing I had been busted a long time ago. "I won't say that I won't get a few licks in, but he'll survive the beating that's coming his way and be arrested before the night's out."

"Why do you have to hit him?" she murmured against my lips, staring at me with tear-filled eyes.

"Because he hurt you." I tightened the hold I had on her face.

"It was an accident, Frisco," she muttered, my name sounding like a curse coming from her lips.

"He's not a good guy, Georgia."

She backed away, and my lips instantly missed her touch. "Take me home."

I nodded, unlatched the door behind her, and helped her inside. It wouldn't be an easy sell. I knew where her fear came from. She worried that things would get out of hand and that something would happen to me. It was the same fear that had gripped me last night.

As I drove, Georgia stared out the window and didn't speak a word. The silence was deafening. Georgia never seemed the type to hold her tongue, but I didn't dare push her.

When we arrived at her place, she exited the car and headed toward her front door. I watched through the window, shocked by her stubbornness and hating that she was pissed at me.

Before she could open the door, I jogged to her side and took the keys from her hand. "Let me."

"I don't think you should come in," she said, yanking the keys out of my grip.

My body recoiled, feeling the blow of her words as if she'd hit me. "You can't mean that."

She bowed her head as her hand with the keys dropped to her side. "I just don't know. I guess I don't know you as well as I thought I did."

I put my arm around her waist, holding her body flush against mine. "I'm still me."

"But-t-t," she said, her body shaking in my arms, "you're going to hurt someone because of me."

"Because of him," I corrected her, brushing my lips against her face. "He did this."

"Why not let the police handle this?"

"He has a rap sheet longer than your arm, Georgia." I peppered kisses down her jawline, finding the spot I loved most on her neck. "Would City do the same if someone had run Sunshine off the road?"

She tipped her head back as her breathing quickened. "Maybe."

"Men want to protect what's theirs," I told her and sank my teeth gently into her skin. "You *are mine.*"

Her body shivered in my arms. "Yes," she moaned, angling her head to the side, and giving me more access.

I licked her flesh, feeling her pulse beat under my tongue. "I'll protect you until my last breath, Georgia."

"Lie down and hold me for a little while." Her voice was airy and filled with want.

I nodded because, hell, there wasn't anything I wanted more in the world than to hold her in my arms.

After taking the key from her hand and unlocking the door, I scooped her into my arms, and carried her inside. Letting the crutches drop to the floor, she kissed me as I kicked the door closed.

CHAPTER 17

OLD-SCHOOL BEATDOWN

When I pulled into the office at ten thirty, I could still hear her voice in my head.

"Frisco, don't leave me. Please," she said, gripping me like her very life depended on it.

"I have to go, Georgia. But I'll be back," I told her before giving her a kiss and walking out the door.

Guilt clawed at my insides. The way she looked at me, the sadness in her eyes when I told her I had to leave, would haunt me for a lifetime.

Thomas, James, Morgan, and City stood in a circle outside James's black SUV and were deep in conversation. Even though I'd told them I wanted to do this alone, I'd lied. It wasn't that I couldn't, but I needed someone there to pull me off the fucker and stop me from killing him.

I'd learned in the military that sometimes, when coming face-to-face with the enemy, emotions often got the better of me. I couldn't easily remove myself from a situation once it started, but the guys would make sure I didn't get carried away.

"Hey." I climbed out of the car and approached them, feeling jittery as I walked.

James gave me a chin lift. "We're waiting for a few more."

"More? I thought I said no one else."

"I know what you said," Thomas told me as he walked in my direction. "But we don't know what we're in for. More men equals safety."

"Well, I—" I shook my head, but I knew he was right. "Okay."

"Here he is," Morgan said when Sam pulled into the lot.

"Tank's with Bear and will be meeting us there." James pulled out his gun and checked the chamber.

"Where?"

"Neon Cowboy." City came to stand next to me. "That's where the fucker knew Tank from. He's been coming into the Cowboy on and off for years."

"Fuck," I said and ran my fingers through my hair. Of all the places in the world the guy could hang out, why did it have to be my spot... our spot?

"I have a plan." City rested his hand on my shoulder. "Want to hear?"

"I'm all ears." In actuality, I knew I was going to hear his plan either way.

"Tank is going to lure him into the parking lot, and we're going to take care of him outside."

I scowled and didn't try to hide my annoyance. "That's your plan?"

He nodded.

"We're going to jump him like a bunch of punks?" I asked, shocked that City had come up with the idea.

"No." He shook his head. "You're going to do what you want while we have your back."

"So I'm going to jump the asshole?"

"What were you going to do before?" City laughed and backed away. "Were you going to knock on his door and have a chat first? Like, 'Hey, I wanted to talk to you about the car you drove off the road. Do you have a moment?'"

I punched him in the shoulder. "No, you prick."

"Then shut the fuck up and get in the truck. We have ass to kick."

"Fuck yeah!" Morgan yelled before climbing in the back.

Sam settled in the middle. "I'm all in."

"Let's go. We have women to get home to," James said, pointing at the backseat.

"I hope I still do."

James and Thomas climbed in the front seat. "Everyone have a firearm, just in case?" James turned the key in the ignition and paused.

"Check," everyone but me answered in unison.

"Frisco?" Thomas turned to look at me.

I shook my head and made tight fists. "I'm not killing the guy. I just want to beat the fuck out of him."

"Always bring a weapon. You never know what's going to happen. Got it?"

I nodded but paid his little advice no heed. The last thing I needed to do was have a firearm with me. Because, knowing my anger, I'd shoot the motherfucker in the head if he said something shitty. I'd rather use my fists to beat the living shit out of him and leave him reeling in pain.

I sat quietly in the backseat and stared out the window as the guys chatted on the way to the Neon Cowboy. Even though I had enough anger inside me to fuel a thousand fires, I couldn't help but smile. This amazing group of guys had my back. I knew if something went wrong, they'd make sure that Georgia would be taken care of and would do what was necessary to protect her.

Just after eleven thirty, we pulled into the Neon Cowboy.

"I'll text Bear," Thomas said and hit a few buttons on his phone.

Moments later, while we sat in silence, Thomas's phone beeped. "He said to go out back. They'll meet us there."

This was it. Twenty-four hours after I thought Georgia had been ripped from my life, I'd get a little revenge before this guy received justice.

As we walked around the back of the bar, we took positions around the perimeter. Everyone evaded the single light that lit the back parking lot, hiding in the shadows, waiting for Tank and Bear to bring him outside. My heart pounded so frantically in my chest that I thought it would burst as the seconds ticked by.

"Thanks for getting the estimate done so quickly," the man said as he wobbled into the light.

"Anytime, man. Are you sure you hit a deer? It's a lot of damage for such a small animal."

"I hit something. I didn't stick around to see what the hell it was." He laughed. "I was fucked up and probably shouldn't have been driving."

Bear looked around, trying to find us in the dark. "That shit isn't cool, dude."

"Eh, fuck it. I lived," the scumbag said.

I couldn't take it anymore. The rage inside me had boiled over. My body hummed with fury. The coldhearted bastard didn't care if he killed someone as long as he survived.

I stepped from the shadows with my hands already clenched into tight fists, coming to a stop in front of him.

He stepped back and snarled. "Watch it, fucker."

I took a step forward and invaded his space. "I think you need to learn some manners, asshole."

"Fuck you, man," he said, waving his hand in my face.

I swatted his hand away. The guys stepped out of the darkness, standing behind me. The man looked around, and his eyes filled with terror. The same fear I felt when I saw his car coming straight for Georgia.

"What the fuck is this about?" he asked with wide eyes, stumbling back another step.

Reaching out, I grabbed his shirt, fisting it in my hands before pulling him closer. "You fuckin' ran my woman off the road last night."

He shook his head and swallowed hard. "It was a deer. I swear." His hands clawed at my fist. "You have the wrong guy," he pleaded, his entire body shaking in my grip.

I didn't wait. I couldn't listen to his lies. My right hand connected with his jaw, snapping his head back sharply as his bone cracked with the impact. When he grabbed his jaw, I dropped him to the ground.

"Get up!" I roared. My anger had grown since I'd stepped out of the SUV. It had morphed into something more…something bigger than I thought possible.

He rubbed his jaw and tried to push himself up but failed. "That was a cheap shot," he complained, sounding like a little bitch.

"Get up and fight." I kicked his feet, trying to get him off the ground quicker. "You want to hurt someone…try to hurt me, motherfucker."

He pushed himself up and put his hands in front of his face, making fists. "You're going to kick my ass over some bitch?"

I cracked my neck and soaked up the adrenaline that coursed through my system. It had been far too long since I'd felt the thrill of beating someone's ass, and I would enjoy every fucking minute of it. "She isn't some bitch. She's mine. You fucked with the wrong people."

His eyes were glued to mine as he spat, and a stream of blood landed next to my shoes. "Let's see if you can do it when I'm waiting for you. You don't look that tough. You even had to bring a gang."

He bounced from foot to foot. "Come on. You hit like a pussy," he said with a cackle.

The guys took a step forward, closing the circle around us. "I got him," I told them and waved them off.

"Kick his ass," James barked.

The anger inside me was raging and my fists flew, landing one punch after another until he swayed and finally fell to the ground.

"Let's get the fuck out of here," Sam called out and moved toward the SUV.

Standing here, I looked down at the guy and felt nothing. I wasn't sorry for what I'd done. He deserved every blow, and tomorrow he'd wake up in jail.

"Come on, man. He won't forget that ass-beating for a long time," Bear said, placing his hand on my shoulder.

I glanced at him, my breathing heavy and labored. "What if he does?" My chest heaved with the anger moving throughout my body more than from the exertion of knocking the guy's lights out.

"He won't, and when he wakes up tomorrow in jail, he'll wish you would've killed him."

Tank stood next to me with plastic zip ties in his hands. "Get out of here. Bear and I will load him in his car and deliver him to the police station."

"Fuck, I wish I had a bow," Bear joked.

Tank kneeled down next to the dirtbag. "Hit it. We got it from here."

Slowly I walked toward the SUV, not caring who saw what had happened. The knot that had settled in my belly last night had vanished, and I knew I'd done the right thing when I saw Tank and Bear loading him into the back of his smashed-up car.

When I settled in my seat and closed the door, Morgan nudged me. "How are you going to explain your bloody knuckles to Georgia?"

She knew I'd left her tonight to take care of something. Since she was a smart one, I knew that she'd put two and two together. I just prayed that she'd understand why I did what I did and forgive me. Hopefully, knowing that I left the prick alive would be enough when combined with her feelings for me. We needed to ride out this storm and emerge stronger on the other side.

Take it or leave it, this was who I had always been. I classified myself as a nice guy, but I had a bunch of asshole hidden beneath the surface. When someone threatened or hurt someone I loved, I happily took him out.

Love.

I gasped.

"What?" James asked, looking at me in the rearview mirror.

"Nothing," I said, feeling my pulse quicken to the same frantic pace it had kept when I had been fighting.

"Sure? You look a bit white."

I clenched my hands in my lap. "I'm good."

Did I love Georgia?

It had taken me months to say those words to Jeanine. They'd been wasted words, because her treachery showed that she didn't feel the same.

But Georgia wasn't Jeanine. They couldn't be any more opposite. Even though they were yin and yang, could I honestly say I loved her?

The answer was simple.

I did.

CHAPTER 18

MAKE AMENDS

Thankfully, by the time I returned to her place, she'd passed out and was sleeping too deeply to wake up when I crawled into bed. I lay here, listening to her breathing and thinking about everything that had transpired since the day I'd met her.

Everything blurred together except for the moments I spent with her. I could play them over and over again in my head, reliving every second.

She was unlike any other woman I'd ever met.

Her kindness.

Her smartass mouth.

Her intelligence.

Her integrity.

Her beauty.

Our shared heartbreak.

The funniest part about it was that I couldn't muster any reason why I'd loved Jeanine, but with Georgia in my arms, I couldn't think of a reason why I didn't love her. I just had to laugh.

"You're home." Georgia's groggy voice made me still.

I pulled her closer, running my fingers through her dark hair. "I'm sorry I woke you, babe. Go back to sleep."

She snuggled into my side, mumbling something that I couldn't make out. Within moments, her breathing deepened.

"I love you, Georgia," I whispered. "I'd do anything to protect you." I drifted off to sleep reliving the moments I'd spent with her.

Every smile, kiss, and touch we'd exchanged in our short relationship. I couldn't imagine a day without them now.

<hr>

WHEN THE SUNLIGHT hit my face, I cracked open an eye and saw her form looming over me. She sat on the bed, the leg with her cast out straight and off to the side, with her other leg tucked in front of her. This wasn't going to be good. Before I closed my eyes, I took notice of her posture. Her back was straight, her arms were crossed in front of her chest, and she wasn't moving.

"Your knuckles are bruised."

Without opening my eyes, I replied, "I got in a few punches." There was some truth to it, but maybe "a few" wasn't entirely accurate.

"You did it, didn't you?"

I reached out and rested my hand on her cast. "He's in custody now."

She swatted my hand away and let out a loud breath. "Is this what you've been cookin' up with my dad?" she asked.

"No," I lied. In all actuality, it wasn't. He'd wanted to kill the guy.

She poked me in my ribs. "Don't lie to me, Frisco."

"I was with the guys last night, and he's in custody and completely alive."

"Damn it."

I sat up quickly, turning my body to face her. "Listen—" I started, but she shook her head and frowned.

"I don't need you to fight my battles."

"I know." I placed my hand on her cheek and caressed her skin. "I had to do it."

She stared at the ceiling. "I can't believe you did that."

Pulling myself closer to her, I wrapped my legs around her body, trapping her. "I want to explain."

"That you beat a man?" She narrowed her eyes at me.

"Georgia."

She drew in two deep breaths, and I waited for the okay. "What?" She glared at me.

"I love you," I blurted out and instantly lost all the air in my lungs.

"You what?" She moved her ear closer, not believing the words I'd muttered as much as I did.

"I. Love. You."

"Ohmygod, ohmygod," she repeated with wide eyes. "You do?"

"I do." I laughed and grasped her face in my hands. "I love you, Georgia."

She closed her eyes and rubbed her cheek against my hand. "Isn't it too soon?" she asked with a soft, raspy voice.

I grazed her lips with my thumb, needing to feel their softness. "I didn't know there were rules."

Her eyes flew open. "There aren't, but damn, I don't want to be one of those clichéd couples."

"We can be whatever we want. You need to know how I feel about you. I'll protect you until my dying breath." I leaned forward, kissing her gently. "Even though we've only known each other for a short time, I can't imagine my life without you."

"Did you kill him?" she asked and stared at me as our lips touched.

"No," I told her and shook my head.

"Thank God," she whispered and rested her forehead against mine. "I don't think I could get over that, Frisco. Promise me that's not who you are."

"I'm not that man anymore, Georgia. That I promise you. But…" I paused, brushing my nose against hers. "If someone hurts you, I will hurt him."

She searched my face, finally landing on my eyes. "Fair enough, but know that I can fight my own battles. Not everyone deserves a beating."

"He did."

"I'm not new to my daddy's brand of justice. He's been trying to protect me since I was a little girl. I don't need another protector, Frisco. I need a partner."

"So, are you saying you wanted to help me kick his ass?" I bit my lip to hold in my laughter.

She shoved my chest and laughed. "You're an asshole."

"But ya love me?" I grabbed her back and pulled her closer.

"I do." She sighed. "For some odd reason, I do."

"Just one thing, babe."

"What?"

"Don't call him 'Daddy'."

Her eyebrows shot up and the corner of her mouth curled. "Do you want me to call you 'Daddy'?"

I nuzzled my face into her neck and smelled the richness of her skin. "No. Don't ever use that word again."

"Only if you promise to let me fight my own battles like a big girl."

"I'll try," I spoke against her pulse, feeling it thumping under my lips.

"I'll try too." She scooted forward, still entangled in my legs, and kissed me. It was unlike any kiss we'd shared before. Our lips moved together, perfectly in sync, and conveyed every emotion I'd felt since the day I met her.

"Frisco," she whispered after breaking the kiss.

"Yeah, baby?" I pulled her so close that no space was left between us.

"I'm happy you saved me."

"I'll always save you. You're mine."

CHAPTER 19
SET STRAIGHT

A loud knocking on her front door woke us.

"Stay here." I moved her off my shoulder and rolled to the side of the bed. After I slid on a pair of shorts, I walked to the living room, and peeked out the front window.

Her dad's car sat in the driveway. *Fuck.*

I swallowed down the lump that had returned and become lodged in my throat before I opened the door.

"Frisco," Mr. Phillips said with a tight jaw. "Did you do it?"

I stared him straight in the eyes. "It's done."

"He alive?"

"Yeah."

"Good job, son."

I swear, we had the oddest conversations. It was a back-and-forth, much like tennis but without the grunting. He barely moved; I didn't dare show weakness as we bantered.

Son. Oh my God, he called me son.

A slow smile spread across my face. "He's taken care of, sir."

He ran his hands through his hair and glanced around her yard. "I can sleep a little better."

"Sir, I think it was the only way it could go."

He took a step forward. "I've never killed someone, but I'd do it for my family. Remember that, Frisco. There's nothing more important to me in this world than them. I'd give my life if it meant they'd be safe."

"I'd do the same, Mr. Phillips. I'd never let anything happen to Georgia. I took care of him. He won't hurt anyone for a very long time, and hopefully, he'll think twice before he has the chance to do it again."

He nodded and placed his hand on my shoulder. "How's my girl today?"

At least he didn't say kid. "She's good. Sleeping."

"I didn't like you, and I still reserve the right to hate you in the future, but for now I'll leave you two in peace."

"Thanks, sir. You're growing on me too." I laughed.

"As long as you make Georgia happy and will protect her with your life, I won't have you whacked."

"What?" I asked, thinking I'd heard him wrong, even though I knew I didn't.

"Nothing. Tell Georgia hello and I'll bring Rosie over tomorrow to see her. She's worried about her, but she knows you're taking care of her."

I crossed my arms in front of me, wondering where he was going with this. "I am."

He winked at me. "Just not too well, got me?"

"Loud and clear, sir."

"Good." He nodded. "Back to the grind."

I nodded back and waited for him to make his way to his car. He stopped before opening the door, turning toward me, and smiling. "I was wrong about you," he said and tipped his head at me.

"Okay," I mumbled, unable to stop my eyebrows from drawing together. I knew what he thought. He'd seen my tattoos, knew my line of work, and probably thought I had been a criminal.

"You're honorable."

"I am."

"Keep that shit up," he said before climbing into the car and slamming the door.

The man always had me on edge. I didn't know if that feeling would ever go away, but I hoped eventually it would pass.

"Was that my dad?" Georgia asked and looked over my shoulder as I closed the front door.

"Yep."

She eyed me with suspicion. "He hassle you?"

"No." I rubbed the back of my neck and closed my eyes. "He's just…"

"Scary?" She laughed.

I walked toward her and wrapped my arms around her, smelling my scent all over her. "Something like that."

"He's all bark and no bite," she said, balancing on her crutches even though I held her.

"Sure," I mumbled. That man could bite, and it could be deadly.

Every girl thought her father was the sweetest man in the entire world. That fact was true of Georgia, but it was a complete and utter lie. Any man who used to carry a weapon for work couldn't be discounted.

"I want to shower, but this damn cast makes it so fucking hard. Can you help me?"

"You know what makes me hard?" I whispered with my mouth buried in her hair as I rubbed my already hard dick against her stomach.

"We're going to get dirty before we get clean, aren't we?"

"You bet that sweet little ass of yours." I lifted her into my arms.

She dropped the crutches and they clattered to the floor before she wrapped her arms around my neck and kissed me.

The cast was a problem. We'd have to make use of the counter before I wrapped her cast in plastic and helped her clean up.

I carried her to the bathroom and sat her on the granite counter, which earned me a yelp. "Jesus," she mumbled, "that shit is cold."

"I'll warm you up." I nudged her legs apart, dropping to my knees, and burying my face in her pussy.

We spent the rest of the day making each other dirty and loving every minute of it.

CHAPTER 20

SIX WEEKS LATER

We walked into City and Suzy's on time. Georgia had gotten a little frisky in the car; her newfound freedom of being cast-free had turned her into a tiger and had almost made us late.

The Gallos, the guys of ALFA PI, and our friends from the Neon Cowboy were there.

"We were getting worried about you," Sunshine said, approaching Georgia with open arms and just about ignoring me. "You look…"

"Don't say it," Georgia warned her and laughed.

"Slut," Sunshine said and wrapped her arms around Georgia's neck. The ladies hugged each other and continued laughing.

"What are we celebrating?" Georgia asked when they finally let go of each other.

"You'll find out soon enough," Sunshine told her before giving me a wicked smile.

"Do you know what this is about?" Georgia glanced up at me.

"No. This is all them. I swear."

She placed her hand on my chest and laughed. "'Cause if you were planning to pop the question in front of all these people, I'd have to kick you in the balls."

I swallowed hard, and in a way, I felt sad that she even thought I would do it here in front of everyone. "No, babe. Tonight has nothing to do with us."

"Good." She adjusted my tie and tightened it. "'Cause there would be pain involved if you did."

City had called a couple of days ago and invited us over for a barbecue. He said there would be friends and family and that we'd be celebrating, but he didn't elaborate and I didn't push.

Mrs. Gallo finally broke the silence. "Why don't you just tell us already? The suspense is killing me."

City and Sunshine glanced at each other and laughed.

"You tell them."

"No, you tell them, sugar."

"For fuck's sake, one of you better start talking," Izzy demanded.

City nodded at Suzy. She covered her face, slowly shaking it back and forth.

Mike stood behind his wife Mia with his hands clasped over her stomach. "Spill the damn secret."

"We're pregnant," Sunshine said and bounced from foot to foot.

Mrs. Gallo leaned forward and looked like she might tip. "You are?"

"We are." City pulled Sunshine against his side.

"With twins," Sunshine added before she grimaced.

Mr. Gallo paled. "Twins?"

"Twins," City repeated and kissed the top of Sunshine's head.

"Oh my God. I couldn't be more excited." Mrs. Gallo practically vibrated in her chair.

"For fuck's sake," Bear complained and glanced toward the ceiling. "Haven't you people heard of birth control?"

Tank slapped him on the back of the head. "Shut the fuck up."

"Hit me again," Bear challenged with a smirk.

"When are they due?" Max asked, rubbing her belly. She'd had a baby recently, but she was barely showing the aftereffects.

"In six months."

Mrs. Gallo's mouth fell open. "Six months?" she whispered.

City puffed out his chest. "Yep."

"Do you know the sex?" Thomas asked.

Sunshine started to laugh. She covered her mouth, trying to hide her excitement. "We found out yesterday."

Izzy put her head in her hands. "Oh, God, no! It's so unfair."

"What is, babe?" James asked, wrapping his arm around his wife.

She pinched the bridge of her nose and frowned. "They're having girls. I can tell. Why the hell do I have boys and they get girls?"

"Karma," Anthony stated flatly. "We all got the shit end of the stick."

City threw a sugar packet at Anthony, but he dodged it, letting it drop to the floor. "Speak for yourself, bro."

Mrs. Gallo began to cry. "There are so many babies. I swear I'm the luckiest lady in the world." Her lip trembled when she wiped away her tears. "I'm so blessed."

"Congrats, son."

"All this sweetness," Georgia whispered in my ear. "It makes me long for the days when we have a family."

"You want a family with me?"

We hadn't talked a ton about marriage, but I already knew I'd be popping the question. I'd never loved anyone like I did her. My entire life, I'd searched for someone to be my equal and never thought it was possible. Until the day I met her.

Even though I tried to push her away, coming up with bullshit excuses, she was the one for me.

I'd pop the question, but it would be a surprise. I wanted it to be on my terms. I already had a ring waiting to slide on her finger at home, but I wouldn't do it until the moment felt right.

"I want lots of babies," she said, rubbing my cheek with her hand.

"Lots?" I swallowed hard, feeling my mouth go dry.

"Lots." She giggled. "I want to sit around a table like this someday with our children."

I looked around. She was right. Thinking this could be us with our kids someday made my body warm. Being an only child had left a sour taste in my mouth, and I'd do everything in my power not to do the same to my children.

"Anything you want, babe."

"You two better hurry up and have boys. I want our kids to get married," Sunshine blurted.

City laughed and gave me a sympathetic look. "Sugar, let's not push things."

She rubbed his belly, making giant circles with her hand. "Shush it."

"Woman, don't make me teach you a lesson," he warned her with a smug grin.

"You know I love when you teach me things," she said playfully.

"I love you," I whispered in Georgia's ear.

"Love you too," she whispered back and settled in the crook of my arm.

I spent the rest of the barbecue thinking about our future and the perfect way to make her mine forever.

When we left, I knew where I wanted to take her. It had been forever since I'd watched the sun setting over the Gulf of Mexico, and I wanted to experience it with her.

She nestled between my legs on the sand and stroked my knee. "Frisco, I've been thinking."

I had one hand wrapped around her belly and held her close. "What's up?"

She peered up at me with a soft smile. "I'm ready?"

I glanced down, completely confused. "For?"

She didn't mean that. No. It couldn't be. We'd been together for almost two months and we rarely spoke about it. I knew when the moment was right she'd tell me, but there was no way I'd push it on her.

"I love you so much," she said and bit her lip.

I touched her chin and pulled her lip free. "I love you too, Georgia."

"I want you to make love to me." A funny smile spread across her face like she was worried I'd say no.

I exhaled slowly and brushed my nose against hers. "I would love to make love to you, but only if you're sure."

She turned in my arms and rested her hands on my knees. "I am. After Brent, I couldn't imagine having sex with anyone. I hated men for a while after him. At that point, it was easier to stay chaste than to open myself up to greater heartache. But then you came into my life."

"It's a big decision," I told her before I grasped her face in my hands.

"I know." Her eyes dipped down and she swallowed hard. "I know it's a big decision. I've spent a long time thinking about it. I can think of no one more worthy than you."

My grip increased and she melted into my touch. "Why me?"

She closed her eyes and took a deep breath before speaking. "Do you love me?"

"Yes." I smiled, more to myself because her eyes hadn't opened yet.

"I love you, too." She opened her eyes and stared into mine. "No one has ever treated me like you do. You saved my life not so long ago. I know you'd do anything in your power to protect me and would never hurt me."

"I'd never let anything happen to you. I'd give my life to save yours."

"That's the thing. I know you love me. Not because you tell me so, but because of how you treat me. I see it in your eyes every day. I even saw it that night when you pulled me out of my car. You were petrified."

"God," I said before sucking in a breath. "I can't even explain how I felt that night. I was terrified and I couldn't do anything to stop it from happening or help, Georgia."

"But you did," she said and shook her head. "You pulled me from the car, comforted me, and stayed with me until I was well enough to take care of myself."

"Anyone would do that."

She shook her head vigorously. "No, they wouldn't, but you did. I want you to be my first."

I kissed her long and deep, conveying everything I felt—joy, elation, horniness, hunger, and more love than I'd ever felt in my life.

When I broke the kiss, I told her, "I'd be honored to be your first."

"Tonight," she said before turning back around and facing the ocean.

I didn't say anything, just pulled her close against me and stared at the sun as it disappeared below the horizon. My entire body was buzzing. Excited about what the night held, in awe of the beauty of Mother Nature, and just having my girl in my arms. I was on top of the world and had everything I ever wanted.

SHE SCOOTED CLOSER and rested her hand on my leg. "I know you're nervous, but I really want this."

Reaching out, I cradled her face in my hand. "I'm not nervous. I just want to make sure you're sure about this. There's no turning back."

"I'm sure." She climbed into my lap. "I want you."

The hard-on in my pants agreed. I thanked the Gods that she no longer had the cast. I wouldn't want to deal with working around it and worrying about hurting her the first time. There were too many variables before this moment that complicated everything.

I wrapped my hand around the back of her neck and brought her lips to mine. She moaned against my lips as my tongue swept inside her mouth, craving more of her sweetness.

She leaned into my kiss, bringing her body closer to mine. The heat from her pussy permeated my jeans, caressing my hardened cock. I grabbed her waist with my free hand, halting her movement when she started to grind against me.

I broke the kiss and stared into her soft, dark eyes. "Let me control this."

I wouldn't rush this. Having her ready and relaxed would be key in making this evening a complete success. As I stroked her skin with my finger, I could feel the nerves I had denied creeping up inside me.

I slid my hands down her body, cupped her ass, and squeezed. I inhaled her exhale, losing myself a little more with each sweep of my tongue. I lifted her from my lap, adjusting myself as I laid her down on the couch, and rested myself on top of her.

My mouth slid down her jaw, finding the soft skin of her neck and tasting her flesh. I felt the thumping of her heartbeat under my lips as I kissed a trail down her throat. She shuddered, digging her claws into my back as I licked the thin veil of perspiration that covered her body.

She wrapped her legs around me, digging her heels into my back as she started to grind against me. Clearly I wouldn't be able to stop her unless I used other means.

I inched down her body, breaking free from her hold. She whined, missing the contact as much as I did, but I didn't let it stop me.

Trailing kisses from her throat to her collarbone, I paid particularly close attention to the muscle that connected her neck and shoulder. As soon as I sank my teeth into that spot, her back arched as she cried out.

I smirked against her skin. The V-neck dress she wore tonight gave me quick access. The buttons down the front made my life even easier as I started to pop them open one by one while I planted kisses against her naked flesh. Once they were undone, I pushed her dress to the sides, exposing her chest.

This was where she spilled the beans last time, telling me that we couldn't do it because she was a virgin. If she did the same this time, I thought my head would explode.

Her tiny moans, almost sounding like a purr as my mouth found her nipple, caused me to hum my happiness, the vibration of my pleasure flowing from my lips into her skin.

I took my time, touching every inch of her body with my mouth, caressing her skin with my fingertips before I even thought about sticking my cock into her. I brought her close to the edge of orgasm time and time again, making her pant with need.

"Frisco," she said, her voice laced with want.

"Shh, baby." I sat up on my heels and stared down at her.

Lying before me almost naked, her body glistened from the lost climax. Her hair cascaded over the couch, her cheeks were bright pink, and her lips were slightly parted as she sucked in air.

When I stood from the couch, she whined, but I shook my head as I started to undo my pants. "I'm not done with you yet, Georgia."

Before I inched my jeans down my legs, I grabbed the condom I'd placed in my back pocket before leaving my house. She watched as I placed the condom between my teeth.

I pulled my shirt over my head, kicked off my boots, and lost my jeans in a hurry. Her nakedness had my dick aching for relief. I couldn't wait any longer to feel myself inside of her.

"Sit up," I told her after I tossed my boxers in a pile on top of my other clothes.

She did as I asked without saying a word. I took a step forward, leaned down, and scooped her into my arms. There was no way that I'd let her lose her virginity on her couch. I nestled my face into her neck as I carried her to her bedroom.

Sliding her down my body, I placed her feet on the floor and gave her another chance to back out. "You're sure?" I asked, praying she wouldn't change her mind.

"I'm sure." She stood before me with her arms down at her sides, looking up at me.

I nodded, touching the straps of her opened dress and pushing them down her arms.

As the dress fell to the floor, she exhaled. "Are you?" she asked, staring up at me through her veiled lashes.

"I am." My voice was confident; I almost believed it myself as I tore the condom wrapper open.

I'd give my left leg to feel her without the piece of latex between us. But I would never ask that of her.

"Is it going to hurt?" She gnawed on her lip.

"I think you'll be okay," I told her as I slid the condom down my cock. "But I'll go slow."

Fuck, I didn't know. I didn't have a pussy. I knew it wasn't going to hurt for me. It would be the most glorious feeling to slide deep into her sweet, tight cunt.

I stepped forward, wrapping my arm around her body, and bringing her lips to mine. Slowly, I led her backward toward the bed, the room illuminated by nothing but moonlight, our mouths connected as we moved.

When her body flattened against the mattress, I crawled between her legs, laying my dick flat against her pussy.

She moaned and broke the kiss. "Are you any good at this?" She grinned.

I laughed, caught off guard by her question. I couldn't believe she'd asked that. "I'm pretty damn good."

She ran her fingernails up my back as she stared up at me. "Just good, or great?"

I shook my head, trying to control my laughter. "You're going to bust my chops when I'm about to stick my cock in you? Really?"

Although Georgia was young, she had an attitude that could rival any woman I'd ever met. She didn't mince words, and she sure as fuck wasn't timid.

"I'm just sayin' that I'll remember this night for my entire life. I hope it's good, because I'd hate to remember you as being the one who didn't live up to the hype."

I sat up on my heels and stared down at her, dumbfounded. My dick wasn't fazed by her comments. It twitched, aching to get closer to her pussy. "I'm going to fuck you so good that no other man will ever satisfy you."

Her smirk turned into a smile. "I like the sound of that."

I positioned myself over her again, but this time I didn't kiss her. I trapped her nipple between my teeth, flicking it with my tongue until she moaned and her body began to shudder. When she started to pant and rub herself against me, I knew she was ready.

Grabbing my shaft, I slid the tip of my dick through her wetness, coating it. I knew she could take me.

As I nudged her opening with my cock, she tensed.

"You okay?" I asked, leaving the tip against her.

"Yeah." She wrapped her legs around my back.

"Just relax."

"I'm trying, but if you keep talking, I may change my mind."

"Fuck, you're so damn bossy." I started to push the tip of my cock inside her.

She hissed, her pussy clamping down against the tip. "Fuck," she muttered after her legs jerked.

"Got any other smart shit to say?"

"Nope." She shook her head. "I'm a big girl. Give me your best."

"Babe, if I did that, I'd break your pussy for a lifetime."

"Oh." Her eyes roamed my face. "Okay. Well... Um..."

"Don't worry. I'm going to make sure you feel so good that you'll beg me for more."

I had been known to be confident, but the bullshit coming out of my mouth was a bit much. She wouldn't know the difference. I knew I was good in bed. I'd never had a complaint, and women asked me to fuck them again. I didn't know why with her I made myself out to be larger than life.

Instead of putting my lips back on her breast, I kissed her. I figured it was the best way to stop her from talking. I eased the tip back out and began to stroke her clit with it. Gliding it back and forth, I brought her close to the brink of orgasm again. Too much time had passed since we'd been in the living room. I needed to have her on the edge, with nothing on her mind but getting fucked.

When her body began to tremble and she pushed her pussy against me, I took the cue and nudged her opening once again. This time she didn't tense.

As I pushed inside her, I captured her gasps and swallowed them. Her body adjusted to my intrusion as I pushed deeper. Once fully seated, I stopped moving and gave her a moment to get used to the feel of my hard length inside of her.

Hell, I needed to give myself a time-out so I didn't come in thirty seconds. It wasn't that her pussy was so tight that I was going to lose it —it was the fact I was fucking Georgia that had me teetering on the edge.

I toyed with her nipple and kissed her until she relaxed.

"Okay?" I asked against her lips.

"I think so," she murmured into my mouth.

"If I hurt you, just tell me." I prayed that if she uttered those words, I'd be able to stop myself.

I slowly pulled out, letting her insides get the feel of my cock.

Jesus, please don't let me come.

I pushed back in with a little more force and felt the air vanish from my lungs. "Fuck," I said into her mouth as my arms began to shake.

My entire body was overcome with so many sensations and feelings that I thought I'd collapse on top of her. I reared back, trying to steady my breath and find the strength to go forward.

Georgia moaned into my mouth, digging her fingernails into my skin with each stroke of my dick. The sounds weren't those of pain but of complete and total pleasure.

I trailed my lips down her jaw to her neck, making it easier for me to hear her pleasure. I wanted to memorize every sound she made, the small gasps and stolen breaths—they were mine.

Her pulse beat against my lips as I peppered her throat with kisses. My dick grew harder, which I would've thought was impossible, but it proved me wrong. I kept my pace, trying to maintain a steady rhythm as I fucked her.

The importance of the event wasn't lost on me. Maybe I was a fool.

When I felt my balls about to crawl up my throat, I dipped my head down and captured her nipple between my teeth. I wanted more than anything to bring her to climax at the same time I did.

Finding all the strength I could muster, I balanced myself on one arm. I licked my fingers, wetting the tips before I placed them between us. I worried that the pain and nerves from it being her first time might make it harder for her to relax enough to come.

Gently, I stroked her clit, rubbing my fingers around the hardened nub in tiny circles. I focused on her breathing and mine, speeding up as her gasps increased and her body began to tremble.

"That's it, baby." I tightened the circle and applied a little more pressure with my fingertips.

"Oh," she moaned, pressing her head into the pillow. Her mouth fell open and her eyes fluttered shut as she got lost in the moment.

"Let go." I felt my orgasm about to rip through my system.

As her body grew rigid, her breathing faltered. I increased my pace, driving her over the edge with me. Our joint moans sounded like a chorus as we rode the wave of pleasure together. Both of our bodies shuddered and jerked in unison.

Her pussy contracted around my cock, squeezing the life out of it in the most delicious way. As she sucked in a breath, I slowed my pace.

Our bodies, covered in sweat, slid against each other as we drew in ragged breaths.

"Fuck me," I whispered against her neck after my arm gave out and I collapsed. In all honesty, it had been the best damn orgasm of my life.

"Gimme a minute," she said, running her fingers through my hair.

I chuckled when my insides flipped. "I'm the one who needs a minute."

As my dick softened, I let it slide out naturally. I rolled off her, pulling her in my arms. "Are you okay?"

She nuzzled into my side and glanced up at me. "I couldn't be better."

I pulled her closer. "Thank God."

Her fingers traced the ridges of my stomach muscles. "Was I okay?" she asked in a small voice.

"Were you worried?"

"Well, was I?"

"Georgia, was I okay?"

"You were fantastic." She smiled up at me. "Not that I can compare it to anyone else." She laughed.

I shook my head as my face softened. "You were amazing. There's really no wrong way to have sex."

"I thought there was," she said.

"I don't know about that, but I do know you were amazing, G."

"Good." She bit her lip. "Maybe you'll want to do it again. I think I need to practice."

I laughed softly at first before it grew louder and I held my stomach. That was the thing about Georgia. She kept me on my toes and a smile on my face.

SURPRISES

Three Weeks Later

Just as I started the coffee, the doorbell rang and I froze. Who the hell would come to my place at eight in the morning on a Sunday?

"Frisco!" the small voice called through the door as they laid on the doorbell.

"Mom," I said, opening the door and ready to fall over from shock.

"Baby," she said with one suitcase in her hand. "Surprise!"

I stared at her, thinking maybe I was still asleep. "Ma?" I asked, shaking my head to clear the sleep from my head, but she still stood there.

"It's me."

She hadn't changed. It had been at least a year since I'd seen her, but she looked exactly as she had when I'd left her in California. Her black hair was pulled into a bun without a hair out of place on the sides. She was wearing a beautiful blue dress and matching heels. She still believed people should dress up when taking a plane, and she looked like she could have stepped out of an episode of *Mad Men*.

"What are you doing here?"

She pushed past me and almost knocked me over with her suitcase.

"I missed you," she said as she bent down and placed it on the floor. The thing was fucking huge. I didn't know how she carried it. For such a little woman, she had more strength than many men I knew.

I closed the door and turned toward her, glancing down the hallway to see if Georgia had heard the doorbell, but luckily she hadn't. "You could've called."

"Didn't you miss me?" she asked as she snaked her arms around my stomach and laid her head just below my chest.

I kissed the top of her head and rubbed her back as I stared at the hallway. "I'm sorry, Mom. Of course I missed you."

"I wanted to see how you were."

"I told you I was fine."

"You've just been so busy. I had to come check on you," she mumbled into my bare chest.

I sighed and knew what was about to come. I hadn't told her about Georgia. Mom had never felt anyone was good enough for me in the past. She was the pickiest woman I knew, and telling her about Georgia would just cause more of a headache than keeping my lips sealed.

Just then, the bedroom door creaked and Mom's eyes flashed up at me. "Is someone here?" she asked in a whisper.

I grimaced. "I have a guest."

"Another one of those whores?"

"Mom." I dropped my arms to my sides. "She's not a whore. She's a good girl. I expect you to be nice to her."

She shook her head and scowled at me. "What kind of girl stays the night at a man's place when they aren't married?"

"This is America, not China."

Georgia peeked out from around the corner, and her eyes grew wide. "Who is that?" she mouthed.

"Mom," I said, loud enough for her to hear, "let me get you a hotel while you're here."

"I'll be fine in your guest room," she said before kicking off her shoes and dropping two more inches. Without her heels, she verged on little-person status, barely making it to the five-foot mark.

Glancing over my mother's head, I noticed that Georgia had disappeared. I didn't blame her. I hadn't told her the nicest stories about my mother, and I sure as hell wouldn't have wanted this to be the way I'd met her father.

"Mom," I said when I dropped my eyes to her.

She narrowed her gaze. "I'm staying here. Your women will have to stay elsewhere."

I started to walk toward the kitchen, taking an extra look down the deserted hallway on my way. "I don't have women, Mom."

She followed close on my heels and glanced down the hallway too. "You don't have a wife either."

"Keep your voice down," I told her before reaching for three coffee cups.

"Why?" She went around to the other side of the kitchen island, and I could feel her eyes on me as I poured the coffee.

When I slid the cup in front of her, I confessed, "I'm going to marry this girl. Do not mess it up for me."

She gasped and her body recoiled. "Married?" she asked and stared up at me with her mouth hanging open.

"Married." I brought the coffee to my lips.

"Finally," she said, collapsing into the chair, and letting her arms hang down at her sides. "I thought I'd never have grandchildren."

"Jesus," I muttered with my lips still around the rim.

"Hello," Georgia said when she entered the kitchen wearing a baggy T-shirt and loose-fitting sweatpants.

My mother turned, her eyes roaming over Georgia's body. "Hello," Mom said in the sweetest tone, shocking me for the second time today. She slid off the stool and walked toward Georgia. "Let me get a good look at you."

Georgia looked at me like I'd save her, but I didn't. My mother had never reacted this way to someone, and I was curious about what was about to happen.

My mother walked around her, grabbing at her sides, pinching her arms, and treating her like livestock. But I knew what she was doing. She wanted to be sure that Georgia had the right body to carry my child, her grandchildren.

"What do you do for work?" Mom asked, standing behind Georgia.

Georgia's jaw tightened. "I'm a librarian."

I was amused by the situation in front of me. Georgia had a mouth on her, but I knew that she wouldn't mouth off to my mother. Plus, I knew if she did, my mom would swat her.

"A smart one." Mom peeked around Georgia's side and smiled at me. "Finally."

"Finally?" Georgia asked, glancing over her shoulder at my mom.

"Those other girls were bimbos."

Georgia laughed. "Oh."

Mom grabbed Georgia's hips and squeezed. "Nice."

"What are you doing?" Georgia asked with a red face.

"Making sure you can have babies. Nice wide hips."

"They're not wide," Georgia barked, swatting my mother's hands away.

"You better hope they're wide enough. When Frisco was born," Mom said, turning to look at me and laugh, "he got stuck. They had to come in with big metal things and pull him out by his head." She moved her hands like giant scissors. "I've never been the same since."

"Dear God," Georgia whispered, and the redness of her cheeks lightened. "I don't want that."

"It won't happen to you. You have nice wide hips."

"Mom," I said, gently pulling my mom away from Georgia by the shoulders, "women don't like to hear how wide their hips are."

"In China—"

"Mom, drink your coffee." I moved her little body back toward the stool.

"Jesus," Georgia mouthed and stared at me.

I grinned even though I wanted to laugh. "How long are you staying?"

"A week," Mom replied into her coffee cup.

I rubbed my face, trying to contain my nonexistent excitement. A fuckin' week with my mother would feel like a month. She'd be in my shit and never leave the house without me.

"Where's Dad?" I asked, hoping he wasn't following behind.

"He's hunting with his friends."

"Huh," I mumbled. Didn't know he was into that.

"He has a new hobby. Really, he just sits his lazy ass in the woods and drinks beer."

Georgia and I both laughed. "Nice."

"So, what are we doing today?" she asked, turning the coffee cup in her hand.

"I don't know," I told her, pulling Georgia into my arms. "I didn't really plan on getting out of bed." I chuckled into Georgia's hair.

My mother choked, spitting out her coffee into the cup.

Georgia's phone rang and she walked out of the room.

"Who calls so early?"

"Who comes by so early…unannounced?"

She nodded, knowing I was right, but she didn't give a shit.

"Hey, Mom," Georgia said, sauntering back into the kitchen. She paused and stared at me. Taking one hand, she placed it on her face and slowly dragged it down her cheek.

"Tonight?" she asked in a whiny voice. "We're kind of busy."

Oh shit. Her mom was inviting us to dinner. This couldn't end well.

"Well, Frisco's mom surprised us with a visit."

There was another pause as her eyes bounced around the room, and she shifted from foot to foot. "Okay," she said into the phone as all color drained from her face. "We'll be there at six."

Fuck me. The nightmare hadn't even begun, but I could see it plain as day. Her father and my mother together would be a clusterfuck of epic proportions.

Georgia dropped her hand to her side, still holding the phone. "We're to be at my parents' for dinner at six, including your mother."

My head dropped into my hands and I tried to steady my breath. It could be fun, right? I mean, it couldn't be that bad. They'd have to meet at some point, especially if I planned to marry Georgia, which I did.

"I get to meet your parents?" Mom asked with the biggest smile I'd ever seen her have.

"Seems so," Georgia replied with the corners of her mouth turned down.

"It'll be fine," I lied to her before I walked over and hugged her. "Just fine."

"You're not a good liar," she whispered into my chest.

"I'm hopeful. It's different." I laughed.

With my back to my mother, Georgia grabbed my dick. "You better work wonders."

"Baby, I always make you see God with that."

She squeezed a little harder. "You know what I mean."

"It'll be great," I lied again and tried not to let my voice crack.

This could make or break us. Even if she didn't castrate me after tonight, the collision of families could make for a very interesting future. Thank God my mother lived on the other side of the country.

CHAPTER 22
COLLIDING WORLDS

The initial meeting didn't go as badly as Georgia and I thought it would. Everyone was on their best behavior. But then Rosie brought out the wine and everything changed.

"This can't be good," Georgia whispered in my ear after Rosie poured my mother another glass of wine.

"Nope," I said in a clipped tone.

She'd never been a drinker, but now that she was on her third glass of wine, things would get interesting. "I think the kids should get married in California."

Mr. Phillips spat out his wine, spraying the coffee table. "Married?" he asked in a strangled voice.

"They're getting married," Mom replied, waving her hands at us violently.

"News to me," he lied.

I'd talked to him last week and asked for Georgia's hand in marriage. I thought she'd like that I went the old-school route and got his permission. I'd marry her anyway, but I figured I'd earn a brownie point or two.

Georgia squeezed my knee, digging her fingernails into my jeans so hard I could feel their pinch. "Uh-oh," she mumbled.

I patted her hand. "We will not," I said. "First, we're not even engaged. And second, we live in Florida. We'd get married here if anywhere, Mom."

"Why aren't you engaged?" Mrs. Phillips asked, giving me the stink eye as her eyes crossed slightly.

Two half-drunk moms did not equal fun.

"When we're ready," Georgia told them, digging her fingernails in farther.

"He's getting old. He needs babies. You get married." Mom's short sentences were thick with her Chinese accent.

"He is kinda old," Mr. Phillips chimed in.

I took a deep breath, wishing I could escape. "I'm not old."

"You need to get working on my grandchildren." Mrs. Phillips pointed her finger at me.

"Not before marriage, of course," Mr. Phillips added.

"Oh, please. She was in his bed this morning."

"She was?" Mr. Phillips asked with a red face.

"She was. Their clothes were in the living room," Mom added, thinking she was the funniest person in the world as she laughed.

I grimaced when she finished. Mr. Phillips looked like he wanted to rip my balls off, and Georgia bowed her head. I didn't think my mom had noticed the clothes behind the couch, but obviously the woman missed nothing.

"Georgia," her father barked, gripping the armrest of his chair so tightly his knuckles were white.

"Daddy."

I squeezed her hand as my stomach flipped. I hated that word.

"She's a good girl, Mr. Phillips," I said, snarling at him. I wouldn't let him make her feel bad for anything we've done.

"She's not like those tramps he's been with before."

Way to go, Mom.

"Oh, my baby is finally a womannn," Mrs. Phillips slurred and poured more wine into her glass.

"Fuck," Mr. Phillips said.

"Oh God, this is so embarrassing," Georgia mumbled into her hands.

"Everyone needs to stop talking. Georgia is a good girl. She's not like any woman I've ever met. What she and I do is our own business. I love her and she'll be my wife. She's mine and always will be. I will not allow you—" I pointed at her father and tried not to yell, "or anyone else to make her feel bad."

Her father sat there, stunned into silence. He sighed before speaking. "You're right. My daughter has the gentlest soul on earth."

I bit my lip because that shit was a complete lie. Georgia had a side to her like a cobra. Get her going and her fangs would come out. Typically, they came in the form of fingernails that dug into my balls like a vise.

Mrs. Phillips threw her husband a challenging look. I was sure Georgia had learned the death claw from someone, and I'd put my money on it being Rosie. "She's a grown woman."

"I still think of her as a little girl. My little girl."

"Let go already," Mrs. Phillips said and sipped her wine. "We'll have grandbabies soon."

"I'm pregnant," Georgia blurted out and laughed.

My heart stopped. "What?" I asked with eyes wider than they'd ever been.

"What?" her father asked, but he leaped from his chair.

"Oh, honey," Mrs. Phillips said, smacking herself in the face.

Georgia's dark eyes sparkled with mischief. "Kidding!" She laughed. "See, now sleeping with him doesn't seem as bad as a baby out of wedlock."

"You about gave me a heart attack," I said, gripping my chest as I felt my heart begin to beat again.

She nudged my shoulder, almost knocking me over. "Come on. That shit was funny."

"Like hell it was."

"Georgia, you are not funny," Mr. Phillips said as the color returned to his face.

She let out the sweetest laugh I'd ever heard. "You know I am, Dad. Lighten up. Life's short."

"Another bottle of wine?" Mrs. Phillips asked.

"No," I answered quickly. "I have to work tomorrow. We better get going." I glanced down at my watch and noticed it was after nine.

"Me too," Georgia added before standing.

My mother turned the wineglass in her hands. "It's not a real job."

I pinched the bridge of my nose, ready for an argument.

"I wanted him to be a lawyer. It's a noble profession, but noooo," she said, drawing out the word. "He had to join the military, and now he's a private dick."

Mr. Phillips choked on his wine and glanced at me.

"Mom, this isn't the place to talk about your disappointment in me." I took the glass from her hands.

After Mr. Phillips cleared his throat, he leaned forward in his chair. "I think it's damn noble that he served in the military and became a SEAL, Mrs. Jones."

I could've caught flies with the way my mouth hung open. Shock flooded me that Mr. Phillips had actually stuck up for me to my mother.

"All that training he went through. He could still be in the military and be retiring soon," Mom whined before rising.

When I entered the Navy, I didn't hear the end of it. She constantly complained about my decision, reminding me that she'd always planned for me to be a lawyer. Now that I had left, she wished I'd stayed. I could never win with the woman, and this was another prime example.

"If he'd stayed, he wouldn't have met our baby," Mrs. Phillips said, rising from the couch before giving Georgia a hug. "We've never seen her so happy."

Georgia smiled at me as her mother squished the life out of her. I smiled back, glancing at Mr. Phillips, who actually had a smile on his face.

Mom stood and looked me up and down with unfocused eyes. "True, but he wouldn't have been with those whores."

"Mom," I said, moving toward her to herd her toward the door. I glanced at Georgia and pleaded with her to leave using nothing but my eyes.

"We better go. I think Mrs. Jones has to be exhausted," Georgia said before kissing her parents.

"Thanks for dinner," I called over my shoulder, pushing my mother toward the door.

"I need to say goodbye," Mom complained, digging the heels of her feet into the carpet.

"Oh, you've said enough, Mom."

Moving quickly, she ducked my arms and walked behind me, making a beeline for Georgia's parents. "Thank you for everything," she said and held out her hand to Mrs. Phillips. "I can't wait to see you at the wedding."

Mrs. Phillips grabbed my mother and hugged her. I wanted to laugh, but I didn't. Mom wasn't the most affectionate person in the world, and I blamed it mostly on her heritage, but Mrs. Phillips was the complete opposite.

"You can bet your ass on it," Mrs. Phillips told Mom when she released her.

"You're welcome," Mr. Phillips said and shook her hand instead of hugging her as his wife had.

"Thanks," I said as I held out my hand.

He glanced down and placed his hand in mine. "You're welcome, kid." He winked.

Ever since we'd had "the talk" when I asked for Georgia's hand in marriage, we'd come to a mutual understanding. He dropped his dick routine and treated me as an equal. It was either because of that or because of the way I handled the asshole who ran Georgia off the road, but things between us had shifted.

Georgia walked toward the door with my mom next to her and me following close behind. "Night."

Once outside, Mom walked in front of us down the long drive toward the car.

"We survived," Georgia said, lacing her arm with mine.

"Barely," I grumbled.

"Could've been worse."

"How?"

Mom leaned against the car and yawned. "How far away does Georgia live? I'm tired and don't want to drive far to drop her off."

I peered down at Georgia and laughed. "She's not going home, Mom. She's staying the night with me."

"But I'm staying the night," she said with wide eyes.

"You're in the guest room."

"You better take me home," Georgia whispered, since we were within earshot.

"Nonsense," I whispered back and looked at my mom. "She's staying in my bed."

My mother's mouth twisted, but she didn't say anything. I opened her door and she climbed in. "Hussy," she murmured as I closed the door.

I closed my eyes. My mother had a sharp tongue and always knew how to horrify and embarrass me. Her behavior had to be stopped. I wouldn't let her decide who shared my bed with me.

Georgia began to laugh.

I opened my eyes and stared at her. "What's so funny?" I asked and sighed.

"Thank fuck she lives on the other side of the country," Georgia said through her laughter.

"That shit ain't no lie." I laughed too before I kissed her, holding her in my arms until my mom began to knock on the window.

"We going?" she yelled inside and continued to knock on the glass.

"We better go," Georgia murmured against my lips. "We have a long night ahead of us."

I shook my head and grinned. "She's had so much wine, she'll be out as soon as her head hits the pillow."

"It's still going to suck." Georgia glanced over her shoulder at my mom, who hadn't let up.

"Babe, tonight you're going to learn about how fantastic sex can be when there's a risk you might get caught."

"Oh, no. We can't." Her eyes grew wide.

"Oh, yes, we will."

"Fuck," she said.

"I plan to," I said, and I chuckled before opening her door.

She climbed in silently and stared straight ahead. I'd planted the seed and given her something to think about. Tonight, whether my mom was there or not, I needed to be inside her.

Mrs. Jones had cock-blocked enough pussy in my time, but tonight wouldn't be another opportunity for her.

CHAPTER 23

CAUGHT

When I walked into work on Monday, I had the biggest damn smile on my face. Just like I thought, Mom passed out, and Georgia and I fucked until we both collapsed from exhaustion. Thankfully, when we left for work, my mother was still fast asleep. I left her a note and told her to call me when she woke up.

Through the entire Monday morning meeting, I could still smell Georgia on my skin. The smell of her sweet perfume had memories of last night playing over in my head and helped the minutes tick by.

I decided one thing during the meeting. With all the talk of marriage, I planned to wait on popping the question. I wanted it to be a surprise, and right now, it would feel too convoluted and like people had forced my hand.

I'd pick the time and place. Georgia wouldn't have a clue when it would happen.

After the meeting, I retreated to my office to make a ton of phone calls I'd saved until today. Calling back clients to inform them of the progress I'd made in their case and to tell others I had everything they needed and they should stop in during the week to meet with me about the details.

I'd been so consumed with my work and thoughts of Georgia that I hadn't realized it was well after one in the afternoon.

"I'm here." Georgia walked into my office.

I jumped from my chair and headed straight toward her. "You're early." I wrapped her in my arms.

"It's the last week of work, and I just had to tie up some loose ends. We get out early all this week."

I buried my face in her hair and smelled the scent I'd enjoyed all morning. "I thought I'd take you to lunch if you haven't had it already," she said and rested her head on my chest.

Placing my fingers under her chin, I tipped her head back and forced her eyes to mine. "There's only one thing I want, and it's not lunch."

She blushed and her eyes slid sideways. "Here?" she whispered.

I motioned toward the desk with my head. "There."

"But it's your work."

I smirked and put my mouth over hers. She kissed me back, dipping her tongue inside my mouth long enough for me to taste her. "No one is here. They're all at lunch for another half hour."

"But—"

I put my finger against her lips and quieted her. "I've never done it in here."

"Well…" She swallowed hard.

"Stop thinking." I brushed my hardened dick against her. "I want you."

She stood on her tiptoes and snaked her arms around my neck. Before she could protest, I captured her lips with mine. Picking her up in my arms, I walked toward the desk before setting her on top.

With my lips still on hers, I pushed her dress up her thighs. Placing my hand between us, I brushed my fingers against her pussy and found her dripping wet.

She liked the idea. Maybe it had been the night before that sold her on the idea of being caught, but it always heightened the pleasure. Georgia was like an unexplored book, and I planned to turn the pages chapter by chapter and give her every experience possible.

Her hands undid my buttons before she quickly lowered the

zipper. With her mouth still on mine, she palmed my cock and stroked it. I flinched and moaned from the contact and warmth that her hand provided.

I needed more. Wanted it more than anything.

I rested my forehead against hers and steadied my breath. "Put my dick in you," I told her.

She peered down at my cock. "There's something so damn sexy about seeing my hand on your dick."

"You can look later," I told her, grinding my teeth. "Right now, I want to fuck you."

"Yes, sir." She pulled me toward her with my own dick.

She rubbed my dick through her wetness, taking her time and moving it up and down. Each time it slid over her clit, her eyes would roll back slightly.

"You're killing me," I whispered, grabbing a condom, and sliding it over my granite dick.

"Pussy," she murmured.

"I want it, yes. Fuck me, Georgia."

She placed the head of my hardened cock against her opening. Unable to wait any longer, I pushed inside her and felt my legs tremble.

Her head tipped back, and I took the opportunity to kiss and bite her neck as I fucked her. My strokes quickened and I dove deeper with each thrust.

"Yes!" she whisper-yelled and bit her lip to quiet her moans.

I placed my hands behind her and tipped her back on the desk. Hammering into her, I closed my eyes and buried my face between her fantastic tits.

The door opened. "Yo!" Bear yelled. "Holy fuck!"

Georgia jumped into my arms and shrieked.

I froze, leaving my cock inside her. "Out!" I yelled without turning around.

"Nice ass, man." Bear laughed. "Can I watch?"

"Get the fuck out!"

"No, really. I can just sit here. Pretend I'm not in the room."

"Excuse me." I heard my mother's voice.

Georgia's eyes were the biggest I'd ever seen as I looked down at her.

"Oh my God!" my mother yelled, and she must've seen my bare ass on full display.

"Please let me die," Georgia whispered and slammed her head into the desk repeatedly.

"Everyone get out of my office!"

"Oh my God!" Mom repeated in the same shocked voice.

"Want to watch?" Bear asked her, not knowing she was my mother.

"What's wrong with you?" Mom asked Bear, and I heard a slap.

"Nothing," he mumbled.

"Everyone, get the fuck out!" I roared.

As the door closed, I heard her say, "Hussy."

"Fuck me," Georgia said and hit her head one final time before closing her eyes.

"That's what got us into this mess," I told her before sticking my face between her breasts as my dick slid out of her.

She started to laugh until she broke out into hysterical giggles. Her body shook underneath me.

"Glad you find this funny," I mumbled into her cleavage before standing straight up and looking down at her.

"Your mom thinks I'm a total slut." She laughed again, holding her stomach.

"If she only knew," I whispered before pulling off the condom, tossing it in the trash, and zipping up my pants.

Georgia sat up, grabbing the edge of the desk, and kicked her feet back and forth. "Hey. I know what it's like to get caught now." She bit her lip.

"Fuckin' great."

I helped her off the desk, and she smoothed her dress before I opened the door.

"Mom, what are you doing here?" I asked as I walked into the hallway.

She pushed off the wall and walked toward me quickly. "What kind of people do you work with?" she asked and glared at me. "I thought I could take you to lunch." She poked me in the chest. "But I can see you're busy."

"Hey." I grabbed her sharp little digit. "I'm not too busy. Georgia stopped by to take me to lunch too. We can all go."

"I don't know," Mom said and pulled her finger from my light grip.

"I want to talk to you in the conference room, and then the three of us will go eat." I ushered her toward the room.

"Want me to keep Georgia company, bro?" Bear yelled down the hallway.

"No!" I shouted before closing the door. "Sit," I demanded and pointed at the chair.

My mother held her purse against her legs as she sat down slowly. "What?" she asked with a sour look on her face.

"We have a few things we have to get straight about Georgia."

I pulled a chair in front of her and sat down. "You don't know anything about Georgia, Mom. She's not a hussy like the other women I've been with."

"She's not?" She tilted her head, calling bullshit without saying it.

"She was a virgin when I met her, Mom."

Her mouth dropped open, and she looked like a goldfish trying to find oxygen.

"So stop treating her like a common whore. She's a good girl."

She leaned forward and whispered, "She was a virgin?"

"Yes."

I heard a loud thud at the door. "Lucky bastard," Bear said. If I weren't having a talk with my mother, I'd laugh.

"Be nice to her. I'm going to marry her, and she's going to be the mother of your grandchildren."

She straightened her back and smiled. "You finally found someone worthy of the title."

"Title?" I asked and scrunched my nose.

She pinched my cheeks, and I didn't think I'd ever seen her so happy. "Yes, the next Mrs. Jones."

"Promise to be nice?"

She nodded vigorously. "I will be on my best behavior."

"Why do I not believe you?" I mumbled when her hands dropped from my face, leaving a tingle where she'd pinched.

"Let's go to lunch and celebrate." She popped up from the chair.

"Celebrate?" I asked before pushing myself up.

"I convinced your father that we needed to move here to be closer to our grandbabies."

My knees grew weak at her words. No. No. She couldn't move here. There was only so much Mom I could take. I had hit maximum overload after only one day.

"But you love California," I said in a weak voice, still in shock with my heart fluttering wildly in my chest.

"But I love my son more—and the babies Georgia is going to give me. Now, let's go celebrate." She patted me on the chest before leaving me in the conference room.

I watched as she walked down the hallway and into my office. I couldn't move. I didn't think anything in my life had me as on edge or in as much of a panic as knowing my parents were going to live nearby. I'd moved to the opposite side of the country for a reason.

Georgia walked out of the office and turned to face me. My mother was at her side. Georgia caught one glance at me and broke out into laughter.

"Fuck," I said before taking off toward the two women in my life.

Six months ago, I never would've guessed that things would change as much and as quickly as they had. If the price I had to pay for having Georgia in my life was my parents, I'd deal. Maybe I could get them to live on the other coast of the state.

"Keep laughing," I said when I took her hand in mine.

We followed my mother down the hallway toward the front doors. "See, it could get worse," she whispered.

"How?" I asked and shook my head.

When we climbed in the car, my mother leaned forward from the backseat and stuck her head in between us. "Oh, Frisco. You know that house for sale next door to you?"

I grimaced and paled. She wouldn't. Georgia laughed so hard, tears began to stream from her eyes.

"Your father put in an offer this morning."

Yep, shit could get worse.

CHAPTER 24
THREE MONTHS LATER

A week after my parents moved to town and I'd hit my limit of family time, I took Georgia on a surprise cruise. We'd spend six days and five nights cut off from the entire world, but mainly from the four people who made us the craziest.

I booked us the biggest suite I could. It had a Jacuzzi tub, huge living room, and a private deck. I wouldn't skimp. This would be the trip where I'd ask Georgia to marry me. I'd waited, much to the dismay of her parents and mine, but fuck them. This was for us.

When we docked in Jamaica, we spent the morning at a private resort and basked in the sun. Halfway through the day, raindrops began to fall and we headed to town to shop and dodge the water. Her eyes twinkled every time she passed a diamond ring, but nothing she saw compared to the one I had in the safe in the room.

I'd chosen Grand Cayman as the place I'd get down on one knee and ask her to be mine forever. But much to my dismay, we couldn't get off the boat and head ashore. A huge front had settled over the island.

That left Cozumel, and I didn't want that to be the thing she remembered about our engagement. It was too touristy and lacked the private place I had originally selected in Grand Cayman.

We stood on the balcony, watching the waves crash against the boat, and gazing at the shore. "I'm going to schedule you a massage," I told her.

"That sounds fantastic." She laid her head on my shoulder. "Why don't you come?"

I pulled her closer and kissed her hair. "You go and enjoy. I'm going to read," I lied. "Let me go inside and see if they have an appointment."

She nodded and I walked into the room and placed a call. I had a plan. A new one and maybe a better one, but I needed a couple of hours to make it happen. I ordered her the works—massage, pedicure, manicure, and whatever else the lady recommended.

After walking her to the spa, I headed straight to the onboard florist. I bought every red rose they had available and the flameless candles they sold.

I spoke with our room attendant and made him part of the plan. While we were at dinner, he was to cover the bed and floor with rose petals and have a bottle of the best champagne chilling in the room. When she and I were alone after dinner, I'd pop the question. I made reservations at the steakhouse on board and asked for an ocean-view table. Tonight I wanted no detail left overlooked.

I slipped the ring into my pocket while she dressed. She raved the entire time about how amazing and relaxed she felt after her hours at the spa. Whereas I felt butterflies doing somersaults in my stomach. I didn't have any doubt that she'd say yes, but damn, it was still such a scary thing.

The last time I'd popped the question I didn't feel this nervous. Jeanine forced it out of me, would be a more accurate way of describing it. She crushed my dreams the day I caught her with her legs spread and another man between them.

I glanced at Georgia while she finished applying her red lipstick and took a deep breath. She was nothing like Jeanine and would never do to me what *she* had done. Georgia was everything I ever wanted and more. She was my equal and wise beyond her years.

"You ready?" I asked and smoothed out my tie, giving myself one final look in the mirror.

"Ready." She walked out of the bathroom looking more beautiful than I think I'd ever seen her. "What's wrong?" she asked and placed her hand on my chest, right over my heart.

"Nothing, babe."

"Your heart is beating kind of crazy. Are you feeling sick?" She moved her hand to my forehead.

I shook it away and pulled her into my arms. "My heart is beating for you. I still lose my breath every time I see you. I can't believe you're mine, Georgia." I nuzzled her neck and kissed the delicate skin where her pulse beat.

"You are a lucky man." She laughed and dug her hands into my hair. "Let's stay in tonight." She held her face against her neck. "I'd prefer to have dinner naked."

"But you took so much time to get ready." I'd rather stay in our room and make love all night, but I already had everything planned.

"True," she whispered and released my hair. "We'll make it quick. We'll have dessert when we get back."

"Perfect."

I'd be lying if I said I remembered a thing that happened as we ate. I couldn't recall a single word. The only thing I knew was how she looked. It would be forever burned in my mind. Her smile. The way her cheeks rose when she laughed. The sparkle in her eyes when she said something wicked. Her innocence.

By the time we walked back to the room, I could feel my body shaking. It wasn't that I feared she'd say no, but I'd just never thought I'd get down on one knee again.

"Thanks for tonight," she said before slipping the keycard into the door.

"Anything for you, babe." I coughed, hearing the quiver in my voice.

She looked at me as she opened the door. "Are you okay?"

"Couldn't be better," I replied honestly and slipped my hand in my pocket.

She walked two steps into the room and gasped. "Oh my God," she whispered and brought her hand to her mouth.

I walked around her, noticing the tears in her eyes before I dropped down on one knee before her. "Georgia," I said, holding the ring between my two fingers and inhaling. "I don't know when I fell in love with you, but I've fallen deeper and harder for you than anyone else in my life. You've become my world. I can't imagine a day without you at my side, an hour without your smile, a minute without hearing your laugh, and a second without you in my life."

She opened her mouth and I shook my head.

"I will spend my life protecting you and being worthy of being yours. I've never wanted anything as badly as I want you to be mine. Walking through life together hand in hand and waking up with you next to me each morning makes my life so much sweeter than I ever thought possible."

I inhaled deeply, trying to catch my breath as my heart pounded and my palms began to sweat.

"You're kind of babbling, love," she said with a giggle.

"Quiet, woman. What I'm trying to say is, will you be my Felicia?"

Tears began to stream down her cheeks and her lip quivered. For a moment, my heart stopped until she screamed, "Yes!"

I leaped from my knee and lifted her into my arms, spinning us around in a circle. "You made me so damn happy," I whispered in her ear, and I felt my eyes begin to water.

"I love you." She held my face in her hands and peppered me with kisses. "I thought you'd never ask."

I laughed, loving the feel of her hands on me, along with her lips. Our chests touched and our hearts beat together, quick and erratic. "I wanted to make it perfect."

"I don't need perfect." She backed away from my face. "I just need you."

I sealed my mouth over hers and carried her to the bed. I needed to make love to her. I set her down on the edge, kneeling before her, and beginning to help her undress. Taking my time, I slipped off her heels and began to ease her from her dress.

"Wait." She grabbed my hands. "I want us to undress each other."

She leaned back on the bed and stared at me while I undressed. "I don't think I'll ever get bored staring at you," she said before licking her lips.

Gripping my already hardened dick in my hands, I pulled on the shaft and moaned. I tipped my head back and let my mouth fall open. "You just want to stare?" I asked, dragging my hand up slowly, and toying with the tip of my cock.

"There's nothing sexier than watching a man as he touches himself," she whispered.

My head snapped forward and my hand stilled. "You don't want to feel me inside you?"

"No," she said, waving her hand in front of her jiggling tits. "You seem into it, and I'm fine just watching."

I stalked forward with my dick in my hand and stopped inches from her face. "You don't want to touch it?"

The corners of her mouth turned up, and I could see a small bit of her white teeth behind her smudged red lipstick. "Let me watch how you touch yourself, and maybe, if you're good, I'll touch it."

I gripped the shaft a little harder, pumping my dick in my hand. "You got that all wrong. If you're worthy, I'll fuck you."

"Worthy?" She sat up. Her mouth came so close to the head of my cock I could feel her hot breath caressing the tip. "Two can play at that game."

She licked the tip of my cock and my entire body lurched forward, trying to get more. "Damn," I said, ready to beg for her mouth.

She laughed and lay back on the bed, spreading her legs. Her eyes never left mine as her fingers glided down her stomach and stopped just above her mound. She closed her eyes, letting her hands dip lower before she moaned.

My lips parted and my breath vanished at the sight of her spread-eagled, legs hanging over the edge of the bed, as she touched herself. The light from the sunset streaming through the window glistened off her already drenched pussy. My mouth watered and my cock stiffened even more in my hand.

Her eyes opened and she glanced at my face before her gaze dropped to my dick, becoming mesmerized. We watched each other, driving ourselves closer to the edge. Her fingertips circled her clit, pinching it lightly before she slid them down and slipped them inside her pussy.

I closed my eyes, unable to take the visual. No matter how hard or fast I stroked my dick, it wouldn't match the feel of her cunt wrapped around my shaft.

"Frisco," she moaned.

I couldn't take it any longer. Jacking off just wasn't going to cut it. I needed to be inside her. Everything in me wanted to crawl in as deep as possible and never leave.

Before she opened her eyes, with her fingers still buried deep inside herself, I positioned myself between her legs. I nudged her legs apart gently with my knees.

"What are you doing?" she asked, thrusting her fingers inside.

"I'm taking what's mine," I told her as I bent down, pulled her hand away from her pussy, and placed her fingers in my mouth. Her eyes rolled back before closing. I licked every ounce of her wetness from her fingers before I slipped the condom on my shaft.

I stroked her clit with the tip of my cock. Her hips lifted from the bed as her back arched. "Don't tease me."

"Fuck, what were you doing?" I laughed, letting my hardness poke her opening, coating it in her wetness.

Slowly I pushed inside her, inch by inch, making her feel all of me and reminding her whom she belonged to. She'd asked me to be hers, wanted more than I had been willing to give, but I'd given in. I met my match the day she walked into my life, and I wasn't about to let anyone else have her.

Her warmth surrounded me, sending tiny shock waves through my system.

I leaned over, taking her lips as I let her body adjust to my length. "Do you feel me?" I murmured against her lips.

"I do," she replied with her body trembling.

"You're mine, Georgia." I began to pull out and heard her whimper. "Mine." I pushed back in, with more force this time.

Toying with her nipples, I felt her pussy clamp down against my dick, wanting more than I'd given. "Tell me you want this."

"I want this," she moaned.

I pulled my dick out and slammed back into her. "Tell me you want me."

"I want you!" she cried out. Her hands dropped to the sheets and fisted them in her palms.

"Tell me you're mine!" I growled and thrust into her again.

"I'm yours!" she yelled when her head pushed deeper into the mattress.

Reaching between us, I swept my fingertip across her clit. "Tell me to fuck you."

Her eyes shot open and she glared at me. "You're going to make me beg."

"I want to know you want this."

"Fuck me, Frisco. Make me know I'm yours," she whispered as she stared up at me.

I pulled out and drove my cock so deep inside her, I was sure I bruised her insides. She cried out and her knuckles turned white as she gripped the sheets a little harder.

"You're fuckin' mine," I roared as I pummeled her, licking her inside with my dick. "No one can take you from me."

Her head thrashed back and forth against the sheets. Feeling the slow sizzling of my passion turn into something more, my spine tingled and my body began to quake. I gripped her thighs and tried to stave off the orgasm that threatened to rip free at any moment.

My finger found her clit and began to circle in the same pattern she'd done to herself earlier. With each pass of my fingertips, her pussy clamped down against my length.

"Come for me, Georgia. I want to feel you as you come on my cock." I gave her clit a light pinch.

Her body began to tremble and a light sheen of perspiration coated her flesh. "Oh, God."

I increased the speed and pressure just enough to tip her over as I battered her pussy with my dick.

"Yes!" she cried out.

"That's it, babe." I changed the motion of my fingers, using a back-and-forth motion as fast as my hand could move. Within seconds, she was screaming unrecognizable words and her body shuddered.

When her cunt squeezed my dick, I followed her over the edge. The orgasm that ripped through my body was so intense that my knees weakened, but I remained upright and thrust into her until she milked my cock dry.

She sucked in air, gasping for breath, and I followed suit. My entire body felt satiated and weak. I leaned forward on trembling arms and kissed her lips.

"Being yours has its perks." She laughed against my mouth.

"As long as you're mine, I'll always protect you and love you like you deserve," I murmured against her lips.

Everything I loved about her would be with me forever. Even on my deathbed, when our bodies would be riddled with wrinkles, I'd think back to this night and the woman I fell in love with.

The one who made me weak in the knees with a simple glance and the one who stole my breath every time she walked into the room. I'd live my life with no regrets and love her as she deserved for eternity.

She was mine and only mine. Tonight and for the rest of my life, I'd do everything in my power to earn that honor.

EPILOGUE

Six months later

As I stood at the altar, waiting for Georgia, I looked out into the crowd. Years ago when I moved to Florida for college, I didn't have anyone. But today, I had enough that I could fill an entire church.

Although I would have said that my life was full before I met her, I didn't really start living until I made her mine. She brought the smile to my face each morning, gave me a reason to come home at night, and always made me feel loved.

My parents sat in the front row and stared at me. My father sat up straight, beaming from ear to ear, and looked prouder of me than at any other moment I could ever remember. And Mom. What could I say about her? I could almost see the corner of her mouth turned up, but she wouldn't give me that satisfaction. It wasn't her way. It never had been.

Behind me along the altar were my groomsmen. Using that term wasn't entirely accurate. Each of them had played an important role in my life. They were my family. The only one I'd had for so many years. City, Bear, Morgan, Thomas, James, Tank, and, last but not least, Flash rounded out the group.

City was my best man, much to the dismay of Bear. I had to explain to him that City and Sunshine were the reason we were getting married in the first place. That alone earned him the right to be my best man. Bear stomped around for a little bit, but eventually gave in, though not before being a dick for a little while.

I wiped the sweat from my brow and tried to steady my breathing. Shaking my hands out, I exhaled slowly and emptied my body of all air. I rolled my neck and inhaled before closing my eyes for a moment.

I could do this.

There hadn't been a day that I'd rethought my proposal or regretted meeting Georgia. She was mine. She was everything I had wanted but tried to avoid. I wouldn't change a moment of my life.

It brought me to her.

All the heartache and the loneliness put me on a collision course with her. Without Jeanine cheating on me, even though I'd never forgive her, I would never have met my girl.

When the music began to play and the doors in the back of the church opened, my heart started to pound faster and beat with such ferocity I thought it would burst out of my chest. It was finally happening. I was getting married. Georgia was mine…forever.

I squeezed my hands into tight balls as I tried to see behind the line of bridesmaids and catch a glimpse of her, but she remained hidden. I pulled at my tie, trying to cool myself off.

Be calm. I just needed to stay calm.

Fuck. I didn't think I would be so nervous. I wanted this. I was sure of it. There was nothing that made me question standing here waiting for my future wife to come to me—to say yes and be my forever.

City rested his hand on my shoulder and gave me a firm squeeze. "It's normal, man. Just breathe," he said softly in my ear. I nodded and kept my gaze fixed on the back of the church.

Gigi walked down the aisle in the cutest pink dress, throwing pink rose pedals with such determination to every toss. The wedding guests all giggled and smiled at the cuteness, and Gigi, being Gigi, ate it up. She was a ham and totally her parents' kid.

One by one, the women walked toward me, and I strained to catch the smallest glimpse of my girl behind them, feeling my heart beat a little faster with each passing second.

Until I saw her.

Georgia.

I sucked in a breath, stunned by her beauty. "Jesus," I whispered. *Why was I such a lucky son of a bitch?*

Her hair was half up, with dark curls cascading over her shoulders and framing her breasts. She'd muted her makeup so that it almost looked like she hadn't applied any. I always told her I loved her natural beauty, and today, at our wedding, I fell in love with her a little more than I had been the day before.

As she walked down the aisle, the long, lace train of her dress flowed over the floor with each step. The dress had a plunging, deep V neckline, but not enough to show a ton of breast—stunningly sexy and beautiful how it draped her body.

Our eyes were locked as she walked toward me. I couldn't drag mine away from hers. It had sunk in that we were getting married, but the enormity and finality of the situation suddenly hit me like a ton of bricks.

A calmness came over me that I'd never felt before. This was what I wanted. She was who I wanted and nothing else in the world would ever change that.

In the beginning, I'd thought she was too young and had too much life to live to be with me. But I'd never been so wrong about anyone in my entire life. Thankfully, our friends didn't allow me to walk away. They pushed and pushed until I didn't have any choice but to admit I had feelings for her.

Somehow, I put aside my bullheaded, asshole thinking long enough to realize that the best thing to ever happen to me was right in front of my eyes. Actually, it was the cocksucker that ran her off the road. That single event changed everything.

"Breathe," she whispered as she took my hand and walked up the altar steps.

I didn't know I'd been holding my breath the entire time she walked toward me. I couldn't stop replaying our time together, what brought us together, and how solid our relationship had become.

When she reached the final step, I kissed her cheek. "You look so beautiful I couldn't help but hold my breath. I thought that somehow I had been dreaming this moment, and that if I even blinked, it would all disappear," I whispered into her ear before righting myself after the priest coughed.

She mouthed "I love you" before we both turned and took our places in front of the priest.

I couldn't even pay attention as the priest spoke. I had no idea what he said, nor did it matter. I knew what the words meant, but the thing I focused on the entire time was the girl by my side and the vows I'd written to explain my love to her.

My knees shook as we stood, ready to say the words that expressed our love to each other. I grasped her hands in mine and slowly stroked the backs of her hands with my thumbs.

I was given the cue to begin my vows and I stared into her eyes.

"Georgia, today I devote my heart, body, and soul to you. Before you came into my life, I was a shell of a man, searching for a purpose. You are my reason to live, to breathe, and to be the best man I can be. You make me want to be worthy of your love. I will spend my entire life showing you how much you mean to me. The day my eyes locked with yours, I knew I wanted you, but I thought it would be too selfish to cage a free spirit so young. I was wrong. Love doesn't stop someone from being who they were meant to be, it only makes them a better version of their former selves. I will love you even after I take my last breath. Today, tomorrow, and for the rest of eternity, I will be yours."

Her eyes had filled with tears as I spoke, but they hadn't fallen. She hadn't even blinked during my words, just stared back at me with her lips parted and barely breathing.

I swallowed hard and inhaled. I'd rattled off the words, everything that I'd felt, without taking a deep breath.

After a short pause, she wiped her eyes and began to speak. "Frisco, when we first met, I thought you didn't like me, but that didn't stop our friends from pushing us together. The more time I spent with you, the more I liked you. I realized that you'd closed your heart and were scared of anything that resembled a relationship. Slowly, I gained your trust, and eventually, your heart. But the thing you don't realize is that I knew, from the moment I kissed you, you'd be mine forever." She paused and inhaled quickly before starting again. "You're the first man to make me feel completely loved for who I am. I will never forget the day you saved my life. Not just by pulling me from my car, but the day you asked me to be yours forever. Not only had you given up on love, but I had too. No longer will I be a poorer version of Miss Havisham—spending my entire life alone. No, Frisco, our love is like those in the greatest love stories told throughout history. But our whole story has yet to be written. I will, from now through all eternity, be yours and only yours." She took another breath and smiled. "Until the sun no longer shines in the sky and the world as we know it no longer exists, I will always be your Felicia."

I squeezed her hands and began to laugh. That was the reason I loved her the most—the way she could take a serious situation and make me feel so much joy that I thought I could die from happiness.

"By the powers vested in me, I now pronounce you husband and wife." The priest nodded to us, but we were too busy gazing into each other's eyes to even remember that we were supposed to turn toward the crowd. "You may now kiss your wife," he whispered.

I wrapped my arms around her back, drawing her flush against me, and kissed her. Not the same way I had yesterday, but as the man who now owned her heart. Forever.

Love doesn't make the world go 'round.
Love is what makes the ride worthwhile.
~ Franklin P. Jones

WICKED IMPULSE

ALFA INVESTIGATIONS BOOK THREE

WALL STREET JOURNAL & USA TODAY BESTSELLING AUTHOR

CHELLE BLISS

CHAPTER 1
BEAR

I fucked up.

It was a fact I could never deny.

My life had been a never-ending string of bad decisions and complications. Molly was just the latest—but not the greatest by any means.

The only thing I did right was marry the love of my life, Jackie. She was the most beautiful thing in the world and sweeter than any honey a bee could make.

When we found out we were going to have our second baby, we were over the moon excited. That was where my fucked-up journey began. Jackie didn't make it through childbirth; she hemorrhaged, and the doctors couldn't stop the bleeding.

Losing her altered me forever.

Not only was she taken from me too soon, I had a newborn baby boy to raise, along with a one-year-old daughter. I knew a little about kids, having two younger sisters, but I wasn't ready to do it alone.

Most of their life I was absent, in and out of jail for petty charges—things like stealing cars and being in possession of stolen property. My crimes never hurt anyone, except for my kids. They paid the price by not having me around and being left in the hands of my sisters.

It took me years to clean up my act.

Hell, decades, if I was being honest. Eventually, I pulled my head out of my ass and surrounded myself with true friends. City, Tank, and Frisco became my family, pulling me off the path of self-destruction.

If Jackie had made it…everything would've been different. We would've been a family, I would've stayed clean, and I wouldn't have been here with freakin' Molly.

I swatted her hand away when she reached for me. "Molly, doll, I appreciate the pussy, but you know this is nothing more than a simple fuck. Yeah?" I was bent over, pulling on my boots. If I put my ass on the bed, she would try to touch me again—and that shit was not happening. "So let's not make this a habit."

Pulling the sheet over her tits, she glared at me. "Bear," she whispered in a gravelly, smoked-too-long tone.

I cut her off, nipping that shit before she started with her bullshit tears to guilt me into giving her my cock once more. "Nope. I never had planned for anything more than what this was—a dirty, sweaty fuckfest."

"You're a bigger asshole than I thought, Bear." She crouched against the headboard with her arms crossed.

"Babe." I laughed at the stupidity of the situation. "When I said 'Wanna fuck?' I wasn't asking you to be my ol' lady. A fuck is a fuck—cock, cunt, and hopefully an orgasm or two. It doesn't make you mine."

She scooted forward and let the sheet drop from her chest. "I didn't even get one, you bastard," she seethed.

I didn't even bother glancing down at her tits, even though she wanted me to look. "Your greedy cunt latched on to me three times, sweetheart. Don't give me shit that you didn't come. You moaned my name like a bitch in heat every time too."

"Get the fuck out!" she yelled as I yanked the shirt over my head.

Using the palm of my hand, I smoothed down my shirt and smiled. "Thought you'd never ask." I waved on my way out, leaving the door open before I headed down the hallway.

She cursed me something awful, and it sounded like something out of a horror movie, but I kept on walking and paid her no mind.

When I walked outside and the wind blew, I caught a whiff of her cheap perfume mingled with cigarettes and sex. Usually, the stench of my sexual exploits didn't bother me, but for some reason, this time was different.

I'd been thinking a lot about Jackie lately. All the things I'd lost the day she left me. I hadn't opened my heart to anyone since then. People in love surrounded me, and it gutted me—knowing I missed that in my life.

Even though I'd had an ol' lady or two in the last twenty-something years, they didn't compare to Jackie. I was sure I'd never given them a chance, but it was hard for them to overshadow the perfection of my wife in my memories.

My phone beeped as I was about to climb onto my bike.

Tank: Get your dick out of her and come to the Cowboy.

I wanted to go home and wash away her scent, but Tank came before ridding myself of Molly's stench.

Me: On my way—be there in 10.

When he asked for a favor, I didn't question him. If Tank wanted me to drive into hell with him at four a.m., I'd show up to fuck shit up with him in a heartbeat.

WHEN I WALKED through the doors of the Neon Cowboy, Tank was seated at our usual table and surrounded by the crew—Frisco, City, Morgan, Thomas, James, Mike, Anthony, and Sam.

They were deep in conversation from the looks of it, leaning across the table in close formation. I didn't even need to hear a word to know that something major was going on.

"Yo," City called out when I was only a few feet away. "Sit your ass down, we have a lot to talk about."

Joseph "City" Gallo had been the other part of our trio. Tank, City, and I had grown close over the years and become more like brothers than just friends. City was younger by ten years, but he was wise beyond his years. When he flashed his perfectly straight, toothy smile, people responded. It didn't hurt that he had a pretty-boy face either.

I pulled out the chair, turning it backward, and straddling it. "What's up?"

"It's Johnny," Morgan replied with his hand in a tight fist on top of the table. "I'm going to kill him if I ever find him." He slammed his fist down on the table, making all the drinks bounce and come down with a loud clatter. Morgan looked frazzled. His dark brown hair was all over the place and hanging into his eyes.

I'd never liked that prick, Johnny. Since the day I met him at Race's track, there'd just been something about him that seemed off. Race raved about how helpful he was, but I just had a feeling about him. After Race bought the track from him, she hired him to stay on and help her get everything up and running in tip-top shape. He quickly cozied up to Fran, Morgan's mom, and the rest was history.

"He stole fifty thousand from the track's account and disappeared." Tank placed his hand on Morgan's shoulder and gave it a firm squeeze.

I was surprised by his balls but not shocked by the audacity. "When?"

"When he didn't show up at work today, Race knew something was fishy. Then the bank called because some checks she wrote bounced."

"Terrible," I muttered and shook my head. This wasn't the time for an "I told ya so."

"We're working this one off the books," Thomas told me with a raised eyebrow. "I'm sure you have no problem with that."

As the owner of ALFA PI, Thomas was my boss. He was also City's brother and ex-DEA. Thomas was the first person in decades who gave me a chance at real employment. I'd finally felt like I'd found a home with him and the guys.

"None," I said firmly. "But if I find him, I get to beat his ass first."

"He's all yours, buddy," James said before he looked around the table. "We're going to gather information and try to find a few leads, then we'll plan our attack." James, the co-owner of ALFA PI, liked to go rogue—that was what I loved most about these guys. No one wanted to call the cops or pussyfoot around a problem. Johnny was going to wish he had never been born by the time we were through with him.

Thomas leaned back in his chair and crossed his arms in front of his chest. "I know tomorrow is Saturday, but we need everyone at the office and working on this."

I grabbed the pitcher of beer and poured myself a glass. Molly was still lingering in my mouth, and it wasn't pleasant. She was like a bad pill, and her aftertaste was stuck in the back of my throat. "I got nothing else to do."

"I'll be there too," Sam finally piped up in the conversation. "I'm always there when you guys need me."

Sam had changed since I'd first met him. He was still a cocky fucker at times, but I'd learned to deal with it. In the past, there wasn't a day I didn't want to punch him in the face, but he'd grown on me. He'd grown up a lot, and he'd always had our backs. Tough fucker even took a bullet without whining like a little bitch. I even dared to say he'd earned my respect—which wasn't easy to do, especially after you'd already been classified as a shithead.

City glanced at his watch. "I know it's late, but let's be there by noon. We don't want to give this guy too much time to get very far."

"There isn't a place in the world he could hide from us for long, brother," Mike said, rubbing his chin with the biggest smile on his face.

Mike was an interesting character. When he wasn't piercing people, he had spent time in the ring. He'd become a UFC champion before finding the love of his life and retiring. Or as I said…becoming pussy-whipped and quitting.

"How's Fran?"

"She's devastated and pissed off. My mom is downright scary when she's mad. Johnny better hope you find him first and not my mother," Morgan replied and grimaced. "We can't let her get involved. She's going to try, but it's a no-go, fellas."

"Understood," James replied.

"I have no problem telling her to butt out," I said and shrugged. "Want me to handle her?"

Morgan's blue eyes sliced to mine. "You will not *handle* my mother."

I couldn't help but laugh. "Kid, you don't have to worry about me. I'm just sayin' she and I are equals. She'd listen to me."

"Bear," Tank whispered at my side and elbowed me in the ribs.

"What? I'd never touch the woman. Jesus. What the fuck do you guys think I am?"

"Seriously," Morgan said through gritted teeth. "You can never keep your shit in your pants. You're getting nowhere near my mom, Bear. Don't even think about *helping*."

I laughed it off, but I'd be lying if I didn't admit it bothered me a little. Fran was a fine piece of ass, but never had I thought about bangin' her silly. Wait. That was a lie. I did imagine it…more than once. I'd just never act on it.

"I'm a perfect gentleman," I told the table, and they all burst into laughter. "Bros before hoes." I shrugged.

"Dude." Morgan dragged his hand through his already messy hair, and he was struggling to stay in his seat.

I shook my head and set shit straight. "I'm referring to anything with a pussy, my friend. You guys—" I glanced around the table "—always come first."

Morgan continued to mumble under his breath, but he dropped the bullshit. Everyone agreed we'd meet at ALFA PI at noon, and then they slowly disappeared until there was only Tank and me left.

"Another?" I asked and grabbed the pitcher that was almost empty.

"I'm good." He waved me off. "You better watch what you say about Fran around Morgan."

"Come on," I groaned before I topped off my glass. "You know me better than that."

He glared at me when he stood up, hovering over me. "That's exactly what I'm afraid of, Bear. She's off-limits. Got it?"

I threw my hands up in the air and pushed back from the table with the pitcher still in my hand. "Fuckin' A. I'm not tapping that shit, Tank. Get the fuck off my back already."

"I've seen the way you look at her, dumb fuck. You're lucky Morgan hasn't caught on."

I slammed the pitcher against the table and narrowed my eyes. "Shut the fuck up already about this shit. I'm not going to fuck Fran."

"Uh-huh," Tank muttered before he left too.

Fuckers.

I might be an asshole, but I had morals. Didn't I?

CHAPTER 2

BEAR

Thomas tapped a stack of papers against the conference table, peering around the room. "Good, everyone's here. What do we have on Johnny?"

We had been at it for three hours—making phone calls, tracking down leads, monitoring his digital footprint, and any other information we could get our hands on about John McDougal.

"McDougal isn't his real name," Sam spoke first and pushed a sheet of paper toward Thomas. "It's O'Sullivan, and he could be using either name."

"What about his cell phone?" James asked.

"It's been turned off," Morgan told us as he rubbed his temples.

"Have your buddy keep on it in case he turns it back on. We just need a few seconds to find his location," James replied like we were all new to the game.

"Already done," Morgan said.

"Bank accounts?" Thomas asked, raising an eyebrow.

"Empty," I told him.

Thomas tapped his pen against the table and leaned back in the chair. "Can someone interview Fran and see what she knows about

Johnny? She may think a detail isn't important, but it might give us a lead."

Morgan dragged his fingers down his face. "I'll do it."

"I got it," I told him because his mom might not open up as much to him as she would to someone else…someone like me.

Everyone at the table turned to me with weird looks on their faces. "What?"

"You want to do it?" Morgan stared at me with narrowed eyes.

"Well, yeah." I shrugged.

"Why?"

"She may not tell you everything you need to know. Parents don't like to be as open with their kids as they would be with a friend."

He gawked at me. "You're my mom's friend?"

I hid my snarl and talked to cover up my annoyance. "I'm your friend, asshole, and by extension, your mother's too."

"Fine," Thomas interrupted before Morgan could say something else. "Bear will interview Fran."

Morgan's glare didn't leave me as the meeting continued. I ignored the stink-eye he gave me and listened to everything I could about Johnny. He was a slippery motherfucker. He hid in plain sight, underneath our noses, and we were never the wiser. I knew every man around this table felt like me—a complete fool.

"Where's the last place he used his credit card?" Frisco asked, making a new bullet point on his fancy legal pad.

Kids. They wrote stupid shit down or put it in their notes in their fancy-ass cell phones. I only wrote down the most important information.

I was old-school and used my memory with most shit. I didn't have time to flip through pages when I was working a case or trying to track someone down. I swear, technology had dumbed them down about ten pegs in the evolutionary chain.

"Yesterday, just outside of Gainesville," Sam answered.

"Morgan?" James called out.

I glanced out of the corner of my eye and realized he was still staring at me. "Morgan," I said, finally turning to look at him with a serious face.

"What?" Morgan replied, his eyes growing narrower.

"Are you listening or giving Bear the evil eye over there?" James laughed, and I couldn't help but join in.

Morgan's face didn't change. "I think someone else should interview my mom."

Thomas cleared his throat before speaking. "It's already decided. Bear will do it."

"Come on, kid," I said with a smile on my face. "I promise to be a complete gentleman. You're like family to me."

His upper lip snarled, and I was about to say "Down, boy" when his face finally softened a bit. "Fine, Bear. I'm trusting you with this."

I nodded, and guilt gnawed at me because I *did* want Fran. I'd always pictured her naked underneath that tracksuit. She was an enigma to me. I could tell she had a smokin' body, but for some reason, she wanted to hide it like she was a Golden Girl. I didn't know what happened to some women when they matured; they felt the need to hide what they had when they should have been showing it to the world.

"Bear, can you meet with her tonight?" James asked.

"On it," I said as I nodded, trying to hide my excitement. "Let me go call her now." I stood and excused myself, feeling Morgan's eyes on me as I walked out of the room and closed the door quietly.

Instead of calling her from my cell phone, I decided to use the office line so it was more official. I sat for a moment and collected my thoughts before I dialed her number that I had scribbled on a tiny scrap of paper I'd hidden underneath my desk calendar.

It rang twice before Fran picked up. "Hello."

"Hey, Fran." I cleared my throat, suddenly feeling nervous. "It's Bear."

"Hey, hot stuff." Her voice was cheerful under the circumstances. "I thought you were Morgan."

"Sorry to disappoint you, sweetheart."

She giggled softly. "You're never a disappointment, Bear."

"I wanted to know if we could sit down tonight and talk about Johnny."

"That fucker. I have a lot to say. Come by tonight, and I'll cook you dinner."

"Franny, you don't have to do that. It's too much work. Why don't you meet me at the bar for a drink?"

"Nope," she said quickly. "I feel like cooking. It keeps my mind busy. Be here at six."

She hung up the phone before I could answer, and I was left staring at the phone, shocked. It'd been ages since anyone had cooked me a meal. I couldn't show up empty-handed. I knew the guys thought I was an animal, but there was a time when I'd had manners.

I stalked back into the room, keeping my eyes down and away from Morgan as I took my seat. The guys were talking more about Johnny and where his next move would be. There was very little we knew about the man, but I figured in the next twenty-four hours we'd have a clearer picture of who the pissant really was.

"Did you get in touch with Aunt Fran?" Thomas asked from the head of the table.

Fuck. Franny was related to almost everyone at the table and so far off-limits that I might as well not even have a dick. To put a beautiful morsel like that in front of me, dangling her like a piece of meat, and not to allow me to touch her was just plain cruel. "Yeah. I'm meeting her at six to talk about Johnny."

Morgan's eyebrow rose. "At the bar?"

"No." I shook my head while I crossed my arms. "She wanted me to come to her place."

"Uh-huh. Maybe I'll drop by." Morgan mimicked me and crossed his arms.

I turned to face him. "Let's get one thing straight, kid. Your mom isn't going to want to talk in front of you. Keep your ass away."

He leaned forward and invaded my space. "Why wouldn't she talk in front of me? She tells me everything."

"Has she called you to tell you everything she knows?"

His lips twisted. "No."

"That's my point. She's embarrassed she didn't realize he was a lying scumbag. Let me talk with Fran. She'll be more comfortable."

He exhaled loudly before leaning back in his chair. "Fine. Don't get too comfortable."

"Oh, shut up already. We've known each other for years. Have a little trust, will ya?"

"That's the problem, Bear. I know too much about you."

He did too. He'd been around for far too many escapades and antics than I'd like to admit. But Morgan didn't know the real me. No one did. I shut him away a long time ago, putting up a steel fortress around my heart to protect myself. They all saw the wild, careless me but not the real man underneath.

I paid his comment no attention and turned back to the conversation at hand. "Let's go over the information one more time so it's fresh in my head."

After another rundown of the information we had on Johnny, the conference room started to look more like a war room. Phones were ringing off the hook, people were jotting down notes, and we used the whiteboard to draw connections to important leads we needed to follow up on to catch the thieving bastard.

By the time I walked out of the office, I had just enough time to head to the little Italian bakery to grab some dessert. Fran probably worked her ass off on the meal, and it was the least I could do—plus, I wanted to make her smile.

CHAPTER 3
BEAR

I pushed the empty plate away and rubbed my belly. "That was so damn good, Franny. I don't remember the last time I had a meal this great."

She beamed at me with the biggest smile. I couldn't recall when I'd seen her so happy. "I like spoiling you." The woman could cook like any of those fancy-ass chefs on television. She didn't just make a dinner, she made an entire meal. Course after course, she carried out of the kitchen, dishing it out onto my plate before I could protest.

"Spoil me anytime, babe." I caught myself and didn't say anything else because I was already verging on flirting, and Morgan would have my balls.

"Cooking relaxes me, but you know I'm really no good at it. Right? I mean, I'm no Maria."

"Well, you must really be stressed." I glanced around the table filled with dish after dish of different foods. "As for being a good cook, I don't remember the last home-cooked meal I ate, so it tasted delicious."

She burst into a fit of laughter. "No one likes my cooking, not even Morgan. Want a drink?" She stood quickly and headed to the tiny cabinet against the wall. "I need something strong to get through this."

"I'm sorry," I said, feeling guilty about putting her out. "We could do this another time."

"Sit down," she commanded me without a thought. "I want you here. I need to talk about it. Alcohol helps. Want one or not?" Her bossiness was definitely a turn-on.

"Yeah, I'll take a gin and tonic."

Her dark, shoulder-length hair parted as she reached into the cabinet and grabbed three bottles. The tiniest patch of exposed skin on the back of her neck peeked out, and my cock started to stir. *Off-limits, Cujo. Don't even think about it.*

"Ice?" she asked with her back to me.

"Two cubes, please." My eyes traveled down her body, focusing on her ass, and trying to see the outline through the flimsy material of her blue tracksuit. Why couldn't the woman wear jeans like other people? Her outfit did nothing for her body and made it so hard for my imagination to run wild. I couldn't even tell if she had on panties, but in my mind I pictured her without.

She set the drink down in front of me and caught me off guard. "Are you feeling okay? You look flushed."

I chuckled softly and hoped she hadn't caught me staring at her ass. "I'm fine. Just a bit warm," I lied my ass off.

"Want me to turn on the air?" she asked and started to move her track jacket away from her skin. "It is a bit warm in here." She stood quickly, removing her jacket, and placing it on the chair before heading to the hallway.

My eyes zoomed in on her chest instantly. The white T-shirt was partially see-through, and all I could focus on was the outline of her black lace bra. *Why did it have to be black?* It didn't match the tracksuit. I highly doubted that the ladies in the *Golden Girls* wore black lingerie underneath their clothing.

"You should feel better soon. I turned it down a bit." She sat, moving the umbrella around in her pink drink. "Sex on the Beach," she said innocently.

I started to choke on my drink at the mention. "What?" I asked in a strangled voice.

"My drink. It's a Sex on the Beach."

My mouth formed an "O" before I started to cough again. All of a sudden, I pictured Fran running around in the sand with beads of water dripping off her while she was clad in a string bikini. *What the fuck was wrong with me?*

"Where do you want to start?" she asked before bringing the drink to her lips and staring at me over the rim.

What I wanted to say and what I needed to say were so opposite, but I went with work. "So today we learned that McDougal isn't Johnny's real name. It's O'Sullivan. Other than that, we don't have a ton to go on, but you may be able to give us some clues."

"O'Sullivan?" she asked, setting down her drink on the table in slow motion. "I've heard the name before."

"You have?"

"Yeah. His cousin who always called was named O'Sullivan."

"Do you remember the cousin's first name?"

"Kate."

I pulled out the tiny tablet I'd stuck in my back pocket before I walked out of ALFA and started to jot down notes. This was one time I wanted to actually write shit down. I needed to go back to the office with a full report. Plus, I'd figured Fran would distract me and I'd probably forget half the shit she'd told me by the time I walked out the door.

"Do you know where she lives?"

"Somewhere in New York."

"Anything else about Kate?" She couldn't have had any more of a plain name. It would be like finding a needle in a haystack in the entire state of New York.

"She's a hairdresser or some shit in the Bronx."

That narrowed it down a lot. Couldn't be too many Kate O'Sullivans doing hair in the Bronx. "I'll start checking her out as soon as possible."

"Now that I think of it..." She placed her face in her hands. "Oh God," she wailed softly. "I'm a fool."

I reached out and pulled her hands away from her face. "Don't feel like a fool, babe. Just tell me."

She sighed before dragging her dark brown eyes to mine. "He

always said I love you to her before they got off the phone. I didn't think anything of it. But he claimed they were cousins. How many cousins do you know who say that every time they talk?"

"I don't know." I shrugged.

"I bet she's his wife or some shit. That's just how my luck is."

"Don't jump to conclusions. Maybe it was his cousin."

She gave me a "don't be an idiot" look. "Let's be real here, Bear. He used me to get comfortable and stay under the radar at work."

"Now you listen to me, Ms. DeLuca, manipulators know just what to say and how to act to get their way. There's nothing you could've done to change things. He knew exactly what he was doing."

"Maybe." She shook her head. "Or I'm just a fool."

"Didn't he work at the track for years?"

"He owned it, and Race bought it from him."

I knew that, but it had slipped my mind. Something wasn't adding up. Why would a man sell a track and then steal from the very person he'd already had a windfall from… It didn't make sense.

"It's highly unlikely that she's his wife, Fran. Maybe she's his sister. If he lived down here for years, running a business, someone would've known about Kate. A man can only hide a wife for so long."

"True," she said in a soft voice and twisted her fingers together on top of the table. "She knew we were a couple. I actually spoke to her on the phone a few times."

I placed my hands over hers. "If that was you on the other end, would you want to talk to the woman sleeping with your husband?"

"I'd track that bitch down and kick her ass."

"Exactly." I laughed loudly. "So she's probably not his wife, but she's definitely a lead. Did Johnny act any differently lately?"

"He seemed more paranoid than normal." She stirred her drink, staring at the liquid swirling around the ice cubes. "He'd look out the windows a few times, double-check locks, and shit like that, but I thought he was just being cautious."

"Did Johnny gamble?"

She shook her head, and her hair skimmed across her shoulder, glistening in the light. "Not that I knew of."

"Who else do you remember him talking to? We're trying to get an accurate picture of who he is and who his associates were."

"Hmm." She paused and chewed on the inside of her lip. "He'd get texts all the time from someone named Trout, but I don't know if it's a nickname or a last name. I heard him reminisce about an old friend named Sawyer too. I'm sorry," she said and rubbed her forehead with her delicate fingers. "I guess I didn't know as much about him as I thought."

"Some people are just guarded, Fran. Usually, it's just out of habit, but sometimes, like with Johnny, there are other reasons why someone doesn't open up about who they really are." I took a large swig of gin, but I kept my eyes trained on her.

"You're kind of like him, Bear. You're very private. I don't even know your real name."

My hand stilled with the glass still pressed against my lips. I never hid my name, but I also never told people openly. My closest friends knew it, and my family, but years ago I stopped answering to it. I set down the gin and licked my lips, taking a moment to debate telling her. When I looked across the table at her sad smile, I couldn't stop myself from answering. "It's Murray."

Her smile widened, like I'd let her in on a very private secret. "I like that name. It suits you." Even though I cringed, she whispered, "Murray."

Usually, hearing my name would bring back too many memories, but coming from her mouth, it sounded as sweet as the most beautiful song. "That's me." I played it off like an idiot.

She placed her hand on my forearm and stroked my skin, sending chills skidding up my arm. "Do you mind if I call you that? Bear is cute, but Murray is more...manly."

"Cook for me again, and you can call me whatever you want." I smiled at her, relishing the feel of her skin against mine.

"Shit. I forgot about your beautiful dessert. Let me grab it." When she removed her hand and stood, I instantly missed the connection.

She disappeared into the kitchen, leaving me alone in the dining room. "What the fuck am I doing?" I whispered and glanced toward the ceiling. Closing my eyes for a moment, I took a deep breath and told myself, *Fran is off-limits, asshole.*

"You okay?" she asked, catching me off guard.

I peered over at her as she stood in the doorway, holding a tray of freshly made cannoli. "I couldn't be better. Good food and great company, but I wish I were here under different circumstances."

She placed two powdered-sugar-covered, chocolate-dipped cannoli on my plate. "Well, let's talk about other things besides Johnny. Ever have any kids?"

I tried to hold back my cringe. My life was something I didn't discuss with many. "I have two," I told her, which was surprisingly easy.

She sat down and placed one cannoli on her dish before setting the napkin in her lap. "How old?"

"Ret's around thirty now, and Janice is just a year older."

"Do they live around here?"

"Last I heard, he lived somewhere in Texas." I took the largest bite of the cannoli, hoping my mouth would be too full to answer any more questions. "And she lives nearby."

"Jesus, I couldn't imagine my kid living so far away. He's my only baby and has been my life since my marriage ended."

"How long ago was that?" I asked with a mouth full of ricotta filling sticking to the roof of my mouth like wallpaper paste.

"He left right around the time Morgan graduated from high school, but the marriage was over long before that." She mindlessly traced the chocolate on the tip of the cannoli tube, and my mind went into overdrive.

It was like something out of a wet dream. Fran's tongue moved slowly across the dried chocolate, the pink beautifully contrasting with the darkness of the treat. Her eyes closed, savoring the taste, and for a brief moment, I pictured my cock in her hand with her making the same motion. When she let out a tiny moan, I almost fell off my chair.

"Anyway," she said before biting off the end and ending my fantasy. "Ray was a piece of shit. He's never had any contact with Morgan since that day. He served me with papers, and I haven't seen him since."

"I'm sorry."

"Eh." She waved her hand. "It was years ago and the best thing that ever could've happened. He was an asshole, straight up. Murray, what about your wife?"

"My wife, Jackie," I said and felt a pang of sadness. I rarely said her name anymore because it was still an open wound that hadn't fully healed. "She died during childbirth."

Her hand flew to her mouth, and her eyes widened. "I'm so sorry." When she dropped her arm, her hand found the same spot on my forearm, stroking me gently. "I can't imagine how hard that must've been."

"Even though it's been almost three decades, the pain is still like yesterday."

"It's different when someone is taken from you. I can't imagine what you went through with a newborn baby and dealing with the loss of your wife."

"I didn't deal well. I was a shitty father, Fran."

She gripped my arm tighter, the bite of her fingernails grounding me. "Men aren't meant to raise babies alone."

"Maybe," I whispered, pushing the cannoli around my dish. "I could've been a better father. Instead, I got involved with the wrong crowd, drank too much, and left Ret and Janice in the care of my sisters. I couldn't look at his cute little face every day. He was a constant reminder of what I'd lost."

"You can't correct the past, but you can try to make amends for the future." She patted my arm softly. "Do you talk to him now?"

"We talk, but I wish he were closer." I shrugged.

She smiled sweetly at me with the softest brown eyes. "Well, why don't you convince him to come here? Who doesn't love Florida?"

"I don't know," I mumbled before shoving the rest of the half-eaten cannoli in my mouth.

"Time is something you can never get back. At our age, it's the most precious thing we have, Murray."

"Fran." Pieces of the cannoli fell from my lips, and I scooped them into my hand and dropped them on the plate. "I love when you say my name, but when we're not alone, can you call me Bear?"

She winked playfully. "Sure. I know you have an image to maintain."

I couldn't hide my smile. "Something like that."

"So..." She dragged her drink in front of her and settled back into her chair. "That makes you about how old? Fifty?"

"Somewhere around there." I winked. "How about you?"

"About the same."

I dabbed at the powdered sugar that I was sure had fallen into my beard with each bite. "I didn't think I'd ever live to see the big five-oh."

Fran licked her finger and scooted forward. "Let me get that." She raised her hand, and I nodded.

My body froze the closer she came with her arm outstretched, running her fingers through my beard. Each hair that moved sent tiny prickles through my system. "There," she said and stroked my face before pulling her hand away.

"Thanks." No one had cleaned my face since Jackie. The small gesture made my heart ache with sadness. "It's getting late. Let's finish up about Johnny so you can get some rest."

"Oh, okay," she said, and I could tell my response wasn't what she expected.

I didn't veer off course for the rest of my visit. We only talked about Johnny and the track. After an hour of jotting down notes, I thanked her for the dinner and made my way to the door.

"Are you sure you don't want to stay a little longer?"

I let out a fake yawn. "I need to get to bed. Thank you for a lovely meal and even better company, Fran." I leaned forward and kissed her soft, round cheek. "I had a good time tonight."

She placed her palm flat against my chest, and I could feel her warmth through my T-shirt. "It was nice to cook for someone who actually likes to eat what I make."

"Whenever you need company, just call." The words just came out of my mouth without a filter. If Morgan were here, he'd punch me right in the back of the head for coming on to his mom.

"I may just take you up on that offer." She smiled and backed away through the door. "Have a safe trip home, Murray."

I had started to jog down the driveway, but I stopped when I heard my name. I turned, smiled at her, and waved. "Sweet dreams, Franny."

I couldn't wipe the stupid grin off my face as I pushed my bike down her driveway to avoid pissing off her neighbors. I kept my eyes on her in the side mirror, watching her watch me from the doorway.

Don't look back.

I was in so much trouble at this point, I'd let Morgan get in a free shot or two without even defending myself. I broke the guy code. He was my buddy and coworker, but Fran… She was a real woman who made me feel something for the first time in as long as I could remember.

CHAPTER 4
FRAN

The phone rang before the sun even shone through my sheers. "Hello," I said in a groggy voice, still half asleep even though the call had startled me.

"Late night?" Maria, my sister-in-law, asked with a small giggle.

I rolled onto my side and squinted to see the numbers on the alarm clock. "What the hell are you doing awake at this ungodly hour?"

"It's almost eight, sleepyhead. We have tennis this morning, but it's raining."

"Ugh," I groaned because I fucking hated tennis, but I played it with Maria weekly to make her happy. The only bright side was that my body had never looked better since I started chasing that stupid neon ball around the court.

"Let's meet for coffee and breakfast instead."

Resting the phone against my shoulder, I rubbed the sleep from my eyes. "Fine. That sounds better than tennis any day. I'm too tired today to actually do much else."

"I heard Bear came over last night."

"From whom?"

"I talked to Tommy last night."

I grabbed the pillow from the other side of the bed and placed it over my face, muffling my voice. "You're already gossiping about me?"

"No."

"Hmph," I mumbled. "Sounds like you were."

"Stop being a baby. Get your ass up and meet me at the diner in an hour."

"Fine," I told her before kicking off the covers. "Bye."

"Don't keep me wait—"

I hung up the phone before she could keep talking. I hadn't even had a cup of coffee, and the last thing I wanted to deal with was Maria and her questions.

After I rolled out of bed and made my way to the kitchen, I dialed Morgan while I waited for the coffee to brew. "Hey, baby," I said when he answered.

"Morning, Ma. How are you today?"

"It's too early to form an opinion. I'm just waiting for the coffee and thought I'd call to check in with you."

"How did it go?"

"Fine," I said, keeping my answer short.

"That's all you have to say?"

I heard the annoyance in his tone. "We had a little dinner, talked, and then he left."

"You made him dinner?" His voice cracked on the last word.

"It helped keep my mind occupied."

"But, Ma," he replied with a deeper tone.

"No buts, Morgan. It was a nice evening."

"It was work."

"I know, son. Trust me, Bear was a complete gentleman."

"Doubtful," Morgan mumbled into the phone.

"He even complimented my cooking."

Morgan was silent for a moment. "Now I really don't trust him."

"You trusted Johnny and so did I, and where did that get us? Bear is a good man. He was kind to me last night."

"I'm sure he was," he grumbled.

"Stop with the shitty attitude, mister."

"Just be careful."

I laughed as I grabbed the half-filled pot and poured myself a cup. "You have nothing to worry about. I just hope I gave him enough information about Johnny to help."

"I'm sure you did, Ma."

"I feel responsible, Morgan. I mean, Johnny and I didn't go steady, but I spent enough time with him that I should've seen the signs. I should've known he wasn't a good guy." I took a sip, savoring the warmth and caffeine.

"Don't be ridiculous. He manipulated everyone. But that's what I'm saying about Bear. You never really know someone until it's too late. Don't think he's a good guy, Ma. He's not."

"Morgan DeLuca, I raised you to think better about people. He's your friend and a friend of the Gallos. Don't confuse your feelings for Johnny with Bear."

"I'm just putting it out there."

"Well, you've said it now. I'm a big girl and can make my own decisions." I placed the mug on the counter and glanced at the clock. "I have to run. Maria is waiting for me to have breakfast. Have a good day, honey."

"We're not done talking about—"

I hung up on him. It was becoming a normal thing for me. When I didn't like what someone was saying, I'd hang up the phone before they could finish. Although I loved Morgan dearly, I was a grown woman, and I didn't have to justify my life to him. I'd made it this far without his "wise words" and worry.

By the time I walked into the diner, Maria was already seated and sipping on a cup of coffee. "Nice of you to finally make it," she said with a lopsided smile. "Bear wear you out last night?"

I slid into the booth and set my purse at my side. "Don't be ridiculous."

She giggled like a teenage girl. "I see the way you look at him, and he's always watching you."

I waved my hand across the table in front of her. "You're imagining things, Mar."

"Am I?"

"Coffee, Fran?" Martha asked, holding an empty cup in her hand.

I smiled at her because I couldn't have timed the interruption any better. "Yes, please."

Maria and I stared at each other while Martha poured a full cup, but we didn't speak. When the waitress was out of earshot, Maria started right where she left off.

"So did you at least kiss him?"

My sister-in-law was a nosy thing. She and Morgan could form their own little club. "No." I rolled my eyes as I brought the mug to my lips.

She pursed her lips and raised her eyebrows. "Did you want to?"

"Maybe," I said, drawing out my answer.

"He's a bit rough around the edges, but he's one of the nicest, most loyal men I've ever met."

"Morgan says he's trouble."

"If Morgan had his way, you'd enter a convent and be celibate the rest of your life."

"You got that right."

Martha came back, pulling the pencil from behind her ear. "You ladies want the usual?"

"Yeah," we answered together before Martha walked away.

"We're really getting predictable, aren't we?" I asked Maria.

"You can think you're old, but I feel like I have a new lease on life. I plan to live with no apologies and no regrets." I smiled and glanced out the window just as I heard the sound of a motorcycle. For a moment, I hoped it would be Bear barreling down the street, just to catch a glimpse of him. But it was a girl in short-shorts and flip-flops, with her long blond hair waving in the wind. "I figure I have twenty good years left in me. I don't plan on spending them crocheting and watching soap operas."

Maria rubbed her face with her fingertips, making tiny circles near her temples. "You just depressed the hell out of me."

"Why?"

"Twenty years? I want to turn back the clock and go back to my youth. Time moves so fast now, it'll pass in the blink of an eye."

"I know, girl, I know. That's why I don't plan on spending it at home—what a waste that would be."

She cupped the dingy cream mug in her hand and leaned back in the booth. "Do you have a plan?"

"No, but I know just where I'm going to start." I rubbed my hands together with the biggest smile on my face.

"I feel there's going to be a rocky road ahead."

"Morgan forgets who the parent is in this situation. He's not the boss of me. He'll just have to deal."

"Oh, this is going to be fun." Maria laughed. "You know..." Her voice trailed off.

"What?"

"We should really get you a new wardrobe if you plan to whore it up."

I glanced down at my favorite pink tracksuit and pulled at the collar. "Why?"

Maria's eyes traveled around my top before connecting with my eyes. "You look like you live in an assisted-living community and are about to play bridge. You certainly don't scream 'fuck me' in that ratty old thing."

"But it's comfortable."

"So is an old shoe, but there's a time when you need to replace it."

"Fine," I muttered. "When do you want to go shopping?"

"I'm not doing anything today," she replied quickly with a partial grin.

"Let's do this, then." I shrugged. "I'm ready for a change." I lied right through my teeth. Some change, I could deal with, but the way I dressed was more of a security blanket to stop the advances of men.

"Fuck, this is going to be epic!"

"When did you start using the word epic, Mar?"

"Izzy seems to like it, so I figured I'd try it out."

I giggled, and Maria quickly followed. As soon as Martha delivered our breakfast, we ate quickly before heading to the mall.

Maria had my head spinning the way she shopped. She twirled around the department store, plucking pieces off the racks, and holding them against me.

"What size are you?" she asked, with a top that looked more like a scrap of material pressed up against my chest.

"Medium, maybe." I cringed because I hadn't bought anything new in so long, I wasn't quite sure.

"And your pants?"

"Medium too."

Her eyebrows drew together as her eyes flicked to mine. "Real pants don't come in medium. What's your actual size?"

I glanced down at my track pants and pulled at the elastic. "Last time I checked, these were real pants."

She laughed softly at first, but every time she looked at my face, her laughter grew louder. "I can't." She tried to catch her breath but couldn't. "Those aren't—"

"Can I help you?" a saleswoman asked after hearing Maria laughing like a hyena.

"We're good," I told her, already embarrassed enough by my sister-in-law. "Thank you, though."

"Can I start a dressing room for you?"

With all the ugly tops piled high on my one arm, I couldn't say no. "Yes, please. I don't think she's done yet."

Maria cleared her throat to try to get rid of her giggles. "No, we're far from done," she said in a strangled voice.

I rolled my eyes and handed over the pile of "real" clothing, as Maria would've called it, before the saleswoman scurried away.

"Are you done laughing at me?"

She shook her head, walking away from me quickly, but I could still hear her laughter as I followed behind. She grabbed some pants in various sizes from the rack to cover the bases before we headed to the dressing room to try on the first round of items.

She stood outside the door, tapping her foot against the cold, white tile. "How does it look?" she asked.

My arms didn't want to go into the tiny opening in the long-sleeved top she'd picked out. I kept sticking my hand through the cutout near the shoulder. "Great."

"Let me see."

When I finally got it on and looked in the mirror, it wasn't as bad as I'd imagined. "Gimme a minute. I have to put on some pants." I grabbed the size eight, figuring it was my best bet, and pulled them on easily. "Wrong size."

"Which one?"

"Eight."

"Too small?"

"Too big," I admitted, feeling slightly ashamed that I didn't know my right size. Track pants were easy. They always fit. Even if I gained a few pounds or lost a few, the elastic always made them right. I threw the eights to the floor and grabbed the size six from the hook. "What the hell are skinny jeans?"

"Just put them on," she said in an annoyed tone.

"I'm doing this for you, so you better drop the attitude, Mar."

"Shut up, Franny. This is for you and that poor, lonely vagina of yours. Put the jeans on, and get your tiny little ass out here."

My vagina wasn't lonely. The thieving bastard Johnny had taken care of it for some time. I just wasn't a talker like Maria. I didn't have to share my sexual experiences to validate that they actually happened.

Once I had the jeans on, I turned around and looked at my ass in the mirror. My bottom never looked so nice. The soft denim had a bit of stretch, making it easy to breathe, and it was comfortable. They looked more like leggings from the way they clung to my body. The outfit was pretty, but I looked younger—too young, in fact.

"I look stupid," I whined, but secretly I liked the outfit. I didn't look like a grandma anymore, but like a woman.

"I'm coming in if you don't come out."

Damn her. She was so damn pushy. Years of being with my brother had turned her into a bossy little thing. "Don't!" I yelled before finally turning the handle and walking out for her inspection.

She clapped the moment she saw me. "You look hot," she said with the widest smile. "Turn around." She twirled her fingers in a circle. Instead of fighting her, I followed her command.

She whistled loudly when my ass faced her full on. "You can bounce a quarter off that thing."

"Please," I groaned in horror. "It's aged too much for that shit."

"You're getting that outfit."

"I don't know. The top really isn't me."

She smacked my ass, causing me to jump. "That's the point. We're retiring the tracksuit. It's too you, and that shit ain't working."

I turned, glaring at her for a second. "Fine." I wanted the outfit, but I'd never admit it to her.

"Go try on the next one."

I closed the door and turned around in front of the mirror, smiling as I did. I really did like the way the outfit hugged my body and showed my curves.

"We have to get you a new bra."

"Why?" I called out when I started to pry the shirt from my body in the most ungraceful way.

"Your boobs shouldn't be near your elbows."

As I tossed the top to the floor with the size-eight jeans, I stared in the mirror and turned to the side. She was right. They were hanging low. The bra I had on was the same style I'd worn for years.

"They're fine."

"No, they're not. Does it even have underwire?"

I grimaced at the thought of wearing something so constrictive. "Underwire?"

"You need a push-up bra to get those girls back toward your chin."

"For the love of God," I muttered, pushing up my tits to the spot they'd sat twenty years ago.

"Let's find more clothes, and then we're on to raising those babies a few inches. You need to show off that cleavage."

In my head, I kept hearing Morgan. He was going to flip his lid the moment he saw me. The entire thing might be worth it just to freak him out.

But then I thought of Bear. What would he say when he saw the new me?

CHAPTER 5
BEAR

"I got a lead!" James yelled from the hallway around noon. "The bastard's in Raleigh."

"Conference room," Thomas said as he walked by my office.

I grabbed my laptop and followed him down the hallway along with the other guys so we could figure out what to do from here.

"Want me to head up?" I asked, sitting down at the table.

"Not yet," he replied.

Once everyone was inside, James asked, "Who do we know in Raleigh?"

"I have a buddy who used to be in the FBI there. I can call him," Sam said quickly.

"Do that. Get eyes on him and verify that it's Johnny. If it is, have them keep him under surveillance until we can get there," James told him, rubbing his chin with one finger before Sam pulled out his phone and sent a text.

"I'll head up," I said again. There was no point in waiting for confirmation. "Raleigh's only nine hours away."

Thomas shook his head. "I don't want to waste the manpower if it's not him."

I grumbled. "You're the boss," I bit out through gritted teeth. Sometimes working for someone else left a sour taste in my mouth. The guys at ALFA had their shit together though and made the right call.

Thomas leaned back in his chair and rocked back and forth. "If it's him, we'll be there within hours by plane. We won't let him slip from our sights. Do you agree, Morgan?"

Morgan rubbed his hands together and thought a moment. "Yeah. Get eyes on him first, and then we'll handle him. I don't want to chase after a ghost."

"It's him," Sam said when his phone started to ring. "I'll be back in a few."

Angel cleared her throat in the doorway as Sam brushed past. "Um," she mumbled and peered over her shoulder. "Mrs. Gallo and Ms. DeLuca are here."

Our entire table turned with the same perplexed looks on our faces. They'd come to visit separately, but never together. There must be something wrong.

Thomas's eyes narrowed on his wife. "Show them in, Angel."

She smiled and glanced behind her again. "I have to warn you—"

"What's wrong?" Morgan asked, wondering the same thing I had been thinking.

"Nothing. They just dropped by to say hi," Angel said and giggled as she walked back toward reception.

"This oughta be good," Frisco added after finally looking up from his laptop.

"Those two cause more trouble..." Thomas muttered.

Mrs. Gallo came into view first, smiling wildly. "Hey, guys. Just wanted to say hello."

Thomas walked over to his mother and kissed her on the cheek. "What are you two doing today?"

All I could see of Fran were her feet. From the angle I was sitting and with Maria in the doorway, I couldn't see any more. Maybe she regretted our dinner last night and didn't want to see me. The thought made my heart a little heavy, although I'd never admit it to anyone.

"Holy shit, Aunt Franny," Thomas said.

I sat a little straighter in my chair and tried to get a better glimpse without being obvious.

"Oh, God, now what?" Morgan said from my side.

Maria held up her hand to stop the hysteria before it started. "We went shopping."

"I'll say," Thomas said and held out his hand to his mother to move her to the side. "Looking good, Auntie."

I craned my neck a little more and kept my ass glued to the chair because I didn't feel like getting into a brawl with her kid. He already didn't like that I had dinner with his mom. He'd made it very clear when I came into work today, but I told him what I always did—we're adults and nothing happened. It wasn't his business anyway. She may have birthed him, but she was a grown-ass adult.

When Fran stepped into view, my mouth dropped open. She had on the sexiest pair of dark blue skinny jeans and a white top that showed just the right amount of cleavage. My mouth watered at the sight. I'd only seen Fran in her tracksuits and thought she was still a stunner, but now… Now she was drop-dead gorgeous.

"Holy shit!" Morgan jumped up from his chair and almost covered her body with his. "What are you thinking, Ma?"

Maria slapped him in the back of the head, and he flinched. "Don't make a big deal out of this. She looks wonderful."

"Where did my mom go?" he asked while he rubbed the spot she'd just hit.

"I'm here, baby. Do I look bad?" She glanced down and swept her palm over the front of her shirt.

"Well," he mumbled and shook his head. "No. You look different."

"Different bad or good?" she asked, looking for validation.

"Good."

Her eyes wandered around the room and locked on mine. For once in my life, I was speechless. Fran DeLuca had it going on. Who knew underneath that frumpy shit she had a killer body?

I sure as fuck didn't.

I couldn't stop my mouth from hanging open as I checked her out, letting my eyes cascade over her body, and imagining the dirtiest shit that I reserved for the naughtiest women.

Frisco elbowed me in the arm. "I'd stop looking at her like that if I were you."

I righted myself and snapped my mouth shut. Fran kept staring at me, ignoring everyone else in the room.

"Let's go to my office." Morgan tried to usher her from the room and probably my view.

"Don't be silly." Fran swatted his hands away. "We wanted to say hi to everyone and see how the investigation was going."

"Everything is good here. Nothing to see and no new information." Morgan couldn't be any more uncomfortable.

"We wanted to show off Fran's new look too. I figured, where else is better than in an office full of men?" Maria smiled directly at me, and I knew instantly that I was really the target of the fashion show.

"You look great," James said.

"Fantastic," Frisco added.

I was at a loss for words, and I was never out of shit to say. Usually, it was some sarcastic comment, but I had nothing.

"Now's the time to talk," Frisco whispered. "Dumbass."

"You look very nice," I said, even though I wanted to say so much more, and Fran's eyes sparkled at the compliment.

I glanced to her side and caught Morgan glaring at me. I must not have been as under the radar with my reaction as I'd thought. I squirmed in my chair—not from Morgan's look but from the sexiness oozing off Fran DeLuca.

My cock approved.

"Well, boys," Maria said and looked right at me, "Franny and I are off to get all sweaty playing tennis."

I realized in that moment that Maria Gallo was a wicked woman. My head filled with images of Fran bouncing up and down, her tits following suit, and covered in a thick veil of perspiration.

"Have fun," James said as he stood from his seat and went to give his mother-in-law a kiss on the cheek.

I couldn't speak because I was too lost in my fantasy.

"Don't overdo it," Morgan told his mother. "It's hot outside."

She placed her hand on his chest and leaned in to kiss him, but her eyes were on me. "Don't worry. I'm in great shape and can last for hours."

"Fucking hell," Morgan groaned and hugged his mother.

I swallowed my tongue and started to choke. Fran was just as rambunctious as Maria. If I was going to make it through the day, I needed to wipe all mental images of Fran running around the tennis court, grunting with each hit, and glistening in the sunlight.

Fran gave me a mischievous smile as she backed away from Morgan. "Don't work too hard today and keep me posted about Johnny."

"We will," Thomas assured the ladies before they walked out of the conference room.

All I could see was Fran's tight little ass swaying back and forth as they made their way down the hallway, following Morgan out.

It would be impossible to work today. Fran made sure of that by putting the images in my mind that would leave room for little else.

"You better get that shit under control," Frisco said.

I turned to face him and snarled. "Mind your own business."

"Morgan's going to have a fit."

"I didn't do anything."

"If I could read your mind, I'm pretty sure it would be X-rated, brother."

I scrubbed my hand down my face and tried to wipe the vivid images from my mind, but all I saw were her perky tits and jiggling ass.

Fuck.

I was in so much trouble.

CHAPTER 6
FRAN

"Did you see the look on his face?" Maria said over the phone as I wiped the kitchen counter.

"Who?" I feigned ignorance.

"Bear. He almost swallowed his tongue." She chuckled.

"I know," I finally admitted. The poor guy—he did look like he was about to hyperventilate when he finally caught a glimpse of me.

It had been a long time since I'd seen a man look at me that way. Ray used to, but that was before he became an uncaring asshole. It felt like as soon as the wedding ring slipped on my finger, he lost his manners and stopped courting me.

But Bear made me feel sexy again. My belly did that weird thing where it flipped a few times, and my fingers tingled just from the way his eyes crawled across my skin. It wasn't lost on me, and based on Morgan's reaction, it wasn't lost on him either.

"You should invite him over for dinner again."

"Maria! I just had him over yesterday." I was protesting too much, but the thought had crossed my mind since I walked out of ALFA PI.

"So what? Live a little, Franny."

"What about Johnny?"

"Were you two even dating?"

"Not really. We'd go to dinner, and sometimes, we'd end up in the sack."

"There's your answer. It's not like you're rebounding or anything."

She was right, but I couldn't give in so easily. "But what about Morgan? Bear's his friend."

"Now you're just making excuses."

I was, too. Bear wasn't normally my type. I don't even know if I had a type anymore. "We'll see. Let me figure out what to do and do it in my own time."

"Fine. Be a pussy."

"The mouth on you."

She laughed loudly. "Your brother taught me well. Speaking of the devil, he just walked in. I got to run."

"Bye, Mar. Say hi to Sal for me."

"Will do. Bye."

With the dishrag still in my hand, I stared out the windows overlooking my backyard and thought about what to do next. Last night had been nice. Bear wasn't exactly the man I thought, and I wanted to know more about him. But was it the right time to go down that road?

Maybe I'd read the signals wrong. I'd never chased a man. Not even Ray. It wasn't my style, but my daughter-in-law Race told me it's what women do in the twenty-first century. My mind was still stuck back in the seventies where there were rules and proper etiquette.

My phone rang before I even had a chance to put it back on the charger. "Hello," I said after seeing it was Race calling.

"I heard you made quite a splash today."

"He already called you."

"He's worried, Ma."

"I'm an adult, Race."

"I know. I think it's cute."

"It's payback from that brat."

"Are you going to ask Bear out?"

"I don't know. I was just thinking about it."

"Do it. He's a great guy."

It seemed like the women in the family were conspiring against me. If Morgan knew Race was calling me, he'd be livid. "How would Morgan feel about that?"

"Who cares? You deserve to be happy too."

"Someone's at the door, Race. I gotta run." I lied because I wasn't ready for this conversation. Everyone was chirping in my ear, and I didn't need their opinions.

"Maybe it's Bear," she said through her laughter.

"Bye, busybody."

"Bye, Ma."

The sky was dark in the distance as the usual afternoon thunderstorms started to roll in. I walked to the mailbox, trying to beat the rain, when my neighbor Meredith caught me before I could sneak back inside.

"You're looking nice today," she said, her eyes raking over me, but not in a complimentary way.

"Thanks, Mer."

Her tiny mouth, one so small I wondered if she was ever able to suck a dick, pursed. "I saw a motorcycle in your driveway last night. Did you have a man over?"

Living in an older-resident community had its disadvantages, and this was a prime example. It was filled with a bunch of bored, nosy people who had no life but to spy on their neighbors.

I plastered a fake smile on my face. "Just a family friend." Thunder sounded in the distance, and I saw my out. "I better get inside before it storms. Take care." I started to walk away, waving over my shoulder at her.

"Bye," she grumbled from behind me, still standing near the driveway where I'd left her.

After I walked inside and flipped through the mail, I tossed it on the countertop and noticed I'd missed a phone call. My eyes widened when I saw the name. *Bear.* Maybe I hadn't interpreted his vibes wrong. After all these years, maybe I still had the ability to read a man.

I couldn't wipe the smile off my face as I waited for his voice mail to play. "Hey, Franny. It's Bear. I wanted to touch base with you and let you know that we may have a possible lead on Johnny. I know you're upset and would want to know what's going on. Call me back...ya know...if you want."

For a moment I was sad because I was hoping for something a little bit more...flirtatious. Even though it wasn't what I'd hoped to hear, I called him back anyway.

"Hey, Bear. It's Franny," I said as soon as he answered the phone.

"I know." He laughed softly.

"I wanted to say thank you for the update." I paced around my living room. "Morgan hasn't really been telling me much."

"He's just busy. Cut him a little slack."

"I know."

"Hold on one second."

The phone became muffled, and I could hear voices in the background.

"No go?" Bear asked and then a pause. "Fuck."

A few more things were said, but I couldn't make them out no matter how hard I pressed the phone to my ear.

"I'm back," he told me. "False alarm on the lead, but don't worry... We'll find him."

"I know you will. Was that Morgan?"

"Yeah."

I smiled because Bear hadn't told him that I was on the other end of the phone. "Well, I better let you go. I know you guys are busy."

"Hey, Franny?" he asked softly.

I stopped pacing, and butterflies filled my stomach. "Yeah?"

"Want to grab a beer tonight?"

I moved the receiver away from my mouth and took a few quick, deep breaths. "I'd love to." My feet started to move on their own, breaking out in a cross between a happy dance and the running man— but more of a senior version.

"Great. I'll pick you up at seven."

"I'll be ready."

"Later."

"Bye," I said, and when the call disconnected, I stared at it like maybe I'd heard him wrong. But when I realized I hadn't, I broke out into a full-on celebratory dance in my living room.

Wait.

Was this a date?

Fuck. I didn't know how shit worked anymore. I'd spent my good years at home after Ray left me. I couldn't even look at another man for a long time. Then Morgan joined the military, and all I could do was think about him. I didn't have time to get involved in a relationship, and I figured, why bother since I was in my forties.

I thought Johnny and I were dating in the beginning, but he made it quite clear that he didn't want any type of relationship. I couldn't understand why, but now it's completely clear.

I guess, with Bear, I'd just have to wait and see. Maybe he was only being nice to me because I was Morgan's mom, and I was feeling so much guilt for not seeing Johnny for the lying, cheating asshole he was.

I'm either going to have to grow a pair and ask what his intentions are or just wait it out and hope that he wants more than just a drink and a hot meal.

WHEN I HEARD his bike pull into the driveway just before seven, I ran into the bedroom so it wouldn't seem as if I'd been waiting for him. I had been. I'd been ready for a half hour, and I'd been pacing back and forth in the living room, checking outside for any glimpse of him.

"This isn't a date," I told myself as I waited for him to knock. "It's just a drink."

My heart leapt when he knocked on the door, and I took one last look at myself in the mirror. I had on the same jeans from the office earlier today, but I had changed my top to something a little more revealing.

I leaned forward and checked my cleavage, heaving it up with my hand, and giggling. The bra Maria picked out really did help them reach a height I hadn't seen since my twenties. Bear was probably used to women much younger, and if this padded, underwire-lined thing ever came off in front of him, he'd be shocked at where they swung.

I hummed the tune to "Swing Low, Sweet Chariot" as I walked toward the door. When I finally worked up the nerve to open it, I was pleasantly surprised by what I saw.

"Good evening, Franny." Bear held out a small bouquet of flowers as his eyes traveled down my body. "You're looking stunning."

I graciously took them and gave them a quick sniff. "Thank you. They're beautiful," I told him. "Would you like to come in while I put these in some water?" My voice wavered.

He nodded. "Sure."

I tried not to skip to the kitchen from excitement. Bear brought me flowers. I don't think anyone, not even Ray, had ever brought me a bouquet. "I'll be quick." I bent over and grabbed a vase from under the sink and caught a glimpse of Bear standing behind me. His eyes were glued to my ass, and I slowed down to give him a longer look.

He cleared his throat when I started to stand and turn around. "How was your day?" he asked as I started to arrange the flowers in the clear vase, and I noticed the redness in his face.

"Busy. Yours?"

He turned his body, adjusting himself, and trying to be discreet but failing completely. "Busy too."

"So where are we headed?" I couldn't stop myself from chattering because I was so nervous. There was an awkwardness tonight I hadn't felt before.

"I thought we'd head down to the little place by the beach."

I smiled because the sun would be setting soon, and it'd been too long since I'd watched it descend below the horizon of the Gulf of Mexico. "That sounds lovely." Suddenly, I sounded more like June Cleaver than Fran DeLuca.

"Ready?" he asked, jostling back and forth on his feet, just as nervous as I was.

"Yeah. You?"

"Yep." His answer was short, and he was heading to the door before the vase was entirely filled with water.

I heard him mumbling to himself in the front room. He was giving himself a pep talk, and I could only make out a few words. I couldn't wipe the smile off my face as I set the flowers on the table near the window. A man like Bear never seemed to have a problem with self-esteem, and I found it endearing that he had to give himself a talk.

"Let's hit it," I said as I breezed into the living room to a pacing Bear.

When we went outside and I locked the door, he asked, "Are you good with being on a bike?"

"It's been a while, but yeah."

I hated bikes, but I didn't tell him that. I knew the man rode his faithfully, and who was I to stop him? Ray had one too, but after my third time on the bike, I never went on it again. I ended up punching him in the ribs when he took a turn a little too sharp for my liking. After that, he never asked me to go with him on another ride, and I was perfectly happy riding in my car instead.

After Bear got situated, he held out his hand like a perfect gentleman and helped me climb onto the back. I set my hands on his shoulders and waited.

"You have to wrap your arms around me," he said, glancing over his shoulder at me. "And hold on."

"Sorry." I smiled, and as soon as he turned around, I swallowed hard, looked up toward the sky, and said a silent prayer.

Wrapping my arms around Bear was like anchoring myself to a mountain. His chest was so wide that my fingers barely clasped in front of his chest. The muscles underneath my hands flexed when my arms tightened. The butterflies that had fluttered in my belly earlier started to move as if they were on hyperdrive. My body slid forward, pressing my chest against the warmth of his back. I wanted to lay my head against him and close my eyes, but I didn't want him to think I was a weirdo—even though I was.

"You good, babe?" he asked and patted my hands.

"I'm good," I whispered softly, shimmying my body so there wasn't a sliver of space between us.

He slid on his glasses that had been hanging near his handlebars and started the bike. The roar of the engine caused the entire machine to vibrate, sending tiny shock waves of pleasure through my system.

I wondered if that was part of the charm of a motorcycle and having a woman on the back—the closeness, the large vibrator in the form of a bike, and the wind through our hair. It was like an aphrodisiac that couldn't be replicated by anything else.

As we pulled out on to the street, I couldn't stop myself from resting my head against his back and closing my eyes. The mix of fear, adrenaline, and lust had me light-headed.

CHAPTER 7

BEAR

The last woman who had wrapped her body so tightly around me on the back of the bike was Jackie. It felt like home the moment Fran put her head against my back, and I took off down the road.

The ladies from the bar that I'd sometimes take home on my bike were so comfortable they'd barely hold on, let alone plaster themselves to my body.

I forgot how nice it was too.

"Tell me more about your wife," Fran said after our first beer.

We'd spent the last half hour talking about our pasts, something I rarely did with anyone. "She had one of those smiles that could light up a room. When she laughed, no matter what was happening around me, I couldn't help but laugh too. Sometimes I try to remember the sound of it, but it's so faint that it just brings me sadness."

"I'm sorry. It sounds like she was a great girl."

"She was one of the best."

She moved the empty glass around on the table and avoided my eyes. "Why didn't you ever remarry?"

"I went to a dark place when I lost her." I picked at the label on my beer and stared out into the ocean, watching the waves roll in and crash against the shore. "I wouldn't have been good for anyone."

"It's been almost thirty years, Murray. I'm sure you're settled by now."

My eyes flickered to her. "I'm an old bastard now, Fran. Why didn't you get hitched after Ray?"

She frowned, dropping her gaze. "He was a mean fucker. When he left, I swore I'd never fall in love again. I've been really good at not getting close to anyone."

"Put all your effort into the kid?" I asked with a small smile.

She laughed softly and bit her lip. "Yeah. Poor Morgan. He was eighteen when Ray left, and I became what they now call a 'helicopter parent.'"

"Ain't nothing wrong with that," I told her and reached out to touch her hand. "I should've been that way with Ret and Janice. They deserved to have me in their life, but I was too self-absorbed and lost in my own sadness to be there for them."

"We all have regrets. But time isn't up yet. You can still make amends for the past." She curled her fingers around mine. "Just don't wait too long."

"Eh," I muttered, caressing the tender skin on the back of her hand with my thumb. "It'll probably cause more hurt after all this time. Sometimes it's better to leave things unsaid."

"Is this a date?" she blurted out with a nervous smile.

I froze for a second and began to laugh as the waitress arrived with our food. "I suppose it is."

Her lips curved up, almost kissing the corners of her eyes. "Good to know."

I was suddenly curious about the tracksuit-loving feisty woman I'd admired since the day I'd met her. "Go on a lot of dates?"

Her hair skimmed her shoulders as she shook her head. "Not really."

"Me either."

She laughed so hard she snorted. "Don't lie. I heard you're quite the ladies' man."

I chuckled softly as my face heated. "I wouldn't say that."

"Well, I've heard the stories."

"Fran," I said, suddenly feeling guilty and whorish.

"You don't owe me an explanation, Bear. I'm just making a general statement."

I stabbed at my pasta, capturing a few flimsy noodles on my fork. "Oh."

"I bet you're pretty good in the sack," she said just as I put the fork in my mouth. I stared at her for a moment, chewing as fast as I could so I could respond, but she kept talking. "Probably a wild man." She made a small roaring noise in the back of her throat.

The fork fell from my hands and clattered against my plate. A noodle lodged in my throat, and tears formed in my eyes as I tried to cough it away.

"Are you okay?" she asked, starting to stand.

I grabbed her hand and kept her in the seat as I cleared my throat. "You have to stop doing that."

Her eyebrows rose, and she smiled innocently. "What?"

My grip tightened on her hand. "Talking about sex with me."

"Sex with you or sex *with* you?" She smirked.

I closed my eyes and muttered a few curse words under my breath. "Both."

"Isn't that what usually happens on dates?"

"How's everything?" the waitress asked, interrupting us at the worst moment.

"It's great," I told her without looking up. "Thank you." When she finally scurried away, I continued. "I'm trying real hard not to think about banging the fuck out of you, Fran. I've never tried so hard not to think about something."

She leaned forward, giving me a better view of her spectacular cleavage. "Why would you do that?"

I licked my lips, my mouth watering from the view more than from the food. "Because we should take things slower. Morgan would kill me if he knew I even said this was a date."

"He doesn't have to know." Her words came out quickly and quietly.

I laughed and rubbed the spot where my hand had held her down before releasing her. "I don't really like to keep secrets from him, but..."

"There are some things he should never know."

She piqued my curiosity. "Like what?"

Her smirk turned into a wicked grin. "I'll save all my secrets until another day. We'll see if you earn the right to know them."

"Fuck," I muttered softly before picking up my fork and stabbing my food with a little more force. She had me on edge and needy.

We sat in silence, exchanging glances as we ate. I couldn't drag my eyes away from her mouth and the way her lips slid against the fork when she pulled it out. I kept thinking about my dick being in the same spot and the softness of her skin sliding against my shaft while the back of her teeth pressed against my head.

"Are you okay?" she asked after catching me adjusting myself in my seat for at least the tenth time since we sat down.

"I'm fine." I wiped my mouth, tossing the napkin on top of my plate, and watched her in absolute heaven.

"This is so good," she said and let out a loud moan.

Vixen. She knew exactly what she was doing when she made that sound.

"Hey, will you take me to the Neon Cowboy for a drink after this? I've heard so much about it, and I'd love to finally step foot inside."

I should've said no. Morgan and the guys were often there and taking his mom there was a huge risk, but I couldn't say no. She looked too excited, and I wasn't ready to take her home yet. "Sure."

I knew I'd regret it the moment the words left my mouth.

"ARE YOU FUCKING CRAZY?" Tank asked when Fran excused herself and went to the ladies' room.

"Clearly, I am."

"What the hell are you doing with Fran DeLuca?"

"Just having a drink." I shrugged and feigned innocence.

Tank's hand connected with the back of my head, and my body lurched forward. "Don't be a dumbass."

I turned and glared at him, balling my hands into tight fists under the table. "You got a free shot—the next one I'm hitting back, fucker. We're adults. She wanted to have a drink so I brought her."

"What are you going to do when Morgan hears about it?"

"He won't, and if he does, I'll handle him."

Tank started to laugh so hard that he almost fell off his chair. "You're a dumber shit than I thought."

"I really like her, Tank," I admitted to him, feeling a weight lift off my chest from finally saying the words out loud.

"You're fucked, buddy. Totally fucked."

I glanced toward the ceiling and exhaled. "I know."

"Hey, guys. What did I miss?" Fran said as she sat down, brushing her hair back off of her shoulders, and smiling.

"Not a thing," Tank replied before taking a slug of his beer and diverting his eyes.

"This place isn't really what I thought."

"What did you think it would be?" I asked.

"I thought it would be more like a hole-in-the-wall honky-tonk."

"Nah." I laughed and pulled my beer a little closer. "It's just a good ole-fashioned biker bar."

She looked around the bar, slowly taking in the crowd. "Do people dance?"

"Sometimes," I lied.

"Will you dance with me?"

"Um…"

"Come on, ya big baby. I'm sure you have some moves," she teased me while nudging me in the ribs.

"Okay," I said, unable to resist her even though I knew every set of eyes in the place would be on us.

"Dumb fucker," Tank muttered under his breath so only I could hear.

Rising to my feet, I glared at him before holding out my hand to Fran. She slid her hand in mine with the biggest grin on her face. Just as our feet touched the empty area of the bar that was typically the dance floor, Brantley Gilbert's "If You Want a Bad Boy" started to play.

"I love this song," she said as I wrapped my arms around her and pulled her closer, but I still left a little space between us. As if she knew what I was doing, her arm hooked around my neck and she closed the tiny gap.

It took me a minute to find my footing because I couldn't get Tank's words out of my head, and having Fran's tits pressed against me only made things worse.

We locked eyes, our feet moving with the beat, and everything else seemed to disappear. All I could see, feel, or hear was Fran. Her tiny laugh when I spun her around, and the feel of her body crashing into me when I pulled her back.

The only time my eyes left hers was to glance down at her cleavage. No girl wears a bra like that without wanting to be noticed. My hand slid lower down her back, just above her ass, when something caught my attention.

More like someone.

Standing near the doorway with his arms crossed and a very pissed off look on his face was Morgan, flanked by City.

"Fuck," I grumbled and closed my eyes, but I didn't let go of Fran.

"What's wrong?" she asked, rubbing my back gently with her palm because she hadn't caught sight of them.

Very slowly, I slid my hand up her back and spun around so she could see them too.

"Fuck," she groaned, finally catching a glimpse of them. "This is a shitshow."

My thoughts exactly.

I'd hoped to keep this evening to us so I didn't need to deal with Morgan, but now I had to face him and hope he didn't flip his shit. "Let's get this over with."

City leaned over, whispering in Morgan's ear as we approached. Morgan's face was unreadable, but his body language wasn't.

"Hey, baby," Fran spoke first, leaning forward to kiss his cheek.

"Mom." He glared at me as she kissed him.

"What are you guys doing here?" she asked as she backed away.

Morgan's eyes hadn't left mine. "The real question is what are you two doing here?"

Fran came back to stand next to me, but I didn't dare wrap my arm around her. Not that I was worried that Morgan could take me, but because I didn't want to get into a fight with him. He was Fran's baby. If I punched him in the face, it wouldn't be pretty and would be the end of us before we even started.

"I was talking to Franny about the case, and she wanted to come for a drink. Who am I to say no to her?" I shrugged, hoping that it would pacify him.

"A word?" City asked and motioned toward the bar with his head.

"Sure," I replied before glancing down at Fran.

She nodded her approval. "Morgan, buy me a drink and sit with me."

"I think we should leave."

She stepped into his space and smiled. "Baby, I'm an adult. I want a drink with my son. Now shut the fuck up and buy me one."

I bit my lip and tried to stifle my laughter. It wasn't the time or the place to laugh my ass off at the way Fran handled him. Morgan wasn't the type of guy many people fucked with, but as with any big man, they were brought down to size when their mother was around.

"One drink," Morgan replied as I walked away to meet an already waiting City.

"What the fuck is wrong with you?" he said before I had a chance to say anything.

My head jerked back in surprise. "What?"

"Why the fuck would you bring her here?"

City had been my friend for years. We'd walk through fire for each other, but his response shocked me. "Where am I supposed to bring her?"

"You knew word would get back to me."

"No one knows her."

"Sure as fuck do."

"How?"

"She's been to all my parties. The guys here know her, stupid fucker."

"So what? We're having a drink. It's not like I'm banging her on the table for everyone to see."

He dug his fingers into his eyes and shook his head. "I can't unsee that image."

He turned to the bartender. "Tequila."

"Make it two," I mumbled before he could walk away. "How pissed is he?"

"I'm lucky you're still alive." City chuckled softly and grabbed the two shot glasses as soon as the bartender set them in front of us. Handing me one, he said, "I may need more than one if I'm going to get through the rest of tonight."

"You know I can't fight back if he hits me."

"I know. After a few of these, you won't feel the pain when he punches your fucking lights out."

As I lifted the shot glass to my lips, I watched Fran and Morgan talking at the table. Her hands were moving wildly as she spoke, and I knew the conversation was heated but it looked like Fran had it under control.

"Were you really talking about business?" he asked, slamming his shot glass down on the table. "Because your hand on her ass made it seem…"

I cut him off with a wave of my hand. "She's a big girl, City."

"I know you'd never hurt Fran on purpose, Bear, but she's my aunt. You're my best friend in the world, but she's family."

"You think I'm going to bang her and treat her like shit."

"It's what you usually do," he said flatly.

How could I explain to him that this was different? Fran wasn't a club whore or a barfly. She was a good woman and reminded me of Jackie. For years, I'd found the trashiest girls, ones I knew I wouldn't feel anything for, and had a good time until they became too clingy and I'd kick them to the curb.

"It's different with her."

He raised an eyebrow, calling bullshit on that statement.

"It is!"

"Uh-huh."

"Fucker, listen to me. I can't explain it, but I really like Fran. She's like a breath of fresh air in my fucked-up life."

Thin arms wrapped around my waist. "Hey, baby."

City's eyes widened, matching my own as soon as I heard the

voice. Fucking Molly. Peeling her hands from my body, I turned slowly and pushed her away gently.

"Molly."

"Wanna have some fun, big boy?" she said with a slur, hanging on to the word boy a little too long to be classified as sober.

"No. I told you I didn't want to see you again, and I meant every word of it." When she reached up to touch me, I grabbed her by the wrist and stopped her forward progress.

"Come on. I can make you feel good." Her eyes dipped to my cock, and she smirked. "I know just how you like it."

"Molly," I said quieter. "I'm not going to explain this again, so listen carefully. We're nothing. Nada. Zip. Zilch. So move along and find your next victim."

She pouted before a small smile spread across her face. "I love when you're like this. It's so hot. I know you want it rough, baby. Take out all that stress on me."

I glanced toward the ceiling and caught a glimpse of Morgan watching me. Quickly, I released Molly's wrist and put some space between us. "Lose my number and forget I exist," I told her because I didn't know what else to say. The woman clearly didn't understand the word no.

"City can join us if you want." She smiled brightly, running her eyes over his body.

City was over a decade my junior. His large body and chiseled good looks made it easy for him to bag the ladies—at least, before he found the love of his life, Suzy. His eyes darkened, and his body stiffened next to me. "I'm out. You clean up this mess and come over to the table," he said.

"Don't fucking leave me here," I told him and reached for his arm.

He took a few steps and turned to face me. "Get rid of her," he mouthed with a snarl.

As if this night couldn't get any worse—Molly had to show up, drunk off her ass, and wanting something I wasn't willing to give her again. With Morgan and Fran here, it added a whole new dimension of fucked up.

Could this night get any worse?

CHAPTER 8

FRAN

"Girlfriend?" Morgan asked as Bear took a seat next to me and set a new pitcher of ice-cold beer on the table. I kicked him under the table because it was none of his fucking business.

"No," Bear replied, but it wasn't exactly convincing.

"Clusterfuck," Tank muttered so quietly I barely heard him. His dark caramel eyes shifted, giving Bear the side-eye.

"What?" Morgan asked, turning his attention to someone else. My handsome son fit right in with this group. In his beauty and darkness, he was one of them.

Tank ran his hand across his jet black hair, which was cut in the most perfect military flat top I'd ever seen. "Nothing, man." His unusually wide shoulders hunched forward, making his neck disappear.

In the murky lighting of the seating area of the Neon Cowboy, Bear looked rougher than the man who'd sat across from me at dinner earlier. There was a darkness in his eyes I hadn't seen before.

"You okay?" I asked, leaning over, and speaking softly so only Bear could hear.

He glanced down at me, his steely gray eyes connecting with mine. He gave me a quick nod, grabbing my hand underneath the table, and giving it a tight squeeze. I smiled up at him, but I wasn't convinced.

"Well, it's getting late. I better get you home, Ma," Morgan said, interrupting the little moment Bear and I were having.

"No." I didn't even look in his direction. It was time that I put this boy in his place. I may be his mother, but that didn't give him the right to dictate my life.

"It's too dangerous for you here."

I turned to face him and narrowed my eyes. "I'm surrounded by four strapping men. I highly doubt anyone will fuck with me, Morgan. So just zip it and have a beer—relax a little bit, and enjoy your friends as much as I am." Bear's hand tightened around mine underneath the table.

The last statement didn't earn me a smile, but I hadn't expected it to either. The boy had some serious control issues. I never really realized it before tonight, but then again, I never hung out with *his* people.

He dragged the pitcher across the table and started to pour himself a glass. "Fine, but I'm driving you home."

My eyes didn't leave him, and I waited a moment to answer. "I'm going home with Bear."

He slammed the pitcher against the table, and some of the beer splashed out onto the table. "Like fuck you are!"

"Morgan, put your pencil dick back in your pants and calm the fuck down," Bear said, moving his arm from under the table, and sliding it across the back of my chair. "Your mom is a grown woman, and we're just friends. Would you rather her be home watching reality television?"

Morgan's face turned the brightest shade of red. "Bear, you know I love you, man, but you better keep your paws off my ma. She's off-limits, and she doesn't need your kind of friendship."

Bear stood quickly, tipping his chair over, and Morgan did the same. I could see that the conversation was becoming heated and that I was the only person who could calm the situation.

"Boys," I yelled, standing up, and placing my face between theirs. "Both of you sit your asses down. Now!"

They didn't move initially, just stared each other down in the ultimate pissing contest. Morgan moved first, snarling at Bear as he sat down slowly. Bear growled in response, easing down into the chair with his eyes still locked on Morgan.

"You two are ridiculous," I scolded them like children. "Morgan." I paused, waiting for my lovely son to give me his full attention. When he did, I continued. "Bear has been kind and respectful to me. He's been nothing but a gentleman. I asked him to bring me here because I didn't want to sit at home alone tonight. Would you rather I use that Tender app I have on my phone?" I tapped my foot, still hovering above them.

Morgan's face scrunched up, and his head jerked back. "Do you mean Tinder?"

I shrugged and rolled my eyes. "Whatever it's called. Would you rather I use that to go out for a drink? I was told all I have to do is swipe, and voilà, I'd have a date."

He rested his elbow on the table and covered his face with his hand. "Tinder is not a dating app, Ma."

"Yeah, it is," I told him and put my hands on my hips.

"Fran, it's not," Bear said, giving me the sweetest smile.

"Well, what the hell is it, then?" Glancing around the table, I saw Morgan was horrified and the other guys at the table were almost in hysterics. I threw up my hands and finally sat my ass down with a huff.

"It's a hookup app." Bear smiled indulgently.

"A what?"

"Oh, God," Morgan groaned, dropping his hand to the table with a loud thump.

"It's how people find each other for one-night stands. It's not to find a long-term relationship."

"That can't be true."

"Sorry, Aunt Fran, it is," City said, clearing his throat to hide his amusement.

"Well, fuck. I'm glad I didn't 'hook up' with Fred last week," I said, using air quotes. "I thought he meant hooking up to have a drink. I didn't know he wanted to have sex with me."

"When the hell did you download Tinder?" Morgan asked with a suspicious look that made me want to spank him like he was a little boy.

"Newsflash, kid... I'm a woman, and I'm single. I can't sit at home alone for my entire life."

"But you had Johnny," Morgan replied quickly.

"Johnny was just a..." My voice trailed off.

"A what?" Morgan's eyes widened.

"We were never a couple."

"I can't." He waved his hands in surrender. "Let's just have our beer and talk about something else."

My mouth turned up into the biggest smile. I'd finally worn his ass down. Maybe now he'd learn to zip it. "I'd like to finish the dance you so rudely interrupted."

"Fine, Ma. I'll dance with you," he grumbled.

"I wasn't talking about with you. Bear," I said, turning to the hot guy sitting next to me.

"Anything you want, Franny." He held his hand out, and I slipped mine into his, loving the roughness of his callused skin against mine.

Morgan sat like a petulant child, gawking at us as we rose and made our way to the same spot we were in before he walked through the door.

"You know this isn't going to end well," Bear said as he wrapped his arms around me, but he didn't dare put his hand anywhere near my ass.

"I'll handle him."

"Babe, you're his mom and you have some sway, but there's a man's code I have to deal with."

"Murray, sweetie, he'll calm down. Just ignore him." Taking my own advice, I rested my head against his chest and followed his lead.

The beat of his heart matched the slow, steady rhythm of the music as we moved. I couldn't wipe the stupid grin off my face while we danced. He smelled too good, and he felt even better pressed against me. Bear had that animal magnetism I'd always found sexy. There was nothing soft about him, except for the way he spoke to me.

I could see the man underneath and sometimes a hint of the man who had deeply loved and lost. In the years I'd known him, I'd never really taken the time to get to know him. I just knew that he worked with Morgan, and he was City's best friend. He was always in the middle of a shit storm, willing to put himself in harm's way for his friends.

I liked that about him. He wasn't a pussy and knew the meaning of loyalty.

When the song started to come to an end, I said, "This is nice."

His hand tightened around my waist, and he buried his face in the top of my hair. "I haven't felt this at peace in years, babe."

"Are they staring at us?" I asked into his T-shirt.

"No, not anymore."

I peered up at him and smiled. "I enjoyed myself tonight."

His eyes softened, and I fought not to reach up on my tiptoes and kiss him. "Me too. Want to do it again?"

"Yes, please."

"Wanna get out of here?" he asked, quirking an eyebrow at me with a mischievous smile.

"Thought you'd never ask."

When we made our way back to the table, I cleared my throat until City, Tank, and Morgan looked up at us. "We're going to go. I'm exhausted." I faked a yawn. "Bear's going to drop me off."

"I'll take you home, Ma," Morgan said again, even though I'd shut that conversation down before.

"No, Morgan. Bear's going to drive me home. You go home to your wife."

"Night, Aunt Fran," City said with a deep, low laugh.

"Night." Tank tipped his head and gave Bear a funny look.

"Ready?" Bear asked behind me but not close enough to feel his body heat.

"Yep."

As soon as we made it outside, a woman dressed more like a washed-up hooker approached with a wild look in her eyes—the same woman Bear had spoken to at the bar with City.

"You're taking this old bitch home?" she seethed as her eyes raked over my body. "What the fuck, Bear?"

Bear placed his body between us. "Shut the fuck up, Molly. Go back to the hole you crawled out of."

Her hand slid over his shoulder. "You know I can make you feel good. She's all dried up."

Bear wrapped his hand around her arm and pushed her away. "Watch your mouth. I'm in no mood for your shit tonight."

She peered around his body and glared at me. "I just fucked him. If you want sloppy seconds, he's all yours."

"I think the man asked you to leave." Somehow, I tried to be diplomatic, when the woman really needed a punch in the face.

"He'll come back… They always do."

Bear glanced at me over his shoulder and looked up toward the sky. "Molly, if I have to tell you again that we're not a couple, you're going to regret it."

"Whatcha gonna do, Bear, spank me?" She laughed loudly and licked her cracked lips, trying to be sexy.

Bear reached behind him and took my hand. "Get a fucking life and leave us alone," he told her as he guided me toward his bike.

"You're going to regret not being with me, Bear!" Her frizzy hair flopped around as she stomped away from us, talking to herself like a crazy person.

"I can't believe you stuck your dick in that."

He turned and grimaced. "Would it make it any better if I blamed it on alcohol?"

"It's the only way I'd ever believe you'd do it."

"It was only once." He pressed his body against me, and using his fingertips, pulled my eyes to his. "I promise."

I searched his eyes and knew he spoke the truth. "She sure seems to be head over heels for you."

"She's a crazy bitch, Fran. Ignore her."

Placing my hand on his arm, I swept my thumb against his skin. "She's forgotten."

He smiled down at me as his fingertips brushed against my cheek. All I could think was, *kiss me, kiss me, kiss me,* but it didn't happen.

As I climbed onto his bike and wrapped my arms around him, I felt a pang of jealousy. Skanky Molly had a piece of Bear that I never did.

I wasn't sure I ever would either.

CHAPTER 9

BEAR

As soon as I shut the engine off, Fran asked, "Want to come in for a nightcap?"

This was where I should've declined and been on my way, but that had never been my style.

"Sure." I knew it was a dumb-ass move, but I didn't give a fuck.

I liked Fran.

More than I should, actually.

I never mixed business, friendship, and sex together. That combination could be nothing more than a recipe for complete disaster. But I'd hit a point in my life where I didn't give a fuck what anyone thought.

I trailed behind her up the walkway, watching her cute little ass swaying back and forth and her sleek black hair matching the rhythm as it swished through the air. She glanced over her shoulder and smiled as she placed the key in the door lock.

For a woman of her age, she had very few wrinkles, and her skin almost glowed, even with her caramel Italian complexion. She had just a few lines near the corners of her eyes that made them seem more mysterious, giving her more character, and intriguing me even more.

"What's your poison?"

"Anything you got." I didn't care if she brought me a glass of water. All I knew was that I wasn't ready to go home to my empty place and say goodnight to her.

I watched her while I sat in her living room as she moved around the bottles in her cabinet, bent over with her ass in the air, and all I could think about was seeing her in the same position without the jeans.

"Gin?" she asked without looking in my direction.

"Sure," I replied, unable to drag my eyes away.

She straightened and finally glanced over her shoulder. "Ice?"

I nodded without speaking because I was at a loss for words, and to be quite frank, I was still lost in the fantasy of bending Fran over in the same position.

"Sex?" she said quietly as she carried two glasses in my direction.

My eyes cut to hers in complete shock. "What?"

"You're looking at me like you want to eat me, Bear." She laughed softly and blushed.

I rubbed my neck, trying to ease the tension, but it wasn't the right part of my body that needed relief. "To be honest, Fran, the shit I want to do with you is illegal in about forty-five states."

She handed me the drink and sat down next to me, smoothing back her hair. "Only forty-five?" she teased.

"Fran." I set the drink down on the coffee table and turned to face her. "I'm trying to be a good guy here, when everything in me wants to be bad. You're not making it any easier, sauntering into the office in clothes that scream sex and a dirty-ass mouth to boot. I'm hanging on by a thread, babe."

She swallowed hard, placing the cold glass against her neck. "Why do you have to be good?"

Rubbing my hands together, I exhaled loudly. "There are a dozen reasons I shouldn't be here right now."

"Don't you dare name my kid."

"He's the first reason." My palms started to sweat, and I knew that the further we got into this conversation, the harder it was going to be to come up with excuses.

"Would you let your kid tell you who to fuck?" she shot back with a smug look because she knew she had me.

"Hell no."

"Well, I'm not going to let mine either."

"I'm not good for you," I admitted. But it was the truth. My police record read more like an issue of *Reader's Digest*, filled with stupid-ass antics that I knew were bad ideas, but I did them anyway.

"There's that word *for* again. I've spent the last twenty years being 'good.' I'm over it." The Fran sitting next to me didn't look like she had an ounce of angel in her. She was a sex kitten with the mouth of a truck driver. The black eyeliner around her chocolate eyes made her seem even more naughty. Gone was the tracksuit, replaced by a wardrobe that said she was on the prowl.

Had she done it for me?

I wondered if I was the cause. I had one dinner with the woman, and the next day, she made a grand entrance at the office, sporting an outfit that would have most men's tongues wagging like a dog in heat.

She didn't give me a chance to respond before she crawled into my lap and straddled me with her legs squeezing my thighs. "Bear," she whispered while she stared down at me with a look that could only be described as lustful. "Kiss me."

I thought about it for a grand total of two seconds before I reached up and cupped her face in my palm. The heat from her pussy had my cock hard a few seconds later. I could no longer deny myself what I wanted—and what she wanted too. I dragged the rough pad of my thumb against her soft, plump lip. "Are you sure, Franny?" My voice was deep, yet gentle.

She nodded with a tiny smile on her lips. I took a deep breath, already light-headed at the thought of tasting her. Instead of leaning forward to kiss her, I wrapped my fingers around the back of her neck and pulled her down to me. Without hesitation, my lips connected with hers. A soft moan escaped her throat, vibrating into my mouth as her body relaxed, and her pussy ground against my already aching dick.

Tasting her was like sinking my teeth into the sweetest fruit for the first time. Describing the feeling of her against my body was impossible. Her soft to my hard had my head spinning and my body in overdrive.

She rocked against my body as she opened to me when I tried to deepen the kiss. I couldn't do gentle with her. The need to touch her was more than I had prepared myself to deal with, but I stilled her body by holding her hip and stopping the through-the-clothes fucking she was giving me.

My fingers tangled in her hair, and her mouth opened more. Our tongues danced together in a perfect harmony, our moans the chorus to the most beautiful kiss I'd had in a long, long time. It wasn't soft. It wasn't hurried. There was nothing but need and lust between us, and I couldn't slow down the momentum even if I wanted to.

Tugging on her hair, I tried to pull her backward, but it only poured fuel on the fire. "Don't stop," she moaned against my lips before her tongue plunged back into my waiting, greedy mouth.

My hand slid from her hip to the middle of her back as I pushed her body against mine, leaving no space between us. She smelled like a mix of beer and flowers, but when my mouth finally blazed a trail to her neck, I caught a whiff of her perfume. The sweet, musky smell made my cock twitch, the familiar scent one I'd smelled somewhere before but couldn't remember where.

When I sank my teeth into her neck, hard enough to make her shiver but not enough to break the skin, she tipped her head back, following the pull of my fingers, and exposed her neck to my mouth more. The position made her core press harder into my cock, making my breath catch.

Her silky fingertips slid underneath my shirt, slowly raking over my sides before tangling in my chest hair. When her fingertips bit into my back, I grunted in approval and wanted more.

Like horny teenagers, we quickly dispensed of our shirts before my mouth found a way back to her bare flesh and her fingers dug into my sides. When our lips found each other's again, our hands started to roam, caressing the other's skin frantically.

My hand cupped her breast, kneading the lushness through her bra. Everything about Fran was soft—except her mouth. Her mouth was harsh and brash and drove me fucking wild.

Scratching her skin with my beard, I kissed my way to her chest, lingering where her tits met, and losing myself in the plumpness. The velvet of her skin met my lips, softer than any silk I'd ever touched, and I groaned softly.

Her eyes were closed when I peered up at her before pulling the top of her bra down and exposing the most perfectly erect nipple I'd ever seen.

I lowered my head and closed my lips around her nipple, stroking the stiff peak with my tongue, and moaning. She shivered in my arms and melted against me, lowering her even farther, and bringing her chest to an easy to reach level. I took my time, not wanting to rush having my face pressed against her chest, buried in her cleavage, and praying I'd die just like that.

When her hands started to tug at the button of my jeans, I pulled back. "Fran, I didn't bring protection."

Her eyebrows shot up, shocked at my admission. "You didn't?"

"No. I wasn't planning on fucking you tonight."

"Oh." She chewed on her bottom lip and cleared her throat. "I'm clean. Are you?"

"I am. I get tested regularly and haven't been with anyone without protection since…"

She frowned, probably knowing I was going to say since Jackie. I had always been prepared, but tonight I didn't even think about it. I planned on dinner and a kiss—because Fran was different.

God, I sounded like a pussy. I sure as fuck thought like one. Fran did that to me.

"Well, lucky for you, big boy, that I can't get knocked up." She giggled softly as her hands roamed my bare chest, toying with my nipples on each pass.

"You can't?"

"Nope." She shook her head with a smirk. "Menopause. It has its advantages."

"Oh, fuck. I didn't even think about that." Fran seemed too young to be in menopause. I don't know why it didn't even dawn on me before that moment. Most of the women I'd been with were younger, and it wasn't a conversation we had. Typically, I'd take what I wanted, wear protection, and be done with it.

"I trust you," she whispered, pressing her chest against mine. Her lips lingered just above mine as she stared into my eyes. "Do you trust me?"

I wouldn't have said I was a trustworthy guy when it came to pussy. I was unapologetic and greedy, but with Fran, I felt that I'd do anything in my power never to hurt her, including never lying to her about anything.

"I trust you," I whispered back before crushing my lips against hers.

It was like someone opened up the floodgates with those words. I lifted her off me, depositing her on the floor, and rising to stand in front of her. Although I wanted to undress her fully, there wasn't enough time or patience to make that a reality.

Watching each other, we unbuttoned our pants and threw them to the floor. The entire time, we were appraising each other, drinking in the other for the first time. I took in her entire beauty while Fran stared at my stiff cock, bobbing and weaving like it was in a boxing match.

The ravages of time and having a child hadn't affected Fran's body much. I couldn't see more than a few scars left as remnants of the baby she'd once carried. Her naturally tan skin shimmered in the dim lighting of her living room.

My hands itched to touch her, my dick ached to be inside her, but my mind kept reminding me that I was about to open up a can of worms that I could never put back.

But I didn't listen.

I never did.

It was how I got myself into half the shit in my life. It was how I ended up in jail and let my life spiral out of control.

Fran was just another notch in that belt.

"Come here," I told her and motioned for her with my hand.

She took tiny steps, tiptoeing her way to me. "Yes, sir," she said with a smug smile and laughter. My cock waved, loving her response.

God, she was beautiful. The way her eyes sparkled when she laughed and the tiny lines near the corners deepened.

I could get lost in them.

The little devil on my shoulder stabbed me with his spear. "Pussy," he whispered in my ear, but I silently told him to fuck off and decided to show him exactly what kind of man I was.

When she stood before me, shifting nervously on her feet and naked as the day she was born, I wrapped a hand behind her neck and pulled her to me. Before she could speak or I could chicken out, I slammed my lips against hers and devoured her as if my very life depended on it.

Reaching down between us, I slid my fingers through her slickness with ease… Fran was ready for me and just as greedy as me. She wanted it. I knew it. The kissing and touching on the couch made it clear, but there was no denying the need that dripped from my fingertips.

I tore my lips away, gasping for air. "I can't go slow."

"Take me," she proclaimed and waggled her eyebrows.

If my balls hadn't been about to turn blue, I'd have laughed.

Normally, I'd toy with the girl, driving her mindless with lust so she'd be willing to let me do anything I wanted just to get off. But Fran was different. I didn't feel like playing games, and I had a feeling she was just as big of a freak as me—if not, I'd bring it out in her.

I turned her around to face the back of the cushy chair and pushed her down, folding her over it. Starting at her neck, I traced a path to her ass and cupped it roughly.

I leaned forward and rested my lips against her ear. "Ever been taken here?" I asked as I ran my finger over her asshole.

She gasped and turned her face ever so slightly to look me in the eyes. "No," she said, clenching her ass, and looking away. "I haven't."

"Good," I murmured. "Don't worry, sweetheart. That's not for tonight. I have to earn that."

Parting her cheeks with one hand and holding my cock with the other, I nipped at her shoulders until she waggled her ass against my tip. "Careful now, girl."

I wanted to put it in her ass so fucking bad I wanted to jump out of my skin, but this was our first time and hopefully not our last. Before I even had the tip inside her pussy, she slammed back against me, impaling herself. I chuckled briefly, but when she started to move before I could, all laughter fell away.

Fran and I moved in synchronized rhythm like the perfect waves in the most ferocious storm, our bodies ebbing toward each other and flowing away.

As our bodies slapped together, I tried to hold it together. I didn't want to be a two-pump chump. But the way her body responded to mine and clamped down against me, I didn't know how long I'd last.

Reaching up, I placed my hand on her shoulder to take the reins and control the pace. "You have a greedy little pussy, don't you?" I grunted.

She answered with a shake of her ass as she tried to take control again. My grip tightened on her shoulder to remind her who was really in charge. "Bend over more."

She peered over her shoulder with a pout. "But I'll be on my tiptoes."

"Exactly." I smirked.

She started to bend forward, and I pushed down on her shoulder to help her, while my cock was still buried inside of her. I moved too, making sure not to lose the connection.

When she was barely able to stand, I slammed into her as hard as I could, causing her feet to dangle. She grunted her dissatisfaction at the position, and I responded with a growl before pounding into her without remorse.

Fran screamed out a moan, calling my name and dropping a few curse words in there too. My hand wandered to her waist, holding her in place as I repeatedly crashed into her.

And there it was. Her asshole. Taunting me. Teasing me. Beggin' to be taken. I couldn't take it anymore. The torment was too much. She gasped when I pulled my cock out of her, but I filled her with my fingers before she had a chance to whine. I plunged them into her, wetting them with her need, and rubbing her G-spot with each pass.

"Oh, God..." she moaned, dragging out the word as if it were a song.

Instead of pulling out, I kept going. Diving deeper, feeling every inch of her insides, and keeping the pressure on her G-spot as she writhed against the chair. When she gasped for air and bore down against my fingers, trying to push me out—I knew I had her right where I wanted her.

She stiffened, and her legs strained as my fingers assaulted her in the most pleasurable way. Fran DeLuca came for me for the very first time, and it was the most magnificent thing in the world. The way her body tensed and her mouth fell open, breathless and lost.

When her body started to calm, I withdrew my fingers and replaced them with my lonely, needy, and still hard-as-fuck dick. She melted against the chair, pliable and ready, just how I wanted her.

My fingers rubbed the remnants of her orgasm against her asshole, and she moaned softly with her head buried in the back of the chair. Slowly, I stuck the tip of my finger inside, and she moaned louder, clamping down on my finger like a vise.

Fran's pussy fastened itself around me, just as needy as her ass, and I took it as a sign that she wanted more—fuck, I knew I did. Slowly, I added a second finger to the mix, and I could no longer keep my eyes open. Fucking heaven. The feel of her ass wrapped around my fingers and her sweet cunt around my cock, I couldn't imagine anything better.

Working out of sync, I finger-fucked her ass and pummeled her pussy until her body grew slicker with sweat and I couldn't hold out any longer. My balls ached, retracting toward my body as if they knew they were home. The release washed over me, sucking the air from my lungs, and leaving my legs shaking. She followed me over the cliff, pushing my fingers out of her with her orgasm.

"Fuck," I groaned and collapsed against her.

Our bodies stuck together as we both tried to fill our lungs with air. My cock was still buried inside of her but making a slow retreat—being forced out by the aftershocks that racked her body.

"Damn," she whispered with her face still buried in the green fabric of the chair.

"You okay?" I asked, even though I knew the answer.

"Yeah," she muttered and tried to right herself, but she couldn't.

Pulling her by the waist, I helped her find her footing and instantly missed the heat of her skin and the heaven that was her pussy.

"I just didn't..." Her voice trailed off as she began to sway, but she caught herself and held on to the back of the chair. "I didn't know it could be that good." She turned around with a flushed face and sweat dotting her brow.

I cocked an eyebrow and smirked. "Just good?"

"Okay." She laughed. "I just didn't want you to get too cocky."

"Sweetheart, it's only cocky if you can't back that shit up." I turned her body to face me. "The way you came on my fingers and pushed against my cock, I know I did it right."

"Fine. It was fucking amazing."

My smirk grew bigger. "Best sex you ever had?"

She pursed her lips and tipped her head to one side, studying me. "I see you have a self-confidence issue."

"Want to see if I can do a repeat performance? Maybe I just got lucky." I shrugged, but I knew I was good. I'd spent too many years with way too many women to suck at it. Plus, I watched thousands of hours of porn in the name of education.

"I couldn't. I'm too old to do it twice."

"Franny." I wrapped my hand around her neck and rubbed her cheek with the pad of my thumb. "What's the longest any man's ever eaten your pussy?"

Her eyes widened. "I don't know."

"I'm not leaving this house until you pass out from exhaustion, completely spent by too many orgasms and a lack of oxygen."

"Fuck me," she whispered and gawked at me.

"I plan to. A lot. Lie down, spread those legs, and let me feast on that greedy pussy," I told her.

By the time the sun rose, Fran was passed out, with one arm hanging over the bed and the other draped across my chest.

I banged her brains out and mine too. Hopefully, I had just enough energy left to deal with Morgan because he wasn't going to be happy about the way I'd defiled his mother when he found out.

And he would find out.

I knew nothing stayed secret in that family for long.

CHAPTER 10

FRAN

"I want all the details," Maria demanded over the phone before I even had a chance to get out of bed.

"There's nothing to tell." I lied for good reason. Morgan would freak the fuck out, and I didn't feel like dealing with my son's shit first thing in the morning.

"I can keep a secret."

I burst into laughter because nobody in my family could hold on to anything for too long. "Don't lie to me. I've been your sister-in-law for far too long."

She made a *hmph* sound. "Did you fuck him?"

"Yes."

"Did you suck his cock?"

"A time or two."

She gasped. "Two?"

"I wasn't counting how many times his dick was in my mouth." I stretched and felt the effects of one too many orgasms on my muscles. The last few I had to strain for, but I couldn't let them slip away.

"Did you have an orgasm at least?"

"A few," I said coyly and smiled into the pillow I'd placed over my face.

507

"My girl," she said before she whistled.

"I lost count, but I sure as hell feel it. My muscles ache like I ran a marathon."

"When has your ass ever run a marathon?"

"Never." I laughed. "But I'm sure I'd feel something like this."

"Tell me more."

"Want me to draw you a picture, Mar? We sucked and fucked until I literally passed out."

"My God," she said softly. "Bear's a beast."

"Yep. The nickname fits."

"You passed out, passed out?"

"Yeah," I replied and thought about all the naughtiness of last night that almost felt like a dream.

"I did that once. Best night of my life."

"I don't want to know." Sometimes I wished Maria was married to someone else. I wanted to talk with her about sex and relationships, but Sal was my brother, and the thought of him having sex made me ill.

"Why?"

"He's my brother, and I'll vomit."

"Fine. Are you still in bed?"

"Yes."

I felt like I was on an episode of *Family Feud* in the bonus round with the way she was rapidly firing questions off at me.

"Get dressed and meet me for lunch. I think we need to go shopping again."

"Why?" I grumbled and struggled to sit upright. "I don't think I can walk around the mall."

"Get your slutty ass up and get dressed. You need more lingerie and clothes. It's time to throw out the tracksuits and keep that man coming back for more."

I kicked off the covers and stood on wobbly legs. "I don't think he cares about my clothes, Mar."

"He's Bear. He's a badass biker. He doesn't want Sophia standing next to him, with her glasses hanging by a chain."

"Fuck off," I told her as I spotted a note on the floor.

"You know I'm right. One o'clock by Macy's," she told me before she hung up.

I rubbed the sleep from my eyes and tried to focus on the blurry words.

Franny,

I didn't want to wake you. I'll call later. Rest up, sweetheart, I'm not done with you yet.

Bear

When I woke, my heart had been the only part of me that didn't feel battered. But after reading his words and thinking of all the possibilities, it started to beat wildly. I collapsed backward onto the bed and clutched his note to my chest. The scent of him, musky and strong, clung to the paper.

Fuckin' Maria. She was right. I needed to break out of my shell a bit further. I needed to shed my skin, ala my favorite tracksuits, and join the dating world again. To trap a man like Bear, I had to dress like a woman and not a grandma.

***

WALKING THROUGH THE PARKING LOT, I had to stop more than a few times to rub out the aches in my calves. Each one a reminder of the delicious night I'd spent with Bear.

"Jesus," Mar complained before I even had a chance to step onto the sidewalk. "I'm melting out here."

"No one told you to wait outside." I walked past her and opened the door, loving the feel of the air conditioning as it washed over me.

"I need something cold to drink before we start shopping."

It was her code for getting my ass in a seat and prying all the details of last night out of me. "I'm not giving you the details."

"You're a cruel woman, Fran. Cruel," she complained, following close behind me as her heels clicked against the linoleum flooring of the department store.

I stopped walking and spun around, narrowing my gaze. "How did you even know I was with him last night?"

"Joe told me."

"Aha." I pointed at her. "That's my point. Nothing is secret."

"What?" She shrugged before smiling. "He called to tell me that it's all my fault. He knows I took you shopping, and he blames me for setting you two up."

I walked away from her and headed into the mall near the food court. "Tell him to mind his own business."

She caught up, standing at my side. "I did."

I rubbed my neck and tried to ease the stress of the entire situation out of my muscles. "Fucking kids. They're so goddamn nosy."

"Don't I know it."

"I swear they're trying to get us back for being good, caring mothers."

As we were peering up at the coffee shop menu, she said, "You were a little over the top."

"Shut up, Mar. I had one kid to look after. I got carried away. I can't help that you pushed out a small army."

"I hover. I know I butt into their lives, but sometimes they seem to forget that I'm the parent."

"I'll take a trip caf half non-fat mocha," I told the pimply faced teenager behind the register.

She turned around and stared up at the menu. "I'm not sure what that is, ma'am."

I looked at Maria and rolled my eyes. "Order me something sweet, please. I don't know why coffee has to be so fucking complicated."

Maria motioned toward the bustling food court. "Go find us a seat, and I'll get the coffee."

"Fine," I grumbled under my breath as I walked away and found a seat nearby.

I glanced around the food court and felt like I fit in for the first time in a long time. No more elastic-trimmed pants and front-zip jackets. Those were gone and replaced by skinny jeans and form-fitting shirts. I couldn't forget the latest high-tech bra from the store that reeked of too much perfume, just down the way from where I sat.

"Here," Maria said, startling me as she placed some cold, blended beverage in a clear cup in front of me.

"What is it?" I stared at it like it had two heads.

"Some fracka something. I don't know." She pushed the drink closer to me. "It's good. Just drink it."

I wrapped my lips around the green straw and took a sip. To my surprise, it tasted amazing and hit the spot on such a hot, sticky day in Florida. "Thanks," I said after licking the remnants of the concoction off my lips.

"So let's talk trash." She rubbed her hands together and smiled. "Tell me every dirty detail."

I fidgeted with the cup, wiping away the moisture that started to dot the outside. "What do you want to know?"

"Is he big?"

"Um, his nickname is Bear."

"I know, dumbass. I'm talking about his cock."

"It's pretty." I giggled and felt my cheeks flush. "And larger than I expected."

"Really?" She tapped her finger against her coffee. "Tell me more. If you leave anything out, I'll tell Morgan."

My eyes widened in shock. "You wouldn't."

"Try me. I've been known to blackmail a person or two. I have leverage, and I'm not afraid to use it."

I sighed and knew it was futile to fight with her and keep quiet. She'd eventually get it out of me. And I was actually excited also—I needed to share what happened with someone, and Maria was the only option who could possibly keep my secret without judgment.

By the time I finished telling her every detail, down to the way he tasted, she was sweating and holding her drained yet still perspiring cup against her neck. "Well, fuck. That's hot."

"Yeah," I said and drained the last bit of fracka-whatever from my glass, but I still felt parched.

"Are you going to see him again?"

"Yep. He wants to see me again, and I can't say no. Especially after last night."

She straightened in her chair and leaned forward, becoming serious. "How are you going to explain this to Morgan?"

"Um," I mumbled and mimicked her by leaning forward too.

"What is there to explain? I'm an adult, he's an adult, and it's none of his fucking business."

She laughed and bit down on her lip. "It's about to get really interesting around here."

I crossed my arms on the table and lowered my voice. "He doesn't need to find out."

"Keep living in your dreamland."

"Just keep your trap shut."

She pretended to zip her lips. "My lips are sealed."

At least I knew I had a little time until the shit hit the fan. Morgan hadn't even entered my thoughts last night when I'd crawled into Bear's lap. He smelled too good and spoke to me too sweetly for my body not to respond. I hadn't expected it to be…so… so amazing. I hadn't planned on him being a gentleman with a raging sexual appetite more befitting a twenty-year-old. But the only thing I knew was that I wasn't willing to walk away from him just yet.

"Are we going to shop or sit here all day?" I asked when I felt stiffness start to seep into my leg muscles.

"Let's go get my girl some gear that screams 'fuck me.'"

"Great." I rolled my eyes and pushed back the chair, letting it scrape against the tile just to annoy her.

By the time we walked out of the mall, the sun had set in the sky and the cement let off heat in waves that looked like a mirage. "I'm exhausted," I said as I threw ten bags of clothing, underwear, shoes, and bras in the back of my tiny little SUV.

"Go home and nap. Recharge for round two." She snickered while she fished her keys out of her purse.

"I could use some sleep."

She leaned forward and kissed my cheek. "I have to get home and cook dinner. Sal will be home soon from the golf course."

"Make him take you out," I told her as I slammed the door closed on the back of my SUV.

"No way. I'm cooking, and he's eating." She waggled her eyebrows up and down, and I pretended to vomit.

"I've got to go."

"Bye," she said as she laughed and walked toward her car in the next row.

"Talk later," I called out and waved.

"Only if Sal unties me!"

I glanced toward the sky and sighed. She always had to leave me with the most disturbing mental images. I needed to scrub that one from my mind if I was ever to have sex again. "Fuckin' Maria," I muttered as I climbed into my car that felt more like an oven than an automobile.

Even after the air conditioning blasted me in the face the entire way home, looking like some old, haggard supermodel in an eighties' rockband video, I was still hot. But the heat wasn't from the sun. It was from the memories of last night playing in my head like a porn video.

When I walked through the front door with my hands full of packages, the phone was ringing off the hook. Before I could get to it, it switched over to my answering machine.

"Fran?" a man said, but the voice didn't sound familiar. There was urgency in his tone as he spoke. "It's Johnny. I need to talk to you."

I tossed the bags to the floor and went running to the phone. "Hello!" I sucked in a breath, trying to recover from the long run across my living room. "Hello," I repeated when I didn't hear anything. "Fuck!" I stared at the phone, knowing he'd already hung up.

I hurried up and dialed the one person I knew would want to know. "Bear," I said as soon as he picked up. I didn't even give him a chance to say hello. "Johnny just called."

"It's Morgan, Ma."

I pulled the phone away from my ear and glanced down at it, confused. Did I dial the wrong number? "Morgan?" I asked and placed the phone on my shoulder so I could pick up the clothes scattered across the carpeting.

"Yep. It's me. What did he say?"

"Nothing. Just that he needed to talk to me, and by the time I got to the phone, he hung up."

"I really wish you had caller ID sometimes, Ma. I'm going to call my buddy at the phone company and have the number traced. If he calls back, play along and try to get his location from him. Okay?"

"I will. Promise."

"And, Ma?"

"Yeah, honey?"

"We'll talk about why you called Bear instead of me later."

"Bye, Morgan," I groaned and disconnected the call before he could say anything more. I peered around the living room and tipped over onto my ass. "Fuck."

Just like Lucy, I had some 'splaining to do.

CHAPTER II

BEAR

I flipped through a file Sam had gathered about Johnny when I walked into my office and found Morgan talking on my phone. "Why are you behind my desk?"

He held up a finger, but he didn't look up. Sitting down across from him, I kicked my feet up on the desk, and shuffled through the information.

"He just called her." He then rattled off Fran's phone number, and I glanced up at him and narrowed my eyes. "Trace it and get back to me with a location," he told the person on the other line before hanging up the phone.

"Who called your ma?"

He glared at me and leaned back in my chair. "You know her number by heart already?"

"I've called her about the case enough that I have it memorized." I fucking lied my ass off because I wasn't ready for the talk.

"We'll talk about it later. Johnny just called her."

I threw the folder on the edge of my desk and leaned forward. "What exactly did he say?"

Slippery fucker. I couldn't believe he had the balls to call her after running off with fifty thousand dollars of Race's money.

"Just that he needed to talk to her."

"What the fuck is there to talk about? He stole money, lied, and ran away." My hand started to shake and I fisted it, then I released it because I couldn't pound Johnny in the face.

"I don't know. It's funny how she called your phone and not mine."

"What?"

"I was in here dropping off a file when her number flashed across the caller ID."

I rubbed the back of my neck and tried to come up with some bull-shit excuse. "I've talked to her more than anyone about the case, so it's only natural she called me first."

"Listen, Bear. You've been a great friend to me for years now, but what in the fuck were you thinking, taking my mom to the Neon Cowboy?"

I crossed my arms in front of my chest, cocking my head at the man and the question. "What's wrong with it there?"

He scrubbed his hand across his forehead and exhaled loudly. "It's dangerous. It's no place for a woman her age."

I held my hand out and stopped him from continuing. "Hold up. What kind of shitty statement is that?"

"Well, it's true. It's a biker bar. My mom isn't really the typical clientele."

"You go there."

"But I'm a man."

And here I'd thought the younger generation wasn't a bunch of sexist pigs—my mistake. "There's nothing wrong with that bar. Your mom wanted to go, and I had no problem taking her with me." I eyed him with suspicion. I assumed it had more to do with her being there with me than the actual type of bar it was. "Where should she be?"

"I dunno." He shrugged. "Church."

I couldn't hold my laughter in as I doubled over and slapped my leg. "You've got to be shitting me, man."

"Just don't bring her there again. And—" He cleared his throat, and I knew what was coming next. "I'd appreciate it if you kept your rela-tionship strictly professional. I don't need my mom to become another notch in your belt. If you get my drift."

"Kid." I shook my head because I knew he had a set on him, but I wasn't going to cater to his dreams. I wasn't about to confess my love or tell him how many times I'd already fucked Fran either. "Your mom is a grown-ass woman. She can make decisions for herself. I've treated your mother with nothing but respect, and I'll continue to do so, but you don't get to decide what type of friendship your mother and I have."

Leaning forward, he pinched the bridge of his nose, and I was ready for him to leap across the desk. "I've seen you with enough women to know what you do, Bear. I'm trying to be nice and talk to you man-to-man, but I won't stay so cordial for long. Friendship only goes so far, my friend."

The phone rang, but just as I was about to answer, Morgan grabbed it first. "You got it?" he said to the caller and grabbed a pen that sat near the top of my desk calendar.

Fuck, don't look at what it says.

I spent the morning scribbling Fran's name around the edges while I made various phone calls. He didn't give it a second look but jotted down a number on a blank space.

"Thanks, Tim." He tapped the pen against the calendar and stared straight at me as they continued to chat for a few more seconds. "Well," he said as he hung up the phone. "Looks like he's in a small town in Georgia."

"I can leave now," I told him because it was partly my case too.

"No, I'll go. You stay here in case he's already gone."

"Okay." I smiled. "I'll keep Fran busy." I knew that would piss him off and make him sing a different tune.

His face reddened. "Like hell, you will. Get your shit, and let's get out of here."

I got to my feet quickly and grabbed my cell phone off the desk, shoving it in my pocket. "I'm ready."

"Don't you want any clothes? We'll probably be gone at least a night."

"I have a bag just in case of emergencies."

"Of course you do," he grumbled and gave me a sideways glance as he stood.

Although I always loved a road trip, especially when it could lead to some trouble, I wasn't exactly thrilled about being trapped in the car with Morgan. "I'll run and get my car."

"No. I'll drive," he corrected me. "You're just coming so I can keep an eye on you."

"I'm not twelve."

"No, but you're making the moves on my mom, and I can't be worried about you instead of having my head in the game."

I wasn't about to tell him that I'd already made my moves. He'd probably shoot my ass before I even had a chance to defend myself. "Anything you want." I smiled wryly.

WE MADE it to the tiny town outside of Valdosta before sunset. Most of the drive I slept since Morgan decided he didn't much feel like talking to me.

"What a shithole," I said as we scouted the tiny bar where the phone call had originated from.

"I've been in worse."

"Excuse me." I waved the lady bartender over. "Hey," I said with a smile to the almost pretty woman behind the bar. "We're looking for someone and hope you can help."

She looked me up and down, her lifeless eyes drifting over to Morgan for a second. "You gonna order something?"

"Yeah, we'll take two Millers." I slid a twenty on the counter. "Keep the change, doll." I winked.

She smiled brightly before snatching the money away and shoving it in her front pocket with her bony arms. "Lots of people come in and out of here." She dug in the beer cooler under the bar, but she never took her eyes off us. "I don't know if I can help."

"He was just here." Morgan reached into his pocket to retrieve a photo that was taken of Johnny last year at the track. "He placed a call from your pay phone."

Her yellow-toothed smile vanished as she set the beers in front of us. "You two cops?"

"Honey, do I look like a cop?" I laughed.

She lifted her chin in Morgan's direction. "He does."

"He's not. Cops aren't usually my type of people anyway. He's looking for his dad is all, sugar."

She eyed us warily. "I may have seen him." She glanced toward the end of the bar to a group of rowdy guys and frowned. "I'll be right back."

"What the fuck?" Morgan gawked at me. "He's not my father, dipshit."

I shrugged. "He could be. Anyway, she'll help if she thinks he's family. This isn't the type of bar where people go to stand out, and it doesn't seem like the type of town where they welcome outsiders. Just shut the fuck up so we can get the information and head home."

"Sorry," she said, wiping her hands on the rag that was thrown over her shoulder. "So he's your daddy." She pointed to Johnny in the photo.

"Yeah."

She lifted it closer to her eyes and squinted before glancing at Morgan. "He doesn't look like you."

"I'm adopted," he said quickly. "He disappeared last week, and my mother is in a panic."

She slid it across the bar with a single finger. "Usually, people who vanish don't want to be found."

"How much do you want to make your conscience feel better?" I asked, knowing how the game was played.

She leaned forward, resting her elbows on the bar. "A hundred should do it."

I reached into my pocket and grabbed my money clip. "Is he staying around here?" I asked when I held a hundreddollar bill between my two fingers.

She grabbed it quickly and stuffed it in her bra. "He's been staying at the inn next door for a few days. He'd wander in here for a drink each night, but I haven't seen him in a few hours."

"Thanks for the information."

"Sure. Anything else you want to know?" she asked. "Maybe I

could interest you two in something else. Seems like you have more money to burn." Her eyes drifted to my money clip still in my hand.

"No, that's it. Thanks," Morgan said and yanked on my T-shirt after he stood up.

"I get off at two," she yelled out as I followed Morgan through the crowd.

"Do women just throw themselves at you?" he barked before we made it to the door.

"I think she was talking to both of us, kid."

"Yeah, 'cause that's gonna happen."

I laughed behind his back because he was wound so fucking tight I thought that if the right string were pulled, his head would start to spin around like a top. He grumbled, talking to himself as we made our way to the motel next door. The woman called it an inn, but in no way did it resemble anything other than a by-the-hour, dirty-ass motel that I'd spent my fair share of time in throughout the country.

"Hello," Morgan called out after the bell on the door finished ringing.

A man with a wild comb-over that looked more like a gnarly bird's nest sitting on his head walked out of the office. "How can I help you?" he asked, seeing Morgan first and then sneering when he saw me. "Sorry, guys, I can't rent a room to two men. It's not biblical."

He could not be serious. This wasn't the Ritz, and in no way was this anything other than a place to hit it and quit it. "I highly doubt anything that happens in this place is biblical."

He smoothed down his hair, but it didn't help. It still looked a mess. "Then what can I help you with?" he asked as he hitched up his brown polyester pants.

"We're looking for someone who's staying here," Morgan replied and pulled the photo from his back pocket and set it on the counter in front of the man.

He didn't look at the photo as he sat down. "I don't make it my business to remember faces."

Morgan fisted a handful of bills in his hand. "How much to make it your business?"

The man glanced down and took stock of the wad of bills. "Two hundred."

"Here," he said, plucking two bills off the top. "What do you know about him?"

Once the balding man had the money in his hand, he said, "He checked out three hours ago."

Morgan glanced at me over his shoulder, and I shrugged and shook my head. That type of information wasn't really worth the amount he'd paid. "Did he pay cash?" I asked, trying to get as much as we could out of him.

"Cash."

"What name did he use?"

"I don't ask for names," he said quickly. "Sorry I couldn't be more help."

"I'm sure you are," Morgan sneered, but I rested my hand on his shoulder to stop him from saying anything more.

"Thanks for your time," I told the guy and started to back up, hoping Morgan would follow.

"What a cocksucker," he said when we were outside in the sticky night air.

"I didn't expect to get much out of him. Should we head back?"

"Got a hot date?" he asked and quirked an eyebrow. "Wait, don't tell me. I don't wanna know."

"Nah, man. I'm just tired." I waved him off and tried to play it cool as we walked through the parking lot.

"Right answer."

"What the fuck!" Morgan ran toward his car and bent down near the tire.

"What's wrong?"

"It's flat."

"Shit," I groaned because that meant we were going to be in this shithole town longer. "Let's put on the spare and get the hell out of here."

He pointed at the tire and growled. "This is the spare."

"Dude, you didn't replace it?"

He shook his head.

"I can push it to the nearest station." Because at that point, I'd carry the car just to get home.

"I don't even remember where one is. I saw one about five miles back."

I closed my eyes and cursed. "I'll call for a tow."

Pacing the parking lot, I listened to the worst elevator music I'd ever heard as I waited on hold for roadside assistance to answer. When they finally did, their response was that someone would be out as soon as possible, but the expected wait time was close to eight hours.

"They coming?" he asked when I hung up and almost crushed the phone in my hand.

"They'll be here in the morning."

"Seriously?"

"I wouldn't lie about something as sad as this."

He scrubbed his hand down his face and grunted. "Might as well get a beer. It's going to be a long-ass night."

"Aren't you happy I'm here to keep you company?"

"Yeah, couldn't be any fucking happier about anything in my life," he grumbled, walking ahead of me toward the honky-tonk.

Even though it was late, I sent Fran a text because I wanted her to know I wouldn't be back soon and that I was with Morgan. She'd already texted me earlier, worried about my safety, being alone with him. I assured her that I could handle him and that he seemed clueless about anything that happened the night before.

"Two Millers," he said as we sat down at the bar next to each other.

The woman from earlier fished out two beers, but she kept her eyes pinned on us. "Find what you were looking for?"

I shook my head.

"Didn't feel like leaving tonight?" she asked and smiled, sliding our beers across the counter.

"Just grabbing a drink before we're on our way."

"Don't leave so soon." She placed her hand on top of Morgan's and toyed with his wedding ring. "Might as well have some fun while you're away."

Morgan pulled his hand back like her hand had burned him. "We're fine. Just wanted a drink."

"Come on. It's not often we get new blood in here."

"Ma'am, we're not looking for anything other than a drink. We're both taken and have no plans to cheat, so why don't you move it along?" I shooed her away.

She pursed her lips. "You don't know what you're missing out on, handsome," she drawled, sauntering away from us, and swinging her hips wildly.

"She's just…" Morgan started to say but didn't bother to finish before taking a gulp of his beer.

"Yeah," I mumbled, knowing exactly where he was going.

"Well, what do we have here," a man said from behind us in the twangiest Southern accent. "Chase, I think we have a couple of city slickers."

I closed my eyes because I knew where this was going. A couple of macho country shitheads felt the need to mark their territory and give us shit.

"Move along," I said without turning around.

"Big shot here wants us to move along," he repeated my words like a moron. "Should we do that, Chase?"

"Nah, man. They look like some uppity fuckers that don't know this isn't their bar."

God, I thought I dealt with some dumb motherfuckers at the Neon Cowboy, but these backwoods, inbred shitheads took the cake.

"They're not worth the time," Morgan said next to me.

I lifted the bottle to my lips and pretended they weren't behind me. The last thing we needed was to get into a fight in the middle of Bumfuck, Georgia, late at night. We were interlopers in their world, and it wouldn't turn out well.

"I'm talking to you, boy," the guy, not Chase, said and hit my shoulder.

Was he fucking serious? I'm fifty fucking years old and hardly a boy, but I knew he meant it as a derogatory statement, trying to get my blood boiling. He accomplished his goal.

I spun around on my stool to come face-to-face with a redneck. Not just any country bumpkin, but a real-life, moonshine-making, shit-shoveling, cousin-fucking country boy.

"What's your fucking problem?" I barked, already curling my hand into a tight fist, and ready to swing at any moment.

He yanked on his red ball cap, adorned with a Confederate flag and covered in dirt. "You are. You don't belong here." He shoved his stubby little finger in my chest.

I glanced down and laughed. "I don't see your name on the bar. It's a free country last time I checked." I tried to play it cool, but I didn't feel like sitting in jail tonight. Even the fleabag motel next door was preferable to a metal bench in a cell.

"This is my town," he announced and spread his arms out and raised his chin like he was king of the world.

I didn't have to look around to know that everyone in the bar was staring at us. He was talking loud enough that everyone heard him, and the music had been turned down for those too far away to hear over it.

I crossed an arm in front of my chest and stroked my beard. He couldn't be more than 5'10", barely taller than me while I was seated. Probably at some time he had muscles, but his flabby arms stuck out from his sleeveless plaid dress shirt. "I'm just having a beer, guy. Why don't you bother someone more your…" I looked him up and down "…size."

Morgan laughed next to me before finally turning to face them. "Chase, why don't you take your buddy and get out of here before you get your ass kicked by an old man and a city boy."

"Who the fuck you calling old, kid? I can kick your ass with one hand behind my back," I replied to him but kept my eyes trained on Chase and Shithead.

"Come on, Travis, let's leave them alone," Chase told Travis, the inbred motherfucker, and averted his eyes. "They're not bothering anyone."

"Listen to your friend," I told him and cracked my neck, slowly turning it side to side.

"I think you're done drinking here, city slicker. This is my bar, and you're not welcome." Travis snarled and cracked his knuckles.

Here we go.

There was a point in every hostile conversation when you knew what was going to happen. No matter what I said or did, he was going to swing at me. It wasn't that I was in *his* bar, but he wanted a fight and figured he'd pick on the stranger.

I didn't know why I looked like a good mark. I was well over half a foot taller than him, my muscles were still thick and strong, and I wasn't friendly looking. My graying beard and dark, weathered eyes didn't convey softness. Maybe he thought my gray was a sign of weakness, but I knew different. I'd taken on bigger men than him and won. It wasn't all about power, but brains too. Travis clearly didn't have much of either.

"Let's get this over with," I said and stepped down off the stool and towered over him.

"Finally, something smart came out of your mouth," he replied and nudged Chase with his elbow.

"I'm still waiting for you to say something smart. Where's your mama? Or is she your cousin?" I teased him because I was done pussy-footing around. I wanted him to swing on me. It had been forever since I'd knocked some country bumpkin on his ass, and Travis was an easy mark.

His face reddened, and a vein in the side of his neck bulged. "No one talks about my mama."

I waited, standing tall and straight, and watched his hand closely. He swung on me moments later, and I jerked my upper body backward to make him miss. He looked like a child trying to hit a piñata that was way too high for him to reach.

He grunted, but it didn't deter him from trying again. This time, I let him connect with my face, just for shits and giggles. My head snapped to the side, all for show, of course, because I had to fuck with him and let him think he got one in. "Best you got, Travis?" I smirked.

He swung again, but this time, I grabbed his hand and crushed it in my grip. "Hit me like a man or don't even bother, pussy," I goaded him before releasing his fist.

He shook it out and looked around the bar. He wasn't looking like such a tough guy in front of his "friends" at this point. An old-ass city guy was showing him up.

"Want any help?" Morgan asked before he took another sip of his beer.

"I got this," I told him and waved him off before I turned my full attention to a fuming Travis. "I'm going to give you five shots to knock my ass out before I put you down."

He swiped his thumb down the side of his nose and started dancing around, using fancy footwork like in the boxer movies. I couldn't hold back and started to laugh. "You've got to be fuckin' jokin'. Is this kid for real, Morgan?"

"Seems like he's going to give you everything he's got, Bear. If he beats you badly, I'll step in and put him out of his misery."

"Shut up," Travis the douchebag said to Morgan and continued to move around like he was Rocky.

"I'll make it easier for you. I'll put my hands behind my back, give you five shots, and if I'm still breathing, I'm going to take you outside by the feet and beat you bloody. Sound like a deal?"

Again he swept his thumb down his nose, and I wondered if he was high on coke or just trying to act tough. I placed my hands behind my back and stuck out my chin to make it easier. Every set of eyes in the place was on us, and a crowd had gathered around.

He swung once, but my head barely moved. I'd had kids hit me harder than that. "One." I counted each blow, if I could even call them that, taunting him.

"This is ridiculous," Morgan said after I called out four.

"I'm a man of my word." Just one more attempted takedown, and I was going to wipe the floor with Travis and teach him a lesson about southern charm and hospitality.

"You're next," Travis said to Morgan through his heavy breathing.

I laughed but kept still, waiting for number five and my chance to knock his ass out. He hit me twice in the face, once in the ribs, and once in the stomach, but it didn't matter—I didn't feel a thing.

The fifth and final blow landed against my chin. I grunted and gave him an uppercut right in the corner of his jaw. I didn't want to knock him out, not yet. I had a promise to keep and a lesson to teach. Travis stumbled backward and lost his footing, falling to the floor with a loud thud.

As promised, I grabbed his leg and started to drag him toward the door. The crowd parted, giving me room to pull a screaming, cursing Travis toward the parking lot. "It's time you learn some manners, country boy."

An older gentleman tipped his hat and held open the door for me with a smile. Travis's head bounced against the threshold as I pulled him on the sidewalk and finally let go. "Get on your feet and take it like a man," I told him and let him climb to his feet before I tried to punch him again.

His body swayed back and forth, and he tried to put his hands in front of his face to block the blow he knew was coming. Leaving his ribs exposed, I gave him a quick jab, forcing his hands downward and his body sideways.

"Fuck," he howled and grabbed his ribs. The crowd hooted with excitement.

Using his position to my advantage, my fist connected with his jaw —harder than inside the bar. He teetered on his heels, the cowboy boots unforgiving and stiff. Before he could fall backward, I grabbed him by the arm and righted him again because I wanted five blows before I left him on the cement.

He shook his head, probably seeing stars, and tried to grab on to me for support. "You need to learn manners, son." I brushed him off and made him stand on his own two pathetic feet before I hit him again.

But I made an error and hit him harder than I'd planned. He hit the ground with a loud thunk and didn't move.

"Maybe you killed him," Morgan said from behind me.

"Would serve his ass right."

"Well, what do we have here?" a voice said toward the back of the crowd. They parted like the Red Sea, and just when I thought we were going to get out of here without any trouble, a local sheriff dressed in a perfectly pressed brown uniform stepped forward.

"I received a call about a fight, but this seems more like an assault," he said before whistling. "I need you to turn around and put your hands behind your back, sir." His hand was already positioned on his gun, and I knew that nothing good would come from this.

"Fucker," I muttered to Morgan as I turned slowly and placed my palms flat on the back of my neck so the Andy Griffith wannabe could reach.

"I'll get you out," Morgan said to me before the sheriff cuffed me and hauled my ass to jail.

"YOU HAVE A RAP SHEET A MILE LONG," Andy said, sitting at his desk only feet from my cell. Of course, it was my made-up name for the guy, but I didn't feel like learning his real name.

"Yep," I replied, stretching out on the cold metal bench in my lonely cell. The joint looked like something from out of an old Western. Wooden walls, three cells, and a desk were all that made up the police station. I guess Podunk, Georgia, didn't get much action.

"B&E, Grand Theft, Assault." He rattled off my charges and convictions while I sat here, staring at the ceiling, and wondering where the fuck Morgan was—it had been three hours. I could barely keep my eyes open as he went on and on. "I don't think the judge is going to give you bail. You're a menace, Mr. North."

I wanted to argue with him, because I wasn't the same dumbass I was ten years ago, but I didn't bother. It didn't matter what I said; he wasn't going to let me go.

"Served hard time back in the eighties, even. Folks around here don't take kindly to people like you coming here and starting trouble."

I sighed loudly and thumped the back of my head against the bars. "I didn't start anything. Travis hit me six times before I even laid my hands on him."

"You weren't the one on the ground, North. I don't even see a mark on you."

"I can't help it if the guy can't fight for shit." I was grouchy, tired, and not in the mood for any more of his bullshit. Just as I opened my mouth, about to spout off, Morgan breezed through the door.

"Can I help you?" Andy asked him without even standing to greet him.

Morgan gave me a quick chin lift before greeting the sheriff. "I'm here for Mr. North."

"Sorry, sir. He's stuck here until the judge comes in."

"There's a phone call coming for you about Mr. North."

Andy glanced back at me with the most unimpressed look. "Rules are rules, son. He's going to be here for a—" He was cut off when the phone rang. Morgan's eyes slid to mine when Andy answered the phone. "Hello, Lowndes County Sheriff's Department." He leaned back in his chair, rocking back and forth but not speaking.

Morgan walked up to my cell and sighed. "Sorry it took so long, man. It isn't easy getting in touch with everyone at this hour."

I motioned toward the douchebag. "Who's on the phone?"

"I called Thomas, and he got in touch with an old buddy at the DEA. He called in a favor and is getting you released."

I smirked. "Andy isn't going to like that."

"Andy? You guys buds now?"

"Fuck no. I'll explain later."

"Yes, sir," Andy said and swiveled around in his seat, glaring at us.

"Guess he heard the news." I chuckled.

"Fuck him. That asshole deserved to be laid out."

"So I didn't fuck up for once?"

Morgan sighed and shook his head. "I can't say that you did."

"Looks like you're off the hook," Andy said as he hung up the phone. "It pains me to let you out, but when the US government calls and says to release you, I don't have much to argue about." He stalked toward the cell and fished his keys from his belt buckle.

"Thanks," I told Morgan, but Andy thought I was talking to him.

"Don't thank me." He motioned toward Morgan before finally opening my cage. "Thank your buddy over there."

I climbed to my feet and stretched before stepping outside the last jail cell I ever planned to inhabit. If I never came back to this shit town, it would be too soon.

"If I were you, I wouldn't stick around town," Andy warned.

I gave a curt nod. "I didn't plan on staying."

"We're on our way out," Morgan said.

"Good idea." Andy took a seat at the desk and pulled out a manila envelope with my personal belongings.

I grabbed them without a thank you and followed Morgan into the parking lot. "Elvira ready to roll?"

"Yep. I made friends with someone at the bar after you *left*. He fixed it, but it cost me three times the normal amount. I didn't give a fuck. I just want out of this shithole."

"Perfect. Get us the fuck out of this place. Don't stop until we hit Florida."

"On it," he said, unlocking the doors to Elvira, his sleek black Challenger.

She purred like a kitten when he started her engine, and he peeled out of the parking lot, the back tires fishtailing all over the road.

"Yeah, that won't have Andy coming after us."

"He can't catch us. Don't worry. I've done this before." His smile was visible in the dull blue lighting of the dashboard.

"That makes me feel all warm and fuzzy."

"Just close your eyes and shut up. We'll be home before you know it."

"Bossy motherfucker. I'd argue with you, kid, but sleep sounds too good right now," I said as I closed my eyes and thought about Fran until I drifted off to sleep.

CHAPTER 12
FRAN

The doorbell rang just after noon, and I ran to the door, excited to finally see Bear. But when I opened it, it wasn't him filling my doorway but Morgan instead.

"We gotta talk," he barked and pushed past me, walking into the hallway, and kicking off his shoes.

I slammed the front door and turned to face him with my hands on my hips. "Nice to see you too."

He didn't seem amused today. "Drop it, Ma." He stalked off into the kitchen, and I followed close behind him.

"What's the problem?"

"Bear." His voice was flat, and I couldn't read him.

"What about him?" I asked, toying with the cross around my neck.

He pulled a coffee cup out of the cabinet and helped himself to the fresh pot I'd brewed for Bear. "I want you to stay away from him."

I glanced toward the door, hoping Bear wasn't about to knock. I'm sure once he saw Morgan's car in the driveway, he'd wait until the coast was clear. "Why?"

"'Cause he's trouble." He carried the cup to the table and made himself at home.

Sitting down across from him, I rested my chin in my palm. "I'm an adult, Morgan."

He leaned back in the chair and stared out the window. "I can't have my mom messing around with a fellow employee. I have to look him in the face every day, and I shouldn't want to punch his lights out. It's not fair to either of us."

"You know I love you, right?" I tried to be diplomatic, but in no way was my son going to run my life.

"Yeah." He dragged his eyes to mine and narrowed his gaze. "What's that have to do with anything?"

"You need to mind your own business."

"This is my business. I work with Bear. I can't have you gallivanting all over town with him like some love-sick kid."

My head jerked back. "Gallivanting? Is that what I'm doing?"

"What do you call hanging out at the Neon Cowboy with him, Ma? Seriously, you need to act your age."

I placed my hands flat on the table and moved them back and forth across the cool wood to stop myself from slapping his pretty little face. "Should I just move into the nursing home now?" I asked sarcastically.

"No, but don't go to bars and dance with men. At least, the ones I know, please."

Oh, no, he didn't. "So you'd rather me go on Tender and hook up."

His head cocked to the side like he hadn't heard me, when I knew he did. "Tinder?"

"Yeah. Want me to just go on there and find a man? I mean, there are millions of them on there that would love to get a piece of this." I motioned toward my body and giggled.

Poor Morgan looked like he was about to pass out. "Ma, you gotta stop with this shit. You can't go on Tinder. It's too dangerous."

"Bear's dangerous. Tender is dangerous." I mispronounced it just to aggravate him and waved my hands around like a lunatic. "Should I just sit home and crochet until I die?"

He turned the coffee cup in his hand and grimaced. "Fuck! You're so hardheaded."

"Listen, kid. I stopped trying to run your life a long time ago. I know you're worried, but you need to stop your shit. I'm an adult.

Bear's an adult. I'm barely fifty. I'm not ready to become an old lady just yet."

He stared at me as he lifted the mug to his lips. "I want my mom back," he grumbled into his coffee.

"I'm still here, kiddo. For the first time in a long time, I actually enjoy spending time with someone, and you want to shit all over my parade."

"You were spending time with Johnny," he said with a cocky smirk.

"And he was a thief and a liar. Bear isn't any of that. You didn't have a problem when I was with Johnny, so you're just going to have to swallow your pride and move the fuck on, baby." I added the little term of endearment to ease the blow of my curse words.

"Fine, Ma."

"And I had you when I was barely legal and got hitched right away to your piece of shit father. I'm ready to actually have some fun before it's too late."

"Okay, okay." He threw his hands up in surrender. "I get it. Just be careful and tell Bear to keep his hands off you for now. I couldn't handle seeing him paw you."

I stood and took two steps to stand over him. "Sure, sweetie," I lied, placing my lips in his silky black hair. "I wouldn't want to make you uncomfortable."

"Thanks." He smiled up at me when I gave him a pat on the back.

"Shouldn't you be getting back to work?" I glanced toward the door again.

He looked down at his watch and yawned. "Yeah, it was a long night, but I should at least make an appearance."

"Okay, baby," I said, already walking toward the door so he'd be gone before Bear arrived.

Morgan leaned over and gave me a kiss as I opened the door for him. "I'll call later and check on you."

I smacked him on the chest playfully. "I'm fine. Spend some time with your wife and stop worrying about me. I'm playing bridge with the ladies later anyway. I won't be home."

"Have fun." He jogged down the front steps toward his car.

"Yeah, it's going to be a wild night." I laughed nervously and looked down the street for any sign of Bear, but nothing.

When Morgan's engine roared to life, he gave me another wave before backing out of my driveway like a maniac. The boy never did learn to drive slowly. It probably wasn't the best choice for him to get a car with over 400 horsepower either.

I waited for him to pull away before closing the door. Hurrying into the kitchen, I put his coffee cup in the dishwasher and checked my makeup before Bear arrived.

Just as I picked up my phone to call him, there was a knock at the door. "Coming!" I skipped to the door like a kid—at least, feeling like one with butterflies fluttering around in my stomach on warp speed.

I yanked the door open and immediately became shadowed from the sunlight. The man was so large that his entire body filled the space, letting no light inside. I smiled gleefully and squinted up at him. "Hey, handsome."

His gray eyes were hooded as they raked over my body. "Hey, sweetheart. Aren't you a sight for sore eyes?"

I could get lost in him. The years had been fair to him. His eyes weren't large, but narrowed and focused from his life on the road. The tiny lines in his cheeks and near his eyes gave him even more character but were marred by his beard.

"Wanna come in?" I asked like an idiot, but I was too nervous even though this wasn't our first time together.

He leaned in and lowered his voice. "I'd bang you out here, but I don't think the neighbors would appreciate it." My body began to sway with his words, but he wrapped his large hands around my arms and steadied me. "You okay?"

I laughed and my cheeks burned, but luckily he kept his hands on me. "You just get me so..." My voice trailed off.

He leaned forward and kissed my cheek, sending a shiver throughout my body. His lips grazed my ear and he whispered, "Horny, Fran?"

My toes curled from the vibration of his voice. "I can barely walk, Bear."

"It's a good thing you don't need to stand for what I have planned."

"Bear," I said and cleared my throat, trying to get myself out of my lusty haze. "We better go inside before—" I glanced around to see if any of the busybody neighbors were watching.

"Want me to put my bike in the garage?"

"Great idea. I don't need Morgan coming by again and seeing your bike in the drive."

"You go inside and get naked, and I'll stow it."

"Wait," I said with one foot inside the doorway. "You expect me to get undressed now?"

"Fran, sweetheart, don't question me. I only say what I mean, and what I want is your fine self naked and waiting. Hurry or I'll have to spank that pretty little ass of yours for not following commands."

"Well," I said and pulled the cross still dangling from my neck from side to side. If I weren't already going to hell, Bear would make sure to get me a one-way ticket.

I ran to the kitchen to open the garage for him before making a beeline to the bedroom. My clothes couldn't come off fast enough as I contorted to work my way out of the super clingy pieces Maria claimed I had to have. *Dear God.* If Bear had to remove them, it would be a nightmare.

I stood in front of my bed and wondered if I was supposed to lie down or stand here. I fidgeted and shifted on my feet, glancing over my shoulder. When the garage door started to close, I hopped on the bed and tried to look sexy by stretching out on my side with my head propped up in my hand. The girls in *Playboy* always made it seem like a sexy position.

"For the love of God," I muttered when I glanced down and caught sight of my belly flowing into the mattress like a mound of half-melted ice cream.

When he walked into the hallway just outside my bedroom, I flopped onto my back to help hide my fluffy stomach. I sucked in a breath as the door swung open, and I waited.

"I love a woman who can follow orders." He kicked off his boots, and I stared down the length of my body to watch him undress with so much excitement that it was hard to be still.

My chest heaved, and my breathing grew more ragged. The anticipation of what was going to come next was killing me. My heart pounded against my insides so hard I wondered if my old ticker would just give out. God, I hoped he'd at least dress me before calling the coroner to remove my body. My greatest fear had always been to be found like this, sprawled out and naked as the day I was born.

The other night, I didn't really have a chance to take in the beauty of Bear. We were too busy undressing and getting down to business to really appreciate each other. Even though his face was hairy, he only had a smattering across his chest. There had always been something about a man with chest hair that just screamed manly to me. I wanted to run my fingers through it.

I was so lost in the moment, taking in all of him, including his "pretty dick," as I'd told Maria, that I hadn't noticed him stalking toward me. He grabbed my ankles and pulled me down the bed so quick I didn't even have time to squeal my surprise.

My feet were in the air and over his shoulder moments later. When his mouth came down against my pussy, I twisted against the sheets and lost my breath.

"I missed this beautiful pussy," he mumbled against my skin before clamping down hard over my clit.

I fisted the comforter, writhing back and forth because of the way he ate me like a starved man. Two nights ago, he'd spent so much time licking me that my head spun. I'd had some good oral sex in my time, men who took their time and treated my vagina more like a sacred flower that they didn't want to break. But Bear... Bear chowed down like it was the best thing he'd ever had in his mouth. It wasn't that he rushed it. Fuck, he spent over an hour licking and sucking every inch between my legs.

"So fucking good," I moaned and dug my heels into his back to trap him against my body.

"Greedy," he murmured with a tiny chuckle that vibrated against my clit, causing me to spasm uncontrollably.

I ground myself against him and dug my fingers into his hair. I'd always been meek and mild in the bedroom, but there was something about Bear that brought out a different side of me. One that didn't give a fuck what he was thinking, even though I knew Bear wouldn't judge me. For once in my life, I was out for me. Greedy, he called me. And I was. Unapologetically, take-what-I-want greedy.

He watched me, our eyes locking on each other as he worshiped me with his mouth. I'd always been the turn the lights off before we get down to business type of gal, but with Bear, I wanted to see him the way he saw me.

It was written all over his face. His attraction. His need. The want he felt for me was almost electric. Why hadn't I seen it before?

"I'm so close," I said, pushing his face deeper, and holding his mouth hostage against my flesh.

The man had a tongue that worked magic. Swiping to the left, then to the right before making a complete circle that could only be described as magnificent. My feet moved back and forth, my muscles strained as I felt the orgasm building inside me.

His mouth was that good. So good that I wanted him to do it all day, but I also wanted the feeling of euphoria I hadn't ever experienced, except for the few times I'd experimented with drugs.

When two fingers dipped inside me, stroking that spot that made me lose my breath, I couldn't hold it back any longer. Everything inside me seized up, including my ability to see straight.

I stared down at him through blurry eyes as he hummed his satisfaction against me, drawing out my climax, and my inability to breathe. As each wave crashed over me, his fingers still stroking my insides, I let oblivion take me.

"Franny..." Bear's voice was soft at first, almost distant.

Mmm. This is so nice. Heavenly.

"Franny." There was more urgency in his voice this time.

He's just the best.

"Franny!" he yelled as my body began to shake back and forth.

"What?" I asked, finally opening my eyes, and snapping back to reality.

"Fuck," he hissed above me, his eyes serious. "I thought you were dying."

I laughed and cradled his face in my hands, even though my arms felt like they weighed a thousand pounds. "It's the perfect way to go."

"Don't do that shit to me, woman. I thought I was going to have to explain this to Morgan. I kinda like livin'."

My laughter grew louder, and I dug my fingers into his salt-and-pepper beard. "I was in that perfect spot until you pulled me back."

His eyebrow drew down, and his jaw clenched. "What spot?"

Pulling my head up, I kissed his lips softly and tasted myself. "The darkness and warmth where you're alive, but on the edge of nothingness."

"You're crazy, Fran. Simply crazy." He slammed his mouth down against mine, pushing the back of my head into the pillow.

My arms snaked around his neck as I opened to him, letting our tongues tangle together in the most beautiful dance. I felt his passion and need in the way his lips covered mine and in his ragged breaths that fed me.

When he collapsed onto his back and took me with him, I was shocked when he said, "Just lie here for a few and close your eyes. The day is young."

My fingers slid through his chest hair, settling against the space between his pecs. "Don't you want me to take care of you?" I asked softly with my lips against his skin and my hand covering his massive erection.

He kissed my forehead and let his lips linger against my skin. "I had a long night last night. Just lie with me."

Snuggle?

Bear wanted to snuggle me?

Never took him for a man who wanted to cuddle a woman. Hell, I'd never been much for it either. But the pull of the nothingness I'd felt before started to grow heavier behind my eyelids, and the last thing I thought was—*I liked being greedy.*

CHAPTER 13

BEAR

City stood over me and laughed. "You look like shit."

"Thanks," I grumbled, pulling at the label on my beer.

I'd been sitting here for an hour, nursing it, and thinking about Fran. We'd spent the last two weeks holed up at her place or mine to keep from being seen by her kid, and I was done with it.

I no longer wanted to hide.

For the first time in my life, I actually liked someone and wanted the rest of the world to know it.

"Still seeing my aunt?"

His words caught me off guard. I turned, pondering what to say, and stroking my beard. "Yep," I finally answered because, fuck it, I wanted him to know.

"Thought so. She the one making you look like you got one foot in the grave?"

"You really wanna know?"

He blanched but righted himself quickly. "I suppose I don't, but you're my friend, so I'll pretend we're talking about someone I don't share blood with."

"She's in my bed or I'm in hers every night. But that's not the most tiring part. Hiding is."

"I imagine it is. It's like having an affair, but your wife is your friend, and you're bangin' his mom."

"Nice," I muttered with a tiny smile.

"So what are you going to do? Have you felt Morgan out about it?"

"Dude." I leaned back in my chair, kicking my feet out underneath the table. "He made it quite clear that he wanted me to stay away from his mother."

"I don't blame him for standing his ground. You have to remember, Fran hasn't really been with anyone since his father left. No matter who she's with, it won't be easy for him." He motioned toward the waitress, asking for two more.

"That's stupid."

"Eh, men aren't always rational, especially when it comes to our women—even when they're our mothers." He studied me for a moment. "So you really like Fran?"

Once our beers were on the table, I dragged mine toward me and pushed the old one away. "I do," I sighed and scratched at my beard, catching a whiff of her perfume that had been left from when I kissed her neck earlier. "She invited Janice over for dinner tomorrow."

He spat the beer he was just about to swallow all over the table. "What? Did you just say—"

"Yep." I nodded and downed half my beer in one giant gulp.

He wiped his mouth with the back of his hand. "How do you feel about that?"

"I don't know. Janice has never approved of my lifestyle, but maybe, if she met Fran, she may soften a bit."

When I left her with my sisters, she cried. Her wails still rang in my ears, and I'd never forget the look on her face when I kissed her good-bye.

Time hadn't healed the wound either. We were cordial, but by no means did she love me like she had. When she was a baby, she'd sleep on my chest for hours. There wasn't anywhere I'd go without her attached to me in some form.

Being her first heartbreak was something I'd never forgive myself for, and I suppose, neither would she.

"She's a tough cookie," City said and sipped his beer, staring off into the distance. "Maybe you should invite Morgan to dinner too."

My head jerked back at his stupidity. "Are you fucking crazy? He'll just add flames to the fire. She doesn't need any more reason to hate me."

"True."

Like the four horsemen of the Apocalypse, James, Morgan, Thomas, and Frisco came bursting through the front door of the Neon Cowboy. Maybe they caught wind of my tryst with Fran and were all here to kick my ass.

Frisco stopped off at the bar, but the others marched directly to our table and sat down. Thomas spoke first, "We found him."

James continued, "We have eyes on him until we can get there."

"Where the hell is he?" I asked just as Frisco pulled over a chair, twirled it around, and sat.

"Back in Lowndes County. Same spot we went to." Morgan shook his head. "Guess after we left, he popped back up. Probably figured we wouldn't look for him there again."

"When do we leave?" I asked, ready to leave now if needed.

They glanced around the table, avoiding my eyes as the waitress dropped off a bucket of beer. "You're not going," Morgan said and glanced at City.

My fist clenched so tightly around my beer bottle I thought it would burst in my hand. "My ass is going."

"No, buddy, you're going to stay here and man the phones," Thomas told me with a straight face.

"Isn't that what Angel's for?" I just kept shaking my head in disbelief.

"She'll be there too, but you have to keep in contact with the clients. You and Sam will stay behind while we head to Georgia and take care of Johnny."

"But—" I started to say, ready to argue my point, when Morgan cut me off.

"The Lowndes County Sheriff would be happy to have you back in town. I'm sure he'd haul your ass back to jail just for looking at someone funny. We don't have time to deal with the hick cops there.

Just stay here, watch the business, keep an eye on the ladies, and let us handle Johnny."

"Fine," I grumbled. "I'll stay here with Sam."

"Good." Thomas eased back into the chair. "We're out of here first thing in the morning. I'll let the service know to forward all the messages to you or Sam. If we aren't back tomorrow night, you need to make sure your ass is in the office first thing in the morning."

I smiled, even though I was anything but happy. "Sure thing, boss." The sarcasm in my voice wasn't missed by anyone.

"Would you rather sit in jail with Andy?" Morgan remembered my nickname for the asshole.

"Not really, although he was entertaining." I smiled.

"You're lucky I got you out. It wasn't easy with your record." Thomas tried to hold back his laughter. "People don't seem to understand how I hired a convicted criminal to work for me, but I know you're an upstanding dude."

"Wish everyone felt that way," I muttered under my breath.

Morgan glared at me from across the table. "You talking about me?"

I shook my head and glared right back. "Never."

"What's the problem?" Frisco asked because he wasn't in the know about anything between Fran and me. It had stayed "within the family."

"Bear and Fran," James said casually, like it wasn't a big fucking deal.

Frisco spat his beer out. "Come again?"

"Yep, you heard me right. Bear and Fran have a 'thing.'" James used air quotes, driving the point home for effect.

Morgan still held my eyes, giving me the look of death. "We had a drink together." I shrugged off the lie.

Thomas cocked an eyebrow and smirked. "Is that all?"

"Yes." My answer was short, but I was being thrown under the bus right in front of the very person I was trying to hide from.

With a scowl on his face, Morgan peered around the table. "Is there something I don't know?"

"Nah, man. We're just fucking with Bear and you." City tried to stop whatever train wreck was coming, but it was hard to stop one once it was set in motion.

Morgan's eyes bounced back and forth between City and me. "You've been with my ma?"

Before I could answer, City stuck up for me. "What's so wrong with Bear seeing Aunt Fran?" He crossed his arms and stared down Morgan. "He's the best friend a guy could ask for. He sticks to his word and has a level head."

"You want him fuckin' your ma?" Morgan snarled and kept his eyes on me. "I sure as fuck don't. Good friend or not, he's not the right man for her."

"When did you become such a shit in the pants?" James laughed, trying to break the tension but failing.

Morgan turned his scowl on him. "Fuck off."

"I wasn't exactly happy about my best buddy being with my sister," Thomas said, giving James the stink-eye. "But at some point, you gotta let go."

"We'll see about that," Morgan replied before taking a long, slow slug of his beer.

"She's your mom. You can't boss her ass around," City, the usual voice of reason, chimed in.

"Fran isn't to be messed with," Thomas said through his laughter. "She's vicious. You should know better than anyone else."

"If you're worried Bear's going to step out of line, I'm sure Fran will put him in his place, just like she has you," City stated, and his words were true.

Fran wasn't a shrinking violet. She had a wicked tongue and an attitude to match. Maybe that was why I liked her so much. She didn't put up with my shit or anyone else's for that matter—including Morgan.

Morgan eyed me warily. "She's been off my back for weeks. It's been..." His voice trailed off.

"Nice?" City nudged him in the arm.

"Yeah." Morgan laughed.

"When her attention is elsewhere, she'll stay off your ass," Frisco said, knowing firsthand what it was like to have a parent who hovered.

"But I don't like that it's him." Morgan pointed his skinny little finger in my direction.

"When did I become the bad guy? It's nice you're all talking about me like I'm not even here too. Fuckers."

Morgan leaned back and swung his arms out wide. "Look around the room. Which girl hasn't Bear fucked here?"

He had a point, but there were a few I hadn't been with. Fuck, I'd been single for thirty years, and I wasn't a priest. Women offered, I accepted—end of discussion.

"Point?" I asked in defense of myself.

"You're a manwhore, Bear," Morgan said matter-of-factly.

"I've been single almost longer than you've been alive, kid."

"He has a point," City said with a nod.

"I never lied to any woman I've slept with either. I never promise anything more than what it is."

Sometimes they were delusional and thought after a single taste of their pussy that I'd get down on one knee and proclaim them as mine, but that was my fault. I should never get involved with the nutty bitches. They weren't worth the headache.

Morgan leaned forward, his face still serious as a heart attack. "And what are you promising my mother?"

Shit. That was something Fran should be answering, not me. But I had to break the news because I couldn't have this shitty-ass tension between us.

"We're dating," I answered simply.

Morgan's entire body stiffened as his eyes widened. "Dating?"

"Yep, dating."

"When was the last time you dated anyone?" Morgan asked, not realizing the seriousness of my words.

"Once since 1985."

Morgan looked at me funny. "Once?"

"Yeah, dumbass. I don't date unless I'm seriously into someone."

His body rocked backward like someone punched him in the face. "You're *seriously* into my ma?" he asked with the biggest eyes I'd ever seen.

I shrugged it off like it was the most nonchalant statement to make. "Yeah."

Morgan rubbed his face, digging his fingers into his eyes and mumbling under his breath. I couldn't make out what he was saying, but I didn't care either. Nothing was going to change the fact that I did like Fran and I wanted to date her.

"We're happy for you, Bear." Thomas smiled and gave me a quick, curt nod.

Morgan hopped from his chair and glared at Thomas. "Like fuck we are!"

James grabbed his arm and stopped him from leaping over the table at me. "Sit your ass down and stop making a scene."

"Dude," Morgan seethed, keeping his eyes pinned to me as he sat again. "It's my mom we're talking about."

"And it's Bear. He's not going to fuck over your mom." James glanced in my direction. "He knows that we'll all kick his ass if he does."

"I do." I didn't dare smile. It wasn't the time or place. This was serious talk about an important person. "I'd expect nothing less."

Morgan clenched his fists on top of the table, his entire body tense. "If I even think you're doing my ma wrong, I'll fucking end you."

All I could do was nod. It didn't matter what I said. I'd have to prove it through my actions and over time. Lots of time—maybe longer than I had left to live. Morgan saw me in a different light, and I wasn't sure I'd ever be able to change it.

CHAPTER 14
FRAN

Bear didn't spend the night last night and I actually missed him, but I had too much to do this morning to dwell on it. Janice was coming for an early dinner, a fact that Bear wasn't so excited about, but I didn't give a shit about his lack of enthusiasm.

He explained to me that they were cordial, but he'd never been able to work his way into her good graces. He fucked up when she was a kid, and for that, he had to pay penance and make amends.

We all made mistakes as parents. Most weren't as big as his, but it was our responsibility to set things right. When I called Janice to ask her over, I thought she'd decline, but she jumped at the chance.

Maybe she was ready to forgive him. Maybe she wanted to tell him off. It didn't really matter. My only goal was to get them in the same room and let them sort their shit out.

"Janice," I said as I opened the door to the most beautiful pregnant woman I'd ever seen.

She smiled brightly with her hands resting on her belly. "Fran."

"Come on in, sweetheart." I stepped to the side, giving her enough room for her belly. "Aren't you a beautiful creature?"

"Thanks." She peered around the living room and frowned. "Is he not coming?"

"He'll be here. He's really excited about today," I lied as I closed the door, but I didn't want her to think otherwise.

Her eyes grew wide. "He is?"

I nodded as I walked up to her. "He's missed you. Does he know you're pregnant?"

She shook her head and glanced toward the floor. "No, I haven't told him yet."

"He's going to be a grandpa." I couldn't contain my excitement at the thought of little ones running around the house.

"Yeah, I guess he is, technically."

Ouch. One thing I knew was that Bear loved his kids, even when he couldn't take care of them.

"I guess so," I said softly. "Would you like to sit down, and I'll get you something to drink?"

"That would be great. My feet are killing me," she said as I wandered into the kitchen to grab a bottle of water.

When I walked back into the room, she sat on the couch, clutching her stomach again. "How far along are you?"

"Eight and a half months, but I feel as big as a whale."

I handed her the water and sat next to her. "I remember when I was pregnant. I was miserable for the entire nine months." I laughed softly. "It probably had more to do with my husband than my son."

The timer on the oven beeped just as there was a knock at the door. "Come in!" I yelled, knowing it was Bear, but I headed toward the kitchen.

I couldn't fuck up this meal. Everyone knew I was a shitty cook. Maria gave me some homemade sauce to make lasagna. It was the one thing I could cook without fail, but usually, I used some jarred shit from the store. She'd insisted that only the family recipe would do for such a special occasion.

After I took out the lasagna and set it on the stove to cool, I tiptoed toward the living room and watched Bear and Janice from a distance as they stood in the center of the room.

She smiled up at him, a hint of a little girl mesmerized by her dad showing through. He placed his hand on her belly, his eyes bouncing between her face and the point at where their bodies were connected.

"Janice," he said with a sad, soft voice. "I'm so, so…"

"I know, Dad."

"No, baby, you don't." His hand moved away from her stomach to her face. He cupped her cheek in his palm, rubbing his thumb against her cheek.

Her eyebrows drew together, but she did nothing to move away from his touch. I didn't dare move or intrude on their moment. They needed this time. Their relationship had been severed, and words needed to be spoken without me in their presence.

"Let's sit." He guided her toward the couch, his hand gripping her elbow in case she tripped. "We need to talk about something that I've put off for too many years."

I looked back at the lasagna and shrugged. It could wait—that was the best thing about this type of meal. It was pretty hard to fuck up and only got better with time. So thankfully, it would still be edible.

Even though I knew it wasn't right to eavesdrop, I did anyway. I couldn't drag my eyes away from them. She looked like him with eyes that were the color of gray clouds on a rainy day. Her dark hair shimmered in the sunlight, streaming through the window behind her. He still had a smattering of the identical shade in his, but the white had started to overtake the darkness. Even the roundness of their cheeks matched. Somehow, even though they had so many similarities, she was feminine and petite while Bear was big, burly, and hard-looking.

She sat down, smoothing her dress down with her palms. "What's wrong, Dad?"

"Nothing, Jan. We've never had a talk about what happened, and I need to talk to you now before it's too late."

Her hand flew to her mouth, and her eyes widened in horror. "Are you dying or something?"

He shook his head with a faint smile visible beneath his beard. "Not today, but I'm getting older." His large hand pulled hers down from her face. "I don't even know where to start."

"You don't have to say anything."

"No. This needs to be said." He pulled in a shaky breath and then began to speak. "Your mother and I had you when we were young, probably too young to really be parents, but we made the best of it. We loved you so much and never let you leave our side. God." He took another deep breath. "I loved Jackie so much. I couldn't imagine my life with anyone else. We were crazy for each other. So much so that Ret came less than a year after you were born."

Janice placed her hands over his. "I heard that from Aunt Caroline. She said you two couldn't keep your hands to yourself. She called it undignified."

"She would say that," he grumbled just loud enough for me to hear. "We loved you so much we couldn't wait for another baby. My world revolved around my family. I can't describe how much I loved your mother, because I've never felt that way about any woman in my life."

My eyes suddenly filled with tears. I shouldn't be jealous of Jackie and the way Bear loved her, but a tiny, greedy piece of me was and probably always would be. It was hard to compete with the memory of someone taken too soon, even if it was almost thirty years ago.

"Your mom and me had big plans. We wanted to have at least four kids. The more, the merrier because you were such a great baby. We wanted an entire house full. We wanted to build a house in the country and just have our own piece of heaven with no one else but us."

"That sounds…" Her voice trailed off.

"Yeah," he said in the sweetest voice, and I could almost feel his longing and heartache. "When she went into labor, it never even crossed my mind that she could die." His voice cracked.

Seeing him like that, choked up and in pain, wasn't the Bear I'd always seen. He was so full of life and jokes that no one saw the pain hidden beneath the surface. Only in fleeting moments when we were lying in bed would he confide to me all the regret and sorrow he had about his past. He missed Jackie and loved her to this day, but his biggest regret was his children—Ret and Janice. He never got the chance to be a father, to teach them how to do things, and to be there for many of their biggest life firsts.

He clutched her hands tighter, and his shoulders slumped forward. "When it happened, I was in shock. I refused to believe she was really gone. I barely remember the following days. They passed in a blur because my mind couldn't comprehend that she was actually gone."

"I wish I could remember Mom," Janice said to him, her face softer than when they had first started talking.

"I saved a box for you."

"You did?" Tears welled in her eyes and quickly trickled down her cheeks.

"I did, babygirl. I had to save some of your mom's stuff so that someday you'd have a piece of her with you."

"Dad," Janice whispered and placed her hands over his.

"I was a shit father. I know it. I'm not making an excuse for how I acted, but I want you to understand the depths of my despair. Seeing you now, with that baby in your belly… It should be a happy time for me. But it's not. I'm scared for you. Frightened that you'll be like your mother, and I'll lose you too."

She smiled softly before wiping away a tear before it fell from her jaw. "I'm fine. The doctor said everything is good, so don't worry."

"Aunt Caroline watched you right after it happened. She knew I couldn't look after you two because I could barely take care of myself. I thought I'd heal and be able to move on, but I couldn't do it. I wasn't strong enough," he admitted. "I was mad at the world. I hated God and couldn't fathom why he took Jackie from me…from us."

"Things happen. We can't control them." Her hands twisted in her lap as she stared down at them. "But why didn't you come back for us?" She dragged her eyes to his, and the pain in them was heart-wrenching.

He grimaced. "I wish I had a reason that sounded right, but I don't. Nothing can justify what I did. I went off the deep end when the dust settled. You kids were being taken care of, and I got mixed up in some bad shit. I had a death wish after losing your mom. I wanted to be with her so bad that I didn't care if I had to die to do it."

"Dad," she gasped. "That's horrible."

"But you kids would've been fine. Or at least, that's what I told myself. Not long after, I ended up in jail for a bit, and when I got out, I didn't see a point in coming back into your lives. Caroline told me how well you both were doing, and we both decided it was best I stayed away. I couldn't argue with her either."

The tears in my eyes dropped down my cheeks as I plastered my back to the wall. I couldn't imagine walking away from Morgan, but I also couldn't imagine the pain Bear went through losing the love of his life.

"It's my biggest regret in life—not being there for you kids. I should've been a stronger man. I should've been a better man. But your mom made me better. I don't know how to make it up to you and Ret for being a shit father."

I peered around the corner, unable to stop myself.

She scooted closer and placed her hand on his arm. "You can be here for us now, Dad. We're always going to be your kids. Just because we're grown doesn't mean we don't need you."

"Babygirl, what do you need me for?"

"Everything. Jeff left me. I'm all alone with the baby on the way. I'm so lost with no one to lean on. Aunt Caroline is great, but you know how she is."

"I'll kick his ass," Bear barked, his body growing rigid.

"Don't bother. He's not worth the jail time. I need you more than I want his ass knocked out."

"Whatever you want, Janice. I'll do anything you want or need as long as you give me a shot at making up all our lost years."

I smiled, still hidden behind the wall as they embraced. When I invited her over, I'd hoped they'd make up, but I never thought it would be this great. I busied myself in the kitchen, tinkering with the table settings until they were done. Luckily, the lasagna was still warm, safely covered by aluminum foil, and ready to be devoured.

When they entered the kitchen with their arms locked, I melted a little bit inside. This big, hunky tough guy had transformed into someone else—someone better.

"Ready to eat?" I asked, transfixed by the image of them together.

"I'm starving, Fran. Thanks for having me today." Janice glanced up at Bear and rested her head on his chest, leaning against him. "I finally feel like I have my dad back."

"Awww, honey. He loves you."

Her smile widened. "I know."

"Sit down, and I'll serve everyone," I said, grabbing the spatula.

Bear helped Janice sit and then came to my side. "Thanks, sweetheart. I'll have to thank you later." He waggled his eyebrows, and I giggled.

"Not in front of the kid," I whispered and glanced at her out of the corner of my eye.

"How do you think she got that way?" he smirked and grabbed my ass.

I swatted his stomach with the hard plastic utensil. "Behave, big boy."

"I will for now, but when the kid goes, all bets are off."

"Salad?" I asked with a strangled voice, unable to hide my excitement.

"No, I'm craving meat," Janice replied.

"Me too," I mumbled, catching Bear's eye.

He smiled easier, and his entire being felt different...lighter. Usually, my meddling brought headaches, but for the first time in a long time, I did fuckin' good.

CHAPTER 15

BEAR

"Talk to your brother lately?" I asked after we'd finished dinner. Janice had forgiven me, but Ret wouldn't be so easy.

He was too much like me for that to happen.

"I talked to him yesterday. I told him I was coming here for dinner."

I hadn't been able to take my eyes off Janice. She looked so much like Jackie that my heart ached. It was bittersweet. At least a piece of my wife lived on in our girl. "What did he say?"

"He wished me luck." She laughed softly and wiped her lips.

"Funny guy," I whispered and shifted in my chair. "Where's he at?"

"Near Miami, but he's ready to make a move as soon as he finds the job of his dreams."

"What's he doing now?" What kind of shitty father was I? I didn't even know what the hell my kid did for a living. After he got out of the military, we lost touch.

"He's a bounty hunter."

My entire body rocked back in the chair. "No shit?"

"Yep. He's been doing it for a few years. He gets restless though and moves around a lot."

My kid, the bounty hunter. "Is he married?"

"Well," she said with a grimace. "He lives an..." Her voice trailed off, and she looked at Fran. "Alternative lifestyle."

"He's gay?" My mouth fell open.

Janice snorted. "No, he has a girl."

"A girlfriend?" Fran asked, saving me the awkwardness.

Janice scrubbed a hand across her face, but she couldn't stop her laughter. "Yeah, I guess you can call her that."

I looked at Fran, and she shrugged. "Well, what is she?"

"They met at a club."

I held up my hands. "Stop." I couldn't discuss this with my kid, no matter how old she was.

"Like Izzy and James?" Fran asked me.

I nodded. "Just tell me he's the boss, at least."

"Yes." Janice snorted again with the rosiest colored cheeks. "She calls him sir. It's kind of sickening."

"I like the sound of that." My fingers tangled in my beard as I stared at Fran.

"Never going to happen, big boy," Fran replied quickly and swatted my arm.

"A guy can wish." I smirked.

Janice placed her hands on her belly and stared at us. "It's nice to see you're at peace, Dad."

"I am," I said with a smile and placed my hand over Fran's on top of the table. "For the first time since your mother died, I am." Fran sucked in a breath and made a weird, throaty noise. "She's a good woman." I clutched her fingers tighter.

"You're an amazing cook, Fran. Thanks for a wonderful meal."

"Isn't she, though?"

"Oh, stop. All I did was make lasagna. It's not a big deal." Fran blushed before leaning over to kiss me.

Warmth flooded me. Having Fran and Janice with me felt better than I could ever dream. I finally felt at peace with my daughter. So much of her life I'd been gone, but I wasn't going to let that happen again. I had a lot to make up for, and I planned to be around to be the father I never had been to her.

"When are you due?" Fran asked as she started to clear the table.

"Three weeks, but I'm hoping it happens sooner. The Florida heat is killing me."

"Three weeks?" I felt sick. I knew it was irrational to worry that she'd meet the same fate as her mother, but I couldn't stop myself from worrying.

"I'll be fine, Dad. Calm down."

"I can't be calm. In three weeks, I'll be a grandpa. Jesus, *fuck.*" Suddenly I felt dizzy. "Oh, God."

Fran turned around from the sink and rolled her eyes. "You're such a baby."

"That's easy for you to say." I held my stomach, trying to wrap my head around that little nugget of truth. Grandpa. I was going to be a motherfucking grandpa.

I wasn't ready for it.

When I looked in the mirror, I saw an older version of myself, but not a grandfather. Those men were hunched over, half-crippled shells of their former selves. I wasn't that. I still had life. I still had strength. Fuck, my dick still stayed hard without the help of that little blue pill.

"Bear, snap out of it." Fran waved her hand in front of my face as I sat here like a zombie. "For shit's sake," she muttered before touching my cheek with her hand. "You're still you, babe. You're still my Bear."

"Grandpa Bear," I whispered, my eyes bouncing between Janice's belly and Fran's tits. "Grand. Pa."

"Maybe we'll get the baby to call ya Pops," Janice said.

"Pops. Fuck." I hung my head and thought about it. It wasn't as bad as Grandpa and hell, maybe people would think the kid was mine. I sighed heavily. "It's fine. As long as it's healthy and you're okay, I'll be just fine."

Janice stayed for a few more hours and left just before dark. I insisted on her leaving because I didn't want her on the road and driving in the sticks. It wasn't safe, and she had precious cargo on board.

As soon as Fran closed the door, I slammed her against the wall, using my body as the ram. "I want you," I said against her neck, running my lips up the side.

"What got into you?" She wrapped her arms around me, tipping her head back to give me better access. "Have something to prove, old man?" She laughed softly before moaning when I sank my teeth into the corner of her neck where it met her shoulder.

I pulled back, staring into her dark brown eyes. "This *old man* can still fuck until you pass out."

"I was just tired—"

I pressed my lips to her, devouring her words and her bullshit. I knew I still had it. Her lips opened, giving me her sweet softness as I kneaded her breasts in my palm. When she moaned, I knew I had her.

When our lips disconnected, she stood against the wall and panted. Backing away, I narrowed my eyes and took in her beauty. "Strip, Franny. I need to be in you."

"Right here?" she asked, using the wall as an anchor.

I pointed to her and motioned to her clothing. "Right here. Get naked."

She swallowed hard and nodded. Slowly she pulled her shirt over her head, exposing her red lace bra and beautiful tits, and tossed it to the floor.

I drew in a shaky breath, but I kept my eyes pinned to her. "Pants too."

Without hesitation, she yanked off her skintight pants, letting them pool near her feet before kicking them away.

I turned my fingers in a circle. "Face the wall," I told her, taking in all of her beauty and softness as she moved.

"You sure you don't want to go in the bedroom?"

"I'm sure, sweetheart. Stop talking and put your hands against the wall."

I took off my clothes at warp speed, giddier than a kid at Christmas and needing to prove my virility—still not over the fact that I was about to become a grandfather.

Pressing my front to her back, I placed my mouth close to her ear. "Who's your daddy?"

"Tom," Fran said with a bit of chuckle.

But her laughter died when I tangled my fingers through her raven hair and pulled her head back. "A smartass and greedy, but I know how to shut you up."

My lips crashed against hers, stealing her breath and her words. My hand drifted down her body, cupping her ass gently in my rough palms before sliding between her cheeks, and checking her readiness for me.

She moaned softly in my mouth and pushed her body against my hand. My fingers moved to her front, coated in her need, and slowly rubbed her clit in a circular motion.

Breaking our kiss, I growled. "Do you want me?"

"Yes," she said in an airy, wanton tone.

"Bend over and touch your toes."

Her eyebrows drew together. "Do you know how old I am? Fuck me, Bear. I haven't been able to touch my toes for twenty years."

"Fran," I said, trying to hold in my laughter. I hadn't even thought about her age as a factor in the scene I had playing out in my mind. "Bend over and hold the door handle."

"That, I can do." Gripping the door handle tightly, she bent at the waist, pushing her ass against my body.

Wrapping my hands around her hips, I pulled them out, bending her farther to give me better access. Before she had a chance to say anything else, I pushed my cock inside and shivered in ecstasy.

"I love your greedy pussy. So fucking good," I growled, pushing myself deeper until there was nowhere else to go but pull out and ram back into her.

"Fuck me," she moaned and met my thrust with enough force that she caused me to rock backward on my heels.

My hands tightened, stilling her movement as I controlled her motions and mine. I thrust into her with such force that her head tapped the wooden door, making a light knocking sound.

Neither of us cared.

We were too lost in the moment to laugh about it and too close to the precipice to stop. My fingertips dug into her flesh the closer to the edge I came. She hunched over, standing on her tiptoes, and arching her back higher in the air to make me dive deeper and stroke her in just the right spot.

When Fran reached between her legs and touched herself—I lost it. My eyes blurred before fuzzy fireworks filled my vision, my body trembling through the orgasm that stole the air from my lungs. She followed me, moaning, and pushed against me, making my dick slide deeper inside.

"Jesus," I said, holding on to her for fear of falling.

"You did good, Grandpa," Fran said, yanking my proverbial chain, and laughing.

I backed away, my cock coming with me, and slapped her ass. "Not yet."

She jumped, her hand coming around to touch the very spot my hand just landed. "Doesn't matter," she said. "You still fuck like a champ."

"Fran." I started to laugh too and stroked my semi-hard dick. "I may be old, but I can fuck you into oblivion."

She turned around with the naughtiest grin I'd ever seen. "Want to find out?"

I took a step forward and twisted my hand in her hair. "You and your greedy pussy are going to be the death of me, woman."

"You'd only be so lucky to go that way."

She was right too. I'd tempted fate half my life, and with my record in the good and evil columns, I was sure I wouldn't be lucky enough to go out inside a woman. With my luck, I'd be hit by a semi or some crazy-ass shit—something agonizing as payback for being a pain in the ass my entire life.

CHAPTER 16
FRAN

I was absolutely buzzing by the time Bear left my house. The feeling stayed with me until the next morning when the phone rang. "Hello."

"Ma?" Morgan sounded weird. It was a mother thing. I could be hundreds of miles away from him and just know when something was off.

I stopped walking. "What's wrong?"

"We found Johnny," he said an octave lower.

"Good. That bastard," I whispered into the phone.

"He's dead."

"What?" I screeched, thinking I heard him wrong.

"He's gone, Ma."

Nervousness filled me, and I grabbed the sponge from the sink and started cleaning in a manic state. "What happened?"

"Looks like suicide. Shot himself."

The guilt I felt after calling him a bastard started to eat at me immediately. "I can't believe it."

"He left a note. It looks like he wasn't working alone in the theft of Race's money."

My hand stopped scrubbing the black granite counter. "What did it say?" Sometimes getting information out of Morgan was more like pulling teeth than an actual conversation.

"I'll send it to you via text. The cops are taking it into evidence."

"Okay," I said, trying to hold back my tears.

"We'll be home later today. I'll stop by when I get a chance."

"Go home to your wife, baby. I'm fine," I lied.

"I need to talk to you, though, about Johnny and his circle of friends."

"I already told Bear everything I knew."

"I still want to talk with you. I gotta run, Ma. We're about to leave and head out. I'll call you later."

"Drive safely, Morgan. I love you."

"Love you too," he said before he disconnected.

Johnny killed himself. I couldn't believe it. Standing in my kitchen, I stared out the window and clutched my phone.

When it beeped, I glanced down, still in a trance.

> Fran,
>
> I'm sorry. He made me do it. I tried to call and explain, but you didn't pick up. I didn't have any other choice. This was the only way out.
>
> Please forgive me.
> Johnny

I read the note five times, trying to figure out who "he" was and why Johnny felt it was his only way out. The information was too sparse and cryptic for me to really make any type of guess on what the hell was going on.

I couldn't sit here all day and replay everything in my head. There was only one place I could go to figure shit out—only one person who would talk to me like a person.

I grabbed my purse and headed straight for ALFA PI. By the time I walked through the front door, my stomach had filled with knots, and my shoulders felt like iron bricks.

"Hey," I said to Angel as she stood from the reception desk and came to greet me. Her auburn hair bounced with each step like a luscious red velvet blanket.

Her dark eyes didn't meet mine when she spoke. "Hey, yourself." She backed away and studied my face. "You don't look so good."

I waved her comment away. "Have you talked to Morgan?"

"He just called to say he's on his way back."

"Is that all he said?" Even though I was standing still, my foot tapped on the floor because pacing wasn't an option.

"No." She frowned and stared down at the floor. "No, he told me about Johnny."

I looked around her shoulder, down the hallway that led to the offices. "Bear around?"

She nodded and stepped to the side. "He's in his office."

"Thanks, doll." I gave her a quick peck on the cheek before marching straight to the man I knew could help me work through the shit in my head.

I knocked softly. "Bear."

No response.

"Bear," I spoke a little louder this time.

The door behind me opened, and a smiling Sam stood in the doorway. "Hi, Ms. D. How are you today?"

"I'm well, Sam. Yourself?" I took him in—all his beauty and muscles. If I were twenty years younger, I would've taken a run at him. I could've climbed that tall drink of water and swung off his vine like a champion.

"I'm well." His white teeth glistened against his tanned face. His white T-shirt clung to his muscles like it couldn't get close enough. "He's inside." He motioned with his scruff-covered chin.

"I don't want to just walk inside," I told him, still eyeing him like a flesh-colored lollipop.

"Just go in. He's probably asleep. We had a long night."

If he only knew.

"Thanks, sweetie," I said and stood on my tiptoes to place a kiss on his cheek. When I planted my lips against his skin, I inhaled his scent like a creeper.

When I came to ALFA, most of the men were my relatives. I was only left with Bear and Sam as eye candy, but they were more than enough to keep my imagination occupied.

"Anytime, Ms. D."

As I backed away, I debated my next statement in my head a few times before finally blurting it out. "Don't tell Morgan I was here, please."

His smile vanished. "Why?"

"I just don't want him to worry. I need to talk to Bear about the case, and I don't want to hear Morgan's shit. Got me?"

He nodded slowly. "Got ya. Whatever you say."

"Good boy." I waved and touched the door handle, waiting for Sam to go back inside. Once he finally closed his door, I opened Bear's to find him on the phone with his back to me.

"I'm working on it. Just get your ass back here and calm the fuck down," he growled, swiveling around in his chair. His eyes raked up my body before a slow, lazy smile appeared. "I'll keep her safe. I have to go. Someone is here to see me." He disconnected the call and leaned back, staring at me.

I shifted on my feet. "Am I bothering you?"

"Come here," he said, motioning for me with his hand.

I walked around the desk and came to a stop in front of him. "I can go."

His big hands slid around my waist, and he pulled me into his lap. "You all right, sweetheart?"

"I'm okay," I told him as I nuzzled against his chest. "Better now that I'm here." My hand tangled in his white T-shirt, the tips of my fingers digging into his hard pecs.

His hand swept up and down my back, soothing me. "How much did you hear?"

I peered up into his silver eyes. "Not much. I assume you were referring to me in that phone call."

He grimaced. "Yeah. I'm supposed to keep an eye on you, and Sam's going to head to the track to be with Race until Morgan gets back."

I would've argued needing to be watched, but I wasn't in the mood, and it was Bear that would do the watching. "Did you see the note?"

"Yeah." His hand came to the back of my neck and gripped me gently. "You know it's not your fault, right?"

My eyes drifted away from his. "Yeah," I whispered.

"Franny, look at me." My chest tightened as I directed my eyes to his, and his hold on me increased. "Whatever Johnny got involved in had nothing to do with you. Do not feel guilty for his choices."

"But," I started to say, but I lost my train of thought.

"Don't worry," he said in the most soothing voice and pulled my head against his chest, cupping my face. "This isn't your fault."

"Bear, if I would've answered the phone, maybe…" I sealed my eyes shut as my chin began to quiver.

"It wouldn't've changed a thing. He was in too deep. He would've just dragged you into whatever mess he was involved in." His fingers swept my hair away from my face and tucked a few strays behind my ear. "It's bad enough that you're this involved. I couldn't imagine if something happened to you too."

I listened to the steady thumping of his heart and let his words sink in. I probably couldn't have changed anything, but knowing I didn't answer the phone would eat at me for some time.

We sat in silence for a few minutes while I gathered my thoughts. I finally straightened in his lap, staring into his steely eyes. "Well, he's gone now. There's nothing I can do to change it."

"You're stuck with me for the rest of the day."

"That's not a hardship." I smiled, and the tears that had collected in my eyes spilled down my cheeks.

Using his thumbs, he brushed them away. "Want to go see Race? We could spend the day out at the track, and I can talk to some of the workers."

"Sure. I never mind spending time with my daughter-in-law."

"Sam!" Bear yelled over my head. His eyes dropped to mine. "Sorry. Didn't mean to yell in your ear."

"It's okay." I laughed.

"Yo," Sam said as he opened the door, filling the entire frame.

"We're heading to the track. Stay here if you want. I'll keep an eye on both of the ladies."

Sam chewed on his lip and thought about it before finally replying, "Sure."

"We're out." Bear lifted me off his lap and deposited my feet on the floor. "Ready?"

"Let's take my car and leave your bike here."

Bear's eyebrows drew together. "Although that sounds *nice,* I'd be more comfortable with you on the back of my bike."

"That makes one of us," I mumbled.

"I'll get your car back to your place, Ms. D," Sam offered.

"Thanks," Bear replied before I could protest.

"Call me if you need anything," Sam said before walking back to his office, leaving us alone again.

"I don't understand why we can't take my car."

"I have nothing against your sedan, baby." Bear stood and grabbed my chin, forcing me to look up at him. "But I'd rather have you on the back of my bike with your sweet thighs squeezing me like a vise and your hungry pussy pressed against my back."

"Okay," I whispered because I liked it too.

———

"FRAN!" Race ran toward me with her arms outstretched.

"Hey, sweetie," I said to her as we hugged.

With her arms still wrapped around me, she said, "Bear. It's good to see you. I've heard a lot about you lately." She snickered.

I backed away and held her shoulders. "Don't believe a word of what Morgan says. You hear me?"

Her deep green eyes sparkled. "Sure, Mom. Whatever you say."

"It's probably worse than you've heard," Bear said, which earned him a stern look.

"I know you're a dirty dog." Race slapped Bear's chest. "What brings you two by?" She blocked the sun from her eyes with her hand.

"Just wanted to go through Johnny's office once more, and I thought I'd take you two to lunch."

"Hmm." She turned around and glanced down at the track behind us. "I'm sure I can get away for a little bit. We're shorthanded without Johnny, but we can make do."

"You're always working. We barely spend time together anymore." I felt whiny, but I did miss her. She had been consumed by the track and making it a success, and with Johnny gone, it hadn't made her job any easier.

"Good. I'll go with Race, and you check out the office," I told Bear when I looped my arm with Race's and started to walk away.

"Meet back here in an hour, and we'll head out."

"You got it!" I yelled out before glancing at my daughter-in-law. "When are you going to give me a grandchild?" I asked because it'd been on my mind ever since Janice came to my house with her giant belly. Really, it'd been on my mind since the day they were married, but I'd been waiting patiently.

"We're working on it, Mom. I promise," Race said, and I believed her.

I'd learned over the last few years that Race never lied to me. Even when Morgan would complain, she still told me like it was—never sparing my feelings in the name of truth.

We walked toward the maintenance building with our arms still locked. "As long as you're trying, then I'm happy."

She looked at me with a quirked eyebrow. "What about you and Bear?"

I smiled so big that my cheeks hurt. "Oh, girl. It's a long story."

"It's a good thing we have an hour, then."

We gabbed the entire time, mostly about Bear, but also about Morgan. Race told me that he'd complained all week about us growing closer. He worried that Bear wasn't going to treat me with the respect I deserved.

I'm sure some of the feelings had more to do with his father and the way he treated me and left us, but I knew Bear was nothing like him. Ray was out for one person—himself.

Bear would do anything to shield his friends and family from any pain, even if it meant he'd take a hit to do it. He was that kind of guy.

CHAPTER 17

BEAR

By the time we finished eating, my ears were ringing. Race and Fran never stopped talking. I was too used to the guys at the office and our limited conversation usually containing some grunts instead of actual words.

But these two—they talked and talked, jumping between topics so quickly that my head spun. The only other time I experienced something like that was being at a Gallo family function.

Race and Fran couldn't look more opposite. The color of Race's hair reminded me of sunshine and spring days with its yellow, pin-straight strands. Fran's sat on her shoulders, a stream of black silk that glistened in the light. Their builds were similar—tiny, not frail. Together they were a matched set of beautiful perfection with foul mouths to rival any biker.

But their talkativeness allowed me time to think about what I found while sweeping Johnny's office for clues. We did it when he first disappeared, but this time, we had solid proof that he wasn't working alone.

I found some Post-its that had been tossed to the side with phone numbers scribbled on them but no names. Any of them could be his accomplice. There were a handful of them underneath the desk that

567

had been crumpled into tiny balls. All over his calendar, like mine, were notes I snapped photos of to follow up on later.

But there was one clue that had me worried. The name Ray was written in black ink and traced over numerous times. No phone number, no other information, just the name. I immediately thought of Fran's ex-husband. My mind reeled at the possibility that the slimy bastard was involved in some way.

Morgan had to know about this sooner rather than later. I slid my phone across the table and discreetly sent him a text.

Me: Gotta talk. Found something interesting.

"Whatcha doing?" Fran asked right after I hit send.

"Just seeing how the guys are." I turned off my screen, shielding the words from her prying eyes. She should be employed at ALFA, because she could sniff out bullshit like a bloodhound.

"Everything okay?" Her perfectly shaped eyebrow arched when she spoke.

"Great." I smiled and hoped she bought the bullshit. I placed my hand across the screen as I waited for his reply.

She narrowed her eyes quickly at the gesture. "We'll talk later."

Race started laughing, softly at first but grew loud in a hurry. "You two are so damn cute. I can't get over it. It's like a match made in heaven. Morgan has to get over his shit 'cause I need you two together."

"Don't be silly," Fran said to her and wrinkled her nose.

"No. No." Race shook her head, still laughing. "It's like Beauty and the Beast. I've never seen this side of Bear. Usually, he's stalking around, grunting and broody, but with you, Mom, he's like a sweet man with a heart of gold and scared as hell of you too."

"I'm not," I said quickly.

"He is kind of a beast, isn't he?" Fran's eyes moved between Race and me before she smiled. "You should see what's underneath those clothes."

"Get out." Race smacked Fran's arm. "Is he beastly everywhere?"

Fuckin' women.

I moved my hand to the side and read Morgan's message, trying not to listen to what they were about to say next.

Morgan: Meet at the Cowboy at 7.

Me: I'll be there. What about the women?

Morgan: Fuck. Don't leave them alone. Sam can stay outside my house, and bring Mom with you to the Cowboy.

I sat here in complete shock. He bitched me out for bringing her there before, and now he wants me to take her with me?

"What did he say?" Fran asked after she finished telling Race that I was pure man with a huge sword.

"He said we should meet him at the Cowboy at seven."

"Oh, I love it there," Race said quickly.

"He wants you at home." I couldn't look her in the eye.

She slammed her hand down on the table. "Like fuck. That's not gonna happen." She plucked her phone from her purse and started to type like a madwoman.

"I'm just following orders." I cringed when she paused long enough to glare at me.

"I'll be going. Morgan will just have to get over his macho shit."

"That's my girl. We have to stick together," Fran said as Race hit send.

"What time should I be ready?" Race asked, jamming her phone back into her purse.

"Six thirty," I told her and looked over at Fran. "And I'll pick you up at five."

Fran glanced down at her watch. "It's almost three now. Why don't you just come over for a bit? I'll give you something to eat." Her smile sparkled, and the wickedness in her eyes was evident.

"I'm sure you will." I winked at her.

"Well, all righty, then. Since we just had lunch, I know you two aren't talking about food." Race nudged Fran. "Lucky woman."

"You do have a husband," Fran told her.

"I'm too pissed at him. It's going to be a long time until he gets a piece of this." Race motioned up and down her body.

"Oh, Lord." I peered up at the ceiling and exhaled.

They were so filthy. I didn't want to think about Race and Morgan, and I sure as fuck didn't want Race thinking about Fran and me, but the two of them had no problem with it.

"Well, I have to get back to work, and you two have to..." Race's voice trailed off before she winked at Fran.

I didn't respond. What could I say to that? I didn't want to be the creepy old dude. Fran and Race had a relationship more like friends than mother-in-law and daughter-in-law. It was sweet and kind, and way too much information was shared between them. More than I ever wanted to know.

Fran scooted from the booth, letting Race out and coming to stand next to me. She put her arm around my shoulder and stroked my neck with her fingers. "We'll see you in a few hours."

Race smiled down at me before kissing Fran on the cheek. "Have fun," she whispered but not soft enough that I couldn't hear.

"We will." Fran grinned and glanced down in my direction. "Right, tiger?"

"Yep," I said, shifting in my seat, and throwing the money for the check on the table.

After Race was far enough away, I pulled Fran into my lap, and she squealed. "You're trying to get me killed, right?"

"Come on," she said gleefully and slapped my chest. "Don't be crazy."

I nuzzled my face against her neck, kissing a path to her jaw. "Talking about my dick and our sex life with Race is a recipe for my execution at the hands of your son, sweetheart."

Fran tipped her head back and closed her eyes. "Race won't say anything."

"Uh-huh," I muttered against her skin. "If I die, know that I had fun."

"Just fun?" she breathed.

"Fuck," I hissed when my cock swelled in my pants. "Let's get out of here, or I'm going to have to fuck you in the bathroom."

"Ooh," she cooed and moved around just enough to send a jolt through my system. "I've never done it in a bathroom."

Note to self. "Not here." I stood, taking her with me in my arms, and stalked toward the door.

"Bear!" she yelled in protest, but she snaked her arm around my shoulders.

"Let's go feed that greedy pussy of yours before we're in public. I need you sated tonight."

Her eyes grew wide. "You do?"

"Yeah. Remember… I like to live. I don't need you rubbing all over me with Morgan there. I want no chance of anything going wrong."

"I'm going to rock your world, baby," she whispered into my ear.

My eyes rolled back, and my dick threatened to break through the material of my pants. I didn't even give a fuck who was around, seeing the massive wood I was sporting. "Fuck, woman. I can't drive like this."

"I'm sure you've been in harder situations." She giggled.

"I don't know what I'm going to do with you." I placed her on the back of the bike before adjusting my cock so it wasn't so…noticeable.

She plucked at her bottom lip while she pouted. "I've been a bad girl. Maybe you should spank me."

Turning my face up to the clouds, I whispered, "What did I ever do to you?"

"Come on, handsome. Take me home so you can go for a real ride."

"Seriously," I said again to the sky and growled loudly. I climbed on my bike with my cock screaming for relief and started the engine.

Fran slid forward, pressing her sweet little pussy against me, and squeezing her thighs around me. "I need your cock, Bear. I need all of your cock," she said into my ear.

The woman didn't have to tell me twice. When we got back, I was going to fuck her until she could barely walk. She needed to be so sated that she wouldn't give any lip tonight or cause any problems. I'd fuck her into oblivion and then pull her out just enough to function.

MORGAN RUSHED toward Fran as soon as we stepped foot inside the Neon Cowboy. "What's wrong, Ma?"

Fran grabbed his arms and stopped him before he hugged her. "I'm fine, baby." She didn't want him too close because the smell of sex oozed right off her.

Morgan looked at me before staring back at her and narrowing his eyes. "You look…different."

Race snorted. "She's fine. Just been a *hard* day for her."

I gritted my teeth, almost grimacing. "I need a drink. Anyone else?" I asked, trying to find a reason to make an exit from this situation before it got sticky.

"I'll take a strawberry daiquiri. I'm parched." Fran smiled lazily at me.

"I'll take a Dirty Martini," Race told me and brushed the hair off her shoulders.

"Coming right up." I walked away, moving straight to the bar where I saw City standing.

"What's up, man?" I asked and slapped him on the back as he leaned over the bar and sipped on his beer.

"Bear. I see you brought my aunt." He tipped his head backward toward the table where they all now sat.

"Yeah. Problem?"

"Nope."

Sandy, the longtime bartender and a one-time fling, approached. "What'll it be?" she asked, pretending not to know me. I accepted the fact that she hated my guts after I kicked her out of bed. As long as she didn't spit in my drinks, I didn't care what the fuck she did.

"Dirty Martini, strawberry daiquiri, and a tequila with a Miller chaser."

She snarled, but she stalked away without any bullshit.

City laughed. "Sandy still hates your fucking guts."

"Such is life." I shrugged and blew it off.

"Things good with Fran?"

"Couldn't be better."

"Good for you," he said, catching me off guard.

"Twenty bucks," Sandy said, all the while giving me the stink-eye as she set the three drinks down on the bar.

"Twenty?"

"Yeah, you get the douchebag rate."

I growled, and City laughed at my side. "Just pay the woman."

"Fine," I said, slamming a twenty plus three more bucks on the bar.

"Only three?"

I couldn't believe she had the balls to ask me this after giving me the "douchebag" rate. "It's the bitch rate from a douchebag," I shot back quickly.

City laughed harder when she flipped me the bird and stalked to the other side of the bar without another word. "You're smooth."

"Fuck her, man." I grabbed the three drinks, balancing them in between my hands. "She doesn't deserve more. I shouldn't have given her the three. She already pocketed five of the twenty. Her pussy wasn't even worth the hassle."

"You sure you want to be with Fran?" He followed behind me, still laughing. "'Cause when you fuck that up, you're going to have bigger problems than the 'douchebag rate.'"

"I know. I know," I mumbled, but I cleared my throat when we came within feet of the table. "Ladies." I set the drinks down and slid Fran's and Race's across the table.

Morgan and Race were deep in conversation, talking too low for anyone to hear, but it seemed heated.

"Kids," Fran whispered and rolled her eyes.

"Yeah." Under the table, I entwined our fingers before slamming back my shot of tequila. The warmth of the liquid slid down my throat before working its way into my system.

If all the shit with Johnny hadn't been going on, I'd have said this had been the best damn week I'd had in decades. But the shadow of the theft and Johnny's death had sucked a bit of the happy out of everything.

"Bear," Morgan said, breaking my train of thought. "Can I talk to you at the bar?" He stood and leaned over to kiss Race on the cheek, but she ducked out of the way.

"Sure." I gave Fran's hand a quick squeeze before standing. Our relationship was already a bit heated, but with him and Race fighting, this couldn't end well.

As I walked toward the bar, I kept telling myself to stay calm. *For Fran's sake—stay calm.* "What's up?"

He leaned against the bar with his hand hanging over the edge, looking completely relaxed. "What did you find in Johnny's office?"

Reaching into my pocket, I pulled out the tiny scrap of paper and tossed it on the bar in front of him.

Morgan glanced down, and his eyes immediately shot to mine. "You think it's *my* Ray?"

"I couldn't say, kid. It's too coincidental to be anything else, in my opinion."

"It can't be. We haven't heard from my father in over a decade."

"Maybe he's been keeping tabs on you."

He shook his head. "I can't believe that. It can't be true."

"Stranger shit has happened, Morgan. Want me to follow up on it?"

"Nah, I'll do it. He's my dad."

"You got it." I patted him on the shoulder. "Maybe I'm wrong. It's a common name."

"Yeah," he sighed. "How did it go with the ladies today?"

"Piece of cake," I replied, but I didn't elaborate.

He eyed me suspiciously. "And things with my mother?"

"Good there too."

"Bear, baby," Fran said, coming up behind me, and wrapping her arms around my waist. "Dance with me."

Morgan's eyes narrowed, and my stomach tightened. "Anything you want, sweetheart."

"Go," Morgan said with a pained look.

"Thanks," I told him, but I was going to do it even if I didn't have his permission.

Fran grabbed my hand, intertwining our fingers as we walked toward the dance floor. "You looked like you needed saving."

I wrapped my arm around her and pulled her close. "Actually, Fran, that was the most civil he's been in a long time."

"Huh." She smiled up at me. "Maybe he's finally realizing he can't control everything in my life."

I didn't have the heart to tell her that he had bigger things on his mind. Shit that had to do with her alcoholic ex-husband possibly being involved in the theft and Johnny's death.

It wasn't my place to tell her, and there was no point in scaring her yet. She had enough shit on her mind for me to clutter it with more bullshit.

"Yeah, I'm sure that's it, sweetheart." I kissed the top of her head, tucking her closer against me as we spun around the dance floor.

I knew shit was about to get stickier and more complicated before we got to the bottom of everything. Lord help us all if my hunch was right.

CHAPTER 18

FRAN

I woke with my body tangled with Murray's and coated in sweat. The man was covered in fur, and when he slept, he threw off heat like a small campfire.

He'd stayed over for the past week, stating that he didn't want to be away from me, but I knew something was up. Morgan had been acting strange since Johnny's death, and Bear had become overprotective to the point of suffocation.

"Morning, sweetheart." Bear tightened his hold on me.

I kicked off the blankets, trying to find some cool air, but there was none to be had. "Morning, babe. Want some coffee?"

"I'm good just like this," he said as he buried his face in my neck.

Even though I felt like I was roasting in the sun, goose bumps broke out across my skin as he kissed me. "We can't stay in bed all day." I wiggled to try to break free, but I failed.

His cock stirred. "Why not?"

I shimmied away from his hardness. "Oh, no. Not now, mister. I'm going to the hairdresser and then to meet Maria for lunch."

"I'll come," he said, and I knew immediately that there was something no one had told me.

"What aren't you telling me?"

"I don't know what you're talking about. Stay here. I want to have a little Fran for breakfast."

I grabbed his balls and gave them a playful squeeze. "Why don't you roll on your back, and I'll give you a proper good morning?" The men in this family, including Bear, must have thought I was an idiot.

His eyes grew wide, and he quickly flipped onto his back, putting his hands behind his head. "This is the best fucking way to wake up."

I crawled between his legs and settled on my heels as I wrapped my hand around his stiff cock. "You like this, baby?"

"God, yes." He let out a little moan when my hand moved.

"Do you want it rough or soft?" I asked in a breathy, sexy voice.

"Any way you want to do it." He licked his lips and closed his eyes. "I'm up for anything you've got."

He shivered when I dragged my tongue around the head. Placing the tip in my mouth, I grazed him with my teeth, and his hips shot off the bed.

"Gentle, baby," he told me, glancing down his body at me.

Pulling his cock out, I waved it in front of my lips. "You want gentle?"

"I don't want teeth."

My hold tightened on his shaft. "You better start telling me what the fuck is going on, and do it quick before you get a blow job you'll never forget, Murray."

His eyes snapped to mine. "What are you talking about?"

"You've been up my ass, and Morgan's acting weird. You better tell me what's going on, or this is going to be the last time your dick is in my hands."

"Fran, let's be civil about this."

Civil? I was being civil. I hadn't punched him in the gut or kicked him out of my house. I was giving him a chance to explain and make shit right.

I stroked his cock slowly, and his hips moved. "You better start explaining, and do it now."

"Fran," he said my name as a plea.

"Talk." My fingers tightened, and my thumb grazed the tip. When he didn't speak, I leaned forward and placed my lips around the head, sucking lightly.

"Fuck, yes," he moaned.

I wasn't going to back down on answers. The men in my life needed to understand that I didn't need shielding from information. It was only fair that I knew what was going on since it had to do with Johnny, me, and a boatload of cash.

I sucked a little more and brought him close to the edge before backing away.

His hips followed my mouth. "I'm not allowed to say anything, Fran."

I shook my head and licked my lips. "Talk, or you get nothing."

He mumbled something I couldn't make out before throwing his arm over his face. "Fine. I'll tell you anything you want to know."

I smiled and didn't feel one bit guilty. "What's going on with the case?"

His hands tangled in my hair. "He wasn't alone."

I swiped my tongue across the underneath of his head and pulled back. "Tell me something I don't know."

He closed his eyes, and his jaw ticked. "We haven't found anything solid yet."

"Talk, or you're going home with blue balls."

I felt proud of myself. Powerful, even. Women often forgot their ability to control a man with their sexuality. Give men a hard-on, and they're putty in our hands.

"All we found is a note with a name," he said through clenched teeth.

I quirked an eyebrow and glared at him. "Whose name?"

"It said Ray," he said quickly when I squeezed his dick like a vise.

My body went rigid, and my hand opened before his cock fell backward and waved. "My Ray?"

"We don't know," he said in a strangled voice. "Morgan is tracking him down."

I covered my mouth, my eyes wider than if I'd seen a ghost. "He can't track him down."

"Why not?" Bear asked as he sat up and scooted closer.

"He's a bad person, Murray. Whether or not he's involved, he's not someone I want back in either of our lives."

"Fran." He slid his legs around me. "We have to follow up on it. Whoever is involved is bad news. Johnny wouldn't kill himself unless it was too bad to break free of, sweetheart."

"I don't want Morgan finding him. Can't you handle it?"

"It's his case, but I can tell Thomas and James, and maybe they'll handle the search for Ray."

"Please," I begged and clutched his shoulders.

Ray DeLuca was one of the biggest pieces of shit I'd ever had the displeasure of being with. I stayed too long with him too. But times were different then. Once I became pregnant, there was no going back. Being raised a Catholic, divorce was a sin, one that my parents would never allow. I didn't have any way to support Morgan and myself, so I stayed.

Bear placed his soft lips against my forehead, tickling my nose with his beard. "I'll talk to them."

Ray had never hit me. He wouldn't be alive if that were the case, but he'd used his words as weapons instead of fists. Every time he drank too much, another side of him would come out. His sharp tongue would lash my soul with hurtful slurs about my body, my face, and my personality. There wasn't one thing he liked about me. He felt tied to me because of the baby and never liked Morgan from the day he was born.

He stayed, though. Just long enough to see Morgan reach adulthood, and then he took off, leaving me to fend for myself. I never really realized the full extent of the piece of shit that was Ray DeLuca until people started showing up at my door. They were looking for him because he had outstanding loans, mainly with local bookies, and he was a wanted man. We never saw him again, and that was just fine by me.

I often shielded Morgan from Ray's nastiness. Morgan didn't remember all the hate his father spewed, and I wanted to keep it that way. No child should feel unwanted, but if he found his father, he'd realize exactly the type of man he came from.

But it was more than Morgan finding out that his father didn't want him. I didn't want my son to think less of me for staying with such a person for as long as I did. I prided myself on my independence and strength, and I worried that Morgan would question my very sanity once he met the real Ray DeLuca. If Ray was involved in this, in Johnny's death and the theft, it would only cement the level of asshole he truly was and probably still is to this day.

"I need coffee," I said as I scurried toward the edge of the bed.

"But what about me?" He glanced down at his boner.

I giggled. "You do what I ask, and I'll make it worth your while."

A giant smile spread across his face. "Is this me earning the one thing you've never given any man?"

I turned around and shook my ass. "You want this?" I bent over and wiggled it. "Do what I ask, and it's yours." It was the only card I had left to play.

He hopped out of the bed like a kid and grabbed his jeans off the floor, jamming his legs inside.

"Where you going?"

"No time to waste," he said as he pulled up the zipper and buttoned them.

I laughed and watched him get dressed faster than I ever thought possible. "You have time for a cup of coffee, Murray. My ass will be here."

"Fran." He smoothed out his wrinkled T-shirt and shook his head. "Some things are more important than coffee. I'm wide awake anyway." He stalked toward me.

I peered up at him and slid my hand against his cheek. "But it's only 6:30. No one's at the office yet."

He smirked and kissed my thumb when it grazed his lip. "Early bird gets the worm, sweetheart. Or in my case, the ass." Leaning forward, his lips pressed against mine, and I melted into him.

I grabbed his denim-covered cock and stroked it roughly. "Sure I can't interest you in staying?"

He backed away and pulled my hand off of him, lifting it to his mouth, and kissing the back. "I'm a patient man, Franny. I'm not fucking this one up."

Before I could reply, he was already marching toward the front door and grabbing his boots. With one on and the other in his hand, he opened the door and jogged down the walkway.

"Call me later!" I yelled as he climbed on his bike and slid his foot into the other boot.

"I'll call as soon as I know anything."

I waved, and he waved back before he started the bike and took off.

"A little ass and a man could move mountains without being asked twice," I said to myself as he disappeared in the distance.

I always thought blow jobs were the keys to the kingdom, but in Bear's world...a little ass made everything possible.

BEAR

"What are you doing here so early?" Thomas glanced down at the watch on his wrist and back at me.

I shrugged off his comment. "I thought I'd get here early. We've been too busy for me to waste any more time lying in bed."

He walked in and closed the door. "Now I know something is up. What's wrong?" he asked as he sat down in the chair across the desk from me.

"It's Fran."

His eyes widened. "Is she okay?"

"Your aunt is fine. She just doesn't want Morgan finding Ray. She wants me to handle it."

"Fuck," Thomas hissed and dragged his hands through his hair. "He's already tracking him down. What are we supposed to do about it?"

I tapped my pencil against my calendar and thought about her shaking her fine ass in my face. "I promised her I would try to get to him first. Can you help a brother out?"

Thomas leaned back and crossed his arms. "I have Sam working with him on it, but I can reassign him and put you with Morgan. It'll be up to you to get to Ray first."

"That'll work." It would at least give me some control over the situation. Once we found him, I could find a way to sidetrack Morgan and get my hands on Ray before anyone else.

"I'll talk to Sam as soon as he gets here, and you can tell Morgan that you're working with him. He's really pissed at you."

"I know, but he's going to have to get the fuck over it."

Thomas nodded and laughed. "I'm sure he will. Just give him some time."

"Thomas, it's been weeks, and he's still up my ass. I really like Fran, hell, I think I even love her."

It was the first time I'd said those words out loud, and I even shocked myself more than Thomas, even given the look of disbelief on his face. "I'm happy for you, man. Don't let my mother know, or she'll start planning your wedding."

I held my hands up and grimaced. "Let's not get ahead of ourselves." I did love Fran, but marriage was a huge step. I hadn't thought about saying "I do" since Jackie passed.

"You know how my family is. If Maria hears love, she'll have a deposit down on a hall faster than you can blink."

"Well, fuck."

"Just don't be surprised," he said as he made his way to the door. "You'd be my uncle then and Morgan's stepdad. This could be some good shit."

"Shit," I groaned and covered my face when he walked out the door. I could hear him whistling as he walked down the hallway, and all I could do was shake my head.

Unable to sit still after Thomas planted that seed, I headed to Morgan's office to look through his files on Ray. I wanted to get a jump-start before he arrived.

I opened the first folder marked Ray's Record and almost fell off the chair. The man had a rap sheet longer than mine. It read like a timeline of America's Most Wanted. Everything from petty theft, assault, and larceny filled the lines. The man had been busy since walking out on Fran and Morgan.

The second folder was marked FBI Ray. Inside were reports on Ray's activities while he was under surveillance by the FBI about five years ago. They thought he was involved in organized crime in Chicago and kept eyes on him at all times. After a year of coming up empty, they pulled the team from him and dropped their investigation.

Even with my bullshit, I don't think the FBI had a file on me. That was usually only reserved for the lowest of the low or those whose crimes that were on the federal level.

Ray wasn't a good man. I knew that from Fran, but as I sat in Morgan's office reading the multiple folders filled with crime after crime and every sordid detail, I knew he was worse than I imagined. Fran was right not to want Morgan to get involved with him, and I'd do everything in my power to make sure it didn't happen.

"What are you doing?" Morgan asked from the doorway.

I didn't bother to look up. "Just doing some reading."

"In my office?"

"Yeah. I didn't want to take the files back to mine. I figured I'd wait here for you and catch up."

"Catch up?"

I finally looked at him and closed the manila folder in my hand. "Thomas had to reassign Sam, so I'm your new partner."

His nostrils flared. "You're my new partner?"

"Glad to know you can still hear," I grumbled and readied myself for a fight.

"Old man, I can do this on my own."

"Kid," I said in response to his dig about my age and made my way around the desk. "I know you could do it on your own, but with someone like Ray, you could use some backup. I wouldn't let anyone in this office go after him alone, and neither would you. So put aside your pride and hate for a little while, and let's find him together."

"Fine," he said a little too quickly.

I tilted my head, moving my ear closer because I was sure I'd heard him wrong. "Fine?"

"You deaf now too?" He smirked.

He pushed past me. "Little fucker."

"I talked to my mom already today," he said as he sat down and pulled his chair up to the desk.

"Yeah?" I asked and took a seat across from him.

This could be good or bad. I wasn't going to pretend I hadn't been with her. I didn't know what Fran said to him, though, and I didn't want to start the day with a lie after he already had an issue with me being in his office.

"She said you spent the night." I couldn't read his facial expression, so I sat here and waited for him to say more. "She seems..." His voice trailed off.

"Happy," I said, finishing the statement for him.

"Well, yeah." He scratched his head and pursed his lips. "I don't remember the last time I really saw her happy. But for some reason, when she's with you, she's glowing."

I didn't have the heart to tell the kid I banged her brains out to the point that she had so many endorphins running through her system, happy was the only way she could feel. "I really like her, Morgan. I know I went about it all wrong, and I should've talked to you first, but—"

He held his hand up and stopped me. "You didn't have to ask permission. She's my mother and I love her dearly, but I can't control her and whom she falls in love with."

My head jerked backward. Who was this man sitting across from me? Morgan would never just give in so easily.

"Plus, she hasn't been up my ass like she usually is since you entered the picture. My phone only rings once a day instead of five. It's a win for both of us."

I narrowed my eyes. "So you're okay with me dating her?"

"I guess, as long as you don't hurt her."

"You've met her, right? I think I'll need protection from Fran if I fuck it up, not the other way around."

"If you fuck up, you'll have more to worry about than just me. You'll have an entire family coming after you."

"Ah, this puts me at ease—nothing like threatening a man to keep him happy in a relationship. You know... Your mom could break my heart first."

"Anything's possible."

We stared at each other for a minute, silently wondering what this meant for us as friends before I spoke first.

"I've always respected you, Morgan. You're a good kid with a solid head on your shoulders. You're a family man and a good son. I don't want this to change our friendship. I promise to be good to your mother for as long as she'll have me."

"Bear, you've been through more shit with my family and every guy in this office. We've always been able to depend on you and always know you have our backs. I know in my heart you'll never do anything to hurt us or our families. I know you'll be good to my mom. If you aren't, she'll let it be known."

I nodded and started to laugh. "Are we done professing our love to each other? We do have work to do, and I'm a little uncomfortable with all these kind words we're throwing at each other."

"I'm over it." He shrugged and opened the folder that I had been reading when he walked in. "So what do you think of my father?"

"He's a real piece of shit."

There was no nice way to say it. Based on everything I'd read and the way Fran acted, he wasn't a nice guy. How she ended up with him and stayed for so long was beyond me.

"He always has been."

"How did Fran stay with him for so long?"

He leaned back, placing his fingers together in an arch in front of him. "He's not a good man. She claims it was because times were different, but I think my mom was always scared to leave him."

My grip tightened on my leg. It was the only thing I could do to keep myself in my seat. "Did he hit her?"

He grimaced. "No. He'd just become a different person when he drank. He'd say the meanest shit to her and I always worried he'd eventually hit her. I stepped in between them once when he grabbed her by the arms, and I knocked him out. That was the end of him ever laying a hand on her."

Every muscle in my body tensed. "Goddamn it. You two shouldn't have had to deal with a fucker like that."

His arms relaxed on the armrests, and his hands curled around with a tight grip. "I told him the night before I graduated that if he didn't leave of his own accord, I'd remove him from the house myself. I wasn't going to leave her there with him."

"You're the reason he left your mom?" My mouth hung open.

He nodded with a smug smile. "Yep. Mom doesn't know, though, so I'd appreciate it if you didn't tell her, Bear."

"Lips are sealed."

"I gave him twenty-four hours to clear out before I had my uncle Santino deal with him."

"Santino?" I'd never heard the name uttered from any of the Gallos. "Is he on your father's side?"

"No, he's the black sheep on my mother's side. She has two brothers—Santino and Salvatore. But Santino was the only one still in Chicago, and I knew he wouldn't have a problem handling Ray for me."

"I can't believe I've never heard him mentioned." Not even City had mentioned the name, and I'd known him for over ten years.

"Well, you'd have to meet him to understand. He's not like my uncle Sal. Santino just got out of prison recently too."

"Sounds like an interesting character."

"He's different, but I knew he'd have no problem kicking my father's ass and making sure he never went back to see my mother again."

Morgan surprised me with his confession. All these years had passed, but he'd never told his mother the real reason Ray had left. She'd gone through so much heartache when it happened. Not only did her husband leave, even if he was a piece of shit, but her son joined the military. She went from a full house to silence in a hurry, just like I did.

"Your mom is worried you're going to get wrapped up in your father's bullshit. She wanted me to help you find him."

Morgan laughed. "I found him about eight years ago. An old friend emailed me to tell me Ray was sniffing around the neighborhood. So when I came home on leave, I made sure to find him. I wanted to make sure he stayed the fuck away from Mom. He got the message."

I hadn't realized my muscles were still rigid as I hung on his every word, learning something new about him and Fran that I hadn't known before. "Do you think he had something to do with Johnny?"

He rubbed his forehead and winced. "I wouldn't be surprised. He's a total piece of shit and will find any way to get his hands on some money."

I mashed my hands together, squeezing them as tightly as I wanted to squeeze the man's neck. "Then we'd better find him before something else happens. It's time to make Ray go away forever."

"You takin' him out?"

"That's too simple. We'll figure it out once we have confirmation that he's involved."

"I'm going to make some phone calls. I have a few friends in Chicago, and maybe you should call Santino too."

He grabbed his cell phone from his pocket and turned it over in his hand. "I don't know if Ma or Uncle Sal will be so happy about it, but he'd know if Ray was back in town."

"This isn't about making people happy; it's about getting to the bottom of this entire mess."

"I want to hand him over to the cops when we find him, Bear. It's the right thing to do. They have the letter from Johnny, and we have the evidence from his office."

"Sure," I said, but I planned on getting a few punches in first.

"We'll kick his ass, of course, but let the cops deal with the rest." He smirked.

I laughed. "I thought you went soft on me for a second."

"I'm happy my mom has you by her side, man. Seriously."

Although I didn't need his blessing, it meant more to me than he probably knew. "Thanks, kid. I appreciate that," I told him as I stood and made my way to the door.

"Now get back to work. We have an asshole to catch."

I nodded and walked into the hallway. There was more than one asshole at stake in this mission. I wasn't about to come up empty this time. But I knew I wouldn't make Fran pay up on our deal. It wasn't something to be bartered for, but something to be earned and given in trust. Morgan had every right to find his father and deal with him as he saw fit. I didn't have the right to take that away and neither did Fran.

CHAPTER 20
FRAN

"Thanks for coming over. Your brother was about to make me drown myself in the pool." Maria yanked on my arm and pulled me into her house. "I swear to God he's making me crazy."

I kicked off my shoes because her house was too clean to keep them on. She was a bigger clean freak than I was, and that was saying something. "What's going on?"

"Fucking Santino!"

My entire body rocked backward as if someone shoved me. "What?"

She blew past me and headed to the kitchen, grabbing two wineglasses off the counter. "Santino called, and Sal has his panties in a bunch." She held up the bottle of wine, and naturally, I nodded. It may have only been noon, but anytime someone mentioned Tino, it was a reason to drink.

"What the hell did he want?" I slid into the chair and tried to keep my body still. The thought of my brother made my stomach turn.

"Morgan called him," she said quickly as she filled our glasses.

My hands landed on the table with a thud, causing the wine-filled glasses to bounce. "What?" I asked through clenched teeth. "You can't be serious."

"As a fuckin' heart attack. You know I never joke when it comes to that man."

"What would Morgan want with Tino?" I gulped down half my glass in one fell swoop because the entire situation called for liquor and lots of it.

"I guess he wanted to know if Tino knew where Ray was. Sal has talked to him a bit lately. I guess he's trying to get his shit together up there after he finally got released from prison. It wasn't Santino that set Sal off; it was the mention of Ray."

"Huh." I leaned back and took a deep breath.

"Sal will never forgive Ray for leaving you the way he did."

"It was best, Mar. You know how Ray was, and I was actually happy the day he disappeared from my life."

"I know, but Sal doesn't know everything that happened. I never told him, even after all these years."

I stared at her in complete shock. "You better not tell him now. He's going to be pissed at both of us for the rest of our lives."

Mar had never been one to keep secrets. The fact that she held on to the one about Ray and his temper for that long was astonishing. Impressive, even. She had always been known as the blabbermouth. An adorable and caring one, but still she wasn't the one you wanted with you when you buried a body. She would sing like a canary before the cops would even have a chance to question her.

"I know," she groaned and laid her head on her hands. "But now Tino's involved. This is going to be a clusterfuck of epic proportions."

I grabbed the bottle of wine and refilled my glass and Maria's too. "It is what it is now. We have to let the chips fall where they may, Mar. I still can't believe Morgan would call him. Tino back in the game?"

And by game, I meant organized crime. We always used the neighborhood lingo because it sounded more pleasant than the reality. Even prison had a different name too—college. Half the time I didn't know if someone was in school or prison, but I rolled with it.

"He claims he's on the up-and-up, but who the hell knows. Why Betty stayed with him, I'll never know."

"You know they were always explosive, but they had that thing…"

"Insanity?" Maria laughed.

"You know who I feel bad for? His kids."

"I haven't seen them since they were little. It's a shame I have two nephews and a niece that I've lost touch with."

"They're all grown-up now, Mar. Vinnie, the youngest, is in college."

"Shit. I feel even worse. Thanks for the pick-me-up, Fran."

"I'm a people pleaser." I smiled into my glass. "Where is my brother, anyway?"

"He went golfing. He felt the need to beat the shit out of something, so he decided an innocent white ball was the best outlet for his anger."

"Seems normal."

We both started laughing. My brother was a pill. He had that wild mix of Italian temper and gentleness. One thing he wasn't…was an abuser. He and Ray had nothing in common. How I ended up with that worthless dirtbag was beyond me. I knew people always thought the same thing but never asked. Thank God, because I wouldn't have had an answer.

"Feel like cooking?" She raised an eyebrow.

I nodded. "What are you thinking?"

"Everyone has been traveling so much. Let's do an impromptu family dinner tonight."

"Sure," I said, but I needed to see Bear.

"Invite him too," she replied like she'd read my mind.

"Let's do this."

Maria headed to the refrigerator and started to pull out all kinds of things that we could make. Instead of trying to decide on one thing, we started prepping everything. Cavatelli, meatballs, sausage, eggplant, chicken, and a boatload of other family dishes.

No one was going to walk out of this house hungry.

"You and Morgan seem chummy," I told Bear as I stood on my tiptoes and kissed his cheek just above the spot where his beard met a clearing of skin.

He wrapped his arm around my back. "Sweetheart, did you ever doubt we could get along?"

Snaking my arm around his neck, I stared into his eyes and smiled. "You two are both hardheaded, baby."

"We both care for you and would do anything to make you happy."

I raised an eyebrow and rubbed my nose against his. "You know what would make me happy?"

"What?" he whispered with his lips barely touching mine.

My fist connected with his stomach. "Making sure Morgan doesn't get my crazy-ass brother in Chicago involved in this shit too."

He barely flinched at the impact and tightened his hold on me so I couldn't get another punch in. "Why?"

"He's no good. He's been involved in organized crime most of his life. I don't want Morgan getting close to him."

"Morgan's a grown man, Fran. I can't make him do anything."

"You're right."

"I like the sound of that." He smiled against my mouth.

"Don't get too used to me saying that," I murmured before he crushed his lips against mine and stole anything else I was about to say.

"You two are gross," Mike said, walking by us in the hallway as he made a gagging noise in the back of his throat.

Bear pulled away and stared into my eyes with the biggest smile I'd ever seen. "It's nice to finally have someone to kiss." I bit my lip and smiled back.

It had been forever since I'd had this feeling. Butterflies still flooded my stomach when he walked into a room, and my mind buzzed with possibilities every time he was near. Bear had that ability to make everything better.

"Where are you guys in the investigation?" Race asked, pushing back from the dinner table and gathering up the dirty plates that everyone had left behind when they headed into the living room.

"Let me get those." Morgan grabbed the stack of plates from Race's hand. "We have some solid leads, babe."

I looked at them, still in Bear's arms, with pride and accomplishment. The man had manners, and I had no one else to thank for that but myself.

"Think we'll get the money back?" She followed him into the kitchen with the half-eaten bowl of cavatelli—why we made five pounds, I'll never know.

"Poor kid," Bear whispered when I glanced up at him with my lips twisted.

"I know. That's a lot of money for a new business to lose."

"We'll figure something out," he said in the sweetest voice and pressed his lips into my hair.

"Wanna get out of here?" I asked and waggled my eyebrows.

"Fuck yeah!" He smirked and licked his lips. "I've been dying to taste you all day." Releasing me, he grabbed my hand, and we started to tiptoe toward the front door.

"Where are you two sneaking off to?" Sal asked just as Bear's hand touched the doorknob.

"Fuck," I hissed and closed my eyes. Even after fifty years, my brother was still a complete cockblock. "We were just going for some fresh air," I sighed, staring up at Bear with my teeth clenched.

He squeezed my hand before he spoke. "I forgot something outside, and we were just going to grab it, Sal. We'll be right back." Bear glanced down at me and winked.

Sal's eyes grew into little slits before he gave us a quick nod. "Don't be too long. We have *things* to talk about."

"Give us five," I called as Bear pulled me out the front door.

"Five? I mean, I'm all for a quickie, but I need more than five minutes to get my fill, Franny."

"We can't now." I looked around the treelined street in the darkness. "Not here. Someone could be watching."

"Like fuck. Don't be a cocktease, woman. There isn't anyone out here. We're in the sticks, for God's sake." He wrapped his arm around my back and guided me down the front steps.

My feet touched the driveway and my stomach rumbled, but not out of fear. "What if someone looks out the window?" My body tingled, and the thought of getting caught sent a tremor of excitement through my body.

He looked down at me with a smug smile. "No windows on the side of the garage, sweetheart."

"Oh," I whispered and walked a little faster so no one would see where we went.

We were barely around the corner of the garage, hidden from the moonlight by the shadows of the trees, when Bear dropped to his knees and started to yank at my pants. "This is where track pants would be an asset. No buttons." His face was hidden in the darkness, but his fingers worked quickly.

"Can't have it both ways," I teased, placing my palms against the garage, and bracing myself for what was coming next.

His hands worked fast, pulling my jeans down to my knees before his lips came crashing down against my skin. I couldn't move my legs. I tried to make my stance wider and give him better access, but I couldn't. My pants were too tight, but it didn't stop Bear.

He dug his fingers into my ass and held me in place as his lips caressed my clit with precision. My eyes sealed shut, the sensation so overwhelming I could barely breathe. Thank God I didn't have any air in my lungs, or I would've been moaning like a whore and drawing attention to us.

When my eyes fluttered open and I was finally able to catch my breath, Bear was already on his feet. He was licking his lips and staring at me like I was the dessert and he was ready for another helping. I bent over and pulled my jeans up, almost falling over because my body hadn't recovered yet.

"How am I supposed to face everyone now?" I asked, sucking in my stomach so I could button the tight jeans that had become my new go-to pants instead of my comfy track pants. Times like these—I missed them.

"Just act natural." He chuckled softly as the moonlight glimmered on his hair when his body moved out of the shadows.

"Yeah, I'm sure that'll be easy." I rolled my eyes and finally got the top button to close. "How do I look?" I asked as I shimmied down the side of the garage to stand under the light.

"Like you just came." He smiled.

"Fuck," I hissed and bit my lip.

"But no one will catch on. I know what I just did to you, so it's easy for me to see it. Your family won't think a thing."

I poked him in the chest as he slid his arms around my back and stared at me sweetly. "You better hope they don't."

"Whatcha gonna do to me if they do?" He quirked a bushy eyebrow, and his eyes twinkled in the dim light.

"I'll think of something. I'm pretty damn good at paybacks." I smirked, still pushing my finger into his chest.

"I look forward to whatever wicked plan you have in mind."

"Don't be so sure, big boy."

I laughed quietly as I followed him, hand in hand, back to the house. The man was thinking sexual payback, but that wasn't my style. I was more the type to get you in a way I thought you needed but would never do yourself. I already had a few ways churning in my head and none of them that he'd like.

"That was fast," Maria said before I even had two feet in the house. "I figured he would take a bit longer." She winked.

I turned around and glared at him. "Paybacks," I mouthed before looking back at Maria. "He just forgot something outside."

"Uh-huh." She walked toward the kitchen and kept laughing loud enough that it annoyed me.

"You're so paying," I said without looking over my shoulder. He laughed with Maria, but little did he know, his laughter wouldn't last for long.

CHAPTER 21

BEAR

"I found him," Morgan said, crashing through my office door without knocking. "Finally found the old bastard."

I pointed toward the chair because his spazzy ass was too much to deal with this early in the morning. "Well, come on in."

He took the hint, planting his ass in the chair, and started to shake his leg so fast I wanted to jump over the desk and nail his foot to the floor. "Santino called this morning. He found him."

I winced and shook my head. "Don't tell your mom that."

"Yeah, she and Tino aren't the best of friends."

"I had to hear about you calling him for twenty minutes last night."

He laughed loudly. "Ha, I have you beat. Try an hour after Aunt Maria spilled the beans."

"Fuck, that woman can sure talk."

"You mean nag."

I pointed at him with a serious expression. "Your words, not mine."

He saluted me. "Anyway, he's in Chicago. Santino has him."

I raised an eyebrow. "Has him?"

"He's keeping him…" His voice drifted off as he smiled. "Company."

"Well, I'll book us a flight."

596

Cupping his hands, he stroked his cheeks. "I want to get there today before Ray finds a way to…" He wanted to say escape, but he couldn't bring himself to do it.

"Me too." I opened up my browser and searched for flights to Chicago. To my surprise, there were a lot of them. "We can go and come back in one day. Think it's enough time?"

He peered down at his watch. "Let's stay one night. I don't want to rush our talk with Ray."

"Anything you want, kid."

He rubbed his hands together and sprang to his feet. "Let me know what time we're leaving. I'll let Race know I won't be home tonight. I'll handle a place for us to stay tonight too."

"I'm not sharing a bed with you," I teased.

He stood in the doorway, holding the frame in his hands, and glanced back at me. "You're not my type, Bear."

"Hey," I said before he could walk away.

"Yeah?"

"Let's not tell your mom where we're going, 'kay?"

"I have no problem with that. I won't even tell Race. I'll just tell her that we're following a lead. Work for you?"

"Works for me." I rubbed my forehead, thinking about the headache I'd have if Franny found out that we were going to see Santino, along with Ray. My ears would ring for hours by the time she got done chewing my ass out.

I booked us two tickets for noon, and that would put us in Chicago a little after one with the time difference. We'd have plenty of time to deal with Ray and be back by lunch the following day.

"Where are you going?" Fran asked after I told her I was heading out of town but didn't say where.

"Up north."

"As in?"

"Indiana," I lied, but I kept my voice firm so she wouldn't pick up on it.

"Okay. Just be careful. Ray isn't a nice guy. Don't buy his act."

"I'm aware, sweetheart."

"You taking Morgan too?"

"He's insisting."

"Just protect him, Bear. Make sure Ray doesn't fuck with his head."

"It won't be a problem," I told her because Morgan had Ray all figured out and knew exactly how to handle him.

"He's all I've got left. If Ray hurts one hair on his head..."

"Franny, I'll be with him. I'll keep him safe. You know I'd step in front of a bullet if it meant I'd save Morgan's life."

"Don't do anything dumb, babe. I want you both to come back to me."

"I love you," I said to her for the first time because it felt right.

She sucked in a breath loud enough for me to hear it clear as day over the phone. "I love you too, Murray."

"I'll call you when we have any information. Just sit tight and don't worry."

"That's easy for you to say. I'm going to worry until I hear from you that you're both safe."

"We'll be fine. Talk soon."

"Not soon enough," she said in almost a whisper.

"Bye, sweetheart."

"Bye, Bear."

I stared at the phone, almost in shock that I had told her I loved her. I hadn't spoken those words to another woman since Jackie. My stupid ass had to say them over the phone to Fran the first time. I wasn't sure how she'd respond, and I wasn't ready for the reaction face-to-face. It felt right telling her then, just before I was going to board a plane to beat the shit out of her ex-husband.

"Ready?" Morgan asked from the hallway.

"Ready." I nodded and grabbed my phone and wallet from the desk, sliding them in my pockets. "Let's do this."

"TINO SHOULD BE AROUND HERE SOMEWHERE," Morgan said when we stepped outside the airport near baggage claim.

"What's he look like?" I peered around like I knew who I was looking for.

"Me only older and probably more gray."

"Morgan!" a man called out, waving his arms frantically from about fifty feet away. "Down here." He motioned to a waiting black sedan that was parked at the curb.

"That him?" I pointed to a man who looked like he had stepped out of a *GQ* cover shoot. His salt-and-pepper hair was perfect, without a strand out of place.

"Yep."

I followed behind Morgan, making our way through the crowd to Santino. I could definitely see the family resemblance. The features in the Gallo family were strong and unmistakable.

"It's so good to see you, son." Santino hugged Morgan tightly and kept his eyes glued to me.

"You too, Uncle."

When he released Morgan, his dark eyes narrowed. "Is this your mom's new friend?"

"Yeah, we work together too. This is Bear."

"Bear." He held out his hand, and I slid my palm against his. "It's nice to meet you." He tightened his fingers around my hand.

"You too." I squeezed tighter, not wanting to be outdone.

We stared each other down. I could see bits of Fran and Sal in Santino's face. Their connection was undeniable. His olive skin was perfectly tanned but completely natural. His eyebrows hung low— almost covering his eyes if he wasn't looking directly at me. It gave him that shifty appearance.

"You two done?" Morgan asked, watching us in a virtual pissing match via handshake, just like one I'd been in with Morgan at some time in the past.

"Yeah," Santino said, finally releasing his hold as I did the same. "Let's go."

Santino walked around the car, glancing over his shoulder as if he was expecting to find someone or something. "Can never be too careful around here. There are cops everywhere."

"Yeah," Morgan said, glancing back at me and rolling his eyes.

Morgan had filled me in on Santino on the plane. He'd spent time in prison for racketeering and had been part of organized crime for as long as Morgan had been alive. It was one reason why Fran and Sal had distanced themselves from him. Santino's family ran a bar on the city's south side called the Hook & Hustle. He had three children with his longtime partner, Betty. Even though they'd been together longer than Morgan had been alive, Betty and Santino never married.

After we got in the car, Morgan in the front and me in the back, Santino said, "Let's stop at the bar first, and then I'll make sure Ray is ready to see us."

"Where is he?"

"At a warehouse a buddy of mine owns. He owed me a favor, and I called it in."

"I'm sure a lot of people owe you favors, Uncle."

"I spent five years of my life locked away for keeping their secrets… They owe me more than a simple favor, Morgan."

Morgan looked over at him, his eyes appraising his uncle. "You keeping your nose clean?"

"Always," Santino replied quickly and without so much as a flinch.

I knew a lot of men like him. It was hard to change after you'd been in the life as long as men like Santino. You didn't run a racket for over twenty years and then turn into an upstanding citizen overnight.

"Why don't I believe you?"

"I'm smarter now. Five years in the joint will do that to a man."

I sat in the backseat, letting them talk as I stared at the city coming into view through the front window. The tall skyscrapers dotted the sky like giant walls of solid rain falling from the clouds. Tampa had nothing on Chicago. The high-rises were minuscule in comparison.

After weaving our way through countless side streets, so many that I'd never find my way out without GPS, Santino pulled in front of his family's bar.

"We're here," he said and turned the car off.

Peering through the passenger window, I took in the Hook & Hustle. The exterior was painted in red and white with a glossy black front door. The sign spanned half the building with its modern, red-block lettering and black background. The windows lining the front had the blinds drawn, keeping prying eyes from seeing inside.

"Be ready for Betty, kid. She's excited to see her nephew."

"It's been a while since I've seen her." Morgan stared out the window too, his forehead almost touching the glass.

"Let's have a drink, and then we'll get out of here."

A small section in the blinds opened, and a set of blue eyes peered out at us.

"Betty's waiting. We better go inside before she comes out and makes a scene in public," Santino said before climbing out.

The crisp Chicago air swirled the leaves that lined the sidewalk as we stepped inside. Like something out of a movie, every person in the bar turned to look at us when the door closed behind me.

People were everywhere. The counter around the bar was filled, and the tables were packed too. How in the hell did so many people have time to shoot the shit at a bar on a weekday afternoon?

"Morgan!" a woman—Betty, I presumed—screeched and came running toward him with her arms open.

"Aunt Betty." Morgan laughed with his face growing a deep shade of red.

"You look so good." She wrapped her arms around his lower waist and put her head on his chest. Betty was a tiny thing, barely coming up to the middle of Morgan's chest. "Hard as a rock too." She giggled.

"It's good to see you, Auntie."

I felt a bit awkward as I watched them. Being an outsider wasn't something I was used to feeling, but in the Hook & Hustle, surrounded by Morgan's family, I did.

Betty took a step back and took him in. "I've missed you."

"You too," Morgan told her before leaning over and kissing her round cheek.

She glanced at me over her shoulder. Maybe she felt the way I'd been staring at them. "And who's this?" She eyed me warily.

"This is Bear. He's my friend and Ma's new guy." They talked about me like I wasn't here.

She spun around to face me, and her eyes widened. "This is your ma's guy?"

"Bear, ma'am." I held out my hand as her eyes roamed over me.

"Give me a hug," she said and came at me with her arms ready to wrap around me.

The name Betty fit her perfectly. She reminded me of Betty Boop but with fire-engine red hair and blue eyes. The woman was drop-dead gorgeous. Why Santino had never married her, I'd never understand.

She wrapped her arms around my middle, her hands moving a little too low to be completely friendly. "They build them big down south," she said into my shirt as her face was buried against my middle. "Fran must have some fun with you."

I'd never been a blusher, but Betty made my skin heat and my cheeks turn a rosy shade of pink. "It's nice to meet you, Betty."

Santino stood to the side, watching everything, and I stayed a complete gentleman. Even if Fran didn't talk with this part of her family, I still had to be respectful.

"You want something?" Betty asked, staring up at me with her soft blue eyes and her hands resting just above my ass. "A drink?"

"That would be great." I tried to untangle myself from her hold, but she kept her grip tight with her arms locked.

"How is Fran? It's been ages since I've seen her."

"She's great." I smiled down at the beautiful Betty because she had that quality that just brought happiness.

"I should give her a call sometime. I've missed her."

"Aunt Betty," Morgan said, coming to my rescue.

"We'd appreciate it if Ma didn't know we were here."

Betty's eyes sliced to Morgan. "Why?"

"We're here on business, and she can't know about it."

"Kid," Betty said, finally releasing me. "I can keep a secret like nobody's business. Just ask your uncle." She pursed her lips when she glanced over at Santino.

"Thanks, Auntie." Morgan kissed the top of her head and looked at me.

Hopefully, she was true to her word, because Fran would rip me a new asshole and then probably kick me straight in the balls for lying to her.

"Sit here, and I'll get you some drinks." Betty scurried off toward the bar.

"She seems...nice." I laughed.

"They're good people," Morgan said and followed Betty with his eyes. "Well, shit. There's my cousin. Let me go say hello, and I'll be right back."

I nodded, and he was off the barstool within seconds. I watched as he went to the bar, shook a man's hand, and then sat down, and started to chat.

"That's my son, Angelo," Santino said to me as he took the empty seat across from me. "He's my oldest."

"Looks just like you."

Angelo was the spitting image of Santino but with darker and more suspicious eyes. He was a Gallo for sure. I'd be happy to have him by my side during any barroom fight.

"My youngest, Vinnie, is away at college."

"Like college or *college*?" I asked because they were two completely different things. I knew enough guys to know that, in some places, they referred to prison as college because it sounded nicer if people were to overhear.

"Notre Dame. He's a football star there."

"Ah." I nodded. I didn't know what else to say. I hadn't heard much about Santino and didn't want to bring up his illustrious past.

"So, Fran still hate me?"

Santino's statement caught me off guard, but I mustered a laugh. "Hate's a pretty strong word."

"The woman can hold a grudge forever, Bear. Better watch yourself."

"I know how to handle her."

"Famous last words," he said and wrapped his arm around Betty when she set down three beers on the table. "Thanks, babe."

"I'll let you guys talk. Maybe I can make dinner for everyone tonight." Betty smiled.

"They're going to be busy, love. Maybe next time."

Her lips twisted, and she sighed. "It's okay. I understand."

"Thank you for the offer, though," I told her and pulled a beer in front of me. I'd rather sit and have dinner with Betty than what was about to happen.

Spending the night with Ray DeLuca wasn't going to be a party, but

I was sure we'd find a way to make it fun. Well, as much fun as you could have beating the fuck out of an abusive asshole.

I missed Fran.

Her calmness.

Her body.

Everything about the woman made me happy.

As I sat here, surrounded by her family, I realized how much I loved having her in my life.

Ever since I first kissed her, I hadn't thought about the emptiness that had filled my world since Jackie passed. All I could focus on was the fullness Fran brought into my life.

CHAPTER 22
FRAN

I sat here, staring at the tiny piece of paper for twenty minutes and debating if I should dial the phone. After seeing how well the reunion went with Janice, I felt the need to make things right between Bear and his son, Ret.

But that was dangerous territory. Janice and Bear had been cordial for years, keeping in contact but never growing close. There was so much hurt to get over, but with her pregnancy and the passage of time, it happened. Plus, I didn't give them much of a choice.

But his relationship with Ret was different. It weighed on Bear more than he would ever let on. He always said he lived life with no regrets, but I knew that was bullshit. Ret was his biggest regret, and the way Bear had handled the aftermath of Jackie's death was his biggest mistake.

Too much time had passed for them to reunite without a force bringing them together, and I thought it should be me.

I loved the man, and I wanted only the best for him. I knew people said I was a busybody, but it was always with a purpose. I didn't stick my nose in places it didn't belong unless I had a damn good reason.

After I convinced myself that what I was doing was right, I finally dialed the phone. Janice had given me Ret's number and wished me good luck.

"Hello," a man said, his voice gravelly yet smooth. He sounded so much like Bear that, for a minute, I wondered if I had dialed right.

"Hello, Ret?" I asked before I started in on my spiel.

"Yes."

"I'm Fran, and I got your number from your sister, Janice."

There was a scratching sound and a muffled cough. "Hi, Fran. How can I help you?"

"Well," I said and paused because I wanted to craft my words very carefully. "I'm a friend of your father's, and I wanted to reach out to you."

"My dad put you up to this?" he asked quickly before I could continue.

"No, sir. He has no idea I'm calling."

"Is he okay?"

"Yes." I smiled because Ret cared. No one asked that unless there was a tiny piece that wanted to hear that the person was okay.

"How can I help you, Fran?" he repeated the question again, cutting straight to the point.

"I was hoping you were up to a trip to Florida. Your old man would love to see you." I winced and waited for him to hang up.

"Why didn't he call me himself?"

"He's out of town. I thought you could be here when he got back as a surprise."

"I don't mean to be rude, ma'am, but I don't like surprises, and I imagine neither does my father."

"It's not a surprise to you, and who cares if your father doesn't like them? He'll get over it."

He laughed. "I imagine so."

"Your father talks about you often, Ret. Sometimes adults are assholes, and as we grow older and more time passes, it's hard for us to admit our mistakes. But one thing I know about your dad is that you're his biggest regret."

"I'm sure I am."

I winced. That didn't come out right. "He regrets not raising you and for all the time he missed out on being with you. I know it hurts him, and he knows that he's hurt you. I'm asking as a mother, for you to give him a chance."

There was silence, but he hadn't hung up.

"I'm sure your mother wouldn't want you two to be estranged. I think that weighs heaviest on him… Jackie was his world, Ret. There's no loss like losing the only person in the world who made you feel worthy. He fucked up. He knows he did, but he wants to make amends with you before it's too late."

"He's going to be pissed."

"I know," I said, smiling to myself because he didn't say no.

"I'll do it for my mom, Fran. Not for Murray, but for her. He still near Tampa?"

"Yes, we're about forty-five minutes north."

"I'm in Miami, so I can be there tomorrow morning if that's okay?"

I bounced in my seat, pumping my fist in the air, and tried not to scream out my excitement. "That's perfect."

"What's the address?"

I rattled mine off, figuring it was better if everything went down here. I could control it easier. We chatted for a few more minutes before he finally said good-bye.

I did a quick happy dance, followed by the worst impression of the running man before I sobered.

Bear was going to be pissed.

I was going to owe him something.

And there was only one thing left he wanted.

My ass clenched at the thought, but I quickly pushed it out of my mind. There was so much to do before Ret arrived and Bear came back home. I'd make dinner. Food was always a good way to break the ice and fill the uncomfortable silence. Of course, my cooking left something to be desired.

I picked up the phone and called the only person I knew who could rescue me. "Maria, I need you."

"I'll be right over."

When she walked through the door twenty minutes later, I was on my hands and knees, scrubbing the kitchen tile.

"What did you do now?" She had her hands on her hips as she stared down at me.

Falling backward on my ass, I threw the dirty rag on the floor and wiped my brow. "I invited Bear's estranged son over."

Her perfectly plucked eyebrows shot up. "Does Bear know?"

Hanging my head, I shook it but didn't speak.

"He's going to freak out."

"I know," I whispered. "But I did it for the right reasons."

"Franny," she said and sat down next to me. "Your heart is always in the right place." She rubbed my arm. "It'll be fine."

"You think?"

"Sure. What do you need me to do?"

I finally looked up. "I want to make them dinner."

"Good thing you called me," she said and laughed.

"I'm nosy, not stupid." I chuckled. "Will you help me get everything together and started so tomorrow I can finish it on my own?"

"Babe, I'll do anything you need."

I lunged forward and wrapped her in the biggest bear hug. "Thanks, Maria. I don't know what I'd do without you."

She rubbed my back, soothing away my stress. "Serve shitty food and burn everything, probably."

"Very funny, but probably true."

"Let's get off this floor and start making a plan. I want you to wow them both."

"I don't know what I was thinking." I rolled my eyes, shaking my head as I stood.

"You were being you. Look how great everything went with Janice."

"It went better than I thought."

"See," she said as she brushed off her butt after crawling off the floor. "Everything will be fine."

CHAPTER 23
BEAR

After a long talk, Morgan agreed that he'd wait outside and let me talk to Ray first. We both, along with Santino, felt that Ray might be more willing to speak without his son around. Really I just wanted to get in a few licks before anyone else and make him feel a small amount of what Fran must have felt when they were together.

Whether he was involved with Johnny hadn't been determined yet. But…he still deserved a beating. I knew it wasn't civilized, but I didn't give a fuck. Men who did bad shit to women deserved all the bad shit that happened to them.

"Who are you?" Ray asked before spitting blood next to my feet.

"Your worst nightmare." I smiled and flexed my knuckles.

"You're a pussy if you have to beat me with my hands tied up."

Ray DeLuca was probably a decent-looking guy back in the day, but sitting before me, bound to the chair, he looked frail. His face was littered with wrinkles and covered in hair that wasn't neat or groomed.

"I'm not the pussy that stole from my own flesh and blood." I took a step forward, ready to hit him again.

"What the hell are you talking about?" He turned his face to the side, reducing the impact of my fist against his face.

The crunching sound of bone on bone echoed in the abandoned warehouse. Ray's cries of agony continued after the echo died out. "Ready to talk?"

I pretended I was going to hit him again, and he flinched.

Ray licked the corner of his lip, drawing the blood into his mouth from the previous punch. "I'll talk. I'll talk. What do you want to know?"

I pulled over a seat, glancing around the dimly lit building. Instead of calling Morgan in like I'd promised, I prodded Ray further.

"Tell me what happened with Johnny." I crossed my arms over my chest and glared at him.

"That piece of shit," he muttered. "I knew he wouldn't be able to keep his mouth shut."

"I'm going to give you thirty seconds to explain to me what happened, and then I'm going to beat you until you're unconscious. Lie, and I'll make sure you're never found."

I wouldn't have done it, but he didn't know that. All he knew was how my fists felt against his face and that he didn't want any more.

"Johnny worked for my kid. I've been keeping track of him for years—checking in on him and my ex-wife. Well, I got in deep with a bookie and needed some cash. I went down to Florida a few times and thought about asking for a loan, but then I knew neither of them would give me one. So I went to the track and hung out for a few races. I watched carefully and saw that Johnny was close with the family. I thought I could get him to do what I wanted. He looked like an easy mark, and I used it to my advantage."

"Go on," I said, keeping my eyes pinned to his, and straightening my back.

"I did some digging and found out Johnny has a kid. I told him that if he didn't find a way to get me $50,000, I would go after his kid and then I'd start on Fran and Morgan."

"So you threatened him to get what you wanted?" Just needed to be sure I didn't hear him wrong. Plus, the confirmation would be good since we were recording the entire thing.

"Yeah, man. Johnny made it too easy. He was too worried about everyone else that he caved quickly."

"How did he get you the money?"

"I met him in some shitty-ass motel room in Alabama. He brought the cash and fulfilled his end of the deal."

"And what was your end?"

"I promised never to bother anyone else again."

Fucking thief and liar.

The thing about thieves was that a promise was never kept. Once you caved to their demands, they knew they had you for life. I'm sure Johnny knew it too. It was a mistake that too many people made.

Plus, how would Johnny ever be able to face Fran, Race, and Morgan again? He was just trying to keep them safe, but he went about it the wrong way. If he'd only told Morgan, we could've gotten involved and Johnny would still be alive.

"Where's the money now?"

"Joey Two Fingers has it." Ray's shoulders sagged, his torso still secured to the chair.

I rolled my eyes. Damn people with their stupid-ass nicknames.

"Can I go now?"

"The only place you're going is the police station."

"For what? You already beat my ass."

"You'll be safer there. I'm sure Joey will be looking for you once I have a talk with him."

His head snapped up, and his eyes widened. "You can't talk to him. He won't give you shit anyway."

"I have my ways." I smiled and figured Santino probably knew Joey and could help. It wasn't Ray's money to begin with, and once Joey heard the story, I'm sure he wouldn't want the dirty money anywhere near him.

"Bullshit."

I leaned forward and grabbed Ray by the hair on the top of his head, getting in his face. "I'm sure the cops will want to talk to you about Johnny's death too. So between Joey and death row, I'm sure you'll be busy."

He gasped. "What? Johnny's dead?"

"Yep, and he left a note that pointed right at you."

Okay, so I lied a bit, but simple police work could uncover the connection, especially with the recording of him confessing his part. Ray DeLuca was going to pay for what he did.

"Fuck," he grunted and struggled to break free from the bindings. He gritted his teeth, bloodied spit spewing from his mouth as he pulled at the restraints.

"I have one more visitor for you," I said, unable to hide my smile as I stood. "Come in!"

"What is this shit?" he seethed, still moving around but not going anywhere.

"Hey, Ray," Morgan said as he walked in and let the door slam behind him.

Ray flinched at the impact and squinted in the direction of the voice. "Morgan?"

"Can you leave us?"

"Sure," I told Morgan, but I glared at Ray. "If you need my help breaking his legs, just holler."

Morgan placed his hand on my shoulder when I was about to pass him. "Thanks, Bear."

"You're welcome. I'll go talk to Santino, and you can talk to your father."

"He's not my father. He's just a low-life piece of shit."

I wondered if Ret thought the same way about me. I'd never pulled this shit with him, but I was never in his life for him to have a connection to me. I hoped he didn't feel the same. My heart ached at the very thought.

I gave Morgan a nod before walking toward the door. Turning back, I watched as Morgan pulled the stool closer and said something to Ray that made him break down in tears.

Morgan DeLuca impressed me.

The man had his shit together and stepped up when necessary. Even though Ray was his father, Fran was his world. He made sure Ray walked out of her life over a decade ago, but I'm sure Ray was about to pay the price for coming back and stealing from Morgan's wife too.

"That went well," Santino said as I walked outside and he took off the headphones. "You know, if you ever need a job, I'm sure I can get you one within minutes up here."

"I'm good," I said and held up my hand. "I'm clean, man. I only do this shit when necessary, and usually only for family."

"You're an interesting man, Bear."

"Yeah, yeah. What can we do about this Joey Two Fingers?"

He waved his hand and grinned. "I'll talk to Joey and get the money back. Just like you said. For being clean, you know a whole lot about dirty."

I laughed. "I have a past, but I'm leaving it there, Santino."

"All right." He held his hands up. "All right. I won't push you any further."

"Should I go back in?" I asked and glanced toward the door.

"Nah, Morgan can handle him."

Twenty minutes later, Morgan walked out with Ray handcuffed and a little more bloodied than I left him. Ray's feet dragged on the ground as Morgan pulled him by the wrists.

"Ready?" I asked, looking between Morgan and Santino.

"Where are you taking me?" Ray tried to pull away, but Morgan yanked him forward.

"To the cops with the recording and the evidence."

Ray faltered in his steps and almost fell forward. "They're going to hear you beating me and know I was coerced."

"I took care of it," Santino said. "I'm not worried about them believing your story, Ray. You're about as friendly with the cops as I am."

"This is bullshit."

"Well..." Morgan motioned toward me with his head. "I can let Bear take care of you if you don't want me to turn you over to the authorities."

He eyed me for a moment and grumbled under his breath. "I'll take my chances with the cops," he said before Morgan shoved him in the back of the car.

"Meet me back at the bar after you drop him off. I'll talk to Joey and have an answer for you."

"Thanks, Uncle."

"You're welcome, kid." Santino climbed into his car and drove away.

"You okay with this?"

Morgan nodded and blew out a breath. "I finally feel like everything is going to work out and that Ray will be out of the picture for a very long time."

"He's going to have a hell of a time getting out of this one," I told Morgan as I slid into the car and he did the same.

"Fella, we don't have to do this," Ray pleaded before Morgan started the car and turned up the radio loud enough to drown out Ray's bullshit.

The grittiness of Chicago fit the people I'd met since I stepped off the plane. Santino himself was a product of his surroundings, and Joey Two Fingers, I assumed, wouldn't be any different.

The sky was gray with fluffy clouds that were as dark as those in Florida when a thunderstorm was looming. Rain began to fall as we pulled up at the police station, and when Morgan opened the door, a quick rush of cold air filled the car.

"Don't do this," Ray pleaded when Morgan pulled him from the backseat without any hesitation.

I stayed in my seat, letting the kid handle his father. I wouldn't want anyone taking that moment away from me, and I sure as hell wasn't going to do it to him.

Ray didn't go like a man. He screamed and tried to break from Morgan's grip as they moved toward the doorway of the police station. When Morgan opened the door and pushed Ray, he kicked him in the ass to give him a final shove inside.

I'd have felt sorry for the guy if he wasn't such a piece of shit.

My phone rang, and it was Fran. I picked it up quickly before she started to call every five minutes until she knew we were safe.

"Hey, sweetheart," I said, watching the door for Morgan. He'd be a few minutes, turning over the evidence and the perpetrator into their custody.

"I wanted to check in on you guys. You two okay?"

"We're great. We'll be home in the morning as scheduled."

"Great, baby," she said and covered the phone, murmuring something. "Maria says hi."

"Tell her hello. So I'll be at your place around noon to give you all the details. I can't really discuss them on a cell."

"I know, Bear. I'm not new." She laughed nervously and a little over the top. "I'll be waiting for you."

"Oh, yeah?" Excitement filled me. "Am I getting my payback for the other night?"

"You are. Don't be mad if it isn't what you expect."

"I'm up for anything you're gonna give me, Franny."

"Remember that. Love you."

"Love you too," I said and hung up as soon as I saw Morgan walking toward the door through the glass.

Fuck. I was so excited to get back to Fran and whatever kinky shit she had planned that I was about ready to catch the next flight out of Chicago and be there before she closed her eyes.

"How did it go?" I asked when he climbed back in.

"They're going to listen to the tape and review the evidence. In the meantime, there was an active warrant out for him, so he's not going anywhere soon."

"For what?"

"Assault and battery." Morgan shrugged. "A leopard never changes its spots."

"Morgan, I need you to know something."

Something had been gnawing at me for a while, and I needed to get it off my chest.

"What's up?" he asked as he turned on the car.

"I'll never lay a hand on your mother. I know sometimes I get carried away when we're dealing with some bad people, but your mother is someone I love. I'd never do anything to hurt her."

He stared at me for a minute before he finally smiled. "One thing I know about you is that you're a good man, Bear. You're not Ray. The thought never crossed my mind."

My face wrinkled. "It hasn't? I've done some pretty fucked-up shit in front of you."

"Each one of them deserved it. I see how you are with my mom and all the women in the family. I never worry about how you're going to treat Ma. Plus, she's not the same woman she was before. Her revenge will be worse than anything any of us could do to you. That much I know."

"Yeah." I laughed. Fuck. He was right. Fran had a wickedness about her sometimes.

If I ever hurt her, I was sure I'd disappear, never to be heard from again. But not before she tortured me in ways I'd never dream possible. I think that's what I loved about her most—her unpredictability.

I sat in silence, thinking of all the ways she'd exact her revenge as we headed toward the bar. By the time we parked the car, my stomach was in knots.

"You're looking a little green," Morgan said as he stared at me.

"Just thinking about Fran. We made a bet, and I lost. Tomorrow, I get my payback."

"I'd be scared if I were you." He laughed and climbed out, slamming the door behind him.

I sighed and waited a minute before following him. "You think I'm in for some shit?" I jogged to keep up.

"I think you should be ready for the unexpected."

My mind wandered to places I never imagined. Hopefully, Fran had planned something sexy. The one place I didn't expect to go was in her beautiful round ass. I wanted it so badly my entire body vibrated at the thought. Maybe I'd done such a good job with Ray that she'd offer it to me as a thank-you.

I shook my head and laughed.

"It ain't that."

My head jerked back just as we approached the door. "What?"

"If it makes you laugh, it isn't what you're hoping. Ma doesn't work like that."

"You're right," I grumbled, and the hard-on that had started to form immediately vanished.

"Morgan!" Angelo waved us over.

Morgan gave him a quick nod. "Hey."

"Shit go alright?" Angelo asked as he leaned over the bartop.

"Hey," I interrupted. "I'm going to go talk to your uncle."

"He's in the back room," Angelo replied and jerked his head toward the hallway behind him.

"Thanks," I said and excused myself.

Not that I was above small talk, I just wanted to get the fuck out of this bar and back to the hotel. I already knew I wasn't going to get much sleep tomorrow when I got home, and I wanted to be ready for whatever Fran was going to throw at me.

CHAPTER 24
FRAN

"You have a lovely home," Ret said, sitting on the couch in the living room as I sat across from him.

"Thank you." I smiled, but inside I was slowly dying.

What the fuck was I thinking? There was going to be hell to pay afterward. I was known for pulling some shit, but even this was beyond me. I was sticking my nose in places that I never thought I'd be willing to take a whiff and live with myself.

"I talked to my sister," Ret said, filling the uncomfortable silence.

I smiled at the spitting image of Bear. The tiny lines around Ret's eyes weren't near as deep as Bear's, but everything else about him matched. From his wide shoulders, large arms, gruff voice, and hard face—there was no mistaking that they were father and son.

"How is she?"

"Ready for her pregnancy to be over." He laughed softly, and the faintest lines appeared near his eyes.

"I'm sure." I plucked at the nonexistent lint on my jeans. "She's so beautiful."

"She said nice things about you, ma'am. It's one reason why I came. She said it was time I talked to my father and set shit straight."

"She sounds a lot like me." I chuckled, covering my mouth with the back of my hand.

"She's a bossy thing. When we were little, she'd pretend I was hers. My entire life, she's told me what to do."

"Women," I muttered because I knew we caused more shit out of our need to be helpful.

"When's he getting here?" Ret glanced down at his watch and tapped the glass.

"Any minute now." My voice was shrill, and my stomach was jumping around like I had gymnasts inside.

"What has he said about me?"

Even though a man sat across from me, all I saw was a little boy who wanted to hear that he was loved and wanted. It was the basic need of any child. When Bear left Ret with his sisters, it stripped him of that.

"He told me what happened with your mom and how his sisters raised you and Janice. He's never gotten over the regret from that."

"He could've come back for us."

"Oh, honey, your dad went down a dark path. It's hard to come back from how far he fell."

"How far?" He crossed his arms over his wide chest and leaned back into the sofa.

"He was in and out of jail a lot before you were even five. I think he got mixed up in drugs and drank a lot too. He knew he wasn't good for you."

"Fran, I would've taken a fucked-up dad as long as he loved me."

"You say that now, but it's easy to say without living it, Ret."

"I guess," he sighed.

"He loved your mom so much that he didn't think he deserved any happiness. I think he was trying to find a way to join her without actually doing it himself."

"That would've been tragic," he muttered.

"It would've."

"I spent a good portion of my teenage years in therapy, Fran. It's hard to know your mother died when she had you. There's a guilt that comes with that knowledge."

"God," I said and stroked my neck. "I never thought of that."

"Dad could've helped me get over that quicker. His rejection made it easier to believe that I killed her."

My entire body rocked back at the horrific admission he had just made. I'm sure Bear never thought of it that way. He figured he was doing a favor to his kids by leaving them with his sisters, giving them the love of a woman over his.

"Your father never blamed you. He blamed himself, sweetie. I think you've both been feeling the same pain for far too long."

His eyebrows drew down over his eyes. "Why would he feel that way?"

"Men are supposed to protect their women, and your father wasn't able to do that for Jackie. Naturally, he's going to feel like he messed up somehow. You're a man. You should understand the need to fix everything."

He smiled and it was genuine. "I know the feeling well."

I stared at him, lost in his eyes when I heard Bear's bike outside. I froze, my body going rigid, and my stomach kicking back into action.

"Well," Ret said, standing up, and taking a deep breath. "I guess it's now or never."

"It'll be fine. Your dad is easygoing," I lied and walked toward the door, clutching my stomach, and praying that Bear didn't walk back out as soon as he saw I'd ambushed him again.

Instead of walking up to the door, he stood outside, staring at Ret's truck. Slowly, I opened the door and waved with the biggest smile on my face.

"Hey, baby. I'm so happy you're back."

He looked at me and then back to the truck and scratched his beard, silent.

Well, fuck. This isn't going exactly as I'd planned.

"Who's inside, Franny?" His eyebrow was cocked. That wasn't a look that instilled a warm and fuzzy feeling in my already shaking body.

"Just a friend. Come on." I waved him inside, holding the door open but not moving.

"You come here." He pointed toward the ground, his eyes still going back and forth between the truck and me like a pinball in a machine.

"It's too hot outside." I was grasping at straws, and just like the man he was—seeing right through me—he knew the type of woman I was—a trick up every sleeve.

"Fran. Out here now," he demanded and snapped his fingers.

Instead of running, I crossed my arms and glared at him. "I don't know who you think you're snapping those meat sticks at, buddy, but it sure as fuck isn't me."

"Fran," he started to plead, but I kept talking.

"You don't want to come in? Fine. I'll meet you halfway, but you ever snap your fingers at me like I'm an animal again, and I'll break them in your sleep."

Ret laughed, and I turned to face him, giving him a sweet smile. "Just letting him know who's boss."

"Remind me never to cross you, Fran. You'd do mighty fine with a whip in your hands."

I laughed nervously. "Thanks."

"Fine, sweetheart. I'm coming up," Bear said, finally coming to his senses.

I don't know what came over me. Usually, I'm not quite so stern, but goddamn it, he was ruining my fabulous surprise.

"I'm coming down," I told him, glancing back at Ret, and holding up a finger. "Be right back."

"I can go," he offered.

"Sit your ass down," I told him and closed the door behind me before marching my skinny-jean-covered ass down the stairway to Bear.

I huffed the entire walk down to him. My knees were still a little wobbly, but I was too pissed off to really pay much attention to them. "Why won't you come in?" I asked, trying to use my sweetest voice.

"Oh, now you're sweet. You're talking about breaking my... What did you call them?" He tapped his chin and smiled. "Meat sticks. And now you're acting like June Cleaver."

"I have a surprise for you. An old friend stopped over. You're going to want to see them."

"Them?" he asked, his finger stopped on his lip.

"Him." I smiled so big my cheeks hurt.

He sighed. "Fran, you've got to stop with the surprises. They aren't my favorite thing in the world, but you insist on doing it."

"This is your payback, but trust me, you're going to like it." I grabbed his hand and started yanking him toward the house.

He dug his heels into the cement, and his feet didn't move—like there was glue on the bottom, holding him to the ground. "Who's inside?"

Intertwining my fingers with his, I gave them a soft squeeze. "Promise you won't be mad?"

"Fran."

"Well." I swallowed and took a deep breath. "Ret's inside."

"My son, Ret?"

"No, Bear." I rolled my eyes. "Ret, the pool guy."

His eyes widened, and his body rocked back. "My son is here?" He pointed toward the ground.

"No, in there." I pitched my thumb over my back. "Waiting for you and watching your reaction very carefully."

His eyes went to the window and back to mine. "He's here."

I nodded. "In there."

"Shit," he said, releasing my hand, and running toward the door without any more nudging from me.

I turned around, but I didn't move as he flung open the door and walked inside. Through the large bay window in the front of the house, I could see them both clear as day.

Bear stared at Ret for a moment, and Ret stood from the couch. A few words were muttered, and I wish I could've heard them. Bear stalked toward Ret and scooped him into his arms. At first, Ret didn't return the gesture, but a few seconds later, he wrapped his arms around his father.

Tears began to well in my eyes, and I wanted to go inside and listen to the reunion, but instead, I just watched.

I had eavesdropped on his talk with Janice, but I knew this one would be different—more important and more personal.

Bear kept hold of Ret, pulling back every so often for a moment to look at his younger reflection before cocooning him in another hug.

Tears streamed down my face from the beauty of the moment. It was better than I imagined when I concocted my little plan.

My knees were shaking as I leaned against the truck, my nerves still frazzled from earlier. Shaking out my hands, I tried to calm myself, but I needed something more. Spotting the fake flowerpot where I stored an extra key and a pack of cigarettes, I glanced around the yard before making a beeline for my hiding spot.

My fingers shook as I opened the hidden compartment around the back and pulled out the pack and lighter. I could barely light the cigarette through my tears and shakes.

"Jesus," I muttered with the filter in my mouth, struggling to steady my hand.

"Fran!"

Naturally, the moment I was going to give myself chemical solace, Bear walked outside to find me. That was exactly how shit had been going down. Tucking the pack, including my unlit cigarette, and lighter back inside, I took a few deep breaths and tried to calm myself before I started to walk toward him.

"Hey," I said, peeking around the corner, and catching a glimpse of him standing near the doorway.

As soon as he saw me, he jogged down to meet me. "Hey, sweetheart." He brushed the tears from his cheeks. "I don't even know what to say."

Placing my hand on his chest, I stood on my tiptoes and kissed his lips. "Don't say a thing."

He wrapped his hands around my upper arms, gripping me tightly as he stared down at me. "I'm just so...so..."

"I know, Bear." I smiled.

"Why didn't you come inside?"

"I wanted to give you time alone."

"He's so much like me, Franny. It's like looking in a mirror." He looked like a little kid, so excited and full of wonder. "He's me, but not. You know?"

"He's very handsome."

"Let's go in, babe. I don't want you to feel like an outsider. This is your house."

I nodded, staying tucked under his arm as we walked toward the front door. "So you're not mad at me?"

"Fran, I'm never *mad* at you. But you do pull some big shit."

"That's what makes me great." I chuckled.

He kissed the top of my head. "It's what makes you mine," he said into my hair as we walked through the door.

CHAPTER 25
BEAR

Part of me was still in shock. Even after spending two hours with Ret, it was hard for me to wrap my head around the reality that my boy was sitting right in front of me.

"I pulled up your rap sheet years ago."

My eyebrows shot up. "Jesus," I muttered. This wasn't going to be good. The damn thing was as long as I was tall.

"Interesting life you've led." He smiled.

"I'm clean and living on the straight and narrow. I have been for years, Ret."

"You really went off the rails after Mom died." He frowned, but he hid it quickly behind the glass of beer he'd been nursing for an hour.

"I did. I didn't handle her death well. I wanted to die too. I was so angry about what happened that I did everything in my power to let the world know just how pissed I was."

"Lucky for me, you didn't get your wish. But based on what I read, you came pretty damn close."

"She'd be so disappointed in me if she knew what happened, son." I hung my head and rubbed my eyebrows. "She'd beat the hell out of me for acting like a fool."

"What's happened, happened, and we can't change it. I'm not

angry with you. I was hurt for a long time. I couldn't understand how you could abandon Janice and me without a backward glance."

Lifting my head, I choked back the tears that were threatening to come. "I did come back. I visited for the first three years. I'd come and hold you in my arms and tell you stories. I still remember the way you smelled and the sound of your voice when you cried. You were so damn little, and I was scared that I might break you."

"I didn't know that. No one ever told me you came." His eyes darkened. "Why didn't anyone tell me?"

"I don't know. My sisters can be bitches and probably thought it was best if you didn't know.

"When you started to talk, Caroline asked me not to come back. She said that you would start to remember me, and if I wasn't able to take you and Janice that I should keep my distance. I believed her and wasn't in the right place to take you with me, so I did as she asked."

"I wish you would've fought for us."

"Ret, I couldn't even fight for me," I admitted. "I hope someday you'll forgive me and let me make it up to you. As I've grown older, I've come to realize nothing else matters except for family and friends. I surround myself with good people and lead my life like I should've. Like your mother would've wanted me to. She'd want us to have a relationship, and it's the only thing in my life that I want right now. There's nothing more important."

"We'll see, Dad. I have a lot to think about." Ret smiled softly. "I have to head back soon."

"Already?" I wasn't ready to say good-bye. We'd spent enough time away from each other. Too long, and it was entirely my fault.

Ret rubbed his hands together as he leaned forward, placing his elbows on his knees. "Alese is waiting for me at the hotel."

"Why didn't you bring her?"

"I didn't know what was going to happen, and I didn't want to stress her."

"I'm sorry." The amount of guilt and shame I felt were almost overwhelming. No child should ever have to worry about their parent being an asshole, but I did that to my kid.

"Why don't you get her and bring her to my place tonight? You two can spend some time with me."

"I don't know," he said and peered around the room, looking for Fran, but she was in the kitchen washing the dishes. "We don't lead a regular lifestyle."

"What's that mean?"

"I don't know how to explain it to someone like you," he sighed.

I placed my hand on my chest and laughed. "Someone like me? Ret, I'm not a normal person. Nothing really shocks me anymore."

"She's my submissive." He stared me straight in the eyes and waited.

Maybe he thought I'd be shocked or horrified, but I wasn't. "Janice told me. Is she your sub or slave?" I asked, trying to sound like I knew the lingo, and he gave me a confused look. "I'm not new."

"She's just my submissive, and we keep it only in the bedroom when we're around other people."

I laughed and shook my head. "One of the owners of my company does the same with his wife. I wish I could get Franny to be mine, but she'd just kick me in the balls and tell me to go fuck myself if I ever bossed her around."

"Yeah," he said, laughing with me. "She doesn't seem like the lifestyle would work for her."

"I heard you!" she yelled from the kitchen, and Ret and I laughed louder.

I sobered at the thought that it might be a while before I saw him again, and I had to do something to not keep that from happening. "Will you at least stick around for a few days? I'm not ready to let you go already."

"I can stay for a bit. I'm in between jobs, so I don't have anywhere to be."

"Why don't you find a job around here? You can be close to Janice, and we could get to know each other better."

"Let's see how the next few days go together before I start setting down roots here."

"Your aunts are here, I'm here, your sister's here. What other reasons do you need? It's time to come back home, son. It's time for me to make up for all the time I've thrown away."

"I'm not saying no, but I have to talk to Alese. She gets a say in where we live too. I'll think about it."

"I'll give you all the time you need."

He stood and rubbed his palms against his jeans. "I'll see you tomorrow, then?"

"Meet me at my office, and we can talk some more. I'll take you to lunch."

"That would be great."

I wanted him to see ALFA PI. He'd fit right in with those guys, and we could use a bounty hunter. He could use our resources, which were vast, and our manpower to track down his cases. I couldn't think of anything more perfect. I'd have to talk with James and Thomas, but I couldn't see them saying no. I'd just have to get him in the door to make shit happen.

Franny walked out from the kitchen, wiping her hands on a dish towel. "Leaving so soon?"

He nodded and walked toward her. "I have to get back to my girl, but I'll be around this week."

She smiled and tossed the towel over her shoulder. "That makes me happy, Ret. Thanks for doing this," she said, grabbing hold of his arms. "I hope it turned out as you'd hoped."

"Better than, actually, Fran." He leaned in and kissed her cheeks, whispering something in her ear.

She laughed softly, her eyes darting to mine for a moment. "I'll see you tomorrow?"

"You will." He hugged her properly as her hands roamed around his back. She was feeling him up, letting his muscles skate across her fingertips. I knew the moves; she did it to me often.

"Dad," Ret said as he walked toward me, and it sounded like music to my ears. He stuck out his hand, but I didn't want a handshake.

"Come here." I pulled him into my arms for the tenth time since I'd laid eyes on him. "I'll see you at the office tomorrow. Don't leave without saying good-bye. You hear me?"

"I'll be there. Don't worry," he said, gripping my bicep with his fully grown hands.

As I watched him walk out the front door, my heart ached. I longed for the years I'd lost. The days. The hours. The minutes. The seconds. There wasn't a milestone in his life that I had been there for. I didn't cheer him on as he took his first step, learned to ride a bike, or threw his first football.

I'd missed them all.

Everything.

I wasn't willing to miss another moment either.

I had been selfish, and the ones who'd suffered were my kids. While I was out trying to chase down the grim reaper and drowning myself in booze and pussy, my kids grew up without me.

What kind of self-absorbed prick does that?

I did.

Jackie would've been so disappointed in me. I knew that. There wasn't a morning I'd woken up over the last thirty years that I didn't think that. But the guilt never drove me to seek them out and make shit right.

So much time had passed that I didn't think there was a way to repair the damage I'd done. I didn't even know how to make the first move. People knew me as a tough guy. The one who would kick anyone's ass if they were acting like a fool or deserved a beatdown, but when it came to my kids...

I was the biggest pussy on earth.

It was time I paid my penance and made up for everything I'd missed. If I had my way, both kids would stay close, and I'd spend as much time as possible with them.

I wouldn't be up in their shit like Franny was with Morgan, but I'd like to develop a relationship and get to know my future grandchildren.

There was still time, and Fran made it possible.

CHAPTER 26

FRAN

"Hey, Ma." Morgan stood outside my front door, but he hadn't called before he'd showed up.

"Hey, baby. What's up?" I asked with the door open only a little bit while Bear gathered up his clothes and ran down the hallway.

His eyebrows were drawn as he tried to peek inside. "You going to bed?"

"No, just relaxing." I smiled and glanced behind me. "What's up?"

He placed his hand against the door and gave it a little shove, but I had my foot against the back, stopping it from moving. "Can I come in?"

I looked over my shoulder, seeing Bear's naked ass as he streaked out of the room. When the bedroom door finally closed, I said, "Sure."

His eyes roamed around the room as he walked inside, taking in the pillows strewn all over the floor. "Bear here with you?"

"He's in the bedroom," I said, clearing my throat. "He wanted to wash up after being on the road."

"Uh-huh," he muttered as he kicked off his boots, placing them next to Bear's boots. "It doesn't matter."

"You don't care that he's here…naked?" I smiled, waiting to see if he'd flinch, but he didn't.

"Nah. We already had a talk. I'm cool with whatever makes you happy. When he stops making you happy, then we have a problem."

"Want something to drink?" I asked as he followed me into the kitchen.

"I'm good, Ma. Come sit with me." He pulled out the chair next to him and patted the seat. "We gotta talk."

"Oh," I said, my voice almost shrill. Pulling my robe tighter, I sat down and braced myself for whatever Morgan was about to tell me.

"We got the money back for the track."

My hand flew to my mouth, and I gasped. "That's great."

His eyes drifted to the window, focusing on a spot in the distance. "We hit a few snags getting it, though. I wanted to tell you before you heard about it from someone else."

My eyes narrowed. "What type of snags, Morgan?"

His fingers started to tap against the table as he brought his eyes back to mine. "Promise me you won't freak out."

"You're making it worse." I crossed my arms. We'd played this game a thousand times, and he already knew that I was going to freak, no matter what I promised.

"Well, um…" He stopped tapping and began to rub the palm of his hand against the table, making the most obnoxious noise. "Ray was involved, for sure."

"Ugh," I groaned and straightened my back, knowing this wasn't the part I needed not to freak out about.

"So we found Ray. He's with the cops now. They're dealing with him. But…" His voice drifted off.

I tilted my head, thinking I heard him wrong. He didn't just mutter what I think he did. My son wouldn't be so stupid to get Tino and Joey Two Fingers involved. "Repeat that again."

"Uncle Santino helped us get the money back. Ray had given it to Joey to pay back a debt. When Joey heard about the theft and that Ray was with the cops, he wanted no part of the money. I guess even criminals have their limits." He laughed nervously, thinking I was going to laugh too, but I didn't.

Grimacing, I dug my fingers into the soft corners of my eyes. "I can't believe you got Joey involved. What a clusterfuck."

"It was the only way, Ma. I swear. Everything is fine."

"Morgan. Baby." I opened my eyes, letting my hands drop to the table like a ton of bricks. "Nothing is fine when Joey is involved. Not only did both of you lie to me about going to Chicago, you went against my wishes when it comes to your uncle and *his* kind."

"Don't be ridiculous. Ray is one of *his* kind too. It's the only way Race would've been made whole again. Would you rather the track go broke and Race lose her dream?"

Guilt.

He used my own weapon against me. I'd perfected it over the last thirty years. It's something that mothers passed on to each other because it fucking worked like a charm. But Morgan became hip to my shit a long time ago and had been known to use the trick on me a time or two.

Pulling it out during our conversation was beautiful—almost poetic. "Naturally, I wouldn't want that."

He gave me a tilted smile. "Didn't think so."

"So now we owe Joey Two Fingers."

"We do not," he corrected me, the one side of his mouth rising farther. "He owed Santino a favor. So now they're even, and we're free and clear."

It was done, and no matter the consequences, I couldn't change anything. Tino, Bear, and Morgan made the decision without me and against my wishes, but at least everything was settled. "What did Ray say?"

"I let Bear talk with him mostly."

"What's mostly?" I raised an eyebrow.

He averted his gaze. "I only spent a few minutes with him and had a little trip down memory lane."

My nose wrinkled because there wasn't anything in the past I wanted to relive except for the moments with Morgan. "Remembering all the good times?"

"Just reminded him of a promise I made him a long time ago."

I crossed my arms, leaning back in my chair. "What promise would that be?"

"It's not important. He broke the promise, and that's all that matters."

"It matters to me. Spill it, Morgan Salvatore, or else."

He laughed softly and waved his hand at me. "You going to spank me, Ma? I'm a little old."

"I have all the time in the world to plot my revenge." I smiled while he continued laughing.

"You're a cream puff."

I always liked when someone underestimated me, especially him. You'd think after thirty years, he'd know better. "You know that pretty pink house for sale on your street?"

His smug little face wasn't laughing anymore. "You mean, the one next door?"

"That's the one." I laughed. "I think I want to buy it."

"Ma," he said in a stern tone. "Don't kid like that."

"I'm looking for a change. Why not move right next door to my baby?"

"Fuck," he muttered and scrubbed his hand down his face. "You wouldn't do that to me."

"I would, especially if you're keeping secrets. I think I need to keep a better eye on you."

There was no way in hell I'd actually move there. Although I liked being close to Morgan, I didn't want to be within walking distance. Before Bear, I probably would've done it, but now I liked to have my privacy.

"Fine." He rested both hands on the table and reclined back in the chair. "I promised Dad on graduation day that if he came anywhere near you, or me for that matter, that there'd be hell to pay."

My head jerked forward, my ear moving closer to him. "Wait, what?"

"I'm the reason he left, Ma."

"You made him leave?" My mouth hung open, and I blinked repeatedly because I still didn't understand.

"Yeah. I didn't want him beating on you when he drank after I left. I figured it would go back to the way it was when I was a kid when I wasn't there to protect you."

How did I not know? I couldn't believe he'd kept the secret for this long. I always assumed Ray left because he wanted to, not because Morgan made him. The revelation that Morgan forced him out rocked me to the core.

"Why didn't you tell me?"

"I knew you'd be mad and give me the whole song and dance about how you could take care of yourself."

"Well, I could." I shrugged.

"Ma, don't shit yourself. That guy was like a disease. He wouldn't have left if I didn't make him."

"I wish you would've told me about this a long time ago, Morgan."

"I did what I felt was best for both of us. I couldn't go away knowing he was there alone with you."

It was really unfair of Morgan to grow up in such a volatile household. No child should have to worry about a parent's safety or to step in to protect one from the other. Morgan did that, though. He did more than any kid should have had to do. He wasn't bitter about his past, and neither was I—every second I lived led me to this moment and place.

Without Ray, the alcoholic low-life asshole, in my life, I wouldn't be with Bear. He was the best thing that'd happened to me since the day Morgan was born. Finally, I felt like I had someone who was my partner.

"Hey," Bear said as he walked into the kitchen, giving Morgan a casual chin lift.

"Hey," Morgan replied with the same motion.

I looked at Bear and back to Morgan, my hands following my eyes. "So this is fine?"

"Yep." Morgan smiled, and Bear nodded.

Coming to stand next to me, Bear put his hands on my shoulders and gave them a light squeeze. "Everything is great," he said as he leaned down and kissed my hair.

"Huh," I muttered, nodding my head as I worked through the fact that Morgan and Bear had finally figured their shit out. "I'm glad to hear you two have made peace."

"I never doubted we would."

"I just needed a little time with the fact that my friend, someone I trust, was trying to date—" Morgan coughed and shifted his eyes "—my mom."

Reaching back, I placed my hand over Bear's. "I'm happier than I've ever been."

"That's all that matters," Morgan said and smiled, bringing his eyes back to mine. "I better get back to Race." He leaned over and kissed my cheek before holding his hand out to Bear. "See you tomorrow, buddy."

"I'll be there."

After Morgan walked out the front door, Bear grabbed me and stalked off toward the bedroom with me in his arms. "It's time to pay up, sweetheart."

"Not my ass!" I giggled. "Not my ass."

He stopped in the hallway just before the door. "Franny, babe. I'm not taking it unless you're willing to give it. So stop freaking out."

"Okay." I blew out a breath and sagged against him.

"But eventually, you're going to beg me to stick it in your ass."

"Said no woman ever," I mumbled softly.

"What?"

"Nothing." I smiled up at him.

"Liar," he whispered as he leaned forward and kissed my lips as he carried me inside the bedroom.

Every ounce of stress from the day melted away with his lips pressed against mine. It was only us, a man and a woman, together as one, without anything else interfering. Bear made everything feel…possible.

CHAPTER 27
BEAR

"James!" Thomas yelled as James walked by his office.

Thomas and I had spent the last thirty minutes talking about the possibility of them hiring Ret as a bounty hunter and private investigator at ALFA. We always had too many cases and often juggled more than we should. An extra body, and one who knew how to find people, would be an asset.

James walked backward, sticking his face in the doorway. "What's up?"

Thomas motioned toward the seat next to me. "We gotta talk. Have a minute?"

He slapped his hand against the doorframe. "I'm not doing anything," he said sarcastically as he walked inside.

Thomas rolled his eyes. "So Bear found us a possible lead on a new hire."

James looked at me and then to Thomas. "Who?"

"Dude's a bounty hunter and is looking to settle down."

James rubbed his chin and smiled. "Interesting. Could be a great match for our company."

"That's what I think too. We could use another set of hands around here."

"So then it's a yes?" I asked, fidgeting in my chair because I wanted this so badly I could almost taste it.

"How do you know him?" James asked.

"He's my kid." It felt weird to say that. I didn't really talk about either of my children with the guys.

James smiled. "Ah, that makes it even better."

"He's stopping in today to see me, and I thought I'd see what you guys thought before I introduced him. He's looking to relocate, and I thought we'd be a perfect fit."

"Way to be a team player for once." Thomas laughed, and James joined him.

"If it weren't for wanting to keep my kid close, I'd tell you both to fuck off."

Thomas cleared his throat. "Bring him to my office when he gets here."

I pushed myself up from the chair, too excited to let them annoy me. "I'll do that."

"Close the door behind you. James and I need to talk in private."

I nodded, closing the door, and heading straight to my office. Getting work done while I waited was impossible. All I could think about was that my son could be working in the same building as me and I'd never miss another day with him.

"Bear." Angel's sultry voice came through the intercom as I was digging through a pile of papers.

"Yeah."

"A Mr. Ret North is here to see you."

"Send him back," I said in a strangled voice.

My stomach started to flip over, and I jumped from my seat, smoothing down my clothes, and combing my beard with my fingers like I was about to go on a date instead of seeing my son again.

Ret strolled into my office in a pair of dark blue jeans, a tight black T-shirt, and black Harley boots like he'd just walked off the set of the *Fast & Furious*. He definitely looked like he'd fit right in with the other guys here at ALFA. Lord knows I never did.

"Hey, Pop," he said like no separation had ever happened. It flowed easily from his lips and brought the biggest smile to my face.

"Glad you made it." I rounded my desk and pulled him into my arms before he even tried to shake my hand. I'd never been a hugger, but for my kid, I'd hug him every chance I got.

"Impressive setup you have here."

"I wish I could take the credit, but it's my buddies' business."

"Still," he said, pulling out of my arms. "You've done well for yourself."

"It helps to surround yourself with good people. Their family changed my life."

"I talked with Alese," he said and smiled.

"Sit. Let's talk." I motioned toward the chair and leaned against the desk while he sat. "What did she say?"

"She said she's fine moving anywhere as long as we're together."

"And what do you think?" I crossed my fingers under my arm.

"I like the idea of being closer to family and getting to know you and Franny better."

"Her son works here too."

"Oh. How does that work?"

"Now?" I laughed and shook my head. "It's fine, but it was a bit touch and go when Fran and I hooked up."

"Uh, yeah. I can imagine."

"You'll like Morgan. He's former military and a good kid. His wife owns a racetrack not far from here."

"Sounds like my kind of people. And the other guys?"

"Well, there's Sam—he's ex-FBI. Thomas and James are ex-DEA and also brothers-in-law. Thomas is Fran's nephew."

"So this is mainly a family operation?"

I shook my head. "No, but it's friends and family. They only surround themselves with people they know they can trust."

"If they want another employee, then I'm game."

I tried to hold in my excitement, but I failed. "Yes!" Fist-pumping the air, I did a little dance with my upper body.

"Don't do that again."

"What?" My head rocked back.

He waved his hands in the air between us. "Whatever that was. Just don't."

I glared at him. "My moves always impressed the ladies."

"You're lucky your ass is old, Pop. That shit don't work today."

"Little fucker." I laughed. "You're going to fit in here like a glove."

Thomas and James walked past my door and backed up and pointed toward Ret. I nodded, letting them know that he was indeed my son.

"Hey," Thomas said, walking in very casually. "I'm Thomas, part owner of ALFA. This is James." He pitched a thumb over his shoulder. "My partner in the business."

"Nice to meet you. I'm Ret," he said, holding out his hand and shaking Thomas's hand very calmly.

"So we heard you might be interested in a job."

"Yes, sir." Ret smiled, glancing over his shoulder at me.

"Have a few minutes to talk?" James asked.

"I sure do."

"Bear, we're going to steal him for a bit. Is that okay with you?" Thomas asked out of respect.

"It's fine. We'll catch up when you're done," I told them, but the three of them were already in the hallway.

Thomas pulled the door closed behind him, and I broke out into my dance again. The same one Ret told me never to perform again. But now the audience was just me, and nothing made me want to dance more than the thought of having Ret near.

"So how'd it go today?" Fran asked before I had the chance to kick off my shoes.

"Fucking perfect. Ret starts in two weeks. He just needs to go back to Miami and pack up his things."

She ran across the room and jumped into my arms. "That's amazing."

"It is," I said into her neck, taking in her scent, and closing my eyes.

She tipped her head back, giving me access to the entire side of her neck. "We should celebrate."

"Am I getting anal tonight?" I murmured.

"No," she said in a breathy tone.

"Not even if I eat your pussy for an hour?" I smiled against her skin.

"Hmm." She laughed. "That's a tempting offer."

My fingers dug into her ass cheeks. "I want you so bad, Franny," I growled when her ass clenched in my palms. "Do this for me."

"What do I get out of this?" she asked, digging her fingernails into my shoulders.

"A killer orgasm that'll make you black out."

"Uh, I have those without you sticking it in my ass, babe."

"Sweetheart." I pulled away so she could see the need in my eyes. "It was worth a shot."

"My ass is the tightest thing I have on this old body. I'd prefer for it to stay intact."

"You're the boss, Franny. You're the boss." I laughed.

One thing Jackie taught me is that the women run the show. Hell, I'd watched the Gallo family closely over the years too, and Fran and Maria had that shit running like a well-oiled machine.

Men did not rule the world.

Men did not make the decisions.

It's just how shit was, and I knew it was how Fran planned on being. She couldn't hand over the reins to me. It went against her nature and probably her genetics.

"But," I said, moving my hands from her ass to her beautiful face. "I want you to make me a promise."

"What, Bear?"

"No more talkin' bad about yourself. Your body is beautiful, your face is stunning, but the thing I love about you most is your heart." I rubbed my nose against hers. "Even if you are a nosy little thing sometimes."

"But I brought your kids back." She smiled.

"You did." I kissed her lips softly. "And for that, I'll always love you."

I never expected there to be another woman on this planet who got me. But Fran DeLuca did. I needed her in my life, and she needed me. We were the perfect mix together.

Her nosiness came from a place of love. She knew that I wanted my kids in my life but didn't have the balls to do it myself.

She made it happen.

And for that, I'd always be by her side.

Eventually, maybe I'd get in her ass too.

CHAPTER 28

FRAN

Months later…

Morgan grabbed my leg. "Ma, get down!"

"Oh, honey. I'm having too much fun," I said, looking down at him, and laughing at the look on his face. My beautiful son was stressed out and embarrassed, but you know what? I didn't give a shit.

"People are looking at you," he begged.

I twirled in a circle, breaking free from his grip. The table moved with me, making it more like dancing on top of a pogo stick than a tabletop. "It's my wedding day, goddamn it."

"Leave her alone," Maria said as she pulled out a chair and used Morgan's shoulder as leverage to dance on the table with me. She grabbed my hands and started to jump up and down when Aretha Franklin's "Respect" began to play.

"Old people," Morgan muttered and rolled his eyes.

"Go find that pretty wife of yours!" I yelled over the music, holding on to Maria tightly so neither of us would fall off the wobbly table.

We danced like teenagers, pretending our almost arthritic knees didn't ache. It didn't hurt that we'd consumed a good percentage of our body weight in alcohol before we cut loose.

"I freaking love this song," she said with the biggest smile.

"R-E-S-P-E-C-T!" we screamed together, making moves like we used to in the old days when we'd go to the discos.

Half the room was on their feet dancing and singing along. If I weren't so hammered, I'd have tears in my eyes. Surrounded by my entire family, I felt so much love—more than I'd ever felt in my entire life.

The day Bear asked me to marry him, I thought my mind was playing tricks on me. Never did I expect that man, the one who said he'd never settle down, to ask me that question. I mean, he always asked for anal sex, but I told him he hadn't earned it yet. Maybe it was his way of staking his claim and *earning* the right to conquer all of me.

He was really kind of old-fashioned about some things. He even talked to Sal to ask for my hand in marriage because he was officially the patriarch of the family since our father wasn't here to ask. I found it endearing and sweet, but Bear swore me to secrecy. He didn't want his credibility as a badass to be ruined.

Not even Morgan knew how Bear popped the question. Hell, I didn't even tell Maria because then everyone would know. I might as well have published it on the front page of the newspaper. We kept it our little secret and told the family that he asked me over dinner.

But the truth of it was much different. He took me to Honeymoon Island to watch the sunset, bringing a blanket and cooler filled with champagne, cheese, and fruit. He held me in his arms, whispering sweet things in my ear as we watched the sun fall below the edge of the ocean.

When the sky turned the most brilliant shades of red and orange, he said four magical words that stole my breath. I turned in his arms and straddled him before I said yes. I'd be lying if I said we didn't get a bit frisky in public. It wasn't something I'd done before, but Bear brought out that side of me—he made me want to do things I never thought I'd do.

"You did it!" Maria yelled, wrapping her arms around my neck when the song ended. "You're Mrs. Fran North."

"That sounds so weird," I said and gripped her waist as the table started to shift underneath us.

"Ladies," Bear, my husband, said from behind me. "You two better get down before that table breaks."

"We got this," Maria said over my shoulder and waved him off.

"I'd like my wife to be in perfect condition tonight for what I have planned."

Maria's eyes slid to mine, and her eyebrows shot up. "Is he talking about what I think he's talking about?"

My lips twisted and I nodded, closing one eye as I thought about the pain and the promise I never should've made.

"Well, shit," Maria said in my ear and laughed. "We better have more to drink."

"Fucking hell," I groaned.

When I turned around, Bear held out his hand—the one with the shiny new shiny gold wedding ring—and helped me down.

"Are my two favorite ladies having fun?" he asked when he reached for Maria and helped her down with just as much care as he did with me.

"I have a feeling you're going to have more fun later." Maria winked, and I wanted to crawl under the table out of embarrassment.

He just laughed and whisked me into his arms, placing his lips against my neck. "I won't do anything you don't want."

My belly flipped as his words skidded across my skin. "I'm yours now, Bear. There's nothing I want more than to give you a piece of me that I've never given to anyone." Clearly, the alcohol made me answer him in that way.

That was Bear. My husband didn't often show it, but when it came to family and friends, he had a soft spot.

If I were younger, I'd have little baby Bears running around the house. If he were given the chance to really be a father, I could almost imagine what he'd be like.

I'd been able to catch glimpses of it since Janice had her baby. When Bear walked into the room and saw the little girl for the first time, I thought he was going to turn into a puddle of goo. The man lost it and started to cry when Janice told him she had named her Jackie.

In all my life, I'd never seen a more involved grandfather. I thought Sal was bad, but Bear was a complete sucker for that little girl. He was probably overdoing it because of the time he lost with his kids, but it didn't matter. After seeing him with a baby in his arms, it had me longing for the days of having a little one in the house.

"Well, I better go find Sal. I'm sure he's getting into trouble somewhere." Maria kissed Bear on the cheek before wrapping me in the biggest hug. "Use lots of lube and do at least three more shots before you go upstairs."

"But I'll black out," I whispered in her ear.

"You want to be half unconscious your first time. Trust me. Or your ass is going to pucker up like no one's business. Thank me tomorrow."

I started to giggle, covering my mouth, and glanced back at my husband.

"I don't know what you two are talking about, but are you ready to say good-bye to everyone?"

"Remember… Do more shots," she called out over her shoulder as she started to walk away.

He quirked an eyebrow at me. "Sage advice from a pro?"

I nodded, still laughing as I looped my arm around his back. "Let's have a drink with our boys, and then we can say good-bye to everyone else."

"Just one?" He smiled and pushed on the small of my back, leading me through the crowd.

I shrugged. "However many it takes."

"Are you sure about this? Before you get too shit-faced, Franny, I need to know this is what you want." He looked so cute when he had that super serious, concerned face going on.

I nodded quickly as my hand slid lower before giving him a quick ass squeeze. "I'm completely sure." I smiled up at him and sighed. "Bring on the tequila, baby!"

Morgan saw us first and nudged Ret with his elbow. They were handsome devils, especially dressed in tuxedos. "Hey, guys." I smiled and looked back and forth between them.

"Ma," Morgan said, leaning forward, and kissing me on the cheek before shaking my husband's hand. "Bear."

"Morgan," Bear replied, pulling him into a hug, and lifting Morgan off his feet. Instead of being a stick in the mud, Morgan hugged him back.

As soon as his feet were back on the floor, Morgan punched Bear in the shoulder. "I'm so fuckin' happy for you."

"Fran, you're a beautiful bride." Ret kissed my cheek, making my toes curl a bit.

Down, girl. He's your husband's kid. Every time I saw Ret, I imagined a young Murray. Even in his fifties, Murray was sexy as sin, but in his youth… *Meow.*

"Thanks, Ret. I'm happy to have the entire family here," I said as Janice approached from the other side of the bar.

"I brought a bottle," she said, waving the tequila bottle in the air. "Who wants a shot? Jackie's with a sitter all night, and I'm not letting this opportunity pass."

"Well, damn. Let's drink, mama," I said, rubbing my hands together as I winked at Bear.

"Don't drink too much, Franny."

"Oh, shush it, buddy. Just two for the road." I smiled and pressed my hand against his chest and motioned with my fingers for him to give me his ear. "You want ass, I get shots."

"Mom!"

My head snapped to Morgan. "What?"

His eyes bulged out of his head. "You may not realize it, but you most certainly did not whisper that."

I chuckled, feeling my cheeks turning pink. "Sorry." I grimaced. "Let's just drink until you all forget what you just heard."

"Not enough liquor in the world for that," Morgan muttered, looking like he was about to vomit while Ret and Janice laughed.

Bear poured the drinks and handed them out. We formed a tight circle, Morgan to my left and Bear along with his kids to the right. "To family," Bear said and held his glass high in the air.

"That's all ya got?" I asked.

"Does anything else matter?" he asked, peering down at me with an adorable smile.

"Not really. To our kids and the future," I said, raising my glass too.

"Salute," Morgan said, followed by Janice and Ret.

My entire body tingled as the tequila slid down my throat. Not just from the warmth of the liquor, but at being surrounded by my family. Our family. Over the last year, I'd grown to love Bear's kids as much as I loved the man himself.

After years of loneliness, my life had become full.

"One more," I said and held my glass in front of Bear, shaking it.

He just laughed and refilled all the glasses.

"To Fran and Bear," Ret said and clinked his tequila to his father's.

I quickly clinked my glass before downing the shot. My legs felt a little wobbly, and I knew I needed to get off my feet. "Love you, baby," I said to Morgan before he put down his shot glass. "I'll see you tomorrow."

"Not if I have anything to say about it." Bear wrapped his arm around my waist from behind.

Morgan narrowed his eyes. "I can still knock you out, old man."

"Now, Morgan, let your mother enjoy herself and her new husband," I told him.

He scrubbed his hands down his face. "Go. Have fun."

"Bye," I said, quickly hugging Ret and Janice.

Bear waved to everyone as we walked away. His arm was still looped behind my back, which I needed to give me support with my liquor-induced sway. I giggled most of the way up to the room—over what, I'm not sure.

Bear couldn't wipe the smile off his face, kissing my neck, and groping me as the elevator dinged with each floor.

The door to the honeymoon suite wasn't even closed before Bear had me against the wall, hiking my dress up my body, and feasting on me like a starving man.

"Bear," I moaned and dug my fingers into his hair.

He didn't stop. His hands slid down my body and groped my bare ass in his hands before lifting me off the floor. My feet dangled for a moment and then instinctively wrapped around his waist.

Sometimes, I wanted to pinch myself because I didn't believe he was mine... But feeling our bodies pressed against each other reminded me that we were forever part of each other.

"You sure about this, Franny?" he asked as he paused in front of the bed and I climbed down his body.

"I'm sure," I said, or at least, I think I did. It's what I meant to say if I didn't. My brain started to get fuzzy from the mass amounts of alcohol I'd consumed.

I stood still while Bear undressed me, kissing the skin he'd exposed until he knelt down in front of me as the dress hit the floor.

He pulled my body closer and leaned forward, placing his fur-covered lips against me. My body jolted from the warmth. I gripped his hair again, but this time to keep myself from falling backward. I closed my eyes and savored the feel of his mouth on my clit.

"I'm so close," I said within minutes. When his mouth pulled away, I gasped. "What are you doing?"

"Just getting warmed up, sweetheart." He smirked.

I blinked slowly, my lopsided grin growing wider. "Ravage me," I proclaimed like I was part of some trashy romance novel.

His hands gripped the sides of my waist and held me tightly before tossing me onto the bed.

"You're lucky I didn't break a hip," I said in the worst, slurred, drunk-off-my-ass tone.

He moved quickly, ripping off his tux in record time. "I wanna break you, Fran," he said as he climbed on top of me. "But only in the most sinful way."

I gasped when his huge erection settled between my legs. "I don't think it'll fit." I wiggled underneath him.

"Baby, it'll fit. I'll go nice and slow. You've taken my fingers like a champ. My cock will be nothing." There wasn't a man on the planet who hadn't used that line in some form to try to get into their girl's ass.

I wasn't stupid, but lucky for him, I was inebriated enough to say, "Yeah." To which I got a smirk before he went down on me again.

My eyes grew heavy and even blinking became a struggle, but every time I started to feel the weight of sleep begin to pull me under, Bear would dig in harder or fuck me deeper.

But when he flipped me onto my stomach, I immediately woke up. "Oh, God," I moaned. "This is going to hurt."

I glanced over my shoulder, using one eye to try to focus as he lifted a bottle of lube in the air. He was nestled between my legs as he squeezed the bottle, letting the lube trickle down my ass crack.

When his finger touched my hole, I puckered, along with every muscle in my body going rigid. "You want this, sweetheart?" he asked as the tip of his finger glided across me.

Fuck, it felt amazing once I let myself relax. Bear had magical fingers, and he knew exactly what to do to get me going.

"Keep going," I said, sealing my eyes shut. "Don't stop."

He growled and dipped the tip of one finger inside. My body melted into the bed, except my abdomen which stayed high from the pillow he'd placed underneath my belly.

Slowly, he worked his finger in and out, and once I adjusted, he added a second. "So good," I moaned. With two fingers buried inside me, coldness slid down my ass. *More lube...thank God.* "You better lube that giant dick of yours," I told him because Maria's advice still played on repeat in my mind.

"I gotcha," he whispered.

I could hear the mass amounts of lube he was coating his cock with. The sound of wetness filled the air along with my gasps as his other hand never stopped working me—driving me closer to climax.

When he pulled his fingers out, I grabbed on to the comforter as if my life depended on it and closed my eyes.

"Breathe, Fran. It'll feel so good."

Bullshit. I grunted as the tip of his cock pushed against my opening. At first, it felt like his finger when he'd rim my ass, looking for permission.

"Bear down," he told me, and I did.

The first inch was the hardest and felt different than I'd imagined. I felt full. Not just a little full either. If he put any more inside of me, I thought my body might split in two.

"So fuckin' tight," he growled behind me and pushed in deeper. "Jesus, I'm not going to last."

Bear had the most stamina out of any man I'd ever known. Maybe my list was short, but the man could fuck like a champ. He wasn't known as a manwhore for no reason.

My mind grew fuzzy.

The darkness began to take me until he reached around and started to tweak my clit between his thumb and index finger. He'd spent at least an hour working me up, always denying me the orgasm I wanted, until now.

But my hand to God—he wasn't inside of me for twenty-five seconds when he cried out. "I can't stop it! You're just too tight."

I gasped for air. My mouth was open like a guppy, but nothing was getting in. It was like his cock had been jammed so far inside me that it punctured my lung, making it impossible for me to breathe.

Within seconds, my body started to tighten, even my ass around his cock clamped down, and I tumbled into the most wonderful darkness. Suddenly, explosions of colors filled the void as my body twitched through the most spectacular orgasm of my entire life.

"Franny." I heard him say, but I couldn't move. My body and mind were paralyzed from the aftershocks.

"Franny," he said again.

I mumbled something, but I didn't know what the fuck I said. When he pulled out, my body jolted—partly missing the fullness and the other part shocked by his size. My eyes were still closed, and I concentrated on my breathing after going so long without air.

The bed dipped, and his footsteps softened. "Here, baby," he said before touching my bottom with a warm, wet washcloth and cleaning me up.

I'd never had a man who cared for me afterward. The first one…the one who shall not be named…was more of a wham, bam, thank you, ma'am kind of guy.

But my husband knew just how I wanted to be treated. "I love you," I murmured into the plush comforter.

"I love you too, Fran." The bed dipped again, but this time, he pulled me into his arms and pressed my back to his front. "Sleep, wife," he whispered in my ear.

As I drifted off, I thought about how much my life had changed. I was no longer a divorced, tracksuit-wearing woman who sat home and played bridge. I was the wife of a badass biker man who looked more like a lumberjack than a private investigator. I felt loved, protected, and content for the first time in my entire life.

It was funny how things worked out. Sometimes good things happened when we least expected it. Especially when the person who came to my rescue was a sexy hunk of man who always kept me on my toes with his smart mouth—and satisfied in the bedroom with his glorious cock and talented tongue.

Tucked against his body and feeling like the sexual beast I knew I was—I slept in my husband's arms for the first night after saying I do.

CHAPTER 29

BEAR

Fran almost pushed me out of the house and ordered me to meet the guys at the Neon Cowboy. She muttered something about cleaning out the spare bedroom. I guess my extra things were cluttering the garage—and maybe we needed our alone time.

Going from bachelor living to being married had been an adjustment, but one I'd actually enjoyed. I'd spent most of my life single and bed-hopping that it was nice to finally settle down and live like the other half did.

"The ol' ball and chain let you out to play?" Tank asked with a chuckle as I sat down and grabbed a beer from the middle of the table.

"I wanted to stay home with my wife and enjoy my birthday, but she insisted I come spend the night with you miserable bastards."

"Smart lady," Ret said and slapped me on the shoulder.

Ret had fit in better than I ever could've imagined. He'd only been at ALFA PI for a short time, but I almost couldn't remember a time without him.

"Where's Morgan?" I asked.

Everyone looked at each other, waiting for someone to respond, but no one said anything.

"Is he okay?" They were acting weirder than usual. None of them were "normal," but usually they answered simple questions.

"Yeah, he's fine. He'll be here in a few. He's just handling a few things," Tank said, but he didn't put my mind at ease.

After being friends for as many years as we had, it was easy to read him, and there was definitely something he wasn't saying.

"Haven't seen you much lately. My aunt keepin' you busy?" City asked.

"She has been dragging me to some classes and shit," I muttered, trying to make it seem like I was still the same miserable, brooding bastard.

"Basket weaving?" He raised an eyebrow and smirked.

"That isn't Franny's style." I laughed, turning the beer bottle in my hand.

Mike leaned forward with a serious look on his face. "You can't just drop that knowledge in our laps and not tell us what you're learning, old man."

"Well..." I shrugged. Fran would absolutely murder me if I told them the truth.

"Just drop the shit," City said, narrowing his eyes. "You're learning to knit. Just admit it."

"Fucker. It's a dance class," I lied. It was a white lie. There was dance, but it involved a pole and very little clothing.

She'd seen an ad online about staying fit and learning new moves, and she'd begged me to go with her. Never in my life did I think I would go to a stripper-pole dance class. It sounded like bullshit. But I didn't expect there to be benefits like a sex-charged wife by the time the sessions were over.

Tank laughed first, and then the others followed suit. "I can't fucking believe it. We have Fred Astaire sitting at our table." Tank shook his head in disappointment. "I never thought I'd see the day you'd be a twinkle toes."

"It ain't that kind of class, dumbass."

"Oh?" he asked, challenging me to answer.

"What kind of class is it, Uncle?" City asked. It was his new way to annoy me. Technically, I was his uncle, but he used every opportunity to remind me just how much older I was than him.

"I can't say." I bit down on my tongue and imagined Franny's face if I spilled the beans.

"I know," Anthony teased with a sinister smile that I wanted to smack right off his face.

"Shut the fuck up," I growled.

"Auntie Fran tells Mom everything." Anthony stuck out his tongue and gagged. "Trust me, I know too much."

Thomas looked from Anthony to me with a scowl and threw up his hands. "I don't want to hear it."

"Now I gotta know. Spill the beans, kid," Tank said to Anthony, rubbing his hands together, and peering at me out of the corner of his eye.

"Assholes," I grumbled before taking a swig of my beer.

Anthony put his hands up and laughed, tipping back in his chair. The cocky little fucker. "All I'm going to say is that there's a pole involved."

One by one, each set of eyes looked over at me with their mouths hanging open. I shrugged. "I can't help if I have a girl who likes to mix shit up."

City started to rub his face and groaned. "I shouldn't know this shit about my aunt, man."

"You asked, he told." I smirked.

Mike sat there, still looking a little green around the gills. Thomas laughed his ass off and grabbed another beer like we weren't talking about his aunt.

"Fran's a wild woman," Ret said and shook his head. "She's perfect for you." He nudged me with his elbow.

"Best woman I've ever known besides your mom." I gave him a bittersweet smile. He nodded, knowing exactly how I felt. "I'm having one more drink, and then I'm outta here."

"Oh, no, you don't," James, the bossiest SOB in the group, said. "We have plans tonight."

"Plans?"

"Yep. So sit your ass there and drink your beer. Fran isn't expecting you until we're done with you."

My entire body rocked backward, taking the chair with me. "Done with me?" These "friends" who sat around the table definitely had something up their sleeves, and they weren't sharing.

"It's your birthday, you old fucker." Tank looked at me like I had three heads.

"Fran doesn't want me out all night." I was making excuses, but it didn't matter. I wanted to be home with my sweetheart. I'd spent too many years in bars and going home to an empty house to want to spend my birthday the same exact way.

"Mom's meeting us at the next stop," Morgan said, walking up from behind me, and placing his hands on my shoulders. "So stop the bullshit. Drink your beer and enjoy your seventieth birthday."

"Fifty-second," I corrected him.

"Still old as fuck," Morgan teased before he took a seat across the table. "Everything's in place."

"I don't like surprises."

"Just shut up," Tank sneered. "Always gotta ruin everything."

I crossed my arms in front of me and scowled. "Fine, but I don't gotta like it."

My phone beeped with a text.

Fran: Stop being a pain and follow the program.

I couldn't wipe the stupid grin off my face as I typed back.

Me: Fine, but only because I love that fine ass.

"Where are we headed for my extra special celebration?"

"The Pink Panther." Tank smiled.

"Eh, I've seen enough tits and ass in strip clubs to last a lifetime." I slammed back the rest of my beer and grabbed another because if I was going to the titty bar for the night, I sure as fuck needed to be drunk.

"So, Ret, how are you settling in at ALFA?" City asked, ignoring my unhappiness about the itinerary for the evening.

"Fucking great, man." Ret leaned forward and gripped the beer bottle in both hands. "Never worked any place where I actually liked the people."

"Smart thing to say since everyone is here."

"Not Sam. Where is that prick anyway?" I asked.

"He's getting something important," City replied and exhaled in annoyance.

"Getting something?"

City nodded. "Stop trying to find a way out of it, Bear. Your ass is ours tonight." He turned back to Ret. "What case are you working on now?"

When there weren't any active PI cases for Ret, he was given free rein to track down wanted criminals. He was a bounty hunter, after all, and the rewards brought in big cash for ALFA. Since he used their resources, he split the money with the company, but he kept the bulk of it.

"Tracking this asshole on the FBI Most Wanted list. He killed his family and took off about fifteen years ago. I'm going to find him and put him exactly where he belongs."

Anthony finally put his phone down to join the conversation. "How much does something like that pay?"

"Hundred grand."

Anthony's eyes lit up. "Fuck, I need to change professions."

"It's risky as fuck, man," Ret told him. "It isn't something you can do without accepting the possibility that they will kill you to keep their freedom."

"Eh, I don't have to worry about that at the shop."

"Smart man, Anth." Mike elbowed him. "Plus, where else can you work where you see tits and ass all day besides a strip club?"

"Dude." Anthony winced. "Some of those tits and ass should never see the light of day, let alone be exposed in front of me."

"You're a real tool," City told him before turning to Ret. "You don't go after guys like that alone, do you?"

"Sometimes. But he's going to be a pain in the ass, so I'll probably rope someone at ALFA to go with me once I get a lock on his location."

"I'll go," I offered because I took every opportunity I could get to spend more time with my son.

He glanced over at me and nodded slowly. "I'd have you at my back anytime, Dad."

Man. It never got old hearing him call me Dad. No sweeter word in the English language. Every day, I felt less guilty about my past and the way I'd left my kids. They seemed to accept me and forgive me for what I'd done, but it'd taken me longer to forgive myself.

"One more round and we're outta here. Sam's on his way," Thomas said.

"Fucking great," I muttered to myself.

"THANKS FOR BEING the designated driver tonight," James told Sam as we climbed off the party bus.

"Eh, with Fi being pregnant, I try not to drink. She gets jealous that she can't have one."

"You're smarter than you look." I laughed.

"You're still an asshole," he replied with a smirk.

The kid had grown on me. Who the fuck knew? I hated him when I first met him. Thought he was a weasel, but he's not. He was a stand-up guy and had our backs more times than I could count.

"Happy Birthday, old bastard." He smiled.

I straightened my back and rubbed my chest. "You only wish you could look this good at my age."

As I started to walk away, he said, "Too bad you won't be around to see that I look better when I'm as old as you."

I turned quickly, narrowing my eyes. "I'll still be here, fucker. Heaven won't take me, and the Devil's too scared to have me down there. I'd take that shit over."

Sam rolled his eyes. "Yeah, I forgot. You're a badass."

I socked him in the shoulder with my knuckles. "Keep it up, and you'll be there before me."

"You two done with your bullshit?" James asked, holding open the door to the Pink Panther.

We both started to laugh, and I grabbed Sam around the neck, locking him under my arm. "We're coming!" I yelled back and then started to mess up Sam's hair. "Even though you're a dick, I still love you."

He punched my ribs, trying to break free. "Not the hair, man," he grunted, pushing against my ribs.

I released him and laughed when he frantically tried to fix his hair that looked like a bird's nest on top of his head. "You're still like a chick."

"You're lucky it's your birthday."

"Fuck off."

"We're late. Get your asses inside and shut up," City said and shoved me in the back.

We had just been here for my bachelor party, and some things were meant never to be discussed again. Explaining to Fran why I had bite marks on my chest the next day wasn't a pleasant conversation, but she eventually forgave me. She mumbled something about her son and nephews being with me so it couldn't have been as bad as she had imagined. I wasn't saying shit because my big mouth would just get me in more trouble.

"Ah, the smell of pussy and desperation," I said when the door closed behind us. "Nothing like it."

"It's a smell you know well." Mike laughed, holding his stomach, and thinking he was the funniest fucker ever.

"I do," I admitted.

James walked ahead of the group, motioning for us to follow. "Let's get a table up front."

"Bossy bastard," I mumbled.

The Pink Panther was one of the seediest strip clubs in the area, but it was centrally located between our houses. Keeping with the name, the lights shining on the stage were pink, casting a hue that made each of the dancers appear to be sunburned.

Epic fail.

Instead of licensing the logo for the Pink Panther, Crater, the owner of the joint, created his own version with a cracked-out pink cat and stuck it on the wall. Whoever was his designer for the logo should be shot.

"I hate this place," I groaned as I sat on a weirdly sticky stadium chair in the front row between Ret and City.

"I've been in worse," City said and eased back in the chair.

The speakers squealed, and I covered my ears. "Next up, we have the divinely delicious Cupcake. Are you ready to sink your teeth into her, gentlemen?"

Hoots and hollers could be heard from the back of the room as the music started to play and the lights lowered. First, a leg appeared, lit up by a spotlight, before the rest of "Cupcake" emerged, covered in a faux fur coat and high heels. I could barely look at her—she was so young, I wondered if she was even really legal.

Ever since spending more time with my daughter, I couldn't look at younger women the same way. They no longer did anything for me. Janice fucked that shit up.

Ret leaned over. "Cupcake lookin' a little young, or is it me?"

"Yup. Just thinking the same thing."

"Either I'm getting old, or she's way underage."

Cupcake showed a shoulder first, shimmying up and down the pole in rhythm with the music. I squirmed in my seat because the entire thing made me uncomfortable. I could almost be her grandfather, and it creeped me out.

"Lap dance?"

I looked up to see Carly, the same girl who gave me all those pretty chest decorations at my bachelor party.

"No thanks." I waved my hands.

"Come on," she said, grabbing my hands, and pulling me forward. "It's already been paid for." She grinned. "I promise I won't bite you this time."

"I'll pass." I didn't feel like going home to a pissed off wife. She'd told me to go out, not come home smelling of pussy and covered in more shit that I didn't want to explain.

"Go, dumbass," City said and pushed my shoulder. "Trust me, you want to go."

I gave him the stink-eye. Why would my supposed best friend push me to go with Carly? It didn't make sense.

"Come on, Dad. Man up." Ret challenged me and joined City's side.

Carly yanked on my hand again. "I have something special planned for you."

"Oh, goodie."

"Pussy," City coughed.

"Fine," I said and finally stood up to follow Carly, pointing at City. "But if Fran gives me any shit, I'm sending her straight to you, and then she's coming for Carly."

Everyone laughed. They didn't know what it was like to love Franny. She had balls bigger than me, and that was pretty hard to do.

"Let's go in a different room," Carly yelled when we passed by the speakers blaring "Cherry Pie" by Warrant.

I shrugged because I didn't care where we went; I was not going to enjoy this. Well, I would enjoy it, but not the aftermath it caused.

She opened the door at the end of the hallway and stepped aside. "Sit down, and I'm going to turn off the lights. I want to try a new routine out on you."

"I don't know if I'm the best judge, Carly."

"You're perfect, Bear." She smiled up at me. "Now, in you go."

I did as she asked and sat down on the chair in the middle of the room before she switched the lights off and closed the door. I could hear her heels click against the tile as she approached, and I held my breath.

One of my favorite songs started to play—"Addicted" by Saving Abel—and I couldn't help but think of Fran and smile.

When the lights turned on, my mouth fell open.

I was dumbfounded.

Standing before me in fuck-me pumps, a lacy G-string, and nothing else was my girl.

"Franny?" I mouthed, but the music was too loud for either of us to hear.

She shook her head, placing her index finger over my lips. Her body started to move with the beat, circling around my chair, and touching my body as she walked.

Fuck, my wife is hot.

Still in shock, I stared at her, watching as she danced around me and put into use all the moves she'd learned at our dance class.

She backed up, straddling my legs, and hovering over my cock as she ground her body against me. *Jesus.* My cock had already perked up when I'd seen her, but now she was about to give me a hard-on that wouldn't go away without fucking her.

My hands slid around her body, gliding up her stomach, and just when I was about to touch her tits, she slapped my hand away. "No touching," she said with a shitty smirk.

"Come on!" I yelled, trying to grope her again, but I ended up getting my hands smacked.

The entire thing made me laugh, but I wasn't laughing at her. I couldn't believe that Fran would do this for me. Her dark hair swayed with her shoulders as her hips moved the other way. I kept reaching out to touch her every time she got close, but she made sure I didn't make contact.

Before the music ended, she sat in my lap with the biggest smile, her body sweaty and glistening. "Did you like your birthday gift?"

I wrapped my arms around her body and pulled her closer. "Best fucking present ever, sweetheart."

"I'm not done yet." She giggled and slithered off my lap to the floor.

Her fingers worked quickly, unfastening my button, and pulling my stiff cock free. My belly fluttered, and my cock waved in anticipation as her tiny hand wrapped around the shaft.

She licked her lips, blowing gently on the tip. "You want me to suck your cock?" she asked, sending chills down my spine.

I freaking loved when she talked dirty. "Fuckin' A."

Her lips slid over the head of my dick, and my hips jumped from the chair, trying to shove myself deeper. She placed her hands on my legs and pushed me back down without missing a single stroke against her tongue.

In the short time we'd been together, she learned every trick to make me come apart at the seams. I said it was to make me come faster so she had to work less, but she claimed it was just to drive me wild with lust. I ain't buying what she was selling.

Her hands twisted back and forth, resting against her lips as she moved up and down. Her tongue flicked the spot that gave me goose bumps, and every time I moaned, she sucked harder.

I dug my fingers into her hair, needing to ground myself to something as my mind became fuzzy. I looked down at her, and there wasn't a sexier sight in the world than seeing your woman with her cheeks caved in, working your cock like a pro. Every time she pulled away, my body went with her.

I needed this.

I wanted this.

I wanted her.

I loved Fran's unpredictability. Sometimes it was a bit much and verged on sticking her nose where it didn't belong, but it always revolved around love.

"Franny," I called out as my body shook through the orgasm. My toes curled inside my boots, and my head tipped backward as I gasped for air.

When I came back to my senses and finally glanced back down to her, she dabbed the corners of her mouth and licked the remnants of me off her lips. Before I could catch my breath, she tucked my cock back into my pants and zipped me up before climbing into my lap. Planting a giant kiss against my mouth, she whispered, "I love you, baby."

"I love you, sweetheart." I gave her a lazy smile.

"Ready to go out there?"

"In a minute. I need to get my legs back."

She tipped her head back and giggled. "I'm excited to finally be at a strip club. You know, I've never been to one?"

My eyes widened. "What?"

"Yep. Never stepped inside."

"We're getting you a lap dance."

"Why?"

"It'll be fun." I'd never share Fran with anyone, but it would still be hot to see another woman rubbing against my wife.

"Then what are we waiting for?" She smiled and rubbed her nose against mine. "Let's get out there."

I chuckled and lifted her off me before standing on wobbly legs. "Didn't you see them dancing when you came in earlier?"

"Nope. I came in through the back door."

"We're going to talk about how you pulled this off later."

"Shh, baby. It's all good." She bit her lip.

"Uh-huh." I knew Fran had tricks, but she didn't know Crater. But Morgan did, and he probably helped her. I trusted her, and that was all that mattered.

We walked down the corridor, the music growing louder the closer we came to the main room.

She whistled, and her eyes bulged when she got her first look. Carly was dancing, half dressed, and hanging upside down from the pole. "I want to do that."

I glanced up at the ceiling. I could already envision a trip to the emergency room in our near future. "I'll teach you," I told her and wrapped my arm around her shoulders.

"You?" She smacked my chest. "I'll talk to my girl, Carly."

I didn't need Carly and Franny becoming best friends. "We'll talk about it later."

City was making a beeline for us, and he didn't look happy.

"What's up?"

"Ret left."

"Where?" I looked around, even though I knew he wasn't anywhere in here.

"He got a tip on that dude he was talking about earlier. I begged him to wait for you or let one of us come, but he wasn't having any of it."

"He just left?"

City ran his hand through his hair and grimaced. "Yep. You better call him."

"Fuck!" I pulled out my phone and dialed. I stared at City as it rang and flipped over to voice mail. "He's not answering."

"Call him back," Fran said, gripping my sides tightly.

I pressed redial and waited.

He answered on the third ring. "I know what you're going to say."

"What the fuck are you doing?"

"I'll be fine, Dad. I had to go tonight. You stay with everyone and enjoy your birthday party. I got this."

"Not alone, Ret. You need backup."

"I've done this a hundred times, Dad. Don't worry about me."

"Ret," I started to say, but he hung up.

I pulled the phone away and stared down at it. "He hung up." My mouth gaped open at the audacity of my kid.

"What did he say?" City's eyebrows were drawn down.

"He said he had it and not to worry."

"That fucker," City growled. "Thomas and James are going to be pissed."

"Let me break the news," I told him and placed my hand on his shoulder. "I'll handle everything."

"I have a bad feeling about this, Bear. A really bad feeling."

"Me too, buddy. Me too."

Ret was too much like me—hardheaded and too macho to ask or wait for help. He shouldn't be out there on his own, tracking a killer who had been on the run for over a decade. There was too much that could go wrong.

"If you gotta go tonight," Franny said, resting her head on my chest, "I understand. You can't let him be out there alone."

"I can't sit here and worry. I'll go talk to the guys, and we'll head out."

James and Thomas must've figured out what was going on because they were jogging toward me. "We heard. You ready?" James asked.

"Let's go." I looked toward my best friend. "Can you take Franny home?"

"Sam will get us all home. Don't worry. Go get Ret."

"Baby, I'm sorry I have to leave," I said, wrapping my hand behind her neck, and pulling her lips to mine.

"I love you, Bear. Be careful and keep your boy safe."

"I will," I told her and kissed her. "Thanks for the best birthday ever. I love you, too." I smiled, staring into her dark eyes.

"Let's hit it," Thomas said and yanked on my T-shirt.

"On it," I said and followed behind him as he pushed open the exit doors.

My night of calm relaxation had gone out the window hours ago, but I never thought I'd be chasing after my kid who seemed to have a death wish by going after a murderer on his own.

Surrounded by my friends and leaving my wife behind, we headed to the office to get a fix on where Ret was headed.

"Let's fuck shit up," James said with a wicked smile as we climbed into a waiting taxi.

"I'm all about it." I wanted to smile, but since my kid's life was on the line, I couldn't. If anything happened to Ret, I didn't know what I'd do with myself.

GUILTY SIN

ALFA INVESTIGATIONS BOOK FOUR

WALL STREET JOURNAL & USA TODAY BESTSELLING AUTHOR

CHELLE BLISS

LETTER FROM CHELLE

Hey there ALFA lover,

So, here's Guilty Sin. Ret's story.

But... this one comes with a WARNING.

Guilty Sin is about LOVE. Unconditional, uncontrollable, fall-to-your-knees-can't-live-without-the-person LOVE. But it's also about LUST, passion, and pleasures of the flesh.

This is one spicy story.

I hope you love Guilty Sin as much as I do. Sometimes the words come out and I have no control over where the story goes. That's how Guilty Sin happened.

Enjoy,

Chelle, xoxo

RET

Dropping my bag to the floor, I collapsed backward onto the mattress. I focused on the stain on the ceiling, wondering how in the hell anything got up there.

"Dude, I thought you were smarter than this," James pleaded on the other end of the phone, unhappy because I took off without bringing someone as backup.

"I've been after this guy for far too long. I know his kind, and I can't risk someone fucking things up."

"When do *we* ever fuck things up?"

"We don't, but Solease is far too dangerous. I don't want anyone else getting hurt."

Martin Solease had been on the FBI's most wanted list for over twenty years, and in the last five, he'd climbed to the number one spot. He'd skipped bail while awaiting trial for murdering his entire family, and then he'd racked up a handful more deaths while eluding the authorities over the last two decades.

"But it's okay if you do?"

He had a point. Being in harm's way wasn't anything new to me. I'd spent my life tracking down assholes, first for the military and then as a bounty hunter. It's what I did. All I knew. The one thing I couldn't get used to was putting those around me, people I cared for, in danger too.

"If I get killed, it's no big deal, man. I don't have kids to worry about like the rest of you."

"Dumb fuck," he hissed. "Alese will have my balls if you die. You know that, right?"

"True that." I laughed, picturing her marching into ALFA and grabbing James by the nuts. "I'll check in with you tomorrow. I'm going to get some shut-eye before I head out tomorrow."

"Bear's coming after you."

"Call him off."

Damn. My father was the last person I wanted hot on my trail and swooping in to save the day like he always tried to do. He wasn't smooth or stealthy like he thought he was; he came in basically announcing himself like a wrecking ball.

"Nope. This one's off the books and doesn't fall under my jurisdiction. Bear's your problem, not mine."

I narrowed my gaze on the stain. "That's bullshit, James."

"I have to run. Keep in contact, and let me know when you're headed back."

"Yeah, yeah."

I let my phone drop to the mattress as soon as the call disconnected and closed my eyes. Bear might have been headed my way, but that didn't mean he'd catch me before I was on the move again. I was sure, at this point, Fran and Alese were climbing the walls, coming up with crazy ways to punish me for my foolish behavior.

When I finally opened my eyes five hours later, I had ten text messages and two missed calls. James was the two calls, probably to bitch me out again, and all the text messages were from Alese.

"I know you are dead set on going after Solease, but I need you to make a quick pit stop in Atlanta first. Details are in your email. I'll call back in a few hours," James said on my voice mail.

Groaning, I pushed myself upright and blinked away the last bit of haze from my eyes before I attempted to read James's lengthy email waiting in my inbox.

The subject line read *Personal Favor – Important and For Your Eyes*

Only. I figured it was a ploy, something to stop me from going after Solease, but as I scanned the details of the file along with James's notes, I knew I was wrong.

Nya Halstead was a twenty-five-year-old woman who'd cut off all communication with her family two months ago. Her mother, a Tampa resident and trustee of a local charity foundation, had contacted ALFA to assist in locating her daughter without law enforcement involvement.

The last known location for Nya was in Atlanta, as she'd graduated from Georgia State University just before her disappearance. Mrs. Halstead believed her daughter had fallen for the wrong man and was being held against her will, unable to contact her family. The Halsteads were willing to pay ALFA one hundred thousand dollars for the safe return of their daughter.

Included with the email was a photo of Nya, smiling with her diploma in one hand and her graduation cap in the other. Her long, wavy, brown hair flowed out to the side, carried by the wind, glistening in the sun. Her big brown eyes twinkled as the apples of her cheeks almost kissed the bottom. Her wide smile was infectious, framed by full lips and perfectly straight, white teeth. She reminded me of a young Mandy Moore, a natural beauty.

As I zoomed in to get a better look, the shiny silver collar with a diamond encrusted lock that she wore around her neck caught my eye.

The design wasn't something that could be found at a department store or worn purely for decoration. I'd seen the style before, the handiwork of the only well-known BDSM jeweler below the Mason-Dixon line.

James's notes included information he'd uncovered through our contacts in the Atlanta area. Nya had been a member at Charmed, an exclusive BDSM club, catering to the filthy rich socialites with too much cash and a thirst for the dark side. She hadn't been seen at the club since she disappeared, but she had been a submissive to a Diego Lopez for a year before she vanished.

James had been able to confirm that Nya was last seen with Diego and that Diego would be at Charmed tonight, therefore leaving his home unattended, allowing me just enough time for a thorough search of the premises.

I was out of my room in under ten minutes, coffee in hand from the lobby, and headed toward my car.

Just when I thought things couldn't get any more fucked up, my father was leaning against his car with his arms folded, working a toothpick between his lips. "Morning, sunshine."

Tightening my grip on my bag, I stalked toward the car and cracked my neck. "What are you doing here? Go home, Pop."

He pulled the toothpick from his mouth and smiled. "I'm happy to see you too."

I popped the trunk as he pushed off his car and walked toward me. I practically threw my bag inside the back before slamming the lid. "How did you find me?"

"GPS." He shrugged like it was the most logical answer in the world and I was an idiot for asking.

"You have a tracker up my ass?"

"Nope." He gave me a big, toothy grin, thoroughly impressed with himself. "Tracked you through the company cell phone, wiseass."

I made a quick mental note to ditch the ALFA cell phone as soon as I got back so shit like that didn't happen again. "Fuckin' James." Crossing my arms over my chest, I turned to face him and stared him down. "Go home. Be with Fran."

"Hell, son. Fran sent me here."

I glanced toward the brilliant orange and yellow sky as the sun started to peek over the trees. "For the love of God."

"God ain't got nothing to do with me being here—that's all Fran. I don't want to hear that woman's nonstop pecking about you being in danger while I sit at home, drinking beer and relaxing. I'm going with you, and that's all there's to say about it. You got a problem with it, you call Fran and talk to her."

I cursed under my breath, but I didn't dare call Fran. She wasn't someone I wanted to mess with, and the woman had a tongue more wicked than most men I knew. The last person I needed pissed at me was her.

"I'm not going to Tennessee."

"Where are we headed?"

"Atlanta, but you're still not going."

The man had been absent for almost thirty years of my life, but since the day I agreed to work at ALFA, he'd been practically up my ass, trying to make up for lost time. Sometimes I found his attention palatable, but times like this, where he put his nose where it didn't belong, I wanted to sock him square in the jaw.

He arched an eyebrow, not the least bit shocked at the news. "Halstead girl?"

"Yep."

"Sex club shit?" He held his breath.

"Yep."

He pointed to himself with his thumbs, displaying a cocky grin. "Then I'm your man."

"This isn't really your *thing*," I told him.

"I don't have a *thing*." He put the toothpick back between his lips before rolling it with his tongue.

"Fine," I groaned and finally gave in. I wasn't winning this battle. I knew that much. I wasn't burning time with an argument I had no hope of winning. "Get in the car. We'll figure out a plan on the way."

"Hell yeah! Let's go fuck up some shit."

DAD WAITED DOWN THE STREET, watching for any sign of Diego while I headed toward the house.

"Coast is still clear," he whispered into the microphone connected to my headset.

"You don't need to whisper. Only I can hear you." I rolled my eyes as I worked the tension wrench and pick in the back door lock.

When the lock finally opened, I moved quickly, searching for any trace of the girl. "First floor's clear," I told Pop. "Moving upstairs."

"You're good to go, champ."

This was probably just another dead-end lead in a missing person's case because families often went after someone or something they couldn't understand. Fetish lifestyles were usually their first target because it wasn't mainstream enough for them to wrap their heads around.

In the last few years, the stigma attached to BDSM had waned, and the lifestyle had grown more mainstream after a popular fiction series had become a pop culture phenomenon. But there were still people who believed the gruesome, overdramatized, and often misguided facts presented by the media about the dangers of sex clubs and their ties to human trafficking.

I made my way through the upstairs, clearing each room except the last. With my gun drawn and flashlight in hand, I pushed open the door, ready for whoever or whatever was on the other side.

All I found was darkness. I spun around, wondering how our intel had been so wrong. This entire thing had been a waste of time. I should've been tracking down Solease, finally putting that bastard behind bars instead of searching a posh mansion on the outskirts of Atlanta. By now, half the bounty hunters in the country were hundreds of miles closer to him, circling like vultures to get their hands on the reward. I'd never be able to make up enough ground to catch up.

I stalked toward the door and holstered my weapon, ready to get the hell out of there before Diego came home and a waste of time turned into a clusterfuck of epic proportions.

Then I heard it. Faint, but my mind wasn't playing tricks on me. I rushed toward the excessively tall bed and fell to my knees, lifting up the bed skirt and exposing a metal cage underneath. A woman huddled near the opposite corner with her knees pulled to her chest, burying her face. She whimpered as I pointed my flashlight at her, and she scurried farther away, pressing her back flush against the other side.

"Ma'am," I said softly, shining the light on myself so she could see my face. "Your mother, Jeanine Halstead, sent me."

"Mom," she whispered with a shaky voice and peered over her knees, shrouded in a pile of brown hair.

Flashing my light on her again, I could finally see the big brown eyes from the photo staring back at me. "Hang tight. I'll have you out of there in a minute."

Nya scurried across the hardwood floor on her knees with tears running down her face. "Help me," she pleaded and wrapped her fingers around the bars until her knuckles turned white.

Diego was lucky he wasn't home. It would've been my pleasure to torture him slowly and watch him die, begging for his life like a little bitch, after the way I'd found her.

I darted my eyes to hers as she stared at me with her face pressed against the bars while I worked the lock. "You're safe now, little one. You're safe," I told her as I pried open the last chamber inside the lock, popping the metal clasp.

Nya crawled out, wearing nothing except the collar from the photograph. She could barely stand as she tried to push herself off the floor. Without a second thought, I wrapped my arms around her before she collapsed, cradling her. She clung to me, her fingers laced tightly around my neck as I jammed everything into my back pockets.

Running down the steps, I was out the front door and heading toward the car with Nya safely in my arms. She rested her head against my chest, still and silent as I stalked down the driveway toward my father. His eyes grew wide as soon as he saw the girl in my arms.

"The fuck. She's naked," he said in a low tone as I motioned for him to open the door so I could get her inside and us the fuck out of there.

"I didn't have time to dress her." I placed Nya in the back seat and grabbed a blanket I'd kept in the back just in case. "You're safe now," I repeated, trying to get her to calm down as I wrapped the blanket around her naked, trembling body.

"Don't go," she said, her voice soft and laced with fear as I backed away, about to close the door.

"This guy's an animal and deserves to be put down," my father said behind me, pacing next to the car like a caged lion. "I'll drive. You look after the girl." He didn't wait for me to answer as he opened the driver's-side door.

I didn't have time to argue, and with one look at Nya's face, I knew I couldn't sit in the front and leave her in the back, trembling and alone. Getting in on the other side, I maintained a safe distance from Nya—for her sake, not mine. After a traumatic experience, I knew human touch and even nearness could be overwhelming to a person. But instead of staying on the other side of the back seat, she crawled in my lap and wrapped her arms around my neck.

My dad's eyes were glued to the rearview mirror, watching in just as much shock as me as she placed her head on my chest. "Go," I told him, ready to get the hell out of Atlanta.

CHAPTER 2
NYA

"I can't." I gazed up at Ret with tears in my eyes, unable to find the right words to explain how I felt. "Not yet."

I couldn't go home. Not yet, at least. My parents already thought I was a freak, and if they found out what happened, they'd have me committed.

"I promised, Nya," Ret said from the bed next to me.

I chewed my lip and pulled the strings of my hoodie tighter, wishing I could hide. "My parents won't understand."

He rubbed the back of his neck, cursing under his breath. "I don't know if I understand either."

I kicked my feet, knocking the backs of my heels against the box spring and stared down at the dirty carpeting. "Do you know anything about…" I stopped, wondering the best way to approach the topic and to explain BDSM to him.

He nodded with a slight smile, eyes still on me like he could read my thoughts. "I do."

"Oh," I whispered, rolling the strings of the sweatshirt between my fingertips and digging my toes into the carpeting. "Diego was my Dom, and at first, I entered into our relationship willingly."

"Go on," he said softly.

"But after I graduated, I was ready to go to New York. I had a huge job opportunity there, and I thought Diego was coming with me."

"Did he say he was?"

"Not exactly." I closed my eyes and sighed, knowing I was about to sound like a complete idiot. "He said he wouldn't be able to let me go, but I figured he meant he was moving with me even though he never said the words."

"Don't be so hard on yourself. It was an easy mistake to make."

Covering my face with my hands, I laughed into my palms and tried to keep the tears at bay. "Two days before I was supposed to leave, Diego summoned me to his house, and I obeyed, and I never stepped foot outside of his mansion again."

"Your parents understand it's not your fault, Nya. Things like this happen. I wouldn't have a job otherwise."

I turned my head with my hands still covering my face and peeked through the slits between my fingers. "Dumb people like me, huh?" I mumbled.

"I will not allow you to talk about yourself like that, little one." His voice was firm yet kind. "We all make mistakes. Your parents will be happy just to have you home and safe."

I dropped my hands to my lap. "They think I'm a freak." I looked him straight in the eyes. "They'll think I deserved what happened to me and that I'll need Jesus to save me from my sexual deviance."

"There's nothing wrong with enjoying pleasure of any kind as long as it's consensual."

I held in my laughter because he'd clearly never met my parents. They made the Westboro Baptists appear sane. If anything involved pleasure, they were against it...especially sex.

"Your parents can't force you to do anything against your will. If they truly believe you deserved what happened, then you either set them straight, or you need to learn to deal with them from a distance to maintain your identity as well as your self-esteem. You're an adult, and although they're your parents, they're not in charge of your life anymore."

"It's easy to say, Sir, but not so easy to do."

"Ret, please," he corrected me.

"Ret," I replied and paused for a moment. "That man in the other room. He's your father, yeah?"

He sighed heavily and nodded. "Afraid so."

Ret's father, the man with the long beard and weathered face, didn't have an unkind word when he spoke to his son. He was patient, affectionate, and everything humanity should be, especially in regard to family.

"You're lucky to have such an understanding father. Mine is a minister, and sex, especially before marriage, that deviates from the norm is a hard limit for him."

"My father is the furthest thing from understanding, but the man is flawed himself. He can't pass judgment on me when he's messed up so much in his own life."

"At least he doesn't speak the word of God, putting the fear of damnation in you and preach at you every chance he gets."

My father had pounded the Gospel into my head for as long as I could remember. I sat in church every Sunday, the well-behaved daughter, at the side of my perfect mother. My father's sermons were filled with fiery hell and a message of redemption only through true faith and complete submission to the word of God.

Even as I'd sat there, listening to the words, I never believed a word of his speeches. The message of the Bible was forgiveness, generosity, and kindness. We were all supposedly children of God and should be accepted for who we were and not punished for how we were created.

When I'd question my father about faith and the existence of God, in private, of course, he'd go into an hour-long diatribe about my heathen ways and my eventual damnation that no amount of prayers could stop.

Ret's face softened, and he almost smiled. "Oh, he's preached, but his words aren't anything you'd find in the Bible."

I pulled my leg under my bottom and faced Ret. "That's what a good father should do. He shouldn't judge you and damn you to hell."

"True." He finally smiled.

"If I go back, I'll never be the same again," I said, holding back the tears because, even after the hell I'd lived, I didn't want to change into a bible-thumpin' robot. I didn't want to forget who I was, and there was no way in hell I'd become a clone of my parents, even if that meant pushing them out of my life forever.

"You don't know that."

"I do," I told him because I did.

"Maybe the time you spent apart changed them. The worry they felt for the last few months had to wear on them and may have softened their views. I'm sure they'll be more accepting."

I arched an eyebrow, calling bullshit, because I knew my parents better than anyone. "So, when they find out that in order to live out my sexual fantasy, I was a submissive, giving myself fully to a man who locked me up against my will, they'll think what?" I paused, rubbing my palms against the baggy sweat pants Ret had given me, and sucked in a breath. "They'll say 'Hallelujah, at least she's safe'? Come on. We both know better than that."

"Weirder shit has happened." He shrugged.

"Yeah," I muttered and took a deep breath.

I knew people changed, but there was no way my parents' viewpoint had made such a dramatic shift since I disappeared. If Jesus didn't make them nice, my disappearance wouldn't either.

"We better get some sleep. We have a long drive tomorrow," he said before turning off the bedside light.

I crawled under the covers and tried to get comfortable, but I hadn't worn clothing in two months. The feel of it against my skin felt foreign and intrusive.

Most nights, Diego had me in his bed, with my arms secured to the headboard and my ankles shackled to the end of the bed. He'd curl his bare body around my naked flesh, pinning me.

When Diego wasn't home, he locked me in the small, three-foot-tall cage in complete darkness. Those were the times I liked most. I didn't fear the blackness or being alone, because nothing or no one could hurt me. I dreaded his footsteps across the floor, coming to uncage me, only to chain me down again.

Pulling my legs to my chest, I turned to the side and stared at Ret through the darkness. His body covered more than half the bed, and his feet hung off the end, making him look like a giant…godlike, even.

Don't go there. Get your shit together, Nya.

You're free.

CHAPTER 3

RET

"Mrs. Halstead is here," James said from the doorway of my office before I could even get comfortable in my chair.

"We'll be right there," I told him.

Nya sat across from me, twisting her hands in her lap without an ounce of excitement on her face. I didn't imagine there would be any. Not after everything she'd told me. Her relationship with her parents was complicated, but that was typically how it was when children didn't fit into the pretty little mold that had been laid out before them.

I'd never had such issues. With my father off doing his own thing, my aunts raised my sister and me, but never once did they judge me for anything I did or wanted.

"Are you ready, Nya?" I asked, watching her closely and looking for any signs she'd run.

She swept her hand across her cheek, maybe wiping away a tear or as a nervous tic, but she didn't bring her eyes to mine. "I guess so. I don't have a choice."

"We all have choices."

She stood, eyes downturned toward the carpeting, but she didn't say another word. I'd taken part in a few family reunions, but usually,

684

the air crackled with so much excitement before the big moment that everyone in the office was pumped.

With Nya, that was not the case. From the moment she walked into ALFA, she made it quite clear that her parents were no better than the man who'd held her against her will.

The very idea of that was hard for us to wrap our heads around. Each of us had parents who weren't judgmental. They might have been overbearing and a pain in the ass, but they never tried to force us into something or made us feel like shit about our decisions.

Nya followed James down the hallway as I walked behind them, rubbing a knot out of my shoulders. I was ready to collapse after a restless night's sleep, wearing far too much clothing. All I wanted to do was get home and crawl under the covers with Alese, leaving everything behind.

James entered the conference room first, Nya practically hiding behind him. She glanced back at me as she stepped inside, and my stomach twisted from the pained expression on her face.

James stopped near the end of the conference table with Nya almost glued to his back. "Mr. and Mrs. Halstead."

A woman popped up from her chair as she glanced around. "Where is she?"

The woman exuded money with immaculate clothing, perfect hair, and flashy jewelry that was way too big for her small frame.

Nya stayed behind James for another moment before finally moving to his side, making herself visible to everyone. She lifted her face, brushing her brown hair over her shoulders, and straightened.

"Nya," her mother said, slowly approaching her with her arms outstretched.

Nya hadn't looked up and seemed frozen, almost catatonic, as she stood next to James. There wasn't any happiness about this event that should've been nothing less than joyous. Even when her mother wrapped her arms around Nya, giving her a tight hug, she didn't reciprocate.

Nya's hands were at her sides as she stood perfectly straight with her mother still holding her tightly. She stiffened even more when Mrs. Halstead whispered something in her ear.

"Nya," her father said, not moving from his spot, only giving her a slight and very sterile head dip as Mrs. Halstead finally released her.

"We can't thank you gentlemen enough for finding our little girl. We'll take her off your hands," Mr. Halstead said, motioning for what appeared to be a doctor they'd brought with them.

My hands curled into tight fists, and James's went rigid. We were here for a happy reunion, not for giving Nya over from one type of imprisonment to another.

The man stood, moving toward Nya with a syringe in his hands. She stepped back, moving closer to me and putting as much distance between herself and him as she could.

What the fuck was wrong with these people? They were exactly as Nya had described them and even worse than I could've ever imagined.

"Now, Nya. This is Dr. Faraday. He's here from the Biltmore Institute. He's going to help you get better."

"I'm not sick," she finally spoke, raising her head up to face her father.

James stepped in front of Nya, and I pulled her back to my side, blocking the doctor and her family from her.

"You're not well either, dear. Just let the good doctor give you something to help you settle down."

"We can't let you do that, sir," James told Mr. Halstead.

"Shh," I said to Nya who was practically in tears as she stared up at me with the widest eyes.

She wrapped her hand around my arm, tethering herself to me. "Don't let them take me," she begged.

"Mr. Caldo, we paid you for the safe return of our daughter and nothing more. She's ours."

James didn't back down as he squared his shoulders and stood his ground. "She's not property, sir."

"What's going on here?" my father asked from behind me.

I peered back, giving him a look that said there wasn't a damn thing good happening. As if on instinct, I grabbed Nya's hand and passed her off to Bear. He took her without question, ushering her toward his office as James and I blocked the doctor and Mr. Halstead from advancing.

"You have no right to keep our daughter from us." Mrs. Halstead stalked toward the door, trying her best to get past us, but it wasn't happening.

I stepped to the side, obscuring the entire doorway and stopping anyone in the room from leaving or going after Nya. Bear wouldn't let anyone get their hands on her. He'd protect her with his life, and there wasn't a person at ALFA who would let anything happen to her, including me.

"Mrs. Halstead, your daughter doesn't need to be drugged and institutionalized. She's been through enough. I've spoken to her at length, and she's of sound mind," James said.

"Where did you get your degree, good sir?" the doctor asked, syringe still in his hands.

"My job is to know people. I've worked at the CIA, and I have skills you could only dream of, Dr. Faraday. Unless you have a court order to commit Nya, you will not touch her, and she won't be leaving with you today," James told her father.

"How dare you?" Mr. Halstead stepped up to James, but he didn't so much as flinch.

We'd been confronted by men a hell of a lot meaner and more dangerous than this rich asshole. He wouldn't get far, no matter how much he raised his voice and no matter how much he threatened us. Nya wasn't going anywhere as long as she had the team at ALFA behind her.

"We paid you for her return, Mr. Caldo, and you haven't delivered."

"I refuse to take any more of your money. I will not allow you to force her to be committed, and we won't permit her to leave with you today under any circumstances."

Thomas entered the room, and I took the chance to duck out, letting them handle the Halsteads while I went to find Nya and tell her she had nothing to worry about.

When I entered my father's office, Nya was sitting in the corner, holding her knees, and rocking gently with her face buried. Bear looked at me and shrugged, completely lost on how to handle a situation like this.

I motioned for him to step out, leaving Nya and me alone to talk. Slowly, I lowered myself down to the floor next to her, waiting in silence until the door clicked closed.

"Nya," I said, keeping my voice soft and calming. The last thing she needed was something more to jar her, pushing her deeper inside herself. "You're safe."

She slowed her rocking but kept her face hidden, pressed against her knees. "I told you they were horrible people."

"You did." I wanted to touch her, soothe her in some fashion, but I knew better than that. After everything she'd been through, touch was something that needed to be avoided if possible.

"I'm not sick, Ret."

"I know you're not."

"You should've left me with Diego."

My entire body tensed as anger flooded me. Not toward Nya, but her asshole parents for making her feel as though she was better off with a sick fuck like Diego. "Don't ever say that. It doesn't matter what your parents want, Nya. We won't let them take you."

She lifted her head, and her eyes met mine. She blinked, probably figuring I was full of shit. But I hoped I'd gained a small sliver of her trust in the last twenty-four hours so that she'd have faith in my word. "I don't have to leave with them?"

"You're an adult. They can't force you to do anything, and I won't allow them to lay a hand on you. I didn't save your life for you to lose it again."

She chewed on her bottom lip and stared at me. I let her process my words as I sat a foot away, not moving. "Where am I going to go, Ret?"

I hadn't thought that far ahead. None of us had. We saw a woman in need. No one in the office wanted to hand her over to be placed in a worse situation than she was before. "I have a guest room you can use until you figure out your next move."

She glanced at my finger, catching sight of my ring. "But what about your wife?"

Pressing my thumb against the gold circle, I twisted the thick ring around my finger. "We're not married. She's my partner, my submissive, but not my wife."

"Will she have a problem with it?"

"I'll talk with Alese, but I'm sure she'll be okay. She'll understand."

For the first time since I found her, I saw a smile spread across Nya's face. Alese probably wouldn't be overjoyed by the idea, but that was for me to handle.

"Say that again."

Alese's expression was hard to pin down. I knew her better than anyone in the world, but in that moment, I wasn't certain if she wanted to kick me in the balls or not.

Alese and I met a few years ago. I was a Dom and she was a bit lost, not sure if she was a top, bottom, or switch. I had been about to give up my search for a submissive and move to a new city to start over again, when Alese became something of a pet project. My goal was to help her figure out where exactly she fell in the lifestyle, but after spending time with her, I knew I wanted no one else.

She tried my patience at times. Her road to discovering her inner submissive wasn't an easy one, but it sure as hell was entertaining. I couldn't imagine being with anyone else either. She challenged me in so many ways.

"She needed someplace to go. I thought she could crash here for a bit."

"Is the girl damaged?"

I rubbed my hands together and debated how many of the details I should divulge to Alese. She deserved to know everything, but I didn't want to throw it all in her lap at once. "She doesn't appear so. She needs to be treated with kindness after what she's been through, but her parents don't seem to understand what happened or the lifestyle she was trying to enjoy when her world ended."

"Tell me how she ended up a prisoner."

"She met a Dom, much like you met me, and he made her believe they were going to have a relationship. Before she knew it, she was his captive without any communication with the outside world. What started out as fun led to her being locked in a cage under his bed and his sex slave."

Alese peered around me to look toward the car where Nya sat in the passenger seat, waiting for my sign. "That's just awful."

"It is." I nodded as Alese's body relaxed, and I knew she wasn't about to say no.

"Her parents wanted to commit her?"

"Yep. They had a doctor with them, waiting to drug her."

"I can't imagine. She can stay until she's back on her feet."

"Thank you, *piccola*."

Alese stepped toward me, wrapping her arms around my middle and burying her face in my chest. "You didn't even have to ask, you know. I wouldn't have protested if you told me she was staying."

I wrapped my arms around her and held her tighter than usual. "I'm your Master in the bedroom, but we're partners in life, Alese. I couldn't bring a stranger into our home without you having a say in the situation."

"It'll be nice to have another woman around, even if it's only for a little while. There's way too much testosterone in this place for me sometimes."

I laughed softly and touched her chin, raising her face to mine. "I'm sure you two will get along well."

"I'll help her any way I can."

I placed my lips against hers, kissing her as her boyfriend and not her Dom. Our relationship had changed over the years, leaving our play for the bedroom or the club. Alese, although a complete submissive, wasn't my slave. She had her own life to live, and I embraced everything she wanted to do as long as it didn't take her away from me.

I had no doubt that she would be good with Nya. She'd help her through this time, building her up and helping her transition back into society under her careful eye. Alese had a way with people, softer than I'd ever been and more loving toward everyone.

CHAPTER 4

NYA

Sitting in the car, I watched Ret as he spoke to Alese. She kept peering over his shoulder as she stood on the front steps, staring at me through the car window. I couldn't imagine what she thought about him bringing home a strange woman.

The house was three stories, white with gray accents, a stark contrast to the deep, cloudless sky behind the structure. Peeking through the space between Ret's house and the neighbors, the ocean crashed against the sand and sea gulls flew overhead, almost beckoning everyone to follow.

Ret glanced backward and smiled before facing Alese again. Maybe I should've gone with my parents, letting them do whatever they wanted to make me better instead of adding complications to Ret's life since he was the man who saved me. He'd already gone above and beyond his job, making me feel safe when I hadn't even thought that was possible.

Ret and Alese were a perfect pair. His wide shoulders, imposing height, and masculine face were like something straight out of a Hollywood movie. He'd absolutely be one of those badass characters who put down the bad guy with a few kicks and a knockout punch to the face. Alese was the complete opposite. Smaller framed, with deli-

691

cate features, and totally feminine in every way possible. Her large breasts, tanned by the Florida sun, practically spilled out of her tank top.

I was just about to get out and call the entire thing off when Alese walked toward the car. At first, I wanted to sink down into the seat and disappear, but as she got closer, she smiled.

"Hey, Nya." She stood near the passenger door, not too close, yet close enough that I could see the tiny freckles dotting her chest. "You want to come inside?" she asked.

I twisted my hands in my lap, glancing down for a moment. "I should just leave," I whispered, probably looking like a lunatic sitting in the car carrying on a conversation with myself.

"Come on. Let's get you settled and out of the heat before you melt in there, princess."

The handle jiggled, and I snapped out of whatever moment I was having and looked up as Alese opened the door. "Sorry," I whispered. I didn't know if I was sorry I had ignored her so far or I hadn't bothered to climb out of the car myself, but saying the words made me feel better.

"Don't be silly. There's nothing to be sorry about."

I climbed out, inhaling the salty-humid air for the first time in months.

"Beach lover?" she asked.

"I used to be."

I'd missed the ocean. I'd spent countless days lying on the white sand of Florida when I was younger, listening to the waves roll in, crashing against the shore before rolling back out again. I never really appreciated the beauty and tranquility of living so close to the ocean until I didn't have it anymore. There were nights, more than I could remember or wanted to, where I lay inside that cage, closed my eyes, and dreamed that I was lying under the scorching hot sun, soaking up the rays. That was the only way I kept my sanity for so long in captivity.

"I am. I spend time every day listening to the waves. It's therapeutic and soothing."

"It is." I didn't go into any more detail. Didn't tell her that picturing a place like this was the only way I'd kept myself sane while I was locked in Diego's cage or strapped to his bed.

"How about we head down to the beach before we go inside? Would you like that?"

I glanced at Ret, still standing near the front steps, and he nodded. I wasn't really looking for his permission, but I didn't want to impose more than I already was. "I'd like that a lot."

Alese walked toward the side of the house, and I followed closely behind her. "Ret, can you bring us some wine?"

"Let me make a call, and I'll be right out," he said.

"So, you and Ret are..." I left the statement open because I didn't know how to finish it.

Ret had filled me in on how they'd met...much the same way I'd met Diego. Watching them now, I wouldn't be able to tell that he was her Dom or that she had an ounce of submissiveness in her, but Ret told me they saved that for the bedroom. If I hadn't heard it with my own ears, I never would've believed it.

"I love that man with my whole heart."

I didn't know what to say to that, but I was a little jealous I hadn't experienced love like that yet.

"We met a few years back. I was a switch, and Ret told me I was a submissive instead and challenged me. The rest is history."

We came to the back of the house, and touching the horizon was a virtually endless aqua blue sea. For a moment, I wondered if I was dreaming everything and I was still trapped under Diego's bed. Maybe he'd killed me or I was unconscious after one of his rough moments, and my mind had taken me away to a better place. I didn't realize I'd stopped walking until Alese backed up and softly touched my arm.

"Are you okay? Is this too much?"

I shook my head and kicked off my sandals, digging my toes into the warm, dry sand. "It's just so beautiful."

Alese didn't speak, just stood at my side as I took in the beauty in front of me. For a moment, I felt breathless and dizzy, the sensation of freedom finally crashing over me like the waves rolling up the sand just a few feet away.

Leaving my sandals near the grass, I walked toward the water, unable to take my eyes off the rhythmic waves as they swept across the shore as if calling me forward. I moved slowly, taking in every sound and sight I'd missed and dreamed of since the last time I'd stepped foot in Florida.

When I sat down, Alese moved to my side, sitting just a foot away. I drew my knees up to my chin, staring out at the vastness, in awe of the beauty. I almost became overwhelmed.

"Did you want to be alone?" she asked.

"No," I said quickly. I wasn't ready to be alone again.

"I brought the white," Ret said, coming up behind us before he sat down next to Alese.

"Good choice," she said, but I didn't glance over.

My eyes were too fixed on the horizon and the way the sun danced off the water like glitter dotting the surface. I'd never thought I'd see the Gulf of Mexico again. I'd never really thought I'd see much of anything besides the inside of Diego's mansion until he grew bored of me. Being back on the sand, with the sound of the waves and the relentless sun burning brightly overhead, I knew Diego had not broken me. He might have stolen time from me, but he didn't steal my soul. I'd be okay. It would take time for me to get back to the happy girl I once was, but for the first time in a long while, I felt like it was entirely possible.

"Would you like a glass, Nya?" Alese asked and held a wineglass in front of me.

I turned my face, smiling at the beautiful, kind woman at my side before taking the glass from her hand. "Thank you, Alese."

"Let's toast." She raised her wineglass and held it in front of her, waiting for us to join. I did the same, followed by Ret. "To new beginnings," she said. "We've all needed one at some point, and although it's scary at times, there's nothing more wonderful than possibilities."

We clinked our glasses together, but I didn't reply. Her words were true and profound. I once again had a world of possibilities at my feet, and no one, not even my parents or Diego, could stop me from following my dreams.

I sipped the wine, savoring the flavors as they danced across my tongue. For two months, I'd had nothing to drink except water, but even that was when Diego felt like giving me a sip. I held the delicate glass between my two palms, stared out across the water, and drank the wine as slowly as possible because the taste was just as magnificent as the scene before me.

"Maybe we can watch the sunset later," Alese said.

I remembered going to the beach with my parents, watching the sun as it kissed the horizon and the sky filled with the most brilliant shades of pink and orange. There was nothing more beautiful or awe-inspiring than the moment the sun finally disappeared, illuminating the sky in one final light show before darkness descended across the bay.

"I'd love that," I said.

"Whatever you ladies want, I'll make happen," Ret said easily.

God, Alese was the luckiest girl in the world.

CHAPTER 5

RET

"Are you okay with this?" I tangled my fingers in Alese's blond hair as she placed her head on my chest and stroked my skin with her fingernails.

She peered up with her beautiful blue eyes and gave me a small smile. "I am. I wasn't sure at first, but after spending time with her, I can't imagine ever letting her parents get their hands on her."

I turned my head and kissed her forehead, content and happy to have someone as caring and understanding as Alese by my side. "I know. They're not good people."

She curled back into me, stroking my chest again with her hand. "Thank God we don't have to deal with people like that in our lives."

"Sometimes we forget how fortunate we are. I'm sorry I headed out of town without talking about it with you first. I know I promised I wouldn't do that again."

She flattened her palm against my chest and sat up a little, looking me in the eyes. "You were a naughty boy, Mr. North. Maybe I should teach you a lesson." She giggled, sounding just like me when we played.

"Mind your place, woman." I smirked.

"Someone's getting a spanking."

I grabbed her wrist, rolling over and taking her with me, pinning her under my body. "You missed me."

She struggled a little, pretending she wanted to get away. Something she liked to do to make her feel she had some control over the situation, when we both knew she didn't. "I did not miss you." She glanced toward the ceiling, giving me attitude.

"Come on, *piccola*. You missed me…or at least my cock." I smirked, sliding my lower half between her legs. "I bet if I touched your pussy, you'd be dripping for me already."

Her eyes darted to mine for a second, and that was all it took for her to break down and grin. "You locked up all my toys before you went out that night, and then you took off. Do you know how hard it is for me to come using only my fingers?"

Alese had a bad habit of masturbating when I wasn't around. Our agreement was no coming without me, but she hadn't been able to keep her end of the bargain lately. To mess with her a little, I'd lock up every single toy I could find and take the key with me when I left. She always complained, but I made sure she never went to bed without at least one orgasm when I was home.

"Am I supposed to feel bad for you?"

She narrowed her eyes, and any trace of her smile vanished. "You should."

"It was one night. You could've waited."

"You know my sex drive is off the charts lately. Waiting a day is nearly impossible anymore."

"What am I going to do with you?"

She arched an eyebrow, the cocky grin back. "You can fuck me and make me come at least twice."

"At least twice?"

Fucking women. Luckiest sons of bitches on the planet. They could come over and over and over again without a single moment of rest in between. Shit like that didn't happen for men except in fiction and the movies. Our bodies needed time to recover, but not Alese. She could go all night and still beg for more.

She placed her hands on my face and brought my lips down to

hers, gazing into my eyes. "Three times is fine. I'm not picky," she said, grinding her pussy against my cock. "I deserve as much."

I wasn't going to argue with her or deny her what she wanted. This wasn't about play or orgasm denial, something I'd found useful with Alese over the years. Sliding my hand down her side, I glided my fingers across her abdomen as I lifted my body and moved to her side.

I lowered my mouth to hers, sealing her moans as my fingers grazed her clit and slipped through her wetness. She let her knees drift to the bed as she spread her legs as far apart as possible, silently begging to be penetrated. Alese loved to be filled. My finger, cock, toys…it didn't matter as long as she was stuffed.

Moving slowly, I pushed my fingers inside, curling them ever so slightly to press on her G-spot. Her nails dug into my skin and held me in place, rocking with my movement. Every time I pushed my fingers deeper, my thumb would skid across her clit and cause her body to quake with anticipation. I loved that about her. Her body was always so responsive to me, always so ready for whatever I gave, and she never seemed to get enough.

My pace quickened, and I pushed my fingers deeper, moving in and out of her faster as our tongues danced together in a frantic and haphazard rhythm. My cock ached to be inside, surrounded by the lush warmth of her pussy, but the first orgasm wasn't about me and never had been.

I pushed a third finger inside, stretching her to the limit, which earned me a strangled cry of passion as her lips fell away from mine. She pressed the back of her head into the pillow, and her mouth fell open as she gasped for air the closer the orgasm came. My strokes became more focused, the pads of my fingers pushing hard on her G-spot with each swipe before thrusting back into her.

She arched her back, thrusting her breasts into the air and closer to my lips. Her skin glowed in the moonlight streaming in through the bedroom window, covered in a fine sheen of sweat and sex.

Leaning forward, I closed my lips around her nipple and flicked the hardened tip with my tongue. Her pussy clamped down, drawing my fingers inward and pulsating as I sucked the puckered flesh.

I moved my hand faster, fingers thrusting harder and deeper as I closed my teeth around her nipple just to the point of pleasurable pain and sent her right over the edge. Her breathing halted, mouth wide open with her eyes closed, and her body convulsed at my side.

Watching a woman come, especially Alese, was the most beautiful thing in the world. Knowing I could do that to her was the biggest head trip in the world. She was mine entirely...mind, body, and soul. Every orgasm she had was because of me, and mine belonged to her.

____

When I woke in the morning, I rolled to my side to find the bed empty and Alese nowhere in sight. Last night, she'd received her three orgasms, deserving every single one of them. Many women in her shoes would've bitched me out for bringing another woman into our home. But my Alese, she had a heart as big as her libido. I'd move heaven and earth for her if it meant she'd be happy.

I slung my legs over the bed, leaning forward and yawning. The late night wouldn't help me focus today, and I knew the office would be a flurry of activity, especially after the shit that went down with the Halsteads.

A few minutes later, the sound of voices drew me downstairs. When I walked into the kitchen, Nya sat on a stool across the counter from Alese as she danced across the tile floor, singing into a spatula, wearing one of my old T-shirts.

When our eyes locked, she didn't stop her performance either. She swayed her hips to the beat, belting out lyrics about love and staring at me as if she'd written the song just for me. I didn't dare interrupt as I made my way around the counter and kissed her on the cheek before grabbing a coffee cup because it was entirely too early to be that energetic.

As Alese screeched out the final line, holding the very last note longer than necessary, Nya clapped wildly as she rose to her feet, giving Alese a standing ovation. "That was perfect. I'm not sure I've ever heard something so beautiful."

"You need to listen to more music," I said as I poured the coffee into my cup, barely able to see straight.

"Don't listen to him." Alese swatted my ass playfully, earning herself a warning glance. "He's always a little grumpy in the morning."

"I hope I didn't keep you two up too late," Nya said, clearly unaware of the real cause of my sleepiness.

"Nah. We're night owls. Anyway, he'll be fine after he has coffee. It takes him a little while to join the living."

I leaned against the counter and watched them over the rim of the mug. Nya returned to her stool as Alese finally started to stir the hash browns, which were on the verge of becoming cinders because she was more concerned about her performance than their meal.

"So, do you want to go shopping today?" Alese glanced back at Nya.

Nya sighed and sagged against the counter as her brown hair spilled forward. "Yeah, but..."

"There's no buts about it, missy. We need to get you some clothes because my hand-me-downs aren't going to cut it." Alese smacked Nya's ass with her free hand and laughed. "Unless you're going to gain twenty pounds in a hurry."

"If she's eating your cooking, it'll never happen."

Alese turned to me, her blue eyes wide and wild, but we both knew she was a shitty cook. Somehow, she was even worse than Fran, and that crap was hard to pull off. It was like she purposely sabotaged every meal so I'd stop asking her to feed me. Luckily for me, my time in the military had dulled my palate to the point that I could eat sand if it filled my belly.

"I can't believe you just said that." Alese gawked at me as Nya giggled, covering her mouth with her hand.

That was the first time I saw a relaxed Nya, a little carefree and step closer back to the girl she probably had been before Diego got his hands on her. I don't know if it was me or maybe Alese's infectious playfulness that put her at ease, but in that moment, I knew I'd made the right choice. By surrounding herself with happy people, accepting people, she'd have an easier time sliding back into society than in the hands of her judgmental parents, no matter how many antipsychotic drugs they pumped her with.

I glanced at Nya as I slid my coffee cup along the counter. "You'll understand after you have her 'world-famous' hash browns."

"I'm going to stop cooking for you," Alese threatened, bumping me with her hip as she handed Nya a plate of her very well done and totally dry breakfast.

"Baby." I wrapped my arm around Alese's waist and pulled her against me. "Make me that promise again." She smacked me as I laughed. "I'm playing. I love your cooking."

That was the biggest lie I'd ever told in our relationship. Everything else I was truthful with her about, but when it came to her cooking, I just couldn't see the hurt in her eyes. She tried. God, how she tried to cook, but it didn't matter what she made, she fucked it up to the best of her ability.

"Good because I'm making your favorite."

Oh, shit. "My favorite" was really the worst thing in her entire repertoire. It was some sort of dried-out casserole, barely edible, and needed to be choked down with two beers.

"I could help," Nya said quickly. "I used to be a good cook." She pushed her food around the plate, suddenly sad. Maybe it was the *used to* part that made her happiness evaporate, but I saw the change just as Alese did.

"That would be great, but only if you want to. I could always use an extra pair of hands. We'll stop at the grocery store after we go to the mall."

"I'd like to feel that I'm contributing in some way."

I prayed that her version of cooking was better than Alese's. Hell, if it was even just a little better, maybe I could convince Alese to let Nya cook just so she felt useful. Maybe the work would help Nya regain some confidence. I didn't know what I was thinking, but I was willing to try anything to help her find herself again.

CHAPTER 6
NYA

"Let me see." Alese sat outside the dressing room as I changed into another outfit. She'd picked out easily thirty different items, and I didn't know how to process so many choices or even what was in style anymore.

I wanted a few pieces of comfortable clothes...nothing flashy or expensive. I didn't care to wear anything too revealing or formfitting, but Alese had other plans. She said I had to get at least five outfits and two pairs of shoes before we could leave the mall. I didn't really know how she expected me to pay for anything. I hadn't had a chance to get a new copy of my credit card or any identification since Diego had destroyed mine when he'd decided to keep me.

I stepped out of the dressing room in a pair of skinny jeans and a tank top with a built-in bra for support. I felt a little like my old self again, even if the jeans were tighter than I was used to wearing. After a few months of no clothes, material of any kind felt weird against my skin, almost suffocating, but I couldn't very well walk around naked without having my ass thrown in jail for public nudity.

Alese stared at me, tapping her chin before she motioned with two fingers for me to twirl in a circle. I turned slowly and caught a glimpse of myself in the mirror. When I'd graduated from college, I was a size ten, comfortable with my body and with a rock-hard plump ass I had worked hard to get.

But Diego fed me very little, restricting my food when he felt I didn't behave or react the way he wanted. Which, based on my flat ass and the hip bones peeking out below the hem of my tank top, happened more times than not. He was a sick bastard. I'd known I had to get away. Every day I'd planned my escape, waiting for him to fuck up, but the bastard was too calculating to let that happen.

"I look like an anorexic." I pushed on my hips, wishing I could get my bones to be not quite as visible, but only calories would do that. "I want my body back."

"Honey." Alese walked toward me and came to a stop behind me, her blue eyes finding mine in the mirror. "You're beautiful no matter what size you are. You want to go bigger and better? I'm down with that."

"I just want my old life back." Suddenly, I felt a mix of anger and sadness, unsure which one was more overwhelming. Tears filled my eyes as I stared at the waif in the mirror, all skin and bones with no ass or tits.

Alese slowly moved closer and wrapped her arms around my waist. "Oh, Nya. I'm so sorry, love. I'll do anything to make things better."

Tears filled my eyes because her tenderness was almost as unbearable as my sadness. No one besides Ret had shown me an ounce of compassion or caring in months, and I wasn't sure how to process the emotions that came with it. With Diego, I knew how to handle his anger...how to tap out of reality and let my mind drift to a faraway place, practically bringing on an out-of-body experience. But sweetness was something I forgot how to handle.

"Don't cry, love."

I wiped my cheeks, sniffling back the others that threatened to fall. I was not this girl. I had never been a crier. Rarely did I ever let Diego see me affected by his actions. I cried the first week he held me captive, but I quickly learned my tears were futile. He loved my tears, basically got off on my sadness, and that's when I learned sorrow was a meaningless emotion that only fueled his lust for me.

"Tears are useless," I whispered when she didn't let go of me.

"No, they aren't. Don't ever feel that way. When you're sad, cry. When you're mad, I'll take you to kickboxing so you don't break my shit."

I turned to face her, and she finally released her arms from around my waist. "I don't really get mad, Alese."

"You will, Nya. You're going to go through a process now that you've regained your freedom after what Diego did to you. You're going to be sad, then angry, then maybe you'll want revenge. Your healing will be in stages and not overnight. If you want to cry, cry. I'll get the wine, and we can cry together."

"What do you have to cry about?"

She placed her hands on my shoulders and gazed into my eyes with a sweet, sorrowful smile. "I'll cry with and for you. For your loss of innocence. For your loss of trust. For your loss of time. There's so many reasons I'd cry with you. Imagine all the women still trapped in a situation like you were in, but without anyone who bothered to look for them."

"I'm grateful to my parents for hiring someone to track me down, but I can't be with them. Does that make me a horrible human being?"

"It doesn't."

"Thank God. I have enough baggage to deal with on top of everything."

"Nya." Alese held out her arms like she wanted to hug me, but she didn't step forward. "Can I?"

Alese was one of those people who just threw off good vibes. It was hard not to like her. Hard not to find her energy infectious and her carefree attitude calming when everything around me felt foreign. "You may," I told her, but I moved my arms around her first.

She embraced me, gently at first, again careful not to set off any triggers. I tightened my hold on her, almost tethering myself to her body as I placed my head on her shoulder. For the first time in as long as I could remember, I felt something besides fear when someone touched me. Never had a hug meant so much even when it was such an inconsequential gesture that I wouldn't have thought twice about before.

We stood there holding each other for a few minutes. I almost cried again, but I fought back the tears because I didn't want Alese to think I was upset. I wasn't. I felt joy, comfort, peacefulness as I stood in her arms with my eyes closed.

"Can I help you ladies?" the saleswoman asked, interrupting our moment.

"We're fine. We'll take everything," Alese replied and tightened her hold when I tried to wiggle free.

"Fabulous." The saleswoman was beyond excited to hear the news.

"You can't," I said, feeling a little uncomfortable that she was going to foot the bill for all the clothes I had tried on.

"Shh." She gave me a hardened stare. "Everything."

"I'll pay you back," I whispered.

"Cook this week, and we'll call it even."

I gawked at her, confused by the offer. "That's not fair."

"Seriously. I hate to cook. I keep making things worse and worse, hoping Ret will take over, but he never does. He just keeps eating the burned shit like it's the best damn thing he's ever put in his mouth."

I laughed and shook my head. "You do it on purpose?"

She raised an eyebrow, waving her hands in front of her pristine outfit, straight down to her designer pumps. "Do I look domestic?"

"Well." I stepped back, taking in her beauty. Alese was drop-dead gorgeous with lush curves and no sharp edges. Her long blond hair was swept over her shoulder, half pulled back in a braid that looked like something out of a fashion magazine. "You definitely don't look like a boring housewife. I'm super jealous."

Even her makeup was on point, something I'd never been able to pull off. I was a chick, but I sucked at anything girlie. Who knew that was even possible? But somehow, I lacked any skills when it came to makeup and hair. I watched hundreds of online tutorials, which made that shit look easy, but every time, I came out looking more like a train wreck than a runway model.

"I will teach you all my skills. We have the clothes. Now we just need your hair and makeup."

I pulled at the messy braid I'd attempted before we'd walked out the door. Pieces stuck out, making it look like more of a mess than an actual style. Trying on clothes, repeatedly pulling things over my head, didn't help the situation either.

"I'm a disaster," I mumbled as I started to walk back to my dressing room.

"Don't say that. You're a knockout."

My insides warmed with her compliment. It had been too long since I'd heard anything nice said about me. I was never the type of person who needed the affirmation, but after months of listening to Diego tell me I was a worthless piece of trash, hearing the opposite was more than nice... It was exactly what I needed to feel a little more human.

I glanced at her over my shoulder, smiling as she stood near the mirror with her hands resting on her hips. "Thanks, Alese."

She nodded once and shooed me toward the dressing room. "Go get changed. We have a long day ahead of us."

———

I TOSSED and turned for the fifth time before I threw off the covers and moved my legs over the side of the bed, unable to sleep for the second night in a row. Spending the day with Alese made me feel more alive than I had in a long time, but it didn't keep the nightmares at bay.

Every time I closed my eyes and started to fall asleep, I'd see Diego's face and startle awake. My heart beat erratically, and I couldn't seem to catch my breath. I stayed awake until I was so exhausted I practically passed out.

I peered around the dimly lit bedroom, thankful for the night-light Alese gave me yesterday. I told her I wasn't sure I could sleep, and she thought it would be the best way to make me feel a little safer instead of lying in the darkness. She was right, it did help, but not enough to make sleep come any easier.

I padded across the floor carefully, turning the handle of the door slowly to avoid waking up Alese or Ret. They'd already done so much for me, and I didn't want to disturb them more than I already had.

I glanced down the hallway, making sure the coast was clear before I stepped outside my room. The guest bedroom was at the end of the hallway, which was lined with doors to an office and the master suite.

The house seemed small yet perfect, compared to the compound Diego owned. I remembered the first time I walked into his mansion before he decided to keep me. I thought he lived like royalty, and I couldn't imagine what it would feel like to have that much money.

I grew up a privileged child. My parents had more money in the bank than they knew what to do with, but they didn't spend it on palatial mansions, opting to hoard as much as possible for God knows what. There was a difference between being wealthy and being rich. My parents were wealthy, but Diego was filthy rich. A man with his bank account didn't have to be bothered with anything, including the law, and I knew that firsthand.

A tiny beam of light shone from the doorway of their bedroom. At first, I scurried past the cracked door, but I backed up a step when I heard Alese's voice.

Curiosity got the better of me as I peered in through the small opening. Ret sat on the foot of the bed with Alese across his lap, naked and with her hands bound. Ret held the rope between his fingers, stopping Alese from falling over, while his other hand glided across the bare skin of her ass.

I touched the handle, ready to rush in to save her, until she lifted her face and a smile played on her lips.

"What did I tell you about that, *piccola?*" Ret asked, his hand still sweeping across her skin in circles. "Have you learned your lesson yet?"

"I'm sorry, Sir."

He raised his hand, and I held my breath. "You didn't answer my question, little one."

She bucked wildly as his hand came down against her ass, raising her head as her feet kicked in the air. I gasped, shocked to see Ret be so harsh with her after everything I'd witnessed the last two days.

I couldn't move. It was like my feet were glued to the floor. I knew I shouldn't be watching. I knew I should've run back to my room and sealed myself inside, but I couldn't, no matter how many times I told myself to go.

"I learned. I learned," she called out, closing her eyes as his hand went back to her ass, but this time to soothe the skin he'd just battered.

He stared down at her and loosened his grip on the ropes around her wrists for a moment, but I couldn't see his eyes. "You love to be spanked, don't you?"

She nodded, and he jerked the ropes. "Yes, Sir. I love when you spank me."

I gasped for air, forgetting that I hadn't been breathing because I'd been so engrossed in the scene playing out before me.

"Are you wet, my sweet?"

"I'm always wet for you, Master."

His hand drifted between her legs as a low hum came from his throat, and Alese stilled in his lap. She moaned as his hand disappeared. My insides convulsed, a small piece of the sexuality I once felt returning.

Before everything went sideways, when I was just a clubgoer, I loved to be finger-fucked. It was the number one thing that got me off. There was something more demanding about it, more pleasurable than a cock. Or maybe it was the fact that a majority of the dicks I'd had inside me were never big enough to get me off.

"Greedy little cunt," he grunted, working his fingers into her faster, harder.

She mewed, pushing her ass against his hand, wanting more, like I'd asked for a hundred times myself. I stepped back, feeling like an asshole for watching them, but I forgot to remove my hand from the doorknob because I'd been so engrossed.

The door creaked softly, and my eyes widened, panic setting deep in my bones. Ret's head snapped up, but his hands never left Alese. He peered toward the doorway and narrowed his eyes, but he didn't stop. I held my breath again, staying stock-still and praying he'd think it was just the wind or maybe something else. I wanted him to think it was anything except for me watching from the hallway.

When he didn't come charging toward the door and returned his full attention to a very naked Alese, I tiptoed back to my room and locked myself inside.

I crawled under the covers, and I felt something I hadn't in a long time. I slipped my hands under the sheet and into my shorts, closing my eyes as I replayed Ret and Alese over and over again until my muscles tightened and an orgasm unlike any I'd felt in a long time ripped through my system. I gasped for air, rocking in the aftermath until sleep pulled me under.

CHAPTER 7

RET

"How's shit going?" Bear asked as he sat down next to me at the conference table, prepping for our morning meeting.

"Good." I didn't know what the man wanted to hear. He must've thought I was going to bring home a woman who had basically been a sex slave for two months and that we'd have wild orgies.

"You have two women under the same roof, and all you can say is good?"

Bingo. The man never ceased to amaze me. He always had sex on the brain, and I almost felt sorry for Fran. Almost. She was just as much of a spitfire as my father and just as much of a troublemaker.

"Nya isn't mine, Pop. Remember?"

He nodded slowly, pursing his lips. "I know, but come on."

"You saw how she was when we found her? What did you think was going to happen with the three of us?"

He glanced toward the ceiling like he was dreaming up every scenario possible, stroking the hair on his chin. "I dunno, but something."

I shuffled the paperwork in my hands, organizing it in priority order for later. "The girls went shopping yesterday."

"Sounds exciting," he mumbled and rolled his eyes.

As if on cue, the rest of the ALFA team filed into the conference room, looking just as tired as I felt. I hadn't planned to stay up so late last night, but I couldn't get my fill of Alese, and she seemed insatiable. Afterward, I kept thinking about Nya and seeing her outside our door, watching us. I wondered what she thought, how she felt, and if it bothered her in any way.

I didn't let it stop what I was doing. I didn't ease up on Alese because Nya saw something she shouldn't. The fact that I found her fast asleep in her bedroom this morning instead of rocking in the corner was a step in the right direction.

"First off," James said, standing at the head of the conference table and leaning on his knuckles. "I want to talk about Nya Halstead and what has transpired since we didn't release her to her family."

The chatter around the table died down, and everyone turned their attention to James. I was waiting for this talk, wondering if we were going to be sued for some bullshit reason because rich assholes like the Halsteads could make just about anything happen if they threw enough cash at it.

"Last night we received a letter from their attorney for breach of contract. I feel like it's the first step in their offensive to try to regain control of their daughter," James told us.

They were grasping at straws, but I was sure with enough time and resources, they'd find something else to hurl at ALFA to make us pay.

"Ret, I need you to take Nya for a mental evaluation. We need to know if she's of sound mind or if she is any way sick and in need of therapy," James said.

"I'll get that done as soon as possible." I gave him a chin lift before jotting myself a note. It would be the first thing I'd do today and probably the most important.

"Her health and safety are our first priority. We've never experienced this with a case before. As you know, we always return the missing family member, especially children, but the Halsteads and Nya are a special case," James continued.

The rest of the ALFA team sat quietly, listening to James and scribbling on their legal pads. I glanced down at my dad's paper, and he was drawing a stick figure of a woman with very large breasts. The man would never grow up. But then, he wouldn't be the same if he ever did.

"If we know she's of sound mind and can make her own decisions, we'll be able to fight the Halsteads without any issue. If she's in need of help, we'll have to make it happen or else we could find ourselves in even deeper legal trouble. I've put in a call to a doctor and an attorney at my club, and we'll be enlisting them in our fight," James finished.

"Ret." Thomas set his phone down and gazed down the table as James sat down next to him. "Why don't you call Alese and have her bring Nya here? We'll have an appointment scheduled with the doctor this afternoon and get the ball rolling."

"On it."

"Now, let's talk about some of our other cases. Sam, where are you at with the Connor case?" Thomas asked.

"I'm meeting with Mrs. Connor today. I've been able to track all the money her ex-husband stole from her. It wasn't easy, but I have a long enough paper trail for her to bring it to a judge and seize his assets."

While the guys talked about the Connors, I grabbed my phone, shooting Alese a quick message. I knew she wasn't a fast mover, especially in the morning. If I didn't know better, I'd swear the girl had molasses in her veins.

Me: Alese, swing by the office in a few hours with Nya, and I'll take you both to lunch.

Alese: But it was makeup day… Can we do lunch another day?

Makeup day? I didn't even want to know what kind of girl shit that involved, but I was pretty sure it would result in a substantial charge on Alese's credit card. I didn't understand why she bothered with all that crap. She was a knockout without a drop of makeup on her face.

Me: It's more than lunch. She needs to be seen by our physician, and I thought I'd treat you two to lunch as a bonus.

I needed to speak with Nya to get a feel for her mental health after what she saw last night. If it affected her in any way, the meeting with the doctor could be an absolute mess. I only hoped that what she saw didn't bother her and that it didn't set her back or remind her of the time she spent with Diego.

Alese: You got it! We'll be there at eleven, 'kay?

Me: Perfect.

————

Nya and Alese came barreling through the door of ALFA three minutes late in a fit of laughter. If I hadn't witnessed it myself, I wouldn't have believed Nya was ever a victim, let alone captive for over two months. Everything I learned in the military about imprisonment and the toll it could take on someone's psyche didn't seem to apply to her.

Maybe it was the fact that some part of her enjoyed the treatment Diego gave her. The BDSM lifestyle was complicated, and sometimes the mindfuck it offered served the different needs and fetishes of certain people.

She seemed at peace around Alese. I was sure some of that had to do with the fact that they were both women and that Nya's captor was a man. She probably wouldn't be as happy if it were only her and me without Alese present.

Angel raised an eyebrow, looking just as surprised as I was by their laughter. "You two having a good day?"

Alese leaned over Angel's desk, resting on her elbow as Nya eyed me from behind her. "The best. How about you, sweetheart?"

"You know…as well as I can with these guys."

I rounded the corner from the hallway and glanced at Angel, giving her a playful smirk. "I heard that."

"Not you, Ret. You're the easiest one here. The other guys…" She paused and glanced around. "They're a pain sometimes. Anyway, where are you headed?"

"Lunch," I said and wrapped my arms around Alese's waist, pulling her against me.

"Quickie?" Angel asked.

I peered over Alese's shoulder, staring at Nya, who was doing everything possible to avoid my gaze. "No, doll. Today, we're really having lunch."

Alese held me tightly, burying her face in my neck as I laughed. "It's a pity."

James walked into the room and cleared his throat, looming large as he always did. "Hello, Nya."

She lifted her head with no expression on her face. "Hello, Sir."

"Are you well?" He kept his distance, careful not to move too close to her because none of us really knew if she had any triggers.

I should've thought more about that before I brought her home. My need to rescue her from her parents outweighed my common sense. As a Dom, I should've been more cognizant of what she'd been through and spent a little more time getting to know her before I left her alone, especially with Alese. But it didn't even occur to me because she seemed calm and unafraid when we sat on the beach together.

"Yes. I'm well."

"She's great, James." Alese stepped away from me, peering up James's tall frame, and smiled. "We were supposed to have a makeup day, but Ret called us in."

His eyebrows drew downward, but he didn't ask. James had enough women in his life to know better than to ask. "I'm sure you can do makeup tomorrow."

"We can. Maybe I'll call Izzy."

James finally cracked a smile. "She'd probably like that."

"That girl is on point with her eyeliner."

I glanced upward before rubbing my forehead. "Let's get going, ladies. We have to be back at one." I held my arms out, ushering them both toward the door before I had to hear anything else about makeup.

"Have fun," Angel called out, always the chipper one in the office. I was thankful to have her around. There were far too many men around, and we needed a little softness, especially when clients came in.

"We will. Bye, James." Alese gave him a playful smile over her shoulder, which earned her a warning glance from me. "Don't be so serious all the time, baby."

"We'll talk about this later," I told her, tightening my grip on her hip. I wasn't really serious or pissed, but I knew Alese did shit just to get a rise out of me.

"You going to spank me again?" She grinned as Nya's eyes widened.

I raised an eyebrow, following her lead, but keeping my eyes on Nya, who was blushing. "If you deserve it."

"I always deserve it."

I leaned forward, brushing my lips against hers. "You mean you always want it."

"Can't blame a girl for going after what she wants."

She was relentless too. Alese wasn't one to shy away from a situation, especially if she could use it to her advantage. We didn't fight. There was no yelling. Any issue we had, we worked out in the bedroom. It seemed to keep the peace and made for the least complicated relationship of my entire life. The "Make Love Not War" slogan worked for us, and there was no way in hell I was messing that up.

CHAPTER 8
NYA

My face heated as I listened to Alese and Ret. They were being playful and didn't act any different from most of my friends in college. The only difference was I'd never watched one of my girlfriends and her boyfriend like I had the night before. I couldn't stop thinking about the way his hand landed, how she moaned in response, and the noises she made as Ret finger-banged her.

I remembered Diego being with me like that, some kindness and playfulness, when we'd meet at the club and do a scene together. It didn't change until he convinced me to move in with him. I foolishly thought our relationship would stay the same, but I learned quickly that the public persona he displayed was nothing like the monster he became behind closed doors.

"God, everything looks so good. I'm famished." Alese studied the menu at the little diner Ret suggested around the corner from his office. "What are you in the mood for, Nya?"

I glanced down at the three-page menu and didn't even know where to start. Everything sounded delicious, and if I'd had a stomach big enough, I would've had more than one dish. "Maybe a burger."

Ret smiled at me from across the table. "That's their specialty."

I still couldn't bring myself to look at him. Part of it was guilt for seeing something I shouldn't, and the other part... That was more complicated. Something about Ret turned me on, but I knew I shouldn't feel that way after everything I'd been through—and for the simple fact that he was Alese's man.

"That's what I'll order, then."

"I have to go to the ladies' room. Order me a BLT and sweet tea if she comes by," Alese said as she slid out of the booth.

Ret nodded, and I stared at her like a deer caught in headlights. "Want me to come?"

She stood next to me with her hand on my shoulder, squeezing it lightly. "Don't be silly. Stay and talk to Ret. I promise he doesn't bite."

The blush that had started to wane was fully back in place as I laughed off her statement, but my insides twisted into knots. I watched as Alese walked across the restaurant, rubbing my hands together in my lap and avoiding looking at Ret.

My biggest worry was that he saw me last night and was upset about it. Maybe he'd toss me out on my ass, or worse yet, lock me in my room. I didn't know what to think about anything anymore. Diego had robbed me of my ability to read people.

"Nya." Ret's voice was strong but not harsh. "Look at me."

I closed my eyes for a moment as the knot in my stomach grew to what felt like the size of a basketball. As I slowly opened my eyes, I let my gaze flicker to Ret's, and I held my breath.

"We need to talk about last night."

Damn it. He did see me.

"I know you were outside our door last night."

I squeezed my eyes closed again, tighter than before, and gritted my teeth, waiting for him to tell me it was time for me to find some other place to live.

"Nya..." He paused.

I opened my eyes again because I knew I couldn't avoid what was coming next. Not even closing my eyes could save me from my own stupidity.

"It's okay, Nya," Ret said softly.

My eyes snapped to his, the words he spoke surprising the hell out of me. "It is?"

"I hope what you saw didn't scare you. I know you've been through so much, and I'm not sure if it triggered any bad memories. But I want you to know that I love Alese very much, and I'd never do anything to hurt her."

I swallowed, my tongue practically sticking to the roof of my mouth as I blinked at him in confusion. How could he think he scared me? I guess it would be a natural thought after the way he found me, but nothing about what I witnessed made me think Alese was in danger.

"I'm sorry," I said again, at a loss for any other words.

"Did it scare you?"

I felt his penetrating gaze across the table even when I glanced down at my hands still twisting in my lap. "No, Sir. You didn't scare me."

"Did you have a nightmare afterward?"

"No."

"Does Alese know?"

I lifted my head, widening my eyes. "No way. I haven't said a thing."

"It's okay, Nya. We're open about our life, and that includes sex. Alese isn't shy, but I also didn't tell her that you watched us. That isn't my secret to share."

"I didn't mean to watch. I couldn't sleep and was going to get a glass of water. When I heard a slap, I couldn't stop myself from looking inside to make sure she was okay." I wasn't being totally truthful, but I was too embarrassed to say anything else.

"It's understandable, and your reaction was natural."

I gawked at him, shocked that he was so level-headed about everything. I thought he'd chastise me for invading their privacy even though that hadn't been my intent.

"It was?"

"I never want you to feel frightened or ashamed again, Nya. You've been through far too much to ever feel that way again. Right now, we'll keep it our little secret. If you ever want to talk to Alese about our relationship, she's very open and will probably talk your ear off, but her heart's in the right place."

"Thank you," I said just as the waitress walked up to the table, tapping her pencil against her tiny pad of paper.

Alese slid back into the booth, smiling at me before grabbing Ret's hand and intertwining her fingers with his. The tenseness I'd felt about what I saw and how Ret would react had vanished, but I still would never admit that what I saw turned me on. The emotions I felt about the entire situation and had started to feel about both Alese and Ret weren't right, and I knew it. Even after Diego fucked with my head, I could still tell the difference between right and wrong...even if my body couldn't.

I STARED AT DR. VALENTINE, fiddling with the hem of my dress as he spoke. We'd already been talking for an hour, and he didn't show any signs of stopping anytime soon. He did most of the talking, asking me about my experience and how I felt about everything. He questioned me about my sleep patterns, my appetite, and if anything had caused me a massive amount of stress since Ret rescued me.

"No, sir."

"Our meeting is confidential, Ms. Halstead. Anything we discuss will not be shared with anyone, including your parents or the employees here at ALFA."

I nodded, unsure if I could trust his words, but I knew, as a doctor, he wasn't legally allowed to share my information unless I gave him permission. But I'd seen my parents bully doctors into telling them things I didn't want them to know. Dr. Valentine wasn't my first shrink, after all. My parents had always tried to control me and usually enlisted a doctor to do it. That was why I went to college so far away; I needed to break free of their overprotective insanity.

"I know," I said softly, smoothing out my dress near my knees with my fingertips.

He scribbled something on the notepad before bringing his eyes to mine again. "Do you blame yourself for what happened?"

I shook my head, but I wasn't one hundred percent truthful. I played a role in my captivity. Diego didn't kidnap me off the street. I went willingly, giving myself to him, but I never thought he'd keep me from my family and society by locking me away in his bedroom.

"Do you feel like harming yourself?"

"No." My response was swift. In no way had I ever thought of harming myself. Life had always been precious to me. Even at the worst moments, the ones where I let my mind drift away, I never wished for my life to end.

He wrote something down, and it took everything in me to keep my ass planted in the seat and not rip the notebook clean out of his hand. I wondered if he was making a case to have me committed, or if all the answers I was giving him were wrong. "Am I broken?"

"You're much better than most who lived through the same experience. Although you've been through a horrific event, you don't seem to have a fear of others or a distrust that many victims feel afterward."

"Doctor…" I paused, swallowing roughly and squeezing my hands into tight fists. "There's only one man I fear, and he's hundreds of miles away. I can't imagine he'd come after me. He wouldn't risk the possibility of being arrested. In Atlanta, he had the police on his payroll, but in Tampa, he has no pull. When we drove across the state line, I knew I was safe and that Diego could never hurt me again."

"Mr. North has never frightened you?"

"Ret?" I gawked at the doctor because the question was laughable. "He saved my life, sir. Why would I be scared of him?"

Ret was the person I trust most in the world. Maybe I was being naïve, but him and Alese had been nothing short of amazing to me. The way they treated each other was filled with respect and love. Something I wished I found with Diego.

"There's no right or wrong way to respond, Ms. Halstead. Fear is a powerful thing, and even in the best circumstances, it's a very natural response after a traumatic event."

"Do you know about my lifestyle?" I asked, wondering if he was the right man to talk to me.

Often the men my parents would hire to be my doctor didn't have the slightest clue about the BDSM lifestyle, and they would judge me from the moment I walked in the room. I could never explain why being a submissive was a massive high or get them to understand about subspace.

"I do. I've been in the lifestyle with my wife for the last twenty years."

I lifted my eyebrows, completely taken aback by that information. It shouldn't have been surprising, but somehow it was.

"So, I understand the level of trust involved in and out of the lifestyle."

I nodded. "I've been sitting here, trying to figure out a way to explain my feelings about what happened with Diego. I know I should be rocking in a corner somewhere, crying about the time I lost, but I don't feel that way."

"There's no one way to feel or respond in a situation like this."

"I know. The months I spent with Diego, I kept lying to myself, repeating over and over again that he was just playing out an extremely long and sometimes cruel scene. When he became rough, I'd let my mind drift and escape whatever he was doing to my body to keep myself sane. I knew it wouldn't last forever. My parents have always stuck their noses where they didn't belong, and I knew it was only a matter of time before they'd come looking for me."

"Did you find pleasure with Diego?"

"Sometimes. But other times, when he was cruel, my body would respond even though I didn't want it to."

"We can't stop a natural response, Ms. Halstead."

"When I met Diego and we'd do scenes with each other at Charmed, he knew I loved pain just as much as pleasure. I think that's why he picked me. He didn't kidnap me from my house. I willingly moved in with him. In a way, I feel responsible for what happened to me."

"No matter how much you love pain or pleasure, no one has the right to hold you captive and keep you from those you love."

"Yes, sir. I know that. I knew that. Maybe if I were a normal girl who loved softness and had no concept of what BDSM was, I'd feel differently about the situation... Maybe I'd be committed at this point. But for the first time since I graduated from college, I feel like anything is possible, and I don't plan to waste another moment of my life living in fear."

I refused to be a victim. There was no way I would let Diego steal any more of my life after the hell he put me through. Maybe I was insane for not feeling the right emotions after everything I'd been through. I knew I didn't deserve what happened to me. No person, boyfriend, or Dom, had the right to steal my life because I loved to be spanked. Diego may have stolen some time, but he sure as hell wasn't going to steal my life.

CHAPTER 9
RET

Nya's results were probably surprising to the others, but based on just the short amount of time I'd spent with her, I wasn't shocked. Even after everything she'd been through, she didn't seem afraid or fearful of me in any way, and I hadn't found her in the fetal position covered in tears. The doctor wanted to see her for weekly sessions to check up on her for the next month, but he didn't find her delusional or suffering from a psychotic break.

"What should we watch?" Alese asked, scrolling through the on-demand video selection and passing half the things I wanted to watch.

"That one," I said as she scrolled over the latest action movie I'd been dying to see.

She turned to me, raising an eyebrow, because she'd made it quite clear it was ladies' night. "What do you want to watch, Nya?" she asked, ignoring me.

"I've missed so many movies. You pick."

"Romantic or funny?"

"Um," Nya mumbled and twirled a strand of her brown hair around her finger. "I don't care as long as it's happy."

"Romantic it is, then." Alese smiled and clicked on the only one I prayed she wouldn't pick.

The movie already looked sappy, with a couple almost embracing in the picture on the guide, and I knew the next two hours wouldn't go by any faster than the rest of my day. Alese climbed onto the couch, placing herself between us, and made herself comfortable.

"I heard this one is amazing. The guy..." Alese started.

"Alese, don't ruin this one," I told her.

She grunted, but she didn't finish her sentence.

Nya laughed at her side and hooked her arm with Alese's like they'd been best friends for years. Alese rested her head on my shoulder and laced her fingers with mine. I placed my feet on the coffee table, sinking down into the couch and preparing for a long two hours, but it seemed to make the ladies happy. I couldn't ask for anything more than a little peace and quiet.

But as I sat there, watching the horror show on screen, I knew I was going to be in trouble. The cover lied, selling the movie as a happy story about love. The guy, who was in a horrible accident, then had to use a wheelchair, and the girl, who was his employee, had become attached to him.

The girls were already sniffling, and I knew the worst was yet to come. The same thing happened when Alese made me watch that walking movie where the girl died of cancer at the end. She was a blubbering mess, and I'd caught her watching it again more than once because, I swear, the woman loves to torture herself.

Nya gripped Alese tighter as the woman on screen pleaded with the man about his life after she fell in love with him. "How could he do that to her? What a selfish prick."

I understood the guy's thinking. I mean, who wanted to live a life in pain, suffering and remembering what you had but could never have again. As a man, I totally understood and would've probably made the same decision. The guy had his mind made up before he ever knew she existed. He wasn't being selfish, he was being realistic, and he knew what lay ahead for him if he didn't do this.

"I'd fucking rip off your balls," Alese said, squeezing the skin near my knee so tightly, her fingernails almost broke the skin. "I'd straight up tear those fuckers off."

I didn't speak because I wasn't stupid. I was outnumbered and didn't have a death wish. Right on cue, they both began to cry, finally letting their tears flow as the woman in the movie started to yell at the man about his choice.

Tonight was supposed to be relaxing and fun, but by the way the two of them were wailing, I knew I was completely fucked. The entire night they'd be talking about this movie, half in tears and angry as hell. Maybe I'd go for a walk on the beach while they ranted about the choice the man made for his own happiness even if it meant he'd die.

The woman stormed away, but when she came to her senses and the man went away to end his life, the girls cried harder.

"I can't believe he's really going to go through with this," Nya wailed and wiped away her tears that hadn't stopped falling since they'd both realized where this story was going.

"He's an asshole." Alese was pissed, but she'd picked this movie without bothering to find out what happened. "A selfish, greedy asshole."

"I understand him."

Alese turned to me, face covered in tears and full on glared at me with red eyes as she untangled her fingers from my grip. "The fuck you say?"

I motioned toward the screen. "He doesn't want to live that way or trap the girl either. He's doing the least selfish thing in his mind."

"Fuckin' men. He could live a lot longer, but he's choosing to die."

"He's choosing his own destiny…there's a difference."

"Oh my God. I can't watch." Nya covered her face, leaving space between her fingers to see the screen.

Alese interlaced her hand with Nya's and returned her attention toward the television. I slung my arm around the back of the couch, settling in for a long-ass night with two emotional women because I sensed the next part of the movie would completely wreck them both.

"Maybe he won't go through with it," Nya said.

"Yeah. Maybe she'll convince him to stay for her. I mean, love can make people do weird things."

I rolled my eyes, but I kept the words I had on the tip of my tongue bottled inside. I'd already gotten myself in enough trouble. The last thing I needed was to add more gasoline to their tear-fueled fire.

As the man died, they cried harder. I squeezed Alese's shoulder, trying to comfort her as I handed them both tissues.

"That was so…" Nya's voice trailed off as she blew her nose.

"Beautiful," Alese said, finishing Nya's sentence like they were on the same wavelength.

What I'd hoped would be an evening with some laughs and maybe drinks down on the beach turned into an emotionally charged evening with half a box of tissues being demolished and the girls with such stuffy noses they couldn't pronounce anything correctly.

Alese pushed herself off the couch, clutching the used tissues in her fists. "I need wine. Lots of wine."

"'Cause that always helps you stop crying." I couldn't stop myself from saying it. I knew I should've kept my mouth shut, but sometimes I couldn't help myself.

She placed her hands on her hips, staring down at me with puffy, angry eyes. "I cried once when I drank wine. Once."

I jumped up from the couch, needing a drink myself. "I'll get the drinks and meet you on the beach."

Alese wasn't in the mood for any type of humor, and having her tipsy-sad was better than pissed off. By the time I got down to the beach, Alese and Nya had spread out a blanket and lit a few candles near the waterline.

"Thank God." Alese plucked the bottle and wineglasses from my hands and placed them on the blanket in front of her, filling them quickly. "I need this. I've been wound so tightly lately, and that movie did nothing to help."

Nya took a wineglass and dropped her gaze. "Is it my fault?"

"Sweetheart," Alese said and placed her hand on Nya's leg, "it's not your fault."

"I showed up, and now you're stressed out."

Alese lifted Nya's glass to her mouth, nudging it toward her lips. "Drink your wine."

I stayed silent, sipping my whiskey, and watched them. I felt like they needed to discuss whatever was going on, and maybe Alese would have an easier time opening up to Nya and vice versa.

Nya stared over the rim of her glass as Alese continued talking.

"Sometimes I need a really good session to get out of my head. Ret and I haven't been to our club for a while, and I think I'm due for a good old-fashioned ass-whupping."

"Baby, I'm ready when you are," I teased with a playful grin.

There was nothing I liked more in the world than playing with my girl. If she wanted her ass spanked, I wasn't going to tell her no. I'd do anything she wanted, fulfilling her every fantasy and meeting every sexual desire she could dream up.

"Oh. I used to be like that. Well, before…"

"I'm sorry," Alese said, frowning. "That was insensitive of me."

"No. No." Nya shook her head and tried to pull off a smile. "I totally understand. I looked forward to going to the club. Sometimes I'd just watch, especially before I met *him*."

Catching her watching us through the door totally made sense now. She was a voyeur. I think everyone in the world had a little voyeur in them, but some people got off on watching more than others.

Alese's face lit up. "Oh my God. I love watching too. There's something so erotic about seeing two people fucking. Jesus." She fanned her face with her hand. "You should totally come with us if you want. You know, if it wouldn't give you nightmares. I'm sure Ret could get you a temporary membership."

"I don't know," Nya said, glancing at me with red cheeks.

"I can make it happen, but only if Nya wants to go and you're one hundred percent okay with inviting another person with us."

"She's not just another person, Ret. Nya can stay with us all night, even," Alese told her.

I raised my eyebrows, shocked that Alese would allow someone to watch us have a session. We'd never had anything but a private room and never invited another person in to watch. "You sure about that?" I asked.

"It's Nya. Of course I'm sure. If she wants to stay in the common area and watch other people, she can, but if she's too afraid, she can come into our room too."

I grunted before I took a sip of whiskey.

"I don't have to," Nya said quickly.

Alese gave me a look like I was fucking shit up and needed to set things straight. "We'd love for you to come, Nya. I'm just surprised at Alese's openness. It has nothing to do with you. I used to scene only in public before I met her. I'm not afraid of you seeing what we do."

"Well…" Nya licked her lips and looked at Alese. "I have to be honest with you, Alese."

Alese's eyebrows drew down as she tilted her head, waiting for whatever Nya had to confess. "Okay."

"So, the other night…"

"Yeah?"

Nya twisted the wineglass in her hands and took a deep breath. "I was walking by your bedroom. I heard noises, and I may have looked inside and saw you two having…" Nya dropped her voice "…sex."

"You watched us?"

"Yeah." Nya nodded slowly.

"For how long?"

"Just a few minutes," she said and grimaced.

"Well, then why are we even talking about this? You've seen me naked, so going to the club is no big deal."

"Well, if you don't…"

Alese touched Nya's arm and glanced over at me. "We'd love for you to come with us if you're up to going."

"I'm up for anything as long as I'm with you two." Nya smiled, but this time, it was genuine.

I polished off my drink and was about to say something I never thought I would from the day I'd met Alese. "Then it's settled. I'll call ahead and reserve a room for the three of us."

I knew this was opening a proverbial can of worms, but if Alese wanted it and Nya was into it, I was down for anything.

CHAPTER 10
NYA

My stomach fluttered as we walked toward their bedroom. Alese held my hand, peering at me over her shoulder every few steps to help calm my fears.

I asked for this. I wanted what was about to happen, but that didn't make the entire thing any less scary.

After seeing Alese and Ret together and the kiss on the beach, I wanted to remember what it felt like to be touched by someone other than Diego. Ret and Alese offered something different, something gentle and sweet. I may have only known them for a few days, but touching them...kissing them, was no different than meeting someone at a club and spending the evening with them.

No. That wasn't entirely true.

They weren't complete strangers to me. I'd watched them closely since I stepped foot in their home and saw nothing but love and respect between them. Both Alese, for all her craziness, and Ret, with his macho bravado, had a side that called to me.

I'd thought Diego would be that for me. I thought he was the one who would sweep me off my feet and shower me with so much love, all while feeding my sexual needs, that I'd never be with another person. I couldn't have been more wrong.

But I needed to move forward. I wanted to forget the past and go into the future with new memories, amazing experiences, and never take another moment for granted.

"I've never done this before," I said, laying my heart out there because I was worried I'd do something wrong.

Even though I was a kinkster and frequented the club in Atlanta to explore my sexuality, I'd never been with two people before. I didn't know the first thing about what to do, where to put my hands, or even how to start.

Alese turned me around to face them as we stood at the end of their bed. My gaze flickered to Ret, taking in his masculinity and size. He towered over me, covered in muscles, tanned skin, and dark hair. He watched me as he stood next to Alese. I swallowed down my nervousness, knowing I was in good hands even after I'd seen him spank her.

The man rescued me, for God's sake. I couldn't imagine he'd hurt me, especially not with Alese here.

She touched my face, forcing me to look at her. Her smile almost kissed the corners of her ice-blue eyes, causing her high cheekbones to protrude a little more than usual, and somehow making her more beautiful than ever. "We'll only do what you want. If you ever want us to stop, just say pickle."

"Pickle?" I held back my nervous laughter because I didn't want either of them to back out.

"Yes. Pickle. Do you just want Ret to watch, or do you want him to touch you too?" she asked with her hands resting on my shoulders.

"Nya," a voice said as my body rocked. "Nya, wake up." My eyes flew open to find Alese sitting next to me with her hair in curlers. "It's time to get up. You have to get ready, or we're going to be late."

My heart pounded as my dream came back to me. I had been about to have sex with Ret and Alese, and every bit of the vision felt so real.

"You okay?" she asked and moved her face closer. "You look flushed."

I jumped up from the couch in a panic as if she could read my thoughts. "I'm fine. I was just, um, I must be hot from sleeping."

Alese tilted her head, eyeing me. "If you're not feeling up to it, you don't have to come."

I glanced down at the floor, unable to look her in the eye. "No. I'm fine. I just need a shower and to get ready. I don't even know what to wear tonight. I don't have any of my old club clothes."

"Wear the black skirt and the hot strapless bustier we bought the other day. They're sexy enough for the club, and you won't feel overly exposed in front of new people. You were a knockout in that outfit."

I blushed again, loving her compliment more than I probably should. "Thanks, Alese. You're a lifesaver."

"Now go." She shooed me toward my bedroom. "We're leaving in an hour."

"Oh God," I squealed and ran forward, filled with more excitement than I'd felt in a very long time.

"Whoa!" I rocked backward and my jaw dropped as we stood on the top of the stairway leading down into the club.

The common area at this club was beyond amazing and more ornate than the club I'd frequented in Atlanta. The overhead lighting was muted toward the middle of the space and more dramatic near the walls, showing off their deep red color. The public areas were along the walls, fully visible and totally packed with participants and onlookers.

In the center of the room was a bar, lined with people in all forms of dress and undress, including submissives kneeling on the floor near their Masters' feet.

To the right was a section with couches and chairs, and not a single one was empty as people chatted. Some were even making out for everyone in the club to see.

Alese nudged my shoulder with hers. "It's pretty kick-ass, isn't it?"

I was transfixed as I took in every square foot. This was a voyeur's ultimate fantasy come true. I nodded, unable to say anything else because I was still trying to process all that I was witnessing.

The club in Atlanta was small, and not much happened in the public areas of the club. People didn't seem to be as open about their sexuality as they were here.

"How about a drink first?" Ret said, but I barely heard him over the beat of the music.

"We'd love one," Alese answered for both of us when I didn't speak.

I barely blinked as I gawked at the people below. "This is crazy," I said, finally dragging my eyes to Alese.

"Come on. It's more fun to watch up close."

I followed behind her and Ret, careful not to fall down the dark staircase in my new heels. I kept my head downcast, trying to avoid the eyes I knew were on me. I was fresh meat, ripe for the picking, and I'd been in clubs long enough to know that every available Dom had their eyes on me from the moment I walked inside.

When we reached the bottom of the staircase, Ret pulled me close and leaned in, placing his mouth near my ear. "Stay close. Don't wander away without telling us where you're going."

I shook my head, twisting my hands together in front of me. "I won't."

There was no way in hell I was going to wander off anywhere without Ret or Alese at my side. I'd already gotten myself in enough trouble and didn't want to repeat that mistake again.

"Wine, or something stronger?" Alese asked as she slid into one of the empty seats at the bar.

"Stronger," I told her and looked down at the woman on the floor, hanging on to the leg of a pretty well-built man.

My knees hurt just looking at her, but she didn't move a muscle with her hands folded in her lap, head bowed, and completely at the will of her Master.

"Alese doesn't kneel," Ret told me like he'd read my mind again. "Not unless I make her."

Alese glanced at me and winked. "We have an understanding. If Ret wants me to kneel, I will, but tonight isn't about that."

"Oh," I said, raising my eyebrows. "What's it about?"

Alese reached out and grabbed my hand, lacing her fingers with mine. "It's about you, silly."

"Me?" I squeaked.

"Yes. Well, it's about me, really, but you too."

My gaze moved to Ret, who was leaning over the bar, talking with the bartender and oblivious to our conversation. "Are you sure about this, Alese? I can just wait out here while you guys..." I waggled my eyebrows.

"Don't be silly. It'll be hot. I haven't had anyone watch in a long time, but I remember it was exciting."

"What if I can't?" I swallowed hard, almost choking on the word. "What if I freak?"

She squeezed my hand gently. "If you need to step out of the room, you can. We don't want to upset you. Did you like what you saw the other night? Did it turn you on?"

I couldn't just come out and say it was so damn hot I had to go back to my room and touch myself, reliving everything as if I were her. Even if that was the truth, it wasn't something I was comfortable admitting just yet. "It didn't upset me."

Alese smiled. "Did it turn you on?"

"Yes," I admitted and bit my lip, stopping myself from saying anything else.

"Drinks," Ret said, holding out the two glasses of whatever he ordered us on the rocks.

I gulped down two mouthfuls and winced. The burn at the back of my throat was something I hadn't prepared for, thinking it was something other than tequila. I had a checkered past with that liquor, and most of the time, things ended with me not remembering too much.

"It's good, no?" Alese licked her lips like she was savoring the flavor.

"It's good," I lied. Even if it tasted god-awful, I needed the liquor to help ease my fears about what was going to happen.

I'd never watched people I actually knew. They were always people at the club in Atlanta with whom I never had any real contact or connection, but this time was going to be something totally different.

CHAPTER 11
RET

"On your knees," I said the words to Alese as soon as we entered the private room. She gaped at me for a moment, but as soon as I crossed my arms over my chest, she kneeled without saying a word. "Nya, if something becomes too overwhelming, you can step into the hallway, but don't go anywhere else."

"Yes, Sir." Nya nodded as she sat, keeping her eyes trained on us. Alese smiled, staring across the room and seeming to enjoy this more than I would've imagined.

"I brought something for you, sweetheart." I fished a blindfold out of my back pocket and dangled the black material in front of Alese's face, knowing how much she was about to hate me.

"No," she growled.

I raised an eyebrow. If she wanted to argue with me, I'd make sure to hold off her orgasm until she was practically bursting at the seams.

"Yes, Sir."

Placing my fingers under her chin, I lifted her eyes to mine. "If you're a good girl, I'll let you look. But until I think you're ready, you're not allowed to watch."

"It's so…" She grimaced.

"It's so what?" I baited her to finish the statement, but she didn't.

Alese's tongue poked out and swept across her bottom lip as I ran my finger across the top of her corset and over the swell of her breasts. I ached to be inside her, burying myself so deep not even an inch separated our bodies, but this wasn't about me. It was about us and Nya.

I tied the blindfold tightly, making sure Alese couldn't sneak a peek during the scene even though I knew she'd try. I moved behind her, giving Nya a full view of Alese as she kneeled on the floor. I dipped my fingers inside the back of Alese's corset, about to pull the strings, when I glanced toward the couch, seeing Nya scooting forward and touching her lips.

Bending down, I placed my ear next to Alese's and inhaled the sweet perfume she'd worn especially for tonight. "Do you like being watched?"

Goose bumps broke out across her skin as she nodded. "Yes, Sir." Her tongue poked back out again, driving me half insane, but I was sure that was part of her plan.

Her body jerked backward as I pulled the strings of her corset loose. Alese's breath caught as the material fell away from her body, exposing her breasts. Her nipples pebbled immediately as the cool air rushed across her chest.

"So beautiful." I traced the swell of her breasts with my fingers, slowly moving across her skin.

Alese tilted her head back, and she moaned as my hand moved lower and I raked the tips of my fingers across her nipple. Her lips parted, and she swayed backward, giving me a magnificent view of her breasts and better access.

I bent down on one knee, cupping her heavy breasts in my hands and using my thumbs to toy with her nipples. She gasped as I pinched and pulled on her nipples, knowing how much she loved rough breast play.

My gaze moved to Nya as she slowly stroked the tops of her own breasts and leaned forward with most of her body hanging over the floor as her eyes zeroed in on my hands.

"Do you like this?" I asked, running the rough pad of my thumb over Alese's hard nipples, but I kept my eyes locked on Nya.

"Yes," Alese moaned and swayed, gravitating toward my touch.

Nya parted her lips, tongue sweeping out just like I'd seen Alese do a hundred times. Her eyes flickered upward, catching me staring at her as I played with Alese's breasts. Nya pulled the corner of her bottom lip inside her mouth and bit down, looking completely innocent and beautiful.

I slid my hand down Alese's front and between her legs, slipping under her skirt. She was wet, practically dripping with desire, and we had barely started. She opened, pushing her knees apart as my fingers glided against her slick pussy. She shivered and inhaled sharply as my thumb swept across her clit.

"Open your legs wider," I told her, swatting at her inner thighs with my hand.

My dick was as hard as granite as she tilted her head back and rested it against my chest while she pushed her knees farther apart. This was a slow form of sensual torture for me. The entire experience would be an exercise in patience and restraint for Alese as well as me.

I pushed two fingers inside her greedy pussy and curled them upward, pressing against her G-spot. My other hand pinched her nipple, keeping pressure on the sensitive bud as I pulled my fingers out and thrust them in deeper this time. Her breathing became erratic as her insides clamped down around my fingers, sucking them back inside.

Nya watched us, stroking her inner thigh with one hand and groping her breast in the other, completely transfixed and in the moment. The hunger in her eyes made me harder almost to the point of pain.

I slid my fingers out of Alese's beautiful cunt, leaving a trail of her wetness up the middle of her body before circling her breast. "Up," I told her, needing to have better access—complete access—to her entire body.

She complied, stretching out her arms as I swept my hands over her tender skin. I undid the zipper at the back of her skirt, letting the material fall to the floor near her feet. Taking her hand, I helped her step out completely naked for the first time in front of someone other than me. Nya swept her gaze across Alese's body, lingering on her perky breasts before dipping to her pussy.

Taking Alese by the hand, I led her to the punishment bench. The name was a total lie. Strapping her into it was the furthest thing from punishment. She loved every minute of being on full display with each hole ready and willing to be filled. I guided her onto the bench, helping her get on without hurting herself. There was a flash of a smile on her face as I buckled her wrists.

"Are you excited?" I asked, tightening the leather straps so she couldn't move.

"Yes, Sir."

My hand traced the curve of her back before circling her ass. "You love this, don't you?"

She shuddered as my finger slid between her cheeks, running over her asshole. "Yes." There was thirst in her voice.

"You want all your holes stuffed?"

"I'm yours to do with what you want, Sir."

I smiled and sucked in a breath. There was so much I wanted to do with her, and her willingness to please me always sent shivers down my spine. I fastened the straps around her ankles, and she pulled against them, testing their tightness.

"You can't move, my love." My back was to Nya as I dipped my fingers into Alese's wet pussy and groaned. My balls throbbed, and my cock strained against my jeans, begging for some relief.

I thrust my fingers deeper, pummeling her cunt over and over again as she tried to squirm but couldn't. She gasped when I pulled my fingers out, leaving her empty and wanting. I walked to the bag I'd left near the door, digging inside and peering over at Nya for a brief moment.

Her knees were farther apart as she leaned back into the couch with her eyes moving between Alese and me. Her hand stilled under her skirt, watching me closely as I dug into the bottom of the bag to retrieve Alese's favorite anal plug and the bottle of lube.

Nya's eyes widened at the size, but anal play was Alese's specialty. When I'd met her, the girl had an arsenal of anal toys but swore she wasn't into ass play. Testing the waters, I'd quickly learned her statement was a complete lie.

I smiled at Nya and mouthed, "Don't worry," trying to calm any fears she had about what was about to happen as I walked back toward the bench. Lifting the bottle in the air, I drizzled the lube down Alese's ass, letting the liquid slide over her pussy and form a puddle on the floor.

Using my fingers, I spread out the lube before slipping the plug through the wetness, coating every inch completely. Alese moaned, knowing what was coming, practically panting as the tip pushed against her asshole.

"You love having your ass stuffed, don't you, *piccola*?" I said, twisting the tip inside her opening.

"Yes," she panted, pushing her ass toward me and trying to force the plug deeper, quicker.

"All your holes are greedy."

"Only for you, Sir," she said and gasped as the widest part of the plug slid past her opening.

My eyes practically rolled back as the need building inside me grew along with my cock. Movement across the room caught my attention as I pulled on the plug and had Alese shaking.

Nya had lifted her skirt, giving me the full view of her beautiful pussy as her fingers dipped inside, disappearing. I sucked in a breath, overcome with more lust and need than I ever thought possible. Nya's eyes were locked on mine, watching me carefully as I licked my lips and pulled my gaze away and back to my girlfriend.

I bent my body over Alese, letting my cock push on her plug, driving it deeper as I placed my mouth near her ear. "Nya's enjoying herself," I whispered. "She's watching you get filled and fingering herself."

Alese groaned, probably wanting to punch me because she couldn't see. I grabbed the bulb hanging from the plug, giving it a quick squeeze. This wasn't just any anal plug, but an expandable one, making her feel even more stuffed than she already did. Her head dropped forward, and her back arched in pleasure.

Fuck, I didn't know how much more of this I could take. I'd probably blow my load like a teenager at this rate if I weren't careful and didn't restrain myself.

Nya hadn't run out of the room, but besides the anal plug, I'd been gentle on my Alese. This wasn't about scaring Nya, instead about bringing pleasure to everyone involved and letting Nya explore her own body, remembering the pleasure of touch.

This wasn't about me. I kept repeating those words, trying to keep my shit together long enough to give Alese, and maybe Nya too, more than one orgasm.

I straightened, pushing against Alese's plug with one hand while I unzipped my jeans with the other. Nya's eyes were on me, no longer watching Alese as she writhed against the bench, her greedy cunt looking to be filled and pleasured.

"Tell me you want my cock," I said, inching my jeans down my thighs.

"I want your cock."

My hand came down hard against Alese's ass, reminding her of her forgotten word.

"Sir, yes, Sir," she bit out quickly, earning her the palm of my hand against her reddened flesh.

Nya gasped and rocked into her fingers, eating up every minute of this just like me.

CHAPTER 12
NYA

Fuck me. I'd forgotten how hot and erotic it was to watch two people bound by passion in a delicate dance of push and pull. I couldn't take my eyes off them as Ret pushed down his pants, exposing his massive cock.

My heart raced, pounding in my chest faster than before as my eyes swept across his body while he pulled off his shirt and threw it to the floor. *Dear God.* The man had everything and so much of it too. His long body was covered with tight muscles and perfectly sun-kissed skin. A small patch of dark hair had fallen over his forehead, almost covering his blue, intense eyes and making him look younger and somehow less intimidating. The muscles in his arms moved under his skin, flexing as he rubbed a hand over Alese's ass slowly and methodically, following the swell of her cheeks.

There was a playful smirk on his lips when I lifted my gaze to his face. I plunged my fingers deeper, pretending I was the girl strapped to the bench about to be fucked and pleasured until I was begging for him to stop.

My eyes dropped to Alese as she panted, mouth open and wanting to be filled every bit as much as I did. He reached for the bulb on the anal plug, and my eyes widened as my asshole constricted, imagining that thing inside me, stretching me.

I was so turned on my fingers glided through my wetness with no resistance, slipping into my cunt like they were always meant to be there. I licked my lips and swallowed, my mouth dry and thirsty for something more, but not daring to move from my spot.

My breath faltered as he pushed his cock inside, grunting as he slipped past the plug and her body writhed in front of him. I squirmed and plunged a third finger inside, needing the feeling of fullness Alese was no doubt experiencing. Her breasts jiggled, bouncing forward with each thrust of Ret's powerful hips against her body.

I felt each stroke, matching my rhythm with his as Alese's hands wrapped around the bench and she moaned. I was so turned on, more than I'd been in months as I watched Ret fuck Alese silly. She gasped and so did I as he swiveled his hips, touching every bit of her pussy from the inside.

His grunts became louder and more punctuated. I thought he was about to come, following me over the cliff of ecstasy as I squeezed my eyes shut, too overcome with sensation to keep them open. My muscles seized and my breathing halted as the waves crashed over me again and again until I gasped for air, completely spent.

I opened my eyes, and they instantly widened as they fixed on Ret, still buried deep inside Alese and pumping into her like he was more of a machine than a human being.

"Damn," I whispered under my breath, seriously impressed with his skill and stamina.

The only sounds in the room were skin slapping against skin, Alese's moans of pleasure, Ret's grunts, and my harsh breathing, working together to create the most beautiful symphony of ecstasy.

Ret tightened his grip on Alese's hips and buried his other hand in her hair, tipping her head back and giving him more leverage. I watched, completely consumed by the scene playing out before me. Alese's mouth fell open as she gasped for air. Ret's hand loosened in her hair, but she didn't let her head fall forward as he moved his fingers to the material tied around her face.

The blindfold dropped to the floor, and Alese opened her eyes, blinking away the haze and pinning me with her gaze. Lust built inside me, faster than it had ever happened before. My fingers slid against my wet flesh, my eyes locked on Alese and hers solely on me.

She grunted, matching Ret, as he slammed into her body, slapping her ass every few strokes. Her eyes watered as she bucked and begged for relief. I thrust my fingers deeper, watching her eyes follow my movements as I followed Ret's lead and kept perfect pace. My wrist ached at the speed, but I couldn't stop; I wouldn't stop.

I widened my legs, feeling emboldened by the look of lust and want on Alese's face as she watched me pleasure myself while being fucked relentlessly by Ret. I stuck my hand in my strapless top and pulled out my breasts, needing something more to push me over the edge a second time.

I bent my neck, pulled my breast to my lips, and closed my mouth around my hard and aching nipple. Pleasure shot through me, splintering inside my body until my toes curled.

I flickered my eyes to Alese, finding her still staring at me, scorching me with her gaze as I sucked on my nipple and thrust my fingers between my legs. Alese's hands tightened around the bench as her eyes rolled back. Ret moaned, calling her name as he reached underneath the bench and slapped her pussy with a thud.

I gasped, my eyes widening as she tossed her head back and wailed, shaking against the restraints. Her moans came out on a crescendo, echoing off the walls of the tiny space as I followed her over the edge, unable to breathe.

I held Alese's gaze as the orgasm rolled through me stronger than the first—and longer. Alese moaned as Ret slammed into her, drawing her orgasm out longer than I thought humanly possible as he followed.

I lay there, legs open, gasping for air, with my fingers still deep inside me, watching them as the aftershocks had both their bodies quaking. Sweat beaded across their flesh, glistening like a thousand points of light. I wasn't sure how long we stayed like that... Me staring, Alese gasping, and Ret's shaking legs showing he was, in fact, human after all, but it was intense and the single most erotic moment of my life.

No one had laid a hand on me, yet I came as if someone had

flipped a switch, reawakening my hunger for sins of the flesh. I glanced toward the floor, slipping my fingers from between my legs and closing my knees, suddenly feeling overexposed. I didn't know what had come over me as I let the lust and passion take control and all reason escaped me.

I kept my eyes on the floor, covered my breasts with my top, and wondered how the rest of the night would go. I'd never watched anyone I knew and didn't know what proper protocol was for something like that. I mean, did I talk about it? Compliment them on their performance, even? I had no clue if we were supposed to pretend like the entire thing hadn't happened even when it did.

These two people, the man who saved me and my new best friend, showed me their bodies, letting me into their intimate life, and I didn't want to say anything to ruin the amazing thing we had going. If they threw me out, where would I go?

I sat in silence, hearing the rustle of their clothes, and closed my eyes, praying I hadn't fucked up. *Just breathe.* I kept reminding myself there was nothing to fear. This was Alese and Ret, two of the nicest people I'd ever met.

The couch dipped on either side of me. "Nya." Ret's deep voice sent a shiver down my spine. "Open your eyes," he said.

Slowly, I brought my gaze to his, swallowing the fear that had settled in the back of my throat. He touched my chin, lifting my face higher to fully meet his stare. "Are you okay?"

"Yes, Sir," I responded quickly and blew out a shaky breath.

"Do you regret being here?" Alese asked as she placed her hand gently on my leg.

I shook my head, turning to face her with a smile. "No, ma'am. I enjoyed myself."

She grinned and waggled her eyebrows. "Me too."

"We both enjoyed having you here. We know it was a big step for you." Ret smiled, but he kept his hands to himself as he wiped away the sweat that had formed on his forehead with a towel. "I don't remember the last time she lasted that long."

"What about you, tiger?" Alese chuckled and made a noise more like a baby lion, but it was cute anyway.

"I couldn't give in so easily. I wanted to draw it out, but I'm not sure I'll be able to walk tomorrow."

He laughed and I cracked a smile, sitting between the two of them as they teased each other. It should've felt odd, but it didn't. I should've been uncomfortable, but I wasn't. There was a peacefulness inside my soul that I hadn't felt in a long time, and it was present because of Ret and Alese.

Ret climbed to his feet and held out his hands. "I could use a drink. How about you ladies?" I slid my hand into his, just like Alese did, and let him pull me from the couch. My legs wobbled as my knees started to give out, but Ret wrapped an arm around my back, steadying me. "Maybe just a soda for you." He grinned.

"No way, buddy. I want booze."

"Three waters and three drinks, it is, but no more," Ret said as he opened the door for us to walk out before him.

I went first, walking like I knew where the hell I was going, when I didn't have a clue. I followed the deep thump of the bass toward the common room, hoping the music wasn't leading me astray.

"You really went easy on me, Ret. Getting soft in your old age?"

I laughed, keeping my face forward as Alese spoke to Ret.

"Baby, I didn't want to scare the girl. This was about each of us having pleasure, not just you," he told her, and I could hear the playfulness in his voice.

"Sometimes I need a good spanking."

"Your ass says you got it."

"Don't go all soft on me. I won't even have a bruise tomorrow the way you were swatting me," she told him. "Man up."

"Watch it," he warned, dropping his voice so low I barely heard him say, "We still have time."

Fucking hell.

CHAPTER 13
RET

"It's quiet without Flash, ya know?" Pop said, sitting down to our morning meeting to go over the week's caseload. "I kind of hate when that little prick is away on assignment."

"Don't be an asshole. He's not loud," Morgan told Pop as he straightened the pile of files he had in front of him. "Not like you, at least. If you weren't here, we'd probably finally enjoy some peace and quiet."

Pop touched his moustache, running his fingers through the hair that was longer than usual as he stared at Morgan. "You'd miss my beautiful face."

Morgan rolled his eyes. "Don't push your luck."

"Who's your daddy?" Pop teased, elbowing him in the arm.

Morgan grumbled under his breath, hating being reminded that Bear was, in fact, his stepfather. It still felt odd to think I had a stepbrother, but I rolled with it. Even Janice seemed to take it better than I did, buddying up with our new brother easy. Legally, we were an insta-family, but that didn't make family dinner any less weird.

Thomas walked into the conference room a little more dressed up than usual, and everyone noticed. "Hot date?" Frisco teased him before he had a chance to sit.

745

"It's my anniversary, and I'm taking my girl out to dinner after work today."

"An expensive dinner," Angel said from the doorway. "I'm only working a half day today, boys, so you're going to be on your own this afternoon."

"We got this." Pop winked, always trying to be the slick one.

"Does anyone need anything before I seal you inside?"

"We're good, baby. Thanks." Thomas slid the folders down the table like he always did to start every meeting. "Let's start with Matías. Where are we with him?"

Matías was a wanted criminal, specializing in human trafficking. So far, the FBI, Interpol, and other legal entities hadn't been able to catch him before he moved on to his new destination with a fresh crop of victims. I'd been tracking him, working with my contacts in the BDSM community to try to get a jump on his location before even the authorities got a whiff of his whereabouts.

I leaned back in my chair and tapped my pen against the folder, happy with the response I'd received from the BDSM community. No one wanted a guy like Matías on the streets. We had enough bullshit to deal with without a man like him kidnapping people and selling them into the sex-slave industry. "I have feelers out to all my community contacts. I expect to hear from them today. We should be able to move soon."

"Let us know as soon as you hear something," James told me.

"I will, boss."

"Next order of business. What cases are we closing out this week?"

"I have a hell of one that I can finally say is over. Cheating husband and shit got ugly." Pop gave him a big, toothy grin.

My phone started vibrating and dancing across the table, catching my attention. "I have to take this," I said before heading toward the door to take Connor's call.

Connor was the owner of Forbidden in Jacksonville and a longtime friend since we'd crossed paths in our younger days. If the man had intel, I'd jump on it because he was a man of his word and wouldn't yank my chain with bullshit information.

"What's up?"

"I did some asking around. Matías has been here on and off the last few weekends. If you want him, you better get your ass up here before he takes off again."

"We'll be there. Thanks, man."

"If you don't show, I'll handle him myself."

"I said we'll be there. End of conversation."

"Noted."

I walked back into the conference room with a huge, shit-eating grin because we'd finally gotten a solid lead on Matías's whereabouts. "Found the fucker."

"Where is he?" James asked.

"He's been frequenting a club in Jacksonville called Forbidden a few nights a week and has been there the last two weekends."

Thomas leaned back in his chair, swiveling from side to side. "I can't believe he's still in Florida."

James nodded as did everybody else because no one could believe that a criminal mastermind like Matías could be so stupid. "He must not have heard about my trip to Taboo. When should we head out?"

Forbidden was only open on the weekend, and knowing Matías, he'd gone underground already, waiting for the weekend to snag another victim. "Let's get our ladies and head up there Friday. We may have to be gone a few days until he shows up. Is that okay, Thomas?"

"Wait." Thomas straightened, and his face grew serious. "You're going to take Izzy again?"

James shrugged like it was the most logical thing in the world and Thomas was crazy for even questioning him. "Yeah. We need the ladies with us to maintain our cover."

Thomas scrubbed his hand down his face. "I don't like it."

"Have I ever let anything happen to her?"

"I trust you. Just be careful. If there's any sign of trouble, get the fuck out."

"I'll be there with them, Thomas. Nothing will happen. I know the owner of the club, and we'll be in good hands," I told him because I'd protect anyone in that room, including their wives, with my own life.

I just had to break the news to Alese and Nya. I needed Alese by my side just as much as James needed Izzy. Nya would have to stay behind because I didn't dare put her life in danger or put her through undue stress. I just hoped she could cope with being alone for a few days while we caught someone who deserved to be behind bars.

"WHEN DO WE HAVE TO LEAVE?" Alese rubbed her temples, not exactly ecstatic about our upcoming trip. Nya had gone back to her bedroom to grab one of my old sweatshirts I'd given to her as Alese prepped dinner.

"Friday morning."

"What about Nya?"

That was the same thing I'd been thinking all day. We hadn't left her alone yet, not for any extended period of time, at least, and I wasn't sure I felt right doing it now. "Maybe my pop and Fran could stay with her while we're gone."

"Oy," Alese groaned and dragged her hands down her face. "If they're our only option."

"She'll be safe with them." I knew my pop would do everything possible to keep Nya safe and calm while Fran cooked her food that was even more inedible than Alese's dishes.

"I'll break the news to her."

"You make it sound like we're getting rid of her."

"That's the last thing I want her to think. I just want to make sure she's okay with it."

"We'll talk to her together. We owe her as much."

Nya strolled back into the kitchen and froze. She glanced between us, knowing the vibe was off. "Why did you stop talking?"

"We didn't." Alese gave me the side-eye before she grabbed the wine I'd set out for dinner.

"We were just talking about this weekend."

"That's all?" Nya moved toward the counter, but she walked slowly, her eyes still moving between us.

Alese smiled nervously. "Let's sit. Dinner's ready, and I made Ret's favorite."

I scratched my head because I didn't really have a favorite. I preferred something that wasn't burned and dried-out, which she did with just about everything. But tonight was pasta, and it was probably the one thing she didn't make like sandpaper, even if it resembled mush.

"Alese and I have to go away this weekend," I said before everyone had a chance to sit down. There was no reason to delay it and end up ruining anyone's appetite. If Nya was going to freak out, it was better to get it out of the way as quickly as possible.

"Oh." Nya frowned, but she didn't have a meltdown. "All weekend?"

"I have a case in Jacksonville, and I need Alese's help. We won't be gone all weekend. Hopefully, we'll be home late Saturday or early Sunday."

Nya pulled out her chair and grabbed her napkin as she sat down, seemingly unaffected. "That's okay. Really. Don't worry about me."

Alese sat next to her and placed her hand over Nya's as she rested it on the table. "We don't want you to be alone in this big house all weekend. We had an idea."

"I don't need a babysitter, Alese."

"They wouldn't babysit you, Nya." Alese leaned forward and grabbed the giant bowl of pasta that would probably be dinner for the week. "They're Ret's dad and stepmom. I thought you might enjoy spending some time with them. Maybe they can just check on you or something. Fran always likes to feel useful." When Alese got nervous, she got chatty, and she was rambling.

I rolled my eyes. That was the understatement of the century. Fran was up everyone's ass and deep into their business, but she was the reason I was here. If she hadn't called me, I probably never would've reconnected with my father. She was nosy, but her heart was always in the right place.

Nya smiled in my direction as she took the plate Alese had filled with so much pasta Nya would be there for an hour even if she didn't come up for air. "I like your dad. He's such a sweet man."

"That's one way to describe him."

"You're hard on your dad. He could be a total asshole like mine."

She had a point, but Bear wasn't the same man he was years ago.

He wasn't always the Father of the Year, but she didn't need to know our past. "He's a good guy underneath his bullshit."

"And what about his wife? Your stepmom?"

"Fran is… I don't know how to describe her."

"She is a riot. She puts that big mountain of a man right in his place. She's kinda scary like that."

"I'm okay with them stopping by just so you two don't worry, but otherwise, I could use a few days by myself."

"Understood." I nodded. I knew the feeling. I tried to avoid looking at my plate because Alese had loaded mine up too. Nya hadn't had a minute to breathe on her own for so long that I was sure she could use a little time to collect her thoughts.

We'd given her very little time alone since she'd walked through the front door. I wasn't sure what the protocol was for something like what she'd been through, and I didn't want her to have a complete meltdown either. But after the doctor gave her a clean bill of health, including her mental health, I was sure we could give her a reprieve.

"I'll give you their cell phone numbers, and they'll have yours."

"I don't have one," Nya said.

"We'll get you one tomorrow. Don't worry." Alese smiled. The woman loved to shop, even if it was for electronics. Set her loose in any store and she was happy as could be. "We'll have our makeup day."

"Great," I mumbled as I jammed the first forkful of overly cooked pasta into my mouth. I didn't care they were spending money, but I wished they knew how beautiful they were without all the shit on their faces. "I don't know why you two need makeup. You're perfect as is."

They both stopped moving, gawking at me like I had two heads. I thought I was being nice, but they didn't see it that way. I'd thought things were rough sometimes with just Alese, but I could already see the two of them were going to try to gang up on me. It was time to show Alese who was in charge again.

CHAPTER 14
NYA

I opened the front door wearing a new outfit Alese had picked out, feeling like a million dollars and a little like my old self again.

Fran whistled. "Look at her," she said, glancing over her shoulder at Bear, who leaned against the car with his hands crossed over his extra-wide chest. Fran was just how I imagined her after Alese and Ret gave me the heads-up about her. She was an older woman, about the age of my mother, but she carried herself differently.

"Very nice," he muttered, adjusting the toothpick between his lips. "We drinkin' or having a fashion show?"

I closed the door as Fran made her way down the stairs, hiding my smile with my back turned to Bear. There was something about the man that I'd liked instantly.

When Fran called and asked if I wanted to go to their favorite bar to dance and drink, I jumped at the chance. I loved the quiet and serenity of being at Ret's place, but I could use an evening of fun like the old days.

"Don't mind him. He's grumpy tonight."

"Why?" I asked as I tossed the keys into the small black purse Alese had sworn I needed because it matched my shoes.

Fran rolled her eyes and shook her head. "He's upset the guys didn't take him with them."

"Poor thing."

Bear opened the door for me, and I slid across the back seat after pulling my legs inside. He smiled, giving me a quick wink with a smile before closing me inside.

"We ready?" he asked as he settled into the driver's seat next to his wife and started the engine.

Fran shot him a warning glance, and I muffled my laughter because the last thing I wanted was for either of them to regret taking me out tonight. "We're ready."

Bear's eyes found mine in the rearview mirror as he drove. "You settlin' in okay, kid?"

"Yes."

"My kid treating you right?"

"Always. He's a great guy."

"Just like his pop." He grinned.

"Oh lordy," Fran groaned. "The man's already got a big head. Don't make it any bigger."

"Babe," Bear said, glancing in Fran's direction and grabbing her hand.

"What?"

"You love me."

"Yeah. Well…"

"You love my big…"

She narrowed her eyes. "Don't say it."

Bear laughed before bringing her hand to his mouth and placing a light kiss against the top. She snatched her hand away and turned up the radio, blasting some country tune I'd never heard before.

"This song is amazing. Maybe we'll dance to it tonight."

"You know I hate to dance."

"Baby?"

"Yeah?"

"If I wanna dance, we're gonna dance."

"Right," he said quickly, his head bobbing in agreement.

I couldn't control my laughter any longer, placing the back of my hand against my mouth. I muffled the sound. Ret was the luckiest guy in the world to have these two people as parents. I wasn't so lucky. My parents cared, but they also tried to control my entire life. That was the reason I'd ended up in Atlanta to begin with…I wanted my freedom.

Kind of funny that I ended up with the exact opposite after everything was said and done, but I wasn't about to repeat the mistakes of my past nor let them guide my future.

When we pulled into the Neon Cowboy, Fran shifted in her seat to face me. "Don't be scared of any of the guys. They'd lay down their life for you in a minute. The crowd can get rowdy sometimes, but I promise you'll have a good time."

"Okay." I smiled, but my stomach was twisted as the nerves started to take hold. I followed them toward the door and fidgeted with the strap of my purse, all while trying to maintain my balance on the damn high heels

"If anyone gets handsy, let me know, and I'll kick their ass."

"Got it."

Bear held the door open for us. Fran walked in first, me behind her, and him following close on my heels. The bar was dimly lit and filled with so many people, I couldn't imagine we'd ever find a table. The floor was covered in peanut shells or sawdust. It was hard to tell with the lighting and the number of feet, but the crunch underneath my shoes was hard to ignore.

Fran parted the crowd and sauntered through the sea of people like she owned the place. In the distance, there was a table with three open seats where a group of men was sipping beer. Fran stopped in front of the table, her eyes skimming the group. "Guys. This is Nya."

A few of the faces looked familiar. I'd seen them at ALFA, but I hadn't spoken to them. "Hi," I said, feeling like a kid on the first day of school, filled with fear and excitement.

A man nodded his head, looking a little like Keanu Reeves, but hotter. "Hey, Nya. It's nice to see you again. I'm Frisco, and this is Morgan, Fran and Bear's kid."

"I'm not Bear's kid. Wipe that shit right out of your mind." He leaned forward, holding out his hand to me. "I'm Fran's son, and we've met before."

He was a hunk. In another place and time, I probably would've flirted with him and tried to catch his eye. That was, until I saw his wedding band glimmer under the overhead light.

"It's nice to see you both again."

"Take a seat," Fran said, pulling out the chairs. "Bear will get us drinks. Beer?"

"Anything cold and wet."

"Ahh." A man sitting toward the center of the group, older than everyone else but still handsome, laughed. "She likes her drinks like I like my ladies."

"You really are a strange bastard, Tank," Frisco told him, slapping him on the chest.

"Never claimed to be normal. I'm Tank, doll. Bear's oldest friend."

"Older than dirt," Bear muttered next to me before motioning for me to take a seat next to Fran.

Slowly, I lowered myself into the chair, unable to take my eyes off the group and wondering if Fran and Bear hung around anyone who wasn't tall, dark, and handsome.

"We were just debating."

"About what?" Fran asked Morgan as she leaned back in her chair, and he took a slug of his beer.

"About Ret and James."

The mention of Ret from Morgan got my full attention.

"What about them, son?"

"You think the ladies ever get to spank them, or is it a one-way street?"

The table erupted in laughter and I grinned, but it wasn't an easy, carefree grin. I wasn't sure if they were making fun of them and being assholes, or if this was the type of trash talk they always engaged in.

"I'm sure they tried." Fran smiled and grabbed the beer Bear set down in front of her, having returned in record time. "I can imagine Izzy isn't always compliant."

"Hell, I'd let either one of those girls beat my ass," Tank said and smiled.

"Tank, you'd let anyone beat your ass if it meant you'd get a piece."

"Damn straight. I ain't picky."

Morgan waved off Tank. "No. Seriously. We were talking about Matías and if they'd finally catch the sick bastard."

"Who's Matías?" I asked as I turned my cold beer in my hands.

"The bad guy they're trying to nab this weekend. He's a human trafficker. Sells people into the sex-slave industry. He's a bad motherfucker."

I gasped and covered my mouth. Ret and Alese didn't tell me they were going after someone dangerous.

I'd read a lot about human trafficking before I joined Charmed. It was my biggest fear when I'd become a member and started to find my footing in the community. I wasn't lucky when I ended up with Diego, but I could've been sold and shipped to a foreign country, never to be heard from again. The very thought sent a chill down my spine.

Bear spoke quickly, probably sensing my unease because I was shit at hiding my emotions. "They'll catch him. It's James and Ret, after all. Nobody's getting away from them. I just wish I were there with them."

"You can't go on every assignment, ya greedy bastard," Frisco told Bear. "And let's face it, if you walked into a sex club, you'd probably die from overstimulation."

"Son," Bear laughed. "I was in sex clubs when you were still sucking on your mother's tit. I may be older, but I've lived a hell of a lot more experiences than your tiny little brain will ever comprehend."

I took a sip of my beer, watching them over the rim of my glass. I couldn't get the thought of Alese and Ret being at a sex club, trying to find a human trafficker and stop him, out of my head.

What if something went wrong?

What if they got hurt?

I wasn't worried about myself or where that would leave me. I wanted them in my life, and even in the short amount of time I'd known them, I knew I couldn't imagine life without them.

CHAPTER 15

RET

Connor was waiting for us at the door after we walked through the empty parking lot of Forbidden. "Welcome."

I shook his hand, always happy to see an old friend. It had been years since I'd laid eyes on him, and although time had been kind to me, it hadn't been so forgiving to Connor. "Thanks for doing this."

Connor had a partner in the business, a former Navy SEAL named Trent Newsome, who was interested in helping us nab Matías. "Welcome," Trent said with a curt head nod as we entered the lobby. The man looked like stereotypical, hard-core, military special forces personnel. Strong jaw, big muscles, perfect posture, and lacking any type of emotional facial expression as he stared at James and me.

Then his gaze slid to our girls. "It's a pleasure to meet you, ladies."

"I'm Alese." She bowed like she was halfway tame.

"Izzy." Being Izzy, she didn't bow her head, but she looked him straight in the eye, defiant to the core.

"Welcome to Forbidden."

"Thanks for helping us, Trent." I pulled Alese close to my side, staking my claim. James did the same because we both knew there was something not quite right with Trent. It wasn't that he'd try anything, but something was off with him. Maybe he'd seen too much in the military, but I wasn't going to stick around long enough to find out. If Connor trusted him, I'd give the guy a pass because Connor didn't play games.

"The last thing we need is a human trafficker lurking around our club. I'll do anything to help put his ass behind bars."

Connor stepped in front of Trent. "Let's get inside, and I'll give you a tour before you can spend a few hours wandering around on your own."

"Sounds great," I told him.

Connor opened the door, and we walked inside the common area with Trent close behind us. "Matías spends about an hour in this part of the club until he convinces someone to join him in a private room," Connor said as soon as the door closed behind us.

Forbidden was an upscale club with modern touches, having received a complete overhaul after Connor purchased it. A black marble floor and blood-red walls matched the leather furniture that was in the center of the room. On the far right was a viewing platform with a St. Andrew's Cross, one of my favorite apparatuses, and shackles hanging from the ceiling just a few feet away.

"We have a lot of members who are into voyeurism. We make sure to have plenty of areas for them to live out that fantasy."

To the left was the bar, lining the entire wall of the club, with built-in stools and a sleek cement top. Behind the bar was a wall-to-wall mirror that could give any drinker the full view of the action going on behind them, followed by cages and stockades.

"Ah, our area for public humiliation." Connor came to stand next to James. "It's become quite popular lately."

Izzy gripped James's arm, pressing her body flush against him. "Um, fuck that."

"Let me show you the private rooms, and then we'll let you be to do whatever you want."

From the outside, the club didn't look large. But it extended into an endless maze of private rooms and smaller public play areas. Each spot had its own theme or purpose, and everything was top-notch. No cheap, shitty BDSM furniture that looked overused. The amount of furniture and apparatus in the club was mind-boggling. Cages, benches, vacbeds, and bondage chairs were everywhere, along with beds and exam tables in too many rooms to count. This was a playland for anyone in the lifestyle.

"Any questions?" Connor asked after we walked into the last small play area tucked away at the end of the hallway.

We stood around the circular bed that could probably fit ten people easily and must have made for quite a scene.

"How do you monitor everything?" James asked.

Connor crossed his arms in front of his chest and glanced upward. "All public areas have closed-circuit television monitoring, and the private rooms have cameras on the doorways with a two-way intercom in case there's an emergency. We have designated Masters who walk the hallways and public areas at all times to stop anything from getting out of hand."

I stared up at the camera, thankful Connor had enough sense to install equipment in the rooms because the fresh waves of douchebags trying to join the lifestyle were mind-boggling and dangerous. "Can you show us the surveillance room?"

"Sure. We don't keep tapes of anything to protect the security and anonymity of our members, but they're monitored every moment the club is open for business," Connor said, motioning for us to follow him back toward the public area where we'd started our tour.

James whispered to Izzy as Alese clutched my hand, staying close to me as we followed Connor.

"It'll be fine," I told her. "I promise."

She never liked new clubs. She wasn't comfortable around new people and preferred sticking with our own crowd over being more adventurous. I knew tomorrow she'd be fine. She'd slide into her role as a submissive, but tonight she'd let the fear take over.

"Let's hope we catch the bastard tonight, and then we can have one day to play," Izzy told James as we stood outside the nondescript door.

"In here is where we have twenty monitors, along with the intercom system. It's really an amazing thing, and I don't know of a club within three hundred miles that has this kind of setup."

James glanced around the room, taking in the sleek flat-screen televisions lining the one wall. "You've done an amazing job with the club, Connor."

"It's my pride and joy." He smiled brightly. "Now if you'll excuse me, Trent and I have a few things to discuss. We'll let you be, and feel free to holler if you have any questions."

"Thank you," I said, looking between the two men before they walked out.

"Should we set up camp in here?"

James rubbed his face. "I think it's best if one of us is on the floor while someone is in here surveying the entire club."

"We'll be in the club," Izzy said quickly, a little too overeager but completely in step with her personality.

"Works for me. Let's walk through it a few more times until we have the layout memorized, and then we can leave for a few hours. They don't open until eight."

"Just enough time to get ready." Izzy laughed.

James peered down at her and gripped her ass roughly in his hand. "Woman, it better not take you seven hours to prepare."

"Baby," she said, running her fingernail down his bicep. "Not all prep is bad."

He grinned. "Whatever you want, doll."

"Let's do this," Izzy said, walking out of the room before the rest of us.

"You ready for this, Alese? Are you going to be okay?" I squeezed her hand as she stared at the screens.

"I'm fine. I can do this."

"We'll use Izzy as bait. If you'd rather stay here in the control room…"

She held up her hand, silencing me. "I want to do this."

"This place is no joke," Alese said, pointing at the screen where no fewer than ten people were gangbanging a woman as another man watched. "I mean, our club is nothing like this."

"Love, we don't know what's happening behind closed doors at our club."

"Well, damn. It's kind of hot and frightening all at the same time."

I laughed and squeezed her leg right above her knee as my eyes scanned the screens, bouncing back to Izzy and James every few seconds so I didn't miss anything.

Based on the fact that James had tugged on her chain more than once, I'd say she was being mouthy, but that was all part of the plan. Men like Matías didn't want an easy mark. Sometimes, unruly slaves fetched a higher price because men always enjoyed breaking a female.

"Izzy's my spirit animal," Alese said as James pulled on her chain again and she glared at him, sassing something back at him.

Moments later, a very well-dressed man stepped in front of Izzy and James and paused, staring down at her as if he were studying an animal in the wild.

James had already swiveled around on the stool, and Matías motioned toward Izzy with his hand. There was an exchange of words before Connor entered the conversation, standing near Izzy, keeping a watchful eye.

James stepped forward, moving closer to Matías, and spoke again before hooking his hand around Izzy's arm and pulling her to her feet. Everything we'd planned was going off without a hitch, and so far, Matías was taking the bait.

They followed behind Matías, James's hand not leaving Izzy's body as they walked down the hallway toward the private rooms. I was sure Izzy wanted to have James's balls on a silver platter in that moment, but she forged on because the girl was fearless.

Matías pushed open a door, waiting in the hallway for them to enter first. Izzy glanced up at the security camera, and I could see the fear in her eyes.

We were putting her life at risk to catch someone who deserved to be off the streets and to spend eternity behind bars. I wasn't sure I could've done the same with Alese. For as much bravado as she displayed, I didn't think she could've walked into that room on her own knowing what kind of man was following her in.

Izzy froze as soon as she walked inside.

"If shit goes south, call the cops. You hear me, Alese?"

"Got it. Now go," Alese said as I stood near the doorway of the security room.

I ran down the labyrinth of hallways, weaving in and out of people on their way to their own private parties. I didn't have time to fuck around. I had one job, and that was to make it to the room before shit went down and someone got hurt.

I drew my gun before I pushed open the door, pointing it at the spot Matías had stood when I'd last seen him on camera. Matías spun around with Izzy in his arms.

"I'll snap her neck," Matías snarled.

"Fucker," Izzy said and glanced over at James, who was already advancing toward them.

"One more step and it's over." Matías's grip tightened.

I narrowed my gaze, and my finger ticked against the trigger. I wasn't afraid to shoot. My aim was always dead on. My years of military experience had never failed me. I'd been in situations like this before, but never with someone I knew and loved standing at the other end of the barrel, in the arms of the perpetrator.

Izzy didn't wait for me to take the shot; she brought her knee up and smashed her six-inch heel straight down on the top of his foot. He lurched forward just enough for her to break free of his hold and run into James's arms.

"Keep him alive," James told me.

"Can I shoot him at least?" The guy deserved at least one bullet. Not in any place that would end his life. We needed the information only he had in order to even hope to retrieve the thousands of people he'd sold into slavery.

Matías straightened, and his eyes grew colder. "You might as well kill me. I won't talk."

"Orders are to bring him in unharmed unless there are extenuating circumstances."

"This is extenuating." I smirked.

"Just let him shoot the fucker," Izzy said to James.

James grabbed Izzy's arms, untangling her from his body. "Stay here and don't move."

James gave me a look and I knew we were moving on Matías, and I wouldn't be lucky enough to shoot his ass today. We moved fast, overpowering him quickly and closing the shackles around his limbs. Matías screamed, struggling the entire time, but no one outside of our room could hear him.

"Izzy," James said as he stalked toward her.

"Yeah?" she whispered.

"You and Alese go back to the hotel, and we'll be back there as soon as they come to pick him up."

"Okay," she said, nodding slowly and robotically.

He wrapped his arms around her, embracing her. "Are you okay, doll?"

"I'm okay," she said to him and buried her face in his shirt. "I'll be okay. Just a little shell-shocked."

"We would've never let anything happen to you," he said in a soft, deep voice.

"I know. Can we wait here for you? I'd rather have a drink and wait in the common area than walk back to the hotel without you."

He swept his hand across her back. "That's fine." He leaned forward and kissed the top of her hair. "Go wait out there. Alese, if you can hear me, meet Izzy at the bar, please."

"Thanks." Izzy hugged him tighter before breaking the embrace.

She took one look at Matías and stalked forward, her heels clicking against the cement floor. James turned and stared at her, but he didn't say a word. I watched her, my mouth hanging open because her fearlessness never ceased to amaze me.

She raised a hand and slapped Matías as hard as she could, the sound of the impact echoing in the small space. Her fingernails grazed his skin as they swept across his face, leaving a red mark and drops of blood oozing from his cheek.

James looked just as shocked as me, but neither of us said anything as she spun around on her heels and marched out of the room. The satisfied look on her face said everything. I wasn't about to stop her from laying her hands on Matías. He'd done worse to people, and if it made Izzy feel better to slap him or more, I was good with it. I wanted to shoot the bastard, but I knew that wouldn't help any of his victims.

"FBI is on the way," Connor said from the doorway before he jammed his phone back into his pocket. "I'll let them in the back so the customers don't freak out."

"We'll wait with him," James told Connor.

When Connor left the room again, Matías started to beg. "What's your price? I'll double it."

"Shut the fuck up," I barked, wishing I'd put a bullet right between his eyes.

"Ten million. I can have it wired to your account in under two minutes."

James stalked toward him and punched him right in the face, knocking him clean out. "Fucker talked too much."

CHAPTER 16
NYA

I paced around the living room, repeatedly flipping the phone Alese had given me. She'd texted me twenty minutes ago and told me they were almost home. I'd barely slept, and even though I knew they were safe, I wouldn't believe it until they stood in front of me.

Peeking through the front window at an empty driveway, I grunted my frustration. The last forty-eight hours had dragged by. Each minute felt more like an hour as I stared at the clock, waiting for word about their safety.

When their truck pulled into the driveway, I pulled open the front door and ran down the stairs, almost running toward them. I wasn't sure I'd ever been so happy to see someone as I was to see them in that moment.

Alese waved from the passenger seat before jumping out of the truck. Ret watched through the window, a smile dancing on his lips as I embraced Alese.

"God, I've been so worried about you two," I whispered in her ear, burying my face in her hair.

"We're fine. Ret kept me safe, and I was never in any danger."

I stepped back with my hands gripping her arms so I could get a better look at her. "That's what you say."

"He made me stay in the security room. They used Izzy as bait."

I couldn't imagine how Izzy had felt knowingly being used to lure a psychopath. I didn't know her, but I didn't think I could willingly put myself in harm's way in the same situation, even to catch someone as bad as Matías. After what I went through with Diego, I couldn't put my life and freedom at risk again.

"Miss us?" Ret said as he walked toward us.

"Yes." I smiled and released Alese before moving toward him. "I've been worried."

Worried might have been an understatement. I wasn't going to tell them I was practically manic with anxiety as I paced the house all night. During the day, I'd kept myself busy, cleaning every inch of the house in hopes that time would pass quicker.

I wrapped my arms around Ret's middle and pressed my body flush against his. The gesture wasn't sexual, and it wasn't meant to be. I was thankful to have him. Thankful he was safe just as much as I was to have Alese back.

"I'm happy you're okay."

Ret laughed softly, his body hardening underneath mine with the slight movement. For a moment, I hugged him without his returning the gesture, but then he did it. He slid his arms around my back and pulled me against him. Not too hard, but with the perfect amount of pressure.

"We had to come back," he said as his hands splayed across my shirt, practically covering every square inch of my back. "We couldn't leave you alone."

"Thank God. I don't think I could've taken another day alone. I was about to clean the house for the third time."

"Oh, honey. You need an outlet for all that anxiety," Alese told me as we walked toward the house. "It's not good to stress."

"Have you slept?" Ret asked.

I frowned and felt embarrassed. "Not much," I admitted.

I hated to seem weak. I hated that I depended on them and felt like such a needy person when they weren't around. Maybe I needed to find my own place and break away from them, letting them get back to the life they had before I arrived.

They said if you really loved someone you should set them free. There were no two people who walked the earth that I loved and felt more thankful for than Ret and Alese. Ret saved me, and the two of them helped make me feel human again.

"Maybe we should…" Alese's voice trailed off as she came to stand next to me, and Ret raised an eyebrow. "Sometimes I sleep better after an amazing orgasm."

"I dunno," I said, but the thought sounded great.

Although I'd watched them, we'd never gone any further. I craved what I witnessed through the cracked doorway of their bedroom. I wanted to feel the rush of excitement, kneeling at a man's feet, awaiting my pleasure and his. It had been so long since I'd felt that way, but Ret and Alese made me want things I never thought I'd want again.

She touched Ret's shoulder, grazing his neck with her fingernails. "I could use some cock, handsome. I'm wound so fucking tight after this weekend. You game?" she asked, staring him straight in the eye and dead serious.

"Baby, I'm always game," he said, winking at her.

Alese turned her attention toward me as I twisted my hands together, unsure if I should say yes, but wanting to more than anything. "You?"

"Yes," I said as my voice trembled.

"You need to get out of your head for a while. Maybe, instead of just watching, you'll let Ret command you tonight. You need a little subspace and to surrender."

I nodded at Alese, knowing full well what she meant, and I couldn't disagree. I'd been wrapped in fear for so long I hadn't given myself time to process a damn thing or given myself a reprieve from anything I'd experienced. Rest hadn't come easily since I'd left Diego's mansion, except after that night at the club.

Ret lifted his chin toward the door behind us. "Let's go inside."

Alese practically squealed with delight as she took off toward the house, leaving us behind. "Y'all coming or what?" she yelled from the front steps of the house.

I moved quickly, following Alese as Ret walked behind me. I wasn't scared as we made our way down the hallway toward their bedroom. I wasn't frightened that either of them would hurt me. They'd already seen my body, and I'd seen theirs. I'd already lived the worst hell imaginable, and I'd never let myself be a victim again.

I wanted what Alese and Ret had. I wanted the love, kindness, and respect they showed each other. Ret adored Alese. He showered her with affection, always making sure she knew he loved her. I wanted someone to worship me the same way. Someone who would lay down their life for me.

In a way, I had that. Ret had saved me, pulling me from Diego's cage before he ushered me away from my parents. He'd saved me twice, and Alese brought me back to life. I never believed in instant love, the kind that swept a person off their feet and made them do foolish things, but with Ret and Alese, I felt it. I understood it, and I knew I wanted more.

"How are we going to do this?" I asked as we walked into their bedroom, stopping just inside the doorway.

"Do you want to keep your clothes on?" Alese asked as she started to pull down the straps of her sundress. "You can, you know, if you're more comfortable."

I smiled as my stomach fluttered. "No. You've already seen me." I glanced down at the floor and blew out a shaky breath. "I've always been comfortable with my nudity anyway."

"Thank God." She laughed, stepping out of the dress and kicking the material to the side. "I was really getting sick of wearing so many clothes all the time."

I peered over at Ret, who stood there with a wicked smile. "I have no issue with you two walking around naked all the time, but don't expect me not to be affected."

"Be affected," Alese said as she groped his crotch. "Be very affected." She smiled and brushed her lips against his as he wrapped an arm around her bare back and pulled her closer.

"Careful what you wish for, love."

"Nya." Alese peeked over her shoulder at me. "Why don't you lie on the bed with us instead of sitting across the room?"

"Oh." A surge of excitement coursed through me. I liked the thought of that…probably more than I should.

I met Ret's gaze, searching for his approval. "We talked in the car about the three of us. We're good with you being as near as you want. You can touch too or be touched if that's what you want," he said with a smile.

My skin tingled and my belly fluttered again as Alese walked toward me and took my hand. "We just want you to know there's nothing you can do that's wrong. Just follow what feels right and natural." She swept my hair behind my shoulder before resting her hand against my skin. "We're not jealous types. If you want to be touched or want to touch, do it."

"But…" I swallowed hard and moved my eyes between her and Ret, confused and turned on. "You guys are in a committed relationship, and I'm just… Just…"

"You're part of us now for as long as you want to be." She smiled, putting my mind at ease. "Ret and I are committed to each other, and nothing that happens between the three of us will do anything to destroy that. Do you understand?"

"I do." I nodded and finally smiled.

I couldn't imagine letting another man touch me. Ret was different. He rescued me and kept me safe. There wasn't another person I trusted more than him besides Alese.

"Now get undressed and get that pretty little ass of yours on the bed," she said as she walked by and swatted my ass playfully.

All the air rushed out of my lungs, and my heart started to race. Not in a bad way, but in an oh-my-God-this-is-going-to-be-amazing manner. Ret walked past me, shrugging like I should listen to Alese and stop stalling.

Alese sat on the edge of the bed, patting the spot next to her as I walked toward her, dropping my clothes to the floor. She swept her eyes across my body as she licked her lips.

Ret leaned forward, placing his fingers under her chin and forcing her eyes upward. "Undress me," he said.

I crawled onto the mattress, resting just behind Alese, observing as she undid the button and unzipped his jeans. He smiled down at her, watching carefully with his fingers still pressed against her chin.

She yanked at the side of his jeans, pulling them down his legs and freeing his cock. I licked my lips, getting the first real view of his size and shape in the bright lighting of their bedroom.

Alese wrapped her fingers around his shaft, slowly stroking up and down and rubbing her thumb along the underside. His body jerked each time, moving closer and into her touch.

He lifted his shirt over his head, throwing it to the floor behind him as she worked his cock in her palm. "Open your mouth," he told her, and she did without hesitation.

I curled my legs to my side and propped myself up, sweeping my hand across the swell of my breast. I watched in awe as she slid his length against her tongue and closed her lips around the base without gagging.

I'd never been able to take a man that size that deep without some sort of gag reflex kicking in and tears streaming down my face. Her lips slid back and forth, her hand still wrapped tightly around him and pressed against her lips, keeping contact with his entire cock with every stroke.

He closed his eyes as he swayed backward and tangled his fingers in her hair, not letting her forget who was really in control.

I wondered what he tasted like and if his cock felt as velvety smooth as it looked. Alese moaned around his shaft with a hint of a smile like she knew exactly what she was doing and what would happen next.

Ret shivered as he glanced down, and he drew in a sharp breath. "Lie back," he told her, releasing his grip on her scalp.

Alese crawled backward with her legs spread, never turning her back on Ret. The hunger in his eyes deepened, and his cock bobbed and weaved, hanging freely from his body with no mouth or hands to support its weight as he moved.

I kept my hands to myself, but I was dying to touch one of them. I'd missed contact, soft and gentle sweeps across the skin that sent goose bumps scattering in all directions. It had been so long since I'd had that type of touch, and I craved it just as much as I wanted to kneel at someone's feet.

I stayed where I was as Alese lay back on the bed and Ret crawled between her legs, nudging her thighs farther apart with his knees.

He glanced at me, and I blushed when his eyes lingered on my breasts longer than I expected. "Touch your nipples."

I looked up, my eyes wide as he gazed at me. "Me?" I asked like a complete idiot.

He nodded with a slight grin. "Yes, you, Nya. Unless you're not comfortable with me…"

I didn't let him finish the statement as I slid my hand to my breasts, sweeping my fingers across my nipples and showing him I was completely comfortable.

"Pinch them lightly," he said.

I sucked in a breath, knowing my nipples had always been sensitive. I closed the tips of my fingers around the bud and applied some pressure. I closed my eyes as I dropped my head back, loving the tingling sensation that cascaded over my skin.

"Touch only your breasts until I say otherwise."

My eyes flew open, growing wide. Don't touch myself in any other way? That was torture, and soon, with the gentle pull of my fingers, I'd be dripping with need with no relief in sight unless he gave his approval.

"Ret, please," I whimpered and pouted.

"Do as I say, and you'll be rewarded," he promised, keeping his eyes trained on my hands as he made himself comfortable between Alese's legs. "You're so wet already, baby." He flickered his eyes up her body as he skidded his fingers across her core.

"There's something so hot about this," she said, finishing on a moan as his fingers drifted across her clit.

I watched his hand as he coated his fingers with her need, moving so slowly it verged on pleasurable torture. But at least Alese was being touched, stroked in all the right places, while I teased my own nipples, wanting to dip my fingers between my legs but didn't dare.

I sat up, tucking my feet underneath me and needing more as I watched Ret push two fingers inside Alese, slowly filling her. My pussy constricted and ached, wishing to feel the same fullness Alese was enjoying while I rocked back and forth on my knees. Using both hands, I pinched my nipples, yanking on them lightly and rolling the tips between my fingertips, alternating the pressure and sensation to stop myself from going mad with lust.

Alese lifted her ass off the bed, offering her pussy to Ret as he thrust his fingers deeper. "You want to come?" he asked her, and I had to bite my lip to stop myself from yelling yes.

"Come on, baby. Gimme your mouth," she pleaded. "I was a good girl." She turned her head and peered over at me with a sinful smirk.

She was good. Their relationship was equal parts push and pull, both of them using every tool in their arsenal to get what they wanted, while keeping the other person happy too.

Ret followed her eyes, glancing at me as I toyed with my nipples and tried to control my ragged breathing. "Spread your legs. Let Alese see how beautiful you are."

Oh God. In the dim lighting of the club's private room, this was easier...less personal and up close. But in the bedroom, only a few feet away with every light shining overhead, it gave everyone a perfect view.

I gave my nipple another tug, feeling the wetness between my legs and knowing they were about to see how turned on I was. I held my breath and spread my knees, giving them both a full view of my pussy.

"She's breathtaking," Alese said, making my face heat.

Their eyes were on me as Ret's fingers continued to fill her pussy, moving in slower, longer strokes than before. "Look how wet she is," Ret said and dragged his tongue across his bottom lip.

I squirmed and sucked in a breath, wishing his tongue were dragging across my clit, lapping up my wetness.

"Keep your legs open, and keep playing with your breasts," he told me before bringing his mouth down on Alese's clit, closing his lips around it as he pushed his fingers deeper inside her.

I felt my eyes roll back as she moaned. The sensations and need that had been building inside me intensified. I felt like I was ready to pop as my body trembled, and I wasn't sure if I could take much more.

He licked her pussy, not missing a single inch of her flesh as he drove her closer to the edge, thrusting his fingers hard and faster. Her fingers curled into the comforter, fisting the material in her palms. "Fuck," she gasped when he pulled away, leaving her empty and panting.

"You want some?" Ret asked as I almost fell forward, gasping right along with her.

I hadn't noticed I'd started to lean forward, drawn to the sights and sounds of her ecstasy. "Me?" I asked, stilling my hands, but continuing to hold my nipples tightly.

"You can stay there, or you can move closer if you trust me enough to touch you."

God, I trusted him. I trusted them both. I was so out of my mind with lust that I didn't hesitate another second as I scooted closer, unsure what else to do.

"Lie down next to Alese," he said as he sat up, positioning his legs underneath his body like I had done.

His cock was hard, sticking straight up, and I wanted so badly to feel the velvety hardness against my skin. But I was turned on, and I was going to do whatever he asked if it meant the throbbing between my legs would go away.

I glanced at Alese, letting a moment of fear flash through my mind until I lay back and she laced her fingers with mine. "Don't worry, Nya. This is his specialty."

"What is?" I asked as my heart started to pound faster, louder than before.

"Finger-fucking." I formed a perfect O with my lips as she smiled. "He's a master at it."

"If you need me to stop, just say 'Red.'"

I nodded, swallowing down the fear that hid just beneath the surface of my lust. Slowly he lowered his hand to my knee and waited for me to adjust to being touched by someone else and naked.

No one had touched me since Diego, and more than anything, I wanted to rid myself of every memory of him. When I closed my eyes, I didn't want to see his face. I wanted new memories, new sensations, new orgasms to wipe away every remnant of him.

"Good?" Ret asked as Alese squeezed my fingers.

"Yes," I said without my voice cracking.

Ret smiled, and my insides warmed. "Close your eyes if you want. Just enjoy this, and don't hesitate to stop me."

"Yes, Sir, but I'd like to watch," I told him. "And I'm okay."

He gave me a quick nod before looking at Alese. "Same goes for you too, baby. Play with those beautiful tits."

I smiled, loving that I wasn't the only one touching myself. His hand moved, and I sucked in a breath, waiting for the moment when he put his hands between my legs.

The pressure of his grip increased the higher up my thigh his hand moved. Gently he pushed against my inner thigh, telling me to open to him. I'd been so wrapped up in my nipples and the anticipation, I'd almost forgotten to give him access to the one part of my body I wanted him to touch the most.

"Jesus, you're both so wet for me," he said as I bent my knees, touching Alese's.

I licked my lips, dying to feel the roughness of his hands against my skin. Slowly, he moved his hand higher, and just when I thought he was never going to touch me there, he glided his fingertips through my wetness.

I gasped at the softness and the warmth of his skin as he raked his fingers across me. I widened my legs in a silent plea for him to keep touching me. I tightened my fingers around Alese's, and I lifted my bottom off the bed as he skated his finger across my clit, sending shockwaves through my system.

There was hesitancy in his touch. Maybe he was as scared as I was, unsure if this was the right thing to do but unable to stop at the same time. The lust outweighed any anxiety I felt about taking this step. I wanted Ret, needing his hands on me to quench the achy desire between my legs.

The thick muscles of his arms flexed as he moved his hands against my body and Alese's simultaneously. I kept my eyes locked on him, moving across his beautiful bare chest, impressive arms, and handsome face. He was watching me, studying my every movement and trying to find subtle cues that I was panicking, but I wasn't. With

Alese, he was doing the opposite. His fingers were buried deep inside her, rocking in and out of her body in a steady rhythm.

"Touch me," I said, giving him full permission. "I want this. I want you. I want what you're giving her."

His eyes darkened, burning with as much lust as I felt coursing through my system. Those must've been the words he needed to hear because his soft touches became firmer and more confident.

I closed my eyes and just let myself be in the moment, enjoying the feel of his hands against me. He flattened his fingers, sliding them against my wetness and coating them in my arousal. My stomach tightened as a new wave of excitement washed over me when the tips of his fingers explored my middle.

I sucked in a breath, keeping my eyes closed as he pushed a single finger inside. The pace was agonizingly slow, but delicious too. His thumb brushed against my clit, and I squirmed, wanting more. He pulled his finger out, and I was about to complain when a second prodded my opening. I exhaled, tipping my hips upward, inviting him to plunge his fingers inside me.

My pussy ached to be filled, stretched by someone who wanted to bring me nothing but pleasure. The painful throb disappeared as soon as he pushed two thick fingers inside, stretching me.

I moaned as my pussy contracted around his fingers, loving every minute of his touch and wanting more. Slowly, he moved his fingers, curling them upward and stroking my G-spot.

Every fear I had fell away, replaced by the urgency to come, chasing the orgasm I wanted and needed more than air. I opened my eyes, making myself remember this was Ret and not Diego. I had to keep myself in the moment and firmly in reality. Ret's touch alone should've been enough. Diego never touched me so gently, but I opened my eyes anyway.

"Alese, get up and get on your knees," Ret said as his fingers slipped out of her but remained deep inside me.

Alese moved quickly, planting the side of her head against the comforter and facing me. She presented him her ass, smiling and staring at me as I turned to face her. We stared at each other for a second, but I glanced back at Ret just as he pressed the tip of his cock between her legs and thrust into her.

I bit my lip and moaned as he filled her and pushed his fingers deeper inside me too. He rocked against her body, finger-fucking me too, in the same fast-paced rhythm. He curled his fingers inside me, stroking my insides and massaging my G-spot, driving me closer to the edge of bliss.

"Yes!" I chanted as my toes curled and my body tightened. "Yes!"

He sped up his hips, pummeling her pussy over and over again as his fingers rocked against my insides, bringing me more pleasure than I ever knew possible.

Two swipes of his thumb over my clit had my back arching off the bed as the orgasm slammed into me. I gasped for air as colors exploded behind my eyes and every nerve in my body sprang to life, rocking me to the core. Aftershocks rattled through me as his fingers slowed, eventually stilling, but never leaving my body.

On his knees before me with Alese still facedown on the bed, Ret smacked her ass so hard her body lurched forward. It was enough to send her over the edge in a howling orgasm, which he followed. I watched as their expressions morphed, the pull of pleasure too intense to keep a straight face. They were at their most vulnerable, riding the waves of pleasure at my side.

I watched, mesmerized by the scene before me, listening to Ret moan her name before his body stilled. I whimpered when his fingers left my body and he rolled to his side with Alese between us.

I smiled as I stared up at the ceiling, my heart sputtering in my chest and my muscles too weak to move. I'd let another man touch me, and I didn't freak out. But that wasn't hard with Ret.

"Yeah, that was…" Alese said, sucking in a breath and swallowing. "Yeah."

"I know," I whispered, knowing exactly what she meant when she really didn't say anything at all.

For the first time in months, I felt nothing but joy, contentment, and serenity.

CHAPTER 17

CHAPTER 17

RET

"I think I fucked up," I told James, sitting across from him inside his office the next afternoon.

He leaned back, blowing out a long, drawn-out breath because I wasn't the first person to utter those words to him. "What happened?"

"Nya."

He pulled his hand down his face, letting out a strangled groan. "What about her?"

"So." I hunched over with my elbows resting on my knees and stared at the floor. "We may have slept with her." I closed my eyes and grimaced, waiting for James to jump over the desk and knock me on my ass.

The wheels on his chair squeaked against the plastic carpet protector. "We?"

"Yeah." I lifted my head just enough to see he was still seated, which was a good sign. So far, James and I didn't have to come to blows over something I did inside my bedroom.

James and I had an understanding about sex. As members of the same club, often seeing each other and the other's woman in very little clothing, we never talked about sex at work. What happened at the club, stayed at the club. We were different people there. The two lives never crossed, and so far, we'd been good at maintaining the separation.

"The three of us," I said and finally brought my eyes to his. I wasn't scared of James. Not of his power, at least, but he was my boss, and I didn't want to put the business in jeopardy.

"Oh," he said, sounding more shocked than pissed.

"I'm sorry." My facial expression wasn't a frown, but I wasn't smiling either. I didn't know what the fuck to say or how to look because I'd never done something as stupid as that in my entire life. Business and pleasure never mixed in my line of work, but then, I'd never rescued someone either.

"Did she want it?"

"Well, yeah."

"Interesting." His eyebrows shot up as his head jerked back. "She's full of surprises."

"That's one way of putting it."

He laced his fingers together before resting them on the desk. "What happens in your house is your business. The doctor gave her the all clear. We are no longer employed by the Halsteads, and Nya isn't our client either. She is willingly staying with you, and you didn't force yourself on her, right?"

"That's a laughable statement. You know me better than that."

"I know, man. Like we've said before, some shit isn't meant for the office, and it's no one's business but your own."

I nodded in assent because that had always been our agreement, but I felt this situation was different from any other we'd been put in before.

Before James could respond, there was a light knock on the door. Angel walked in, face ashen and without a smile. "Ret," she said softly as I turned.

My stomach dropped as soon as my eyes met hers. "What happened?"

Angel was always our ray of sunshine. The single bright light in the office every day. No matter how crazy shit got, she always kept her cool, sprinkling her happiness everywhere she could.

She stepped into the room, still holding the door handle, and swallowed hard before she blew out a breath. "I just took a call that Alese is being transported to Tampa General. You need to go there now."

I was on my feet, pushing Angel out of the way and ignoring James as he yelled after me. I barely remembered running through the office as everything passed by in a blur.

The palm trees whizzed by like feathers in the wind as I weaved in and out of traffic, heading toward the hospital and breaking every speed limit along the way without giving two fucks about any of it. My hands shook, and no matter how tightly I wrapped them around the steering wheel, nothing stopped the fear from seeping into my bones and simultaneously wrapping around my neck like a noose.

I tried to steady my breathing. "She's fine." I repeated those words to myself as I pulled into the emergency room parking lot, put the car in park, and almost forgot to turn the damn thing off before I sprinted toward the door.

"Alese Winters," I told the nurse, trying to play it cool when I was pretty sure she could see my heart beating right through my shirt.

"Ret!"

I turned and saw Nya running in my direction with her cheeks covered in tears and her eyes practically swollen shut. "Nya." I wrapped her in my arms as she collided with my chest. "What happened?" As I searched her face, I pushed back the hair clinging to her wet cheeks.

"We were…" She sucked in a breath, practically hyperventilating and shaking uncontrollably. "We were walking…" Her voice trembled and her lip quivered as she stared up at me with tears spilling down her face.

"Slow down." I pulled her closer, trying to comfort her even though I'd never been very good at the tender things. "Is Alese okay?"

"A car." She clutched my shirt and held on tight, balling the fabric in her fists. "It hit her in the crosswalk," she whispered so softly, I thought I heard her wrong. "I don't know how it missed me."

I had to remind myself to breathe as my chest seized and my muscles locked. "Is she okay?" I asked again, but this time, my jaw was clenched and my teeth mashed together because I realized the answer to my question might not be something I wanted to hear.

"I don't know."

"Mr. North," a woman said behind me.

Nya and I turned together, clutching each other tightly as if we were the only thing keeping the other upright.

"Yes?" My voice trembled, sounding foreign and unlike myself. I always possessed confidence when I spoke. I always had my shit together.

But then, I'd never loved someone the way I loved Alese. I'd never worried about losing anything in my life before because I spent most of my years alone. Alese changed that. She came along at a time when I wasn't looking for anyone. She kind of fell into my lap when I least expected to find someone, and as they said…the rest was history.

The woman held a clipboard tightly against her chest, clutching it the same way I was holding on to Nya. "Can you follow me please?"

I glanced down, and Nya was staring up at me with wide eyes like I had all the answers and could make everything better. Which I couldn't, but she didn't know that yet.

"Come on, doll. I'm sure she's fine." I told that lie like I was a professional bullshitter because the words slid off my tongue like honey.

Nya stayed attached to me with her arm around my back as we followed the woman in the blue scrubs still holding the clipboard through a bustling hallway to a tiny room.

"Where's Alese?" I asked as we entered the nondescript room with nothing but a few chairs and a small table.

"Please sit." She motioned toward the chairs before closing the door and sitting across from us.

Nya sat next to me with one hand on my leg and the fingers on the other one intertwined with mine. Neither of us spoke. What was there to say at a time like this? We didn't dare speak the words or fears we both felt. Saying them made it true or possible, and neither of us had the ability to face what came next.

"I'm Dr. Hughes. I thought it was best we talk in private before I take you in to see Ms. Winters."

"Doctor, be straight with us. Where's Alese?"

She cleared her throat as she placed the clipboard on the table next to her. "She's comfortable at the moment. You're listed as her emergency contact and next of kin so I can speak openly about her condition, but please know she has a DNR in place."

I jerked back in my chair, and Nya tightened her fingers around mine as she gasped. Alese had not told me about having a Do Not Resuscitate order in place. We'd never talked about things like what we wanted if something should happen to us, but I didn't know she had a plan in place.

"Ms. Winters's body sustained numerous injuries from the impact. Before we knew about her DNR, we resuscitated her when she arrived in the ER. We've been able to stabilize her as much as possible, but she's in grave condition."

"Speak English, Doc." My brain couldn't process all the terms. I still couldn't believe I was sitting here, hearing that Alese was possibly going to die. She already had once, I guessed, but they were able to bring her back.

"Ms. Winters has a punctured lung, a broken leg, and internal bleeding."

I didn't move. I couldn't speak, and breathing became difficult. Nya sobbed at my side, holding my hands so tightly my fingers started to tingle, but none of it mattered.

"We need to do surgery to find and stop the bleeding before we can begin to address her other injuries, but the likelihood she'll survive is slim, Mr. North."

The doctor said everything so matter-of-factly, like she was telling me about her plans for the evening. I was sure she'd done this a thousand times, dropped bad news in laps of other loved ones, but this was something I'd never experienced. The coldness in the way the news was given had me in as much shock as the realization that Alese could very well die.

"If she survives, her recovery will be long and extensive. She might never be able to walk again, and if she does, it will be well over a year before she would be fully mobile again."

The sadness left me, replaced by anger. Anger at the doctor. Anger at the driver. Anger at the world. "I don't care. I just want my girl back. Do whatever you can to save her life."

She stood, grabbing that goddamn clipboard before she straightened. "I'll bring you back to see her now while we prep for surgery."

"Thank you."

We followed her out of the tiny room, back into the hallway that teemed with life. Nya held on to me, practically climbing up my body as she cried.

The doctor stopped outside a room, motioning for us to go in, but I wasn't ready. I turned to Nya and held her by the shoulders, moving her away from me a little. "Nya, listen to me."

She gazed up at me with her swollen face and red eyes, unable to hold back the tears. She didn't speak, but she nodded that she was listening.

"We have to hold our shit together for Alese. Do you understand? We can't scare her."

She dropped her head, staring at the floor as her tears plopped on the floor near her feet. "I can't go in there, Ret. I can't see her like that."

I gripped her shoulders tighter and closed my eyes for a moment. "Stay out here. Let me talk to my girl first. If she seems okay, I'll come get you."

"Go," she said softly.

I released my grip on her and turned my back. I took a deep breath and tried to remember my training from the military to calm myself down, but it didn't work. I was prepared for battle. Send me into hostile territory armed to the hilt, and I could stay level-headed without my hand shaking even a little. But this... This was new territory and one I wasn't sure I was ready to face.

CHAPTER 18

RET

The only sound in the room was the beeping of her monitors, telegraphing her labored breaths and unsteady heart rate. I pressed her hand to my face, taking in her scent and the sweetness that had been the only true home I'd ever known.

Lying in the bed, she seemed so weak and small, but Alese had never been either of those things before, and it didn't feel right. She barely moved as I swept my lips across her skin, closing my eyes and soaking in her softness against me.

She woke up for a moment when I first walked in, staring at me with her big, wide blue eyes before they fluttered closed again. The nurse had told me they had her on a ton of pain killers and drugs to keep her sedated because it was important for her to stay calm.

I tried to keep the fear off my face. I tried to keep my shit together and not let the tears that were threatening to fall overtake me. The last thing I wanted was for her to open her eyes and see me a complete mess. I had always been Alese's rock, and I wasn't about to change now. She needed me to be stronger than I'd ever been, but I wasn't sure how long I could keep up the façade.

I wanted to crawl into bed with her, pull her into my arms, and make her better. It took everything in me to restrain myself from doing just that because I wanted to heal her. I wanted to save her life.

Her hands, arms, and face were covered in scratches and bruises like she'd been in a bar brawl and had come out on the losing end. But I knew the real injuries, the life-threatening ones, hid beneath the surface and were tucked neatly beneath the blankets covering her tattered body.

I placed my mouth next to her ear and set one arm above her head, softly stroking her golden hair as I stared at my girl. "I love you, *piccola*," I whispered without my voice cracking. "Don't give up. I'm not ready to let you go."

But then I realized I'd never be ready for that day. Things like this, shitty events and near-death experiences, made a person realize how precious and fragile life truly was.

"Son." My dad's voice filled the space between the beeps, but I couldn't bring myself to face him.

I couldn't take my eyes off Alese because, any minute now, they'd take her from me. "Pop."

His footsteps were heavy as he crossed the gray linoleum flooring and rested his hand on my shoulder. "Alese," he said softly with a hard squeeze.

"It's not good, Pop."

"Nya filled me in." He took a deep breath, probably on the verge of tears just like I was. The man acted tough, but I knew, underneath, he was a big pile of feelings. He didn't always talk about them, but they lingered, hidden away to maintain his tough-guy persona. "The doctors are outside, and they said they're about to take her down for surgery."

I squeezed my eyes shut, not ready to let her go even though I knew it was her only hope of surviving. How could you say goodbye to someone when you weren't sure you'd ever see them again?

"Gimme a minute."

His hand tightened on my shoulder before his footsteps grew softer, the door closing behind him. I buried my face in her hair, placing my lips near her ear, and inhaled every drop of Alese I could.

"Come back to me, Alese. If you can't, I'll understand and I'll love you forever, but fight."

I wanted to hear her say my name. I wanted to hear the laughter I'd grown to love. I wanted to relive the moment we kissed each other goodbye this morning. I wanted everything I couldn't have at that moment.

When the door opened behind me, I knew what it meant. My time was up, and Alese's fight was just beginning. "I love you," I whispered in her ear again. "I love you, Alese."

"Mr. North," the doctor said as she entered the room. "We're ready for Alese now."

I wanted to tell her to fuck off because I wasn't ready to let her go, but I had to man up and I knew this was the only way I'd get my girl back. I kissed her cheek, careful not to hurt her but hard enough that I hoped she felt it too.

"There's a surgical waiting room downstairs, and we'll keep you updated on her progress."

I stared down at Alese as I stood from the chair beside her bed. Her body was so broken, with her injuries clearly evident all over her skin. The road rash, the bruises, the blood that covered almost every inch of her body.

"She's in good hands, and we'll do everything possible to save her life." I knew the doctor's words were meant to calm me and give me hope, but they did neither.

I didn't move. I couldn't make myself walk away. I wanted to stand over her in the operating room, watching as they saved her life. A team of people entered the room and started to prep her bed for the journey downstairs.

"Son," my dad said again, softer this time, the somberness in his voice unmistakable.

I waited for them to wheel her out, watching as she disappeared behind my dad, before I took a step toward the doorway.

I didn't say anything to him as I stood at his side, staring down the corridor in total shock. My pop didn't say anything either; each of us just as lost as the other. The sound of someone sobbing drew my attention away from Alese for a moment, and I found Nya huddled on the floor in tears.

"Nya," I said as my heart seized, not only for myself, but for her too. Alese and Nya had formed such a quick bond, and this would devastate her too. I reached down, pulling Nya to her feet and tucking her against me. I couldn't save Alese, I couldn't protect her, but I could be that person for Nya.

Pop slid his arm around my shoulder and pulled me closer. "Come on, Ret. The guys are on their way."

I followed his motion, moving down the hospital hallway in a haze. Nya gripped my hand tightly, clinging to me. "She'll be okay," I told Nya, but the words were more for me than for her.

Alese had to be okay.

For six long hours, I paced the waiting room, practically wearing a rut in the floor. The guys sat silently, filling the waiting room and refusing to leave. Every time the doors to the restricted area opened, my heart would jump because I thought it was an update on Alese. I'd badgered the poor nurse manning the desk outside at least twenty times for an update, but she always said they were still working on Alese and to be patient.

Patience. Mine had worn out five hours ago. Somehow, I kept my cool, trying to maintain my strength and hopefulness. I'd begged Fran to take Nya home. She'd been through enough trauma in the last few months, and I worried that the added stress would push her over the edge. Nya refused to leave, though, and Fran wasn't going to push her either.

No one wanted to go. No matter how many times I told them they could go home, they refused to leave my side.

"How 'bout something to eat?" Fran asked as her eyes followed me pacing back and forth for the thousandth time.

"I'm good," I told her because the last thing I cared about was eating.

"You need to stay strong for her."

I nodded, but I didn't miss a beat as I continued my steps. If I stopped, I thought too much. If I walked, I stayed focused, picturing Alese well again and in my arms.

"The doc's coming," Pop said, motioning toward the doorway with his chin.

I stalked toward her, barely letting her step foot in the waiting room before I spoke. "Is she okay?"

She pulled the cap from her head and wiped her forehead with the back of her hand. I was on pins and needles, unable to move even in the slightest.

"We were able to stabilize her. She's a fighter, that's for sure. She has a long road to recovery and she's not out of the woods entirely, but we've stopped the bleeding and she's in the recovery room."

I clutched my chest, finally letting out the air I'd been holding in my lungs. I had expected to hear bad news, figured the universe was trying to pay me back for something I'd done in the past.

"Thank God," I groaned, feeling like the weight of the world was finally off my shoulders.

"We'll know more in a day or so."

I stepped forward, wanting to get to Alese as soon as possible. "Can I see her?"

"She's in recovery right now. When she's ready, we'll let you see her, but she may be moved to her room first."

"Thank you," I said and finally smiled.

When the doctor walked out of the room, I turned to face my family. The ladies were in tears, and the guys were shaking their heads and holding their women tightly. Moments like this made us remember how fragile life really was and how quickly everything could change.

CHAPTER 19

NYA

2 weeks later…

"Please go to work," Alese begged Ret from the couch. "I have Nya. I'll be fine." She tried to move and winced.

Ret practically leaped across the coffee table and placed his hands under her arms to help her. "I can't leave you here like this."

She'd been home from the hospital a week and hadn't had a minute alone. Even when I was with her, he'd be standing nearby, ready to swoop in and save her in case of some major tragedy.

"Nya will watch me."

His watchful eyes turned to me, and I smiled, shifting nervously on my feet. "I'll take good care of her. I swear."

"The guys don't need me back yet."

Alese rolled her eyes as she tried to adjust her leg on the pillow beneath it. "That's not what Izzy said."

Ret snarled and turned his head. "You two talking about me?"

I was about to run into my bedroom and hide because Alese wasn't going to back down, and I was afraid Ret wasn't going to either.

"Go back to work, Ret. Please. I can only take so much mothering. You're worse than Fran sometimes."

I inched backward, knowing she'd just threw down something Ret didn't want to hear. Fran was divine and one of the sweetest people I'd ever met, but she was a hawk, always circling above everyone and micromanaging.

"You didn't." He stepped forward, shaking his head, and waved his arms. "I can't believe you just said that to me."

"I need some normalcy, baby. Go to work. Let us have a girls' day—unless you want a mani-pedi too."

"Nya."

I swallowed down my laughter and straightened my face because he already looked like he was about to blow his top. "Yeah?"

He pinned me with his stare, his turquoise eyes burning. "You call me if anything happens. I mean anything. Got me?"

"Yes, Sir." I nodded quickly, but I didn't dare crack a smile.

"If shit goes south, you won't get me out of here again until you're fully recovered."

Alese waved her hands toward the door as he stared her down. "We'll be fine. Go."

"Fine," he said, walking toward her and not out like she'd hoped. He leaned forward, brushing his lips across her forehead before gazing into her eyes. "I love you, *piccola*. Don't overdo it today."

"I'll be right here. It's pretty hard to overdo it when I can only move my hands." She smiled up at him before pulling his face down to hers. "Kiss me for real."

Ret didn't hesitate as he pressed his lips against hers, soft at first like he was afraid he could break her. I didn't know if he even realized he'd been treating her with kid gloves since the moment we got home from the hospital, but I was sure, even if I pointed it out, he wouldn't give a damn.

She pushed against his chest when he lingered a little too long, the kiss growing deeper as he tried to sidetrack her. We both knew his game, and although he thought he was the boss, Alese always found a way to set his ass straight.

"Go," she said once again, finally pushing him hard and far enough that his lips drifted away from hers.

He growled, moving slowly as he straightened but kept his eyes locked on her. "I'm going. I'll check in every hour."

"I have no doubt." She shook her head and laughed. "I'm not going to tell you again," she warned after he still hadn't started toward the door.

He grumbled something before snagging his keys off the counter and finally walking toward the door. Alese and I stared at each other, waiting for the familiar click as he closed the door behind him.

We both took a deep breath and sighed, finally alone again without Ret staring at us both.

"Geez, he's so intense sometimes."

Alese giggled, grimacing and holding her stomach as her body moved. "I knew the Fran remark would get his ass in gear."

"That was a low blow."

She shrugged with an unapologetic smile. "It worked."

"Can I get you something?"

"Nothing." She patted the couch next to her. "Come sit."

I hadn't realized I'd been hovering over her just as much as Ret had been the last two weeks. We went in shifts oftentimes. He'd sleep; I'd watch Alese. I'd sleep, and he'd do the same. When we were both awake, the poor woman couldn't get a moment to herself.

I sat on the couch next to her, my ass hanging off the cushion because I didn't want to get too close or hurt her. I'd never seen a couch as big as this, but I still made sure to leave plenty of room between us.

"How are you doing? We haven't talked about what happened yet."

We hadn't talked about the accident at all. After I explained everything to Ret, I didn't speak another word about it. But I had played the sequence of events in my head over and over again, reliving the nightmare of watching Alese's body as she flew through the air and landed on the cement.

"I'm okay." I folded my hands in my lap and twisted my fingers together, dreading going over the day once again.

"I didn't think I'd survive. When that car hit me, all I could think about was Ret..." Her voice trailed off as she reached for my hand. "And you too, of course."

My insides warmed because I never expected her to think about me as she lay dying in the mall parking lot. I wasn't even sure what I'd think about if I were in the same situation.

"You don't have to say that." I squeezed her hand gently, careful not to hurt her because Ret had drummed that into my head over the last week. He treated her like a porcelain doll that could shatter if touched too roughly. "Ret was beside himself, Alese."

"I'm sure he was. I hate that you guys had to go through that."

"No." I slid my hand up her arms, stroking her soft, warm skin and feeling completely at peace. "None of that matters. You're getting better, and we couldn't ask for anything more than that."

"Promise me something," she said, placing her hand over mine as she stared at me.

"Anything."

"Promise me you'll distract Ret a bit. You two need to stop staring at me every second of the day."

I laughed and nodded slowly. "I can promise to try to distract him, and I'll stop staring. But I can't guarantee Ret will do the same."

"We'll find a way." She gave me a devilish smile, and I knew she was cooking up a plan to get a bit of normalcy back into our lives. "We always do."

CHAPTER 20

RET

Alese was right. I needed to go back to work. Not just because they needed me, but for my sanity as well as hers. We'd never been so far up each other's ass as we'd been the last two weeks. But I couldn't imagine leaving her behind until I was confident she was better. I knew Nya was more than capable of taking care of Alese while I was gone, but it didn't help ease my worry after coming so close to losing her.

"Dude," Morgan called. "It's been hell without you, man. I didn't think I'd last another day."

I had barely made it through the front door when he started walking toward me. That was what I loved most about this place. It wasn't just a job; we were a family. A very fucked-up one, but still, we loved each other. None of us would ever admit that shit either.

"Pop bothering you?"

Bear didn't have my ass to be up in while I'd been off. The dude seriously needed to find a new hobby. For the first thirty years of my life, I barely heard from him, but now, he was Dad of the Year and had to know every little thing that was happening in my life. It didn't help that we worked at the same place, but damn, the man could give me a little room to breathe sometimes.

"Fuckin' making me crazy. I have enough shit with my mom, but add Bear to the mix, and it's ridiculous."

I laughed and placed my arm around my stepbrother. The word was still foreign on my tongue, and I wasn't sure I'd ever get used to thinking of Morgan as more than a friend. "I'll take some of the heat off. You can have a little break."

Morgan stepped away and glanced down the hallway, probably seeing if my pop was eavesdropping like he'd done more than once. "He's all up in arms about this case he's working on. He wants me to help, but I'm swamped. Think you can do me that solid?"

"I'll handle him."

"Ret!"

I rolled my eyes, but I knew my dad had heard me. I was actually surprised he wasn't in the waiting room already because he always seemed to know when I was near.

"See." Morgan tilted his head toward the offices. "He's going off the deep end without you."

"I'm on it," I told him, giving a quick chin dip to Angel as I walked by the front desk. She waved, laughing quietly as she talked to someone on the phone.

I made it within three feet of my dad's office when he came barreling out the door and wrapped his arms around me. "Thank God you're here. I've missed you, kid."

"Thanks, Pop," I said as I tried to breathe through his bear hug. "You can put me down now."

He lowered my feet to the floor and slapped me on the shoulder, harder than I expected, and I jolted sideways and glared.

"Sorry. Sorry. I'm just so damn happy to have you back. It's boring without you."

"Need help with a case?" I skipped over the sappy shit, preferring to get right down to business. I didn't have all day and night to chitchat like long lost friends catching up after years of separation.

I'd only been gone a few weeks, but everyone acted like I hadn't walked through the front door in years.

"Yeah. We're about to have a team meeting about it."

The man loved anything that involved the team. Most guys his age dreamed about retirement, but not Pop. He wanted action. He craved adventure, and if it involved watching people banging...it was even better. He loved living on the edge and danger. I wasn't sure he'd ever have a peaceful day the rest of his life. I'd figured Fran would've convinced him to retire by now, but even she didn't have the power to get him to sit at home and watch television all day.

"Lead the way," I said, motioning down the hallway, ready to get the day started.

As I followed behind him, I pulled out my phone and shot off a message to Nya.

Me: Things okay?

Pop glanced over his shoulder and eyed my phone. "Texting Alese?"

"Just checking in on the girls."

"Good idea."

That was when I knew it wasn't a good idea. If Pop thought it was...then it wasn't. When in doubt, do the opposite.

Nya: We're both dead. —Alese.

I stared at the phone and shook my head.

Me: I'll text later.

Nya: Very later.

Well, she told me.

She might have been injured and recovering, but that didn't mean there wouldn't be hell to pay. Alese had a short fuse, and after two weeks of nonstop attention, she was done with it.

James, Thomas, and the rest of the ragtag crew of guys sat around the table, shuffling papers around.

"Look who I found," Pop said, sounding like a total cheeseball, but I knew his heart was in the right place.

"Glad you're back. We could use another set of hands." Thomas gave me a quick nod. "Let's get started."

James gave me a chin lift right before he started to speak. "The Almeda case. Bear, update us real quick for those who may have missed what's going on."

The group seemed to be on edge, but I couldn't quite figure out why. I didn't think being away for a few weeks would be awkward, but there was something I was missing, and I wouldn't stop until I found out.

Me: Dude, why's everyone grumpy as fuck?

Sam glanced at his phone before looking down the table as he picked it up.

Sam: Who the hell knows. I think it has to do with Nya. Ask Frisco. He knows more than me.

Nya?

Me: What's going on with Nya?

Frisco: Some bullshit with that Diego dude.

I breathed a sigh of relief that it had nothing to do with her treacherous parents, but Diego… He was an entirely different animal.

Me: What about him?

Frisco: Another girl has gone missing.

My eyebrows shot up. Not in surprise that he'd found a new victim, but that he did it so quickly without thinking it would set off alarm bells in the BDSM community in Atlanta. Even in big cities, the club community was often tight, and information moved like wildfire. I curled my fingers around my phone and growled, earning me a look from James.

"You up to helping Bear on this one, Ret?" James asked, staring at my hands as I tried my best to crush my phone.

I placed the phone on the table and took a deep breath, trying to calm the fuck down. "I'll be his point person on it."

James nodded, but he kept his eyes on me. "Good. Next order of business is Charmed and Diego Lopez."

I gritted my teeth and pictured the smug bastard with my hands wrapped around his neck, begging for mercy when he didn't deserve any. I'd known Nya wouldn't be his last victim, but I'd make sure there wouldn't be another after this new one. If it was the last thing I did, I'd put his ass behind bars.

"The owner of Charmed contacted me two days ago and said another submissive had gone missing. She had some interaction with Diego but hadn't committed to being with him before she disappeared."

I balled my fist against the table and kept my voice steady when all

I wanted to do was yell. "How the fuck did he even get back into the club?"

"He didn't. He lured the girl off site after the owner banned him for life. Another submissive inside the club told her Master what happened, and the information was passed on to us."

"We should've handled him after we found Nya."

Thomas nodded along with James. We all knew we'd dropped the ball on that motherfucker, but it wasn't our case, and we thought the local authorities would follow up on his crimes. But Diego had too much money. He paid off anyone and everyone he could so they'd look the other way, and they did it because they were a slave to the almighty dollar more than they were to human decency.

Thomas stood from his chair and started to pace near the windows at the back of the room. "We can't count on the cooperation of local law enforcement. We'll be calling in some favors with the FBI through Sam and our contacts in the DEA. I'm sure we'll be able to find enough dirt on this man to bring him down so he doesn't have the ability to do this again.

"This is a team project. Once we have enough information and have our contacts in place, we'll be heading to Atlanta to put an end to Diego Lopez. Anyone have an objection?"

No one spoke as they shook their heads. There was nothing that got the team more fired up than a scumbag who hurt women. I had a bigger stake in this than anyone else. I'd seen firsthand the devastation Diego could and did cause.

"Be ready to move by the weekend. We'll be acting quickly on this out of necessity. The man has enough money that he could easily vanish without a trace."

I'd hunt him until the end of time. Eventually, everyone fucked up. I learned that bounty hunting. A person could only stay hidden for so long without a paper trail. In today's day and age, with everything able to be linked electronically, I'd eventually find him. But I wanted to do it before he ruined the life of another girl, or worse, killed someone.

Diego Lopez was going to pay a price, and this time, no amount of money in the bank was going to save him.

CHAPTER 21

NYA

Ret walked through the door in an even worse mood than when Alese forced him to go to work this morning. He'd barely spoken a word to either of us after checking on Alese and making sure we didn't need anything. He retreated to his office, talking on the phone in whispered tones, and hadn't come out for the last hour.

"You worried about something?" Alese asked as I stared down the hallway toward Ret's office.

"He's grumpy, no?" I dabbed the end of the nail polish brush against the bottle before I went back to painting Alese's toes the most beautiful shade of pink.

"He's moody like a chick sometimes. All men are, but they'll never admit it." Alese closed her eyes and yawned. "Just ignore him. He'll tell us when he's ready."

As I dabbed her last toe, covering the tiny nail somehow without getting any on her skin, I felt a sense of accomplishment. "Why don't you rest, and I'll get dinner together."

She didn't open her eyes as she pulled the blanket closer to her face and made herself more comfortable. Well, as comfortable as she could be only able to lie in one position because of her incisions. "That sounds like a plan."

I quietly cleaned off the coffee table, careful not to make too much noise so Alese could get some rest. I had an ulterior motive too. I wanted to talk to Ret without Alese around and try to see what was bothering him before we had dinner tonight.

I never did well when people were upset. I was a people pleaser and would do anything to bring a smile to their face, especially Ret's. When Alese finally started to snore, I tiptoed down the hallway toward his office.

I knocked softly and took a deep breath, nervous that he'd bite my head off for disturbing him.

"Come in," he said quickly, but there was no malice in his voice.

Turning the knob, I shook out my nervous energy before walking into his office with a smile on my face and my shoulders pushed back. I'd exude confidence. Something Alese and I had been working on since that day in the dressing room. "Can I get you anything? A drink maybe?"

Ret sat at his desk, sweeping his eyes over me as he propped his chin on the back of his hand, his elbow resting against the wooden surface. "I have some already." His eyes dipped to the half-filled glass sitting next to his arm. "Would you like a glass?"

I hated whiskey. Nothing about the taste or burn as it slid down my throat appealed to me. "I'd love some," I lied because I figured this was my way in.

He turned his chair, grabbing the bottle and glass off a small table behind his desk. "Sit for a bit. I want to talk to you," he said as he turned back around and motioned toward the chair across from him with a dip of his head.

I relaxed into the chair, watching him closely as he filled the glass with more whiskey than I wanted or needed. When he slid it across the desk, I grabbed the crystal glass and placed it on my knee. "Everything okay?"

I figured he wanted to talk about Alese and her recovery—the long road we both knew was coming the day she was released from the hospital. Once her incisions healed and her cast came off, she'd have physical therapy to regain strength and full movement.

"I don't know," he admitted before taking a sip of his whiskey, staring back at me over the rim.

"That doesn't sound good." I lifted the glass to my lips, letting a small amount of whiskey slide over my tongue. Based on the look on his face and the tone of his voice, I figured I'd need a little something to get me through the rest of the conversation.

"I don't want you to freak out."

I moved the glass away from my mouth and stared at him. There was nothing about that phrase that exuded positivity. Saying he didn't want me to freak out did exactly that. "What's wrong? Oh God," I groaned. "Is it Alese? Do you want me to leave?"

Every bad thought I could imagine crossed my mind. Maybe since she'd been released, he realized I was a drain on their relationship. Maybe my welcome here was about to be revoked, and he was plying me with alcohol so I wouldn't flip my shit and have a complete meltdown.

"No. No. It's nothing like that. Drink the whiskey first."

I took another sip, staring at his beautiful face and turquoise eyes, seeing the storm behind their peace. "You're killing me, Smalls."

Ret cracked a smile. "I have to leave town for a few days this weekend. Think you'll be okay with Alese on your own?"

"Of course." Like I'd say no to something like that. I'd do anything for Ret and Alese, and it wasn't like I had to watch her like she was a child. She was starting to be more mobile, barely needing help getting to the bathroom anymore. "She's a lot better than she was a few days ago."

"I feel confident you can handle things. I know she isn't your responsibility, and I..."

I waved my hand in the air, silencing him. "Don't say that. I love Alese. I would do anything for her and for you too, Ret."

His smile returned, matching my own. Saying the words out loud was easier than I imagined. I'd thought them a million times since the day Ret and Alese welcomed me into their home, making me feel part of something special. "We adore you, Nya. I don't know what I would've done without you the last few weeks."

"You would've managed."

Ret was the type of guy that really didn't need help with anything. He was a giver and not a taker, but it was nice to think that he felt I did my part in assisting with her recovery.

"I wouldn't have gone back to work so soon. I wouldn't have slept in weeks either. You do more than you think. You mean a lot to us both."

I hoped I did. I knew the way they moaned, and I wanted more. The last thing I wanted was not to be part of whatever they had, even if it was a small piece of that special something.

"Thank you. I'll take good care of our girl." I paused for a second and glanced down at the glass I'd rested on my leg, wondering if I overstepped my bounds by referring to her as mine. She wasn't. I knew that, but I liked how it sounded sliding off my tongue.

In reality, I was hers. Ret's too. I owed them everything, including my life, my happiness, my love.

"Good. I'll be headed to Atlanta."

My eyes flew to his, growing wide. "Why?"

Atlanta had been my home for years, but you couldn't force me back into that shithole town. The magic I thought it held had worn off quickly once I'd found myself trapped in Diego's mansion.

"A new case has come up." He tried to hide his face behind the glass, but there was something he wasn't telling me.

"And? What aren't you telling me?"

The tension on his face evaporated and was replaced by a small smile. "Am I that easy to read?"

"I've spent a lot of time studying your face, trying to read your emotions so I wasn't caught off guard."

His face tightened. "Are you worried I'm going to be upset with you?"

"I…" I didn't know how to answer that. I wasn't worried he'd hurt me. Ret would never do that, but after being with Diego, I tried to read everybody so I wouldn't be surprised if they lashed out. "No. It's just an old habit I can't seem to shake."

He slowly turned the glass in his hands. "I'll always be straight with you." He paused and rubbed the back of his neck, dipping his eyes toward the desk. "I have to go to Atlanta because of Diego."

I rocked back in my chair, not expecting his name to roll off Ret's tongue. "Why?" I asked, my voice small and soft.

"Another girl has gone missing."

"Shit," I hissed, imagining and knowing firsthand everything she was going through. I covered my mouth as the whiskey started to claw its way out of my stomach.

He dragged his eyes to mine and dropped his hand back to the glass. "We'll save her just like I found you, but this time, we're taking him down forever."

I swallowed down the wicked mix of bile and whiskey and cleared my throat, trying to find the words, but failing. "God, I hope so."

"I could use your help, actually."

"Just don't make me go back there, Ret. I can't step foot in that house again."

He quickly shook his head, and I felt relief. "Never. I just need to know about the first few weeks you were with him. I want to know what I'm going into and where he may be keeping her. Any details you can remember will help us to get everyone out alive."

I sat in silence, running through the events at the start of my captivity and how stupid I was to believe anything good was going to come out of it.

"You want to know now?"

Ret eyed the whiskey in my glass. "Finish your drink first and have another if you need it, but anything you can tell me may help us stop him forever. I'd like to return this girl to her family in one piece just like we did you."

But I wasn't with my family. They were just as crazy as Diego, only on a different scale. Both hid it behind a veil of love and caring, but they all wanted to control me for different reasons.

I lifted the glass to my lips, watching Ret as I guzzled down the contents, wincing as the whiskey burned on the way down my throat. I knew eventually I'd have to spill my guts about my stupidity, and I prayed Ret wouldn't judge me for any of it.

I placed the empty glass on his desk, tipping my head toward the bottle because I wanted more if I was going to spill the story of how I got myself into such a mess to begin with. It wasn't pretty.

He filled the glass again, this time a little more than before. "Nothing you tell me will leave this room. Not even Alese will know what you say. You can trust me, Nya."

I knew I could. He was the person I trusted most in the world. Next to Alese, of course, but she and I had a different relationship entirely.

"The first few days I was with Diego at his place, it was more of a game. I didn't think much of it because we were leaving for New York in a few days, so I thought I'd play along. He said he was testing my ability and my limits and that I was to think of it all as an extended scene." I took another gulp of the whiskey, letting the burn settle deep in my stomach as Ret stared at me. "I thought it was odd because we'd done dozens of scenes at the club, but looking back, I should've known it was all a sick and twisted game."

I was too stupid then. I was too enamored of the man…his beauty and wealth…to question anything he commanded or did because I thought he really cared about me.

"He started with mind games, pushing me further than he did at Charmed, but this time, there was no monitor to step in and save me when shit got bad."

I blew out a breath and tightened my hand into a hard fist. "He'd locked me in a closet, saying he was punishing me and testing my sensory deprivation limits. He'd leave me in there for hours at a time. When I finally saw light again, I'd be so grateful that I listened to his every command just to keep myself from being locked up again."

"He's a twisted fuck."

I nodded. "We'd discussed my hard limits before we ever hooked up, but as soon as he got me in the house, he made sure to hit every single item I'd made off-limits before."

"Like?"

I couldn't look at Ret anymore. He wasn't staring at me like he was judging me, but I still felt the shame wash over me for my stupidity. "I didn't like darkness and had refused to have my eyes covered during any scene. I think that's why he went there first, locking me up without any light. He knew it terrified me."

Ret twisted his lips, but he remained silent as I took a moment to take another gulp. My vision blurred a little, and the words flowed easier than before as the liquor started to buzz through my system. "When he finally put me in the cage under his bed, I was thankful. How fucked up is that? I was so fucking happy for the bars instead of the dark room. What kind of person is happy about that?"

"It was your fear, Nya. He knew how to manipulate you. Don't ever blame yourself for how you felt. It wasn't your fault."

"Back to the first few days…"

I spent the next hour recounting every moment of torture, agony, and pleasure that Diego gave me, indoctrinating me into his twisted games. Ret sat mostly silent, barely making a facial expression in order to keep me talking. I could tell he wanted to say something, but he didn't as I barely stopped long enough to take a deep breath while I laid it all on the line, and none of it was pretty.

When I finally finished, I dropped my head forward and took a deep breath. "I don't want to say anything more. I'm sure you can imagine what happened after that."

The chair squeaked as his weight shifted, and he rose to his feet. First, his boots came into view and then his eyes as he placed his fingers under my chin and forced me to look at him. "He abused your trust, Nya. Never blame yourself for what he did." My eyes started to tear when I looked up at Ret as he spoke so tenderly to me. "A Dom/sub relationship is about trust, and he made you trust him before he broke his promise. You did nothing wrong. He's to blame, and I'm going to do everything in my power to stop him."

"Just be careful." The thought of something happening to Ret sent a shiver down my spine.

CHAPTER 22
NYA

"Let's surprise Ret for lunch."

I gawked at Alese as she leaned against the countertop for support, standing next to the small electric scooter Ret had had delivered. "I don't think you're up to it yet."

Ret insisted Alese get a scooter so he didn't have to worry about her falling. Crutches weren't easy for her yet because her incisions were still healing, and it would be weeks before the soreness went away. When he ordered the sucker, I didn't think he meant for us to drop by the office quite so soon.

She scrunched her face and let out a strangled snarl. "It's been almost three weeks. I can't be in this house anymore. I need a little freedom before you two make me half insane."

I knew what it was like to feel trapped all too well, and it was awful. "Fine," I said as I slid off the couch and tucked my toes into my flip-flops. "If Ret gets mad, you have to deal with him."

I could already hear him now. He'd never been one to nag, but ever since Alese got hurt, he'd been a little over the top with his overprotective nature. At times, I knew Alese wanted to lay into him, but she didn't have the energy to argue. Now that she was on the road to recovery, I knew fireworks were inevitable.

She smiled and straightened a little. "If he gets mad, it won't matter because he's leaving in the morning. He can only be grouchy for so long."

I laughed and rubbed my face in the palms of my hands as I shook my head. "It'll be the longest twelve hours ever."

"Psh." She waved her hands. "I'm sure we can find a way to make him happy."

"You've been planning this all morning, haven't you? That's why you had me do your hair and makeup."

She gave me that sweet, innocent look, batting her eyelashes at me like I'd seen her do to Ret to get her way. "Maybe. Does it matter?"

I laughed, knowing her game but loving her just the same. "I suppose it doesn't."

Alese had a plan for everything. I think she'd developed that after being with Ret for so long. I could imagine her free spirit always thinking ahead, plotting her next move to make things go her way when she was younger. Sometimes I could almost see the wheels turning inside her mind.

"Come on. The guys at the office are too much fun, not to mention hot, and the weather's too nice for us to sit inside all day."

"Any of those guys single?" I asked, raising an eyebrow. I didn't know why I blurted that out, but I did. I grimaced as her smile disappeared and her shoulders slumped.

"You leavin' us?"

"Well, I…" I shrugged, not knowing what else to do. "No."

"You can never leave," she said quickly, trying to move in my direction, but stopped as soon as she put any pressure on her cast.

I rushed to her side, grabbing her by the arm, and I grunted. "You know you're not supposed to put pressure on it. You need to slow your roll, missy. If you hurt yourself, Ret will never let you out of his sight again."

She let out a loud huff before shifting all her weight to her good foot and plopping herself onto the scooter seat. "Fine. I'll behave, but we're not staying here today. I need some fresh air, good food, and those hot men."

"Let's do it."

"Hey," she said, grabbing my hand as I stood at her side. She peered up at me with a small, sad smile on her face. "Don't leave us. Not yet. Okay?"

"Yeah," I answered quickly, not even thinking twice about it.

"I know someday you'll want to go, but I'm not ready for that yet."

I stared down at Alese, bruised and still broken, but not letting that stop her from doing anything. My injuries weren't on the outside, visible to everyone, but they were there, lurking under the surface. Being with Ret and Alese was easy. They knew almost everything I'd been through and didn't think any less of me. Having to explain my past to someone else would be damn near impossible and almost paralyzing.

"I don't want to go anywhere." I smiled and touched her face the same way I'd seen Ret do when he wanted to get his point across. "I'm here until you don't want me anymore."

She blinked slowly, moving into my touch. "That day will never come, Nya."

I hoped her words were true. It was easy to say she wanted me around forever and that Ret liked having another woman around the house, even if neither of us was a domestic goddess.

"Let's get out of here before it gets too late."

I didn't ask what we'd be too late for, figuring she wanted to change the subject just as much as I did. I followed her out the front door and down the temporary ramps Ret put down last night, and I did my best to keep everyone happy.

INSTEAD OF GOING out to eat, Alese insisted we grab a few pizzas and sub sandwiches on the way to bring enough food for the entire office. She said something about wanting their energy, but I think it had more to do with the pain involved in getting in and out of the car. The scooter was great, but without an automatic lift in the car, the system for her to get around wasn't foolproof.

She grabbed the subs from my hands and placed them in the basket that hung on the front of her scooter. "This thing kinda rocks," she said, laughing. "I just need to borrow one of Fran's old tracksuits, and I'll be halfway to old age."

I slammed the lid of the trunk, balancing the pizzas in one hand and praying I didn't drop them. "Tracksuit?"

"You don't want to know. Let's just say, Fran wasn't always the hot cougar she is today."

"Okay." I smiled, wondering what she'd been like before Bear.

Alese raced ahead, beeping the horn on her scooter as she got closer to the door. Within moments, Angel, the receptionist, pushed it open and welcomed us both inside.

"The guys are going to love you two for this." She smiled, tossing her long red hair behind her shoulder. "They're always foraging."

I hadn't really paid too much attention to Angel the first few times I'd been to ALFA, but today, I soaked her in. She was drop-dead gorgeous. Not surprising considering I'd met all the spouses at the hospital while Alese recovered. There wasn't a bad-looking one in the bunch. Their husbands were hot too. I'd never seen anything like it before.

Bear, Ret's hot-ass father, came stalking down the hallway, rubbing his belly with his head bopping around. "What do I smell?"

Alese rolled toward him on her shiny new scooter, finally catching his eye. "Hey, Pop. We brought you lunch."

I placed the three large and extremely hot pizza boxes on Angel's desk, thankful to get them out of my hands without dumping them.

Bear stared down at Alese and jerked backward, shaking his head. "You got a scooter?"

She nodded, looking pretty impressed with herself. "Whatcha think?"

"Smokin' hot, babe."

"I just need a little more power, and we can race."

He patted her on the head and smiled. "You've got a long way before that bad boy has any chance of beating my bike, kid, but it's cute you think so."

I chuckled and covered my mouth. I loved Bear. Ret had a dash of his father in him, but he was way more serious. Bear was playful, funny, and was easy on the eyes. For an older man, he had everything going for him.

"Alese?" Ret walked out of his office, heading right for us, but I couldn't tell if he was happy to see us or ready to pop his lid.

"We brought you lunch." She smiled so big, not giving two fucks if he was upset as she lifted his favorite sub from her basket as an offering to keep his ass happy. "See?"

Ret crossed his arms, squaring his shoulders and looking more like a big bad Dom than I'd seen in weeks. He narrowed his eyes as he tilted his head, and for a moment, I readied myself for the ass-chewing we were about to get.

"Don't you think it's a little early for you to be out of the house?"

I gnawed on the inside of my cheek as I moved my eyes between them. I knew it was a bad idea to come here, and I should've done everything possible to keep Alese home.

"Darling, I missed you."

He pursed his lips and was about to say something when Bear stepped between them and grabbed the bag of subs from her basket. "We're happy to see you, kid. It's always good not to lie around too much. Gotta stay strong."

Ret turned his gaze to his father, but he stayed silent.

Bear gave Alese a wink before lifting the pizzas off the desk with his other hand. "Let's take this to the conference room. We could use a little more beauty around this place."

I giggled with Alese and Angel because none of us missed the snarl coming from Ret. His father shut him down, which was good because if he hadn't, I knew Alese would have.

"Lunch," Bear announced, gliding down the hallway with both hands filled.

Like clockwork, the men piled out of their offices, sniffing the air like Bear had done. They didn't speak in words, but short, deep grunts as if it were some secret male language.

"You two are the best," James, one of the owners, said after he walked into the room and spotted Alese and me. He gave us each a quick kiss on the cheek.

I stood at Alese's side as the small army of men pawed at the food, filling paper plates that Angel had brought in just behind Bear. After the men had almost cleaned everything out, I grabbed sandwiches for Alese and me before going back to stand near her.

"Ready for tomorrow?" Alese asked as she unwrapped her sub.

The man at Angel's side, Thomas, I think was his name, rubbed his hands together and smirked. "We're ready to kick some ass."

"Yep. That fucker's going down." Bear took another bite of his sub and had a few pieces of lettuce stuck in his beard. "That's a guarantee."

They exuded fearlessness and strength. If anyone could bring Diego down, it would be them. I picked off some of the toppings on my sandwich, hiding my eyes behind my hair as they started to talk about Diego and how they had everything in place to bring him to justice.

I just hoped they knew what they were getting into, because Diego always covered his ass.

CHAPTER 23

RET

Sam glanced up from his phone and exhaled. "Everything's finally in place."

"Thank fuck," Morgan said at my side as we sat inside a blacked-out SUV down the street from Diego's, looking like something out of a movie.

Getting some of our contacts on board had been harder than we thought. The FBI and other agencies were overworked and under-staffed, but a favor was a favor. We knew eventually they'd come around because we'd helped them out of more than one jam over the years.

That was the thing about working for the government. It was all about who you knew and if you'd scratched their back before. Being former military and a bounty hunter, I had contacts all over the country, from local law enforcement to the most covert black-ops agencies. Couple that with Sam's friends in the FBI and James and Thomas's DEA buddies, and we knew someone was bound to come around.

After some digging into Diego's past, we learned he'd been previously investigated in the disappearance of two females in the last ten years. They were never found, though, and there wasn't enough evidence to charge him. But with the recent crackdown on immigration laws due to the new presidential administration, Immigration and Customs Enforcement could toss him out of the country and send him back to Mexico where he was a wanted man. The police there didn't want him—they were as corrupt as the Atlanta cops—but there was more than one Mexican cartel that placed a bounty on his head.

"Pop and Sam, you two find the girl while the rest of us work on securing Diego."

"I'm all about the rescue." Pop rubbed his hands together. "But…"

"You going to just handcuff him?" Sam asked, interrupting my dad.

"I don't know. We'll see how everything unfolds."

That was a lie. After hearing everything Nya went through, I couldn't just hand Diego over to the authorities without making him pay for what he'd done to her. Not just her, but to every unsuspecting and trusting female he'd gotten his claws into over the years.

The sun hung low in the sky, almost hidden by the trees lining the long street near Diego's place. "I'll go in first." I squeezed my hands into tight fists, stretching the gloves I'd bought just for this occasion.

Sure, this wasn't a covert operation, but I was more than happy to fuck up Diego a little bit before we handed him off to the proper authorities. With the cops on his payroll, I didn't want to leave a trace that I'd been inside. There was nothing worse than crooked cops, depending on supplemental income and suddenly at a loss. I was sure heads would roll, but it sure as hell wasn't going to be any of the guys at ALFA on the hook.

"Let's discuss this as a team," Morgan said as he climbed out of the truck.

The fucker was trying to block me, but it wasn't going to work. I'd already discussed the entire operation with James and Thomas, and they were on board.

James swept his fingers through his hair, waiting for our team to join the others between the SUVs. "Let's go over this one more time. I want zero fuck-ups."

"I'm ready to fuck shit up." Pop cracked his knuckles, hungry for blood.

"Ret will go in first. We'll secure the perimeter before he enters. Once he's inside and verifies the girl's location, we'll enter as backup.

Bear and Morgan will retrieve the girl and escort her to safety. The rest of us will be Ret's backup as he takes down Diego."

"Immigration is on the way. They should be here in ten," Sam added.

James gave Sam a quick chin lift and rubbed his hands together. "We better get moving, then. Any last-minute questions or issues?"

"Nope." I shook my head, ready to get moving.

I walked ahead of the group, sneaking around to the back of the property to enter through a rear door I'd seen when I cased the place to rescue Nya.

The lock was easier to pick a second time. Maybe he had a false sense of security with the piles of money he tossed at local law enforcement, but his careless mistake made it easy for me to gain access to the lower level of his home. Nya told me he often spent time in his study, which was located on the second floor near the front of the house.

I took a few steps inside, careful not to make a sound as I moved. The door to the closet Nya told me about had the lock engaged and two dead bolts fastened. What kind of sick fuck would think they actually needed so many locks to keep such a little girl inside? Maybe it was part of a sick, twisted mind game, the sound of each lock closing more terrifying than the last. Maybe it was the sound of them opening to reveal the monster on the other side that got his rocks off.

"Girl's locked inside," I said softly into the microphone so the rest of the team would start to move. "I'm going up."

"We're right behind you."

I moved so quickly, my feet barely touched the floor as I headed up the stairs, straight toward his study. I couldn't stop thinking about the way I found Nya, the sadness and hurt in her eyes as she told me about her time in this very house, and the countless women he'd done the same thing to over the years.

My insides were practically vibrating by the time I pushed the door to his study wide open.

"What the fuck?" Diego jumped to his feet, coming at me with the same burning anger in his eyes as I had raging in mine.

He swung at me, missing as I ducked and jabbed him in the gut. The loud grunt coming from his mouth as he crouched over screamed easy target. The man loved to hurt women, he thrived on their pain, but he couldn't take a small hit without crying out like a little bitch.

My blood boiled as Diego stood in front of me, breathing the same air I did when he didn't deserve to live. No man who did what he did deserved to exist in the same world as the ones he hurt.

Before he came at me again, I lunged forward and thrust my fist upward, connecting with his jaw. His head snapped back, spittle and blood flying from his mouth as he staggered and tried to maintain his footing.

"This is for Nya," I said before striking again, harder than before. He didn't just stagger that time. His body jolted as his feet left the ground, and he fell backward onto the hardwood floor.

I could've stopped then. Just rolled him over and put his hands in cuffs, but I couldn't. The feelings Nya had stirred in me, coupled with my experience as a Dom, made it so I couldn't let that be the end.

I stepped over him, placing my feet on either side of his writhing body, and crouched down. "You like to beat women?" He reached up, trying to push my face away, but I didn't budge. I grabbed his hair, lifting his face closer to mine. "You like to scare them?"

"Fuck you," he spat, blood dribbling down the corners of his mouth.

I laughed and tightened my grip, figuring I'd fuck with his head a little. "I bet the cartel in Mexico is going to love getting their hands on you."

His eyes widened, and he started to swing his arms, trying to break free of my hold. I slapped him, stunning him, but totally loving the wild look in his eyes.

Lowering myself, I sat on his chest, giving him all of my weight and making it hard for him to breathe. "You deserve a slow death, Diego. The cartel may make it too quick for what you deserve."

"The girl's secured," James said from behind me, but I didn't turn around as I glared at the piece of shit below me.

"Can I kill him?" I wanted nothing more than to slowly choke the life out of him. Watching him gasp for his last breaths, knowing they would be his final few, would give me more pleasure than just about anything in life.

"Don't do it. We have too many hands involved now. Let the Mexicans take him out."

I still slid my hands around his neck as he bucked and pleaded with me, with us, to release him. As I tightened my grip, squeezing his neck so hard that his eyes started to bulge and loving every second of watching the sick fuck struggle for air, James placed his hand on my shoulder.

"He's not worth it, man."

I could've argued. I wouldn't feel remorse for ending his life. Trash like Diego didn't deserve any pity or guilt. The world would be a better place without him in it, and if I had to kill him myself...I would.

"Son," Pop said, his heavy footsteps sounding against the hardwood as he came up behind me. "ICE is here."

"Fuck," I hissed, wanting to at least choke Diego to the point that he passed out, but maybe his knowing he was being carted off to the one country he didn't have protection was the way to go. He'd be terrified and maybe feel an ounce of the fear he caused his victims.

I lightened my grip but slammed the back of his head into the floor before I climbed to my feet.

"You'll pay for this," he said in a strangled voice as he rubbed his neck and gasped for air.

The room erupted in laughter because whether he knew it or not, his time for making threats was over and so was his life.

CHAPTER 24

NYA

Alese and I had danced around the topic of my being part of their relationship for days. Sometimes I felt like an interloper, like I'd inserted myself into their relationship without being invited. Not just their day-to-day life, but their bed too.

She'd asked me to never leave, but maybe it was because she was still healing from her accident and couldn't get around. The number of pain meds she was on didn't help her make any decisions either.

"Is this awkward for you?" I asked, sitting next to her on the couch, curled under the blanket.

She glanced at me with her eyebrows furrowed, looking confused by my question. I didn't know how I'd feel in her shoes. Before Diego, I'd had boyfriends, but nothing long term and no one I truly loved. I don't know how I'd feel if I were put in her situation.

"What? The three of us?" She rolled her eyes and curled the blanket closer to her chin. "Don't be silly. I love you being here with us."

"Okay."

"The only thing I'm jealous about right now is that you can come and I can't," she told me, letting her head fall to the side to stare at me.

"I'm sorry," I said like it was my fault.

"I was so close last time. So, so close, but I need my damn muscles to cooperate. It feels like it's going to take forever for me to get better."

"It won't," I lied. The doctors said her incisions would heal, but her leg would take much longer. Once the cast was finally removed, she'd need therapy to build up strength.

"Maybe if my incisions would heal. I don't know." She chewed her lips, glancing back at the television. "God, I love this part."

I glanced toward the screen, watching as the characters fell onto the bed, wrapped in each other's arms in a deep kiss. I smiled, sighing at the easiness they had with each other.

"Fuck, seriously. Even this tender shit is turning me on," she groaned and pulled the blanket over her head. "I can't take it."

I pulled the blanket away from her face. "Can I help at all? Do you think if we…"

"If we what?" she asked, a playful smile on her face.

"I don't know. Maybe if you get worked up enough, it'll just happen."

She looked at me almost cross-eyed, like I was speaking another language. "Like a spontaneous orgasm?"

I shrugged and laughed. "Dumb. I know."

She was quiet for a moment, staring at me as I peered back toward the television, suddenly feeling like a complete moron. "It may work. I mean, anything can happen, right?"

"Maybe. Can't hurt, can it?"

"Seriously?" She gaped at me, and I realized what I'd said.

"I mean, it would suck if it didn't work. Maybe we shouldn't."

"Fuck you. We're doing it."

"Now?"

She shook her head and giggled. "When Ret gets back, silly."

"Oh."

"Thank you," she said quickly, reaching down and grabbing my hand under the blanket.

"For what?"

I couldn't imagine what she was thanking me for. I should've been the one thanking her. She could've very easily turned her back on me and not welcomed me into her home and into her life. But that wasn't Alese. She didn't have an ounce of meanness in her body.

"I don't know what I would've done the last few weeks without you."

I felt the same way and couldn't stop the tears from filling my eyes as I stared at her beautiful, warm face. "I love you," I blurted out, saying the words for the first time.

She smiled, squeezing my hand tightly. "I love you too, Nya. Don't ever doubt that you're wanted and loved. Oh my God. Do you know what this means?"

"No," I said softly.

"I'm going to have a sister wife." She smiled.

The tears came faster, falling harder as she spoke. My parents never even said those words of love to me. No one on this planet had uttered such a thing before now. Just Alese, and although Ret didn't say it, I felt the unspoken words in his touch and burning in his eyes.

"Hey." She brushed away the tears from my face with a tender smile. "Can we watch something else? I can't take all this sex and sappy shit. We need some killing or laughs."

I leaned forward, wiping the tears away from my face as I grabbed the remote. There would be no more tears and no more sadness. I was done being that girl. I was part of something bigger, something better. I had two people who loved me, accepted me, and wanted me in their lives.

My phone vibrated next to me, and I practically jumped from the couch. "Fucking hell, that scared me."

"Is it Ret?" she asked, looking over as I pulled the phone in front of me.

"It is."

We both read the screen and exhaled in unison.

Ret: He's captured. It's done.

She was thankful Ret was okay and so was I, but I was happy to know Diego would never hurt another woman again. What I went through and probably dozens of women had gone through before me, no one should ever have to experience.

I was strong enough to withstand his mental games and torture, but others probably weren't as tough.

She pushed her head back into the couch cushion and smiled. "Thank God he's okay."

"Yeah," I said, staring at the screen again because I was a little bit in shock.

I'd never thought Diego would be brought to justice. Men like him, with more money than any human should be able to amass, usually found ways to skate the law because their bank accounts were so big.

But Ret and the guys at ALFA couldn't be bought.

I WOKE to soft voices mumbling back and forth and blinked a few times, stretching my sore muscles as I yawned. Ret sat on the coffee table, talking to Alese as she sat next to me.

"You're home?" I asked, my voice rough from sleep.

He smiled, leaning his upper body over his legs with his elbows on his knees. "Just got back."

"Everything go okay?"

I'd sat on the couch last night, trying to pay attention to the movie, but couldn't stop thinking about Ret and Diego.

"He's on a plane to Mexico right now. I give him twenty-four hours."

I knew in my heart I shouldn't be happy about someone dying, but if anyone deserved to cease to exist, it was Diego. "That's good."

"It's the best fucking news ever." Alese smiled, pulling herself upright with her hands without so much as a wince.

"Your hands," I said, finally letting my eyes roam Ret's body. His hands were bruised, and his knuckles were swollen.

He glanced down, squeezing his fists tightly. "I'm fine. You should see Diego's face." He smirked. "You ladies do okay without me?"

"Yeah. I think so." My eyes closed for a second, and sleep threatened to pull me back under.

"Nya had a fabulous idea, though."

The sleepy feeling was short-lived as my eyes flew open, knowing exactly what she was talking about.

Ret raised an eyebrow and stared at me. "I can't wait to hear this."

I glanced toward the ceiling, keeping my mouth shut because I was sure Alese could pull off my words better than I could. I'd sound crazy, but somehow, she'd say it in a way that would sound convincing and rational.

"I need to come."

I held back my laughter as Ret smiled and nodded his head. We both knew she could be a handful, and soon, if she didn't get her way or an orgasm, she'd probably be brutal to live with.

"Okay…"

"We're going to try for a spontaneous orgasm."

His eyes darted to me before going back to Alese. "Spontaneous orgasm?"

"Yep." She smiled.

"Want to explain that one to me? Like what… I look at you, and you come?"

She shrugged and laughed. "Not exactly."

Oh God. I wanted to crawl under the blanket and hide because she wasn't pulling off what I told her at all. I wasn't about to enter this conversation to clarify my statement either.

"Nya?" Ret stared at me, but I kept my eyes trained on the blank television behind him, pretending to be in a trance.

"You know how you get me all worked up?"

I breathed a sigh of relief when she started talking because it was becoming impossible to ignore Ret. This was more awkward than any other moment with them, and there were some that should've ranked right up here with this but didn't.

"Yeah." He smirked. "You like when I do that."

"Like sometimes when you only need to blow on my clit and I explode."

"Uh-huh." His smile widened.

"We gotta do that."

"So, lots of foreplay until you don't even need your muscles to push you over the edge."

"You got it." She laughed and folded her arms in front of her. "Just like that."

"I've never heard it called spontaneous orgasm, though."

"It's the best we could come up with in a pinch."

"You love to be pinched," he told her, winking while he moved his two fingers together like he was pinching her nipples.

"Jesus Christ," she groaned.

"What's wrong, baby… Horny?"

"Someone better get me off before I leave wet spots on every damn surface in this house."

I burst out in giggles. I didn't know if it was the crazy expression on her face or the tone of her voice, but I couldn't stop. I tried to swallow it down, but every time I almost got my composure back, I'd look at Alese and lose it all over again.

Alese didn't find it nearly as amusing as I did. "You won't be laughing if he doesn't let you come, ya know?"

My gaze flickered to Ret, and I instantly sobered. "I wasn't laughing at her."

It wasn't like I couldn't come without them, but there was something about being touched by another person that made everything more intense and pleasurable.

Ret stared at me, his face expressionless.

"I swear I wasn't."

The corner of his lip twitched, and I finally took a breath, relaxing a little bit. "It's okay. It was funny. You'll learn that when Alese doesn't get her way, she gets super whiny."

"And bitchy," Alese added.

Ret threw up his hands, still laughing. "Your words, not mine."

"You go three weeks without an orgasm. I bet you'd turn into a complete asshole."

"Babe, let's be honest. I already am."

"Your words, not mine." She laughed.

God, I freaking loved them. I was probably staring at them like an idiot at this point, but I couldn't wipe the smile off my face. I didn't know how I got so lucky to be part of their world. It almost made everything I went through worth it. If it hadn't been for Diego, I never would've found them. Or Ret never would've found me.

"Shall we try this spontaneous orgasm?" Ret cocked an eyebrow, and Alese scurried off the couch faster than I'd seen her move in weeks.

"We aren't leaving the bedroom until it happens."

Ret grabbed her hand and pulled her back down on the couch. "Who needs a bed, *piccola*?" He grinned.

CHAPTER 25
RET

Alese squirmed on the couch, squeezing her thighs together and mumbling something I couldn't quite make out behind the gag. The words sounded something like "I'm going to kill you," but I just smiled at my beautiful girl and pinched her nipple a little harder.

She asked for this. She wanted to get so turned on that she could come without having to strain her muscles, chasing the orgasm she rarely let happen naturally.

"Come here," I said to Nya, motioning for her to move closer. "Alese likes to watch. She told me a naughty secret the other day."

Alese's eyes widened, and she shook her head before groaning. Her hands moved against the ropes binding her, probably wishing she could touch herself.

"She did?" Nya asked as she took off her dress and walked toward me.

"She did, my sweet girl. She's a voyeur like you. She loves to watch. Gets off on seeing other people have pleasure."

Alese mumbled into the ball gag and pressed her thighs together again. She was already getting worked up, and we hadn't even done anything.

I held out my hand, and Nya slid her palm against mine. Her eyes were dark with lust. "She's like me."

"How did you feel when you watched us fucking at the club or in the bed?"

Nya let out a shaky breath. Maybe she knew where I was going as I guided her onto my lap. "It was hot. I was so turned on I could barely stand the ache between my legs."

I smiled and nodded. "Exactly. Alese told me not too long ago that she wanted to watch us having sex." Alese moaned, and I pinched her nipple harder, causing her body to twitch. "How would you feel about that?"

Nya's gaze dropped to Alese. "You'd want that?"

Alese nodded, trying to move her hands between her legs, but I swatted them away. "No touching," I told her.

"I know we've never done that before…made love to each other."

"I'm willing to do it to help out a friend. I offer myself up as a sacrifice." Her words came out quickly, and she giggled softly.

"Do you want me, Nya?" My dick was rock hard, straining against my pants and dying to be buried deep inside one of them.

"I do," she whispered and took another step forward, straddling my legs.

I removed my hand from Alese's body and grabbed Nya around the waist. "We'll go slow and take our time. This is about pleasure, but also sealing our connection, making us one."

Nya set her arms on mine, dragging her nails across my skin. "I'd like that."

With one hand, I unzipped my jeans and lifted my ass enough to slide them down my legs, letting my cock spring free in celebration. "Get a condom," I told her, motioning toward the side table where I'd placed one.

She moved quickly, grabbing the condom wrapper and tearing it open with her teeth. She was an eager little one, hungry for my cock as much as I was hungry to be inside her.

I slid the latex over my cock before stroking the shaft and blowing out a shaky breath. "Come here," I told Nya. "Let me touch you."

She climbed onto the couch with my help, guiding her to place her knees on each side of me, using the cushion as support. Alese grunted and struggled against her bindings, drawing Nya's attention.

"Pretend she isn't here," I told Nya, placing my fingers under her chin and bringing her eyes back to mine.

"That's kind of mean, Ret," she said, but there was a hint of a smile.

"She wanted a spontaneous orgasm, didn't she? I don't want there to be any hesitation in what's about to happen. I want her to enjoy every moment and get herself so worked up she barely needs to be touched to come."

Alese sucked in a breath and moaned, but I knew her better than anyone. We'd talked about this. Went over it a dozen times on how to break through the next barrier with Nya. The spontaneous orgasm thing was a nice touch and worked well to get to our ultimate goal. We both wanted Nya here with us. We enjoyed having her around, and she'd become part of us, inseparable and just as important.

I loved her too. A different sort of love from what I had with Alese, but we had years together wrapped up in those feelings.

Nya hadn't moved, just kneeled on the couch cushions, hovering above my body with her perky tits near my face. I slid my arm behind her back, resting the other just above her hip bone at her waist. "Are you okay with this?" I asked again.

She placed her hand on my shoulder, finally connecting herself to me. "Yes," she said breathlessly and nodded. "I want you, Ret. I want Alese too. I want all of this, all of you."

My fingers tightened against her skin as I pulled her closer. I gazed up at her as I leaned forward, gently placing my lips just below her collarbone. Her fingers curled into my skin as she leaned into my touch, wanting this as much as we'd hoped.

Moving slowly, I trailed a path down her chest with my lips, licking and sucking her soft skin as I made my way to her breasts. I slid my hand up, cupping her in my palm and lifting her nipple closer to my mouth. I paused and peered up at her, waiting for a sign to confirm she was still okay with this. She inhaled and smiled as she nodded ever so slightly.

I dragged my tongue down the middle of her breast before closing my lips around her nipple. She dropped her head backward and thrust her chest forward, offering herself to me completely.

I tightened my arm around her back, holding her to me as I sucked her nipple into my mouth, flicking the hardened tip with my tongue. She moaned, making my impossibly hard cock like granite.

Alese moaned as the couch moved, but I ignored her, giving her exactly what she wanted. By the time I touched her again, she would have that spontaneous orgasm she'd cooked up in my absence.

Nya lowered herself over my cock, rocking against the length and driving me crazy with lust. I pulled her nipple between my teeth, applying pressure as I traced the outline of the tip with my tongue. She shivered against me, moving her hips faster.

I flattened my palm against her back and drew her breast deeper into my mouth, trying to focus on her breast and not the fact that she was riding me. I repositioned my hand at her hip, moving it between us and sliding through her wetness.

"You want my cock in you, Nya?"

"Yes," she moaned, not stopping grinding against me.

"I'm going to go slow. Be gentle and let you set the pace. I don't want to hurt you."

"Shut up and fuck me, Ret."

I jerked my head back, and I couldn't stop the slow slide of the smile on my face. This girl suddenly had some teeth, telling me what to do.

When she lifted off me, I instantly missed the warmth of her skin against my cock, but it didn't last long. I ran the tip of my dick through her wetness, wishing I could feel every drop of her need soaking my cock. I fucking hated condoms.

She reached down, taking my cock in her hands, and gaining control. I placed one hand on her hip, peering down at Alese as she watched, unblinking and totally mesmerized. I wrapped my fingers around Alese's nipple, giving it a hard squeeze and she jolted and moaned. She spread her legs, begging to be touched, but I didn't. I wouldn't. Not until she couldn't lay still and was gasping behind the gag in her mouth. Her pussy glistened in the light, her need clearly evident as she squirmed.

Nya lowered herself slowly, enveloping my cock in her warmth with her hands squeezing my shoulders. Although I hated the condom, I loved it too. If it weren't for the thin piece of latex, I'd probably blow my load within seconds of being inside her tight, wet cunt.

She lifted and dropped herself back down, taking my cock deeper as her fingernails bit into my skin. I stared into her eyes, watching as she fucked herself using my cock. I blew out a breath, trying to keep my shit under control as she slowly fucked me silly, driving me close to the edge before I was ready.

Before I could come, I slid my hand between her legs, pressing on her clit with my thumb. Nya moaned, swiveling her hips as her pussy convulsed around my cock. I couldn't take it anymore. Couldn't stop the freight train from plowing into me like I'd broken down on the track, waiting for the devastation. The slowness was something I wasn't used to and didn't expect to affect me as much as it did.

I pressed my thumb harder, circling her clit as my spine tingled and the orgasm slammed into me, stealing the wind from my lungs. Nya bucked, gasping for air as her entire body twitched and quaked against me and her sweet little cunt milked my cock.

Her motion slowed as her head fell forward, covering my face with her soft, brown hair. I sucked in a breath, coming down from a high I hadn't felt in ages. With Alese being injured, I didn't dare touch her and risk hurting her further. But taking care of myself using my hand was nothing compared to the wet warmth of a beautiful pussy.

Alese grunted, wiggling and squirming at our side. I turned to her, smiling as her skin glistened, her flesh covered in a fine sheen of sweat. Her pussy was slick, ready, and needing some attention. I lifted Nya, placing her on the couch next to me before I leaned forward, hovering my lips over Alese's pussy.

She begged me with her eyes, wanting my mouth to devour her flesh and push her over the edge, giving her the orgasm she so badly needed and craved. I brought my lips down, sucking her clit into my mouth and flicked it with my tongue.

Her back bowed, and she screamed behind the gag. I thrust two fingers inside her pussy, delivering the final blow as I sucked her clit harder and sent her right over the edge. Her body rocked, trembling as the orgasm she'd been unable to achieve for weeks finally crashed into her, stealing her breath.

I stayed like that...my face buried between her legs, flicking her clit with my tongue as the aftershocks rippled through her until she went limp, gasping for air.

She closed her eyes as her chest heaved and her body relaxed. I lifted my face, taking in her beauty and realizing I was the luckiest man in the world. Not only did I have the love of my life, but we had Nya too. A beautiful, selfless creature, not broken, but stronger than she even knew.

I undid the gag, wiping away the spit from Alese's cheeks with the back of my hand.

"I could die happy now," Alese said with a smile.

The thought twisted my stomach. We'd come so close to losing her once that even a casual statement like that made me ill, but I didn't want to bring down the mood, and I let the comment slide.

"I got you ladies something while I was gone."

Alese waggled her fingers near my face, needing help up from the totally flat position and probably completely spent. "Help me," she said when I didn't move fast enough. Pulling her gently, I guided her up before I stalked off toward the counter to grab the tiny black velvet pouch.

Before I left for Atlanta, I'd contacted the jeweler who had made the original collar I'd seen on Nya's neck in her graduation photo. I'd asked him for four things. I wanted a proper and extravagant collar for Alese, but I didn't want it looking anything like the one Nya had. I also wanted something to symbolize the connection the three of us built, and it needed to be beautiful and meaningful.

Even on short notice, the jeweler pulled it off and gave me exactly what I wanted. I carried the bag to the couch and kneeled before Nya and Alese. Patting the edge, I motioned for Nya to sit next to Alese because I wanted this moment to be important and memorable.

"Presents," Alese said, her eyes lighting up as soon as she saw the bag in my hand.

Nya hung her legs over the edge and folded her hands in her lap as she peered down at my hands. I couldn't wipe the smile off my face looking at the two of them, sitting on the edge of the couch like two kids on Christmas morning waiting to open their presents.

"I thought long and hard about this." I undid the velvet tie, moving slowly so I could explain everything.

"You're killing me," Alese groaned and dropped her head forward.

"Eyes on me," I said quickly.

Alese snapped her head up immediately, and I placed two boxes in her lap. She squealed and reached for one, but I made a tsk and she stilled. I held out a single box to Nya, and she blushed, staring at me for a moment before snatching the package from my hands.

I held Alese's hand, needing to tell her how I felt. "I've never loved another person the way I love you. You're not only my lover, you're my best friend and partner. I almost lost you."

"But you didn't," she interrupted and bit down on her lip, stopping herself from saying anything more.

"I wanted to get you something special to symbolize our connection and your importance in my life."

"Can I open it?" She smirked and wiggled her fingers underneath my hand.

I laughed and finally released my hold. "There's no person more important in the world to me than you. This is a small gift, symbolizing my love."

Alese tore open the paper and flipped off the lid, revealing the handcrafted, diamond-encrusted choker I had specially made for her.

The light splintered from the stones, and she gasped, covering her mouth. "Oh my God. It's so beautiful."

Reaching up, I removed her old collar before replacing it with the new one. It was the perfect size. Not too loose and yet tight enough to remind her who she belonged to. I didn't know who I was kidding. I belonged to Alese, not the other way around. Even in the bedroom she fucked with my head to get exactly what she wanted, but it was a beautiful game of cat and mouse.

"This is a constant reminder of our connection," I said as I closed the lock on the collar.

Her fingers stroked the cool metal. "I love it, Ret." She lunged forward, the other box falling to the floor, and wrapped her arms around me, hugging me so tight I could barely breathe. "I love you, baby," she whispered in my ear.

My gaze flickered to Nya as she watched us, smiling and tearful. "Nya, open your box, sweetheart."

She was not as fast as Alese as she pulled the paper away from her smaller box. "You didn't have to get me anything," she said as she ran her finger over the lid. "It really wasn't necessary."

Alese released me, moving back to the spot next to Nya and clapping her hands. "This is so exciting."

"Wait," I said, lifting the box off the floor and placing it back on Alese's lap. "This gift is for the three of us."

"Yeah?" Alese looked at me with wide eyes. "All three?"

I nod. "All three. Open yours too."

They moved a little faster now, ripping into the packages, and pulled out their matching bracelets. Nya held it up in front of her eyes. "It's so...so..."

"Baby," Alese said with the biggest smile. "You did good."

I laughed. Alese knew me better than anyone. Shopping for anything, including jewelry, wasn't something I did well or enjoyed. But there was something different about selecting this gift. I wanted the three pieces to be perfect. "The bracelet has three bands woven together—yellow gold, white gold, and rose gold—to signify each of us. Nya, baby."

Nya lifted her eyes to mine. They were filled with tears, but she was smiling. "You've quickly become part of us, inseparable and important. Alese and I couldn't imagine life without you. This bracelet signifies the connection we have and that we're all bound together, tangled with no beginning or end."

"You mean..." She sniffled and wiped a tear away from her cheek. "You want me to stay?"

I placed my hands against her cheeks and stared into her eyes. "We want you to stay forever," I told her.

Nya covered her mouth and burst into tears. I glanced at Alese, wondering if I'd fucked everything up, but Alese touched my hand, letting me know it was all okay.

"You're one of us. I love you, Nya," Alese told her. "I can't imagine life without you anymore. Please say you'll stay."

Nya wiped her face and laughed, causing more tears to fall. "I never..." She laughed and shook her head. "I'm sorry I'm so emotional."

"You be whatever you want to be," I said and patted her knee.

She took three deep breaths, exhaling slowly on each one before stilling. "Not that long ago, I thought I'd spend my life locked in a cage at Diego's mercy. But then you—" Nya touched my face and smiled "—you saved me. You were like something right out of a fairy tale, Ret. Then you and Alese..." She choked back a sob. "You welcomed me into your home, showing me what real love is supposed to look like, and then made me part of something so special and pure. I love you both so, so much." She stopped only long enough to take a breath. "I never want to be anywhere or with anyone else."

I grabbed the bangle from Alese's hands and slid it over her wrist and then did the same for Nya before grabbing mine. Mine was chunkier, more manly compared to theirs, but matching in every other way.

"My girls," I said and pulled them toward me, wrapping my arms around them. "I'm the happiest and luckiest guy in the world."

Alese laughed. "You are one lucky bastard."

EPILOGUE

ALESE

Bear stopped mid-chew, gawking at me. "You're what?"

"We're together and committed," I told him before taking a sip of the wine Fran had just given me.

He looked at Nya and then to Ret as he set down his fork. "You got them both?"

I laughed over the rim of my glass, loving the look on his face. Bear was by far the funniest person I'd ever met. When Ret said he wanted to move to Tampa and that his father was there too, I was hesitant. I knew about Ret's past and his father leaving him and his sister behind after the death of his wife, Ret's mother.

From what I'd heard about Bear, I was petrified to let this man into our lives. He had a criminal record longer than my arm and hung around with bikers. The last thing I expected was to find this fun-loving, goofy, and even sexy man to come barreling into our lives.

Ret nodded with a grin. He knew, just like I did, this would eat Bear up inside. I wasn't worried about breaking the news to him, but Fran was an entirely different story. "Yeah, Pop. They're mine."

My stomach fluttered with those words. I could hear Ret say them over and over again and never tire of them. Bear glanced around again, mouth hanging open, and pushed back from the table.

"Well, fuck," he said, dropping his fork. "If there was any doubt, this proves you're every bit my son."

I laughed harder, covering my mouth so I didn't spit my wine across the table. The man thought of himself as a playboy, but we all knew the truth. He had eyes for only one woman, and she was standing right behind him, not looking the least bit amused.

I sobered, sitting up a little straighter in my chair. "Hey, Fran."

She leaned forward and wrapped her arms around his chest. "You want two women?" she asked, resting her mouth against his ear.

His eyes widened as he stared at me. "No, baby," he coughed and placed his hands over hers in front of him. "I have you. What more could a guy ask for?"

"We can make it a reality," she told him.

He moved his gaze around the table like he needed validation that what she said was indeed what he heard. "What?"

Fran touched his cheek with her mouth and tightened her arms around his neck. "But if you need two, just know I'm not going to be one of them."

He turned quickly and pulled her down into his lap, wrapping his arms around her. "You're all I ever need, Fran. Don't be ridiculous. I can barely handle you sometimes, wildcat."

She raised an eyebrow with no smile on her face as she stared at him. "Mm-hm."

Bear rubbed his beard against her neck until she finally lost it.

"Stop!" Fran wiggled in his lap, laughing. "Baby, be happy for the kids. I'm excited for them."

Fran finally turned her gaze toward me. "Are you happy?"

"Yes," I said.

She looked to Nya. "Are you happy, sweetheart?"

"Yes." Nya nodded.

Fran eyed Ret and shook her head. "I know you're happy. I'm not even going to bother to ask." Turning in Bear's lap, she pushed his plate aside. "I learned something important a long time ago."

"Here we go," Bear muttered.

He was instantly met with Fran's icy glare. "You got something to say?"

"Of course not, love. Talk to the kids," he said, touching her cheek and turning her face away from him.

Nya had her hand over her mouth, trying to hide her laughter, but I didn't bother. Those two had kept me rolling since the day we moved here. Fran was my spirit animal and exactly how I wanted to be as I grew older. She never held back and definitely didn't pull any punches. If she said it, she meant it.

"As I was saying before I was so rudely interrupted…"

Bear rolled his eyes.

"Love isn't something we can control. We don't get to pick who our heart wants, and sometimes it's not as clean as society wants us to believe. I mean, take your father and me." She turned toward Ret, talking straight to him. "I never thought I'd fall in love with a man who couldn't settle and hopped from woman to woman like it was an Olympic sport. People told me we were doomed and he'd never settle down. But here we are, and we're happily in love and completely committed. Right, honey?"

"Of course." He nodded.

"Do whatever makes you happy in life. It can all disappear in a blink of an eye. Live without regret. Love without remorse. And never let anyone make you feel less than you are because they have a stick rammed so far up their ass the damn thing scrambles their brain when they walk."

I blinked and stared. For a second, I thought Fran was going soft on me. She was almost there with her live and love bit, but then in typical Fran fashion, she went to the stick and ruined everything.

"That was beautiful, baby," Bear said and held her tighter, kissing the back of her neck softly.

"Now, I don't care which one of you does this, but someone better start making some babies. I'm not getting any younger, and neither are you."

"Well, I…" I didn't want to tell Fran I had no inclination of ever having a human grow in my body. It wasn't that I was anti kid, but I liked my body, vagina, and life the way they were. I was completely selfish, but I was okay with that and so was Ret.

But Nya…she was another story. She longed for a baby and was open about it.

"We're trying," I said and didn't say anything more. It didn't matter whose body the baby would eventually come out of, he or she would be loved just the same by all three of us.

Bear smacked Ret's shoulder and grinned. "My boy. I envy the task before you." Fran kicked him under the table, and Bear growled. "I meant I don't envy you at all."

On the outside, our relationship probably looked like it was impossible. But on the inside, it was the purest form of love and respect I'd ever had.

This was my life. Parents that weren't mine but loved me like I was their own. A boyfriend and Master who was selfless and loving. And then there was Nya…a best friend, a confidant, and my other half.

I started to take Guilty Sin in another direction, but quickly changed course. Want to read the deleted chapters? <u>Tap here</u> or visit *<u>https:// BookHip.com/LXDQQT</u>*

Ready for more hot & sexy alphas?

DOWNLOAD FREE MEN OF INKED NOVELS!

Join the Gallos as their lives are turned upside down by irresistible chemistry and unexpected love. <u>Tap here to download Chelle's FREE eBooks</u> or visit *https://menofinked.com/free-books/*.

BE A GALLO GIRL...

Want to be the first to hear about the next Men of Inked book or everything Chelle Bliss? Join my newsletter by _tapping here to sign up_ or visit _menofinked.com/inked-news_

Want a place to talk romance books, meet other bookworms, and all things Men of Inked? Join Chelle Bliss Books on Facebook to get sneak peeks, exclusive news, and special giveaways.

ABOUT THE AUTHOR

I'm a full-time writer, time-waster extraordinaire, social media addict, coffee fiend, and ex-history teacher. *To learn more about my books, please visit menofinked.com.*

Want to stay up-to-date on the newest Men of Inked release and more? Tap here to join my newsletter or visit *menofinked.com/inked-news*

Join over 10,000 readers on Facebook in Chelle Bliss Books private reader group and talk books and all things reading. Tap here to become part of the family or visit at *facebook.com/groups/blisshangout*

Tap here to see the Gallo Family Tree or visit *menofinked.com/gallo-family-tree*

Where to Follow Me:

facebook.com/authorchellebliss1

instagram.com/authorchellebliss

bookbub.com/authors/chelle-bliss

goodreads.com/chellebliss

amazon.com/author/chellebliss

tiktok.com/@chelleblissauthor

x.com/ChelleBliss1

pinterest.com/chellebliss10